UNHOLY WAR

THE MOONTIDE QUARTET BOOK III

DAVID HAIR

Jo Fletcher

BOOKS

First published in Great Britain in 2014 by Jo Fletcher Books
This paperback edition published in 2015 by

Jo Fletcher Books
an imprint of
Quercus Publishing Ltd
Carmelite House
50 Victoria Embankment
London EC4Y 0DZ

An Hachette UK company

A CIP catalogue record for this book is available
from the British Library

PB ISBN 978 1 78087 205 6
EBOOK ISBN 978 1 78087 204 9

10 9 8 7 6 5 4 3 2

Typeset by Jouve (UK), Milton Keynes
Printed and bound in Great Britain by Clays Ltd, St Ives plc

This book is dedicated to Paul Linton. Paul has test-driven this entire series to date, risking his sanity to ensure that the book is safe for you, the consumer. He is a truly international man of the world, with a talent for introducing his friends to the very worst alcoholic beverages this planet has to offer (and some of the best, to be fair). Thanks, mate – and yeah, why not: pour me another shot of Orujo.

TABLE OF CONTENTS

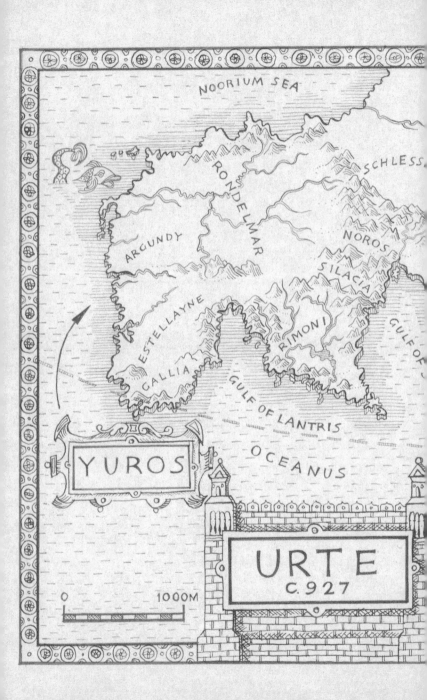

NOORIUM SEA

RONDELMAR

SCHLESS

ARGUNDY

NOROS

SILACIA

ESTELLAYNE

RIMONI

GULF OF

GALLIA

GULF OF LANTRIS

OCEANUS

YUROS

URTE
c.927

0   1000M

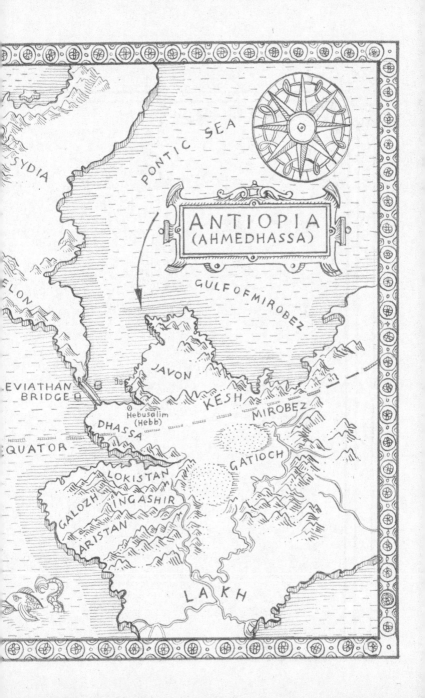

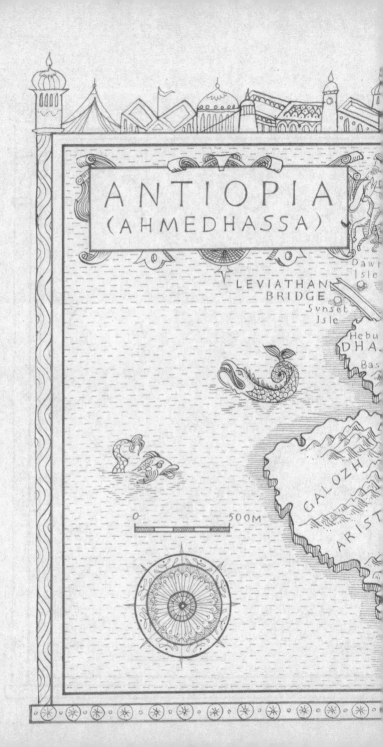

GULF OF MIROBEZ

Hytel
Lybis · Loctis
ochena
Riban
Forensa
VON HARKUM
Intemsa
oz
Krak
Hallikut
Istabad
Galataz
KESH MIROBEZ
Sagostabad · Shaliyah
Ghosh
dishar · Peroz
Vida
EASTERN
KESH
DESERT
ad
Barakabad
Khotriawal
Gujati
GATIOCH
AN
SITHARDHA
DESERT
Ullakesh
SHIR
NIMTAYA
ETERNAL
Kankriti-
MOUNTAINS
pur
Teshwallabad
ALAYAN
NTAINS
Tuklabad
Baranasi

LAKH
idabad · Jeslamabad
Dili

The Vexations of Emperor Constant
(Part Three)

The Rimoni Empire: Emperors

It was many centuries before Rimoni could dare to call itself an empire, and the transformation from republic to empire was bloody and almost disastrous. The lesson it taught: court power as you would court a lover.

THE RIMONI EMPIRE: A HISTORY,
ARNO RUFIUS, LANTRIS 752

Pallas, Rondelmar
Summer 927
1 Year until the Moontide

Gurvon Gyle let his gaze drift around the room while his country-man Belonius Vult restated the plans for the invasion of Kesh and the entrapment and destruction of Echor Borodium, Duke of Argundy, and his army. Two Noromen who'd risen against the emperor only seventeen years ago, sitting in that same emperor's inner sanctum and presenting him with a plan to cement his rule. Who would have imagined such a gathering?

Emperor Constant had been just a child then, and perhaps a life in the shadow of more powerful figures had undermined him, made him the weak-kneed young man he was now, startled by shadows and afraid even of those closest to him. The weight of the crown furrowed his brow and hunched his shoulders. Every few seconds he glanced at his mother, as if seeking approval.

Yet if what we've just outlined works, we'll have destroyed a man who'd make a far better ruler and widowed a quarter of a million of his people – and all in your name, Constant Sacrecour.

It was Mater-Imperia Lucia who dominated the room. She had never needed eye-catching beauty; her sheer presence and veiled intensity were sufficient. Her matronly face was a study in concentration as she listened to Vult, but her eyes roved continually, noting reactions, filing away the tiny behaviours of everyone present. Her attention wasn't on those familiar to her – iron-faced Kaltus Korion, who was to take over the command of the Crusade next year when Echor died; Tomas Betillon, who would troubleshoot the inevitable crises behind the lines; Calan Dubrayle, who would be safe here in Pallas, counting the profits, and Grand Prelate Wurther, who would be wherever the food was. She was studying Vult, and Gyle himself too; occasionally their eyes met, appraising each other.

Mostly though, her eyes were on the newcomer: the alien. The enemy.

Emir Rashid Mubarak of Halli'kut was quite likely the first Keshi ever to enter this room. In contrast to the dour formality of Rondian courtiers, when he'd removed his cloak it had been as if a peacock had unfurled its tail-feathers: his clothes were almost gaudy, with glittering gems woven into the fabric that were nearly as bright as his own mesmerising green eyes. He reminded Gyle of a cobra swaying to a snake-charmer on the streets of Hebusalim.

Rashid had listened patiently, asked good questions, then he had allowed them to question him. He answered with practised ease, replying to some, not all. Most were logistical: could he field an army big enough to destroy Echor's? How many magi did he have? Was he sure he could overcome Meiros' faction within the Ordo Costruo?

The emir didn't give any definitive answers, of course, and Gurvon would have been surprised if he had. They were not allies; just enemies in collusion. Nor did the Rondians tell him all their plan, just the part he needed to know so that he could deploy overwhelming forces against the Duke of Argundy during the crusade. Echor would have inexperienced soldiers and weak-blooded magi, and was travelling into the most inhospitable deserts of the east. None of the

Rondians showed concern that Rashid was any threat to the real army – Kaltus Korion's forces, who would have the best of everything and were nigh-on invincible.

And after that . . .

Gurvon smiled grimly.

. . . then the rest of our plan unfurls. Dhassa, Kesh and Javon would become states in thrall to Pallas for ever, and provide the staging-ground for the full conquest of Antiopia. Rashid's destruction of Echor would be forgotten, except in Argundy itself, where its weakening effect would prevent any possibility of revolt for generations to come. Emperor Constant would become ruler of the known world.

Belonius Vult concluded the discussion with his trademark flourish and turned towards the throne, seeking imperial assent. Constant glanced sideways at his mother as usual before inclining his head. Rashid noticed, of course: a little intelligence of his own to take home: that the Emperor of the West's hands were tied up in apron-strings.

'Emir Rashid,' Lucia said, 'do you have any questions of your own?'

The emir bowed his head slightly. 'None at all, lady. The magus has been most clear.' His voice had a music that would have beguiled one of Kore's nuns.

'You do not find it strange that we would act against our own?' Lucia asked lightly.

Rashid smiled. 'Let me tell you a tale of my own family. My grandfather once invited his brothers and cousins, all those with a claim to the throne of Halli'kut, to a great feast. He lavished them with gifts and sweet things for a week. On the final night, having allayed the fears of even the wariest, he released ten thousand serpents he had collected for the purpose into the sleeping chambers. He wiped out his entire family, except for his immediate kin, and so secured his reign.'

Gurvon saw looks of sceptical disdain creep across Korion and Dubrayle's faces. Betillon was looking appreciative – his own ruthlessness ran just as deep. For himself? It just seemed wasteful. He could have found more elegant solutions to such problems, he was sure. As for Lucia . . . it was as if she recognised a kindred spirit.

'How will your people greet victory over Duke Echor?' he asked Rashid.

Those emerald eyes met his own. 'With great rejoicing.'

'It will be your only victory,' Korion warned.

Rashid smiled faintly. 'All know your reputation, General Korion.'

'Then don't be deluded by the crust we throw you and think you can repeat the feat without our connivance,' Korion snapped, his mouth was shaping the insult 'mudskin', but he had the sense to leave to it unspoken. Rashid was a magus himself, one of a handful of Keshi-blooded magi who were part of the Ordo Costruo, the heretical magi based in Antiopia. Rashid was a three-quarter-blooded mage, and though all present in this room had the gnosis, Rashid was a renowned practitioner of the art.

'The war will unfold as Ahm wills,' Rashid responded mildly. 'We will destroy your enemy the Duke of Argundy, and then all cooperation is over. What will be, will be.'

'As it should be,' Lucia put in. 'Emir Rashid, we are grateful for your presence here. We will ensure you are kept apprised of Echor's movements as the campaign unfolds, and will take care of sending him false intelligence to draw him on to Shaliyah. We trust you will take full advantage.'

Rashid rose smoothly to his feet and bowed gracefully. 'We will have victory, Ahm willing.'

Lucia rose also, and accepted a kiss on the hand from the emir. A flurry of insincere well-wishes from the men across the table propelled the Keshi nobleman from the room. Gurvon followed him, as he had facilitated the emir's travel and participation.

'Well, Magister Gyle,' Rashid said once they were alone in the antechamber, 'did that go as you wish?'

'It did, Emir,' he said, offering his hand.

Rashid studied it, then slowly took it. 'Your Rondian hand-clasps are an odd gesture,' he remarked. 'Impersonal. It says much of your race. Cold lands, cold hearts.'

'I don't think our peoples are so different, Emir. Rulers rule, and the common herd bleat. In the end, the cream rises to the surface.'

Rashid's eyebrows flickered. 'I disagree. Your people are argumentative and sceptical. They question their betters too much. In that small room I saw mother overrule son, generals squabble with priests, and thieves like you – forgive me, but you are a thief, Gyle – dictate the future to an emperor. In my land, Ahm has anointed the kings and they speak with one voice. You are divided, and therefore flawed.'

'Our divisions make us strong, Emir.'

'Your gnosis makes you strong. All else underlines your godless weakness.' Rashid patted his cheek amiably. 'One day, Ahm will strike you all down with lightning from the skies and you will plunge into the fires of Shaitan. So it is written.'

Gurvon chuckled. 'You believe that? I didn't really see you as a fanatic, Emir.'

'I am a pragmatic man, Magister Gyle, but I too do Ahm's work.' Rashid bowed. 'We will not meet again as allies, Gurvon Gyle.'

'A shame.'

Rashid raised an eyebrow. 'Think you?' He bowed again, and opened the door to the palace functionary waiting to guide him back to his windship. He would be gone within the hour.

Gurvon returned to the meeting room to find it quiet and gloomy, as if the departure of the colourful emir had drained the life from it. He saw Grand Prelate Wurther purse his lips as he returned; the clergyman had argued hard against entrapping Echor's army in the coming crusade, claiming it was against the dictates of Kore to involve the heathen Keshi in their plans. He looked no happier to have met the enemy in the flesh. 'Has he gone?' he rumbled. He belched softly. 'We would be better to take him to Headsman Square and end him right now. He will cause us grief, I warrant.'

'The Keshi will rise in their millions when news of Echor's defeat comes out,' Dubrayle agreed. 'It is a risk.'

'It is no risk,' Korion snapped. 'Echor's provincials are one thing; my legions are quite another. Let the Keshi rise – I will stamp them back down.'

Betillon snickered. 'We know how to deal with uppity Noories.'

The room fell silent until Constant twitched and said, 'I didn't like that darkie. He dressed like a woman. Perhaps he is one?'

Gurvon watched the other men laugh at this tired old joke. He glanced at Lucia. *You see what I have to put up with*, her gaze seemed to say. *You and I, we see them for what they are: children*.

Aloud she said, 'Time for the next matter: Treasurer Dubrayle, I believe the floor is yours.'

Gurvon glanced at Vult. This was the one part of the plan he hadn't contributed to. It was something Dubrayle had cooked up with Vult – something to do with the slave trade. Lucia had demanded that the practice stop, not because she had any pity for Eastern slaves, but because she felt that dark skins were becoming too common in Yuros. She wanted a return to using Sydian and Vereloni slaves, who were at least Yuros-born.

The treasurer sat up, shuffled his papers and started, 'My Lord Emperor, Mater-Imperia, gentlemen, may I introduce my own expert guests to this gathering?' He looked at Lucia and after she gave her approval, Constant belatedly following suit, he rapped loudly on a side-door, which opened to reveal an old man in stained robes, bent as if he'd spent his best years hunched over illegible scrolls. He hobbled inside, followed by a man in plain tunic and short leggings, with a shaven skull and the Yothic character 'Delta' branded upon his forehead. His face was vacant, as if he were drugged or a simpleton. He carried a falcon on his wrist. The bird shrieked once, but was soothed into silence as he patted it – but it wasn't that which made Gyle stare at 'Delta'. It was his aura. All the magi in the room could see it: energies roiling and twisting strangely, like nothing they'd ever seen.

'Exalted Ones,' the old man said, 'allow me to introduce myself. I am Ervyn Naxius, at your service.'

Gurvon knew of Naxius: he'd been the head of the Ordo Costruo based in Pontus, tending to Northpoint Tower and the northern reaches of the Bridge. Though people blamed Antonin Meiros for allowing the Crusades to cross the Leviathan Bridge, it was Ervyn Naxius and his followers who'd been bribed to cede Northpoint, in return for support for his own research into fields that Antonin Meiros had forbidden. Few knew the name now; Naxius and his adherents had vanished at the beginning of the First Crusade.

'Welcome, Magister Naxius,' Lucia said smoothly. 'The empire has much to be grateful to you for.'

'And you have repaid that gratitude many times over,' Naxius purred. 'The freedom to work unfettered has been priceless.' He looked at the bald man and the hawk with the joyous ownership of a child with a new pet. 'I have something truly wonderful to show you.'

He pulled a large crystal the size of his fist from a pocket. It was dead-looking, and not of any stone Gurvon knew. 'Do you recognise it?' he asked, and when everyone shook their heads, explained, 'This is a "solarus": a crystal we of the Ordo Costruo developed to give gnos' tic strength to the Bridge. It takes in the rays of the sun, what we call "solar force", and converts it to gnostic energy. A solarus can store more energy than any mere periapt.'

The magi around the table frowned. Each wore a periapt gem to enhance their gnosis. 'Then why do we not all have one?' Belonius Vult asked. 'If this is an enhanced periapt, surely it should be made available to all worthies?'

'Would that we could,' sighed Naxius. 'Sadly, the energy these suncrystals radiate is so intense that it is debilitating. I am certain such eminent magi as yourselves are aware that the solarus crystals on the Bridge are deadly in prolonged doses – even a mage wearing protective wards can endure them for only a few minutes at a time. Once filled with solar force they cannot even be touched. We've tried using them as periapts, but unless they are sealed in lead they infect the user immediately with destructive humours that kill in months – and the lead destroys their effectiveness.'

'Then what are they good for?' Korion grumbled.

Naxius beamed. 'Ah, what indeed? You will be amazed, great general: amazed! We have found a use for individual gems such as this that no mage could ever have predicted.'

7

'So what is it?' Betillon demanded impatiently.

The Ordo Costruo renegade held up a hand. 'First, let me introduce my fellow demonstrator.' He turned to the branded mage. 'This is "Delta" – not perhaps the name he was born with' – he indicated the man's branded forehead – 'but it is the obvious name for him now.' He puffed up proudly. 'He is a Souldrinker.'

The room was filled with gasps and scraping chair-legs as Betillon, Korion and Wurther jumped to their feet, aghast. Even Belonius Vult looked startled, and in truth, Gyle had barely managed to restrain himself from a similar horrified reaction. *A Dokken in Pallas? Unthinkable!*

The Ascension of Corineus had changed the world, for it had resulted in the creation of the magi – but there had been a number of acolytes of Corineus who had failed to become magi despite drinking the ambrosia. Instead, their gnosis was triggered afterwards by inhaling the soul of a dying mage and fed thereafter by the consumption of human souls. The reaction to this horrifying revelation was immediate and fatal: most had been hunted down without mercy. There weren't many left now, but their deadly trait perpetuated through their descendants and they remained the magi's most hated enemies – and their only real rivals.

'Peace, be at peace!' Naxius exclaimed as Korion, Betillon and Wurther's gnostic energies flared.

He was echoed by Dubrayle, who cried, 'Delta is no threat to you. He is a slave and his powers have been contained.'

The old mage cackled gleefully. 'I've placed such bindings upon his mind that he can scarcely place one foot before the other without my permission.'

It was true that the Dokken's eyes were chillingly empty. Gurvon glanced at Lucia, who was watching with calm equanimity. Clearly she had already been briefed and had no qualms at whatever Naxius was doing. He took his cue from her and sat back to watch.

Korion and Betillon belatedly looked at Lucia too, then slowly sat, but the Grand Prelate remained standing. 'My lady, I must protest.

The presence of an Amteh worshipper in this place was barely tolerable, but this is clear blasphemy.'

Lucia looked at the churchman disinterestedly. 'You can always leave us, Grand Prelate. But this session will continue, with or without you.'

Wurther's protests floundered. 'My lady, I feel that I must remain, but under duress—'

'Sit down, you old windbag,' Betillon growled. 'Your point's made.'

'Save your wibbling for Holy Day,' Korion added scornfully.

Wurther glowered about him and settled ponderously back into his chair. It creaked in protest.

Naxius resumed his presentation, his voice childishly happy. 'My lords, noble Lady, thank you for your attention. It is with great excitement that I will demonstrate this remarkable thing we have discovered.' He clapped his fingers loudly and the door behind him opened wide enough for a soldier to shove a pale-skinned, skinny young man in torn and dirty clothes into the room. Naxius caught the boy's shoulder with fingers like talons and held him immobile. 'Let me introduce Orly: a thief, I'm sad to say.' The mage displayed the youth's left arm, which ended in a stump at the wrist. 'Young Orly had his left hand removed for stealing two years ago. A few nights ago he was caught again and yesterday he was convicted. He will hang next week.'

The boy's eyes were wide with terror as he fell to his knees. 'Please, mercy,' the young Pallacian started, but Naxius held up a hand to silence him.

'Do not fear,' the mage purred. 'We are going to give you a reprieve – one you could never have dreamed of.' He handed the inert solarus crystal to Delta.

The boy looked about the room. He clearly had no idea in whose presence he was, but he sobbed in gratitude, 'Oh thank you, thank you, good sirs, madam, thankyouthankyou—'

His torrent of words ended as Naxius made a peremptory gesture and channelled kinetic gnosis. The young thief's neck audibly snapped and he slumped to the floor, his face going from shock to bewilderment to betrayal before falling slack.

The falcon on Delta's wrist shrieked as if marking the moment.

Gurvon stared, surprised to find himself mildly shocked, though Naxius' reputation preceded him. *Well, he's got our attention* . . .

Delta bent over and seemed to kiss the dead thief on the mouth. The watching men winced in distaste, but Gurvon also sensed curiosity; he doubted any of them had ever seen a Souldrinker in action. He certainly hadn't.

The crystal in Delta's hands lit faintly and Naxius' voice took on a declamatory tone, as if he were lecturing to students.

'Observe,' he ordered. 'Delta has now inhaled the soul of the young man, but he has not absorbed it himself. Instead, because of the presence of the solarus crystal and the gnostic inhibitions I have placed on Delta, Orly's intellect is now preserved intact *inside* the crystal.'

Holy Kore! Gurvon looked at Vult, feeling his own eyes going wide.

'And now!' Naxius said theatrically, with a sweep of the arm.

Delta held up the crystal in front of the falcon on his wrist and it flared again. A stream of white light shafted from the gem into the eyes of the bird. It shrieked piteously, flapped its wings, half rose into the air and then fell from the man's wrist and sprawled across the table. Everyone in the room except Lucia and Dubrayle recoiled from it.

'What have you done?' Korion demanded. 'If there is danger to the emperor I will—'

'Calm down, Kaltus,' Lucia drawled. 'You think I would risk my beloved only son?'

Naxius prodded the fallen falcon. 'Get up, little bird,' he cackled merrily.

The falcon stirred and then pulled itself upright and began to preen itself awkwardly. The watching magi stared.

Finally Vult broke the silence. 'Did he just do what it appeared?'

Naxius giggled in delight. 'Yes! You see it, don't you? The soul of the thief Orly is now in the bird.' He reached out a hand. 'Orly,' he said, addressing the falcon, 'tap three times with your left leg.'

As they all watched, the falcon did precisely as instructed. 'Now fly thrice around the room, then land on the chandelier.'

No one moved as the bird fulfilled these instructions exactly.

Naxius smirked. 'We have found that the transplanted soul is extremely suggestible to command and rapidly falls into the habit of complete obedience.'

Calan Dubrayle, clearly Naxius' sponsor, took up the narrative. 'Imagine our cavalry, mounted on constructs that can follow precise instructions. Imagine winged venators with human intelligence. Imagine beasts of burden that need not be driven, just instructed where to deliver their loads. Imagine plough-horses that can work the fields alone. Imagine birds scouting miles ahead of the army and reporting back. Imagine rats and snakes able to slip beneath castle walls and attack the defenders. Imagine the unimaginable.' He tapped the map of Dhassa and Kesh on the table. 'All we need to make such miracles in the numbers we will need are animals, constructs – and thousands of human souls.'

Constant's jaw worked but only little squeaks came out. Korion and Betillon were pale, their expressions torn between horror and greed. Wurther looked outraged. But Vult was fascinated, his fingers tapping rhythmically as no doubt a hundred more uses for such creatures ran through his mind.

Mater-Imperia Lucia looked as if she'd just gorged on chocolate.

And me? How do I feel? It's very, very clever. And it's probably the most horrifying thing I've ever seen.

'Well,' said Emperor Constant, 'the Keshi are just beasts anyway. They shouldn't mind a whit.'

Low laughter rippled about the room and Gurvon took care to join in, though he was staring at the face of the man called Delta. Now he could recognise something in those empty eyes: utter self-loathing and despair.

'Have we done well?' Naxius asked the throne.

Lucia smiled. 'Magister Naxius, you have surpassed yourself.'

Waking to a Changed World

The Dawn to End All Night

The Rondians call it 'The Dawn to End All Night': the morning when the Blessed
Three Hundred awoke and began to realise the gift they had been given. Imagine
that sense of possibility, the sense of holding Urte in your hands! But it was a
false dawn! They replaced Rimoni oppression with Rondian oppression! The true
dawn of the Age of Light starts here, and now!

GENERAL LEROI ROBLER, ON THE EVE
OF THE NOROS REVOLT, 909

Eastern Dhassa, on the continent of Antiopia
Zulhijja (Decore) 928
6th month of the Moontide

Vann Mercer was startled awake as his horses snorted and danced
sideways. He hauled on the reins to pull them back into line, then
cast about for what had startled them. He didn't have to look far: a
despatch rider was alongside his wagon, peering at him intently.
'Vannaton Mercer?' the man asked. His accent was clearly of Noros.

The man's voice invoked *home*: snow-capped peaks, verdant forests
and sudden storms, lush grass and tumbling rivers. It was so far from
Vann's present reality that for a moment his guts ached. The hori-
zons were straight, the land here flat and brown. At least the
temperature was bearable – Decore in the East was the onset of what
passed for winter here; cold by local standards but akin to early
spring in Noros.

'Who's asking?'

'My name's Relik Folsteyn, of Knebb. You won't remember me, sir, but I was on the mountain, back in nine-ten. Part of Langstrit's legion.'

Vann smiled sadly. *The brotherhood of veterans.* 'Good to meet you, Folsteyn.'

'Honoured, Cap.' Folsteyn glanced at the wagon. 'Fuckin' hot place t'be selling wool bales, sir.'

'It's all I've got – but you'd be surprised, the weavers here snap them up.' Vann took the proffered envelope. It looked official: the seal of the Norostein Watch was scuffed but unbroken. He recognised Jeris Muhren's writing. It didn't feel like good news.

'Might I beg some water, Cap?' Folsteyn asked. 'It's been a thirsty ride.'

Vann indicated the water tank on the side of his wagon. 'Help yourself – I've plenty.'

'Thank'ee,' the rider said. He looked at Vann worriedly. 'After you read that, we'll be needing to talk.'

Vann was travelling with two dozen other traders; they'd all crossed the Bridge together once the military traffic had lessened. There was still trade to be had, mostly here in eastern Dhassa, away from the path of the Crusade. Vann's family's future was depending upon his success here, and his thoughts turned often to his wife Tesla and his son Alaron, waiting patiently at home in Norostein. He and Tesla had been estranged, but recent events had thrown them together again; despite everything, he still loved her. He still clung to the memory of the person she'd been. And his mage-son Alaron, naïve and impetuous but honest at heart, was the centre of his life.

He pulled his wagon to the side of the road, shouting to his fellow traders not to worry, that he'd catch them up. Then he looked down at the letter, filled with foreboding.

Perhaps if I never open it, nothing it contains will have happened . . .

He cursed the foolish notion and broke the seal. The letter was dated Junesse – six months ago. Even allowing for three months to traverse Verelon and Sydia on the coast road it had taken a long time to find him. But then, he'd always kept a low profile while travelling.

My dear friend Vann

I pray this reaches you promptly, and is the first word you receive of this matter. It is with utmost sadness that I must tell you that Tesla has passed away. She died 11th Junesse, of natural causes. Alaron is well and looking after your affairs in Norostein. He will write when he is able, but do not be concerned if you do not hear for some time. He sends his love, as do I. Take care on the road and avoid Imperial contact. May good fortune be with you, and may we meet again soon.

In haste

Jeris Muhren

written 12th Junesse, in Norostein

He read it again, carefully, then bowed his head. Tears threatened, but never quite came.

Tesla, my dearest, you would have gone to death with open arms.

When he looked up, Relik Folsteyn was watching him carefully. 'Captain Muhren and your son left Norostein the same day the letter was written, Cap,' he said, gruffly sympathetic.

'What?' Vann asked sharply. 'Why?'

'We don't know, sir. But all along the Imperial Road from Brekaellen to Pontus, there've been Imperials looking for them – and you.'

A chill that overrode the sullen heat of the desert prickled his skin. 'I wasn't going to cross the Bridge this time, but when I got to Pontus I realised I had no chance of turning a profit unless I did my own trading.' He swallowed. 'Why are they looking for me?'

'We don't know, Cap. But it was Quizzies doing the asking.'

Inquisitors . . . Kore's Blood. 'Who sent you, Relik?'

'The Merchants' Guild – when they heard about the Inquisition, they decided to find you first. Jean Benoit sent us. His orders were that whoever found you should get you to safety.'

Benoit family had been disgraced for embezzlement and stripped of their titles and lands; the punishment had driven them into trading and young Jean Benoit, a pure-blood mage, had risen quickly, pulling many lower-blooded magi into his following as he swiftly rose to Guildmaster in Pallas. It was he, forty years ago, who had advised rich merchants to seek out and marry into impoverished mage families, and as a result Benoit's influence was now immense. The Imperial magi took a different view; to them, Jean Benoit was kin to the Lord of Hel himself.

Vann licked his lips. Benoit was no friend to Noros or to provincial traders, though he had been instrumental in brokering the peace after the Noros Revolt. Civil wars were bad for trade, after all. The Pallas Merchants' Guild had been bullying provincial traders for centuries; it had become worse under Benoit. 'I don't suppose I have much choice,' he said wryly.

'Not unless you enjoy chatting with Inquisitors,' Folsteyn agreed.

'Then I suppose I'm in your hands.' He cast his eyes skywards and breathed a silent prayer for Tesla, his damaged and broken wife, finally at rest, and for Alaron, wherever on Urte he was.

Near the Isle of Glass, Javon coast, on the continent of Antiopia
Zulhijja (Decore) 928
6th month of the Moontide

Alaron dreamed of home and of his father, laughing and happy. Even his mother was joyous, her burns gone and her whole body restored to youth and beauty. He should have known from that alone that he was dreaming, but it seemed so real. Then a hand on his shoulder pulled him from sleep's clutches and he jolted awake into a terrifying reality.

He was wrapped around a tiny girl with a hugely distended belly and skin the colour of dark coffee, and they were lying in the stern of a tiny skiff that was hovering above the ocean. The sun blazed through seaspray and the air was full of a watery roar.

'The sea is rising again,' the girl said, and he stared at her dumbly until his memory supplied her name: Ramita, Lord Meiros' seventeen-year-old pregnant widow. They'd fled the attack on the Isle of Glass together, leaping into the skiff to escape Malevorn Andevarion, his old nemesis from college, and an unlikely bunch of shapechangers and Inquisitors. Then another memory emerged and he groped inside his jacket, sighing in relief as his hand fell on a long, hard scroll-case.

The Scytale of Corineus.

More memories surfaced: they'd plunged into the sea, he and Ramita, though he'd been sure it would be the death of them – but the little windskiff, *Seeker*, was steeped in spells and it had sealed over and kept the water out long enough for them to reach the surface. After that, they'd endured a dizzying, sickness-inducing horror ride, going under time and again, clinging together, soaked and frozen, frantically trying to get Air-gnosis into the drained keel, enough to stay above the waters, all the while expecting each moment to be the end.

Somehow they'd survived, though the waves had swept them so far from the Isle of Glass that the rocky pinnacle was no longer visible. About midnight he'd found the strength to lift the skiff from the waves, but without a mast or sail they had no way to propel it, so they'd just hovered above the waves. It was at the very least a respite, a chance for sleep.

The Lakh girl crawled awkwardly along the hull. She was steady-eyed, despite her obvious exhaustion. 'The waves are getting higher each minute,' she said. 'We need to fly away.'

There was no land in sight and the waves, black-green spume-encrusted mountains, were indeed churning up towards them. Alaron cast his mind back to the previous night and their escape. Keeping them alive beneath the waves had used up most of the gnosis stored in the keel and now they were barely managing to hover above the ocean. Without any means of propulsion they were just delaying the inevitable. 'I can put more Air-gnosis into the keel,' he told Ramita, 'though my affinity isn't strong. But we need a mast and a sail.'

His eyes went to the hole where the mast should have been: the wooden shaft was now buried in the body of an Inquisitor, a glorious blonde girl with the cold eyes of a killer, back at the Isle of Glass. He had no qualms about the Inquisitor's death – she'd been about to kill him, after all – but he would have loved to have had that mast back right now.

Ramita looked around thoughtfully, then with surprising strength she wrenched off a piece of the bracing from the hull. *Then again,* Alaron thought, *it's not that surprising, is it? She threw that mast nearly thirty yards, and with enough force to penetrate a pure-blood Inquisitor's shields as if they didn't exist.*

'We must . . .' She fished for a word in Rondian, and when it came she spoke it like a spell: 'We must *improvise*.'

He nodded, grateful to be able to throw himself into the task at hand, because back on the Isle of Glass, Cymbellea di Regia was a prisoner, or dead. He blinked back tears, reached for his gnosis and began to recharge the keel.

It didn't take Ramita long once she worked out what needed to be done. Working with wood and plant matter was one of her strengths: her *affinities*. She liked the word. It sounded magical. The gnosis had frightened her once, but now she realised she could not contemplate being without it. Her family would barely know her: pregnant to the greatest mage in the world, alone with a strange ferang boy in the middle of the ocean, and yet she wasn't afraid.

I am Lady Meiros. I can do anything.

She made a mast by growing it from the piece of bracing, then made a canvas sail from the material that had been used to cover the stores – not that they had any stores; a little water was the only thing left. They'd not expected to be needing the skiff, so they hadn't got around to restocking it. A big mistake.

She grew more rope from the existing ones and Alaron, who knew how these things worked, fixed them to the corners of the new sail. Together they lifted the mast into place, then she helped him replenish the skiff's keel, gripping his hand and feeding him energy for him to convert to air-gnosis. They weren't used to working together and she could sense most of it being wasted, but enough got through to make a difference.

At last they rose from the grip of the reaching waves and using the position of the sun, turned the bow south, where there should be land, if they remembered the charts aright.

Thank you, Great Goddess.

Thank you, Creator and Protector.

Thank you Darikha-ji, for protecting us from the agents of death.

She flinched inwardly, trying not to remember that dreadful moment when Huriya, once her best friend but now an enemy, had pierced Justina Meiros' defence by telling her the terrible truth: that the death of Antonin Meiros, Justina's father, had come about because Ramita had betrayed him. That one piece of knowledge, hidden so carefully, had undone her dead husband's daughter. Though she had never meant to deceive her husband, the deed could not be undone, and nor could the consequences. She had tried to be a dutiful wife, but instead she had betrayed all trust and brought ruin to the Meiros family.

She tried to hold the tears in, but still they flowed, even as her children stirred in her belly.

Vishnarayan, Lord of Light, show me what to do. Send me a sign.

Near the Isle of Glass, Javon coast, on the continent of Antiopia
Zulhijja (Decore) 928
6th month of the Moontide

Cymbellea di Regia woke with tears in her eyes, still seeing the face of her mother Justina, the way it had changed from composed strength to floundering bewilderment as each word uttered by the tiny Soul-drinker Huriya struck her like a blow.

What had she said?

Then Zaqri, the lion-headed shapechanger, had swiped his clawed hand across Justina's throat and all but ripped her head off.

Mother!

She lifted her face and found she was lying on her stomach across an unmade bed. She began to move, but a heavy weight landed on her back. She craned behind her to see – and froze. A lion was lying beside her on the bed, one forepaw across her back, pinning her down.

Zaqri?

He looked at her and growled. His paws were licked clean of her mother's blood, but they still glinted in the half-light.

He killed my mother.

She remembered what she had sworn last night: a sacred vow to visit the same suffering on him. *I will, Mother. I promise you.*

At the doorway she spotted a dark-furred jackal with a scarred face, watching them. It yowled, a sound full of displeasure, aimed at her she was certain. Zaqri growled again, more menacing this time, and the jackal dropped its head and left them.

Cym tried to pull clear, but couldn't, not without having her skin torn to pieces. 'I need to piss,' she told the lion, hoping he spoke Rondian.

Zaqri's shape flowed from beast to human in an eye-blink. He was naked, of course, and built like a Lantric hero: golden, beautiful, and terrifying. If gods walked the lands, they would walk as he did. 'I will go with you,' he told her in a voice that sounded rusty from under-use. 'You are not safe alone.'

'I'm not safe with you,' she retorted, averting her eyes from his body with some difficulty, despite her fear.

'You are,' he replied shortly. 'I have watched over you all night.'

She tried to show defiance, but couldn't. He terrified her. Instead she rose and hurried to the door. They were in a bedroom – Alaron's, judging by the clothes piled on the floor. The chamber was deep inside a cylinder of rock that Antonin Meiros himself had turned into a hideaway. That they'd been found here was entirely her own fault: her lack of gnostic skill had given away their position. It was only the fact that two groups of enemies had arrived at the same time that had given them any chance, and it was beginning to look like Alaron and Ramita, Lord Meiros' Lakh wife, had escaped. The Souldrinkers had triumphed over the other attackers: the Kore Inquisitors were gone, defeated.

Outside the bedchamber she'd unwittingly shared with Zaqri she saw the rest of the Souldrinker pack was waiting. Most were in human form, and the dark jackal was changing shape herself, to a tall, angular Lokistani woman with a beak-like nose and short-hewn hair. Her name was Hessaz and she was a new widow; her husband had been cut down by the Inquisitors. Zaqri, she knew, was also widowed. His wife Ghila – this Hessaz's sister – had also been slain during the fight. It was clear Hessaz wanted to take her sister's place, and it was evident the pack expected that also.

Hessaz glared at Gym and rasped, 'Why is the gypsy still alive?'

'She is under my protection,' Zaqri replied. 'Touch her and you answer to me. Any of you.'

'She is magi,' a male growled. 'You cannot protect her.'

'I have a son who is yet to awaken,' another man said. 'Give her to him, to awaken his gnosis.'

'When we return to our village, I may allow this,' Zaqri said. His emotionless words made Cym shudder. 'But for now, she has my protection and you will not touch her.'

'You slept with her,' Hessaz spat. 'If you can use her, why forbid others? Lie with me if you require comfort. As your widow's sister it is customary that I take her place.'

'I did not use this girl – and Ghila is only one night dead. May I not mourn she whom I loved?'

'Allow me to comfort you,' Hessaz demanded. Her whole demeanour was as far from comforting as Cym could imagine.

'Respect my grief, Hessaz, as I respect yours.' Zaqri turned away, but the quivering tension of the pack didn't lessen.

'How noble,' tinkled a girl who appeared at the door. She was barely five foot tall, though her body was ripely mature. 'We all grieve for you, Zaqri.'

Zaqri bowed his head. 'Seeress Huriya,' he greeted her.

The seeress sashayed into the middle of the pack. Her rank carried authority, clearly, but though the pack bowed their heads before the girl, their eyes still followed Zaqri. Cym tried to read the balances of power, but couldn't. The pack seemed closer to beasts than men, and they all looked at her with uniform hunger.

'Mourning is not our way,' Huriya said. 'Our kind are surrounded by death, but we cannot immerse ourselves in it. We move on without looking back. You know this, Zaqri.' She swayed up to him, stroked his chest. 'Do not mourn overlong.'

Zaqri shifted uncomfortably. 'Seeress, Ghila and I . . . we were as one being. Without her, I am only half a man.'

'Then if any of us can help you become whole, you have only to ask.'

Cym was grateful that the attention was elsewhere as the memory of the awful slaughter last night returned. Her mother, whom she had barely known, was lost for ever. And the others . . .

Where's Alaron? she wondered. *And Ramita?*

'Gone,' the Keshi girl said, turning to her and answering her thought as if she had spoken out loud. She spoke Rondian tentatively, as if for the first time. ' "Alaron" . . . ?' she tittered. 'Al'Rhon: the Goat! How amusing! He is gone, and Ramita also. For now, we cannot follow, not with so many wounded or exhausted.' She studied Cym. 'Of what value are you, Gypsy? Are you worth ransoming?'

Cym swallowed. *Ransom? Might I buy my life somehow?* To her shame, she found that she still wanted to live. 'My name is Cymbellea di Regia-Meiros.'

Huriya cocked her head. 'A Meiros? How wonderful. But of little use.' She glanced at one of the shifters. 'Kill her to replenish yourself.'

Before Cym had time to realise just what was happening to her, the fingers of the man holding her had sprouted inch-long claws – but someone else had clamped a hand around the shifter's wrist, stopping him from ripping out her throat then and there.

'I claim her,' Zaqri growled.

Huriya looked at him petulantly. 'Zaqri, I have said they may kill her.'

'And I say that we will question her, and after that we might use her to awaken one of our children. Think of the wider gain, Seeress.'

Huriya acquiesced regally. 'Very well, dear Zaqri. She belongs to you.' She looked Cym up and down and added, 'Do with her as you will. But if she cannot fly with us when we leave here, then she must die. You have three days.'

Cym blanched. The island was hundreds of miles from the mainland, much further than she could fly using air-gnosis. Only someone in bird-shape could do that, but she'd never changed shape – she didn't even know if she could. 'Three days?' she spat. 'Just kill me now!'

'Shut up, girl,' Zaqri growled. <*Don't tempt us.*> He stared into her eyes and the weight and skill of his gnosis dismantled her mental defences with assured strength. <*Be still, girl. I need to appraise your gnosis.*>

Though terrified, she summoned her defiance and tried to resist. <*You killed my mother.*>

<*And your companions slew my mate,*> he countered bitterly.

They stared at each other unflinchingly, until she couldn't help herself asking, <*Is . . . is my mother inside you?*>

He shook his head. <*Only her energies. We don't absorb memories or personality.*> His eyes flickered to Huriya. *Normally*, she heard him thinking.

<*Is my mother . . . aware?*> she asked tremulously.

<*Gone,*> he replied, with no attempt to soften the blow. Then he focused, and she felt his mental penetration go deeper. He spoke aloud. 'Open to me, girl, or this will hurt.'

If she did not open up, she would be crushed and left broken. She let him into her mind. He was like a torch in a darkened room, filling her absolutely, his lion face shining like the sun as he studied her. She forgot how to breathe. Then she found herself humiliated as private moments were dredged up for his study: memories of family, friends, moments alone, her first kiss . . .

Then his eyes went wide and he dropped from her mind and turned to Huriya, shaking with excitement. 'Seeress, I have learned something,' he announced.

Huriya walked slowly back to him. 'Yes?' she asked.

Cym could only just make out his words as Zaqri bent his head down to whisper in Huriya's ear, 'You have Sabele's memories so you will know of the Scytale of Corineus. This one has held it in her hands!'

Near the Isle of Glass, Javon coast, on the continent of Antiopia
Zulhijja (Decore) 928
6th month of the Moontide

The Fist awoke as the windship drifted aimlessly across the skies.

Malevorn Andevarion heard someone moving in the darkness: his bunkmate Dominic, dressing himself for his turn on watch on the decks above. Poor, dedicated Dom, drifting about like a lost sheep now their invincible Fist had been all but destroyed over the past few months. And his illusions that the Inquisition was a force for truth and justice, and virtue was rewarded and sin punished, had been shattered too. He had discovered that life was far from fair.

Malevorn had outgrown such childishness before he was ten.

He feigned sleep now, having no desire to converse, listening instead to the noises of the windship at night: the timbers creaking, the wind tugging futilely at the remaining stumps of masts on the half-burned hulk. None of the surviving Inquisitors had strong enough sylvan-gnosis to effect swift repairs. They were adrift, and would remain so for some time unless rescue came. The ocean crashed far below. Moonlight shone dimly through a small porthole barely six inches in diameter as he went back over the encounter at the island, worrying at the questions it had raised.

How could Alaron Mercer have escaped? Who was that mudskin girl with the terrifying strength? What about the shapechangers: were they really the dreaded Dokken? Were they also pursuing the Scytale?

The cabin door opened, as he had known it would about now, and Raine Caladryn, her goblinesque face alight with mischief, sidled through. He watched as she disrobed. Her breasts were as much chest muscle as anything else, and her waist was fleshy, her bottom slab-like. Her shoulders were broad and her thighs solid. Her face was ill-formed and she was quite the least feminine woman he'd ever had – but there was something in Raine's glowering hatred of the world that he related to. They were alike in that: both driven by bloody-minded greed and lust.

Beauty is a myth, he thought. *Compatability is more important. I like the way she tastes and smells and thinks.* His cock was rigid well before she slid into the bunk and gripped it, purring appreciatively. Her mouth was sour, but it tasted sweet to him as they kissed and groped, his fingers inside her wetness while she stroked him. He mounted her and stabbed deep into her, and they pounded into each other, sweating and grunting, until at last she clawed his back and spasmed beneath him, and that brought on his own climax. He sagged onto her, his skin as slick and flushed as hers.

'Can't imagine why that silly cunt Virgina thought chastity was divine,' Raine panted in his ear.

'The Noorie woman skewered her with a mast,' Malevorn said, still marvelling at the feat. 'I saw it: a forty-yard throw, hard enough to penetrate her shields and armour. Impossible.'

'Ordo Costruo?' Raine suggested.

'She looked too dark – even the darkest Ordo Costruo are half-bloods. This one was black as a peasant.'

'Revolting. Have you ever fucked a mudskin?'

Malevorn shook his head violently. 'Kore, no! The very thought disgusts me.'

Raine guffawed. 'Get away with you. You men will fuck anything with a hole.' She grunted, looking down at herself. 'Luckily for me.'

'I'd take you ahead of anyone else.'

'Liar. First pretty girl we meet, you won't even look back.'

'Not true. You and I are cut from the same cloth, Raine Caladryn. We want the same things, we have the same scruples. We're kindred spirits.' He looked down at her mockingly. 'You'll fall in love with me. Everyone I screw does.'

'*Love?*' she snorted. 'Go to Hel, pretty boy. I don't believe in it.' She scratched herself thoughtfully. 'So, this Alaron Mercer of yours has the Scytale of Corineus.'

'Not for long. He's an imbecile.' Malevorn scowled. 'We'll take it off him soon enough.'

'And then?'

'We'll give it back to the emperor . . . Afterwards.'

'After what?'

'After using it. I want to be an Ascendant. You too. Both of us will be, with all the powers of the mighty. Then I'll make those bastards who rejoiced when my father killed himself wish they'd never been born.'

Mount Tigrat, Javon, on the continent of Antiopia
Zulhijja (Decore) 928
6th month of the Moontide

Elena woke to the wind on her cheeks to find herself huddled inside her skiff, the *Greyhawk*, in the foothills west of Loctis. She and Kazim had flown all night, then slept all day in the shadow of the hull. Kazim was snoring gently, his body warm against hers, even through the layers of clothing and blankets. They were near the snowline and their breath steamed in the clear, cold air.

She wanted to stroke his cheek and pull him against her. He was so handsome, his bronze face perfectly formed, and so alive, so determined. He could have abandoned her, but instead he'd come back and fought tooth and nail against his own bloodbrothers to prevent her rape. She owed him. And he wanted her too: she could see it in his eyes, feel in his judicious concern and his closeness.

But she held herself back.

He's a Dokken.

His aura was quiescent now that he'd killed and fed on the souls of his former colleagues, but she could still sense the way it reached for her, like tentacles of light, expressing his yearnings. Its touch was not unpleasant, but it frightened her. She could sense it was linked to his desire for her.

What if we make love? What would happen? The little lore about magi and Dokken was troubling; she knew only the Brevian tale of Nasette Ledoc, a young mage-woman born three hundred years ago.

Nasette had gone missing, and a woodsman claimed to have seen her with two wolf-men, lupine creatures who ran on all fours and also walked erect. After months of searching, Nasette's father, Heward, also a pure-blood, tracked her down. Finding that her captors were Souldrinkers – Dokken, as they were called in the north – he killed them both and freed Nasette. But he was too late, for the girl was pregnant – and worse, she had become a Souldrinker herself. Heart-broken, Heward had no choice but to kill his only daughter as well.

Heward was desperate to understand what had happened to Nasette, and he spent years researching. According to the story, he read every written account of the lives of the Souldrinkers – but no one could explain Nasette's transformation, for there were no records of Dokken and magi ever lying together, and Souldrinkers were becoming increasingly rare as the constant purges took their toll. At last Heward concluded that any female mage who fornicated with a Dokken would be infected by their curse, for there was no other explanation for what had happened to Nasette.

Over the years, the story became a popular cautionary tale for mage-children, and with each retelling the truth became increasingly shrouded in myth.

Elena watched Kazim sleep and fearfully wondered where legend ended and fact began.

Kazim woke to find Elena's eyes on him. Her functionally short blonde hair was matted from sleep and she looked pale and bleary, sad-eyed in the dawn. Her nose and cheeks were dotted with freckles and her skin was wind- and sun-chafed. His fingers itched to stroke her skin, to soothe it gently and draw her close, to kiss her chapped lips . . .

She is my Cause now. She is my shihad. She took me in when my brother Hadishah abandoned me. She taught me when she could have killed me. She trusted me even when she found out what I did and what I am. I am assassin and Souldrinker and I owe her everything: above the holy war, above my family, above Ramita. Elena is my Cause.

'Ella.' He felt his whole face smile. He freed his arms from the blankets, pulled her against him, nuzzled her neck. All he wanted was to . . .

'Kazim,' she said, her voice strange enough to make him pause. 'We have to talk.'

He stopped, slapped by a premonition that life was yet again going to take away the thing he wanted most.

Her voice sounded regretful, even bitter. 'Kazim, I want there to be only honesty between us.'

He nodded slowly, carefully. 'Of course?'

She held him close and told him a tale of a girl called Nasette who became a Souldrinker, like him.

He tried to pretend he understood.

Brochena, Javon, on the continent of Antiopia
Zulhijja (Decore) 928
6th month of the Moontide

The axes fell and the heads rolled, bouncing wetly on the stones. Octa Dorobon's henchmen looked bewildered by this aberrant behaviour. *We are magi!*, their heads cried. *We are the rulers of Urte! We cannot die!* Then in seconds their flesh rotted away, leaving their chattering skulls bleaching in the sand.

Cera Nesti woke, heart pounding, tangled in sweaty sheets.

A dream – it's only a dream.

But yesterday it had been real: violently, vividly real, and it had been her own life at stake. The dim room harboured too many shadows so she emerged from the bedclothes and wrenched open the curtains. The sun was rising over the mist-shrouded city: Brochena in winter, wrapped in a morass of fog and wood-smoke. But the light calmed her. She fell into a chair, wrapped her arms about herself and tried to slow her heart.

It was still impossible to grasp all that had happened: the mesmerising eyes of a Lantric witch ensorcelling her; sending her to Gurvon Gyle's chambers though she loathed him. Octa Dorobon bursting in. A dungeon cell, rank with damp filth, a forced confession, the taunts of the guards.

Mudskin whore . . .

Octa had seized the initiative from Gyle, tried to entrap him and wrest back control over her son Francis, the king. It had been a brutal and clumsy attempt to smash over the house of cards Gyle had built.

You'll beg to die . . .

And just as abruptly: the counter-strike. Octa was dead and Gyle free. King Francis was blinking dazedly as he emerged from the shadow of his tyrant mother, flushed with new power and completely blind to the fact that all he had was Gyle's to take away. His sister Olivia was simpering beside him, eyes on Gyle and no one else, while Gyle himself, relishing his new control over the court, was as calmly confident and sardonically vicious as ever.

Cera found herself enthroned again, alongside her fellow-queen Portia, her secret, illicit lover. All she wanted was to hold Portia close and block out the world, but they'd been made to watch the execution of Octa's henchmen and then sit through a banquet where Francis Dorobon had cavorted as if some great victory had been won. His imbecilic self-obsession left her breathless.

She pulled on a gown and went to the balcony, enjoyed the faint heat of the coppery sun. The Godsingers were wailing their summons to prayer as the city awoke, most probably unaware of the coup that had taken place within Brochena Palace – outwardly at least, the Dorobon flag still flew and their soldiers still manned the gates and walls. City-folk had more immediate worries – how to find food and work in a land in turmoil.

Where do I stand now? On the face of it, little had changed, but

Octa's death now gave Gyle an almost free hand. His counter-coup was in Francis' name, but anyone with any brain could see it was entirely for his own benefit. The Dorobon magi, knights and soldiers, outnumbered by Gyle's mercenaries, were confused and anxious. Their seizure of Javon was unravelling and the kingdom was rumbling like a volcano set to explode. She'd heard them talking in the banquet hall, wondering aloud if it would still be safe for the next wave of Dorobon settlers due to arrive – which included the soldiers' families.

What am I to do? I was regent here. My little brother is the rightful king but I don't even know where he is now. We're trapped and helpless.

Then she thought about that.

I am a Nesti. I refuse to be helpless.

So she stared out over the city, studying the movements of the tiny shapes below, and made her plans.

The pitiless sunlight burned away Francis Dorobon's illusions of safety, shafts of unbearable brightness piercing the uncovered windows and slapping him awake.

The last thing he remembered after the banquet was swaying down the corridors with Craith Margham and Jedyk Luman, belting out 'Let the Bells Ring', an anthem about the fall of Rimoni. He'd been intending great feats of amatory congress with both of his Noorie wives, but the celebratory wines had struck him low. It had begun with a foul bilious surge as his stomach rebelled, followed by a horribly liquid spell of farting. With his belly cramping painfully, he collapsed to the stone floor and crawled to the privy while Craith and Jedyk, oblivious, sang on. While he had his head down a privy, vomiting uncontrollably, they were tunelessly bellowing the old favourites – 'Death to Tyrants' and 'Light the Gold Lantern'. The chorus of the latter, 'We are free now, free forever', echoed inside his skull as he struggled upright, rolled off the bed and crawled to a copper basin. It was half-filled with Kore knew what, but he didn't care; he dry-retched until he could think again, then knelt and peed into the basin. Gagging on the stench, he crawled back to the bed, pulled a sheet from it and wrapped himself in it, then sat in the corner, shaking uncontrollably.

It wasn't for several minutes that he realised that he was crying. *Mother is dead.*

Last night he'd been jubilant, elated: the tyrant bitch who'd dominated his every waking moment, dragging him wherever she wanted as if the umbilical cord had never been severed, was gone. Let the bells ring! He, Francis Dorobon, was now truly the king, the uncontested ruler at last, free to do whatever he wanted.

Except he wasn't free at all.

Somewhere beneath the haze of the celebration he'd already begun to realise that he'd merely exchanged one master for another, like a horse whose rider is slain by bandits, but finds himself the bandit chief's new steed. It had began to dawn on him as he'd looked down the banquet table and seen Sir Roland Heale, his swordmaster. The look on Heale's weathered face, of pity and contempt when every other face around him was filled with jubilation, had stung him. Then he looked around and began to recognise the calculating hunger in the eyes of Gurvon Gyle's adherents. He caught measured looks between Endus Rykjard's mercenary magi, as if they were already weighing up the Dorobon men and had found them wanting. He saw the cold eyes of his two queens, who were ignoring him and instead leaning together and whispering to each other. Even his sister Olivia, who should have been sharing his joy, was fawning upon Gyle as if this was *his* moment. And Gyle himself, cool and composed in Imperial purple, was suddenly frightening, like a glimpse of fang in a fox's mouth.

They all think I'm a buffoon.

He'd wanted to shout at them, to proclaim his victory: *The Tyrant is Dead! I am free! Let the bells ring!*

Instead, as if his subconscious had admitted the truth his conscious mind dared not confront, he'd reached down blindly, seized a goblet, drained it, and pitched himself into the middle of his carousing friends, desperate to cling to his fleeting moment of joy and too scared to look beyond it again.

But it was morning now and he had a kingdom to rule, even if his head was pounding and his stomach muscles were aching. He dragged himself to his feet and found the water pitcher. He guzzled water until he'd washed away the vile taste, then emptied the rest over his head.

Then he rang for service.

It was Sir Roland Heale who opened the door. 'So you're awake at last,' he noted, then added, 'Sire,' with the faintest echo of irony.

'Sir Roland,' Francis croaked. *He's always been honest with me. Even when I didn't want honesty.* Perhaps he needed that right now. 'What are you doing here?'

The old swordsman looked about the room, sniffed and took an involuntary step backwards. 'Kore's Blood, boy! What are you doing to yourself?'

'She's dead,' Francis muttered, half-apologetic, half-defiant. 'You don't know what she was like.'

'I know exactly what she was like. But everything she ever did was for House Dorobon, and if she thought it right to move against Gurvon Gyle, then it was right.' Heale scowled. 'You've got the second Dorobon legion arriving in three months, lad, along with thirty thousand immigrants. They have uprooted their lives and are even now marching across the Leviathan Bridge to follow you – the Dorobon family – into the East. My own family is in that column. You must secure the kingdom for them. Francis, give me leave to move against Gurvon Gyle.'

Heale should have been head of the Dorobon knights, Francis knew that, but he'd been passed over again and again; he harboured grudges against most of Octa's coterie. But now he was undoubtedly the most senior surviving knight, both in age and experience. By rights he should at last be made knight-commander.

But I promised Craith Margham that position. Craith was his best friend, his companion for most of his childhood. He couldn't promote another above him, not when they shared so close a bond. *If I give Sir Roland this, we're declaring war on Gurvon Gyle. Look how that turned out for Mother . . .*

'No, Sir Roland,' he said at last. 'The situation is too delicate.'

'But your Majesty,' he protested, 'Gyle is weak at the moment – we may never have another chance—'

'Gurvon Gyle is the legally appointed Legate, the representative of Emperor Constant himself!' Francis cried. 'My mother was wrong to order his arrest and execution, and she has paid the price – the emperor will be furious at her perfidy! What happens if he withdraws his support of our family?'

'Octa would not have moved without Mater-Imperia's consent,' Heale retorted. 'Francis, please—'

'There was no consent,' Francis countered. 'I saw nothing.'

'Mater-Imperia wouldn't have committed it to paper, but you can be sure it was given. Octa would not have acted without it.'

'Then there is no proof.' Francis hauled on a shirt. His stomach growled and he had to steady himself against another bout of dizziness. *Kore, I need a drink.* 'I refuse to sanction an act of treachery against the Imperial Legate.'

Heale bowed with ill grace. *Like the rural bumpkin he is,* Francis thought as his pride reasserted itself. *How dare he come in and judge me for having celebrated too much?* To drink was manly – it showed one had vitality and virility, both attributes Heale had clearly lost. 'Leave me, Sir Roland. I must ready myself for the new day.'

The old knight bowed stiffly, failing to conceal his disappointment.

At midday Gurvon Gyle gathered those he could trust in a side-room adjacent to the Imperial suite. He was still wiping sleep from his eyes, but most of the court were still abed; the palace would not come alive until mid-afternoon after such a night. He studied the gathering: just five people, including himself. Endus Rykjard was nibbling on bread dipped in oil. Beside him, gigantic Mara Secordin was gorging on ham and apples. Rutt Sordell, sitting beside her, inhabited the body of a pure-blood Dorobon mage named Guy Lassaigne, one of Francis' friends. His control was still imperfect; he was having trouble speaking and moving naturally, but that would come quickly. Beside him was 'Symone', the current guise of the shapeshifter Coin. The adoration on Symone's face whenever he spoke was causing him some discomfort, especially as Endus didn't know the shapeshifter's true nature; the mercenary was giving them both decidedly odd looks.

The tiny gathering represented most of his resources in the kingdom of Javon, something he wasn't at all comfortable with. Elena Anborn's treachery had cost him most of his best agents here. He had dozens more, but they were scattered far and wide throughout Yuros, all carrying out essential missions. It meant he was dependent on Endus – he trusted the mercenary captain as much as anyone, but it still left him feeling profoundly uneasy. Octa's unexpected strike had left them having to show their hand too early, well before he was ready.

'If the emperor decides to come down on Octa's side, they'll dismiss you as legate, Gurvon,' Endus was saying. 'If he does, we've no choice: it's war against the Dorobon.'

'That really would be a disaster,' Gurvon agreed. 'We're not strong enough to win, and nor are they. We control the Krak di Condotiori, and we control the palace here in Brochena, but the Dorobon have a whole legion here too, as well as several maniples of Kirkegarde propping up the Gorgio family in Hytel.'

'If Francis brings the Kirkegarde south, we could be in trouble.'

'Francis and his friends are nothing, but the Kirkegarde mean business,' Rutt slurred. It usually took weeks to completely master control of a new body, especially if the victim was a mage – but at least this body was male, unlike his last.

Endus tapped the table. 'Adi Paavus has control of the Krak, and we've two more legions coming, but they won't get here until Febreux. That's two months during which the Dorobon could try something.'

'The Dorobon also have reinforcements coming, lest we forget,' Gurvon reminded them. 'They've got at least thirty thousand settlers crossing the Bridge into Antiopia even now. They're expected in three to four months.'

'Settlers,' sneered Mara. 'Worse than useless.'

'The settlers will all be young families or single men, and they have two full legions protecting them,' Endus pointed out. 'Those are numbers that count.'

'Hans Frikter and Staria Canestos both have almost two legions each,' Gurvon replied. 'And Adi has his legion in the Krak. That will be the key: we can keep control of the supply route.'

'Staria's people will be a liability,' Endus observed testily. 'They always are.'

Gurvon frowned. 'She's got the best part of two legions, and twice as many magi in each than a standard legion. We're lucky she bought into this venture. We'll tolerate the issues she brings.'

'Yes, but—'

'I know,' Gurvon acknowledged, 'but she's a part of this and we need her. Accept it.'

'What's the problem?' Symone asked in a fluted, childlike voice.

Endus' nose wrinkled a little. 'I dare say you won't find them a problem at all, shisha.'

Symone looked puzzled. 'Shisha? What's a shisha?'

Mara and Endus snickered while Rutt rolled his eyes. 'You'll find out sooner than most,' Endus said, glancing at Gurvon as if to say, *Why is this idiot even here?*

They were interrupted by a rap at the door. 'I'll explain later,' Gurvon told Symone. 'Answer that.'

Symone sashayed to the door – at times the hermaphrodite shifter forgot what gender 'he' was currently pretending to be – then returned and whispered in his ear, 'It's Sir Roland Heale. He's alone.'

Gurvon blinked, then looked at Rutt. 'Leave us now by the side door, so he doesn't know "Guy Lassaigne" is a friend of mine. Listen outside, intervene if there's trouble.' He waited until the necromancer had gone, then gave Symone permission to allow the Dorobon knight to enter.

Sir Roland took no time in coming to the point. 'Imperial Legate,' he said stiffly, 'I won't pretend to be delighted at what happened last night. I am a Dorobon man, and always will be. I was not involved in Octa's move, but if she'd triumphed I'd not have mourned you. But that didn't happen and now we must deal with the aftermath. If you wish to avoid a confrontation that would ruin us all, we need to reach an arrangement. I warn you, it will not come cheaply.'

Well, well. Gurvon glanced at Endus, then slowly nodded. 'Well then, Sir Roland, why don't you take a seat and we will see what we can do.'

Shaliyah, Kesh, on the continent of Antiopia
Zulhijja (Decore) 928
6th month of the Moontide

Dawn. Ramon Sensini rose, gently extracted himself from the blanket he shared with Severine Tiseme, smoothed the hair from her face and went to piss from the ruined battlements.

Outside, the landscape had changed. Where there had once been a rocky plain dotted with stunted trees, now dun and grey sand rippled in frozen waves, like the surface of a pond after a stone had been thrown. The sun was a pale apricot disc, barely visible through layers of grey cloud. The wind, which had howled all night, was utterly still, as if the whole of Urte was holding its breath.

When he was done with watering the desert, Ramon wandered along the wall towards the nearest guard post. 'Magister.' The guard saluted, fist over heart. He was Pallacios XIII, a Tenth Maniple man, one of Ramon's own. There were a cohort of twenty slumped against a ruined wall, their faces drawn and strained. The one who spoke had a new respect in his voice. Ramon had got them away from the destruction of Duke Echor's army – not by any great feat of heroism or some mighty deed; he'd just known when to run. Clearly survival instincts were valued highly by the rankers.

Ramon tried to project calm as he asked, 'What's been happening?'

'Bugger all – er, begging your pardon, sir. Storm only quieted down an hour ago. Now it feels like rain,' the guard added doubtfully, 'if'n it can rain out 'ere.'

'That storm yesterday was gnosis-fuelled,' Ramon told him. 'It'll have rukked the weather completely. Anything could happen – might be it blows for months on end, or we get more rukking sunshine.'

The ranker sniffed dourly. 'We gonna make a run west, sir?'

Ramon had been wondering that himself. 'We'll see.'

The guard pointed north, towards the sand-covered battlefield. 'I've seen lights, sir. Just when it's quietest, they shoot into the air and head west. Look, there's another!'

Ramon saw a tiny dot, like a shooting star, rise in the gloom, light immediately flashing about it. It ended in a scarlet flash, and winked out. His gnostic senses reported the distant fizz of discharged energy.

'What is it, sir?'

He weighed his words carefully, then decided to tell the truth. 'It's a mage, trying to escape the battlefield. And failing.' He could imagine the scene – some battle-mage whose unit was destroyed, hiding amidst the fallen as long as he could, then trying to make a run for it before full daylight. But evidently the enemy magi were lying in wait. *The Keshi have magi!* He wondered how many more were out there.

'Why don't they come here, sir?'

'They probably don't know we're here.' *Or don't care.* 'Have any escaped?'

'A few. The biggest balls of light usually make it across the sky. Pure-bloods, eh, sir?'

'I expect so.' He looked the ranker up and down, saw him make up his own mind – that Ramon was a Silacian low-blood and was probably little better off than himself. *And he's probably right. Though if I could get to a skiff . . .* His own was lost on the battlefield.

'Who's in charge, sir?' the ranker asked. 'Any other plumes make it out?'

Plumes, the rankers slang for their commander-magi: *Not exactly reverential, is it?* Ramon shook his head. 'Not many. We've got all manner of stragglers here, what's left of five legions, I reckon. But no senior magi. The Keshi were buzzing around the centre like flies yesterday.'

'So how many magi have we got, sir?'

Ramon eyed him steadily. 'Enough to get us home, soldier. What's your name?'

'Magro, sir. Penn Magro.'

'Well, Magro, you tell everyone that General Korion's son is in charge and we're going to get home.' Ramon put all the calm coolness he could fake into the statement. *Because I'm damned if I'm going to die here. And I've got to see Sevvie and our child safe.*

Magro seemed to see something in Ramon's face. His backbone straightened and his jaw strengthened and he punched his breastplate in salute again. Ramon realised that other men had been listening; he saw the frightened faces taking heart, merely because someone with rank seemed to be in control.

He raised his voice. 'All of you, listen. We're going to be moving soon – but not in the way our enemies think. Keep watch and gather your things. Seth Korion has a plan.'

The Hel he does! But I do.

He saluted them all as the desert skies swirled darker and the first rain-drops, large as walnuts, began to fall. The skies turned black in seconds, and the heavens emptied.

Taking Flight

Souldrinkers

Rumour reached us from the East, that our gnosis could be awakened in a terrible way. We had all been able to see them: the ghosts of the fallen, rising from bodies, then fading away. It was Vorn who tested whether the rumour was true. He kissed his dying wife and inhaled. Then he produced fire from his hand, just like the Keepers. Soon we were all doing it, without a thought of what it was we were actually doing: consuming one of our kind's immortal soul!

NOTES FROM THE TRIAL OF JORGI HARLE,
SOULDRINKER MAGUS, PALLAS 488

Dhassa, on the continent of Antiopia
Zulhijja (Decore) 928 to Moharram (Janune) 929
6th and 7th months of the Moontide

Alaron and Ramita struck the coast of Dhassa during the night, somewhere east of Southpoint Tower, and kept going. They steered well clear of the line of torches below marking the road from the tower to Hebusalim. It would be packed with soldiers and traders commissioned to supply the army.

Food and water were their first priorities. Alaron had vague intentions of buying supplies, but he spoke neither Keshi nor Dhassan and had no coin. Neither he nor Ramita wanted to steal; they were both from trading families.

Away from the road the land looked empty until Ramita pointed out that the mounds he'd thought natural were the huts of poor farmers who were eking a living from the apparently barren desert. He picked out a small cluster of them near a small domed edifice and brought the windskiff down. Distant figures stared at them, someone screamed – a frightened woman calling for her children – and a bell started clanging. A man with a hunting bow appeared from behind a hut, but when he saw the skiff, he froze.

Alaron raised his shields, but tried to appear nonchalant as he helped Ramita from the skiff. The little Lakh girl was like a doll – a very plump doll, who walked with a waddling gait and still managed to look dignified.

An arrow rattled against his shields, but he didn't react.

A young man burst shouting from a hut, waving what looked like a spade. Alaron gestured, and his kinetic-gnosis blew the young man over onto his back. The youth clambered to his knees, scrabbling for his spade again: he was brave enough to be prepared to die for his family. This time Ramita blasted him over backwards. The youth moaned, clutching his head dazedly as the two magi walked past him, heading towards the domed building.

Another attack came, four men at once, but they never got close. Ramita and Alaron made sure not to kill or wound them, though one farmer had to be subdued four times before he finally stopped trying.

When they got close enough to hear what the people were shouting, Ramita answered them in what Alaron presumed was Keshi. At her words the attacks stopped and the villagers gathered warily. There were some seventy people or so, mostly aged, mostly women or children.

They went to the tiny Dom-al'Ahm, where Ramita produced a Lakh sari, a gem-encrusted wonder from the markets of Aruna Nagar in Baranasi, and took control of the bargaining. The expensive cloth was worth far more than a bit of food and water in normal times, but these weren't normal times. Alaron might not have understood the words but from the tone of Ramita's voice as she argued it was clear she was a tough bargainer.

The women produced dried chickpeas, lentils and curry leaves while Alaron pumped brackish water from the well, far more than they needed, and Ramita used Water-gnosis to purify it all, so that the villagers would have some more useful gain from the transaction.

'Tell no one we were here,' Ramita told them.

Fat chance, Alaron thought, looking at the wide-eyed wonder and dread on the faces surrounding them.

Alaron managed to get her back to the skiff and airborne before she hunched over, wracked by another bout of internal cramping. She wasn't due for another month, but apparently she had entered the period where over-exertion might trigger early labour. He spotted a dried-up riverbed with high banks that offered some shade and pointed the skiff towards it.

Once they'd landed he covered the skiff with the dun-coloured canvas sails, then gathered enough wood for Ramita to cook the lentils. It was plain fare, but it tasted like a feast after two days with no more than a few sips of water.

They resolved to fly only at night now – the Inquisitors would likely repair their windship quickly and the Dokken were shape-changers, so also capable of flight – and their pursuers would soon be hot on their tail. Before they bedded down, he scanned the expanse of brown around them and the dome of clear blue overhead. High-circling vultures were the only signs of life in all the world. Alaron's last conscious thought was that one of them needed to stay alert.

Ramita woke to find Alaron sound asleep, slumped over like a corpse on the ground beside her. She studied his face: rather naïve and earnest when awake, childlike in repose. It was a pleasing face, she decided, despite his pallor – no wonder the Keshi called white people 'slugskins'! Even his hair was fair: a light reddish-brown colour, flecked with gold – she'd never known people whose hair was not jet-black until Antonin Meiros brought her north. She wondered how many other strange things there were in the world, and then, *Will I live to see them?*

As if aware of her scrutiny, Alaron blinked awake and immediately clutched at the cylinder in his belt. *He looks so young to be bearing such a responsibility as this 'Scytale',* she thought as he rubbed his eyes and visibly collected himself. *He doesn't know what to do – and neither do I.*

She had asked the Goddess for a sign, but there had been none. *Parvasi-ji,* she prayed quickly, *don't forget me, please.* She tipped a little water away as an offering.

'This is so alien,' Alaron said eventually, looking around. 'I've seen a lot of the world this year, but this place – just look at it! It goes on for ever but it's a wasteland – there's nothing out here. What do people eat?'

'This is desert,' Ramita replied, 'but all around Hebusalim there are wheat fields. And there are slave mines in the mountains to the east. Hebusalim trades with the east and the south. Trade is the blood in the veins of the world, my father always says.'

Alaron crinkled his brow. 'My da once met a Lakh man; he told him the same words.'

'Really? When did your father meet a man from Lakh?'

Alaron looked at her and smiled awkwardly. 'I hadn't wanted to mention it. Before he became a trader, my father was a soldier. This was in the First Crusade, you see. Da had no quarrel with the Dhassans, but they had to follow orders.'

Ramita felt her heart flutter. Her father's voice echoed inside her head: *Orders, the Rondian captain told me. They did it because of orders.* 'Your last name,' she asked, her voice trembling a little, 'what is it again, please? And your father's name?'

'Mercer. Vann Mercer.'

Her hand went to her mouth as a strange feeling enveloped her. She couldn't believe that she and Alaron had not spoken of this before, but then, she'd been busy laughing at his first name – Al'Rhon; in Keshi "the Goat" – and she'd paid no attention to his family name. And anyway, what would be the chances that her father and his might have met, and then their children?

This is the sign I was seeking! Oh thank you, Parvasi-ji! A thousand blessings!

'By all the gods—' she started.

Alaron looked at her uncertainly. 'What's wrong? Are you all right?'

'The Lakh man your father met? He was my father, Ispal Anke-sharan. My father met yours . . . it is incredible!'

They hurriedly swapped accounts, and the fate of Alaron's mother, blinded by her own spells, confirmed the tale.

'Unbelievable!' he murmured, awestruck.

'Do you know what this means?' Ramita asked him. 'It is Fate!'

'There's no such thing,' Alaron said with surprising vehemence.

'But this is living proof – I tell you, Aum is watching us. This is Destiny.'

He stuck his chin out and declared, 'No such thing.'

She snorted. 'The gods are watching us, Alaron Mercer. Your father met my father in the middle of war-time and talked of peace. That is *Fate*. That is *Destiny*. We are Her instruments.'

'Her?'

'Fate is a goddess, a woman. This is known. The Goddess of Fate is Makheera, who has six eyes and six arms so that she can watch and manipulate past, present and future. She had brought us together.'

To her confusion Alaron looked increasingly upset. 'It's only a coincidence, that's all.' He jabbed a finger at her. 'I refuse to believe that everything I do is determined by any god.'

'Makheera is a grim but malleable goddess,' Ramita said, to reassure him. 'She can be bribed, by sacrificing sweets.' A programme of prayers and sacrifices bloomed in her mind.

'For goodness sake, listen to yourself!'

'People sacrifice to Makheera all the time. Often she grants the person's wish.'

His lip curled. 'In other words, a fifty-fifty chance comes off about half the time.'

'I don't know why you are angry – this is very auspicious. We are favoured by the gods.'

'Tell that to my mother: she had her eyes burned out.' He turned his back on her and stared out at the barren landscape.

Your mother was sinning, she went to say, then thought better of it.

It seemed rude, even ignorant, to make such a judgement. 'Your mother still gave birth to you. This is the mirror of the story of my Kazim: his father burned, but his wife stood by him, just like your father did.'

He turned back and said angrily, 'No! That's just too trite – what sort of "higher being" would contrive so much pain just to prove a point? It's *disgusting*. You're just an ignorant peasant!'

'*Peasant?* So that's what you think of me!'

'You know *nothing* about what my mother and father have been through.'

'Yes, I do,' she said patiently. 'I've seen it first-hand. I've bathed Raz Makani's burns myself. His children shared our house.'

'Then you must have had your eyes closed the whole time,' he said bitterly before storming away.

Alaron stared out over the featureless sands, seeing nothing, locked in memory. He remembered his mother's rages, the nights when she would set fire to the bedclothes whilst in the throes of a nightmare, and the way she always tried to hide her marred face from her only child. Tears stung his eyes and he wiped them away angrily. He was aware that Ramita was watching him like a parent waiting for a child to calm down.

We can't afford to argue. Kore's Blood, I've got the Scytale of Corineus in my belt and the widow of Antonin Meiros in my care. But she'd better not talk about Destiny again. He inhaled deeply until he could speak calmly again. 'I'm sorry. It still hurts.'

She did her Lakh head-wag, which could mean a lot things but today he thought meant 'fair enough'. 'What shall we do?'

He studied her as she spoke. Her Rondian was stilted, and she spoke in a thick Lakh accent, with heavy emphasis on the first syllable and a sing-song lilt that was accentuated by the way she waggled her head slightly as she spoke. She was about as tall as a fourteen-year-old in Noros, but apparently in her land she was full-grown.

But what she did to that Inquisitor . . .

He had learned of pregnancy manifestation in college: a human woman could develop a weak form of the gnosis from bearing mage-children. But Ramita Ankesharan was bearing the children of Antonin Meiros and there was nothing weak about her gnosis!

She's going to give birth soon. The weight of his responsibilities felt enormous. 'I don't know,' he said at last. 'Cym took the Scytale to give to her mother – that was as far as our planning went.' He shuddered at the memory of Justina Meiros' death. 'That's all gone now.'

Ramita nodded composedly. 'My husband told me that if something happened to him, I should go to Vizier Hanook, the adviser to the Mughal of Lakh, so that is my intention. But I am aware that it may not be yours.'

Alaron bit his lip. 'When we were in Norostein trying to work out what to do with the Scytale, we pledged to protect it, and only let people we trust use it. There was General Langstrit, Captain Muhren, Cym, Ramon and me. Just the five of us. Langstrit and Muhren are dead now, Cym's either dead' – he swallowed – 'or she's a prisoner, and I have no idea where Ramon is.'

'I too have lost everyone. I do not even know this Hanook. But my husband trusted him and that is enough for me, at least until I can go home.'

Home. Alaron was almost overwhelmed by the mere thought. He pictured lush green fields, and mountains glistening with snow. Familiar faces and voices. Buildings hewn from the rock, cobbled streets. His father. *Where's my father?* For the first time it occurred to him that Vann Mercer might be in trouble too – if the Inquisition were hunting one Mercer, surely they'd be hunting them all … Ramon too, perhaps. *But what can I do? If I try to warn either of them, I might draw the Inquisitors to us.*

He quietly kissed goodbye to the lingering daydream that one day he might return to Silacia, to find a certain girl. A cheeky face with smiling eyes danced into his mind: Anise, whose life he'd saved. *I've got Inquisitors after me, and there is no way they'll let me live, even if I go to them of my own free will and hand them the Scytale. There's no way I'll ever be able to have that life …*

He quietly resolved to go on and hope a solution presented itself, though that meant going into an alien land where he knew nothing and no one. 'Ramita, whomever I give this Scytale to will become like a god. I don't know how it works, but there are people out there who do and if they got hold of it, they could become as powerful as the Emperor of Yuros. So I can't just give it to a stranger, just to be rid of the burden. And you need my help, for now at least.'

'I do,' Ramita said softly. She took his hand. 'Al'Rhon, I know you don't believe me, but Destiny has brought us together. My husband was very wise, and a great prophet. He told me to trust Vizier Hanook with his own children – might not the vizier also be the right person to trust with the Scytale?'

'I don't *know*,' he burst out, 'I don't know *him* – I've never even heard his name before! He's not even from Yuros.'

'Does that matter?' she asked sharply.

He coloured. 'No . . . I suppose not. But the Scytale could create a monster – if I give it to the wrong person . . .'

'Then come with me and find out. My husband foresaw me going to the vizier. Come with me to Teshwallabad and at least see if he is the right man to trust with your burden.'

He stared away into space for a few moments, then made up his mind. 'All right. I'll come with you.'

They slept the remainder of the day. Ramita was awakened first by painful stirrings in her belly. *It's too soon.* She clutched the tight mound of her stomach, fingering her belly button, which had popped out during the night flight from the Isle of Glass. Her whole womb was quivering; her skin was tight as a drum. But this was only the start of the ninth month. It was too soon. If the twins came early, they would likely die.

Stay safe, little ones. Stay inside your mother.

She had been frightened many times in the past year since Antonin Meiros had brought her north. She'd dreaded what awaited her in Hebusalim. She'd felt utter terror when Kazim and the Hadishah had murdered her husband. She still feared violence and imprisonment. Keeping her sanity intact through those long periods of doubt and stark seconds of terror had been a severe test – but fear of the impending births was worse than all the rest put together. Her husband had been a tall man – all these white people were giants – and she was sure his twins would be too big for her. If a woman could not push the babies from her belly, she had to be carved open, and that usually killed them. Every girl in Aruna Nagar grew up knowing that pregnancy would be the greatest trial of their lives. Some women were lucky and popped out children easily, but for most, every new child meant risking their lives all over again.

She glanced across at the unruly tuft of hair poking from beneath the blanket. Alaron's head had flopped sideways, but his breathing was regular. He was so young – not much older than her – but she could see the adult beginning to form beneath the puppy fat. He didn't look like a mighty jadugara, but during the fight at the Isle of Glass she had glimpsed someone more impressive emerging. There weren't many she could trust just now, but he was one. She was glad he'd agreed to come with her.

Beneath the sheet she could make out the leather case that held the Scytale, this magical cylinder that could turn men into magi. She imagined how the Mughal's court might receive such a thing, the desperate avarice it would engender. They were sailing into a storm. She prayed to the goddess, but no divine guidance came; there were no insights or brilliant new ideas. Eventually she drifted back to sleep while the sun spun above and jackals yowled in the distance.

During the nights that followed they flew south, flying by vague memories of the maps Alaron had seen. They took it slowly, not taking to the air until the sun was well gone and the sky was black. Some nights Ramita was too distressed by the internal convulsions to fly at all, but despite the discomfort, the babies stayed inside her and the days passed in travel, sleep and awkward conversation. Luna and her entourage of stars wheeled overhead until the fugitives realised that almost a month had passed. They were somewhere in south Dhassa, the empty lands far from the eastwards march of the Crusade. This time when they ran short of supplies they hid their skiff and approached the lonely settlements on foot, offering the meat of wild animals Alaron had managed to snare using beast-gnosis in trade for vegetables and rice. Many settlements were almost deserted and the crops gone to seed because the menfolk had been taken by the shihad, but they found enough food to get by. No one tried to scry them and they saw no pursuers, but every day Ramita's cramps and convulsions became more frequent.

Only when they hit the ranges in the south of Dhassa did they begin to believe that they might just escape . . .

After some debate, they decided to continue south through, aiming for gaps in the coastal ranges. Under a waning moon the ground gave way to sea, boiling beneath them with a ferocity beyond even that of the northern seas about the Isle of Glass.

Alaron shouted above the winds, 'What is this place?'

Ramita felt a surge of pride because she knew this. 'It's called the Rakasarphal,' she shouted back, staring down at the waters churning below. She couldn't see the shape of the land from the skiff, but she knew it from the maps her husband had made her study and the legends her parents had told her. 'That means "tail of the demon-serpent". When the gods slept after making the world, the rakas-demons crept into it and hid. One was immense, called Kadru, the Mother of the Nagas. She seduced Sivraman by taking on the appearance of his wife, and she conceived. She tunnelled beneath the earth, where she gave birth to one thousand children who were half-man and half-snake: the Nagas.'

Alaron raised an eyebrow. 'Half-snake? Like a lamia?'

She didn't know what he meant, and carried on, 'Vishnarayan the Protector heard her birth labours and went hunting beneath the earth. He slew many Nagas, but some escaped. Suddenly he was confronted by Kadru, whose head was as large as a mountain. She reared up from the earth, creating a huge gouge in the land, and tried to swallow the god whole. But Vishnarayan used his magic to grow as well, and then he grabbed Kadru and pulled her out of the ground, just as the sun rose. The sun struck her and turned her to stone. Her body became the mountain range we crossed, and the place where she'd lain filled with water and is now the sea below. It grows narrower and narrower as you travel east until it meets a great river, the Efratis. The Naga were overawed by the god and became Sivraman's servants. They helped build the world.'

Alaron smiled as if this were a child's tale, which annoyed her, but all he said was, 'In our lands, your Naga are called lamiae: the snake-people I told you about back at the Isle of Glass.'

Oh yes, his *story.* He and his friend Cymbellea claimed they had met snake-men on their journey. *Perhaps they did.* 'The correct name is Naga,' she told him firmly.

'Do we keep going south?' he called. The winds were very strong from the northeast and it would be a real struggle to fight them. The windskiff was already being viciously battered by updrafts from the sea.

She pictured the map in her mind; her recollection was that the Rakasarphal was somewhat to the west of where they wanted to be. 'We should go east from here,' she called back. 'To the south is Lokistan. They are all insane Amteh fanatics there.' Her guru had told her so. 'We should not go there.'

He tried to swing the craft about, but the air-currents picked them up and hurled them south. 'It's too strong,' he shouted. 'Let's cross the sea, then head east once these winds have dropped.'

She might have argued, but she could feel the beginnings of another bout of belly-cramp so instead she nodded weakly, braced herself and prayed that this sea-crossing would not trigger her labour.

We are not ready yet, my sweet children. Go back to sleep.

Cymbellea stared at her bared arms, willing them to change. She sucked in her breath as spiny feathers broke through and spread, giant replicas of the feathers of the gull that lay at her feet. She'd been studying it for hours, imprinting the shape onto her mind, but now that it came time to try it, she couldn't manage. They were on the highest point of the Isle of Glass, whipped by wind and spray on a chilly but clear day, trying to unlock her inner shapechanger within the three days Huriya had allowed. Below, the rest of the pack either went about their business or slept and recovered.

'I can't do it!' she snapped.

'You can,' Zaqri replied tersely. 'The problem is you're trying to force it. Let go of yourself. *Become* the gull.'

Become the gull! Rukka mia, what does that even mean? She scowled at her self-appointed guardian, wishing she had a knife. She owed him his death for what he'd done to her mother. The last thing she wanted was to rely on him for her survival.

This isn't working . . . Though she couldn't blame him for that. Zaqri knew so much and she so little. It was becoming increasingly clear that there were huge gaps in her gnostic education, and not enough time to fill them.

Why is he helping me? Perhaps he felt sorry for her? Or guilty, for killing her mother? She decided she didn't care, as long as he taught her enough to get away. With any luck she'd be leaving his corpse as a warning not to follow. But damn his black heart, he was a fine sight with the sun on his golden shoulders and the wind in his blond hair. And his mental touch was as masterful as his body – she felt like she already knew him far too well, thanks to this forced companionship. He might be older than her – decades older, she sensed – yet he was obviously in his prime.

'You are half-blood, Cymbellea: you can do this,' he told her. 'Animagery might not be your strength, but you have enough gnostic power. You just have to *believe*.'

Although as a teacher he wasn't as haphazard as Alaron and Ramon, whose well-meaning but erratic instruction was all she'd ever had, she couldn't grasp what was needed – the letting go, the abandonment of shape, trusting in the gnosis to let her mutate her very body while believing she could find the way back. She *didn't* believe, in other words.

The fact that Zaqri was grieving made it harder for Cym to hate him – but not much. He was her only protector against the still hostile pack: to survive – and not just survive, but find a way to strike back – her vengeance would have to wait. The way of her people had always been an eye for an eye, but she had to be patient.

She looked around the viewing platform, listened to the sea thundering and licked salty spray from her lips. The gulls had fled, sensing that the birds that now lived here were not natural. *Bide your time*, she told herself. *Get off this rock and opportunities to escape will come.*

'Try again,' Zaqri urged. 'Let me guide you through it.' He put his fingers to her temple and entered her head like a conqueror, completely sure of himself and his right to go where he willed. She had no choice but to endure the mental intrusion. Her senses were flooded with a tactile sensation of feathers, how bird-shape *felt*, how it was achieved – how her arms might become wings, how her chest and shoulder muscles must alter . . . She accepted the mental imagery of the gull he gave her and tried to flow into it as he directed. For a moment it looked like she could do it, then she yowled as her arms bowed and bent, the bones cracking and reforming, racking her with instant agony. Her shoulders twisted and remade themselves and she screamed, crying out as much in panic as pain as she saw her arms hanging twisted and useless. She almost blacked out, but Zaqri stepped inside her head again and, soothing and healing, showed her the way back to herself.

She was still recoverng from the agony when she heard a sly female voice from the top of the steps that led to this upper platform. 'Well, Zaqri, will she fly for us?' Huriya enquired, striking a pose with the wind ruffling her long black hair. 'She's running out of time.'

'Then give us more,' Zaqri replied, going to her. 'She's had next to no instruction in the gnosis. Self-taught magi can do the basics, sometimes well, but she needs detailed, intense teaching to do this.'

'We can't wait, packleader!' Huriya answered waspishly. 'You know the prize at stake! We cannot delay, and I cannot leave you behind. This is your pack, these are your people, and they are angry enough at the time you waste on this gypsy.'

Zaqri clenched his fists in frustration. 'She can be an asset to our search, Seeress. She knows the quarry.'

'As do I,' Huriya replied. 'Ramita Ankesharan has been my bloodsister since birth.'

'But you have failed to scry this Ramita, Seeress. And what if this Alaron Mercer is no longer with her? We must have the option of finding him, and for that we need her.'

'She will not aid us, packleader!' Huriya swatted the air dismissively. 'She will slow us down; she will obstruct us. The injured are almost healed and the pack flies soon! Ready her, or she dies.' She shot Cym a pitiless look, then turned to go.

'Seeress!' Zaqri grabbed her arm. 'Let her and I catch you up. Two, three days and I swear she'll be flying.'

Huriya looked at his hand, then up at him. It seemed bizarre to Cym that this little woman, tiny as a child before the giant packleader, might have the greater authority, but he hurriedly removed his grip. 'It demeans you in the eyes of your pack to be sniffing her nethers so obviously, Zaqri. She is magi: our oldest enemy. Treat her as such!' She spun and stamped away.

Zaqri bowed his head, then slowly rejoined Cym, his face grim. 'Well?' he snapped at Cym, 'you heard her!'

'Why are you helping me?' she blurted. 'I won't betray my friends.'

'I know that,' he told her steadily. He frowned. 'You are Rimoni. Once, so was I.'

Cym glanced at him in surprise. Normally her people were dark-haired, not blond, and his voice had no hints of such ancestry. But it was true there were blond Rimoni in the north of the country, where mixed blood was not uncommon. It could be so. It didn't feel like a complete reason though.

He just wants the Scytale. Nevertheless, she was resolved to live through this if she could. 'Let's try again,' she said, already wincing at the thought of going through that horrible change all over again.

But despite renewed determination, she got no further by the time she was exhausted and collapsed into her bed.

At night Zaqri guarded her. Though he shared her bed, he did so chastely, in lion form, literally keeping the jackals from the door. Hessaz watched them both with bitter eyes, but Cym soon realised that she was not alone: all the women of the pack wanted Zaqri. *They are more beast than human*, she thought. *He is the alpha male and must have a mate.*

When she dreamed it was of him, and she was a bird flitting about his giant jaws. A dozen times a night his teeth clamped on her fluttering wings; a dozen times a night she awoke with hammering heart to find a lion lying next to her, never sleeping, his eyes on the door.

In some dreams he lowered himself onto her, his fur soft on her skin, his meaty breath hot on her neck: the lion and his lover. In her dream she welcomed it, but when she woke she could scarcely keep from vomiting at the notion.

Next day he made her strip to her underclothes, a humiliation, but he claimed he needed to see her body as she attempted the change. Not that Zaqri made her feel overly uncomfortable about it. He remained proper toward her, gave her no further reasons to hate him, not that any were needed. Her frustration grew through the day at her lack of tangible progress. The more she tried, the worse she got, and still the change wouldn't come. Eventually she stormed away, screaming, 'Just let me sleep! I'll do it tomorrow!'

Despite her mind-numbing exhaustion, she lay awake for hours, agonisingly conscious of his proximity; when she eventually slept, she dreamed of him and woke jaded, nowhere near ready for the day to come. Breakfast was a spicy meal similar to Ramita's cooking, full of alien flavours and tongue-stinging bite.

She threw some Rimoni words at Zaqri, to test his story, but he fielded them easily. 'Northern barbarian,' she sneered anyway. 'You're no Rimoni.'

But none of that could put off the appointed moment. The pack wrecked Meiros' lair and tipped most of the debris into the sea, then gathered on the roof. As she looked around she was met only by blank hatred.

Calmness, girl, Zaqri whispered in her mind. *You can do this, I know it. Shed your inhibitions as you shed your identity. Become the gull.*

'How's she going to shapeshift fully clothed?' someone laughed, and the pack tittered contemptuously. They were all naked as they waited to change shape; whatever possessions they carried were packed into satchels strapped to their shoulders or waists.

'Does the gypsy think she's got something we haven't?' Darice, a big Brician woman, cackled.

'Too good for us, eh?' sneered another woman.

Cym felt her skin flush darker and tossed her head angrily. 'No, I'm the same as you,' she snapped back. 'Just better looking.' *A Rimoni backs down to no one.*

A few of them chuckled, appreciating her spunk. 'She's certainly a damned sight prettier than you, Darice,' one of the men called.

Another leaped up and waggled his cock at her. 'Hey, girly, this'll be waiting for you when we land.'

'How'll she find that little thing, Kenner?' Zaqri quipped, to more laughter.

'It'll be towering above Southpoint,' Kenner the cock-waver boasted.

'It'll be mistaken for a tiddy-worm and eaten by a gull, more like,' Darice responded. More banter was flung about, all voices shouting at once, as much laughter as hostility present.

'She's still got to fly,' Huriya said sourly, her voice killing the merriment. 'Or someone gets a free meal.'

Cym glared at the tiny Keshi girl, whose voluptuous breasts stood proudly high on her chest as she stood with her hands on her hips. Small as a child, worldly as a whore.

Little bitch. I'll show you.

'We're waiting, gypsy,' Huriya trilled.

<Calmness, Cymbellea.> Zaqri's silent voice filled her mind, his mental touch like warm fur. <Don't fear. Concentrate. Remember. Then just let go, and the rest will follow.>

She gave him a contemptuous look and walked to the far wall. She touched a panel and the wall opened. Inside it, right where her mother had told her, was a large rolled-up carpet and a pouch containing the gemstone that powered it. The only pity was that Zaqri had been so attentive of her that she'd not had the chance to slip up here alone.

Who says I need wings to fly?

She removed the gem from the pouch and hung it about her neck beside her own periapt, then she dragged out the carpet and unrolled it. Justina had told her the gem converted other types of gnostic energy into Air-gnosis, but she was an Air-mage and shouldn't need it, she hoped.

Some pack-members started guffawing with laughter as they watched her place her few belongings in the middle and sit down.

'Wait,' Huriya snapped. 'I said you must learn to shape-change – your life is still forfeit, girl!'

'No,' Cym said calmly, 'you said I must fly. And so I shall. I won't slow you down.' She looked at Zaqri, who was grinning broadly, to her surprise. 'The question,' she added, 'is whether you *animals* can keep up with me.'

Before the Dokken could react, she threw all her stored energy into the carpet and willed it into the air.

In a few seconds, the shrieking howls of outrage were dulled by distance, but she felt a sudden flaring of the gnosis behind her and a vast force gathered as if to swot her from the air. She looked back fearfully and saw Zaqri had seized Huriya's arm and just in time deflected whatever attack the tiny girl had launched. She felt her skin flush at the exertion, and poured more energy into her flight.

Hey, maybe I can outrun these bastards? she thought jubilantly.

She couldn't, though. A few minutes later a giant golden eagle swooped onto the carpet and gripped the fabric in its claws to steady itself before resolving into a naked Zaqri. He had a satchel tied to his waist. His eyes were a mixture of fury and amusement. 'Damn you, girl, why didn't you tell me?'

'You killed my mother,' she said. 'I'll never tell you anything I don't want you to know. Anyway, you've been inside my head: you should have worked it out for yourself.'

'It doesn't work like that. I'm not a strong mystic: I just got glimpses – emotions mostly, and a few big memories. Huriya wanted to rip you limb from limb for that little trick.'

Cym smiled at that.

'Girl, she is our Seeress. She has the power of an Ascendant, and Sabele still dwells inside her, she who was present when Corineus died.'

That wiped the smile from her face. *No wonder the little bitch thinks she owns the world.* 'Why do you resist her?' she asked Zaqri snarkily. 'Shouldn't you be honoured that she wants to rukk you?'

'I still grieve for my wife,' he replied flatly. 'I loved her, whatever you think of *animals* like us.' He pointed southwards across the sea. 'That way.'

She willed the carpet to turn and it did so. It was taxing, and not as efficient as a windskiff, being neither aerodynamic nor assisted by sails, but she set her jaw and powered on, aware that she was burning through energy fast. The wind whipped at her face and made a banner of her hair, but the worst of the headwind was deflected by unseen shields. She glanced over her shoulder to see a stream of gulls following, shrieking angrily. She wondered which was Huriya. *Probably the smallest, with the best plumage . . .*

'Are all Dokken beast-magi?' she wondered.

Zaqri's eyes narrowed at her tone. 'We call ourselves Brethren, or Kindred. And no, we have a mix of skills, but we tend to clan together according to our major affinities. My pack are, as you can see, mostly animagi. You can judge us for our rough manner if you must, but remember that we must live on the fringes because the most powerful beings on Urte have pledged our annihilation.'

'I'm Rimoni – they pledged ours too,' she retorted, though she couldn't deny his words had struck a chord in her. 'They destroyed our cities and turned us into wandering beggars. If you're really one of us you'll know that.'

'I know my heritage, girl. I was born on the Metian border and Rimoni was my first tongue. But my father was Brethren, and he took me into the pack. Our forebears were at the Ascension of Corineus. The Blessed Three Hundred ascended, but they didn't, and for that crime they named us apostates.' He glanced at the nearest gull, a dark-hued bird with red eyes. *Hessaz*, Cym guessed. 'The Brethren found Ahmedhassa before even the Ordo Costruo.'

Cym noted that he said 'Ahmedhassa' – the local word for the eastern continent, not the Yurosian 'Antiopia'. 'Did most of you come here?'

'Those who could. It took morphic-gnosis, animagery, Air-gnosis or Water-gnosis. Most of those who couldn't use those affinities stayed in Yuros. The Ordo Costruo were no friends to us, nor us to them: we preyed on them to gain more souls and awaken the gnosis in our children. It was war.'

Cym imagined untaught Dokken against Arcanum-trained magi. 'You lost.'

'We lost. We had to go into hiding, even here in Ahmedhassa. The locals believed us to be Afreet – the demons of their legends. We could not live or train openly, so we could master only the simplest gnosis: elemental magic and body-magic. Only a rare few, like Sabele, can do more.'

His words echoed the plight of her own people too closely. She willed away her empathy. 'So you really were Rimoni.'

'My mother was. My father was Brician . . . and Brethren. He's long dead. I am older than I look.'

She studied him, his timeless eyes and weathered, ruggedly handsome face. He had the commanding manner of someone who knew himself, had come to terms with what he was, but there was a haunted aspect to his eyes that suggested it had been a long battle. 'How many people have you killed?'

He looked at her steadily. 'I don't know. I lost count long ago.'

How revolting, she thought, surprised she had felt any pity for him. That angered her. 'I guess being a packleader justifies everything,' she jeered. 'You killed my mother. Does that make you as strong as she was now?'

His face was grave but unrepentant. 'It does: purer blood strengthens our own gnosis. I gained her strength, though not her skill.'

'Quite a coup for you,' she said harshly. '*Murderer.*'

'We were in combat, and she fell. What was I to do?'

'Grant her passage to the afterlife! Let her die! Don't pretend you have a conscience, you piece of dung. If you did you'd hang yourself.'

'No, I wouldn't. I want to live as much as you do. I want to be able to walk free without being hunted down for the nature I was born with – *born with*, not chose. Sol made me what I am; he had to have a reason.'

'You should have been drowned at birth.'

'I go on as I must, for my kindred. Sabele has prophesied that we will find a way to cure ourselves; we will become equals with the magi.'

'The magi don't want any equals,' she retorted.

'I know. We are not fools, but we have to hope. Until then I guard the humanity I still have.'

It felt harsh to mock such a dream when her own people harboured much the same aspirations, but he had ripped her mother's throat out and drunk her soul. *There is no way to forgive that.* 'Why are you protecting me?'

'Cymbellea,' he said in his rough-smooth voice, 'I'm not a murderer, whatever you think. When my gnosis was awakened I didn't even know what was being done to me. I've tried to kill only enemies in battle, or someone who is dying already. Your mother's last thoughts were of you: she begged me to protect you. I swore to do so, to the last remnants of her soul. I hold that oath sacred.'

'How dare you try to make killing her sound so rukking noble. Go away: I don't want to talk to you.'

He didn't go, though. They fell silent as the air rushed by. Below, the sea churned, menacing even at this height. There was still no sign of the coast and she was beginning to feel her strength flagging. She was going to have to ask his help soon, and that gnawed at her pride.

In the end she didn't need to ask. Almost as soon as she began to falter he reached out, plucked the gemstone from her throat and sent his own gnosis powering into the carpet. At once it gained speed.

She looked away, unsure how to convey gratitude and hating this ambivalence she felt when things needed to be clear between them. But she was so tired, so drained from the grief and exertion and the stress of hating, that she just rolled into a bundle and closed her eyes. *If he can't reach the coast, let us drown instead.*

She awoke to find herself covered with a thin blanket. She was still lying on the carpet which was spread on the sands beneath vast open skies. A vivid sunrise pierced the gaps in the mountain ranges on the eastern horizon. She blinked uncertainly and sat up.

Beneath a spindly tree a few yards away, a lion rumbled, its amber eyes on her. Zaqri. Not far off, a black panther prowled, watching her with hooded eyes, and beyond that menacing shape, many more, perhaps a hundred, far more than had left the Isle of Glass. Some were in human form, others still in beast shape, jackals mostly. In their midst was Huriya, wrapped in a shawl and hunched over a luminous bowl of water, scrying.

The Keshi girl sensed her gaze. 'Ah, you're awake.' A pulse of energy stirred about her and the pack came awake as one, leaping onto their feet or paws, shaking and grunting and snuffling their way to alertness. So many eyes, hemming her in as Huriya called to her, 'Clever girl. Do you have any other surprises for us?'

Cym clambered stiffly to her feet. 'That's for you to find out.'

'Such pretty defiance. You know, I could almost come to like you, girl. But you're magi.' The blanket fell from one shoulder as Huriya stalked forward, swaying hypnotically, a cobra in girl shape. 'That makes you more useful to us dead.'

Cym glanced uncertainly at Zaqri. 'He said—'

'Zaqri is packleader. I am Seeress of the Western Reaches. Our authorities are different. But Brethren laws say that a mage must die, to strengthen us. The only thing preserving you is Zaqri's whim.' She flashed from ten yards away to one in an eye-blink without apparent effort, and the Rimoni girl recoiled in shock. 'I'm feeling quite whimsical myself.'

Zaqri stood and flowed into man-form. 'Lady Huriya, I—'

'Hush, dear Zaqri. I'm not going to kill her just yet. I merely have some questions for the *prisoner*.' Huriya's gnosis pierced Cym's brain like a lance. <*This Scytale, girl: I want it. Who is this Al'Rhon Mercer and where was he taking it?*>

She couldn't fight. It was like trying to hold back an avalanche with a blade of grass. She was dimly aware of falling to her knees, and someone big with warm hands holding her up. She tried to scream as all she'd gone through in the past six months or more was ripped from her mind with brutal, overwhelming power: from the discovery of the Scytale, her flight across Yuros, her capture by the barbarian Sfera tribesmen and rescue by Alaron, to the terrifying fight at the Isle of Glass. It felt like Huriya had taken a giant claw and reached inside her head to pull out whatever she wanted. Time and again the Keshi seeress came back to Alaron, searching for some kind of recent contact, but there was nothing to find.

When her vision cleared, she found herself in a small rocky dell, away from the pack: just her, and Huriya and Zaqri. Huriya had moved her and she'd not even been aware. Her skull throbbed from the intrusion, filling her with nausea. She rubbed her temples.

Huriya *tsked* in annoyance. 'She doesn't know where this Al'Rhon Mercer has gone.'

'Please, Seeress,' Zaqri said, his voice as low. 'We need her memories to find him. This is an opportunity beyond dreams, and we must move carefully. The Inquisition also hunt this prize.'

Huriya's face turned cunning. 'Indeed. For now it must remain our secret.'

'We should tell Wornu,' Zaqri argued.

'No. No others, not yet.' Huriya turned and snapped at Cym, 'Girl, I do not like being made a fool of.' She eyed her speculatively, then looked back at Zaqri. 'I would like to ensure her loyalty: by giving her Nasette's choice.'

Zaqri pulled Cym behind him. 'No. She can and will aid us without that. I take full responsibility.'

Cym wondered what they were talking about. It didn't sound

good, not if Zaqri was so adamantly against it. She felt a real surge of relief when Huriya pouted, but backed down.

'I will hold you to that, packleader. She may keep her carpet for now, but she is your responsibility.'

Adamus Crozier used relay-staves to summon aid, but it was still a week until another windship pulled up alongside their drifting hulk and allowed the remaining Inquisitors of Dranid's Fist to resume the chase. They didn't bother with repairs, just set the abandoned craft on fire. As they sailed away it plummeted like a comet into the sea.

Malevorn joined his fellow survivors for the formal introduction to their rescuers. They were all in full dress uniform: over their armour their black and white tunics bore the Sacred Heart, and they carried dragon-helms under their arms. He knew the new Commandant's name at least; Fronck Quintius' clan was prominent in Pallas.

Another name was also familiar: a young Acolyte with distinctive duelling scars slashed across his right cheek. Malevorn himself had put them there when Artus Leblanc was fourteen. He'd been twelve.

Commandant Quintius continued the introductions. 'Acolyte Artus Leblanc,' he announced.

'Brother Artus,' Malevorn chorused with the others, staring into his eyes and seeing that he hadn't been forgotten. Artus Leblanc glared balefully and stepped back into line. *I guess he hasn't forgiven me either.*

Duels between magi were illegal in Pallas, and doubly so amongst children, but Artus Leblanc's persistent malice had become unbearable and in the end they'd gone at each other behind the stables, their carving knives hot with gnosis. The magic-burns had made the scars doubly bad; even with gnostic healing, Leblanc's face had been marred for life.

After the introductions, Adamus Crozier went below with Quintius, leaving the Acolytes free to mingle. Artus made straight for Malevorn. 'Andevarion. We meet again.'

'What a treat,' Malevorn drawled.

'I'll admit I'm surprised to see you. I thought you'd have given up and slit your wrists by now. Just like Daddy.' Malevorn felt Raine's warning hand on his forearm. Artus took in the gesture and ran his eyes over her. 'Remind me, what's this troll's name again?'

Raine answered for herself, her voice calm.

Artus Leblanc curled his lip. 'Caladryn? I don't believe I know your family.'

'And I don't know yours,' she retorted.

Artus snorted. *Everyone* knew the Leblancs. 'I think you're possibly the ugliest quim I've ever seen in uniform, Raine Caladryn. Are you of pig-farming stock? Did your mother climb into the pen one night?'

Malevorn grasped Leblanc's collar and yanked him close. 'You'll retract that.'

Artus didn't blink. 'I can say what I like: "No brother or sister may raise a hand against another. Any insult must be borne." So say the Scriptures. So you can go fuck yourself and your hog-faced whore too, *Brother.*'

Malevorn glared, knowing he was right: while politeness was expected, it certainly wasn't enforced, but violence against a fellow Inquisitor was expressly forbidden. He shoved Leblanc away, pushing the edges of those rules. 'See you in training, Artus. Perhaps we'll use knives?'

Hands went to sword hilts, but Elath Dranid appeared and the Acolytes, eyeing each other warily, moved apart. Dranid was a legend in battle and still had rank, even in the depleted Eighteenth Fist. 'Step away, Andevarion,' he ordered.

Artus Leblanc went to talk to his colleagues at the far end of the windship. Malevorn stayed by Dranid, seething. 'Where are we going?' he asked eventually, once he was certain his voice would be steady.

'Back to that cursed island. If the shifters are still there, we'll destroy them. If not, we'll seek clues.' Dranid was ill at ease: though he'd been recently promoted to Fist Commandant of the Eighteenth, it obviously weighed uncomfortably on him. He hadn't tried to deal as an equal with Quintius, Malevorn thought. He would have asserted himself, but Dranid was out of his depth in matters that couldn't be dealt with using a blade.

It took another day to find the Isle of Glass, and when they arrived everything of value had been stolen, destroyed or thrown into the sea. Adamus was visibly disappointed, though unsurprised. He ordered the Acolytes to search for any bits of Dokken fur or feathers so they could resume the search; Brother Geoffram, the new Farseer from Quintius' Fist, thought he could use Dokken traces to guide the pursuit. It was the only viable option they had left right now.

Hopefully they will lead us to Mercer and the Scytale. But I'll be damned before I let Artus Leblanc lay hands on it, Malevorn thought.

3

Desire

The Morals of the Ordo Costruo

The Ordo Costruo have long made a practice of seizing the moral high ground in debates, their high-handedness nowhere more evident than their criticisms of the slave trade. The truth is that the Ordo Costruo have been exploiting their status as the only magi in Antiopia to subtly subjugate all Antiopia. The number of mixed-race half-blooded magi in their order speaks eloquently of their own moral degeneracy.

ARCH-PRELATE DOMINIUS WURTHER,
CORINEUS DAY ADDRESS, PALLAS, 899

Northern Javon, on the continent of Antiopia
Zulhijja (Decore) 928 to Moharram (Janune) 929
6th and 7th months of the Moontide

Kazim fell asleep some time after midnight as Elena piloted the *Greyhawk* over a featureless plain somewhere northwest of their old lair. His last conscious sight was of mountains to his right, plains on the left. When the rising sun blazed through his eyelids, he woke to find himself surrounded by red rocks, carved by millennia of sun and wind and rain into strange shapes, like clay moulded by a blind sculptor. He stared at them for a few bleary seconds until he realised that they weren't moving, that they had landed. He glanced back at her, his mouth forming the question.

'Yes, we've arrived,' Elena told him cheerily, baring her teeth and crinkling up her eyes. Her hair was tied against the wind. It was gleaming blonde from days in the sun practising combat and gnosis together in the monastery. It had felt like an idle pursuit then, training for the sake of excellence or personal enlightenment, like the original Zain monastics who'd built the place. Now they were going to war for real.

'Where are we?' he asked blearily, looking around. They were in a little hollow, sheltering below a rock wall that had been split aeons ago by a dried-up river. A goat-path jinked away out of sight above the banks. The air was cool and hazy. 'Is this the place we discussed?'

'It is. We hit the northern road from Brochena to Hytel during the night, and I've been following it until an hour ago.'

'I don't know Javon at all,' he confessed.

'I'll draw you a map. I've brought a little parchment and ink.' She looked at him steadily. 'Are you ready for this, Kazim? We're going to war.'

'You know I can fight,' he said soberly.

'Of course! You're the best young swordsman I've ever seen. But this won't feel like fighting. We'll be killing with the gnosis – most of those we face won't stand a chance.'

He flinched at that. Using the gnosis against ordinary men felt somehow wrong, *unsporting*. He knew he shouldn't be thinking like that but he couldn't help himself. He'd played too many kalikiti games in Aruna Nagar; fairness *mattered*.

'I can kill,' he said quietly. He'd proven that too. 'I can do what you require.' *Because it is you who requires it.* 'This is the holy war,' he added.

'War is never holy.' She looked away, exhaled heavily. 'Come, we need to hide the skiff and get settled in before dark.' She gestured towards the crack in the rock face. 'Through there. Sorry, it's not as nice as the monastery.'

They dragged the skiff up the dried riverbed and draped it in its dun-coloured sails before throwing sand over the top so that it would be invisible from the air. Then they hefted their packs and entered the narrow defile. It twisted and turned for a hundred yards, until they reached a flat area with a little three-sided mudbrick building, barely twelve paces square, at the centre. It looked deserted.

'It's a shepherd's hut,' Elena said, shrugging off her pack. Sweat clung to her back and Kazim saw the bloodstains had run; they'd had no chance to wash after the battle at the monastery. 'I set it up as an alternative bolt-hole two years ago. There's some equipment buried nearby. The river fills for three months or so after monsoon, but there's a cave further upstream with a pool. The shepherd only uses the hut at midsummer, so we're safe until Junesse, should we need to stay that long.'

He put down his pack and looked around: no windows, but a recess in the wall for a cooking fire with a smoke outlet in the roof above. The floor was filthy with dried dung, dirt and dead insects. There was a blackened metal tripod holding a battered pot, a bucket, a wooden bowl and a couple of spoons on the hearth, and a wooden bed-frame. Nothing else.

'I guess I'll fit, but where will you be?'

Elena chuckled. 'We'll make it work. We've got a cot, a fireplace and a cooking pot, and I've got stores buried behind the hut. There's water in the next cave, about a hundred yards upstream.'

It didn't take them long to get set up. Elena drove a family of cobras from their lair behind the hut, killed them with mage-bolts and gutted them so they'd be ready to roast, while Kazim used Air-gnosis to scour the hut of loose debris. Then he took the bucket to find the water cave Elena had mentioned. He found jackals lurking there, but a quick blast of Fire-gnosis was all it took to drive them off. The cave wasn't deep, more like a deep overhang, but it sloped inwards to a pool that looked to be fed by a slow drip from the walls. The level was not high enough now to reach the narrow race into the riverbed, but from the way the rock was worn, Kazim guessed it would overflow in the rainy season and almost fill the gully. He lowered his bucket into the water, which was pleasantly cool.

He took it back, and while Elena washed the floor he dug up the stores. He found rice, lentils, nuts and chickpeas wrapped in greased canvas bags, and cured meat and dried fruits too, as well as various spices. Exploring further, he found a good pile of dried dung cakes stored behind a narrow cleft which the shepherd evidently used as a pen for his flock.

Finally, Elena showed him her watch-point, a place above the pool-cave that offered views over all the possible approaches. The day was beginning to heat up and in the distance the land shimmered.

'I'm going to go and wash,' she announced, her voice still husky from an old throat wound. She complained that she hardly knew her own voice, but to Kazim it was just the way she sounded and he couldn't imagine her sounding any other way. 'I've been dreaming of just being clean again,' she added.

Kazim understood just how soiled she must feel – and he knew she wasn't just talking about blood and sweat. She'd not had the chance to wash since she'd been almost raped by Gatoz, the fanatical Hadishah captain. And they had not yet even talked about that.

'Elena,' he said awkwardly, 'what Gatoz was going to do ... you must believe me when I say there is nothing in the *Kalistham* that justifies that. He was wrong and evil – please do not judge all Amteh by one man.'

'Kaz, I've met men like Gatoz before – most of them Kore-worshippers, actually. Not surprising, I guess, as I've lived most of my life in Yuros. No religion has the monopoly on evil or good.' She shuddered a little. 'I've survived worse. But thank you for arriving on time. What he was going to do ... I'll never forget how much I owe you.'

He bowed his head, a lump in his throat because he didn't know how to have someone feel indebted to him. He owed her too, in ways he couldn't express. So he changed the subject. 'Can we both drink and bathe in the pool?'

She understood, and also let the subject go.

'I'm a Water-mage: I'll purify our water before drinking.' She flashed him a wan smile. 'Your turn after me.'

She returned almost an hour later, hair tied up and her damp clothes clinging to her. She smiled as he passed her and climbed to the cave. He too was relieved to finally remove the days of sweat, grime and blood from his skin. It was blissful, to enter the cool water and feel it soak into him. He floated on his back and closed his eyes, just as he used to do when bathing in the Imuña River at Baranasi, seeking peace amidst the clamour of ten thousand Lakh praying and washing and laundering all round him. He felt human again: his gnosis fully replenished after all the killing at the monastery, erasing the gnawing hunger he felt when it was low. He felt at peace . . . *almost* . . .

Elena brought the rice to the boil and added some of the cured meat and the last of their greens. Her time in Brochena and Forensa as Royal Protector to the Nesti family, when all her meals had been prepared for her and she had been waited on hand and foot, felt like another life. She glanced up to see Kazim walking back from the pool-cave, his wet clothing clinging to his damp skin, and her throat went dry.

For four months they'd been living and training together, trying to find a way through all the cultural and religious barriers that divided them: Yurosian and Ahmedhassan; skin colour; religion; Crusade and shihad; mage and Souldrinker; youth and age; man and woman . . . She could not imagine two more opposite people, and yet here they were. They'd argued, sulked, fought, laughed and cried. They'd found compromises when others might have come to real blows; they'd worked out what mattered to them both and what they could work round. They'd found a cause they could both believe in. They'd saved each other's lives. But every day still brought new challenges.

Think of all the common ground, she reminded herself. *I speak his tongue. And we're both warriors. We understand the language of blades. We have a cause, to free Javon from the invaders. We have common enemies.*

She admired his smooth, powerful gait. With the hunger of his condition currently abated, his aura was quiescent, almost normal; if you didn't know what to look for you wouldn't know he was a Souldrinker.

Damn Nasette and her rukking transformation.

He put his back against the hut and sat, facing her, his gaze direct and straightforward. It was one of the many traits she liked in him.

Not to mention looking like an eastern demi-god and having an honest heart. He might be no courtier – he had neither sophistication nor a Western education – but he was smart. And too young for her, really . . .

But since when has any lover of mine been perfect?

Lover.

That was the crux of it. He wanted her, and she wanted him.

Damn Nasette to Hel.

'What are we going to do?' he asked.

It could have been a question about their next move, or their long-term goals, but it wasn't.

'Nasette was wounded when the two Dokken shifters captured her,' she said. 'That could have been the source of the infection, if it was an infection that made her change. Alternatively, one of them got her with child – if a human woman becomes pregnant to a high-blooded mage she can develop the gnosis, so it's not unreasonable to think that being impregnated by a Dokken could have altered her gnostic abilities. It might have been a temporary thing, but she was put to death so we'll never know.' *Poor cow. What kind of father butchers his own daughter?* 'Or there might have been some other factor at play. We just don't know.'

He listened to her quietly, then pointed at the cot. 'That's too small for me. I can sleep outside.' His voice had an adult maturity that showed the type of man he was becoming.

She shook her head, shuffled closer to him, threw a leg over his hip and straddled him. He went utterly still, as if afraid that if he reacted, she'd stop. She cradled his head and whispered, 'Here's what I think. The wound is a red herring—' She stopped, then said with a snigger, 'Pardon the pun.'

'What has a red fish to do with anything?' Tentatively, he put his arms about her. She felt her skin flush and her breath quicken.

'Nothing. Forget the herring.' She laughed nervously, feeling like a young woman again, the girl she had been before the Noros Revolt, before she'd met Gurvon Gyle. She had almost forgotten that girl: earnest, determined, straightforward, all innocent single-mindedness. That girl was a lot like the young man in her arms. 'I think the pregnancy caused Nasette to alter. So I think we just need to be careful.'

'You are willing to risk it?'

She nodded.

'Why?'

'Because I want you too much not to.'

She kissed him as he opened his mouth to reply. He hesitated an instant, then responded, his mouth equally hungry for hers. Long minutes vanished as they clung to each other, tasting each other, nipping at lips, flicking with tongues, then his lips slipped to her neck and his hands slid inside her shift and up the silken skin of her back.

She murmured encouragement, all the while kneading his shoulders, feeling the strength in his solid muscles. Then it was too much and she raised her arms over her head and whispered in his ear, 'Pull it off.'

He pulled her shift over her head, then put his mouth to her left nipple and began to suckle it, hard, drawing a moan from her lips as she held him there, arching against him.

Only once did the ugliness of Gatoz and his threats intrude, a brief flash that she pushed aside. Done was done, and there was no point in dwelling on it. If there was one thing her career in the shadows had taught her, it was how to forget. Life was always renewing itself: that was its lesson. She let the pure physical pleasure of his touch lick her soul clean, then murmured, 'Let's try out that cot anyway, shall we?'

Kazim undressed, and then she let him pull her leggings off. The afternoon sun was brilliant outside, but inside the tiny shepherd's rick, there was shade enough to make it a haven. All he could see was Elena as she lowered herself onto her back and pulled him down onto her. Her hair shone palely as he stopped, poised above her, then he had to catch his breath as she grasped his shaft and pulled him towards her. She lifted her face to meet his and his mouth locked on hers. She tasted salty, as if she'd been drinking tears, and her lips moved as she sighed. His hand found her breast and he cupped it, his fingers stroking the nipple into a hard little nub while he pushed into her wetness, into her warmth. Memories of Ramita flashed momentarily before him, then they were swept away by the here and now as Elena gasped and made a sobbing sound as he thrust into her. Her hands gripped his buttocks as he found his rhythm, *in-in-in*, and the heat inside him rushed to his loins and suddenly all control was gone, borne away on the tumult that flooded through his lingam and into her yoni. A moan burst from his throat and he found himself sobbing tearlessly into the soft triangle of her neck.

When his breathing had come back to something like normal, he slid out of her and rolled back onto his side, his eyes never leaving her face. 'I love you,' he whispered, because that's what the boys in Aruna Nagar said you were supposed to say, and right now, it was very possibly true.

She giggled, a girlish sound that made him quiver. 'Thank you. I'm rather fond of you too. That was ... mmm, *passionate*.' In the soft light she could have been sixteen. Then her eyes narrowed and her rasping almost-cough voice sounded more its usual acerbic self. 'However, it was also exceedingly *brief*.' Her mouth twitched and she stroked his hair affectionately. 'Young men ... no control at all.'

'Don't I please you?' he asked anxiously.

'You please me very much. You have a face like a demi-god, and the body of a mythic hero. You rescued me from an awful fate and I adore you for all of these things.' She rolled over to face him and propped herself up on one elbow. 'However, one minute of lovemaking is not enough. But you're young: there's still time to knock you into shape.' She smiled, reached out and grasped his softening member. 'I've had to teach you war, magic and cooking. I will very much enjoy teaching you this as well.'

He cuffed her gently, growling. 'I'll show you how to—'

She smiled softly, putting a finger to his lips. 'No, *I'll* show *you*. Listen! I have some good news for you: we're magi and that comes with some very nice side-benefits. Now, start by closing your eyes, and thinking of an incredibly desirable woman. Obviously I'd like to think it's me,' she added with a giggle. 'Now, let those thoughts swirl about, then wrap them around your gnosis ... got it?'

He concentrated and his imagination roaming over her body gave him all the stimulus he needed. He began to feel a warm, erotic glow.

'That's it,' she whispered in his ear. 'Now, send those naughty thoughts coursing into this fellow.' She stroked his slick member with one fingernail, sending a shiver up his spine, and to his amazement it began to grow turgid again. 'Mmm,' she murmured, 'that's the way.'

He felt a painful throbbing as flesh that had only just convulsed in orgasm was forced to harden again, but that was almost immediately overwhelmed by a return of aching desire – then the full effect of the gnosis boost hit his groin and his lingam went so hard he gasped in shock.

She pushed him over onto his back. 'Now,' she purred, sitting astride him, 'let's try this again, shall we?'

Elena lay naked on the rock, baking in the sun. She felt perfect. Her body was as limber and lean as it had ever been, and even in winter the air was warm through the middle of the day. Her pale skin was slowly turning brown. Her limbs ached from training and her loins from lovemaking. The warm glow of amatory satiation suffused her with rare happiness. She felt utterly divorced from what might be happening in the world; only occasionally did her mind prickle with a lingering discontent that those who had wronged her were still prospering.

Yes, yes, we will move soon – we will bloody our swords. But I will enjoy this first.

She turned her head and gazed at Kazim, basking on the rock beside her. It was a month or more since they'd first made love and those early days had been intense, as if they had been making up for lost time. Her loins had taken a battering, but she'd been as insatiable as he was. They rukked the days and nights away: in the pool or beside it; on the cot or under the sky. She lay above him, beneath him, beside him, and whichever way she revelled in him, and in the power of their lovemaking. It even succeeded in banishing her lingering sense of loss for Lorenzo di Kestria, her previous lover; she would always wonder what might have been, but time had passed and Kazim was a young man and full to bursting with life. Even now she marvelled to see his muscular golden body lying beside her; she had to physically quell the urge to crawl onto him and start another bout – but it was darkmoon this week, her bleeding time.

Managing the risk of pregnancy might have made their sexual explorations a little tricky, but they'd managed to be inventive. During her fertile period they put their energies to other uses: scouting the area, flying at night, then moving on foot during the day, checking the road and marking the best ambush points. They slept rough under the starlit skies and used fingers and tongues to pleasure each other, and other tricks to ensure their bliss didn't lead to conception. Such acts were 'nefara' under the Amteh code, but Kazim said he didn't care. 'Rape is the greatest act of nefara, and Gatoz had no qualms about that,' he growled. 'I don't believe in that *bok* any more.'

This was a significant moment for him: a renunciation of the last vestiges of fanaticism. *But then again, he's a young man and preternaturally horny*, Elena thought with a grin. *I suspect he'd renounce anything for sex!*

The following week took them into Janune and they spent the month watching troop movements in the Hytel area, identifying places they could lie low and preparing those sites with caches of food and equipment. She bled as the new moon rose, to her huge relief. She'd never wanted a child with Gurvon, and she certainly didn't want one now, not to a Souldrinker, in spite of all she felt for him. Her theory appeared to be correct too: her gnostic abilities were unchanged, though sometimes she noticed his aura clinging to hers, and she had to forcibly sever those bindings, an odd and uncomfortable sensation. She started to worry that the intermingling of auras might be what turned a mage into a Dokken, but weeks passed and she decided that it too was a false concern.

When her courses passed, they were at each other again like rabbits until fertility once again enforced caution and gave her battered purse a respite. Now, though, she felt ready to draw steel once again.

'Kaz, Janune – Moharram – is almost gone,' she whispered now. 'It's time we acted.'

He nodded, not opening his eyes. 'I am ready.'

'Are you? To kill men you've never met?'

'They are invaders and infid—' He grunted. 'They are enemies.' He rolled onto his side, which gave her a wonderful view of his magnificent physique. 'You are the one who will be fighting your countrymen. How do you feel?'

'They're not my countrymen. Noromen don't like Rondians either.'

'Neighbours always make the worst enemies. It is like that everywhere.'

'True enough.' She sat up and drew her knees to her chest. 'I just wish we could stay like this for ever.'

He sat up too and studied her face. 'Because we two are at peace does not mean the world is.'

'I know. Gurvon is out there, and Rutt and Mara too. They deserve death many times over.' She shifted a little uneasily, then added, 'Cera too.' *Oh Cera, I still don't understand why you turned on me.* 'The Dorobon think they can turn my spiritual home into their own pig-trough. I'm not going to let them.'

'You don't need to persuade me. All my life I was raised on the evil of the Crusade,' Kazim murmured. 'My father was all but burned alive in it.'

'As was my sister,' Elena commented. 'Strange coincidence.'

Kazim raised an eyebrow, but didn't follow up the thought. 'My point is, I must do my part, as any man must. I will not fight alongside the Hadishah, because they are corrupt. But I must still fight, and I will do that at your side. Because I love you.'

She smiled at him a little sadly. 'I'm twice your age, Kaz.'

'You are timeless,' he replied. 'You will never grow old.'

She looked away, thinking about the lines on her brow, the crow's feet and dark shadows about her eyes – and about the fact that swordplay was a young person's game and some days she felt every one of her forty years. 'I wish that were so.'

'My adopted mother, Tanuva Ankesharan, used to say that a

woman is only as old as the men in her life,' Kazim told her. 'That makes you as young as me.'

'Good, because I've never wanted to grow old.'

'You will. With me, and our seven children.'

She pulled a face. 'Seven?'

'Or eight. Maybe more. Enough for a kalikiti team.'

She laughed. 'You might need to marry more than one woman if that's your ambition.'

'Fortunately, I am Amteh – this is permitted.' He grinned wickedly. 'You would always be my favourite wife, of course. At first, anyway.'

'I should bloody think so!' She cuffed him lightly and they kissed, then she pulled away before she was turned from more serious matters. 'We need to decide on our first target. There is a way-station on the road to Hytel, twenty miles from here. The Dorobon caravans are coming through on the same day every second week.'

'I know the one,' he said thoughtfully. 'There is usually only one mage and a cohort of legionaries to guard around a dozen wagons. Small enough for us to take on.'

'The next one is due the second week of Febreux – Safar – and that's next week. If we move tomorrow, we'll have time to properly prepare.'

Kazim looked around the arid landscape and she could almost see his blood pump just that little bit harder. He was excited, but not with the innocence of the unblooded. He knew what killing was, and the cost that exacted. But he was eager for the test.

She was well past such emotions now. She saw only an unpleasant job that had to be done.

Gurvon. Rutt. Mara.

And Cera.

Oh, Cera . . .

4

Beggars' Court

Alms-Giving in Brochena

Queen Lilludh has instituted a new custom: she doles out leftovers each morning in the gardens of the zenana. Hundreds of women and children are fed there now, and they are all so cheery. It's rather sweet, and of course it does give the poor dear something to do.

SARNIA DI KESTRIA, ROYAL MISTRESS, JAVON 743

Brochena, Javon, on the continent of Antiopia
Moharram (Janune) 928
7th month of the Moontide

There was a small courtyard at the back of the Royal Palace in Brochena, a place they called the Beggars' Court. It was near the kitchens and over time had become the place where alms were distributed – mostly leftover food, but on holy days it was the tradition to give out coins too. A clerk had been assigned to ensure that the alms went only to the genuinely needy, and it was all done in the name of the queen, as the Beggars' Court backed onto the rear gateway of the gardens of the zenana, the queen's suite within the palace. It was rare for the queen herself to attend; it was only expected at the New Year celebrations. As she had been only a regent last year, Cera had never done it.

But every day, women gathered in the gardens, and the distribution of the leftovers represented the opportunity she craved to return to public life.

I am a queen of Javon, she reminded herself, lowering her circlet onto her brow and examining herself in the mirror. She wore a violet dress, the colour of her family, House Nesti, and her thick braids were bound in gold chains and looped on top of her head. Glowing amethyst earrings and a larger gemstone set in a solid gold torc completed her dress. A long, serious face stared back at her, older than she remembered. She was too plain for beauty, but she could allow that she now had a dignity about her; her matronly look echoed her dead mother, as if she'd bypassed childhood and gone straight to middle age.

But it was not unbecoming, she allowed. She looked queenly, and that was what was required today.

And she was attractive enough to tempt Gurvon Gyle, apparently – sufficiently so that when she'd thrown herself at him whilst under gnostic influence he'd not pushed her away. He still looked at her in the way men looked at prettier girls. But the very thought of him filled her with loathing, even though she had flirted at times to try and get her way, both because he was the man who'd murdered her parents, and because all men left her cold.

Accepting this truth about herself, that she was safian, still made her deeply uneasy. It was a stoning offence under al-Shaar, the Amteh law, and Sollan law would see her locked away in a convent for the rest of her life. But she knew herself now, knew what she was. It didn't mean that suddenly she was lustfully eyeing the breasts or buttocks of every women she saw, but she finally understood why the men at court had always left her unmoved, even in happier times. There had been something missing, and now she held that missing piece.

Not that self-knowledge had made life – or love – any easier.

Portia Tolidi had revealed her secret to her, seducing and unravelling her with gentle patience, each of the painfully few opportunities a scary and beautiful ecstasy. But deep inside she knew that Portia was not safian herself, merely generous enough to give succour to a lost young woman.

She is the most beautiful woman in the kingdom; what rational reason is there for her to make love to me out of anything but pity?

Portia was also Francis' favoured queen; he bedded her almost nightly. Recently she had succumbed to a bout of illness that Cera was certain was morning sickness. If she really was with child, their own fledgling relationship would soon be tested by separation as well as secrecy: the Gorgio's arrangements with the Dorobon was that Portia would be sent north to give birth in her family home in Hytel.

The thought of being alone with her own longings unfulfilled ate at her sleep and tainted her thoughts. She'd always been contemptuous of those who became so overcome with adoration for another that they ceased to think; to be this lovelorn herself felt both ludicrous and heartbreaking.

So instead, I will throw myself into this new thing and see where it leads, she thought firmly.

The door slid open and Tarita, her young maid, poked her head through. 'Are you ready?' she asked, her pert face alive with mischief, no hint of subservience in her demeanour. She was Cera's eyes and ears in the city, able to go out where Cera could not; it was her daily descriptions of life in the city under Dorobon rule that had given Cera this idea. 'The crowd is gathering.'

'Where is the king?' Cera asked.

'Asleep,' Tarita replied with a wink.

'And Gyle?'

'Meeting with the senior Dorobon knights. Again.'

Cera nibbled her lower lip. Gyle had been seen a lot with the Dorobon knights recently; she thought they had cut some kind of deal, but she had no idea what. She'd tried to talk to Francis about it last month when they were alone, after he'd bedded her in his usual perfunctory manner, but he'd become enraged and stormed out of the chamber. *It was as if he was too frightened to think about the consequences,* she thought now. She turned her attention back to Tarita.

'Well then, we should not be interrupted too swiftly,' she said, trying to sound light-hearted. She stuffed her purse with the copper coins Tarita proffered and went to the alms-giving.

'Sal'Ahm, Holy Queen,' the woman said. 'Light be upon you.' It was early morning still, and the breath of the crowd made a steam that hung in the cold air.

'His blessings upon you also,' Cera replied formally, reaching through the iron bars of the gate to press her last copper into the woman's upturned hands. Beside her, scullery maids were handing small loaves of bread through the grilles to the women who waited with mouths open like baby birds. There were three dozen of them at least. 'What is your name?'

The woman seized her hand, kissed it, touched it to her forehead. 'I am Mukla, Holy Queen.' She was wearing a bekira-shroud – all the women were – but here in the Beggars' Court only women were permitted, so they were allowed to lower their hoods. Her deeply wrinkled face had been eroded by poverty and unending work under the harsh sun; her teeth were broken stumps and her nose was running in the chill air. Her tangled oily hair was fast turning grey.

'How come you to be here?' Cera asked. The woman still had not let go her hand.

'My husband has cast me out for siding with my daughter over a matter of honour,' Mukla replied, her voice simmering. She kissed Cera's hand again. 'The Godspeakers condemn her. You are her only hope.'

Cera glanced at Tarita, who lowered her gaze. This was the woman the little maid had told her to talk to.

This is it. If I have the nerve to go through with this plan, then it begins here.

Mukla too glanced at Tarita, her own face anxious. She had been primed, but it was clear she did not truly believe her prayers might be answered. She dropped Cera's hand and waited expectantly as Cera returned to the throne on the plinth behind her.

She seated herself and clapped her hands for silence. 'My people,' she said, pitching her voice to fill the courtyard, 'I have given you what alms I can, but there is another gift I can give you: my attention. I would hear from you of those injustices you suffer, the reasons you are here in the Beggars' Court, instead of home with your family.'

An immediate clamour rose from the small gathering. 'I'm constantly beaten, for no reason!' one woman shouted.

'They took my child away!' called another.

'My husband is missing – his brother killed him, then paid the Godspeaker not to investigate!'

'My son is to be stoned for buggery, but it is a lie!'

'They cut off my hand for theft, but I didn't steal anything!'

'The Godspeakers won't listen to cases brought by women!'

Cera raised a hand. 'Please! Please! I will hear you all, but you will sit, and I will listen to your stories one at a time.' She watched as the women reluctantly complied, jostling for position then sitting cross-legged on the ground before the grilled metal gate.

When the hubbub had died down, she pointed to Mukla and said, 'You – please, step forth now and tell me your story.'

Mukla stood and came to the gate. Clinging to it as if for strength, she started, 'Please, Holy Queen, I am Mukla, daughter of Rabab the sandal-maker, and I am married to Hazmani the belt-maker. We have six living children. My Oviya, the eldest, is now fourteen and she has newly been blessed with the sacred blood, so we began to arrange suitors.'

The seated women murmured amongst themselves: when a girl began to bleed, it was a delicate time for the whole family. They were expected to marry immediately, but they were often moody and changeable at this time. Cera thought it an inhumanly young age to become a wife and mother, and she was eternally grateful that her own parents had been of the same mind.

'One young man – a metalworker, like his father and uncles – looked to be a match, but my daughter did not like him,' Mukla continued. 'We asked about and found that he was known to be intemperate, and that his father was not as well-off as he pretended, so we curtailed the courtship.'

A hum of worried anticipation filled the courtyard: such a scenario was often a precursor to unpleasantness.

'The young man came to our door, asking to see our daughter one last time, to beg forgiveness, and we foolishly admitted him – but as soon as my daughter appeared, he pulled out a waterskin and squirted liquid into my daughter's face, then ran away.'

The woman broke off speaking and wailed out loud, and Cera shuddered at the grief in her voice. After a moment she said gently, 'Mukla, I must have the whole story.'

One woman put her arms around Mukla, and she wiped her face on the sleeve of her bekira-shroud before saying brokenly, 'The liquid was acid, used for decorative etching of metalwork, and before we could wash it away the left side of my daughter's face had been burned right through to the bone. My beautiful girl lost her left eye, and her skin was burned from the acid which splashed all down her front . . .'

Cries of sympathetic anguish filled the courtyard, frightening the pigeons and crows into the air, and it was several minutes until Mukla could speak again. She could not stop weeping now. 'At first, my husband Hazmani and I were united: the young man must be arrested and punished.'

'Vaii!' the crowd shouted, 'vaii!!' *Yes, it must be so.*

'But the Royal Court would not hear us!' Mukla shouted, indignation giving her the strength to continue. A pregnant hush fell over the crowd and the women eyed Cera warily, waiting to see how she would took this.

And this is the heart of the matter, she thought, *right here. This is why I am here.*

Octa Dorobon had demanded the constitutional laws be redrafted in her bid to legitimise Dorobon rule, and Don Francesco Perdonello, the rigorous and upright head of the Grey Crows, Javon's bureaucracy, had to comply, meaning he could no longer staff the justice courts adequately with clerks who knew the statutes and could advise the young King Francis. And Francis had no interest in the law anyway – his idea of kingship was all war, banquets and hunts. So instead of the royal courts settling civil cases, such matters were now falling into the hands of two feuding factions: those seeking to mete out religious law and those looking to administer vigilante justice.

The Javon nobility had spent centuries trying to wrest control of civil justice from the Amteh Godspeakers, whose arbitrary inter-pretations of the ancient holy scripts were not only a mass of contradictions but, more worryingly, enshrined racial, sexual and gender bigotries endemic in the religion. The justice administered by the nobles might not always be better, but at least it had been rela-tively consistent and understandable – and now Francis Dorobon's lack of interest in justice meant those hard-won rights were falling back into the Godspeakers' hands.

Which was why Cera had selected this case specifically for the Beg-gars' Court. Few there would know that she had no authority – even a queen could not administer justice unless she was sole ruler in her own right. But she could listen.

'Your queen is hearing you now,' Cera said loudly, and as a sigh ran through the gathering, Mukla looked up at her, gratitude and belief on her face: belief in the magic of titles and authority to make things happen.

'We had no choice but to go to the Godspeaker,' she said, her head bowed as she gathered her courage. 'But the Godspeaker did not give us justice.'

The gathering exhaled as one, and again their eyes searched Cera's face, looking for signs of reproof. Criticising a Godspeaker in public was not something done lightly.

'Tell us,' Cera invited.

Mukla's hands tightened on the iron bars. 'The family of the young man lied! They claimed that my daughter had committed indecen-cies upon the boy, to lure him into marriage!' Her voice was shaking with anger, each sentence ringing through the court. 'They swore on the holy *Kalistham* itself and then told their wicked lies!'

'Were the boy and girl ever left unsupervised?' Cera asked gently.

'Never! There were always uncles from both families present,' Mukla said.

'And why would this boy harm your daughter?' Cera asked loudly, wanting the answer to be heard by all. This was becoming too com-mon in Javon: that a young man would seek to harm any girl who rejected him, because it hurt his pride and damaged him in the marriage market; too many refusals and the whole family might be affected. Some tried to blame the prospective bride to protect their own reputation, but the worst were those who sought to exact retribution like this boy, using acid or knives to mutilate faces and breasts.

'He ruined my daughter from spite!' Mukla shouted. 'He was ashamed of being refused!' She burst into tears. 'She was so beautiful, my Oviya, the light of my life! She deserves justice! *Justice!*'

Cera threw up a hand as the call for justice echoed from the palace walls and as silence fell, asked, 'How came you and your husband Hazmani to fall out?'

'At the Godspeaker's court Hazmani took money from the boy's family to withdraw the charges,' Mukla said.

Cera had to suppress the urge to growl in disgust. This too was disgracefully predictable – the sort of thing that happened far too frequently ... which was why she and Tarita had selected this case. No doubt the father could see no point in defending the honour of a ruined girl, so why not take a few coins, allow the girl to bear the guilt and no doubt hope she would become another's problem. She was now unmarriageable, nothing but a burden on her family, so unless some man could be found to take her in out of pity, her fate was either slavery or, if she converted, a place among the Sollan sisters. That wasn't an option for most Amteh. Many girls in such a plight took their own lives – though Cera suspected that many such suicides were assisted, and involuntary.

'You refused to agree with your husband?' Cera asked gently.

Mukla nodded, tears streaming down her face. 'I stood before the Godspeaker and denied these lies, even as my husband was changing my daughter's plea. So he cast me out without my dowry, and my daughter too, and now I can live only through charity. If I cannot have justice, my daughter must be sold into service or we will starve together.' She made begging gestures with her clasped hands, and repeated, 'She was so beautiful, Holy Queen–'

'Is she here?' Cera asked.

Tarita had spent a day persuading Mukla that it would be

necessary to display her daughter to the queen. A small figure completely covered by her bekira-shroud was ushered to the front. Her mother turned to her and slowly lowered the hood. The crowd hissed as her left side was presented to them, but Cera at first saw only her right side: a sweet, sad face; she could have been any pretty girl in the market.

Then the girl turned and Cera saw the whole of the left side, from above the hairline to the jaw, and the neck below, was livid red and glistening wetly. Where her left eye should have been was a sightless white orb oozing yellowy pus. The ear was half-eaten away and upper and lower teeth were visible through holes in her cheek. Though she'd been prepared for something horrible, Cera was still aghast.

I should not forget that this might be a move in a game, but it is also about real people – real crimes, she thought, trying to keep her face impassive.

'Holy Queen, you are our only hope,' Mukla pleaded. 'Please, give us justice!'

The call was taken up, and throughout the Beggars' Court the women chanted, 'Adaala, Adaala, Adaala!' – *Justice, justice, justice!*

She could feel their anger building and at last she raised her hands for silence. 'My people,' she cried, 'I am only a queen. I may do no more than beg my husband the king for justice.'

The gathering fell silent, then let loose a hissing sound of displeasure. 'The king will not listen!' someone from the back shouted. 'He does not care!'

'But I care,' Cera shouted in response. 'Your tale breaks my heart and I too wish to see justice!' She looked theatrically at the towers above, where the Dorobon flags flew. 'My people, justice is something all people crave. Disagreements happen, crimes are committed, but it is how we deal with them that defines us. Fairness must be seen for the king to retain the love of his people! This is why in his role as Justiciari, the king listens to both the accused and the accuser equally. This is why his judgements must be rooted in the statutes, not in arbitrary whim and selective use of scripture – this is why justice cannot be neglected. And it will not be!'

She paused, and the crowd, growing all the time as people slipped in from the market streets outside to see what was happening, fell silent expectantly.

'I will tell you a story,' she said, dropping her words carefully into the silence. 'Once there was a robber from Hytel who came to Brochena because he thought the people of Brochena foolish and easy to steal from.'

The story was well-known; it had been told many times when the nobles had wrested control of the courts from the Amteh. It was almost certainly made up, but she told it anyway.

'This robber was wrong, and the vigilant people of Brochena seized him and turned him over to the Godspeaker for punishment. But the robber told the Godspeaker he had much gold hidden away, and he agreed to hand it over in return for his freedom. So the robber was freed, and the Godspeaker profited.'

The gathering hissed angrily, though they had all heard this tale before, and plenty of others besides; the Godspeakers themselves had their own variants, designed to show the perfidy of noblemen.

'However, the people who saw this injustice were not happy, so they found and captured the robber and they surrounded the Godspeaker outside his own Dom-al'Ahm and demanded the gold with which the robber had bribed him. The robber they hanged, and the Godspeaker they sent on his way. They took the robber's gold and distributed it to his victims. And thus is it known that true justice lies in the hands of the people.'

She felt the *frisson* of tension in the court grow as the crowd took in her message, none too subtle: that they were not powerless.

Sol et Lune! I can't believe I'm advocating mob justice. She took a deep breath. *But if that is what it must take . . .*

'My people,' she said, her voice intimate, confiding, 'from the time I was a child, my father ensured that I was well versed in law. He knew that there might come a time when I was forced by circumstance to hear such cases. You may have seen me sitting at my father's knee as he heard your problems.' She'd been known as *La Scrittoretta* – the Little Scribe-Girl – as she'd sat beside her father's throne jotting down notes during his cases and writing up his verdicts as he spoke. She saw several of the women smile at the remembrance.

'So while I might not be permitted to hear cases, I am permitted to listen. And if at times I venture an opinion, you are not obligated to accept it, but my views might give you some . . . *consolation*.'

She studied the upturned, hopeful faces; she saw understanding grow.

Yes, come to me, tell me your complaints and hear my opinions. Act on them as you see fit, because there are many, many ways to ensure that a person suffers if the community at large agrees that it should be so . . .

'So hear me, my people. I cannot legally sit in judgement, but I can give an opinion, which you can choose to ignore. In this matter I believe that Mukla's husband should take his wife and daughter back. I believe the boy who perpetrated this offence should be punished.' That meant being hanged, everyone here knew that. 'And I believe that this boy's family should support your wronged daughter for the rest of her life.'

Murmurs of agreement, and anger directed at the boy and his family, filled the courtyard. Mukla fell to her knees, her daughter beside her, their hands clasped in thanks.

Cera swallowed, and wonder whether any of her decree would come to pass – after all, she had no formal authority, and no power to enforce her views. But word would spread, that she knew.

She looked around, and at Tarita's nudge, beckoned forward another woman, who spoke on behalf of an already dead daughter, stoned to death for adultery after being raped by a married man who had been acquitted of any crime; another bereaved mother spoke of another rape by the same man; an act which had driven her only daughter to suicide.

'Such a man deserves no protection from the Godspeakers, if his guilt is known,' Cera ventured. Heads nodded, and more cases were raised. Next she heard from the daughter of a woman sold into slavery for a theft she had not committed and who had then been denied freedom even when the true thief had been caught. She heard from servants abused by masters, mothers whose girls had been abducted and sold into prostitution in neighbouring towns; victims of property disputes, confidence tricksters and false doctors. Some of the tales were heartbreaking, others just made her furious. And some were disputed, as relatives of one side or other came forward to tell their versions of the truth.

Once Cera had heard both sides of the case, she gave an opinion. The first time she ventured her view, that the plaintiff might be entitled to compensation, the accused, who had knowingly passed off used cooking oil as a herbal remedy, read the mood of those about her and suspecting that her life would not be worth living if she did not comply, paid up immediately and apologised, her head bowed low. It set a precedent, and more people began to gather, and more cases were raised.

Cera sat all day without a break, soothing her throat with tea brought by silent servants. Some time after noon she became conscious of a grey-clad man on the battlements above, watching silently. The crowd, growing all the time, saw him too, and a few brave souls jeered at him. Cera smiled inwardly as he disappeared, but outwardly, she ignored the interruption.

As the sun went down, she called the session to an end. 'My people, thank you for telling me your tales,' she said, rising from the throne. 'I thank you for your generosity, and your indulgence in hearing what are nothing more than my opinions.'

'Holy Queen, when will you come here again?' Tarita asked loudly, and the cry was taken up throughout the yard.

'Tomorrow morning,' Cera said tiredly, 'from the third bell.'

Gurvon Gyle found Queen Cera Nesti on her balcony, wrapped up in herself, her eyes closed and her whole body shaking. It was evening, and the banquet about to commence below awaited his presence. Cera had already cried off, pleading illness.

Exhaustion is more likely, Gurvon thought. *She's been holding informal court all day*. He studied her, still faintly stirred by her combination of serious intellect and womanly dignity. In the two weeks since the fall of Octa Dorobon he'd been deliberately avoiding her; he was disturbed by how easily he'd fallen into Octa's trap. Cera had been mesmerised with the gnosis and sent to his rooms to seduce him, which would have given Octa Dorobon the chance to lay charges of adultery against him. It was a simple, almost banal plot, and it had so very nearly worked.

Mesmerism works best when you're persuading someone to do something they are inclined towards anyway . . . That hinted at vulnerabilities he could exploit.

Her black hair, still braided and caught up in gold filigree, gleamed in the setting sun. She wasn't a statuesque beauty like Portia Tolidi, but she was by no means ill-formed either. If she did not develop a taste for exercise she would run to fat in middle age, but for now she had an attractive face and a full but pleasing figure. But it was her mind that interested him: Cera was a dispassionate thinker, cool under pressure and willing to take risks. She'd been regent for less than a year, but she and Elena had been a formidable team and that hadn't been down to Elena entirely. Her name still had power among the people of Javon, something she was only just beginning to realise. His agents told him that many Jhafi and Rimoni commoners believed she would escape and unite them in rebellion, but without her, her people were paralysed.

That was something he could put to good use. His own bridges, if not burned, were certainly on fire. Octa Dorobon had been a favourite of Mater-Imperia Lucia and Octa had to have moved against him with Lucia's blessing. But the fact that Lucia had kept her name out of the matter hinted at a way back. The bankers Jusst & Holsen had his gold in transit, and Francis Dorobon was pliable. Javon was still the haven he needed post-Crusade, but it was becoming volatile again. The Godspeakers were speaking against him, and the Javonesi nobles were meeting soon to discuss disinheriting the boy-king Timori Nesti and choosing another to lead them in rebellion. He needed to regain full control before war broke out, and that included the Dorobon court and its queens.

So what was Cera Nesti doing in her little courtyard? he wondered. *And how can I use it?*

'Cera,' he said softly, speaking in Rimoni, the tongue they shared. He raised a placatory hand as she jerked around, frightened at his sudden appearance. 'Peace, girl. I mean you no harm.'

'I don't wish to see you,' she said loudly. 'Not without a chaperone.'

'Don't be ridiculous. Octa's dead, girl. Show some gratitude: I saved you from the axe.'

'Really. Where's my brother? I want to see Timori.'

'You will, as soon as it can be arranged. Right now I have more urgent matters to attend to.' Which was true: he had to reassert control over King Francis, mollify Mater-Imperia Lucia and get his mercenary friends inside Javon as soon as possible. 'What were you doing in the courtyard today?'

'The Beggars' Court? I gave alms. And listened to my people.'

'Really? What for?'

'Because I care.'

He studied her face. She sounded in earnest, but she was also an intelligent young woman who was politically adept. 'Inciting rebellion is treason.'

'I didn't incite anything. I listened to complaints, that is all.'

'You heard civil cases?'

'I listened. I did not judge: I don't have the right, as I'm *only* a woman.'

Gurvon was dimly aware that Francis had stopped hearing civil cases, because constitutional reforms were sucking up all the legal resources. But the clergy were stepping in, surely? That had been something he'd been happy to allow Francis to relinquish, as it had taken the heat out of the Godspeakers' incessant preaching against the Crusade. 'Acmed al-Istan has been hearing the civil cases recently.'

'He has no constitutional right to do so,' Cera sniffed. 'And his Godspeakers don't rule according to the facts. They favour the pious and the generous over those who've been wronged.'

He couldn't deny that. His spies told him that the al-Shaar Courts were as barbaric as any Inquisition Court in Yuros. 'His judgement in some matters has been . . . hmmm, rather extreme, I admit.'

'He's a Godspeaker: his only standard of judgement is a book written hundreds of years ago which demands maiming or killing for every crime.'

'That's what happens when you leave priests in charge of the law.'

'Javon has used the Rimoni Empire system of adversarial justice for centuries,' Cera told him, lifting her head proudly. 'But perhaps you prefer allowing the same people who declared shihad against you to settle your civil cases now?'

He looked at her, his interest piqued. *Perhaps there is something going on here I can use . . .* Civil law hadn't been a priority of his, and it was the blade you ignored that invariably got you where it hurt. 'Once Perdonello has completed the reforms, civil law will be given to the bureaucracy, where it belongs under Rondian law.'

'And when exactly will that be?' she enquired archly. 'Six months for Don Perdonello to complete his redrafting, a year, maybe? Then his people will have to *learn* the law: his Grey Crows are not trained as legalae; they don't as a matter of course learn the things I've been taught.'

'You have no authority to judge cases,' he reminded her sharply, annoyed that she was right.

'No, I don't. Not legally. But some people listen to what I say.'

He'd seen that. Though he spoke no Jhafi, he'd heard the tones of the voices, felt the mood of the gathering. He had sensed the growing bonds, formed of indignation and anger and now he extrapolated that in his mind, imagining crowds in the thousands, women and men alike, all hanging on this girl's words and then going forth and applying them in the alleys and slums surrounding the palace.

What would you make of that, Acmed al-Istan?

'When Francis is told what you are doing, he may demand that you stop,' he said levelly.

Cera's lips tightened. 'Perhaps.'

If she is allowed to do this, she could a problem – but an unchecked Amteh clergy is even more dangerous. 'I could put in a good word for you,' he said, meeting her eye. 'If I felt so inclined.'

'What are you insinuating?' she asked, her voice loaded with disgust.

He found himself colouring. 'I'm not *insinuating* anything. I'm *saying* that I could allow you to play Justiciari, if I thought it was in the best interest of the empire.'

'Then if you want your empire to rule over a kingdom that is not tearing itself apart piece by piece through negligence, put in your "good word" without sounding like a whoremonger,' she snapped.

He bared his teeth. 'You're getting well above yourself, you little Noorie bint. It's time Francis put a child in your belly so we can lock you up in the nursery where you can rule over swaddling and lactation routines.'

'At least I'd be suited to that by nature. You're not fit to rule anything, spy.'

'I have a kingdom at my feet: yours!'

'Even so. You might understand all there is to know about *gaining* power, but you know nothing about how to *use* it, and therefore you will lose it.'

'Think you so?' His temper flashed. 'I am newly appointed as Imperial Legate here.'

'An empty title that your emperor could revoke in an instant.' She quoted from an old Rimoni philosopher: 'He who disdains the will of the people must rule by fear, and live in fear.'

'I am a Rondian mage: fear is for lesser mortals.'

'We both know the truth of that, Magister. I'm sure you enjoyed the cells as much as I did.'

He glared. 'You might think standing up to me is brave, girl, but it's not. It's foolish in the extreme.'

She half-turned her head, as if offering a cheek to his hand. The smugness of the gesture infuriated him, but even as the thought that she deserved a beating crossed his mind, a voice intruded.

'Cera?'

He turned as a tall woman with tangle of red ringlets cascading across her porcelain-pale shoulders entered Cera's suite. Combat reflexes had kindled mage-light in his palms before he recognised Portia Tolidi, Cera's sister-queen.

'Haven't you done enough damage?' she snapped, brushing past him as if he were a disobedient child. She gathered Cera into her arms like a protective older sister. 'Leave her alone!'

He hadn't yet got Portia worked out. She was the undoubted beauty of the realm and Francis' favourite wife, but to Gurvon she seemed a hollow thing. Her family had commanded that she give herself to the young Dorobon king and so she did, but she feigned her affection for Francis. He'd spied on the royal bed and seen her move like a *galmi*, the stone construct of Brician gnostic lore; her body present but her soul faraway. He could never tell what she was thinking, or how she really felt. This was the most emotion he'd ever seen in her, and even now it seemed reserved and calculated, as if she were nothing more than a mediocre actress delivering poorly written lines.

Nevertheless, he had botched this scene. 'I had news of her Majesty's illness,' he said stiffly. 'I am here merely to assure myself that the queen is well.'

'I am well,' Cera said from within Portia's sheltering arms. 'But not well enough to dine publically tonight. I wish only to sit quietly with my sister-queen.'

There was something intimidating in their defiance, as if they took strength from each other. 'Then I wish you both good day,' he said curtly, and left openly by the bedchamber door, startling the guard outside who'd not seen him enter. He strode blindly down the corridors to his own suite, and once he was certain he was alone, he kicked a stone wall until his toes were bruised and his annoyance had receded.

'Gurvon?'

He looked around, angry to be seen in this mood but trying quickly to soften his face for Coin. The shapeshifter was wearing Olivia Dorobon's form, as it was still important to keep Francis from discovering that his beloved sister was dead, slain by Coin herself. Poor fat, boring Olivia, who thought only of food and fleshly pleasures. Gurvon had been screwing the real Olivia as much to annoy Octa as to secure

Francis' support, but he had not enjoyed the liaison and had stopped it the moment Coin had assumed Olivia's persona.

'Gurvon,' Coin said in Olivia's sing-song voice, 'they're looking for you downstairs.'

Sighing, he joined her in the entrance hall to his suite. The last thing he wanted was another stupid banquet. 'Then I suppose that is where I must be.'

She put a hand on his arm. 'We could be a little late,' she said slyly.

'No.' He removed it gently. 'That fiction is over. I've told you before.'

'Francis liked that you were bedding his sister.'

'I don't care what that child prefers. He is my puppet, and he'll think what I tell him to.'

'Then what good do I serve pretending to be this gross cow?' Coin whined. She clutched her Olivia-sized stomach. 'You think I like waddling around like this? I feel like a pig in a trough.'

'You're doing important work,' Gurvon said, trying to keep his temper. *I'm getting utterly sick of women who don't know their place.* 'He's only getting through this because he thinks you're with him – he's lost everyone else he cares about–'

'Hogshit! He spends most nights carousing with his knights – he doesn't even summon Portia to his bed any more, not now he thinks she might be pregnant. He certainly doesn't give a shit about his sister.' Abruptly, Coin altered herself, flowing smoothly from shape to shape in a way that only an absolute master of the art could manage. This was her magic: she was the most perfect shapeshifter of mage history, capable of becoming either gender, flawlessly and with perfect control.

She'd put on Elena's face and form and he flinched as she sashayed towards him, her small Elena-breasts revealed as the dress, too large for the smaller body, slipped off her shoulders. 'Would you rather I looked like this?'

'Yvette!' he snapped, hoping her given name would focus her erratic mind. Her instability made it too easy to forget that she was a pure-blood mage capable of ripping him apart. Her devotion had been hard-won and right now it – and his safety – were at risk here.

93

'Or maybe you'd prefer this?' she added maliciously, as with a twist of meat and bone, Coin became Portia, radiantly beautiful, the dress slipping to her hips, the breasts growing into perfect orbs. Coin had evidently been creeping about at night as well, studying the shapes of the palace women. She seized his limp hand and placed it over her right breast. 'Want to be king for a night?' she purred.

'No, Yvette,' he said, though his mouth had gone dry.

'Or maybe Cera is more your preference: you were crawling all over her when Octa found you both.' Now her voice had dropped to a bitter whine.

He grimaced and looked away as Coin became the Nesti queen, perfectly rendered.

'Yvette, I have a role to play, and so do you. *Please.* We will resolve these . . . personal matters . . . another time.'

She met his eyes and he recognised madness and desire.

For six months he had tended her devotedly while she had lain at the very threshold of death. He had seen it as an investment; if he succeeded, he would have a powerful – and unsuspected – agent at the court, one who owed him *everything*. He wasn't entirely heartless, no matter what Cera Nesti might think, and he could not deny feeling a smidgeon of pity for the hermaphrodite. But he didn't want her adoration, just her obedience. He took on the persona of a father gently upbraiding a beloved child: 'Yvette, I do not respect neediness. I admire intelligence and capability. I know you feel you owe me, that you are looking for ways to repay that debt. I know you're lonely and desire solace. But I can't give you that until you have *earned* it, by showing the qualities I admire. Wearing another person's face won't achieve that.'

For one horrible second he thought he might have to fight for his life. Her eyes hooded and her face became another, seldom seen: her own. She was thin to the point of emaciation, her features bland and indeterminate, her thin ginger cut close to her scalp. Her teeth seemed to grow as her lips parted.

Then she . . . he . . . *it* . . . calmed. 'You resurrected me!' she bleated. 'You saved my life! How can you be so indifferent?'

'Yvette, I *do* care about you – and I know you know that, deep down. But what you want can't happen. Did Octa's strike teach you nothing? We are on a knife's edge here. Play your part, be Olivia a while longer, and everything we want will come about, I promise.'

He'd made such vague promises all his life, words that seemed to say one thing but in reality said little at all. Coin was still naïve enough to be placated by such baseless promises, though.

'Very well. I won't let you down,' she swore, solemn as a child.

'I know you won't,' he replied, straightening her dress for her, a pretence of intimacy. 'Now, be Olivia for me, and attend upon her brother.'

Her body reformed once more, back into the voluptuous shape of the king's sister, and she smiled winningly at him before waddling off with new purpose.

Gurvon watched her go while adding her to his growing list of worries. *For now, she's still useful.* He sighed. *But I'm going to have to kill her eventually.*

Cera waited until the door was shut behind them, before she turned and gave Portia the welcome she had wanted to give the moment she'd stepped into the room. She kissed her lips, pressed herself to her, trembling in the warmth and feel of her. 'Amora,' she breathed.

Portia pulled away. 'That man Gyle frightens me,' she whispered. 'At any moment he could drag us down. I was so frightened when they locked you away. I begged and pleaded but Francis did nothing.'

'I won't let Gyle hurt us,' Cera swore, rashly and against all reason.

Portia's lovely face was clouded with doubt and fear. 'What can we do against him?'

'We are queens. We're not helpless.'

'Queens married to a stupid lustful boy,' Portia said, her lips curling, 'who thinks only with his dildus.'

'I know.' Cera stroked her lustrous hair, kissed her perfect ear lobe. 'But who controls that, my darling? You do.'

Portia's face became clouded. 'He knows that my bleeding is late. In a few days he will announce that I am with child.'

They both knew what that meant: Portia would be sent to Hytel until she came to term.

'Perhaps when I am also with child, he will send me to my family in Forensa,' Cera joked bitterly. Hytel was a Dorobon-controlled territory while Forensa remained free. 'I wish I could go with you.'

'I wish Mater Lune would kill the child in my belly,' Portia cursed. Her hands crept over her still-flat stomach. 'I can feel it in there, like a serpent.'

'Nonsense,' Cera whispered, ignoring the blasphemy. She didn't blame Portia for feeling that way. 'You won't feel anything for ages.' She hugged her sister-queen and tried to kiss her, but Portia pulled her face away.

'Don't, Cera. I don't feel loving right now.' Her voice was sour. Then she looked at Cera properly. 'You look pretty tonight.'

Cera put her head against Portia's breast, leaned into her, desperately wanting to be held, to be touched with a loving hand, but she could feel the mood slipping away. 'I don't feel pretty, just tired. I was in the Beggars' Court all day.'

'Why did you put yourself through that?' Portia asked.

She adored Portia, but Cera couldn't understand her lover's total disinterest towards what was happening outside the palace walls. 'They're suffering, *amora mia*. Someone needs to hear them. Francis won't.'

'The poor are always complaining, darling.'

'They have much to complain about. You should hear their stories.'

Portia shook her head, making her ringlets ripple like liquid gold. 'Let the Crows deal with them.'

'Perdonello's Crows are too busy and the clergy are botching it. Someone has to listen.'

Portia stroked her shoulders. 'But not you, *amora*. All that time outside is bad for your skin – and your clothes smell of smoke from the street. You really must look after yourself better.'

Cera smiled up at her sadly. *She really doesn't understand – or care. But I know she's a good person.* She went up on her tiptoes and kissed her mouth, but again Portia pulled away. 'Cera, please. I'm too scared. You know what was going to happen when they found you and Gyle together – imagine what they would do to *us*.'

Cera didn't have to imagine anything. Safians were always stoned to death publically, and sometimes no one even produced any proof; the mere suspicion of perversion was enough.

'I'm sorry,' Portia whispered. 'I'm so afraid when we're together, ever since that awful night.' Her eyes dropped. 'And now I have a child . . . perhaps it is for the best that I'm to be sent away . . .'

Cera felt her eyes sting suddenly. 'What are you saying?'

Portia stroked her cheek. 'Darling, you knew this couldn't last. It was something you – *we* – needed, at a terrible time in our lives. But now . . . it's just too dangerous.'

'Amora, I–'

'We shouldn't use that word,' Portia said sadly. 'It's too dangerous for us to be lovers.'

Cera clutched her arms. 'Dearest Portia – making love is the least important thing we do together. It's your *company* I need. Your *support*. Your *insights*. Your *smile*. Your *hugs*. All of these things matter far more to me than anything we might do in bed.' She felt her voice crack, but she pressed on, 'I can live without lovemaking, but I can't live without your love.'

'I'm sorry.' Portia looked away. 'I'm not brave like you, Cera.'

'You *are* brave!' she said fiercely. 'You have to go to that pig every night and pretend you enjoy it – I couldn't do that.'

Portia laughed humourlessly. 'Rukking is just rukking – it doesn't matter what man it is with. But I don't want to die. Pater Sol and Mater Lune have seen my sins – will they be merciful? Will they know that I had no choice?'

'They'll know,' Cera replied firmly. 'How could they not?' She took a deep breath and stepped slowly, painfully, away from her lover's arms. 'Portia, will you come to the Beggars' Court tomorrow? It would mean so much for you to be there too. Please? For me?'

Portia's eyelids fluttered rapidly. Her eyes were moist. 'I can't,' she whispered, and fled.

The next day, twice as many women filled the Beggars' Court and the Dorobon palace guard were deployed in the zenana to ensure there was no breach of security. Cera heard about every crime she could imagine, and some she couldn't. Some of the women were clearly lying, or just attention-seekers, but the crowd itself seemed to know who they were, and if their story didn't ring true they were shouted down. Gyle watched from above from time to time, his eyes narrowed. Neither Francis nor Portia came near at all.

By the end of the week there were thousands awaiting Cera in the plaza outside. By the end of the month, the Godspeakers were sending Scripturalists to warn her to cease what she was doing or risk open conflict.

Cera took that as a sign that she was making progress.

<Magister Gyle?>

Gurvon Gyle opened up his mind as he felt the contact. He used a mind-cleansing spell that would give him a few minutes of clear thought, though the price would be the redoubling of his headache later. It had been a long and trying month, and one of the things hanging over his head had been the question of if and when he might receive this contact.

<Mater-Imperia. I trust you are well tonight?>

< We are at the Winter Court in Bres. It is near dusk and the snow has settled. The torch-dancers are lovely.> Lucia Fasterius, Living Saint and Mother of the Empire, sounded like a sentimental aunt tonight, but Gurvon wasn't fooled.

<Bres is beautiful this time of year, Holiness.>

<Indeed. And I can wear my furs without sweating. But enough small-talk, Magister. Let us speak of my late, dear friend, Octa Dorobon . . .>

He stiffened nervously, though she was thousands of miles away. <Mater-Imperia?>

<Octa counted herself a favourite of mine.> Lucia's voice dropped into a

hard, matter-of-fact tone. *<But she was a bore, and she got above herself. When she resolved to bring you down, I knew the loss of one of you was inevitable. You won that duel with her, and I congratulate you. I appointed you my Legate. Your victory over Octa has strengthened my reputation as much as it did yours.>*

She's backing down, letting me have my win. He smiled warily. *<She made the first move, Mater-Imperia, I assure you.>*

<You are my Legate, Magister Gyle. You have my sanction.> She paused, then added, *<For now.>*

That sobered him up. *<I know this, Mater-Imperia. You have my gratitude.>*

<However, Magister Gyle, the Javon situation concerns me. It is vital, not just for the duration of the Crusade, but beyond, not least because the Dorobon were charged with supplying the Crusade with produce and equipment. Those supplies concern me far more than who is nominally in charge.>

<The supplies will continue to be delivered, Holiness; I assure you of that.> He scarcely heard his own reply, for his mind was still flip-flopping over what she had just said: *Those supplies concern me far more than who is nominally in charge.* That was tantamount to handing him control of the kingdom, should he be brave enough to reach out and grasp it.

There's a logic in that, he mused. *She knows as well as anyone that a conflict between my people and the Dorobon would effectively hand the kingdom back to the locals. She also knows by now that I have mercenaries on the way, so if she was going to intervene, it would require substantial resources, and she can't spare them from the Crusade.* He smiled again, more deeply this time.

<Has news of Shaliyah reached Javon yet?> she asked. *<I know how primitive things are there, with so few magi to relay news.>*

Gurvon doubted Lucia had any idea what 'primitive' even looked like. *<Mater-Imperia, the news reached us tonight. There has been rioting, but nothing we can't handle.>*

<General Korion reports similar unrest in other major cities as news of Shaliyah spreads. Some garrisons have been hard-pressed, but this was anticipated and losses have been low.>

<Here in Brochena the city has emptied significantly since the Dorobon

arrived, so we are under no real threat. The riots may cause damage to some of the poorer sectors, but they'll kill more of their own people than ours.>

<No loss, then.> Lucia's voice took on an edge. <Magister Gyle, let me be frank. Kaltus Korion reports that three mercenary legions have deserted and are marching north through the Zhassi Valley toward Javon. One is alleged to have seized the Krak di Condotiori. Korion wants your head, and so does my son. I, however, am minded to be practical for now – but I will remind you, Magister, that I am a patient woman. No one who has wronged me has ever prospered in the end.>

He chose his words carefully, to begin mending bridges. <Holiness, once I had escaped from Octa, I realised that the only way I could function as your Imperial Legate here was to have soldiers of my own. Francis hated his mother and he supports me, but many of his people don't. I called in favours with those mercenary commanders solely to preserve the empire's stake in Javon.>

Lucia's mental voice became sharp. <You know, Gyle, one of the things I like about you is your constant plausibility. But I fear that there are times when that credibility becomes stretched. I have it on good authority that these mercenaries of whom I speak are – shall we say, 'friends' of the mercenary captain Endus Rykjard. And that same Captain Rykjard is currently in Javon and ostensibly under Francis' command. And that same authority describes you and Rykjard as 'thick as thieves' – a singularly apt description, I thought. I also understand that you yourself recommended Rykjard to Octa Dorobon in the first place. So, Magister Gyle> – her voice pierced Gurvon's aching head – <when exactly did you conceive stealing Javon for yourself?>

He didn't hesitate, not for an instant. <I am not stealing Javon, Holiness. I am preserving it for you and for the empire, as I was ordered to do.>

Her laugh was brittle. <As I said: always plausible.> He could hear the sound of her fingers drumming. <So, you are manoeuvring your pieces onto the board, Gyle. It is a pretty little plan. I suppose you see yourself as King of Javon come the end of this game?>

<Of course not. Me a king? I don't have the breeding.> He was pretty sure he managed to keep the sarcasm out of his voice.

<You certainly don't, Gurvon Gyle.> She fell silent again, and Gurvon

pictured her pleasant, matronly face silently fuming. <*Were we not paying you enough, Gyle? Or is your greed truly without bounds?*>

This was it. If he couldn't persuade her now, he could measure his lifespan in hours. <*With all respect, Mater-Imperia, Javon is on a knife-edge. I have said all along that two legions would never be enough to control it. We have postponed an uprising thus far only because we have Timori Nesti as hostage and we have secured Cera Nesti as queen – both my initiatives, I will remind you. But the usefulness of these hostages will end as soon as the Javonesi nobility elect a new king. So however it happened, it is fortuitous that those mercenaries are coming here.*>

<*You think you can dictate policy to me from Javon and present it as a fait accompli?*> Her mental voice could have frozen birds in midair. <*Those mercenary legions were protecting vital supply lines! Kaltus Korion's army is fighting as we speak – and not mudskin peasants with pitchforks and dinner knives but a real enemy, with magi of their own. He needs those supply lines open!*>

<*If we can't hold Javon the supply lines will be cut anyway. They are better deployed here.*>

Lucia tsked angrily. It felt like she was about to lose her temper – but then she recovered herself. <*By Kore, Gyle, you can twist words. Very well, damn it, I will authorise the transfer of those mercenary legions to Javon. Let it all appear planned. But you had better deliver: do you understand?*>

<*I understand, Mater-Imperia. Completely.*>

<*Then you will promise me this: your guarantee of the safety of Francis Dorobon whilst you are my Legate in Javon.*>

<*But any mischance—*>

<*Will be blamed on you. I mean it, Gyle: I want your personal guarantee!*>

He scowled. <*Of course, Mater-Imperia.*>

She went silent for a time, then abruptly she changed subject. <*You know, I never actually believed that Salim would defeat Echor. I thought at best Echor would be badly bruised, enough to keep Argundy weak – but so comprehensive a defeat? All of Argundy is in shock . . . Kaltus even lost his only legitimate son.*>

<*I'm sorry* . . .> Gurvon paused, and then said carefully, <*You mean that Kaltus Korion put his only son into Echor's army, knowing what was planned?*>

Lucia smiled faintly at his incredulity. <*Kaltus was disappointed in young Seth. I believe he is planning to legitimise one of his bastards – he has forty or so to select from, and one or two are pure-blooded, I gather.*>

Gurvon ran his fingers through his hair. That was the true definition of cold-hearted. <*Well, I suppose the Shaliyah part of our plan has worked perfectly, Mater-Imperia.*> He studied her image, and got the sudden feeling that she was troubled by something. <*Surely you have no regrets, Holiness?*>

<*Of course not. But* . . .> Suddenly, unexpectedly, she burst out, <*Where did all these damned Keshi magi come from, Gyle? You and Vult introduced Rashid Mubarak to the Imperial Council: did you know he had such resources at his finger-tips?*>

<*Sainted Lady, I swear I didn't,*> he protested, completely honestly. <*I thought the same as you. But the reports I've seen – of hundreds of magi – you must believe me when I say I am as shocked as anyone.*>

<*Are you? Survivors who reached Peroz say the Keshi had Dokken among their army. Kore-bedamned Souldrinkers, Gyle! Has Rashid allied with our oldest enemy?*>

Gurvon almost lost the connection. <*Dokken?*> The blood drained from his face and he felt his mouth go dry. Despite all his years of spying, all his guerrilla warfare, he'd never encountered a true Dokken other than the tame one Calan Dubrayle had displayed at the pre-Crusade council in 926. In his heart he had believed them to be little more than rumour. <*The reports are certain?*> he said at last.

<*Very certain. Salim and Rashid had at least a hundred Dokken with them at Shaliyah. My observers – those who escaped and were able to report back – are adamant. Our magi were fully engaged, allowing our legions to be overwhelmed. Salim has hundreds of Dokken, when we believed there to be no more than a few dozen outcasts eking out their existence in the wild. Rashid will move north next. Kaltus will have a real fight on his hands. The whole Crusade is in danger, Gyle.*>

He rubbed his forehead, trying to take this in. *Rashid has outma-noeuvred us all.* He took a deep breath, and sought a positive slant on this news. <*Mater-Imperia, if Rashid has allied with Dokken, it is fortunate he revealed them against Echor and not Korion.*>

<*Indeed – I suppose we can be thankful for that. But now Salim is stronger than ever. After being cowed into submission by two Crusades, his people will believe they can win. Salim's army is reportedly flooded with new recruits.*>

<*What is Korion doing about it?*>

<*Kaltus is doing what Kaltus does: killing people and burning things. He has all the resource of the empire at his disposal – construct-beasts, windfleets, khurne-riders, Inquisitors, pure-blood magi– and he will overcome, I am sure. But your plan was for Echor and Salim to destroy each other, leaving Kaltus in complete control of northern Kesh for when the final phase begins.*>

<*Kaltus Korion is the empire's greatest general,*> Gurvon said. <*He controls its mightiest army, Mater-Imperia. I have no doubt he will prevail.*> He was suddenly sure that that the mighty Lucia Fasterius was actually afraid. <*My Lady, no plan survives first contact with the enemy. I am confident that we hold all the major cards.*>

Her mental voice dropped to a whisper so faint he barely caught it. <*Would that we did.*> Then with a jolt he realised that he wasn't supposed to have heard her at all. Her words were accompanied by a genuine sense of palpable fear, which she instantly masked. When she spoke again, she was brisk, and eager to be gone. <*Very well, Gyle. You may continue as Imperial Legate and work out the control of Javon with Francis in whatever way you can. Just keep him alive and ensure the supplies keep coming, because if there is a problem, I am going to send in Tomas Betillon to fix it, understood?*>

<*There will be no such a need, Mater-Imperia, I assure you.*>

<*See you make good on that promise, Magister.*>

Then she was gone.

He blinked and stared about him slowly, his mind repeating those half-heard words: *Would that we did.*

'What is this major card she doesn't hold?' he wondered.

5

Lost Legion

The Conquest of Yuros

By 280, the year of the Ascension of Corineus, the eight-hundred-year-old Rimoni Empire had entered a period of stability. Military supremacy enabled all the luxuries of civilisation. Higher education and prosperity decoupled the State from the Sollan religion and a period of medical and scientific exploration resulted. But when the Blessed Three Hundred emerged, the legions were powerless, and within a few years the great edifice the Rimoni rulers had constructed was destroyed. The subsequent reconquest of the old Rimoni Empire by the Rondians took longer, requiring as it did the military defeat of former allies. Most of the magi were Rondian, though, so the outcome was never in doubt.

ORDO COSTRUO COLLEGIATE, PONTUS

*Eastern Keshi Desert, south of Shaliyah, on the continent of Antiopia
Zulhijja (Decore) to Moharram (Janune) 928
6th and 7th months of the Moontide*

Ramon Sensini and his little delegation found Seth Korion beside a gap in the ruined walls, staring blankly at the sheets of rain. Visibility was thirty yards at best and they were all saturated, despite their heavy cloaks. Seth stood anxiously as he recognised those with Ramon. Fridryk Kippenegger and the two Argundians, Jelaska Lyndrethuse and Sigurd Vaas, were not amongst those Seth would count as friends.

'What is it?' he asked, trying his best to sound haughty.

'We need to discuss the situation of the army.'

Seth winced and said morosely, 'It's trapped in a ruin by an enemy who can summon storms and defeat pure-blood magi. What else is there to say?'

Fridryk Kippenegger had shed his legion garb sometime during the battle; he was harnessed in a Schlessen kirtle over his chainmail vest. His bare arms were muscled like a warrior-king of old. He nodded at the torrential downpour outside. 'Gut rain, yar? Just like home.'

'Oh, it's not so bad as that,' Ramon said. 'And as far as I can tell, thanks to the weather the enemy don't even know we're here. This storm is our friend. We can move while it lasts, using it as cover to wriggle out from under their noses.'

Seth glowered at him. 'What do you care, Silacian? No doubt you'll just fly away as soon as the storm lifts.'

Ramon had been expecting just such a remark, which helped him keep his temper over it. '*No one* is running away, Seth. I wouldn't, even if my skiff wasn't lying broken somewhere on the battlefield. We've all got too much invested in this army to just walk away.' *About three hundred thousand in gold in my case, though I'm not telling you that.* 'We're going to get out of this, and find a way home.'

Seth looked at Jelaska and Sigurd. The Argundian pure-bloods had vast experience. Jelaska looked like an eccentric aunt, with a bony face and unruly tangles of grey hair, but she was a skilled and indomitable battle-mage who'd fought against the empire in the last Argundian wars. Sigurd had no less a reputation as a warrior – and as a drinker. He was a sturdily built man with a greying red beard.

'Why talk to me?' Seth asked bitterly. 'I'm nothing more than a novice battle-mage.'

'The survivors – the rankers – need someone to believe in,' Jelaska said, her voice smoky. 'We've done a quick count and we reckon there are two, maybe even three legions-worth of men hidden among these ruins and the surrounding slopes. That's ten to fifteen thousand men. Pallacios XIII – your legion – is the only one that's mostly intact. We've got Argundians, Noromen, even some Estellan archers and cavalry, as well as provincial Rondians from at least seven legions. If we're to pull them together, we need a name.'

'The name of Korion,' said Sigurd Vas, his voice gruff, his face dour.

Ramon watched Seth's eyes flicker nervously. The general's son hadn't been his friend at college. *In fact you were a bullying, supercilious, arrogant pezzi di merda, truth be told. But I know you, a little.* He suspected Seth would do anything to live up to the brutal demands of his fearsome father, never mind that he lacked the aptitude, personality or experience for the role.

We need the name of Korion if we're to keep this army together.

Ramon was new to the military, but he'd kept his eyes wide open and made it his business to learn how it all worked since arriving, and the one thing he was certain of was that leadership was crucial. If the men believed that the man in charge of them was competent and would see them right, they'd do as they were told. Men who didn't believe in that leadership did as they pleased and destroyed the cohesion of the whole. It was why Kip was a popular battle-mage who got instant obedience, though he was a Schlessen low-blood, while Renn Bondeau was loathed despite being a half-blood Rondian noble.

Ramon had come to the conclusion that the commanding general was primarily a figurehead, but his role was still vital – a bit like Pater-Retiari, his familioso head, who inspired absolute loyalty, even in people who'd never met him. A general required a legend of success. Soldiers didn't care whether that legend was won with fairness or brutality; they just needed to know that the man in charge was a *winner*. And there was no name higher in the arena of war than that of Korion.

Seth, the youngest of that name, stared at the ground and muttered, 'I'm not a general. I'm barely a battle-mage.'

True enough.

'You'll have plenty of advice,' Ramon told him. 'Sigurd and Jelaska have both commanded front-line maniples in Argundy against the Rondians.'

'Then put them in charge,' Seth spat, glaring at the Argundians.

'My reputation is in fighting against your empire,' Sigurd replied coolly. 'The bulk of the survivors are Rondian – they will not accept me as commander.'

'Nor would they accept me,' Jelaska put in, adding dryly, 'I have no cock, so clearly I'm not fit to command.' There was no particular answer to that which wouldn't lead to a shouting match, so the men just looked uncomfortably away.

'What about Renn Bondeau?' Seth asked morosely.

'Bondeau is a dim-witted, arrogant *figlio di puttana*. He is the last person we should put in charge.' Ramon jabbed a finger at Seth. 'Accept it, Korion. You know it's what you've always dreamed of.'

'What do you know about my dreams?'

Ramon gave him a knowing look, and Seth coughed and dropped his head. 'You don't know what it is like, to have my father's eyes fixed on you,' he whispered. 'Do you know that poem by Carriticus, about the last moments of a deer trapped by wolves: "*Transfixed by the amber glare.*" My father has eyes like that. You can't breathe, you can't think – all you want is for those eyes to smile, for him to say, "Well done" – but he never does.'

Ramon saw Sigurd's eyes narrow and he looked at his fellow Argundian. Poetry and self-pity were not things either valued. He shook his head faintly at them both. *Be patient, give him time.*

'I thought when I graduated I would gain his approval. But instead . . .' Seth looked at Ramon. 'You know, you were there. It was me they should have failed, not Mercer. *I* was the failure.'

Ramon nodded. *I do indeed know, Lesser Son.*

Seth's voice sounded hollow as he went on, 'When I got home after graduation, Father wouldn't even see me. I wrote him letters – *from my room next door to his* – begging to see him. I was not invited to the hunts or the balls, or even to dine with him. Then he just flew away. I had to apply to join the Crusade myself, and I ended up in a disgraced legion. You must have thought it hilarious.'

Well yes, actually . . .

But watching self-flagellation wasn't a pastime Ramon enjoyed. 'Seth, we wouldn't be here if we thought there was no substance to you.' That might not be quite the truth, but even as he said it, he decided that maybe it was so. 'Listen, no one believes being the son of an arsehole like Kaltus Korion is easy.'

Seth glared hotly at Ramon. 'My father is not an *arsehole*. He is a *great* man. I would not expect someone like you to understand him.'

'Most fathers allow their sons a little imperfection,' Ramon retorted. 'Just not him. But you can still grow into the man *you* want to be. Whether that's someone your father would approve of, well, I neither know nor care, and neither should you. You've got a backbone in there. I do believe that.'

It's amazing what you can talk yourself into believing.

Seth inhaled, exhaled. 'Of course I've always wanted to be a general – a hero, like my father. But I wanted to *earn* leadership, not be given it as a stopgap. I wanted to *prove* myself, to learn at my father's side. I'm not ready yet. I've never even led a charge.'

'Seth, a general doesn't *lead* charges. He organises people; he makes decisions; he sets the strategy – and then he lets others work out how to implement it. Most of all, he is calm, confident, and never wrong. And he is *visible*.'

'It is as Sensini says,' Sigurd Vaas put in. 'Your father has not fought in combat for decades.'

Seth blinked. 'But he led two Crusades, and he broke the Noromen, and quelled the Silacian revolt, and the Argundy-Estellayne border war, and—'

'He trotted around on a horse giving orders. Others fought and died,' Ramon replied, having to fight really hard to keep the scorn from his voice. 'Mostly he just drank wine and raped serving girls.'

Seth stiffened, his eyes suddenly blazing. 'You will retract that, or I will have satisfaction.'

Ramon met his eyes fiercely. *You really want to fight me?* Then he exhaled. *That would be counterproductive.* 'I retract it. He *seduced* serving girls.'

Kaltus Korion's reputation as a womaniser was too well known for Seth to take him up on those words. He bowed his head. 'You know, they say my father has fathered forty bastards. And one legitimate son.' He raised his head. 'I will make my father proud. And I will learn to be a real general.'

'There's nothing like learning on the job,' Ramon replied.

Seth took another deep breath. 'Is this your idea, Sensini?'

'It's our idea. And it's better than having Renn-rukking-Bondeau in charge.'

'Kore's Word,' Sigurd Vaas breathed.

Seth bowed his head. Then he lifted it. 'Very well. I accept.'

Seth Korion stood beneath the half-ruined platform of stone they'd chosen for the address, sweating and shaking. As many of the twelve thousand or so survivors of Echor's army who could squeeze in were gathered around and above him, perched on the old battlements, filling every nook and cranny of the ruined fortress. They were frightened men who'd never thought to see a true defeat. Most of them probably hadn't drawn a weapon until now except to extort plunder from frightened civilians. Now they were vividly confronted with the true fragility of life, trapped in a harsh land thousands of miles from safety.

Seth felt his knees tremble, and confessed to Ramon in a shaky voice, 'I don't know what to say.'

Renn Bondeau scowled in disgust and turned away. He'd spent the morning telling whoever would listen that he was the only one truly fit for command.

'I'll tell you the words,' Ramon Sensini hissed in Seth's ear. Seth glanced at him nervously. The little Silacian had been a figure of contempt at college, a victim for him and his friends to pick on, but in the six months of the crusade he'd grown in ways Seth didn't begin to understand. There was an air of capability and subtle menace about him now – as if he knew exactly what he wanted to happen, and how to make it so. The men respected him and his hulking Schlessen shadow, Kippenegger. Somehow he'd usurped control, and got the girl too: Severine Tiseme was watching them, her hands folded across her swelling belly.

'H-how?' he asked shakily.

<I'll feed you your lines,> Sensini whispered into his head. *<Now get up there and repeat what I tell you.>* He shoved Seth towards the steps.

Here goes ... Seth tottered up and found himself confronted with thousands of upturned faces, all with big, scared eyes. They swarmed closer and he swallowed and opened his mouth, but it too dry to speak.

Silence fell. He groped for his water-bottle and realised he'd left it below. 'I need a drink,' he croaked, and his words boomed off the rocks and walls. He flinched.

A ripple of grim laughter ran through the crowd of sweating soldiers. 'Yeah, me too,' several guffawed. Someone tossed him a metal bottle, which he barely caught. He unstoppered it, took a swig – not of water, but some kind of whiskey. He winced, and the men laughed at the face he pulled.

<That's strong stuff,> Ramon Sensini whispered his head. *<Say it.>*

'That's strong stuff,' he parroted awkwardly.

<Like us,> Ramon added.

'Like us,' Seth said, managing to get more firmness into his voice. More words flowed, and Seth began to feel calmer. He'd been a fair mage at the more sedentary and passive Studies. He might have been a poor fighter, but he'd always been competent at speaking – and whilst that might have been mostly addressing his ranked toy soldiers in his nursery, now he instinctively dressed up Ramon's terse comments into something more, turning the relayed phrases into the bones of a real speech. 'We're still here!' he shouted, eliciting more cheers. 'We got out – some of us by the barest whisker. Some of us hacked our way free of hordes of screaming Keshi. We left brothers behind us, dead in the sands. But we got out!'

'Yeah, we did,' someone shouted. 'In Kore we trust,' another added.

'But we didn't escape that Hel to huddle in here, did we! We have people at home, loved ones, waiting for us! In Pallas and Bres! In Estella and Argundy! In Noros and Schlessen! Our wives and children, our mothers and fathers, our families are waiting for us. Are we going to let them wait for ever?'

'No damned way,' a ranker shouted, and others echoed agreement, crying out in half a dozen languages. He looked about him and saw dark-haired men of Estellayne and spade-bearded Argundians standing in clusters among the more numerous brown-haired Rondians and Bricians. There were scatterings of Brevian tartans and groups of blond Hollenians. Banners and standards were draped above their units, heavy with rain.

'My father wouldn't leave a single man behind!' he boasted, ignoring Sensini's suggested next lines. 'I too am a Korion, and I too am honour-bound to do the same!'

Big cheers – *huge* cheers – at the magic name *Korion*. He cursed it silently as he felt the raw, desperate hope these beaten men invested in it. So much to live up to. He took a moment to glance at Tyron Frand, the one person here he thought of as a friend. The chaplain gave him an approving nod.

<*You're doing well,*> Ramon told him, <*but stick to the script. I want you to tell them we're going south.*>

<*South? But that's—*>

<*I know. Just say it.*>

'Move your fuckin' arses, you soft-cocked scrotes! Move it!'

Ramon winced as a centurion stalked past him, throwing a loose salute in his direction. 'Wit' all 'spec', sir,' the man added. He had a face of badly moulded clay and a voice that could shred timber as he bellowed into the faces of the nearest rankers, 'Move your shit-holes!'

Ramon grunted approval and waved the men on, his eyes running back down the line of trudging men, or what he could see of it as they wound their crooked path away from the enemy. The rain was hammering down on them for the third day solid and visibility was barely a hundred feet. The scouts reported the plains below had turned to lakes, so he'd sent Coll and the others to pick a route through the low hills south of Shaliyah. At least there was no one in the air: the storms hadn't abated for a moment and lightning blazed every few seconds – anyone stupid enough to fly would be turned into blackened shisha in the blink of an eye. Flash-floods were their biggest peril right now: sudden torrents rushing from unseen gullies would sweep everything away in their path. They'd already lost men that way, gone in an eye-blink.

But as Kip says, it's no worse than summer in Schlessen.

He stroked Lu's wet flank, then tapped his heels to get the mare moving, working his way up the slope and back down the line. Fog rose about them, the gauzy clouds ripped to shreds by the rain. More and more men loomed out of the downpour, all staring up at him as they passed, one or two reaching out to touch the horse for luck. It still unnerved him a little, that to some of them at least, he was sacred: a mage, one of the Blessed. One seized his reins and he went to berate the man when he recognised him. 'Storn? What's happening? Where are the wagons?'

Tribune Storn, commander of Pallacios XIII's Tenth Maniple and the second richest man in the army after Ramon himself, looked a worried man – or rather, Ramon realised as he sneezed with all his body, worried sick. He steadied himself by clinging to Ramon's horse, then looked up at him and croaked, 'Magister, they're secure. And your goodwife also.'

'She's not my wife, Storn.' Ramon picked out a dark shape rumbling out of the gloom – midday was as dark as twilight in this weather but he thought it late afternoon. 'We're going too slowly, Tribune.'

'There's no proper roads through these hills and the gullies are overflowing. It's madness, sir!' He lowered his voice. 'There's so much gold in those wagons the horses can barely move them.'

Ramon leaned closer and whispered, 'We're going to need every fennik if we're going to get out of this, Storn.'

'If one of the wagons tip, the whole damned army's going to know about it, sir. There'll be a riot.'

'Storn, right now the rankers aren't seeing anything beyond their next footstep. Just make sure the wagons keep up, all right. Now what about the stores?'

Storn dissolved into another bout of coughing, then hawked up great globs of mucus until his throat was clear enough to reply. 'Sir, we've got about three week's worth, and that's only because you got our maniple out in good order. That's about fifteen wagons of rice and Noorie food, sir. There's nothing from home.'

'It's all edible, Tribune.' Ramon patted his shoulder and said firmly, 'Go and hitch a ride in one of the wagons, Storn. You're too valuable to be out in this.'

Storn nodded gratefully and shuffled away while Ramon touched his heels to his mount's side and trotted on, his mind busy calculating as he compared half-remembered maps to the terrain about them. He had two and a half legions'-worth of survivors from the sixteen legions annihilated at Shaliyah four days ago: twelve thousand men strung out in a line, with no idea where the enemy was.

We're probably still only about twenty miles south of Shaliyah – half a day's ride in good weather. If the Keshi cavalry find us, we're dead. So let's hope they aren't looking.

Another wagon loomed out of the mud and spray, a covered one with a giant XIII emblazoned on the canvas cover. He nudged his horse closer. 'Shh, Lu,' he told her. 'Night's coming, lass. You'll rest soon.' He wiped his face and peered into the wagon. 'Sevvie?'

He spotted a huddled shape perched amidst the stores. The head turned and Severine Tiseme's cowled face appeared: soft white cheeks framed by a shock of dark curls, squinting at him through the rain. He took a deep breath and tried to gauge her mood. Severine, high-blood dissident that she was, could be Heaven or Hel. But pregnancy might be mellowing her ...

'Darling' is that you?' she called, making the passing soldiers snort with laughter.

Would it hurt her to at least try to sound like she was in the military? 'It's me.'

'Are we stopping soon, Lovebug?'

Lovebug? Sol et Lune!

The nearest rankers were grinning ear to ear.

'There's a small plateau, half a mile on, where we're setting camp.

I think the rain's finally beginning to peter out.' He could feel it: the deluge wasn't natural, but the after-effects of the enemy magi's monstrous tampering with the weather. At last those effects were dissipating as the hours passed and they drew further from the epicentre at Shaliyah.

'Thank Kore!' Severine exclaimed. 'Come inside, darling – it's the only dry place left in the world!'

'I can't, Sevvie. I've got to find the rear and make sure we're not being followed.' He didn't pause to hear her reply but nudged Lu back into motion. He was pretty sure someone in the ranks muttered 'Lovebug' behind his back. The mare snorted irritably as she kicked into a trot, splashing past another staggering column of sodden rankers. 'Pick it up, lads,' he called, then asked, 'Where's your tribune?'

Most of the men just stared past him, their eyes glazed with exhaustion. The column had been marching twelve hours a day for the past three, and that after a headlong flight from a catastrophic defeat. One of them slowly raised a hand and jabbed his finger towards the rear. 'Dunno. Dead?' He shrugged, dropped his arm and stumbled on.

'What unit are you?'

Another man cast him a dark look. 'We're what's left of Noros VI.'

Ramon cast his mind back to a day last year and five young magi holding battle-standards aloft in the cathedral at Norostein. 'Silver Wolves. Where's your standard?'

One or two of the men blinked at his recognition of their legion's nickname. 'First Maniple had it when the storm hit,' one responded. 'Ain't seen it since.' He looked Ramon up and down, and slowly added, 'Sir.'

Ramon flipped a thumb back the way he'd come. 'One more mile, soldier, and there'll be rest and hot food.'

'Thank Kore,' several of the men chorused, listening in. The man Ramon was speaking to looked up. 'I seen you, sir. In Norostein. You was at the college there. Seen you an' your mate watching us drill.' He threw a sheepish salute, and hurried on.

Me and my mate . . . Alaron. Where are you, amici? No doubt somewhere far away, and no doubt in trouble. He laughed at himself, then pulled his mind back to the present. The next troop were Estellan archers with their longbows unstrung and wrapped in canvas, their quivers covered over to protect the fletching from the rain. The Estellan tongue was rooted in Rimoni, so he was able to converse a little with them. Then Fridryk Kippenegger came past, marching alongside a troop of rankers from his own Ninth Maniple, carrying a pack and shovel like any common soldier. He even had them singing, some call-and-response marching song about Lantric girls and their proclivities. After them came a troop of heavily armed Argundians with their distinctive conical helmets and two-headed axes.

Jelaska Lyndrethuse was riding alongside them, her leathery face framed by tangled grey curls. 'Sensini.' She greeted him with a small ironic salute. 'Have you come to take me away from all this?'

'I'm afraid not, Jelaska. Where's your Air-mage?' he asked. 'I'm hoping he can scout behind us to—'

'He's gone,' the woman interrupted dryly.

Ramon blinked. 'Where?'

Jelaska ran fingers through her sodden tresses, combing out a cascade of raindrops. 'Caleb decided to make a run for it on his own. I've no idea whether he got away.' Her voice was bitter. 'I really thought the fucker would stay.'

'It looks like all our Air-mages are flying away.' He'd not seen Baltus Prenton, the Thirteenth's windmaster, since before Shaliyah, when he'd been sent west to guide the next supply caravan. He was trying not to think ill of the Brevian for that. 'Except me, of course.'

'Well, aren't you the hero. Though your skiff was left on the battlefield, wasn't it?' She winked at him.

'I'm sure I'd have stayed anyway. Who wouldn't want to be here?'

'Ha!' She patted his arm. 'I like you, boy. Do you have a plan for when we reach the end of these hills?'

'Sure. I always have a plan. I'll tell you about it over a merlo tonight,' he added, fluttering his eyelids.

Jelaska laughed, which was oddly girlish but somehow pleasing. 'I like your spunk, boy. But don't flirt with Argundian women until you know who they're seeing. Sigurd would bury you for that.'

He couldn't tell if she was joking, which was funny in itself. *So she's seeing Vaas . . . I guess most of the women in this army will be seeing someone by now. There's only half a dozen of them anyway. I'm lucky I've got one of them in my tent.* It felt odd to be kidding around with a female battle-mage twice his age, but nice too. It probably would never have happened in normal life, but the army was a great leveller. They shared a laugh, then he tugged on Lu's reins. 'There's hot food a mile on. Probably some merlo too. Enjoy!'

'Thanks be to Kore!' Jelaska said, gesturing to the heavens.

After the Argundian unit, there were more wagons, more soldiers, including his own Tenth Maniple, the logistics unit, with their supply wagons and equipment, all that they'd been able to salvage in their headlong flight. The rearguard was a troop of archers, constantly checking behind them as they marched stolidly along.

Ramon waited another twenty minutes to ensure there really were no Keshi on their trail and was just about to leave when more men loomed out of the rain. Their commander wore a lion's head cowl over his head, making it look as if he were peering from between the jaws of the dead beast. He shouted a loud 'Halt!', and his unit snapped to order as smartly if this were all a training exercise. 'Hail, Magister!'

Ramon saluted, feeling almost intimidated by the commander confronting him. He bore the insignia of the Thirteenth, to Ramon's surprise. 'I thought I was the last in the line,' he commented. 'Who are you?'

'I am Pilus Lukaz, First Cohort, Second Maniple, Pallacios XIII.'

Rufus Marle's men. Marle had been the only real soldier among the magi of the Thirteenth – Ramon had seen him go down at Shaliyah under a swarm of Keshi, still blazing fire as he fell. 'I'm impressed you made it out, Pilus.'

The cohort commander met his eyes. He was clearly exhausted, but he also looked prepared to march from here to Hebusalim and still be ready to fight at the end of it. Marle had drilled his maniple hard and these men were testament to that. 'We're all that got out from the Second Maniple, sir.' He pursed his lips, considered his words, then said slowly, 'When the sand-storm struck, the Keshi went to ground. We managed to stick together and take shelter like they do, in sand-caves. We kept mum and let them leave, then we followed. We've been trailing you through the storm.'

Ramon felt his throat tighten. He glanced at the waiting men, their eyes facing forward, not looking at him, but visibly straining their ears. 'That's good work, Pilus.'

The pilus shook his head. 'We lived by the will of Kore,' he said devoutly. He was clearly Vereloni, tall with dark-tanned skin and curly black hair and stiff-backed formality. His men were a mixture, most pale-skinned, several with the blond hair of the north, but they all shared a look of grim competence. Lukaz jabbed a finger at a chunky Pallacian behind him, who unfurled the standard he carried. From the crosspiece hung a crimson pennant with XIII embroidered in gold. It was stained and tattered, but it gave Ramon a real thrill to see it. 'Baden retrieved the standard when Commander Duprey fell.'

Ramon had been above and behind the lines when the Keshi overwhelmed the front line. It had been a tumult down there, thousands of bodies pressed together, all hacking at each other, while the magi blasted at each other and whoever got in their way. Anyone who could have plunged willingly into that maelstrom in search of a piece of wood and cloth was insane.

'Baden is a hero,' he said, a little awed.

The bannerman shuffled uncomfortably. 'T'others what went with me din't get out,' he muttered, barely audible above the rain. 'They was t'heroes, not me.'

'Baden doesn't like being singled out,' Lukaz said softly, just for Ramon to hear, 'but he did well.'

Ramon nodded his understanding, then lifted his head and looked about him. Stories like this could be used to lift the men, to give them belief. 'Most of the Thirteenth got out,' Ramon told them, to low cheers. 'The battle-standard's return will be very welcome indeed.'

'A meal would be welcome too, Magister,' someone called from the rear.

'There's hot food up ahead. About a mile.'

The men emitted low cheers, until Lukaz's stern eye silenced them. 'Where is your guard cohort, Magister?'

'I'm only the mage of the tenth maniple,' Ramon replied. 'We're just logisticalae and archers. I don't have a guard cohort.'

Lukaz frowned. 'With respect, it is not right that a mage is unescorted, sir.' He looked apologetic but insistent. 'We must protect the Blessed of Kore.'

Ramon went to protest, but Lukaz's solemn face dissuaded him. All of the other magi had a cohort whose task was to guard them, at least nominally, though such measures had been largely unnecessary. Until Shaliyah. And Lukaz sounded determined.

Well, the rest of his maniple are dead. And likely I'll need them.

'Very well, Pilus,' he said, saluting formally, 'I am honoured to accept your offer.'

Ramon led his new guards into the camp as the dull glow of the setting sun was occasionally glimpsed through the curtain of rain. He left them to settle in and went looking for the command tent. This was the first attempt by the remnants of the army to form a proper defensible camp – they'd spent the previous nights after the battle huddled in whatever shelter could be found from the torrential rain, strung out over two miles of rugged trail. But the scouts had found this small plateau, which they estimated covered half a square mile, and already the traditional interlocking squares of a legion camp were taking shape around him as he headed for the centre.

When he arrived at the command pavilion, the first voice he heard was that of Renn Bondeau. The young Pallacian mage was on his feet, jabbing a finger at Seth Korion as he snarled, 'At least I actually know which end of a sword to use.'

Seth went to say something, floundering as the rest of the magi watched dispassionately. Only the chaplain of the Thirteenth, mild Tyron Frand, appeared to be taking Korion's part. The rest were subtly distancing themselves, unconsciously forming a ring as if readying themselves for a duel. The Keshi had specifically targeted the Rondian magi in the battle, and many of those who'd escaped had abandoned their units and run. They had started with two hundred and forty magi – fifteen per legion – and there were now only twenty-one of them left in this column. That was a catastrophe by any measure.

Ramon was under no illusions about the remaining magi either: most were still here only because they weren't equipped for flight, being neither Air-mage nor shapeshifter nor animagus. Should the chance arrive, most would likely seek to escape; he doubted many felt any true loyalty to the rankers.

'What are you proposing to use this sword of yours for, Renn?' Ramon threw into the silence. 'Picking your nose with the hilt? Or loosening up your constipation?'

A few of the circle about him sniggered. Ramon sought Severine and found her safely tucked in beside Kip's massive frame. He winked at her, then scanned the rest. The Thirteenth dominated, though Duprey and Marle were dead and so were Coulder and Fenn, and Lewen, one of the three Andressans. They had no idea where Baltus Prenton was; he'd been guiding the supply trains before the storm hit. That left Seth Korion, Renn Bondeau, Ramon, Severine, Kip, the remaining Andressans, Hugh Gerant and Evan Hale, Chaplain Tyron Frand and the healer Lanna Jureigh. The remainder were a mixture: three Noromen magi, three Argundians, including Jelaska and Sigurd, two Brevians, a Brician chaplain and one man each from Hollenia and Estellayne. Seth, Jelaska and Sigurd were the only pure-bloods.

Renn Bondeau whirled to face him. 'So you're back. About time!'

'What man of worth would be anywhere else?' Ramon quipped, quoting from a famous play about a Rimoni general facing overwhelming odds during the Schlessen wars.

'You think quoting some play makes you a general?' Bondeau sneered, eliciting a laugh from those about him: Seth Korion quoted poetry all the time. 'I can just about take Korion as a figurehead, but

I'm damned if we're going to all play second fiddle to you. I'm the only one here fit to command this army.'

'The very fact you think so proves you're not,' Ramon replied tartly. 'Do you even know where we are?'

'South of Shaliyah, near the Efratis River. Which will be impassable for a week after this rain. It's the biggest water-course in the region, which you'd know if you'd read the briefing notes before we left Peroz.' Bondeau slapped the table triumphantly. 'The gnostic storm at Shaliyah has triggered an early rainy season. If we continue south we'll find the river in flood and no way across. We'll be trapped.'

'I read the briefing notes, and I spoke to traders too,' Ramon said calmly. He walked into the middle, noting that the Brician and two Brevians appeared to be favouring Bondeau. 'If you'd really done your research you'd know about a town called Ardijah. It's about here.' He jabbed his finger at an unmarked part of the map. 'If this map wasn't so badly drawn, you'd know that Ardijah has an Ordo Costruo-built bridge that lies above the highest flow of the river. The Efratis can be crossed there.'

Renn tutted impatiently. 'The town will be fortified! And even if we could cross, it only takes us into Khotriawal – we'll be trapped between two enemies, rather than staying ahead of one! We should be marching back to Peroz—'

'Peroz is four weeks' hard march from here, across a searing desert. This rain is localised, don't forget. It was hard enough the first time, but we don't have four weeks' stores, and worse than that, most of the men have worn through their shoes. Have you seen how many are limping along on bleeding feet? And that's not even stopping to consider what the enemy are doing. If I were them, I'd have pushed cavalry west already to block the retreat of anyone who escaped Shaliyah. Ardijah is our gateway to freedom, not Peroz.'

'The enemy don't care about *us*,' Bondeau scoffed. 'They'll be sending men north, to take on General Korion.' He glanced at Seth and added witheringly, 'That's the *real* General Korion, not *you*.'

For a moment Seth looked as if he would take umbrage, but once again he did nothing. It was as if his reaction was muted by something – fear, Ramon guessed. For all that he was a pure-blood, Seth had always been weak-willed. He looked Korion in the eye. *<You can't let him say such things to your face.>*

Seth visibly quailed. *<He's right, he outranks me. I don't have the right of it.>*

<You've got every right. You're our general now – so act like it!>

Seth shook his head faintly. *<I can't . . .>*

Ramon rolled his eyes. 'You should take that back,' he said evenly to Renn Bondeau. *I'll corner you into standing up to him, Seth. See if I can't.* 'His honour demands a retraction.'

'Oh, you speak for his honour, do you?' Bondeau stepped towards him. 'Maybe he's just your puppet, Silacian? Do you have your hand up his arse to make him talk?'

Ramon's hand went to his sword-hilt, but before he could open his mouth, Seth finally broke his silence. 'You will retract that, Renn,' he blurted, his face turning crimson.

Bondeau smiled triumphantly. 'Or what?'

'Retract, or I demand satisfaction,' Seth blurted again, his eyes widening as if in horror at what his mouth was saying. 'It is my right.'

'How about we duel for the leadership of this army?' Bondeau suggested in a sly voice. 'That will show us who is more fit to lead fighting men.'

'Brother magi may not duel,' Jelaska growled, and most of the room murmured firm agreement, to Bondeau's obvious displeasure. 'Least of all when we're caught behind enemy lines. We will find another way to resolve this.' There was a mutter of agreement from the unaligned.

'Pah!' Renn stabbed a finger at Ramon. 'This sneak seems to think he can play us all. Neither of them are any use in a real fight. All they did at Shaliyah was run.'

'Seth is the ranking mage,' Ramon retorted, putting aside the slur to his own courage. *For now.* He tapped the table. 'More than that: he's a *Korion.* I think we all know that his name is pretty much all that's keeping this army together right now.'

'There is a rukking world of difference between *Kaltus* Korion and *Seth* Korion,' Bondeau snarled.

'I know it,' Ramon responded, before Seth could. 'We all know it. But for forty years, the name Korion more than any other has been associated with victory. Those men out there are running out of hope, and the only thing we can do for them is to tell them that someone with the magical name of Korion is in charge – and that this fact might bring his father to the rescue.'

The magi were all nodding at this, even Bondeau's supporters, if grudgingly. Bondeau read the mood and threw up his arms. 'We've been over that already,' he said dismissively. 'You may be right about the common herd needing to have a Korion in charge, but we've got to agree in this tent about who is *really* in command. I nominate me. I'm better qualified for it than any oily southerner.'

'You're not even a career battle-mage,' Sigurd Vaas retorted. 'I've served in the legions for thirty years.'

'Mostly spent fighting the empire,' Bondeau sneered. 'I'm neither a rebel nor a mudskin.'

Ramon felt hackles rise about him. To his surprise, Seth Korion waded into the middle, sweating profusely but with jaw set. 'Stop this,' he said angrily. 'You all put me in charge and I'll be in charge. I'll listen to advice, but I'll give the orders.'

Ramon wondered if this was some sign of stepping up to his role – or perhaps he just wanted the glory. He glanced about the room, counting, and decided that Seth might have the numbers, if only because Bondeau was so unpopular. 'I can live with that,' he said finally. 'Let Seth decide whose advice to follow.'

If I can't outmanoeuvre Bondeau, I deserve to lose.

There was a murmur of assent. Ramon looked at Jelaska, who gave a faint smile of satisfaction. Bondeau glared about him, then his shoulders dropped. He spat disgustedly and made one last effort. 'All right, *General*, here's my advice: march to Peroz! It's garrisoned, it's safe and it's in the right direction. Any other course is rukking madness!'

To Bondeau's utter disgust, Seth looked at Ramon questioningly.

See, Renn? I win again. Ramon hid his smile as he walked back to the map. It was rough, poorly drafted and probably completely unreliable beyond very basic detail, but it was all they had. 'We can't go west without ending up in a trap, or death by sun and sand: whatever Renn thinks, we won't make it. Anyway, don't you think the people of Peroz know of Shaliyah by now? Echor left one legion to garrison it: anyone want to take odds whether they're still intact?'

He let them digest that thought, then moved on. 'To the south of us is a region called El Efratia, named for the river that runs through the heart of it. It's a floodplain. The currents are deep and strong in the rainy season, but it dries up swiftly to a much narrower flow during the remainder of the year. On the far side is Khotriawal, ruled by the Emir of Khotri. Do any of you know of it?' He looked about at the shaking heads. 'As it happens, I do. When I lived in Norostein, I billeted with the Mercer family. Vann Mercer was a trader and a soldier. He spent time in Hebusalim and other cities, and asked a lot of questions. He used to talk of Kesh all the time at dinner. In fact—'

'Get to the point, Sensini,' Sigurd Vaas rumbled.

Ramon raised a hand. 'Sorry. Right. So: Khotriawal. The thing is: it's a free city. The people don't consider themselves Keshi, and they don't answer to Salim – in fact, the Mughal of Lakh is from the Khotri royal family.'

The faces about him were blank. 'So what?' Renn demanded.

'So,' Ramon replied, 'we should go there. Salim can't follow us without violating the border and starting a three-sided war, and I think even he would hesitate to do that while Korion Senior is pillaging the north.' He looked pointedly at Seth. 'So General, what do you think?'

Seth Korion sat uncomfortably on his horse and watched the army march past. It was dawn, and they had broken camp and were heading south. Making a decision the previous evening had been simple: only Ramon's idea made any sense to him. Even though it felt utterly wrong to be marching south when home was north, it seemed to be the only way they stood a chance. Renn Bondeau was sulking, but even he'd been forced to concede in the end.

As each battle-standard and maniple banner passed, Seth gave his most impressive salute, and the soldiers raised their arms and pummelled their breasts in response. It felt like a dress-up game, not the fulfilment of a lifelong ambition, and yet here he was, general of an army.

Liar. You're no real general. Father would die laughing at the very thought.

Beside him, Ramon Sensini waited for the opportunity to talk. Seth let him stew for a while longer, because it troubled him to rely so much on the little Silacian. *He doesn't mean me well, I swear.* Occasionally he glanced sideways at Chaplain Frand – *Tyron* – the only person he trusted in this whole army. His calm presence gave him the strength to turn to Ramon.

'All right, Sensini, what is it now?'

The little Silacian hissed impatiently and nudged his mare forward. 'I'm so delighted you could make time for me,' he said tersely. 'Some of us have a rukking *baggage train* to organise.'

'You're the battle-mage of the Tenth,' Frand replied mildly. 'You got the supplies out in the midst of a rout – you're clearly in the right role.' He gave a sideways nod, the courtiers' acknowledgment of a point scored in a verbal duel.

Go Tyron! Heartened, Seth demanded again, 'What is it?'

'There are decisions you need to make.' Sensini lifted three fingers, began counting them off. 'One: we've got just enough food to get to Ardijah and that's all. If we get baulked there, we're in trouble. And—'

Seth interrupted with a snort, 'As if mudskins could stop us from crossing.'

Sensini frowned. 'I wouldn't be so sure. It's likely to keep raining heavily for some time now and a defended ford is hard to cross. What if the Khotri also have magi?'

Seth went to open his mouth then paused. *The enemy have magi. We don't know how many or where. Frightening.* A few days ago he would have said that was impossible.

He looked at Tyron, who frowned. 'Who's to say if the fords will be as treacherous as you say? It can rain anywhere, anytime,' the chaplain said.

Sensini shook his head. 'Not here, chaplain. According to the veterans it rains here twice a year, lightly in Janune and more heavily in Junesse. The storm at Shaliyah has brought the Janune rains early.'

'In Yuros—' Tyron began.

'We're not in Yuros,' Sensini retorted, his eyes narrowing. 'I thought you'd have noticed by now, prete.'

Tyron flushed, then closed his mouth.

Seth looked at Sensini crossly. 'What was your question?'

'There are two roads from here to Ardijah. One is shorter, but we're likely to run out of water on the way. I want us to take the more southerly route, which is significantly longer but will bring us alongside the Efratis River. Then we can refill our water barrels as we make our way to Ardijah.'

Seth pulled a face. *How would I know what to do?* Yet this decision could cost lives. He reached out mentally to Tyron. <*Yes? No?*>

The chaplain glanced vexedly at the Silacian and admitted, <*He's probably right.*>

Seth sighed. 'Very well, the river road it is.' He saluted the next battle-standard to pass. Fridryk Kippenegger was riding beneath it. *I'm surrounded by barbarians and low-lives.* 'What else?'

Ten minutes of rattled-off requests followed, far more than the promised three: where in the column the baggage would go, the order of march, where to scout and who should form the rearguard, and a multitude of trivia that Seth was appalled to find a general needed to think about. He did the best he could off the cuff, and finally the irritating Silacian nudged his horse into motion and bounced away.

'Anyone would think he's enjoying himself,' Tyron observed. 'You were at college with him, weren't you? How did he ever get into a proper Arcanum?'

Seth curled his lip. 'He arrived with a sack of money and some mysterious note from his real parent, or so we assume. The principal never even told the other staff about it. His mother was a tavern girl – he never made any secret of that. But his father . . . who knows?'

'The by-blow of some rich noble?'

'Or some mage criminal. In Silacia the only magi are army men and their by-blows.' Seth stared after Sensini as he trotted away. 'Every time he speaks, it makes my stomach churn.'

'Why is that?'

Seth hung his head guiltily. 'The truth is, my friends and I were cruel to him. Regardless of his baseborn nature, I'm not proud of the way we bullied him and his friend Mercer. One shouldn't whip animals for the mere pleasure of it.'

'Trials make us strong,' the chaplain responded, quoting the *Book of Kore*. 'You were probably doing him a favour, beating the devils out of him.'

Perhaps that's why Sensini appears to be coping with this better than the rest of us? Seth shook his head. What had happened at the Arcanum hadn't been right; he'd known it then and could see it even more clearly now. 'What do you think the enemy are doing?'

Tyron shrugged. 'I don't know. None of us do.' He gestured towards the northeast. 'I've sensed gnosis being expended from the direction of Shaliyah, but not a lot, and not near.'

'It's not supposed to be like this,' Seth complained. 'We're magi – we're not supposed to be blind. But now we're all too scared to try our powers, in case it brings the enemy to us.' He squeezed his reins tighter. 'What if we're walking into another trap? What if I'm going to get us all killed?'

'I believe in you,' Tyron Frand said encouragingly.

That just made him feel the responsibility even more deeply.

Salim Kabarakhi I, Sultan of Kesh, sat beneath an embroidered canopy, sipping cool sharbat and nibbling on sweets as the victory parade wound its way past his balcony. He looked attentive, as if he was watching every movement avidly, but in truth, his mind was far away. Trumpets blared and people bellowed thanks and praise to Ahm and every apsara in Paradise; the cacophony was deafening, but he barely noticed it. The shimmering sea of rejoicing could have been a thousand miles away. Behind him, two dozen courtiers chattered softly in each other's ears, little jokes and asides, little stabbing knives of wit. But he was above and apart, as always.

We won. Ahm be praised indeed . . .

His eyes drifted down a line of spears planted all along the route of the parade. They were stabbed butt-first into the earth, and impaled on the spearhead of each were the gore-caked heads of the fallen magi, eighty-three of them, including Duke Echor Borodium himself, pulled down by Souldrinkers while trying to flee. Salim had the duke's crown and signet in his treasury, along with a few other personal effects. About a third of the enemy magi had died in battle; any captured by the Souldrinkers were dead and emptied and the rest were now prisoners or fled. The prisoners had been handed over to Rashid's Hadishah for breeding.

Never have we seen such a victory . . . But without the Enemy's connivance, could we have done it?

Salim looked towards the lower balcony, where Rashid Mubarak, Emir of Halli'kut, sat amidst a more martial retinue of cloaked magi. It was his Ordo Costruo renegades who'd conjured the mighty storm that had carved into the Yuros army and aided its destruction. Most were almost as white-skinned as the men they'd fought, lured to the side of the shihad by Rashid's cunning persuasiveness. He looked the very embodiment of greatness, sitting among his retinue with the majestically beautiful Alyssa Dulayne at his side. His glittering robes outshone all but Salim himself.

In truth, it was your victory, Rashid. He considered the man's demeanour. Did the emir still know his place? *Or will his magi turn on me next?* They had always had a strange understanding. Rashid was a mixed-blood mage, and that made him hateful to the common Keshi. He needed a ruler who was prepared to support and protect him. But he was also ambitious – some might say exceedingly so – and to have to defer to a higher authority, especially a human, rankled with the emir, though he tried to hide it.

As if sensing his regard, Rashid's head turned to him and he raised a goblet in silent toast, then turned back to the parade. Salim watched him silently a moment longer, then followed the emir's gaze to the opposite side of the parade-route, where a lower balcony faced his. On it stood a more motley collection of men and women, rough-dressed, laughing and cavorting uncouthly, pointing at sights in the parade like children. Not all were Keshi, or even of Antiopia, though most were as dark-skinned as peasants. They had a feral look to them, as if more used to sleeping beneath stars than ceilings. In the midst of them sat a powerfully built figure clad in robes the colour of a scabbed wound. His powerful, sensuous face looked carved out of granite; his skull was shaven but for a black top-knot bound with jew-elled ribbons. Gold loops hung about his arms and neck.

Yorj Arkanus. Our so-called ally.

A tall, voluptuous red-haired woman with coppery skin sat at Arkanus' feet: his mate, apparently: a Fire-magus named Hecatta. To command the Souldrinkers, one had to consume the soul of one's predecessor, he was told – and in a barbaric twist, mated pairs fought for supremacy together. Arkanus and his wife were the Souldrinker warleaders.

I think perhaps I can still trust Rashid and his magi, but what of these? They are slugskins, for the most part, for all they claim to hate the magi more than we do . . .

This had been his greatest gamble, sending Rashid to Pallas to try and reach accommodation with the emperor over Duke Echor. The idea had been proposed by a Rondian spy who offered the deadly deal: take on Echor's army under advantageous circumstances to win a victory that both Rondians and Keshi would celebrate. And it had worked, exactly as planned.

But now came the aftermath: the news of this unprecedented vic-tory would spread and people would rise up against the Rondian garrisons. Some might even be successful, where they massively out-numbered the Rondians. But Kaltus Korion was still in the north, and his far more powerful army was well-entrenched, with strong supply-lines.

The victory at Shaliyah marked the end of the arrangement with the Rondians, leaving him free to go after Korion. But did he dare? Kaltus Korion had destroyed Ahmed hassan armies before. Was it better to wait out the Crusade and then rebuild as usual, this time with the glory of Shaliyah to immortalise his fame?

Salim knew how others saw him; he had cultivated his public persona as carefully as a farmer cultivates his crops. He was a tall man, still only in his mid-twenties, and extremely well-educated. Women sighed over him, but they were not a passion for him: they were for breeding and little else. His was a male world, and he'd grown up learning to read the men around him, assessing their relative threat. His courtiers feared him, something he had deliberately promoted with little acts of dominance as he became confident in his authority. His soldiers loved him. He had been trained to rule with sword and intellect, and thanks to magi-training he could mask his thoughts. He knew how to balance risk with reward, and how to pursue a goal without remorse.

But the decisions to come would be like trying to negotiate a maze filled with cobras. And the first of those decisions concerned the Souldrinkers.

He turned to the small shaven-haired secretary on his left, and whispered, 'Have Rashid and Arkanus join me in the royal suite immediately this parade is over.'

'What is left of Echor's army?' Salim asked, speaking Rondian for the sake of the Souldrinkers. Both were of Yuros ancestry and still favoured the common tongue of the empire. The suite was illuminated by lattice-patterns of orange-pink light from the falling sun. Precious carpets covered the floors; the walls and low tables held trophies and ornaments. Mute servants stood like statues holding trays of iced drink. 'Did any escape?'

Rashid Mubarak pursed his lips. He too spoke Rondian easily. 'Our storm came across the front from north to south, with our men and war-elephants shielded within. We crushed all of the enemy except those on their southern flank, who fled into the hills.'

'Echor's forces were rabble,' Alyssa Dulayne purred, stroking a blonde tress from her brow. 'Just as I said.' She and Hecatta, Arkanus' woman, exchanged a look. Two beauties of very different types: one the embodiment of the courtly lady, the other filled with primitive sensuality. They pretended friendship, but Salim could see the rivalry clearly.

Arkanus rolled his powerful shoulders. 'The survivors have gone south,' he grunted. 'No more than ten thousand, my scouts say. Only the deluge following the dust-storm prevented a complete massacre.'

'The laxity of your watchers allowed their escape,' Rashid said coolly.

'Visibility was less than ten yards at the worse of it,' Arkanus rumbled. 'Your magi didn't see them either. Anyway, they can't have gone far.'

'They're heading south,' Rashid reiterated. 'Towards Khotri. That is a problem.'

'Let them,' Hecatta said in her deep cat-purr. 'Why should we care?' She picked up a handful of nuts with her left hand – the social gaffe made Salim wince – and stuffed them into her mouth. These Souldrinkers had apparently dwelt secretly in Ahmedhassa for years, but their manners were barbarous. 'We can follow wherever they go.'

Salim tapped the table, silencing them all, though the deference from Arkanus and Hecatta seemed grudging. 'The Emir of Khotriawal has an army permanently stationed across the Efratis River, camped outside the town of Ardijah. Khotri refused to heed the shihad, and they will not tolerate any incursion. If they cross into Khotri, we cannot follow without provoking the emir.'

'We cannot afford war with Khotri at this time,' Rashid said.

'My people acknowledge no borders,' Arkanus sniffed.

Rashid raised his voice. 'We must move the bulk of our army north to confront Kaltus Korion, but this matter must be resolved before these blundering Rondians trigger a border war with Khotri.'

Hecatta whispered something in Arkanus' ear. The Souldrinker warleader nodded thoughtfully. 'My mate reminds me that our agreement to aid you ended with this great victory, Sultan. My people have done our share, and we have harvested well. We lost many, but gained far more. Dozens more of our youth now have the gnosis. If you wish our service for longer, we will require additional concessions.'

Rashid frowned. 'Do you indeed? Fighting for Ahm's holy shihad is not enough for you?'

'It is of great comfort.' The corner of Arkanus' mouth twitched with sarcasm. 'However, our lineage and ways are traced to Yuros and the Ascension of Corineus, so it does not pull our heart-strings quite so strongly as yours. We have been persecuted here as well. We are your "Afreet" in the flesh.'

'What is it you want, war-leader?' Salim asked.

'Land of our own.'

Salim glanced at Rashid, who'd gone still. To give these beings land to rule could create a monster for future generations: a new enemy with the gnosis, and the need to constantly consume souls to sustain that power. It was such a deal as Shaitan himself might offer.

And what about you, Rashid? What do you think on this? The emir gave no sign either way. Arkanus and Hecatta waited, their eyes predatory.

Alyssa Dulayne stroked Rashid's arm and shared a look with him. No doubt they were communicating silently in the way of the magi. Salim envied that, but he would fear a mage wife, and that his thoughts were not his truly own. A ruler had to rule his own bed first. He wondered if either Arkanus or Rashid could truly claim that.

'I hear you, Arkanus, my friend,' he said eventually. 'I value all you have done and all you could do for the shihad, but what you ask is a great deal. I will need to consider it.' He drew himself upright, looked about him meaningfully. 'Alone.'

Arkanus looked at Rashid, then at Hecatta. Something passed between them, then both men nodded simultaneously. Rashid had once said that the Souldrinker warleaders spent so much time in each other's minds that it was hard to know where one began and the other ended. All the Souldrinkers Salim had observed were like that: more dog-pack than human group. But it had been Rashid who'd come to him with the Souldrinkers' offer to aid the shihad, almost seven years ago. It had cost a lot of gold, and now it looked likely to cost land as well.

And perhaps damn my soul in the eyes of Ahm for ever . . .

A few minutes later, Rashid slipped back into the room. He bowed low to his sultan before saying, 'Appear reluctant, but give them what they want. We still need them.'

Salim looked through the lattice-work of the shutters towards the sunset. 'My friend,' he started, musing aloud, 'I am wondering who is worse: these afreet, or the Rondians? These Souldrinkers feel no remorse at killing the innocent to replenish themselves. My captains are uneasy about our current arrangement. Many of them saw the strings of half-starved slaves who were led into battle by the Souldrinkers for one reason only – to provide more "fuel" when their powers burned low. At the end they were still chained together, and all dead. What sort of monsters are we allied with?'

'I have been creating monsters for decades, Great Sultan,' Rashid said. 'I have kidnapped female magi and sent them to breed until their bodies gave out. I have had male magi chained to pallets and sent fertile human women to them, again and again, and I have forged their gnosis-wielding offspring into killers. That is what having magi for enemies has done to us.'

'The Rondian Emperor sent his own uncle to die at our hands. You are saying we should be as ruthless?'

'Indeed.' Rashid walked over to the mounds of exotic fruit, plucked a grape from the bunch and swallowed it, a liberty none but he would dare in the presence of the sultan. 'Dangle a prize before Arkanus and it will blind him to his peril. Offer him . . .' He paused, then smiled wolfishly. 'Offer him Khotri.'

'Khotri is not mine to offer.'

'All the better. You won't miss it.' Rashid chose another grape. 'We must march north to confront Kaltus Korion. He will raze Halli'kut if I leave him unchecked.'

Kaltus Korion. Salim had never met the fabled Rondian commander, but he had seen sketches. The man looked like a hawk. 'What of the soldiers who escaped the battle? If Arkanus is right, there may be at least two Rondian legions out there somewhere.'

Rashid considered. 'Conventional wisdom says the only way to defeat the Rondians is by strength – we must outnumber them five to one – but now we have magi of our own. I would keep thirty thousand men here, local men by preference, with magi support from Arkanus' people. Make him divide his power.'

'And if the Rondians flee into Khotri territory?'

'Then let Arkanus follow them. We need to start thinking as the Rondians do, Great Sultan. We have our own magi now, enough to destroy the Khotri if they don't bend the knee to you. It is high time we demonstrated our new power to the Emir of Khotriawal. It will be a message to his kinsman the Mughal of Lakh as well. Let us not forget that during the last Crusade, the Lakh raided our lands behind our backs. Vengeance is still owed on that account.'

Salim considered his words, then gave his assent. 'Let it be so. But as the situation may become delicate I believe it will be best if I stay here in the south, to ensure that Arkanus does not attempt to take more than is offered.'

Rashid bowed. 'You can trust me to act always in your interests in the north, Great Sultan.'

'Yes, my friend, I can,' he said. 'Take the bulk of the army north – after Shaliyah, I believe many more will rally to our banner. Here in the south, I will ensure that the remainder of the Rondians are crushed, and that Arkanus deals with Khotriawal.' He picked up his goblet. 'And what price does the Emir of Halli'kut wish? Do you also desire your own kingdom?'

Rashid shook his head. 'The Rondian magi rule through terror – that is the only way they can rule at all. I do not desire such a kingdom. My magi will be tolerated by ordinary people only if we are aligned to them in service of Ahm and of you, Great Sultan. And once we have ensured that the Rondians have been driven from Ahmedhassa for the last time, we will watch as Arkanus' kingdom collapses about him, and then we will finish off him and his entire misbegotten brood for good.'

Salim noted the burning hate behind the emir's words and asked mildly, 'It took much for your people to fight alongside these creatures?'

'Great Sultan, the Souldrinkers are a foulness that must be expunged. They are as much the enemy as the Rondians, and one day it will give me great pleasure to exterminate them. But right now, they are a necessary evil.'

'Then we have made a bargain with Shaitan?'

'We have indeed, Great Sultan,' Rashid said quietly. 'We have indeed.'

6

Retreat

Mage-Children

The offspring of a mage usually gains the gnosis as they enter puberty, the most turbulent period of change in both body and psyche. Until then a mage-child is like any other, though of course their special destiny elevates them above other children. It is common practice to segregate them from lesser children, though I do sometimes wonder if this is entirely beneficial.

MARTHA YUNE, ARCANUM TUTOR, BRES 877

*Lokistan, on the continent of Antiopia
Safar (Febreux) 929
8th month of the Moontide*

Alaron stared morosely at *Seeker*'s battered hull, and in particular at the sheared-off stumps of the landing struts. Examining the damaged windskiff was a good distraction from looking at the Lakh girl lying moaning on the blanket and clutching her belly.

Brilliant. I've probably put her into labour. He groaned and buried his head in his hands, but that didn't help.

He had no idea where he was, only that it was Lokistan, a place he knew nothing about. The few maps he'd seen at Turm Zauberin had the considerable swathes of blank space filled in with lots of jaggedly artistic mountains and pictures of winged serpents. He was really hoping that was just artistic license and that the cartographer had had no real idea either.

The gales that had swept them southwards across the Rakasarphal had then hurled them against the rearing walls of stone on the south side of the huge inlet; it had taken an almost superhuman effort to gain enough altitude to avoid *Seeker* being dashed to pieces against the coastal range. But though they'd won a brief reprieve, it wasn't long before they were enduring a harrowing ride through sheer-sided ravines that had been hacked into the mountain range as if by the cleavers of murderous giants. They'd skimmed cliffs and narrowly dodged treacherous overhangs, only to explode out into this valley, coming in too fast and too low.

The result of their precipitous landing was spread out before him: the skiff had skidded into the rocky slope, shearing off struts and cracking the hull; now it lay there quietly amidst the vermilion poppies that covered the scree and danced in the late afternoon wind. He could see the darkness rushing towards them: the sun was already lost in the clouds that swirled about the peaks looming above them.

'Al'Rhon,' Ramita gasped weakly, her eyes clenched shut, her hands groping for him blindly, 'help me!'

He hurried over to her and clasped her small hand. They were the hardest hands he'd ever touched, rough and callused from a life of manual labour. She was less than half his size, even with the pregnancy, but there was something solid about her, something earthy and tenacious. Her skin was slick with sweat and her eyes were clenched shut as she forced herself to breathe through the contractions.

'I'm here,' he whispered, dropping to his knees beside her. He felt helpless and useless as he wiped the sweat from her brow with his sleeve. 'What do you need?'

She didn't answer but clutched at his arm. She was breathing fast, her whole form quivering. A stream of words in her own tongue tumbled from her mouth as she exhaled like a bellows, then she sagged against him as this latest wave of pain let go.

'Hurts,' she whispered in Rondian, shivering.

'I don't know what to do,' he told her. 'Can you use gnosis to dull the pain?'

'I'm trying,' she replied. 'It's so cold.'

Cold – she's cold. Now she mentioned it, he too could feel the wind biting at his flesh. High overhead he caught flashes of the stark white of fresh snow. *She needs heat.* 'I'll light a fire,' he said, then thought, *What the Hel can I burn?*

He wrapped her in their blankets as she prepared for the next onslaught, then he scurried about looking for wood, but they were so high up he could find nothing but grass and rock. In desperation, he gathered up the broken stumps of the landing struts and lit them with Fire-gnosis. The orange blossom was stark against the darkness, the swirling winds making the flames dance chaotically.

Ramita leaned towards the heat, beads of perspiration running into her eyes and blending with tears as she fought another great wave of agony. She finished the last of their water and moaned, 'Thirsty.'

Thirsty. Great Kore, what do I do now? There had been a stream running down the ravine they'd flown up. He muttered words of reassurance as he held her through the next bout, then disentangled himself. She was increasingly detached, almost delirious, and didn't appear even to hear him as he prised himself loose. 'I'll get more water,' he promised.

He headed down to the darkening cleft below, sure he could hear water rushing amidst the groaning wind. Using the gnosis for light, he found an icy stream trickling down the narrow valley and filled their water-bottles. When he returned, Ramita drank greedily. 'It's passing,' she whispered, shaking. She let go of his hand and looked at him with a brave little smile.

'Is the baby coming?'

'Not tonight – no waters yet. But soon.' She reached out and flicked his fringe from his forehead. 'Shukriya, Al'Rhon. You are a good man.'

He squirmed. He didn't feel like a man at all – and for all her adult manner and earthy pragmatism, she was younger than he was, and about to face the greatest killer of her gender. There were female magi – the Sisters of Assarla – who dedicated their lives to childbirth in Yuros. He remembered his mother telling him that without such healer-midwives, as many as one in three women died giving birth. That was worse than going to war. He wished there was an Assarlian sister here, right now. He'd have kissed her hem in gratitude. 'Are you hungry?'

She shook her head and closed her eyes. 'Husband,' she whispered, pressed against her side, 'I will make you proud.'

He frowned, then realised she wasn't talking to him. That her children were the progeny of Antonin Meiros redoubled his anxiety. But her breathing was becoming more regular, and at last she fell asleep.

There was no real way to get comfortable. The ground was hard and rocks jabbed through the blankets. Ramita's head fell into his lap and the stale, damp smell of her sweating body wafted past his nose. Neither of them had washed in days, but he was getting used to the ripe smells and the itching of soiled skin. He draped an arm across her and without thinking, he bent down and kissed her forehead. 'I'll look after you,' he promised.

Time dragged as a crescent of light climbed over the eastern peaks, sharp as a scimitar: Luna, rising over this desolate place. *No one will ever find our bones if we die here.* He wondered where his father was. Vann Mercer – Da – was indestructible ... but what if Inquisitors found him? Would they care that he knew nothing of the Scytale? And what about Anise? Or Cym? Had the Souldrinkers killed her? And where was Ramon?

For the first time it occurred to him that everyone he cared about could be dead.

For a long, long moment he just stared into the darkness and wished he was anywhere but here. His free hand stroked the scroll-case containing the Scytale. It didn't make him feel strong or powerful, just frightened and alone.

Maybe I should just bury it? he thought. *Or throw it down the ravine? Maybe I could just drop it into the sea?*

He knew he wouldn't, though. For one thing, the artefact had enough wards woven into it to survive pretty much anything. More importantly, it represented his one chance to make this world different, for his life to mean something.

These were just abstract notions though, as wispy as the mists rolling down these bleak mountains. They were certainly less tangible than the dark-skinned girl pressed to his side, snoring and cradling her belly protectively. Right now, it boiled down to one thing: *I'm here for her.*

He twisted until he could rest his head into a fold of the blanket, then he cradled Ramita and closed his eyes.

He woke with sunlight streaming into his eyes, orange-clad men standing all around them and Ramita in labour.

Alaron held onto Ramita's hand as her contractions built towards a new crescendo. There was nothing else he could do. They were in Kore's hands now. *Or whoever's,* he added silently, eyeing the monks who came and went with heated water and soft cloths. Their chants echoed distantly through the monastery.

The past few hours had been a blur, since he'd awakened to find the saffron-robed men with long hair tied up in top-knots, and knotted beards that fell to their waists, bending over them. At first he'd thought he would have to fight them, though they looked harmless enough, until Ramita found she could understand their tongue, a variant of Lakh. They were Zain monks, and they'd helped Alaron turn one of *Seeker's* sails into a stretcher and carried her carefully a mile up the valley to their monastery. He doubted they would ever have found the place themselves, so well camouflaged was it, for it had been carved out of the rocky peaks themselves.

The monks had installed Ramita in a small candlelit cell and immediately summoned a midwife from a village in the valley below. The middle-aged woman had a weathered face and the businesslike air of a farmer during calving, but Ramita was not alone in finding her quiet confidence a great comfort – Alaron was embarrassed at how relieved he was to be able to hand over the business of birthing to a competent woman. Ramita didn't have to ask him to stay. She was his responsibility and he wouldn't leave her side until he knew she was safe.

Hours went by, with Ramita screaming like a torture victim one moment and panting softly the next. He felt he knew her to her very core by now: he could number every pore sweating out her exertion, every lank black hair plastered to her forehead, every anguished expression her face would pull. He could never forget the immensely strong grip of her small leathery hands, or the downy softness of her cheek, or the silken tautness of her slick, drum-tight belly. She babbled constantly, incomprehensibly, but he felt as if he was learning that language too. There had always been a part of him that wanted to protect vulnerable things; that need almost overwhelmed him now. He was bound to her; if he could have taken on her pain, he would have, but he couldn't even ward her from it – a healer-mage probably could, but he didn't know how.

In the lulls between contractions, her mind wandered. Sometimes she called him Jai, sometimes Kazim, and often, when she remembered to use Rondian, 'Husband'. So when she finally remembered his own name, it woke him from his dazed reverie.

'Al'Rhon?' Ramita's hand searched for his and he seized it and held it tightly, sending what strength he could. Healing-gnosis wasn't his affinity, so he just sent energy – she was burning through hers at a colossal rate. He was relieved that her loins were covered by a cloth – he was afraid that what he might see would put him off women for life.

'Al'Rhon – the baby is crowning!'

'I'm here! I'm here! Are you all right?' He had no idea what else to say because he had no idea what crowning meant – except that whatever it was, it was just the *first* baby. She'd told him proudly that twins and triplets ran in her family, and he'd breathed a huge sigh of relief when she'd assured him that she was only carrying two – as if birthing twins thousands of miles from the nearest healer-mage wasn't bad enough!

'Where are we?' she groaned huskily.

'Safe.' He got her to sip some water before the next wave of pain came. The midwife jabbered excitedly and Alaron clung to her hands as Ramita's whole body arched. It was agony to watch her, but he couldn't look away – it was the least he could do: to bear witness to her terrifying ordeal.

And finally, with an almighty effort, she forced a tiny child out of herself and into the midwife's waiting arms.

Even then, it wasn't over. As the infant wailed lustily, protesting this bright and cold new world, Ramita gathered what remained of her strength for one last effort. Only then would she be able to rest, only then could she sleep ... And just a few minutes later another screwed-up, screaming little face appeared

Good lungs on the pair of them, Alaron thought, and an enormous grin plastered itself over his face.

Ramita looked up into his eyes with a look of dazed happiness, and he leaned over and kissed her cheeks and hugged her, totally overcome with emotion and exhausted relief. He felt as proud of her as if she were his sister or his wife. Then the midwife shoved Alaron and the monks towards the door so she could clean up Ramita and the babies.

Outside, he realised the monks were congratulating him as if they were his own children. He tried to explain, then realised the futility and just thanked them, still grinning widely. He fell asleep while waiting for food.

Ramita blinked through a haze of exhaustion and stared down at the two tiny bundles at her breasts. She was naked, but the midwife had washed her and made up the pallet with fresh linen. Everything below her waist hurt, but they must have given her something – poppy-juice, most likely – because she was floating in a dream.

I'm a mother ... Sweet Parvasi be praised!

The children were neither white nor dark but something in between, a pale gold, and completely gorgeous. *Two boys.* The first-born was sleeping now – she could tell him by the tiny birthmark on his neck. His little brother still suckled at her right breast, fiercely hungry. Her left nipple was sore, the breast still swollen, but she hardly noticed as she cradled them to her, filled with wonder and disbelief.

My children. Antonin Meiros' children. Our special babies.

She closed her eyes and thought of her husband: his strong face, his shaven skull gleaming in the sunlight, a wry smile on his face as he chuckled over some little incident. Would they take after him, or her? Or would they be something in-between, something entirely themselves? She could not stop the tears, thinking that they would have no father in their lives.

Milk came naturally, to her relief, and so did love. She'd heard of women who could not bear to be near their own children; it was the fear of every pregnant woman, her mother had once told her. But she was not so cursed: she adored them both, and she carried their tiny faces down with her into the trackless paths of sleep.

When Ramita awoke again, someone had clad her in a shift with a long buttoned slit in the front, to make feeding the twins easier. Alaron was beside her, his anxious face shining, and she smiled, remembering his attentiveness. She wished she could hug him, but she wasn't sure if a Rondian would find that proper.

'You're awake,' he said, stating the obvious as if it were a miracle.

She had to struggle to remember her Rondian. 'Yes. Awake. Thirsty.'

He gave her a cup of water, and she drank deeply. 'Are you in pain?'

'Everywhere,' she admitted, 'but especially . . .' She waved a hand towards her groin, and smiled when he looked embarrassed. He was so easy to tease.

'Are you hungry? You should eat – I'll ask them to bring food, if you're up to it?'

Her stomach gurgled eagerly, answering his question, and they both laughed. 'Shukriya, Al'Rhon,' she whispered, and when he looked at her quizzically, she added, 'Shukriya means "Thank you" in my tongue.'

'I – uh – um . . . sure,' he burbled, and went to fetch food. He returned with a bowl of steaming broth, and she managed to finish it before the babies started stirring. She hadn't realised how starving she was, but seconds would have to wait.

She got him to pass her the babies, one by one, smiling at his aghast look when she undid her shift in front of him. 'You'll be seeing a lot of these things, so get used to it,' she scolded him gently.

He still averted his eyes though, which was polite, and rather charming. *He is a well-brought-up young man*, she decided.

'What are you going to name them?' he asked.

'I don't know – I've not really thought about it,' she admitted. 'My husband gave me no names to use.' She pondered a while, then announced, 'I will call them Nasatya and Dasra. Those are the names of the twin sons of the sun god Surya. They are healers, and very playful.' She showed him Nasatya's neck. 'This is the eldest, the one with this mark.'

'Nas and Das.' Alaron grinned. 'I like it.' Then he bent closer and, dropping his voice, asked, 'Ramita, who are these Zains? Are we safe here? Can we trust them?'

Don't they have Zain monks where he comes from? she wondered, a little shocked, then realised, *Of course they don't!* The Zains came from Lakh originally, and over time had spread over most of Ahmedhassa. 'Al'Rhon, they are holy men,' she chided. 'Of course we can trust them.'

His face clouded. Trust was clearly something he was learning to dole out sparingly. 'I don't think taking anyone or anything on trust is a good idea right now. It's us against the world, don't forget.'

A faint cough sounded from the doorway and they started guiltily, then flinched in embarrassment when the old monk with the wispy beard and long, top-knotted grey hair bowed and greeted them in Rondian. His accent was odd and his phrasing archaic, as if he'd learned the language from an old manuscript. Perhaps he had. 'Humbly I apologise, and greet thee formally now that you have recovered. Welcome to Mandira Khojana. My name is Puravai, which means "East Wind". I am the head scholar of this order of Zain.' He bowed from the waist, his beard touching the floor as he bent in half. 'Everything here is at your disposal.'

'Everything?' Alaron echoed doubtfully.

'These are Zain monks, Al'Rhon,' Ramita told him. 'They are sworn to the sanctity of life. This is known.'

'Not by me it's not.'

'But it is so, nevertheless,' Puravai said without rancour, bobbing his head. 'Are your children well?' He asked the question of Alaron.

Alaron glanced at Ramita and sent her a silent message: <*They think the children are ours.*>

Ramita bit her lip, then waggled her head: *So be it.* She asked the Goddess to forgive the lie.

Alaron swallowed, took her dark little hand in his big pink one and kissed it. 'My . . . uh, wife and I are eternally grateful to you,' he mumbled unconvincingly.

Puravai bowed again, though his eyes seemed to narrow a little. Ramita could guess why: she did not have a wife's pooja mark, nor was she wearing dowry bangles. Her arms and wrists should be adorned with gold – a married woman in Lakh would always wear them – but she'd not worn them at home. In fact, she couldn't remember seeing them since Meiros had died. But she was grateful for Alaron's protective nature. *Puravai will think we are refugees from the Crusade, illicit lovers fleeing the wars,* she told herself. *But surely that is safer than the truth.*

'I'm so tired,' she blurted out. She met Alaron's eyes. <*I think he knows you're not my husband. But I am sure he means us no harm.*>

Puravai was apologetic. 'I am sorry to disturb you. The midwife will check on you, then you may rest.' He turned to Alaron. 'Will you walk with me, Magister?'

Alaron agreed hesitantly. He let go of her hand and she felt a little regret at that loss of contact. She'd grown used to her husband's affection and the past months had been characterised by an aching loneliness – Justina had been many things, but affectionate was not one. She realised that she liked being near this odd young man from Yuros.

As he said: there is just us. And the three most precious things in the world: my babies, and that scitally-thing. The Scytale.

Alaron left with the monk as the bustling midwife returned. She had so many things she needed to ask, but she was too tired. Once again she found herself drifting slowly back into sleep, her questions unanswered.

Puravai led Alaron through dimly lit passageways and onto an unexpected balcony bathed in stark sunlight. The air was cold, and their breath trailed them like wispy spirits, haunting their every exhalation. The sun's rays glinted dazzling on the white snow, casting blacker shadows on the dark, barren landscape; the monochrome palette was broken only by the saffron robes of the monk next to him.

Alaron peered over the wooden balcony railing, taking in the dizzying drop below. Narrow waterfalls tumbled from the precipices about them. Though the sun was at its zenith, it hung low in the northern sky and gave little heat.

'I sent a party to retrieve your conveyance,' Puravai said eventually, breaking the awkward silence.

'The skiff?' Alaron said in surprise. 'Thank you. May I see it?'

'Of course. It is yours.' Puravai looked sideways at him, appraising him. 'Do you know of our order?'

'No,' Alaron admitted.

'There was once an Omali holy man named Attiya Zai, who realised that achieving moksha, the release from the cycle of life, required divorce from all earthly matters – the pursuit of wealth, of power, of women, these things which absorb most men. He taught that those seeking moksha must set aside such things and retreat from the world into a simpler existence. This is one such place. Here a man's only cares are for his immortal soul.'

Alaron thought of all the things his father used to say about Kore monasteries back in Yuros. Parasites, he used to call them. It seemed a little churlish to argue with someone who'd more than likely saved Ramita's life and the lives of her babies, but the words came out unchecked nonetheless. 'Must be nice. Who provides your food and clothing?'

Puravai looked at him wryly. 'The nearby villages barter with us.'

'What do you trade them? Prayers?'

'We share our knowledge and wisdom.'

Alaron raised his eyebrows. 'Yeah, I bet. That's why you live so close to them, I expect.'

Puravai frowned slightly, but his eyes sparkled a little, as if he liked a good debate. 'Let me tell you a tale of Attiya Zai. He was very rich, the son of a noble, but he took off his gold and fine silks and went to Imuna, the holy river. He wished only to empty himself of all his cares. He meditated for days, oblivious to all discomfort. His rivals at court came to jeer, but he gave no sign that he even heard their cruel words. One man struck him, and he gave no sign of feeling the blow. Eventually they grew bored and left him there, thinking him mad. Days passed, and only one thing sustained his life: a young boy, who brought him water and a little rice. The boy asked nothing in return, and Attiya Zai had no coins to reward him, so instead he told the boy a great secret.

The boy listened, and as he grew up, he used this secret knowledge and became wealthy beyond all measure. And yet in his last years, he put aside his wealth and after telling his son Attiya's secret, he retreated to a distant monastery to see out his last days. That boy was born as a peasant, but he died as the Emir of Khotriawal.' Puravai bowed his head. 'Wisdom is power, Alaron Mercer. Priests often say that this world has no value, that only the next life is worthy of attention, but Attiya Zai knew that this life is equally as vital.'

'So you people secretly rule the world?' Alaron asked lightly.

Puravai laughed. 'The villagers bring us food and water and we teach their young to read and write, and to count. We study things that take our interest. We prize knowledge, but we also share it. Zain monks advise all the great rulers of Lakh.'

'What do you tell them?'

'How to be the best version of themselves they can.'

Alaron was impressed despite himself. *The best version of myself . . . would I even know what that is?* 'Do you think magi worship demons?' he asked.

Puravai chuckled. 'No, I do not. Magisters of the Ordo Costruo have walked these very halls. Antonin Meiros himself has stood where you now stand.'

Alaron swallowed. 'Really? Antonin Meiros!' He almost blurted that the great man's wife was in the room below, but just in time he checked himself. 'Er . . . can I ask, is that how you know Rondian?'

'Indeed you may. Knowledge was shared, and both parties enriched.' Puravai looked sideways at Alaron. 'We are isolated here, but news does reach us. We are saddened by that noble lord's death.' He touched Alaron's shoulder. 'Tell me of you and that poor child.'

'You mean Ramita?'

'Yes. What is the true nature of your relationship?' Puravai's voice took on a steely tone. 'Did you force her? Or beguile her with your gnosis? And before you answer, you should know that our observations of the human body and mind have made us particularly aware of the nuances of truth and deception.'

'No! I would never do such a thing!' Alaron looked away, trying to frame his story. 'She was abandoned and alone. I felt sorry for her,' he started, then, looking at Puravai's face, he gave up any attempt at lying – though he still resolved not to mention the Scytale. 'She's not my wife, but I will protect her as if she is,' he said firmly.

'Where did you meet her?'

'A place Antonin Meiros built: a hideaway. She's Lakh, but he brought her north.'

'I am not surprised: he stopped here on his journey south.'

Alaron felt his eyebrows go up. 'Really?' *What does he know?* He tried to slide a probe into the man's brain, but to his shock the old man blocked him easily. He turned to face him warily, in case this old man revealed other surprises. 'The Ordo Costruo taught you.'

'They did, but we are not magi,' Puravai said carefully. 'Lord Meiros found that his ideals had much in common with ours. His people taught us skills to better equip us for the royal courts, where lies and deceits are common. This relationship of monk and mage began many years ago, before even the completion of the great bridge.'

Alaron felt a weird sense of Destiny, whatever that might be, unfolding before him. *To be here, with Antonin Meiros' widow, at a place her husband has stood ...* It made all his questions feel wrong, and for a long time he just stood there, stunned into silence.

The Zain master waited silently with him, unperturbed. 'How did you come to these mountains?' Puravai asked eventually.

'I was trying to take her home,' Alaron answered, which wasn't too far from the truth. 'How do you make people the best they can be?' he asked, trying to sound sceptical, though it felt important for him to know.

Puravai looked him up and down. 'By breaking them down and then remaking them, piece by piece.'

'Even magi?'

'Most magi believe they are already perfect.' Puravai's eyes narrowed. 'Are you?'

Hardly. Alaron swallowed. 'I'm going back to Ramita now.'

Puravai smiled, and let him go.

7

Interrogation

Theurgy: Mesmerism

*Do not meet an enchanter's eyes. Recite prayers or mantras inside your head.
Repeat your own name internally, or concentrate deeply on a single thought.
Your mind is the king in an elaborate game of tabula. Protect it well.*

JULIANO DI TRATO, SILACIA 555

*Eastern Dhassa, on the continent of Antiopia
Safar (Febreux) 929
8th month of the Moontide*

From his vantage place at the door Malevorn Andevarion stared down
at the hunched form strapped to the chair, then looked away, out
across the rocky ground and waste-heaps. The Fist had arrived
in another Dhassan town that was trying to scratch out an existence
in a desert. What passed for the rainy season here was already over: a
few weeks of light rain that vanished into the parched earth. Salty
haze filled the air from the ocean, a good sixty miles west – it was all
that allowed the main crop, some type of peppercorn, to grow at
all. Deep wells provided what little fresh water they had, and the
villagers spent most nights hauling it up in buckets to feed their
straggle-leafed crops. The amount of labour required just to survive
was appalling.

Why do they bother with these pointless bloody lives? he wondered. *Surely
even slavery in Pallas would be preferable to this.*

The arrival of the Fist's windship had paralysed the village. The warbird dwarfed even the largest houses and left the villagers awe-struck and unresisting. The Inquisitors had taken all their food and as much water as they could carry. *The villagers will have to move or die soon, in all likelihood*, Malevorn thought. From what he could see, that was a kindness.

'Well?' he heard Adamus Crozier ask, and he returned his attention to the room. Raine Caladryn was bending over a Rondian captive, her hand on the prisoner's forehead. Beside her stood Commandant Fronck Quintius and a battle-mage from the local garrison, a stupid young Pallacian named Enott. Enott had been alternately questioning and pummelling the prisoner for a week now.

'He's alive, and still shielding his mind,' Raine reported. She sounded faintly impressed. 'I could break it down, but it'll take time and leave him mentally damaged.'

Quintius considered. 'Is he a mage?'

'No, but someone has taught him how to protect himself.' She glanced at Enott, her ugly face contemptuous. 'This cretin could've killed him.'

Enott ducked his head, humiliated before the Crozier and his Inquisitors.

The Fist had arrived at the village that afternoon, summoned by a patrol which had detained a trader who claimed to know a person of interest to their hunt: Vannaton Mercer. Discreet offers of reward had lured the man out from behind the curtain of silence the Merchants' Guild usually erected to protect their own – typical of the breed, in Malevorn's view. Enott had decided to start the interrogation early – no doubt hoping for the glory if he'd managed to crack the informant before the Fist had arrived.

We're lucky he's alive at all.

Malevorn vaguely remembered Vann Mercer, who'd always attended the family events at Turm Zauberin. Once he'd even brought his wife, who was the mage of the family. She had been left hideously burned from her military service and remained veiled throughout, but Malevorn had glimpsed her arm: the mess of mottled scar tissue made it look as if she'd melted. He remembered how he and his cronies had joked about the unlikely couple, wondering how any man could bear to lie with such a benighted hag, how the Hel he had ever brought himself to mount her. No wonder Alaron had turned out such an imbecile, with parents like that.

Vann Mercer was part of the Noros Revolt. He was traitor-scum and we should've hanged the lot of them.

Adamus Crozier stroked his chin thoughtfully. 'Sister Raine, we need to know where Mercer is now. Extract what we need, as swiftly as possible.'

Raine's eyes lit up, though she hesitated a moment. 'This man is a Guild trader, sir. The Guild—'

'Let me worry about that, Sister,' Adamus said airily. 'Brother Malevorn will assist you.'

Raine ceased protesting. 'At once, sir.'

'Meanwhile, get this imbecile out of my sight,' he added, turning to Enott, 'before I flog him.'

The Crozier waited until Quintius and Enott were gone, then turned to Malevorn and Raine. 'Brother, Sister, this is our first lead in six weeks. Every day the danger increases that the prize we seek will show up in the hands of someone who is a genuine danger to the Empire.'

'Is that likely?' Raine asked.

'It is possible. The Scytale must be understood to be used, and there are few who have the required knowledge.' He preened slightly. 'I do, of course. But we have no idea what these Dokken might know – and there are Ordo Costruo traitors fighting for the enemy too.' He looked down at the unnamed trader. 'Find out what he knows of Mercer. I don't care how.'

As soon as he'd gone, Raine went to the door, locked and warded it, then pulled the thin curtains across the small window. Malevorn followed her, caught her from behind and clasped her to him. Their steel armour ground together as he nuzzled her neck; she turned in his grasp and her hot mouth enveloped his. They kissed fiercely while his heart began to pump with increasing urgency.

'Kore's Blood, I've been longing for you,' she gasped. 'It's been weeks.'

They crashed to the floor, still kissing even as they were hiking chainmail skirts and hauling down breeches. He rammed himself into her, grunting and scrabbling on the wooden floor, every thrust making the floorboards rattle, and came swiftly, the pent-up need impossible to deny. But he used his gnosis to keep his cock hard, hammering into her, all need, no finesse, until she came too, her body going rigid and her eyes glassy as she convulsed, panting and groaning, in his arms.

They lay uncomfortably entwined on the floor until they noticed the trader staring at them with equally glassy eyes.

Raine gave a throaty laugh. 'Ah well. Playtime's over. I suppose we should get on with it.'

An hour later, with the room hastily freshened and their uniforms restored, Malevorn opened the door to admit Adamus and Quintius. They marched in and peered indifferently at the unconscious trader. 'Well?' Quintius asked. He prodded at the body, but there was no reaction. Raine had torn his mind apart and he would likely never regain consciousness.

Raine lifted her chin. 'I am sorry, Holiness. He knows nothing of where Mercer is, or the prize we seek.' She looked ready to be berated for her failure.

'You're certain?' Quintius asked angrily.

'He knows nothing, sir.'

Quintius jabbed a finger at her. 'Your skills have been highly praised, Caladryn. This is a grave failure—!'

Adamus tutted vexedly. 'Oh, come down off your pony, Quintius. If the man knows nothing, he knows nothing. Would you rather the Acolyte invented something just to keep you happy?' He smiled indulgently at Raine and Malevorn. 'This pair are two of our best, Commandant.'

Quintius wrinkled his nose, but he bowed his head faintly, the closest thing to an apology Raine was ever likely to get. 'Then now what?'

'Mercer must have been tipped off,' Adamus murmured. 'Orders to detain him have been circulating through Verelon, Pontus and Dhassa for months now and nothing. So someone is hiding him.'

'Jean Benoit?' Quintius growled.

'Most likely,' Adamus agreed, prodding at the broken trader. 'Kill this fool and burn the body. Hang a few villagers and put it about that they murdered him. I want us gone before sundown.'

'Where?' Quintius sounded dispirited, already feeling the weight of blame settling on his shoulders. The Inquisition did not brook failure.

'South. The Dokken we're trailing are moving that way so all we can do is follow them, and hope.'

Malevorn looked at Raine. *<We're reduced to hoping? Damn Mercer – damn him to Hel!>*

Hopeful or not, the Fist continued the pursuit southwards, seeking anything in the arid landscape that might put them back on the trail of Alaron Mercer and the Scytale of Corineus. By the time they were southwest of Hebusalim, it was as if the Third Crusade did not even exist, and the trail was not just cold: it had vanished completely.

But their luck finally changed somewhere west of Bassaz. Quintius' farseer detected a flare of gnosis where there should be none, discharged as if in distress, and immediately swung the windship towards it. They found a cohort of Rondian cavalry, out on wide patrol from Bassaz, who'd caught something in their steel traps far stranger than a jackal or a desert lion. The beast lay there trembling: a naked figure, half man, half antelope, caught in mid-transformation. His broken leg was still clenched in the vicious jaws of the trap.

The Dokken's mind was warded, but he wasn't Arcanum-trained, and the Inquisition had much experience in such skills. This time the crozier oversaw the task personally, leaving Malevorn and Raine to assist, and the Dokken broke quickly, barely needing the hideous medley of physical and mental agony Adamus had prepared to open the mind of the antelope-man. The Souldrinker was Brician, a strange mixture of feral youth and innocence, as if he were more animal than human and could not believe that one creature could so cruelly use another. He broke swiftly and completely, his mind and body ruined past even gnostic redemption.

'The Dokken travel in similarly skilled packs,' Adamus reported to Commandant Quintius. 'His are all shapechangers. They have a Seeress guiding them, but there are tensions in the pack.' He grinned widely. 'This is clearly the right group: they are hunting a Lakh female – and a Rondian male!'

'Do you recall the Rimoni bint we saw at the island?' Raine added. 'They have her in their hands, and she's the source of a lot of dissent. The prisoner says their packleader is protecting her, and probably rutting her. Apparently these animals don't like any of theirs mating outside the pack.'

'More importantly,' Adamus announced, 'we know where the pack are gathering next.' He looked at Raine and handed her his dagger. 'Well done, Sister Raine. You are commended. You may finish the interrogation.' Raine bowed over the blade, kissed it then carefully pushed it into the Souldrinker's heart, while Adamus turned to Quintius and said, 'We will need steeds for a land attack.'

'And more men?' Quintius asked.

'We have enough for the task. I don't want others involved in this mission, not when our task is so sensitive.'

Malevorn met Raine's eyes. The dead Dokken had spoken of almost a hundred of his kindred gathering. *Is just one Fist truly enough?* But the greed in the air was as palpable as the stink of blood, and he knew that no help would be summoned.

Malevorn and Raine were on deck, standing just out of touching reach, by mutual agreement – there were too many hostile eyes about. Dominic was with them, his eyes downcast, exuding his usual faint reek of shame. They'd been on the Dokken trail for two more days now, flying southeast. Southern Dhassa was spread below, flat and brown and featureless.

They were flying lower than usual, as if seeking a specific place, and Malevorn was contemplating asking Adamus outright what was going on when Artus Leblanc swaggered past, eying the three of them disdainfully and smirking when Malevorn met his stare. There was something in Leblanc's manner recently that he didn't like – it was as if he knew something that pleased him immensely, something that wasn't going to be good for Malevorn.

Then a lookout shouted, pointing towards the ground, 'There, Captain – we've found it!'

Within minutes the ship was landing beside a large corral. As they descended, the creatures in the pen became clearer. 'Great Kore,' Malevorn breathed, feeling a *frisson* of excitement. 'Khurnes!'

The new intelligent horned steeds had been a cause of much excitement in the Inquisition, but Malevorn's Fist had not yet been assigned theirs, so it was a genuine boost to land and be given his new mount. The khurne he was assigned was a bay, with a bronze-coloured twisted horn emerging from its forehead, just above the eyes. The horn was wickedly sharp, but it was the eyes that drew him: they were strangely alert and focused. Around them, the rest of the Fist were making themselves known to their new steeds. Raine's was black with white socks and a blaze, and she was looking at the creature with something like lust in her eyes. He felt the same: the beasts were power and grace embodied.

<*Hey!*> Raine's face split into a wicked grin as she stroked her khurne's mane. <*Do you like my horny beast?*> He sent her a lewd mental image in return that made her blink, then she laughed and in a low voice murmured, <*That is mostly certainly not going to happen.*> She glanced at Artus Leblanc, standing on the other side of the corral next to a white khurne. <*Though he'd probably enjoy it.*>

'Be careful around him,' he warned her softly.

'I can handle him,' Raine replied. 'No problem at all. You watch me.'

They rode out the next day. Windships were a magnificent weapon of war, but they were hard to hide, and Adamus wanted to take the Dokken by surprise. The Souldrinkers' rendezvous point was near the southern coastal range, a week's ride away; that would give them all time to bond with their new mounts. The khurnes were a delight to ride, with a powerful, flowing gait, and they were capable of following even complex mental instructions. There was something disturbing about their intellect, but their obedience was absolute.

Quintius' Fist still treated the survivors of the Eighteenth as outsiders, and Leblanc was wearing that irritating smirk whenever he looked Malevorn's way, but Adamus obviously favoured them still, which gave Malevorn heart as the Fist closed in on the place the Souldrinker prisoner had told them about. They found the shanty he'd spoken of deserted, but filled with signs of recent habitation – by both humans and jackals, the spore so fresh that they could almost smell their prey.

Do they have the Scytale? Or have Mercer and the mudskin evaded them? Malevorn felt his enthusiasm rekindle. *We will find him: this is my destiny: I'm going to become an Ascendant and my family will be restored to glory.* He glanced sideways at Raine, saw similar dreams in her face, saw his own soul reflected in hers. *Yes, this is our destiny, both of us.*

All his life he'd expected – and demanded – the best of all things. That had most certainly included girls. But he'd never felt anything like what he felt for Raine. Pretty girls were shallow. Nice girls were vapid. Well-bred girls had nothing but their title and their posturing. But this one . . .

I want ambition and lust in a woman and I don't care that the package she comes in is imperfect. I want her.

<We're going to be immortal,> he whispered into her brain, and felt a strange inner glow as he watched the way his promise lit her from within. His mind went back to a teasing conversation they'd once had after sex: that she would fall in love with him. He wasn't sure what love was, not really, but they shared a bond, of that he was certain, and it felt stronger than the love that poets warbled of. <You and me, and the rest can go hang.>

8

Personal Growth

The Sunsurge

Every twelve years, the tides drop to their lowest point and the Leviathan Bridge rises from the sea, the most visible sign of the Moontide, which has come to define the epoch. But before the construction of the Bridge, it was the Sunsurge that had the greater impact. This is the two-year period midway between Moontides, when the opposite occurs – the seas rise to their greatest levels, in many places inundating low-lying coastal areas. During the Sunsurge the winters are marked by huge snowfalls, and the summers by incessant rain and flooding. The severity of the Sunsurge can still define the lives of whole generations.

ORDO COSTRUO ARCANUM, PONTUS, 832

Mandira Khojana, Lokistan, on the continent of Antiopia
Awwal (Martrois) to Jumada (Maicin) 929
9th to 11th months of the Moontide

Gradually Alaron's anxiety over pursuit lessened. He was sure the combination of the sea and the mountains would block any attempt to scry them, and he could detect nothing hostile in the Zain monks who were looking after them; no one had asked them anything in the least bit untoward or prying. When he went to check out the skiff, he was offered use of the monks' workshop to make repairs. The wood here was mostly poor stuff, but there was just enough to repair the landing-struts and hull, and Ramita could grow more to replace what he'd used once she was up and about again.

But there was no question of moving on, not yet. Ramita was

plainly exhausted. She moved like a walking corpse, never more than half awake as she stumbled from sleep to feeding and back in a cruel four-hour cycle. The midwife had gone, and though the monks cheerfully brought them food, they clearly expected him to care for Ramita alone. He assumed there was something in their vows that forbade much contact with women. Ramita seemed grateful for his company, even if he was constantly having to avert his eyes. He'd become somewhat inured to bare skin when around the lamiae, but Ramita's breastfeeding was another matter entirely. Thankfully, the Lakh girl soon took pity on him and became more decorous.

As for the newborn children, they were content to sleep and suckle and foul their wraps over and again. Occasionally they vented their lungs, sending piercing shrieks echoing through the vast complex – an utterly alien sound in such a place – but most times they could be quietened easily enough by laying them as close together as if they still shared a womb.

Once the skiff was repaired, Alaron had plenty of time on his hands. He explored the monastery, which had been gradually built up over hundreds of years, like an enormous wasp nest, but he was becoming increasingly restless. He longed to move, though he knew they couldn't, and that made him prickly and irritable.

At last he started practising his swordsmanship, going through the familiar forms over and over again. He thought perhaps he'd improved a bit since Turm Zauberin. There was something about having used the blade for real that made training more focused. It was the same with the gnosis, which he also practised when he knew he was entirely alone – just simple workings, more about releasing energy than anything else. He really missed having someone to talk to. Master Puravai told him there were female Zain cloisters in some of the larger Lakh cities, but the monks here were all male: even so, none of them came near him.

Alaron was working on his forms when Puravai came into the courtyard, followed by a shaven-headed young novice in a dark crimson robe. He was stocky but muscular, and carried a metal-heeled stave taller than himself.

'Master Alaron, this is Novice Yash. Will you accept his companionship?' the Zain master asked formally.

'Why?' Alaron looked worried; was this some kind of attempt to spy on him?

'Because young men require company, and Yash has yet to settle into this secluded life.' Puravai smiled wryly. 'And neither have you.'

Yash ducked his head, and Alaron immediately recognised his unease – after all, he had grown up with parents who felt no compunction about discussing him around the dinner table as if he wasn't there. It made him grin, remembering, and to his surprise the young novice reciprocated, his white teeth illuminating his dark face, and then it was impossible to say no.

Puravai bowed and left, and Alaron looked uncertainly at Yash. 'Do you speak Rondian?' he said, enunciating slowly and loudly.

'Some. I am learn.' He twirled his staff dextrously. 'Ordo Costruo?' he asked, with a touch of the reverence one heard in Yuros, rather than the antipathy Alaron expected.

Alaron shook his head. 'I'm from Noros.'

Hostility bloomed behind the young man's eyes. He spun his staff and slammed it down on the stone with a metallic crack. 'Not Ordo Costruo. Crusader?'

'No. I'm on my own.'

'But you have Lakh wife?'

'She's not my wife. I'm protecting her.' He realised suddenly that Puravai was right: he *was* lonely. Ramita was absorbed with the day-to-day trials of tending to the newborns and recovering her strength. Even this simple conversation was feeding something inside him that he hadn't realised needed nourishment.

'I hear her babies have white skin?'

'So what if they have?'

Yash coloured and looked down. Then he brightened. 'Many Ordo Costruo have mixed blood.'

'Really? Good for them.'

'I have heard they are all dead?'

The Ordo Costruo are dead . . . Alaron nibbled his lower lip. It made sense, if Meiros was dead that many others were too. It didn't seem relevant to his situation, but it made him sad. 'I don't know about that.' He looked at the novice's staff. 'Is that a walking stick?'

'This is not stick. It is called "kon". It is weapon.'

'I thought you were all sworn to peace.'

'Yes – but travelling monk must defend self.' Yash shifted, a beautifully balanced shuffle-and-spin, and the staff whistled through the air. The shift from stillness to movement happened in an eye-blink, and so did the transition back to a standing pose. 'Blades not allowed, but kon . . .' He grinned. 'Is just walking stick, yes?'

Alaron felt his eyebrows lift. 'Kore's Light! You're good.'

Yash gave a shy smile. 'The master is pleased with progress at defence. But not other things.' He sighed regretfully. 'I sometimes fight with other novice.'

Alaron could certainly relate to that. 'What about?'

'Most from wealthy families with too much sons. But I am poor orphan. The monastery in my village – it would not admit me.'

'Then how did you come to be here?'

'I leave village, find other monastery. Was turned away, find other. And other.' He shrugged. 'Almost I die. But Master Puravai find me, bring me here.'

'Why did you want to join the Zains?'

'To learn magic.'

Alaron snorted. 'You have to be born with the gnosis.'

Yash scowled. 'I know this, now. But then, not. We poor, we believe Zain know magic because of their wisdom. Now I know. But this is a good life,' he added, a little too enthusiastically. 'I will be wise monk and teach the poor.'

'Good for you,' Alaron said sincerely.

Yash looked at him, his face lit by a touch of mischief. 'Anyway, kon is better than sword.'

'The hell it is.' Alaron lifted his blade. It wasn't anything flash, but it was good Yuros steel. 'I could cut your twig in half in one blow.'

'Could you?' Yash grinned, and then suddenly he was spinning forward, the metal heel of the staff a blur. Alaron blocked instinctively and found his blade knocked sideways and the other end of the staff jabbing him in the midriff. Yash's face, inches from his own, was slightly smug. 'Blow to kidney, severe pain. You fall. I finish.'

Right.

Alaron went into a fighting crouch. He didn't feel threatened; Yash could have done exactly what he said and he knew it. This was just sparring – but he was conscious that he held an edged blade. He didn't want to hurt the young man.

He never even came close. It was like being back in college and getting flattened by Malevorn – except that Yash didn't use overpowering gnosis to tilt the odds utterly in his favour. He simply used the staff brilliantly, swirling it with dizzying speed. He could block and attack in so many ways that using a sword began to feel cumbersome. And the hardened wood could block even a full-blooded sword-blow and survive undamaged. After five minutes Alaron was dripping in sweat and his sword was sent spinning across the floor yet again.

He swallowed his pride and threw up a hand. 'Enough! Enough!'

Yash stepped back, breathing heavily and beaming proudly. 'You wish rest?'

Yeah, for about a week. Alaron bent over. 'I'm . . . a little . . . out of practise,' he panted.

Yash looked a little worried that he had overstepped. 'You have many cares to distract you. I sorry.'

Alaron wiped the sweat off his forehead with his sleeve. 'Don't be. One thing I learned at my college was how to get the snot kicked out of me.'

'Snot?'

'I mean that I used to lose at college too.'

'Snot is losing?'

'Ha! No, forget snot. I'm just not so good as you.'

'Losing more instructive than winning, Master Puravai say.'

'Then I'm sure your sparring partners must be well-educated.'

Yash smiled radiantly. Then Alaron reached out and used telekinesis to pull the sword back to his hand. The novice's jaw dropped. 'You could beaten me at any time,' he said accusingly.

'And learned nothing.' Alaron flicked a finger and sent a telekinetic punch into Yash's chest. Somehow the novice turned what should have been a ignominious sprawl into a head-over-heels piece of athleticism and was on his feet again, but now he was wary.

Alaron sheathed his sword. 'Peace.'

'Peace?' Yash cautiously lowered his staff and leant on it, trembling slightly. 'That was gnosis? No wonder magi rule world.'

'You've not seen anything,' Alaron told him. He indicated the staff. 'Could you teach me to fight like you do?'

Yash looked troubled. 'I must ask Master Puravai. We do not teach uninitiated such things.'

'I will ask him myself,' Alaron said.

He did too, that night, and permission was graciously given. Puravai sent him a staff, and a crimson tunic too. Alaron felt ridiculous in it, until he joined the rest of the novices and forgot his strange apparel, so hard was he concentrating on not getting the snot pounded out of him again.

From then on he spent each morning with the novices, and the afternoons alone in the library, on his own knowledge quest while the novices were studying, learning languages and how to read and count. Evenings were for Ramita and the twins. His days were long and exhausting, but the routine gave his life a rhythm, and a calming peace. He lost track of time, barely conscious of the passing weeks as the moon was hidden behind the constant clouds. It reminded him of the months he'd spent alone at Anborn Manor, building the skiff – was that really only last year? But this was different: here he was learning new things, not just practising old skills. He had always known that he was no warrior; he'd never been blessed with the balance and grace of body that Yash had. But he wasn't the worst, either, and that did surprise him: at Turm Zauberin he and Ramon had always been the lowest of the low.

Gradually the other novices lost their shyness and started enthusiastically practising their Rondian lessons on him, treating him as one of their own, though he was a foot taller than most. Each night he slept as if dead, too drained to dream.

'So,' Yash asked him one morning as they rested between bouts, 'what you think of Zain fighting now? Is different to Rondian way?'

Alaron nodded emphatically. 'Very different. At my Arcanum we learned the sword; it was less fluid, more static – you plant your feet *here*, keep your stance strong, and fight from the shoulders. But you Zains, you're never still, always moving. And we were taught that the sword was the weapon, the blade and hilt: but for you, *everything* is a weapon: not just the staff, but head, hands, feet. It's very different.'

'Better, yes?' Yash grinned.

'I guess. Sure.'

Yash patted his forearm. 'You are getting better, Brother Longlegs. Truly.'

Alaron hoped so. He knew he would never be able to match the best of the novices, let alone the full monks – if someone had told him they had the gnosis, he would have believed it. Even after training with them for days on end he couldn't see how the feats they achieved were mortally possible without it. From slowly contorting into impossible positions, always with precise control, or spinning into the fastest, most impossible pirouettes and landing with their staves at the ready, or leaping gaps he'd have hesitated to attempt even with telekinesis or running up vertical walls, then cartwheeling back off them without looking – he was perpetually amazed.

And if that wasn't enough to absorb Alaron, the library became his afternoon battleground. After spending the morning in joint-popping, muscle-straining exercise, he'd hobble to a chair and try to find clues to unravelling the Scytale.

The library deep in the foundations of the Zain monastery was cunningly vented to keep it dry and the air moving. Bent old men in grey – the oldest of the monks – shuffled about, shelving scrolls of papyrus and paper, and leather- and linen-bound tomes of all sizes.

'What language are they?' he asked Puravai on their first visit. He had asked permission to do some research, without actually telling the monk what he was looking for.

'All tongues.' The master pointed to the far aisle. 'The Ordo Costruo gifted us many texts, including some in the Runic speech of the magi. Perhaps they might help your research?'

'Perfect!' Alaron exclaimed, and as soon as he was certain he was alone, out came the leather cylinder containing the Scytale and he set to work.

The Scytale was made of brass and ivory, but other than a little wearing at the edges, there was no sign of any deterioration from age or use. On the outside were carved symbols, and holes displaying more symbols, which changed if the brass caps at either end were twisted. Four leather straps at one end could be wrapped about it and pinned to the outside in dozens of different combinations. It was an encryption device, deceptively simple and dauntingly complex.

A couple of years ago he wouldn't have known how to even begin deciphering the most prized and secret artefact of the empire. For a start, he would never have believed himself adequate to the task. But he'd been through a lot since then, so he didn't bother wondering if he was good enough; he just got on with it. And his intial hunt for the Scytale had attuned his mind to puzzles as never before.

He started with the known: he recognised some of the exterior symbols: the four etched into the brass beside each of the four straps were the runes of Fire, Earth, Water and Air: the base elements. And in the ivory below the cap was a shape that might have been a phallus, opposite a delta: they represented male and female. On the same level were a sun and moon, which usually meant age and youth. On the cap at the bottom were four more runes, symbolising the four Studies: Sorcery (a star), Hermetic (three interlocked circles), Thaumaturgy (a diamond) and Theurgy (a triangle containing a circle). The rest of the runes weren't familiar, but that was a beginning. He began to play, creating hypotheses as he went.

One evening, Ramita came looking for him. She was tired, but determined to be up and about. She traced the name of Rene Cardien on a tract he'd been reading. 'I met him, at a banquet. He stared at my belly button,' she added with a giggle.

'Please don't explain that,' Alaron laughed. Eager to share what he'd learned, he went on, 'I've been studying the Scytale. Look, if I move the top and the base, different symbols appear in the holes on the outside. And if I pin these three straps to the outside like this, following the trail of runes of the same type, they cover most of the symbols.'

Ramita squinted and frowned. 'So?'

'Well, I've gone through and made a note of every symbol it's possible to make appear. There are eight at each level of holes, and eight levels – that's sixty-four different symbols. None of them are simple runes – they're all complicated, the sort that signify mixtures of different chemicals.' At her look of astonishment he said, blushing slightly, 'I'm only guessing this, because I recognise two from college. One is an anaesthetic.'

'An anastas . . . ? What is that?'

'It's a potion that decreases pain. And the other is supposed to make the mind more receptive to dreams.'

She frowned. 'So you know two of the sixty-four?'

'Yes – but that's not as bad as it sounds. I think I've worked out what the Scytale does. It's a recipe codex. I think it was created by Baramitius to store the recipe for the ambrosia – that's the drink that imparts the gnosis. The Scytale stores that recipe: but I think there are variations, depending upon the nature of the person it's being brewed for. There are probably hundreds of different variations on the one base recipe.'

'Baramitius?' She pondered the strange name for a moment, then brightened. 'My husband once told me that this Baramitius took a lot of notes about the people who followed Corineus.'

Alaron sighed. 'I wish he was here now. He'd understand this thing in minutes.'

'I know,' Ramita agreed sadly. 'But you are clever too, Al'Rhon.'

He ducked his head. 'I've heard that only a third of the people who took the original ambrosia gained the gnosis, and over half those who failed died. The rest became Dokken. I bet that original potion was very basic compared to this. I bet Baramitius worked on it for centuries afterwards to improve it.'

'Can you work out what all the symbols mean?'

'Maybe. Potions were never my strength. I wanted to be a battle-mage, not a healer.'

She looked disappointed, but gave him an encouraging smile and squeezed his hand. 'The rest will come.' She didn't seem to realise that she hadn't let his hand go, and he saw no reason to remind her.

'I hope so.' *I found the Scytale, and guided the lamiae to their new home, and I managed to go into gnostic trance at the Isle of Glass. I'm sure I can puzzle this out!*

'If you can work this out, I can get you the ingredients,' she said. 'I know a place where you can buy anything: Aruna Nagar market, where I grew up.' They smiled at each other, then looked down at their hands. The levity left her face. 'It is time for me to feed the twins,' she muttered and scurried away.

Alaron's father was the hardest-working person he'd ever met. Vann was full of sayings like, *Only hard work brings true satisfaction* – usually while he was doing three things at once, as if it would make him three times happier. For the young Alaron, that had meant a regimen of pre-dawn tasks, and after he'd finished school, whatever was required in the stables, the work shop or just running errands, fol-lowed by evening study – and that was all before he turned twelve, gained the gnosis and went to the Arcanum. He'd always resented it – none of his friends had had to work that hard – but now that he had time on his hands, he noticed that he was doing the same thing: filling his days with never-ending tasks.

As well as the morning exercise regime with the novices and try-ing to unpick the Scytale in the afternoons, he decided it was time he took his gnostic practise seriously too. Late most afternoons, around nine bells, when his concentration on the Scytale research started to waver, he headed for an alcove behind the terraced gardens where he could practise unobserved. He'd thought his activity had gone completely unnoticed, so he was surprised to be met one afternoon by Master Puravai, with Ramita behind him. She was clad in a simple cream-coloured tunic and leggings, her long hair was tied up, and she had a serious, nervous look on her face.

'Brother Longlegs,' Puravai greeted him with twinkling eyes, 'may we join you?'

Alaron stopped in his tracks, feeling self-conscious. He didn't want company – the gnosis was a personal thing and the Arcanum had been bad enough, where his every spell was analysed and criticised by the tutors, then sneered at by the other students. He really didn't want an audience. But it would be churlish to say no – and Ramita was here, and he liked spending time with her.

'The twins are asleep,' she said, when he looked at her questioningly. 'I've been trying to practise the gnosis like Justina showed me, but Master Puravai suggested that we should work together.' The old monk backed her up by nodding at Alaron expectantly.

'I – er, well, I guess so.' Alaron had begun to trust in Master Puravai and his weird methods. One morning, all of the novices had been told to bind each other's favoured hand behind their backs and do everything with their wrong hand. At first it had driven Alaron mad, but faster than he would have believed, his left hand had become more dextrous, and when they had been unbound, much to his surprise, Alaron found he was operating with both far more surely. Sometimes they had to do their exercises one-legged, or spend time sitting on their heads, or perform strange balancing exercises, but he was beginning to see that each came with some unexpected benefit, aiding coordination, control or dexterity.

So he made room for Ramita in the small garden, then turned to Puravai. 'How should we do this?'

'Firstly, what type of mage are you, Alaron?' he asked.

'Fire, with a little Earth; and Sorcery.'

Puravai studied Alaron's periapt, a piece of amber Cym had given him which he had attuned to his gnosis. Then he pocketed it. 'I will look after this, yes.'

'Hey! I need that—!' Alaron reached out, then glanced at Ramita and realised that she wasn't wearing her periapt either. He paused. 'What's happening?'

The Lakh girl gave him a reassuring if tentative smile.

Puravai handed Alaron a bowl of water from the garden fountain. 'Instead, use this.'

'But . . . I can't. It's water! Only a gem can be used as a focus . . .'

Puravai's eyes narrowed. 'What have I told you novices about the word "can't"?'

'You don't know what you are asking.'

'Do I not? I, who worked with Antonin Meiros himself twelve years ago, opening up gnosis to him that he had never previously used?'

He taught Meiros?

He looked again at Ramita, who was nodding meekly.

Any minute now she's going to say something about Destiny.

'Think of it this way,' Puravai told them. He produced a parchment and crudely sketched a man with two cross-shapes on either side of him, one arm of each cross touching him. 'See, here is a typical mage. His primary gnosis, both elemental and conceptual, define him. For you, Longlegs, it is Fire and Sorcery – these two gnostic abilities are fused inside your gnosis, yes? For you, Ramita, it is Earth and Hermetic gnosis. These things are buried in you – deeper for Alaron, because of his training. You understand?'

Both nodded. Alaron had seen similar drawings before. The first thing every young mage did when they gained the gnosis was to undergo a test to determine their affinities: the elements and modes of operating that revealed their strengths and weaknesses. In the Arcanum the Magisters had used sketches like this to show them what their affinities were and weren't. Thereafter, all their training was devoted to their strengths: developing and exploring the magic that came to them naturally. Strong affinities were admired, as that meant feats beyond what most magi could manage. Some – a few – had only mild affinities, like his Aunt Elena. That made them more versatile, but it also meant such magi were thought to be inhibited in their powers as they lacked what the Arcanum tutors called 'clear affinity'.

'Now,' Puravai went on, 'both of you are a little capable of reaching one other point of each cross. Alaron, for you that is Earth; Ramita, it's Fire. Neither of you can reach Water or Air easily, if at all. Similarly, on the other cross – Alaron can reach a little Theurgy, Ramita a little Thaumaturgy. Other things elude you.'

'That's just normal,' Alaron told him tersely.

'Why should it be?' Puravai asked with disarming simplicity. 'What if, instead of a cross, that shape was an arc, with each aspect of the gnosis in equal reach? What if you could access every spell with equal facility? Would you not have a tremendous advantage?'

Alaron stared, while Ramita just looked perplexed. 'Yes, I suppose – but it's impossible.'

'You are quick to say so, but Lord Meiros understood. He agreed that ideally a mage should be in balance, without preference or aversion to any aspect of their gnosis.'

'But we link to our affinities from the moment we gain the gnosis.'

'Because you are conditioned to do so. But what if that is the wrong approach? What if, instead of specialising immediately, you chose to be as diverse in your approach as possible?'

Alaron was just confused. 'We can't help our affinities. The gnosis is an extension of who we are.'

'Is it?'

Alaron had to fight not to shout at the old man. 'Yes! Everyone knows this!'

'Then everyone is wrong. Think on this: people *change*. We form and reform ourselves all the time. But from an early age a mage is forced by your Arcanum system to anchor his . . .' He smiled at Ramita and added, 'Or her gender, makes no difference. So you are forced to anchor your gnosis in a certain way. From there on, that binding is made tighter and stronger, for as you have said, the affinities do reflect personality – but it is not in the way you mean. Let us imagine a hot-tempered young mage anchors his gnosis in Fire. But as he matures and becomes more reflective – more an Air-type, say – does he become an Air-mage? No, because his gnosis is firmly linked to Fire by now.'

Alaron considered this helplessly, but Ramita was head-wagging reflectively; of course, she'd not had a lot of training so far so he didn't think her opinion mattered on this. *I know better.*

'The good thing,' Master Puravai went on, 'is that both of you are ideal candidates for this training. Lord Meiros agreed that most mature magi would be too set in their ways: he believed this requires someone young enough that their affinities were not fully imbedded, old enough to grasp the possibilities and open-minded enough to try. I believe that you both are highly suitable.'

'I don't know about this,' Alaron said doubtfully. 'It contradicts centuries of Arcanum teaching.'

'Brother Longlegs, I travelled widely when I was younger. I have seen idiocy enshrined as wisdom in all corners of the world: mistaken knowledge taught as facts, remedies that are deadlier than the sickness, destructive traditions preserved and sensible ones lost, fools and charlatans revered as gurus and proven scholars ignored. There is always a better way of doing things, if we are prepared to seek it.'

Alaron glanced at Ramita, who met his gaze and said, 'This is destiny, Al'Rhon.'

Arghhh!

Puravai saw the look on his face and smiled faintly. 'Remember, Antonin Meiros unlocked his own gnosis from its Earth and wizardry foundations, after just two months of using the methods he and I devised. He did this after *centuries* of specialisation. I believe he was going to reveal our discoveries to his Order this year, had not death taken him.' The old monk patted Alaron's forearm. 'Will you at least try?'

He gritted his teeth. 'Okay, fine. Let's do it.'

It won't work.

Puravai and Ramita shared a look, which irritated him more.

The first thing Puravai made Alaron attempt was a simple light spell, channelling through water instead of using his periapt. He'd never tried anything like that before. In the opposite corner of the garden, he set Ramita, primarily an Earth mage, a similar task: to channel using nothing but the air around her.

Neither could do it.

After three straight hours he was resenting the lost time and ready to give up; he could have been working on the Scytale or trimming his nails, or doing anything at all and it would have been more valuable than this utter waste of time. Even Ramita was frustrated, which was a mild comfort.

'This isn't working,' he told Puravai eventually. 'A mage is born with their affinities. You can't change them.'

'Lord Meiros did,' the old monk replied, the hint of challenge in his voice.

Alaron bit his lip. *Sure: because he was Lord rukking Meiros! He could do anything!*

But that made it a point of pride: he would show them both that he, Alaron Mercer, could turn his hand to *anything*. He would show Ramita that he could do what her husband could. And he'd do it before Ramita did, because he was Arcanum-trained and she wasn't, and that *had* to have meant something. His father had sacrificed and scrimped for years to get him into Turm Zauberin. It *had* to have been worth it.

But his misery was compounded after days of continued failure when Ramita, with a squeal of delight, produced a faint glow on her fingertip. *I managed more on my first day at the Arcanum,* he thought sulkily. She danced around the garden so gleefully he almost stormed off. In desperation he took to immersing himself in the stream below the monastery, using the gnosis to keep his body temperature up until it felt like he was on the verge of dissolving into liquid himself. The only thing he achieved was a cold.

He didn't give up though. Puravai made suggestions: like trying to visualise an invisible arm holding a tongue of flame, while the core of his gnosis was reserved for pure energy. Then he had to envisage another arm, holding the Water-gnosis. It sounded simple enough when Puravai described it, but of course it wasn't – and he just couldn't do it. Trying to follow Puravai's instructions was akin to being taught to paint by a blind man, in his view.

Am I going to become the first known mage to ever lose the gnosis? he wondered after waking one night unable even to conjure light. The Fire-gnosis had been so central to his being that stripping it out of his core energies left him enfeebled. He panicked, lying there in bed feeling like he'd lost all his senses.

After a moment or two, he managed to attain gnostic sight, which had never been linked to Fire-gnosis, and that settled his dread. Seeking calm, he slowly re-found those gnosis skills that were based upon pure energy rather than an element or Study. Then he lifted a hand and, trembling, conjured light without his periapt.

A glowing sliver of energy coalesced in his palm and he screamed silently in joyous relief. *I did it!*

He turned the light into a glowing ball, grew it, shrank it, threw it and drew it back, shaking with relief.

I really did it.

That afternoon he couldn't wait to get to the garden – where he found Ramita juggling globes of light so happily it almost crushed him.

How can a mere Lakh market-girl be so much better than me?

Then he mentally slapped himself. That thought had been so ugly he could have borrowed it whole from Malevorn Andevarion or Francis Dorobon. It certainly wasn't worthy of someone raised by Vann and Tesla Mercer.

Who do I think I am? he told himself, bitterly ashamed that such a notion had ever crossed his mind. *She's got a brain as good as anyone's. She's had different opportunities to me – most would say a harder path – and yet she's more open-minded and adaptable and willing to explore than I am. Why should I expect that a path created by a Rondian mage must be best?*

Why shouldn't this be better? It was good enough for the greatest mage in history.

He walked quietly into the garden, sat cross-legged before her, conjured a globe of light – not as bright as hers – and tossed it into her ring of whirling light.

She laughed aloud, caught it, and sent half of her balls of light cascading towards him. He dropped all but one, and they tossed it back and forth, then she mischievously pulled a trowel from the garden with telekinesis and threw it at him. He caught it instinctively using kinetic gnosis before he'd realised what he was doing, and a wide grin split his face.

They spent the next hour playing, and if Puravai came past, neither saw him, so wrapped up were they in what they were doing.

Alaron's eyes met Ramita's as they faced each other and let the various garden implements clatter to the ground before sitting back, laughing. He suddenly realised that he'd not been this relaxed for two years, not since the befuddled General Langstrit had appeared at Anborn Manor. But this was better, because there was someone to share the feeling of peace.

'That was fun, Brother Longlegs,' Ramita said.

'Please! I'd rather you called me Al'Rhon the Goat than Brother Longlegs,' he chuckled. She giggled, then looked away shyly.

After that breakthrough, he caught up rapidly, his six years of training finally paying off. He knew the basic gnostic skills intimately: wards, shields, binding, enchanting and the rest were all second nature to him, but new ground for Ramita. But he was fascinated to find that all of these basic skills worked much better once he'd taken the Fire 'taint' from his core gnosis: his shields and wards were stronger, his mage-bolts more powerful and precise.

When he examined his own aura, he could see the change, and in Ramita's too. Where both auras had been crimson or earthen, they now burned pure white. The deep blue patina of his Sorcery affinities were also gone: so he had apparently purged his gnosis, but at the price of losing touch with his elemental and arcane affinities. When he tried to conjure fire, he couldn't.

Instead of panicking, he and Ramita went to see Puravai.

'So, you are now ready for the next step.' The old monk beamed at them both. 'You have cleansed your canvas and now it is time to paint. Let me show you both something.'

They followed him to a small room that contained a very strange statue of a man – or a god, Alaron supposed – with blue skin and a lot of arms. The three-foot-high marble sculpture was finely carved and highly polished. It portrayed a muscular, clean-shaven man with long hair in a topknot, sitting cross-legged. He'd never seen such a bizarre thing, but Ramita gave a squeal of recognition. She fell to her knees before it and immediately began to pray.

Alaron looked at Puravai, puzzled. 'I thought you Zains don't believe in gods?'

'We don't. But we understand that the concept of godhood has been important to man since time began, and it is instructive to look at how men conceive their gods to be. This is a representation of the Lakh god Sivraman, made more than a thousand years ago. It comes from Teshwallabad. I keep it to remind me of my discussions with Lord Meiros.'

He bent and touched Ramita's shoulder. 'My dear, there will be opportunity for prayer later. Please listen now.'

She stood obediently and inclined her head towards the old monk. Puravai turned to Alaron. 'Please, describe what you see.'

'Uh . . . the god has four arms . . . one's held up as if in greeting with a lightning bolt etched onto the palm; one is holding a bowl; another a lamp. The fourth is holding a staff with a snake coiled around it.'

'Correct. What do you think they mean?'

Alaron frowned. 'That the sculptor doesn't know anything about anatomy?'

Ramita threw him a peeved look, but Puravai just smiled faintly. 'What else do you see?'

'Umm . . . he's sitting on a lion pelt. He's got an eye symbol in the middle of his forehead. And . . .' He peered closer, then frowned. 'He's got a woman's breast, on his right side . . . in fact, his face is half-male and half-female too!' He pulled a face. 'That's really weird.'

Puravai turned to Ramita. 'Can you clarify for Master Alaron?'

The little market-girl tossed her head defiantly and glared at Alaron. 'This is an Ardhanari statue, showing the union of Sivraman and Darikha as one being. All gods are one god who is many gods. My guru says this. It is known.'

Yes, but what does it actually mean? Alaron looked at Puravai impatiently. He had quite enough trouble following all the contradictions of the Kore, and he'd had that thrown in his face his whole life. Omali theology was utterly alien to him.

Puravai indicated the statue. 'Let me interpret. This highly symbolic statue is meant to represent the many powers and aspects of the god. There are variants, but this one is a common representation, and it is relevant to your gnostic study. Note his four arms and what they hold: a lamp, a bowl, a snake-staff and a lightning mark. Do you know that in many cultures, the snake is regarded as spiritually linked to the earth?'

Alaron's eyes widened. 'A snake for Earth ... A lamp for Fire ... A bowl for Water. And a lightning bolt – that's Air.'

'So perhaps the sculptor is telling us that Sivraman is a master of the elements. What else?'

'The eye in his forehead ... that could be for Sorcery. And the lion-skin for mastery over living things ... Hermetic gnosis. And Theurgy ... um ... the half-female, maybe? I'm not sure I understand that.'

'Well, as Ramita says this is not purely a statue of Sivraman: it is also partly a representation of his wife, Darikha. Often the Omali make such statues to remind worshippers that the god and goddess are one union, as men and women should be. It is also a reminder that the Lakh believe the soul has no gender and that the flesh is only a vehicle for the soul.'

That rang bells for Alaron. 'The definition of Theurgy is use of the spiritus – the soul, I guess – to perform gnosis that affects other souls, bypassing the flesh ...'

'Sivraman and Darikha-ji created the gnosis when he created the world,' Ramita announced proudly. 'That is clearly what this statue is saying.'

Alaron turned on her crossly. 'No! Baramitius discovered the gnosis—'

'*Discovered*. Therefore it was already there.' Ramita looked at him truculently.

He rolled his eyes and turned back to Puravai. 'How can an old Lakh statue have anything to do with the gnosis?'

The monk looked at them both. 'I am not going to take sides – you may both be right. The real lesson of the statue is this: the god is holding the elements of the gnosis outside his core body, but within reach, yes? Omali statues often have many arms, to show all the powers that the god can reach.' He put particular emphasis on *reach*.

Ramita got it first. 'You are saying that we should hold our core as pure energy and reach for the affinities without pulling them into us?'

'Exactly.'

Alaron stared at the statue and tried to picture himself: a core of gnostic energy with all the Studies in reach, like balls of light linked to him by 'arms' – cords of energy forming conduits to the power. 'I think I see it,' he admitted. *I get it – and I think maybe I could learn to do it too.* He felt his pulse begin to quicken as the possibilities magnified. 'We have to grow arms to hold the elements.'

'And more,' Puravai replied. 'You must open the eye in your forehead. You must master living things and free your soul.' He smiled faintly. 'Best you both get busy.'

They did get busy. For Ramita, it represented a magical, spiritual time. From the moment she had been given to Antonin Meiros, her life had become a strange learning journey, but each phase had been brought to an end in violence. In her married life in Hebusalim she had learned languages as well as how to be a wife, a period ended by her husband's murder. In the next phase, on the Isle of Glass, she had learned about her newly flowered gnosis with Justina, though they'd had little time to do more than teach her a few basics and do some early exploration of her affinities. Justina had told her that her enormously strong gnosis – born from pregnancy manifestation whilst carrying the twins – had allowed her access to powers that often eluded better trained magi, but the fact remained that she was a neophyte.

This third phase, as a mother and a novice mage, was characterised by the alarming exposure to new sensations and experiences. Each day was filled to the brim with wonders and new discoveries. Under Puravai's guidance they teased their affinities back into reach and tried to use them without pulling them inside and changing their core aura. She could scarcely believe the things she was achieving. And with the joy of her twins sharing her room, she'd not been so happy for a long time. She just dreaded that this phase too might end in violence.

Part of her enjoyment was seeing Alaron Mercer blossom. She could see how downhearted he'd been – and even offended – by having a non-mage turning all he had been taught on its head. He'd been upset that she'd made faster progress at first. But now he'd got his head around it, he was enthusiasm itself.

After they had regained touch with their normal affinities, Puravai directed them to concentrate on those elements they'd not previously been able to reach, trying to balance Fire, Water, Earth and Air, never allowing one to overwhelm the others. Progress was steady as days blurred into weeks and she began to think her head would burst. Between caring for her children, regaining her physical health and strength and this new learning, she was exhausted, but she also felt immense fulfilment.

It was a shock to realise that almost three months had passed. It was Jumada already, late spring, and the mountain goats had returned to the slopes to graze the patches of pale green. Every day the villagers brought gifts to the monastery: food and cloth and other necessities. They were small, wiry people with narrow skulls, almond-shaped eyes and unkempt black hair sprouting everywhere; they wore elaborately patterned blankets and shawls.

She caught movement in the garden below: Alaron, practising with his sword. Something in his stance reminded her of Jai, her brother. She thought that they would get on well. And that thought led to wondering where Jai was now – was he still with Keita, and had they got home safely and found Mother and Father? Were they all well? And the twins – they must be six by now! And the two surviving triplets – they'd be eight! *I can't believe I've not seen them for two years!* The next moment she was dabbing at a haze of tears while loneliness welled up.

At least I have someone here . . . He was increasingly pleasing to look at, especially now, clad in a crimson novice's robe that left his shoulders, arms and legs bare. His limbs were muscled now, and as tanned as his face. His chest was broader and his shoulders more square. His face looked different too: older, leaner, the jawline more pronounced, his cheeks more sunken. The effect was, well . . . *manly*. Somewhere in the past months, the last of his boyhood had gone.

She looked away as that nagging temptation to lie beside him returned. He liked her, she knew that, maybe more than just *liked*, and she was beginning to feel pretty again. The dark circles beneath her eyes were fading and she no longer looked so tired and wan. Her breasts were still full – he was sneaking looks at them when he thought she wasn't looking. Her waist was narrowing and her backside was taut again, as it had been in Aruna Nagar Market when she'd worked so hard and never had quite enough to eat. The Zain way of life, the food, the exercise, even the meditating, was making her stand taller. She was stronger and more flexible and her vitality had returned, even her feminine energy, the womanly desire that moistened her yoni on sleepless nights.

He wouldn't say no to me.

But she held back, haunted by all that was at stake.

It appeared that Master Puravai noticed such things too, for he pulled her aside one afternoon after gnostic lessons, not long after she'd shared some of the truth with him: including exactly who she was, and her husband's final instruction, that she should seek out Vizier Hanook. She left out only the most dangerous details: the Scytale, and her relationship with Kazim and Huriya. Puravai had accepted her story as he accepted everything else: with wry equanimity.

Now, as Alaron left to wash, he said quietly, 'Ramita, soon you will be moving on, as we have discussed.'

'We are happy here,' she replied, 'but we know we can't stay for ever.'

'You must go to Teshwallabad, as you planned,' Puravai said. 'I should tell you now that the vizier and I are known to each other. He was a Zain monk – he trained here, alongside me, when we were both much younger.'

Ramita raised her eyebrows at that. 'What's he like?'

'He is a serious man, as he should be, but witty and droll as well. He is a complex, goodhearted person. But I will tell you this: he will ask that you wed someone of power in the mughal's court. That is inevitable: the Lakh royal family have long coveted the gnosis, so long as they can obtain it secretly. How would you feel about such a marriage?'

She had known it would come to that, at some point. 'I am well used to being bartered for, and I know my value. The marketplace of Aruna Nagar teaches such lessons early.'

His face was sympathetic. 'When I see you like today, happy and excited, I see the bonds between you and Brother Longlegs growing tighter and it gladdens my heart. If these other things did not matter, I would rejoice for you both.'

She dropped her eyes. 'Al'Rhon is a good friend. No more than that.'

'But he wishes he were more to you, and so do you. Ramita, I must warn you that the time you spend learning the gnosis together will deepen your affections. As you progress, you will begin to work mind-to-mind, and that will involve sharing secrets and desires. This will drive you closer so that, unless you guard your heart, it will end in either love or hate. You must be careful.'

She looked away, suddenly scared. *Do I want to fall in love again, ever? To a foreign mage?* She wasn't sure. But such questions led to others: *Could I now marry someone who isn't a mage? Could I now marry someone ordinary? I'm not the simple girl who fell in love with Kazim any more. I am Lady Meiros, mage and mother.*

And I like my goat . . .

She blinked back tears. 'It won't be hate.' *For all his irritating, pedantic precision, his annoying superiority and scepticism and his silly competiveness, for all his ridiculous puppy-dog eagerness and his complete inability to do his hair and dress properly . . .* 'He is too good a person to hate.'

'Then if it were love, it would be a dangerous love, and it might ruin the marriage Hanook will arrange for you. The mughal's court is dangerous, and even the gnosis can't protect someone in such a hostile place for ever. No one there will tolerate a Rondian mage as a rival.'

'What should I do?'

'That is up to you. You are a woman now, and your choices are your own. Just be aware of the consequences. In my experience, in matters of the heart what is lost is more damaging than what is gained.'

She wondered whether a matter of the heart might have driven him to this life of celibacy and privation.

'Thank you, Master. I will consider what you say.'

9

Rejoining the War

The Rimoni Empire: The Fall

How did the Blessed Three Hundred conquer an empire? Through the power of Kore.

BOOK OF KORE

Three Hundred Ascendants: more power than any army could contain, let alone one largely bereft of archery or cavalry, and with no experience in dealing with such foes. Though the Ascendants at this time were wielding only Thaumaturgy, and had yet to discover periapts and other tools of the modern gnosis, they were unstoppable.

ORDO COSTRUO COLLEGIATE, PONTUS

Northern Javon, on the continent of Antiopia
Safar (Febreux) to Awwal (Martrois) 929
8th and 9th months of the Moontide

The village was on the road to Hytel, just a cluster of buildings where relay horses were stationed to support the Gorgio and Dorobon supply wagons moving produce south to the capital. It was a way-station of little import, just a few dozen Jhafi servants and stablehands under the dominion of a patrol of Dorobon legionaries. But tonight the best room in the rough tavern housed a Dorobon battle-mage.

Elena crept forward as the light drained from the sky, her mind linked to Kazim's on the other side of the village. There was a guard at the stable doors and another in front of the inn. The villagers had dispersed to their own huts, except for the whoremaster, whose string of Jhafi girls he kept to service the Rondian soldiery were being kept fully occupied.

They'd been watching the village for four days. It was a full night's flight from their base and they'd hidden the skiff nearby, ready to depart as soon as this job was done. *This 'job'*. Even thinking that way conjured up the old Elena, who did such 'jobs' for a living. The coldly calculating and ruthless Elena.

She was wrapped in an illusion of shadows; she passed the corral without the beasts reacting, stealing up on the stable guard, her knife ready in her hand. He never saw her coming.

You join the army knowing you could die.

He was middle-aged, and sweating in the alien heat. She gripped him from behind and flashed the razor-sharp blade across his neck, slicing effortlessly through his jugular vein. Blood spurted; he choked, quivered then sagged. She propped him upright against the feed-trough and moved into the shadows. <*Clear,*> she sent, and felt Kazim acknowledge.

From there, she slid along the outside wall of the stables, around a bend and into another alley on the far side, a narrow space running alongside the rear wall of a barracks. There were no open windows; they'd been closed against the reek of the rotting refuse in the alley. Rats scattered as she crept past. She heard desultory singing from the tavern as she cautiously extended her senses to the rooms above. There was crude laughter emanating from one room and rhythmic grunting from another. It was the third room that interested her. A pale blue light shimmered against the glass and she could sense the discharge of power like breeze on her skin. <*He's upstairs, this side.*>

<*Coming,*> Kazim responded. A minute later he ghosted out of the darkness and whispered, 'That one?' He pointed at the third window. His sense of the gnosis was growing ever more precise.

'Yes. We need to get upstairs with as little fuss as possible.'

'Straight in the window?'

'No. Look carefully – there are wards. See the glow around the frame?'

'I could blast through that.'

'Yes, but it would rouse the whole place. Let's delay that moment as long as we can.' She inclined her head to the next corner of the building. 'We'll go in the back way.' She slipped along the wall to the kitchen door again.

He followed, reaching out to stroke her hip as she paused by the corner. <*Behave*,> she reproved, unable to completely suppress a smile.

The back door led directly to the kitchen. The door was open, revealing young Jhafi men sweating over pots and pans of food. The air was thick with steam and heat. It was too small to pass unseen, and that wasn't the plan anyway. She motioned for Kazim to move ahead of her and he stepped into the kitchen and brandished a metal disc with a jackal's head embossed into it. *Hadishah*. The kitchen hands backed away, and as they passed, Elena jerked her head towards the back door. They took her meaning and left swiftly and silently. No one looked back.

I hope they have the sense to just grab their things and leave.

A staircase behind the taproom led to the upper storey. Elena lowered her hood and took the stairs silently, reaching the upstairs hall unimpeded and spotted a well-muscled, shaven-headed Jhafi man, a handler for the whores, there to ensure the girls weren't beaten and that the soldiers paid. His head turned to her as she came into view and his eyebrows raised as he realised he was seeing a white woman.

She smiled at him as if her presence were the most natural thing and showed him her hands, palms outspread. There was a coin in her right hand. The Jhafi man blinked and rose to his feet. 'Lady, I—'

She used telekinesis to send the coin flashing into his right eye socket and it struck with a nauseatingly liquid *splat*. Blood sprayed and the man slumped back into his chair, the coin lodged in his brain. She darted forward and propped him up as Kazim appeared behind her.

She nodded to the far door. The gaps were leaking blue light.

She knew little about this battle-mage, only that he was from the Dorobon III legion. She'd glimpsed him from a distance during the day and watched him sending a bird south. He was young, brown-haired – reminiscent of her nephew Alaron. The fact that he was handling birds meant he was probably an animagus, and therefore most likely an Earth mage. His blood-strength was unknown and so were his affinities. She didn't like that.

She went to his door and pressed her hand to the wooden surface, feeling energy pulsing through, binding the barrier closed. The wards were competently set, and stronger than she could manage – a pure-blood then: a daunting prospect. She could hear the faint scratching of a pen.

Enough delaying. Let's get this done.

She knocked, while calling aloud in Rondian with a thick Jhafi accent, 'Good sir, good sir. I come.'

The writing noises ceased, and a male voice called, 'Go away.'

'Sir. Manager send me. Free for you.' She knocked again, harder. 'I have tight and juicy yoni, sir. Anything you want, I do.'

'For Kore's sake,' the man inside sighed. Behind her she felt Kazim settle beside the middle door, in case someone came out. She heard a chair shift inside, then footsteps. The door pulsed faintly with energy as the wards were disabled, then it was pulled open a crack.

She rammed her shoulder into the door, slamming it into the man's shoulder and half-turning him while she pushed a dagger through the tiny gap into his chest. It struck personal shields, but tore through his robes and left pectoral muscle. He yelped and staggered backwards.

'Wha—!' He gestured, slamming telekinetic energy at her, but she was already on him and hammering another dagger blow into the middle of his chest. Light crackled like splintering glass across his torso and the blade snapped. He shouted again, and she heard someone call from the next room. His eyes filled with crystalline light and mesmeric swirls wove across his irises as he locked eyes with hers. *<Stillbestillbestillbestill,>* they commanded, tentacles of light reaching for her, trying to freeze her in place.

<No fucking way.>

She reversed the broken dagger and slammed it into his belly with a bolt of energy wrapped about it, and his body convulsed from the force. As his shield shorted and flickered, she pivoted and booted him under the jaw: the timing was perfect and his neck snapped. He crashed backwards and sprawled limply across the floor.

A voice called out from the desk where the man had been sitting, 'Luman? *Luman?*' There was a faint outline of a face in a shifting pile of sand, and eyes searching blindly. The dead mage had been engaged in some kind of communication spell. She blasted it away with raw energy, then snapped the dead mage's periapt chain and pocketed the gem, and took his dagger to replace her broken one. He looked barely twenty, his vacant face all innocent stupidity.

Too bloody easy.

A woman screamed from another room and Elena drew her sword and ran into the hall. Kazim was standing over a naked Rondian man with a bloodied chest. The far door, the one by the stairs, opened and another Rondian emerged, clad in breeches and holding a longsword.

Stupid weapon for an enclosed space, she thought as Kazim blocked the first blow and drove his scimitar straight-armed into the man's stomach, all the way in and out the other side. He kicked the man off his blade and vanished into the room. Elena ran to the stairs, glancing left to see a Jhafi girl on the bed, wrapped in a sheet with her mouth wide open. She screamed again when she saw Elena and hid her face.

Gurvon will know it was me by dawn.

She went down the stairs, Kazim a heartbeat behind her. A Jhafi man was at the foot, caught in an agony of indecision: the whoremaster, she guessed, torn between trying to protect his assets and keeping his hide intact.

She'd never much liked men who sold women for money. It took just one thrust.

She kicked open the doors to the taproom and went through at a flat run. Steel flashed and she parried, then let energy burst from her, throwing the men who'd gathered about the doorway backwards. She dropped another with a mage-bolt that fried his face to the bone, then blocked two swords at once. Suddenly she was pressed, cornered—

Then Kazim burst in. His first blow to the back of one of the men attacking her went into his neck and through his spinal cord. He went down in a boneless heap, blood spraying, and without pausing she spun to face the flanking legionary, blocked his solid shortsword, ducked beneath a roundhouse swipe and skewered his heart. A thrown knife skittered off her shields and more men erupted from the far corner. She picked out the first and raised a hand, ready to blast him, when Kazim stepped across her and threw up his own hands.

Fire blazed from his fingertips: a sheet of heat that washed over the entire side of the room. She knew she'd never be able to survive such an attack herself; the rankers didn't stand a chance. They were torched by the flames that washed over them and up the walls.

'Shut it down!' she shouted. 'Keep the building intact!'

For a second she didn't think he'd heard her. His blood was up, and his face was alive with unsated fury. But he raised his hand again and she watched, impressed, as the flames were sucked back into his palm, fizzling out as they struck it. It reminded her that he had an Ascendant's power, and a growing competence to go with it. He turned to her, his face still impassioned. 'You should stay behind me,' he snapped. 'I'm the stronger.'

'You shouldn't fucking step in front of me in a fight!' she retorted. 'I almost loosed into your back!'

'You're my woman.'

'It's not a bloody joust!'

He reached for her and she knocked his hand away. For a second she saw anger, and then he relaxed. 'I'm sorry. It frightened me, to see you in danger.'

'Okay. I understand. But don't do it again.'

There was shouting outside, someone calling, 'Petar? Langer?'

Kazim pushed her aside and went for the door, surging out through the billowing smoke like a demon erupting from the Fiery Pit, battering down the man's guard and slashing his throat open. Elena followed, fired a mage-bolt into a crossbowman as he took aim, and lined up another. The remaining Rondians must have realised what they were facing now, because they turned and ran.

They didn't get far: the first one to reach the stables vanished inside, only to stagger back out with a pitchfork through his chest. He waltzed sideways and fell on his side, twitching violently. Elena blasted him with a mage-bolt out of pity. The rest of the Rondians took to their heels, running for the open desert as the Jhafi emerged, armed with tools and kitchen knives, first a dozen men, then suddenly many more, women and children too.

The kitchen staff were among them, pointing and jabbering, speaking too fast even for her ears. She went to Kazim's side as the eldest Jhafi man barraged him with questions, then interrupted, 'Do you know who I am?'

The Jhafi shook his head, but the crowd of people behind him were pointing and murmuring, and one of the women jabbed a finger at her and shouted, 'You are Alhana, the queen's champion. I saw you once, in Brochena.'

Kazim looked at her questioningly. *<Shouldn't we be anonymous?>*

<The Rondians who got away will have recognised me anyway,> she told him, then out loud, she said, 'Yes, I am she.'

The Jhafi smiled cautious smiles.

'Is there aught you need?' the spokesman asked carefully.

'Food, perhaps? We have some coin.'

'No coin.' He shook his head.

'I insist.' She indicated the bar, reminded that her throat was very dry. She'd not drunk beer for – what, six years? That was a Hel of a long time for a girl from Norostein. 'Some food and drink, perhaps? And a few comforts?'

The man nodded acquiescence – it wasn't his tavern anyway – and followed them inside, a crowd of his people trailing cautiously behind. Several of the women tried to kiss her feet but she wouldn't let them, pressing coins into their hands instead, then going behind the bar where she pumped a glass full of Easenbeer, brought by the Rondians to give their rankers a taste of home. The strong smooth malty taste was divine on her tongue, soothing on her throat.

We'll take a keg of this if we can . . . Then she remembered what she'd been like when she'd drunk at the monastery, and changed her mind. *No, better we don't.*

While Kazim arranged food, including a sack of lentils, she went upstairs. The girls were gone and the bodies of the soldiers were lying lifeless on the floors in pools of blood. She stepped around them, fished about in the whores' room and found a few comforts: some scent, some soap. The mage's room yielded parchment, quills and ink, and best of all a piece of Brician smoked cheese, the aroma alone enough to make her salivate.

When she got back to the taproom, Kazim was downing a mug of beer himself. One of the whores was hanging about him, a narrow-faced girl with a businesslike manner, but he was ignoring her. *Only just, though, my lover.* He was breathing heavily, and his eyes went straight to Elena's body as she walked up. Fighting for one's life did that to some men, made them randy as Hel afterwards. It was something about the margins between living and dying. It looked like he was affected that way, though it left her cold.

'Get the goods into a handcart,' she told him. She fixed the whore with a cold stare and she fled. 'I need to speak to the headman, then we'll go.'

They returned to the street in front of the tavern, where people were milling about in confusion. The younger ones were becoming boisterous, chanting, 'Death to the Rondians' and other shihadi slogans. She found the spokesman and said, 'Rondian magi will come here, asking questions,' she told him. 'You must all leave.'

'You will not stay?'

'We can't.' *Gurvon will rip their brains out looking for clues.*

He became afraid. 'Stay with us, Lady Alhana – or let us come with you.'

'It's not possible. You must get out of here.'

'When will Queen Cera call us to arms?' a woman asked. 'We are waiting for her call!' She looked fierce enough to be in the front rank.

'One day,' Elena replied, though she doubted Cera had any such intention. 'But for now, you must hide.'

'The queen is married to the infidel now,' another spat. 'She does not care for us.'

'She does care,' Elena replied. *They want to believe in her and I can't damage that, whatever I think.* 'But she is a prisoner, and so is Timori. The time will come, I swear!'

It took a long time to extricate themselves, and then to shake off those who followed them, either curious or just unwilling to let go of this new hope. Finally they were alone, trudging through the desert, Kazim hauling the handcart. They reached the skiff and she sagged against the hull, inhaled the cooling air in relief.

'Well, we've made a start,' she breathed.

At once Kazim was all over her, clutching her from behind, his hands kneading at her chest. She twisted in his arms to face him. 'Hey, no!'

He grunted, a bundle of needs. 'Ella . . .'

'No!' she told him firmly. 'I'm filthy and I need to wash.'

'But—'

She put the flat of her hands against his chest. 'No! I'll not have it.' She scowled. 'Gurvon was like this too. But I'm not, and I'll not have you remind me of him. Understand?'

He sagged, not happy, but the name of Gurvon Gyle soured his mood. 'All right.'

She kissed his cheek. 'Tonight, when we're safely away from here, and clean, I'll be all yours.'

The flight to their camp seemed to Kazim to take for ever, but it was only two hours. They arrived after dawn, but Elena was confident no one had seen them as they flew overhead. They washed, and as she emerged from the pool, Kazim couldn't take his eyes from her. His blood had cooled, but the sight of her, all wet and sleek, rewakened his ardour. She lay on the blanket on her side, turning away from him, and he moulded himself to her back, then pushed himself into her, slowly filled her yoni. Their lovemaking was gentle and his climax mild, yet it felt profound, as if he had poured more than just bodily fluids inside her. Afterwards the dawn sang gently through them, blissful and engulfing.

'When this war is over, what will we do?' he asked, trying to sound nonchalant.

She wriggled about to face him. 'Kazim, we might not have a lot of time together. We're going up against an empire, and sooner or later the odds are going to be against us. I'm not going to think beyond the next mission, and nor should you.'

He hugged her to him. 'I love you,' he told her. *I just thought love would be simpler than this.*

'I know you do,' was the best response he could get from her. She seldom said exactly what she felt and it was beginning to eat at him. She tilted her head, and he felt her gnosis engage as she examined their bodies. 'Our auras keep binding, do you notice? It's like they are growing together. Sometimes it's like I'm the earth, and you're a tree taking root in me.'

'I don't know how to make it stop.'

'It's especially bad right now. Maybe because we just fucked. Or because you depleted your gnosis. Maybe both.' She kissed his cheek, just above the line of his beard. 'It's like a sticky spiderweb, your aura; I can feel your tendrils all round me. There are too many to sever. They're too thick.'

He gave her a hopeful smile. 'Perhaps it is because of love?'

'Maybe. I don't know.'

'Whether you love me?'

'Yes – no, I don't know. I meant that I don't know about Souldrinkers.' She stroked his cheek. 'Kaz, for what it's worth, I've never really been good at being in love. The stuff Gurvon and I did together, the plots and the scheming, felt like love at the time but wasn't. Since then, I've kind of had to grow back my heartstrings. Maybe I'm falling in love and I don't know it?'

'You would know,' he told her. 'I do.'

*

Cera stared up at the windship, her whole frame quivering with too many emotions to bear. Lines from too many ballads and poems filled her head, all about love and loss, love and pain, love and parting, love and regret, and *damn all this stupid obsession with love anyway*. Her eyes were stinging and her skin going from hot to cold in flashes. She could hardly breathe around the lump in the back of her throat and if she had to speak she was going to scream.

It was a two-masted windcraft, larger than the single-crew skiffs the air-magi liked to use but much smaller than the trade windships that occasionally came and went. Cera had never been in one, not even Elena's. It was big enough for half a dozen soldiers, two magi and one precious passenger: Portia Tolidi, clutching her barely swelling belly, her downcast face lost in her cascade of russet ringlets.

Francis Dorobon was prattling away in Rondian, a tongue neither of his wives understood, playing to the gallery of stony-faced Dorobon adherents who looked at his 'foreign' wives with utter contempt, mingled in Portia's case with barely concealed lust. The young king was flanked by crafty-faced Craith Margham and dour Guy Lassaigne, the only ones paying him much attention.

The two queens had already said their farewells, stilted words leaving too much unsaid. Neither could be sure that they were not being spied upon, so they could do no more than hold each other in a chaste embrace and whisper. The reasons for sending Portia north to have the child made little sense to Cera; some complicated part of the Dorobon's dealings with the Gorgio clan of Hytel. It felt like some vindictive plot by a cruel world to tear her heart in two. That Portia felt it less only increased the pain. The mother-to-be was closing up like a night-flower at dawn. Already their love-making felt like it had happened to different people in another lifetime.

How will I ever find happiness?

Cera clutched Tarita's hand and gritted her teeth. The little maid was putting on a bravely cheerful face to help her through. *I won't cry.*

She managed to stay dry-eyed, even as the windship lifted into the air and the tethers fell away, or as it climbed and the sails caught the breeze, or all the way back to the palace. *I refuse to cry.*

She did though. All that night and through the next day. Then she rose, moving like a *galmi*, a Brician walking statue. She put her hair up and her violet dress on, and returned to the Beggars' Court.

The halls leading through the zenana were filled with palace maids, who used every excuse they could find to overhear what was said in the courtyard. They dropped to their knees as she passed, brushing her hems with their fingers or their lips. Voices called out blessings. She emerged into the small gardens, the dew steaming in the early spring sunlight. Voices thrummed among the crowds gathered before the iron gates. There were palace soldiers on the walls above, many more than there had been a month ago when she first started this. Servants were handing hard-baked biscuits of grain and honey through the bars, and they were being passed back through the crowd, but that all stopped when they saw her and a wall of shrill noise rose, resounding amongst the walls and towers.

'Cera! Cera! Cera!'

I wonder what Francis thinks when he hears that sound.

'Look! There is a Godspeaker here,' Tarita muttered, pointing out a white-clad man with an imposing beard, waiting by the gates. He stood apart from the women, visibly upset at the press. Half a dozen rough-clad men with staves surrounded him, prodding and poking to keep the women back. The smell of so many people washed over her as she ascended the steps to her throne and the women cried out in welcome, waving their hands in the air, fingers wriggling like grass in the wind.

She raised her hand, and silence fell. There was a routine by now, a call and response that felt inclusive. 'Good morning, my sisters,' she called. 'Sal'Ahm and buongiorno,' she added, though she'd seen very few Rimoni among the women here. Most of the Rimoni in Javon were of a higher caste than the Jhafi working women who filled the courtyard; their families had a tendency to sort out their own legal issues without involving the throne. It wasn't something Cera approved of: Rimoni vendettas were infamous.

'Sal'Ahm!' the women chorused, every day the response that much louder, rolling back through the crowds as those at the back reacted slower to her presence.

'May Ahm and Sol bless our gathering.'

'Sal'Ahm!'

'May Bekira and Luna touch our hearts.'

'Sal'Ahm!'

She put on her public smile, pointedly ignored the Godspeaker beside the railings and turned to her clerk. The scribe looked harassed already, and why not: what was supposed to have been a ten-minute job each morning had become an all-day marathon of note-taking and organising. Cera was vaguely surprised that Don Perdonello had not complained to her, but perhaps Gurvon Gyle had already dealt with that.

The Godspeaker hammered his staff against the railings of the iron gate. 'Blasphemy!' he roared. 'Blasphemy!' He was a big man with a big voice that boomed off the walls, blending with the resounding clangour of his staff. The crowd shrank fearfully from him, as he jabbed a finger at Cera. 'It is blasphemy to invoke great Ahm in conjunction with your heathen Rimoni gods!'

'The royal family are patrons of both faiths,' Cera responded. 'It is our right and duty to invoke both.'

'But the women here are Amteh!' the Godspeaker shouted back. 'They are forbidden to speak the names of your pagan idols!'

'They didn't,' Cera replied shortly. 'I did.' *He could haggle all day over such trivialities, I don't doubt.* 'Do you have a purpose here, Godspeaker?'

The holy man drew himself up to his full height. 'I am Godspeaker Ilmaz, and I come bearing a message from the Maula of Fayeedhar Dom-al'Ahm.' The Maula was the chief Scriptualist, most senior of those Amteh scholars in charge of the preservation and interpretation of the faith. A Maula rarely left his assigned Dom-al'Ahm, but their word held considerable weight.

'Then perhaps you will deliver your message in private to me later today?' Cera said evenly.

Godspeaker Ilmaz looked at her disdainfully. 'The words of the Maula are intended also for those gathered here. They are, after all, the wives and daughters of the men of his Dom-Al'Ahm.'

Cera gave him a measuring look, decided she couldn't stop him and would look foolish if she decided to try. She waved a hand of assent. *This won't be good.*

Ilmaz puffed himself up as he drew out a scroll, ignoring the clamour rising from those at the back without a view of the proceedings who were wondering aloud what was happening. They began to surge forward and the Godspeaker's guards shook their staves warningly. There was a feeling of impending danger in the air and Cera saw the women at the front would have little hope of staying out of harm's way if the jostling got worse, but the Godspeaker paid no notice as he drew himself up and began to declaim:

'Ishemmel, Maula of Fayeedhar Dom-al'Ahm, declares the gathering of women at the Beggars' Court to be un-Amteh! It is a usurpation of the judicial rights of the clergy! He declares the passing judgement on civil cases by a woman un-Amteh! He orders all here to go home and be about their lawful business!' He glared about him at the wall of female faces staring at him with expressions of fear and apprehension.

His words were passed back through the crowd, repeated over and over, and Cera could see the fear and the anger intensifying on the faces of those he addressed. The Rondian soldiers on the walls were looking at each other nervously, and a runner was already scooting along the walls towards the central tower.

'Godspeaker!' she called, her voice cutting through the babble. The women hushed and turned to her. 'No gathering of women is un-Amteh or unlawful! We have the right to be here!'

A murmur of agreement, loudest away from the front line, greeted her words.

'And Godspeaker,' she continued, 'the civil law cases are the prerogative of the royal family and nobility! This is well known! Shall I send your Maula a copy of the statutes?'

Godspeaker Ilmaz stuck out his wire-brush beard. 'Usurper!'

'That is an old argument, which you lost a long time ago! Let rulers rule and priests pray! So said the great King Felix Altamonto more than a hundred years ago. The people wanted real laws for real life, and we have given them this! So go back to your Maula and tell him that the *Kalistham* is his jurisdiction, not the law statutes.'

'You quote a Rimoni king!' Ilmaz bellowed back, hammering his staff against the gates for emphasis. 'We are Amteh here! Women know nothing of the law! You are only a girl!'

'I am *La Scrittoretta*, and I know the laws better than you do,' she called back. The crowd liked that and started chanting her name and shouting at the Godspeaker. His guards ringed him, fearfully jabbing their staves about as the crowd surged forward, barely contained.

'Rimoni laws are un-Amteh laws!' the Godspeaker shouted. 'This court is an affront to Ahm!' He glared about him at the wall of female faces. 'GO HOME, YOU LAZY WRETCHES! RETURN TO YOUR DOMESTIC DUTIES!'

'Don't you call me lazy, you soft-handed bouka!' screeched a woman, skinny and fierce as a jackal, waving gnarled hands, hardened to claws by decades of labour. Others echoed her and the obscenity ran through the crowd: impotent worm, roughly. The crowd's ingrained respect for the clergy warred with their anger at Ilmaz's arrogance and effrontery, and while many backed away, the more volatile women poured into the spaces left.

'Go back to your wormhole, bouka!' another woman shouted, while Cera's heart went to her mouth. The first blows were struck, staves hammered against reaching hands. Indignant cries rang out, and the guards shrank against the iron gate. The Godspeaker was roaring into the crowd, face to face with the crone who had first harangued him. Insults flew, getting more and more vicious on both sides.

I have to try to stop this.

Cera stood, raised both hands and shouted, 'SILENCE, PLEASE!'

Those at the front who weren't directly threatened by a staff-wielding guard turned their heads to heed her, but most, either facing an armed man or being shoved from behind, carried on struggling, and suddenly the wall of bodies washed forward. Staves flailed, screams resounded and swirled around the walls and she saw a woman in the front row having her face battered by an iron-bound staff. Blood started pouring from a hideous gash. A few more aggressive women were wading forward, but most were here for the courtroom stories, not fighting. The clergyman's guards battered more women into the ground, while the Godspeaker was pressed against the iron gate, howling imprecations. The press grew heavier, one of the bodyguards went down and then another, trampled in the thick of the mêlée. The noise was deafening.

Then, suddenly, Gurvon Gyle was on the walls above the gate. He gestured and the locks unbound, the gates went flying open and the throng poured through, led by the Godspeaker himself, storming, furious and indignant, towards Cera.

'You did this, you ungodly bitch!' he shrieked. 'Look what you've started!' For an instant Cera thought he was going to grab and throttle her, but Tarita threw herself in his path and that act brought him to his senses. Meanwhile Dorobon soldiers were pouring along the walls and down the stairs into the courtyard. They dragged the Godspeaker's men, battered and bloodied, from the crowd and ringed them. The women drew back from the line of steel, and some of the pressure was released as many on the fringes took fright and began to flee. But more than a dozen women lay on the stone, some bloodied, a couple unmoving.

Ilmaz glared at her, panting heavily, his beard flecked with spittle, his chest heaving. She stared back, refusing to be intimidated. *I am a Nesti. I am a queen.*

'Godspeaker, go back to your Dom-al'Ahm. You have done enough damage today.'

'You are the one who started this,' Ilmaz began. 'You are not a true woman! You are an unnatural whore! You are a—'

'Oh for Kore's sake!' Gurvon Gyle snapped, appearing at her side and shutting the Godspeaker's mouth with a gesture. 'Get out of here or I'll arrest you for disturbing the peace, Godspeaker.'

Loathe Gyle though she did, she had to fight to hide her delight at the terror in the Godspeaker's eyes as he realised what he was confronting. 'I wouldn't press the issue, priest,' the Rondian drawled.

The Godspeaker found his tongue again. 'This is only just beginning, Rondian.'

Gyle was not in the least perturbed. 'It's time for you to leave. This is the Women's Palace, and I hate to think what being in here is doing to your *purity*.'

The Godspeaker scowled, then swallowed. It looked like he was trying to hold his breath, as if inhaling the air of the zenana might pollute his lungs. Cera snorted softly, unable to contain herself, something not lost on the holy man. 'Rondian-lover!' he muttered. 'Collaborator!'

'You know nothing,' she told him.

He sneered and turned away.

Gyle summoned an officer. 'Take them out by another way, Captain, and escort them back to their Dom-al'Ahm.' He stayed by Cera's side as the men were led away, then prowled over to the gates, behind the line of soldiers. The crowd were pelting the legionaries with bread and insults, but when Gyle raised a hand the crowd flinched and drew away, leaving enough space for his soldiers to pull the hurt women inside. Some were badly hurt and would bear scars for the rest of their lives, but mercifully none were dead.

I started this, from safe behind an iron gate, and they paid the price. Perhaps I should stop.

She immediately rejected the notion. Over the past month she'd heard hundreds of cases, helping women who otherwise would have got no justice at all. The Queen's Hospital, housed in an old stables, now offered a refuge to women running from abusive and violent men. It was overflowing. She sensed that something bigger than her was happening here.

I can't stop now.

Gyle strolled back to the open gates. 'Queen Cera,' he called, refraining from re-entering the zenana gardens, 'might I suggest you cancel the rest of your session today while I regain control in the plaza outside.'

She stood and walked towards him, pointing to the masses still waiting outside. 'These people have come to be heard. I cannot deny them that right.'

'Being heard is not a right. It's a privilege. If it becomes a problem, that privilege will end.'

'I didn't think you were the sort of man who backed down to intimidation.'

'I'm not.'

'Nor am I.'

He gave a wry smile. 'You're not a man at all.'

She waved an impatient hand. 'My people wish to speak and I wish to listen to them. Today.' She stopped a foot from him and dropped her voice. 'You said you'd let me.'

Gyle frowned, considering, then looked up and said shortly, 'All right. Continue, if you so desire. I'm going to have a strong word with the Maula of Fayeedhar Dom-al'Ahm and if he gives me any lip I'll haul the old prick away. I'm told he's been calling me bad names in his sermons and I don't like that.'

'You're using my court as an excuse for your own ends,' she said quietly.

He dropped his own voice. 'Of course. But don't think I'm not a little sympathetic with what you're doing, girl. You see, Rondelmar and the empire went through just these sorts of issues, centuries ago. The thing was, we had female magi, some of them every bit as capable as their male counterparts, and they demanded a voice. That led to a wider debate, and an ongoing struggle for better rights for women. Ironically, even Mater-Imperia Lucia has played her part in that, despite all her sins. Yuros might be a magi-led tyranny of privilege and wealth, but we do have a few virtues.'

She put her hands on her hips. 'What do you want? Applause?'

'No, Cera. I just want you to know that on this matter, we're work-ing together. It can be done.'

'I will continue, with or without your so-called support.'

He looked amused. 'Mob politics is a dangerous thing, Cera. Crowds like simple truths, and law is complex. Remember this: a mob is like an ocean wave: it might bear you far, or drown you. I'll try to keep Francis off your back, and Acmed al-Istan too, but you should know that if things go too far, I'll be the first to recommend that we close you down.'

She simmered, then took a deep breath. *Just be thankful he's not try-ing to do that now.* 'Thank you, Magister,' she said aloud. 'I will take your advice.' She turned from him and addressed the women gath-ered behind the line of spears.

'My people,' she cried, 'in the light of this disturbance, it is not right for today's session to go ahead!'

A few groaned, and shouted denials.

'But I swear that I will be back here tomorrow morning to hear your voices!'

The answering cheers rattled the windows of the towers.

It sustained her through the evening and through the night as she fell asleep wondering where Portia was, what she was doing, and if she still remembered what they'd had.

Portia Tolidi buried her face into the pillow, closed her eyes and made the air snorting from her mouth sound like desperate passion. The man behind her was encouraged to ram himself into her faster, his loins slapping the cheeks of her buttocks harder and louder as he grunted and growled, then roaring as he expended himself. They both fell forward as he collapsed over her, he quivering in some kind of ecstasy, she struggling to breathe as his sweaty weight pressed her into the mattress.

'Uncle,' she croaked, 'my belly.' She twisted sideways and cradled the small bulge until Alfredo Gorgio rolled off her, his softening member sliding wetly from her cleft.

She was twenty-two years old, and for nine years she had been her uncle's sexual plaything – not his only one, but his favourite. From before she'd even bled, he'd marked her out, told everyone what a beauty his sister's child would be. She'd been moved into his household the day her father had died in the war. The morning after her first womanly courses, he'd summoned her to his chamber and began to shape her into his own personal fantasy. There had been no one to complain to: he was the most powerful man in Hytel. He used her when he wanted, trained her in every act he could imagine. He also began to dole her out as a reward: to this noble who gave Alfredo something he wanted; or that young knight who won a tourney. She was the golden prize, sent to the boudoir to seduce his favourites and bind them to him closer.

She'd been through so many phases of hating Alfredo Gorgio that she'd lost count. She hated her loss of childhood, her loss of innocence. She hated the way he'd made her realise that everyone around her was driven to some extent by the same desires; that reason and emotion could be buried beneath animal lust. She hated the way that her body could betray her and take pleasure in the filth. And most of all, she hated that she'd become emotionally numb, unable to feel true affection any more, not even for poor little Cera Nesti, who so needed and deserved it.

Alfredo stroked her shoulders, which she endured silently. 'Four months, si? Your mage-child will be born in Septinon.'

She nodded mutely. This was what she had been raised to be: Alfredo's offering to the Dorobon on their return. Francis had gobbled her up, become as addicted to her as her uncle had prophesied. The only miracle was that it had taken her so long to quicken, when Francis was at her all the time. But pure-blood magi had thin seed, they said, so conception often took longer. It had felt like Eternity, enduring that buffoon.

'I told you that there would be rewards for all you've learned,' Alfredo said to the back of her head. 'And I was right: you are queen, and you have conceived first. Now we need to be rid of the Nesti *cagna*.'

'Cera is not a bitch.'

'She is a *cagna* if I say so.' Alfredo was contemptuously amused. 'Gyle put *her* in Francis' bed; I gave him *you*, after years of amatory training. So much for the legendary cunning of the man, eh?'

Portia wriggled from his arms and sat up. 'I need to pee. And your court is waiting for you.'

'They can wait.' He sat up. 'Show me yourself.'

She spun slowly, lifting her arms, showing her bulging waist and heavier breasts. 'Haven't you already studied me in detail today?'

He wiped his cock on her sheets and chuckled. 'I never tire of the sight. Even doubled in size and waddling, you are beauty itself. Good bloodlines, well-tended, well-trained.' He ran his eye down her legs then back up. 'Smile for me, Portia. Tell me how much you love me.'

It was the one licence he gave her: to truly profess her loathing. '*Love* you? Uncle, I loathe you for the stinking, lecherous rat you are.'

He laughed delightedly.

Oh, but I do hate you, so desperately that one day I will visit suffering on you so profound that it will be remembered for all eternity.

When she was sixteen, one of her uncle's other young protégés had made a pact with her, that when it became unendurable, they would both kill themselves. But then they'd argued over something trivial and the other girl had gone and hanged herself alone. Seeing her purple, swollen face and lifeless eyes had frightened her from taking her own life. Vanity was a sin, they said, but she was not going to die like that. And certainly not before visiting some kind of revenge on her uncle.

'The Nesti girl wrote again today,' Alfredo noted. He'd have read it, of course. 'Clearly she thinks of you as a friend.'

Portia lifted her shoulders, feigned indifference. 'I really do need to pee.'

'I burned the letter,' he murmured. 'It was nothing but girlish prattling. Wash yourself too. You smell like a whore.' He wrapped a robe about him and strode through to his adjoining suite.

She sank to her knees when he left and fought the need to scream.

*

Cera sat at her desk, chose a clean sheet of parchment and inked her quill.

Dearest Sister-Queen

It is evening now, and the city is quiet again. But earlier it was not so quiet. Today was the worst day of all in the Beggars' Court, and I am becoming frightened.

She frowned, tore up the parchment and started again. Gurvon Gyle was undoubtedly reading her mail, and she would not reveal her fears to him, not in such a tangible way. She began again.

Dearest Portia

It is evening now, and the city is quiet again. Earlier it was not so: the Amteh clergy have been preaching against the Beggars' Court, and they chose today to unleash their fury. Sadly, Acmed al-Istan, my former counsellor, is at the heart of the troubles, preaching that husbands should lock up their wives to prevent them attending the Beggars' Court, and 'disciplining' those who do. That frightened some away, but still the crowds grow. Women from the Widow Cells have been attending too – it is shameful that we lock away widowed women when they have so much still to offer. Many young unmarried women of the lower castes are coming as well. The things I hear are increasingly horrific.

Why do men hate women so much?

Today, a mob came from a Dom-al'Ahm and attacked the crowd with clubs and sticks. Several women were badly injured before Gyle's soldiers forced them apart. Gyle then arrested the Maula and that set off a riot. After, there was a march by some women supporting the Maula – women chanting slogans in favour of their own enslavement! They tried to storm the zenana! It is madness here, but I can't stop.

I wish they would let you write to me; I long to read words from your hand. It would be like hearing your voice. I trust your convalescence goes well, and your health remains strong. May Sol and Ahm smile upon you!

Your loving Sister-Queen, Cera

She reread it critically, hoping she could trust Gyle's assurances that her letters were being delivered. She wondered again why Portia had not written back, and whether she would ever see her again. So many women died in childbirth ... but surely a woman bearing a mage-child would receive the very best gnostic aid? And not just any woman, but the Dorobon king's favourite, bearing the king's heir ...

With a sigh she folded the parchment and sealed it with a wax signet, trying not to feel like everything was coming apart.

Then she wrapped herself in a gown and left her suite, taking the stairs to the top floor and her waiting husband.

In the daytime I fight for women to have justice and rights. And then in the evening, this ...

The guard at the door leered as she disrobed at the door to show that she was unarmed, then allowed her inside, naked and humiliated. Francis was sprawled on the sofa, clad in riding breeches and a loose white shirt, his lank hair dishevelled. He grunted disinterestedly when he saw her, then sighed heavily.

'Kneel,' he said. 'Over there.' He jabbed a finger towards the rug before the empty fireplace.

Feeling the colour in her face rising, she did as bade, dropped to her knees and sat back on her heels, waiting for him to join her. He didn't, just glared at her moodily.

'They say that a beautiful woman makes the seed of her man more potent,' he said stiffly. 'That is why Portia conceived and you have not.'

How I loathe you.

He wrestled his breeches off, half rose then sank back again. 'Oh, rukking Hel! Forget it. I don't want this any more than you do.'

She blinked, surprised he'd actually noticed her dislike. She stood, at a loss what to do.

Francis poured himself a goblet of red wine, swirled a little in his mouth then swallowed it. He looked her up and down. 'You have a behind like a cow,' he remarked, 'but your teats are well-proportioned.'

And you are running to fat and you stink of horses.

'Do you judge a woman only by her looks, my king?' she asked, probably unwisely. She cast about for a blanket and covered herself, then knelt again.

'It's the only criteria that matters.'

'Yet a woman rules your empire,' she said softly.

'Her son rules,' Francis retorted. 'The Imperial Mother merely advises.'

'Women have many more skills than that, if you only opened your eyes,' she said, drawn to argue despite the knowledge that it was futile. 'Elena Anborn—'

His face blazed with sudden rage, his hands sparked and he jumped to his feet, shouting, 'Don't you mention that *rukking bitch* to me, never! Never speak her name again!'

She went rigid with shock. *Sol et Lune! What's happened?*

All of a sudden Francis' fury collapsed into grief. His face crumpled, tears overflowed his eyes and the fire in his hands went out. 'Jedyk! Jedyk! She killed him! He was my *friend* and the evil bitch killed him . . .' He stumbled to the sofa, crooning, 'Oh Jedyk, Jedyk!'

Elena . . . Elena has killed one of them! She recalled Jedyk Luman: a babe in the woods, naïve and boyish. Elena would have slaughtered him easily: a hardened fighter against a child. *Elena is out there!* The thought filled her both with fierce joy and deep dread.

'What happened?' she asked, struggling to sound sympathetic, but Francis was so lost in his own misery he paid no attention to her tone of voice.

'Poor Jedyk was on the Hytel Road – she killed him in his bedroom, the safian witch!' His whole frame was shaking. 'What would make a mage betray her own kind? She must be *Evil incarnate*! But I'll hunt her down, I swear!' Then he seemed to see her again, remembered who she was and screamed, '*Get out of here, you stinking Noorie!*'

Cera fled, struggling to mask the new sense of exhilaration that was filling her. She didn't care that Elena must now hate her; this news lit something in inside her that she couldn't deny: a newfound sense of purpose.

And it was reinforced when she observed the fretting in the Great

Hall later that night, the wringing of hands among the Dorobon and the consternation on even Gurvon Gyle's face.

Elena is fighting back.

Then so must I.

Gurvon Gyle, clad in the purple robes of the Imperial Legate, watched the lines of soldiers marching into Piazza Policano, the big military parade ground outside the southern gates of Brochena. Around him the blue-and-white-uniformed Dorobon soldiery were ranked immaculately beneath the watchful eye of Sir Roland Heale. On the dais above sat Francis Dorobon, with his friends around him. Craith Margham's ferret-faced features were taut with anxiety, but Guy Lassaigne – Rutt Sordell's new host – was speaking soothingly, just as Gurvon had ordered him to. If Francis did something stupid today, things could turn ugly.

He glanced sideways at a knight resplendent in black and white, with a yellow wheel emblazoned on his left breast and a circlet of gold on his ceremonial helmet. Sir Etain Tullesque was a Grandmaster of the Kirkegarde; the order of knights formed to protect the Church's rapidly increasing holdings now represented the largest standing army in Yuros. Luckily, Wurther had sent only a maniple to Javon to aid the Dorobons and ensure the Church's investment in the Dorobon conquest. They'd come south at Margham's behest and without consulting Gurvon, which worried him. Margham fancied himself cunning, but he wasn't smart enough to realise that conflict between the king and the imperial legate could destroy them both.

A week ago Gurvon had intervened to prevent a riot at the Beggars' Court, but since then the violence had got worse, not better, and his legionaries were struggling to keep the gangs fired up by the God-speakers apart from the men siding with their women. The body count was rising and the gaols were so full he'd had to commandeer new buildings to stash prisoners. The constitution re-write had stalled as Don Perdonello tried belatedly to regain control of the civil judiciary, but mob justice had taken over the streets. Cera Nesti had criticised a man for beating his wife; an hour later the man's body had been found floating in the canals. The Amteh clergy were in uproar and Gurvon had locked up more than two dozen of them so far: iron-faced men with huge beards and an almost savage hatred for the queen.

On the bright side, civil disobedience against the Dorobon had all but collapsed, subsumed into this new struggle, and he'd had the excuse he'd been looking for to plunder every sizable Dom-al'Ahm in Brochena. He'd confiscated illegal weapon caches, caches of gold, banned books and all manner of surprising artefacts.

It's been well worth my while, but it will need to stop soon.

He glanced back at the thrones, where Cera Nesti sat pensively. She was changing, growing up in the full glare of the struggle she'd ignited. She was blooming: her confidence and poise were increasing, and she far more at ease with public scrutiny. She was clad in violet, the Nesti colours, worn blatantly in the Dorobon court. Her hair was coiled up in gold netting and she was beginning to wear make-up. Even her posture had changed: she was no longer the hunched-over, serious girl he'd first met. It showed her physical assets off to better effect, though he doubted she even realised. He was beginning to be reminded of Lucia Fasterius.

Then trumpets blared and the leaders of the new arrivals trotted forward to meet him.

Adi Paavus had stayed in the Krak, but Hans Frikter and Staria Canestos had marched north. Both had strong, overmanned legions, with many more than fifteen magi in each. Hans' men were well-equipped in a rough and ready way, battle-hardened from border wars in Estellan and Argundy. He was Argundian himself, a solid and aggressive fighter with few airs and graces, and he genuinely liked the man.

Staria Canestos, on the other hand, he would have preferred not to have involved at all, but circumstances had put her in the ideal place. Her sprawling, colourful legions were formidable, and her presence guaranteed that the Dorobon would be outnumbered and cowed into submission, but like their commander, her soldiers came with a set of unique issues.

The Sacro Arcoyris Estellan, the Sacred Rainbow of Estellan, was the fanciful name for Staria's motley collection of outcasts. Some twenty years ago, during a manpower crisis, Staria's aged father Ernesto, the founder of the mercenary legion, had decided to take on men who couldn't find a place in other legions – not only criminals or deserters, who were common but unreliable, but those seen as disruptive, not worthy of the trouble: atheists, migrants, Rimoni and Silacians, Sydian nomads . . . and especially mooners, men who loved other men. Such men were not rare, but they generally hid their curse for their own safety; they tended to be an unacknowledged grouping within any legion. When Ernesto Canestos allowed them to join openly, he was flooded with new recruits, including magi; many deserting from other legions. The new legion had very swiftly disproved the widely held belief that homosexuals were timid fighters. It became a notorious but unassailably strong unit. Staria had inherited command upon her father's death and she had continued the tradition, growing the Sacro Arcoyris in strength and discipline.

The two mercenary commanders reined in their horses – Hans rode a massive warhorse, Staria a lean, graceful mare – and approached the throne with apparent ease, despite the tension on the faces of all present. Hans looked at Gurvon and winked before ducking into a sketchy bow as the Dorobon trumpets blared. Staria bowed too – she had never been the curtseying sort. Gurvon hadn't quite figured out what she wanted, or whether having her here was going to be more trouble than it was worth, but for now she was a powerful piece on a complex tabula board.

'Greetings, King Francis,' Hans Frikter boomed, saluting fist-to-heart. 'I hope you've got plenty of ale,' he added with a smile. No one laughed, but he didn't seem to mind. 'Gurvon: nice rags you got there. Purple suits you.'

All very jocular: but Hans had also reminded all present that he had plenty of men and was friends with the legate. He was like that: apparently casual, but all business. It was a mercenary thing.

Staria mirrored Hans' salute, then scratched her sallow cheek. She was around forty now, an Estellan with greying black hair, thick black eyebrows above a broken nose and dark skin. Despite the composition of her legion and the obvious rumours that ensued, she was not safian – she was not particularly anything, as far as Gurvon knew. She didn't let people get close, and her first line of defence was her prickly personality. 'Gurv,' she greeted him shortly.

'Good to see you both,' he replied, waiting till Staria glanced away then winking at Hans. They all turned to the king, and despite all the preparation for this moment, Gurvon still held his breath.

Francis Dorobon shifted uncertainly on his throne. Even a blind king could not help but notice that his court was filling up with people who had no natural affiliation to him. Francis might be stupidity itself, but Craith Margham and Roland Heale weren't, and so assurances had been given, some of them under the Imperial Seal.

'My lords,' said Francis, reading from a small scroll in his lap in a fluted voice, 'welcome to Javon. I am King Francis Dorobon, rightful ruler of Javon and loyal subject of His Imperial Majesty Constant Sacrecour. In his name I invite you to take the oath of allegiance to my House. Do you so agree?'

Hans Frikter shuffled and Staria Canestos looked like she'd sooner lick dust off Francis' feet, but after a moment, both muttered their assent.

'Let's do it,' the Argundian grunted.

This had been the key point: that the mercenaries would accept a sacred oath of allegiance to Francis himself. Hans Frikter was a lot of things, but he was a devout follower of Kore and wouldn't lightly break a holy oath. Staria was more sceptical, but many of her men were worshippers, even the mooners whom Kore disavowed, so they too would be deeply troubled if she broke such an oath. Mercenaries usually took no vows of service: their contract was their bond. But there had been no other way that Gurvon could get Margham and Heale, the real negotiators, to agree to welcoming the mercenaries. There was a contract too, of course, but that was another matter entirely.

Etain Tullesque stepped forward. 'In the absence of a crozier, I have been charged with offering the sacred oath,' the Kirkegarde Grandmaster intoned formally. 'Do you accept my right and station in doing so?'

'We do,' the two commanders chorused.

Gurvon felt his eyes and mind glaze over as Grandmaster Tullesque launched into a long and tortuously worded oath; instead, he studied their faces. In all likelihood he was going to be sharing a kingdom with this group, after all.

About fifty years ago three legions of mercenaries stationed in Rimoni had rebelled against Imperial rule and seized Becchio, establishing a 'free city'. It had taken eight years of the bloodiest battles in Rondian history for the empire to retake the city, and no one had trusted mercenaries much since – if they ever had beforehand. But this was different: Gurvon and his friends had a kingdom to seize.

Francis and his Dorobon could have the capital and Hytel, at least initially. *Until we kill him.* Staria and Endus would go into the west against Forensa and the rebel cities. Adi Paavus would hold the Krak and Hans would go southwest along with the Kirkegarde to seize Intemsa. Roland Heale understood tacitly what was happening, and he would get Hytel if he behaved. Craith Margham was different: he was slated to die with Francis. And then they would have to decide what manner of kingdom Javon would be thereafter. A loose collective of autonomous republics was what Gurvon envisaged, and the other conspirators were at least pretending to agree.

'Do you, Staria Canestos, swear in the name of Kore Most High, to serve loyally and faithfully the House of Dorobon?' Tullesque asked, his voice clear over the field and drawing his attention back to the events at hand.

'I do so swear,' Staria said, her voice flat, and she knelt at Francis' feet and kissed the ring on his right hand.

Hans Frikter swore next. 'I believe we have a deal, gentlemen,' he said after he was done, with blithe disregard for Staria's gender. 'Now, where's that Kore-bedamned beer?'

Cera sat in a chair beside Francis at the head table, watching the faces and the way they interacted. The tent was filled with senior magi of all parties, and she could almost see the gnostic energies, the subtle protections from spells or steel. They were all unarmed, but they wore their gnostic prowess like weapons. The numbers were carefully even at twenty each. Apart from herself and Staria Canestos, there were no women. The conversation was formal, stilted, and mostly concerning news of the crusade. None appeared at all worried about the news from Shaliyah: it scarcely rated a mention, and when it did, it was only to speculate about enemy magi. That the sultan had somehow gained gnostic aid stunned her, but no one spoke to her, so she could only store up the snippets of information for later. Tarita had told her the tale of Shaliyah was all over the streets of Brochena. The Javonesi were in ferment about it, gangs of youths breaking curfew and harassing the Rondian soldiers, but still open rebellion had not broken out.

She scanned the room, saw that the mercenaries didn't mix with the Dorobon at all. Endus Rykjard clearly liked Hans Frikter, but not Staria Canestos. She heard sneering terms like 'shisha-men', 'froci' and 'mooners', but never in Staria's hearing. There was an intimidating brittleness about the female mercenary that made everyone uneasy.

So she swallowed a little when the woman came and sat beside her, looking her up and down with narrow eyes. 'So, you're the Nesti?' she said in passable Rimoni. The language shared enough words with Estellayne that most people who spoke one could converse with little misunderstanding.

'I am Queen Cera Nesti.'

Staria studied her thoughtfully. 'I hear Francis has two wives?'

Cera didn't want to talk about Portia with this woman. 'My sister-wife has been sent north for the term of her pregnancy.'

'Three in a bed is rarely as much fun as people think,' Staria remarked drily. 'There's never enough room and too many elbows. If you had the choice, which one would you kick out?'

Cera blinked, looked at the mercenary, then away. 'Amteh men frequently have many wives.'

'Francis isn't Amteh and he's not a man. He's an immature, randy boy. I'm told he favours your rival?'

'She's not my rival.' She made herself meet the other woman's crooked gaze. 'Are you married?'

'Me? No. I have a nephew whom I have legally adopted: Leopollo is the best-looking mooner in Yuros. I have an adopted daughter too, Kordea. But I've not shared my bed with anyone for ten years or more, not since taking command of the legion.' She picked at a bowl of nuts. 'Love and leadership do not mix easily, and especially not for a woman.'

Cera nibbled her lower lip at that less than optimistic thought. *Is that what I must also do?*

Staria studied Cera silently for a moment, looking her over as if she was a piece of fruit she was thinking of buying. 'So,' she said, 'what is the Beggars' Court?'

'It's a place where any person's grievances can be voiced and heard. You have heard of it?'

'Gurvon told me. He says that you are on a crusade for women's justice.' She sounded amused at the concept.

'He mocks me.'

'Oh, I don't think so, dear. He admires you.' She added, 'But I see from your face that this is not mutual.'

'He had my parents killed, and my sister too. If I had any way of doing so, I would kill him for those crimes. My Rimoni blood demands it, as does natural justice.'

'Yet still you dance to his tune.'

'*I do not.*'

Staria smirked. 'You are political, I am told. Alliances of expedience happen all the time in that arena.' Her eyebrows lifted. 'Even marital alliances with invaders.'

'I'm not interested in alliances of expedience,' Cera snapped back, angry because her own statement wasn't true: she'd made such alliances too often: with Gyle, and with others. 'One day I will have my revenge.'

Staria's eyes bored into hers. 'You are in earnest, clearly. But how do your people view your marriage?'

'They understand,' Cera shot back. 'Come to the Beggars' Court, see for yourself.'

Staria rubbed her chin. 'Perhaps I shall.'

10

Nasette's Shadow

The Tale of Nasette

The fate of Nasette is one of the most disturbing stories to emerge from the period of the Church's holy crusade against the Souldrinkers. A young mage-maid, captured by Dokken and made into one of them. Was it the rape and subsequent pregnancy? Was it something else? The reason for Nasette's transformation has not become public knowledge, though many whisper that the Inquisition know.

ORDO COSTRUO COLLEGIATE, PONTUS 761

It is still rumoured in Nasette's village that she was not kidnapped, and nor was her liaison unwilling.

ESPAR MOLDEN, HISTORIAN, BRES, 772

Southern Dhassa, on the continent of Antiopia
Awwal (Martrois) 929
9th month of the Moontide

'Who was Nasette?' Cym asked the leonine shape on the far side of the small cooking fire as she stirred the rabbit stew. The name had been on her mind for days, ever since Huriya had said it.

Zaqri looked across the fire, his eyes lit by the flames. He was darning a ripped shirt with a bone needle. 'You do not know the tale?'

'Obviously not, or I wouldn't ask,' she replied sarcastically.

'Nasette was a mage-girl who became a Souldrinker.'

Cym dropped her stirring stick and stared. She felt her skin break out in a sweat. 'Truly?'

'Yes, though how is a secret known only to a few, like Sabele. When Huriya assumed Sabele's soul she gained this knowledge.'

'But you told me that Dokken gain only energy from taking a soul,' Cym reminded him.

'This is so, but Sabele has taken many bodies in her long life. Somehow she has found a way to move her soul from Souldrinker to Souldrinker. At times it has appeared to be involuntary; other times clearly deliberate. Either way, her personality asserts itself eventually.'

Cym felt a faint rush of nausea, despite her loathing of the little Keshi girl. 'Does Huriya know?'

Zaqri shrugged. 'I doubt it, or she would not be so sure of herself.' There was little sympathy in his voice.

Cym had none either. 'So, when she talked about Nasette, she was suggesting turning me into one of you.'

'She still believes it would enforce your loyalty to our Brethren.'

Cym had seen enough of the half-beast lives of these Dokken to know she never, ever, wanted to be one. And to have to kill for the gnosis? *Never!* 'She can't be serious.'

'She is – but I won't let it happen, Cymbellea.'

She studied his face, trying to understand what she felt for him. Her gnostic sight showed her the wrongness in his aura, the strange tendrils and bruise-like discolouration. She'd noticed it got worse when he was low on energy.

'Why?' she asked at last.

'Because you are perfect as you are.'

She spat disgustedly. 'Go rukk yourself, Dokken.'

He snorted mildly, though she could sense his temper rising. She knew she was trying his patience and that wasn't wise. Nor did it make her proud: she'd been raised to give respect, to keep her dignity, even among enemies.

Damn him for his honour – and everything else about him that I can't ignore.

'You can be as nice as you like to me,' she told him, 'I'm still going to kill you. Or your mother.'

'My mother is long dead, and my father too. I have no kin other than this pack.'

'They don't count. It will have to be you, then.'

He didn't react. He never did.

She and Zaqri travelled separately from the pack, using the carpet so she didn't slow him down, though even with the energy crystal she was permanently exhausted. They flew mostly under moonlight, sleeping during the day, and that had its own tensions, for she knew he wanted her; she could feel it. That he was able to contain his desires was something she respected and was grateful for, but it made her uncomfortable too, especially when she found herself lusting for him: lithe, muscular, handsome, regal, everything she'd ever dreamed of. But the oath of vendetta had the stronger claim.

Days and weeks passed and still there was no sign of Alaron or Ramita. The pack had spread out, sweeping the land on a wide perimeter as they moved south. Zaqri occasionally left her alone to hunt in lion form; she noted that animals did not replenish his gnosis. It had to be a human spirit, so when his gnosis ran low, he would haunt some village and return with his aura brighter. It still nauseated her, and clearly he too hated the burden of having to kill to replenish himself; she struggled not to pity him for that.

The pack mustered again in southern Dhassa, beneath the shadow of the coastal range. The rendezvous was a watering hole beneath a rocky outcropping in a landscape strewn with massive piles of shattered and eroded stone. The whole of Zaqri's pack had gathered, and Cym counted eighty-odd adult Dokken in all manner of shapes, and dozens of children. Huriya was there too, bathing naked in the pool, flirting blatantly with the men, but as Cym and Zaqri landed the carpet, all eyes turned to them.

The sensation hit her like a blow: *This is Pack.*

She had spent so much time with Zaqri that she could sense it now. It was something in the nature of the Dokken and the way they lived in such close intimacy: they were gnostically bonded, aware of each other in ways humans could never be. It made them almost one organism, especially when they were gathered like this. They had no concepts of privacy or even individuality; they were able to feed off each other, sharing the gnosis. She could see the links clearly when she engaged her gnostic sight: tendrils of aura stretching from being to being, drawing them into the greater whole. There were no secrets here, no respite from each other. She felt violated just being aware of it and threw up her shields as she looked at Zaqri fearfully.

<How do you stand it?>

<How do you live without it?> He flowed into human form and spoke aloud. 'This is Cymbellea, and she is my mine. She is not to be harmed.'

The rest of the pack took human form too, except for a black panther, which snarled as it stepped towards her. *Hessaz*. Cym froze as the great cat prowled forward, not daring to move. It sniffed at her crotch, then blurred into human form. Hessaz' skin was almost as black as her panther fur, but she was fractionally shorter than Cym, which seemed to anger her.

'They have not mated,' she announced, her harsh voice echoing about the water.

Thanks, tell the world, Cym thought sourly. The woman's manner irked her. 'He still doesn't want you, Kitty,' she snapped, the words coming out without thought.

Hessaz growled as if still in beast form, and raised a hand to slap her, but Cym moved more quickly, catching her wrist and holding on, trembling at the sudden trial of strength. The Lokistani woman was stronger, just, but she gripped her hard and snapped defiantly, 'You haven't got what it takes to fight me.' *A Rimoni doesn't back down*.

'We'll see about that.' Hessaz glowered at her until a low rumble from Zaqri's throat made her go still. She wrenched her hand out of Cym's grip and backed away. 'She will never be one of us,' she said to Zaqri in a low voice. 'She can never replace my sister. Ghila was your mate for *nine years*. She wed you the same day I wed Perno. You pledged that day to care for me if Perno fell, as he pledged to care for Ghila. You promised to love me as a sister. Where is that love now?'

'It is still here, sister,' he said, touching his left breast.

Hessaz looked at him with baleful eyes. 'Then why do I not feel its heat?'

'You are still my sister.'

'I don't want to be your sister,' she shouted, her voice cracking. 'I want more!'

Zaqri shook his head. 'Nevertheless.'

For an instant Cym thought the Lokistani woman might sprout teeth and claws and fly at him, but instead she threw her head and wailed, then she spun round and ran out into the sands.

Huriya whispered in the ear of a man at her side, and he trotted after Hessaz.

<Who is that?> she asked Zaqri, studying him. He was big, older than Zaqri, and heavily scarred. He looked very strong, though less agile than the lion-man. The bleached pallor of his hair hinted at northern Yuros, though his skin was burned dark.

<Wornu. He was also widowed in the attack on the Inquisitors. He is my friend.> His eyes went to Huriya. <Or so I thought.>

<Is he a threat to you?>

<Why, are you worried for me?> His eyes glinted teasingly.

<No, for me. You're my protection, remember?>

<He is my equal, no more than that,> Zaqri said seriously. <We both know it. But if he had a mate . . . >

<What do you mean?>

<A leadership challenge is made by mated couple to mated couple. A pack-leader without a mate is highly vulnerable.> His eyes followed Wornu until he was out of sight. <I must take a new wife soon if I wish to survive.>

She put her hands on her hips. <Well, don't let me rukking well stop you!>

The next morning, Wornu was wed to Hessaz. The ceremony was a simple and barbaric thing: Wornu simply laid claim to her, then they mated before the pack. Their heaving, sweaty coupling replayed in Cym's mind for days after, stirring complex emotions. Hessaz was not pacified by her new mate though: whenever she looked at Cym, her eyes were full of hatred.

Zaqri spent the next few days among his people, renewing old bonds. Cym realised that her presence had weakened his standing, and she was afraid to be far from him, though so far no one had violated Zaqri's protection edict. It wasn't just the ancient enmity between magi and Dokken; Zaqri told her that hundreds of potential Dokken went their whole lives without ever awakening the gnosis for want of a mage to kill – no wonder they all wanted to destroy her, especially those with unawakened children.

The growing tension between Wornu and Zaqri came to a head the next evening as the pack gathered around the central cooking fires.

'We must find these damned magi!' Wornu shouted angrily. 'How has this boy from Yuros eluded us? I'll tell you why: it's because you will not plunder the knowledge inside *her* head!' He stabbed his finger at Cym. 'She knows where the boy is and you're protecting her, packleader! Why?'

Cym felt her breath shorten as a chorus of derision rose. Clearly some of the pack had been primed for this confrontation.

'*Zaqri pants after the gypsy!*'

'*She's stolen the balls from his sack.*'

'*An unmated packleader is no leader at all.*'

'*Kill the gypsy and use her knowledge!*'

Cym looked around for Huriya and found her at the back, a satisfied look on her face. *She's put Wornu up to this.*

Zaqri leapt atop the closest rock and shouted above the hubbub. 'I know all that the Rimoni girl knows! It is not for lack of her information that we have not found the boy!'

'We were promised blood – I have children to avenge!' a woman called.

'If I were leader we would not run from the Inquisitors!' Wornu cried. 'We would fight!'

Zaqri's nostrils flared. 'If *you* were leader – but you're not, Wornu, and nor do you have the support for a challenge!'

'Not got the support?' Wornu shouted back, spreading his arms theatrically. 'Do I not?'

As if primed, an alarming number of voices rose, shouting, 'WORNU! WORNU!'

Cym saw Zaqri's surprise and was shocked he'd not seen it coming. *He's politically naïve,* she realised, *too noble and honest for his own good.* Her eyes went to Huriya, the Seeress. *I bet she foresaw everything . . .*

The clamour grew louder and Dokken started calling, '*A challenge! A challenge!*'

Zaqri drew himself to his full height and shouted for silence. It took several tries, but finally they settled enough to hear him out. 'Listen to me! I swear to you, Cymbellea knows nothing she has not shared, willingly or by force. A challenge would achieve nothing but the further weakening of the pack!'

'It is you who weakens the pack!' Wornu snarled. 'If you wish to strengthen us, share the essence of your Rimoni whore!'

'Aye,' Hessaz echoed, 'kill the gypsy slut! Who here has a child ready to have their gnosis awakened?'

A chorus of hands went up and the noise rose further. Zaqri looked down at Cym and she could read his concern. Any illusion of safety was collapsing around them. He looked around at Huriya and read her smug expression and it finally sank in: Wornu was deadly serious, and Hessaz was willing to kill a man she'd once wanted as mate.

He's my protection . . .

With a sinking heart she watched the inevitable play out in rituals of bravado. Wornu confronted Zaqri, bringing in his head so their foreheads were touching, and snorting like a bull, shouted, 'I will find those we hunt! I'll rip the knowledge from the gypsy's mind!'

'I don't know where they are, *pezzi di merda!*' Cym shouted furiously, unable to stay silent.

Hessaz stalked towards her and shoved her in the chest. 'Shut it, whore!'

Cym staggered, caught herself and cried, 'Tie your bitch back up, Wornu!'

Hessaz slapped her and she slapped back with a resounding great crack. All round her the pack whooped and shouted encouragement. She fed gnosis into her nails, bent her fingers into claws.

Hessaz's whole head shifted to panther shape and she roared in Cym's face.

Rukka!

'Call her off, Wornu!' she warned, backing up, fighting to keep her voice firm.

'Do it yourself, whore,' Wornu sneered, still facing Zaqri nose to nose.

Cym's temper flared. 'I'm no one's whore, you oversized bullock.'

Wornu's face turned ugly. 'Bullock? Zaqri's the one who's been gelded!'

Zaqri shoved, Wornu shoved back, and Cym was confronted by an advancing Hessaz, her panther head full of teeth. She backed up, ready to fight there and then, when an old man stepped between them. Tomacz, a pack elder. To her relief, Hessaz stopped and her head returned to something mostly human. That didn't prevent violence breaking out between supporters of the two contenders behind them, and Cym noted with alarm that Wornu appeared to have at least as many behind him as Zaqri did.

'Peace!' shouted Huriya. She strode between the two men and with a double-handed gesture threw them apart. 'Enough, I say! A leadership challenge is one thing, but a brawl is intolerable!' She looked at Wornu, taking the stance of disinterested outsider. 'You must make your challenge or withdraw your words, Wornu.'

'*A challenge! A challenge!*' the call went out again.

Hessaz pointed at Cym. 'This creature has bent your horn,' she rasped at Zaqri. 'Give her to us and we will withdraw the challenge.'

A growl rose about her and Cym could feel the raw hostility all around her: she was a mage, she was an outsider, she was a threat to pack unity. There were no friendly eyes, no sympathy anywhere. Even Zaqri, beloved as he was by many, could not change centuries of hatred.

He'll have to sacrifice me or face death . . .

Sensing the mood, Wornu spoke again, his booming voice filling the dell. 'Feed her to a deserving recipient, to strengthen the pack!'

Zaqri snarled. 'She's my—'

'Yes? She's your *what*, exactly?' Hessaz enquired. 'You won't kill her and you won't fuck her. So what is she?'

'She is my ward,' Zaqri maintained, but his posture was defensive now. 'She does not come between me and my duties as packleader.'

'Does she not?' rumbled Wornu. 'Yet here you are, a packleader without a mate, and she is your constant companion. Your *chaste* companion. Tell me she has not emasculated you, Brother.'

Zaqri's chest swelled and his chin rose. His eyes blazed. 'Refusal to rape a prisoner is not a sign of weakness, *Brother*.' His eyes flickered to Hessaz. 'Perhaps a man who is being led by the balls is the one who is emasculated.'

Wornu bared his teeth. 'I am my own man, and my woman gives me strength. She does not undermine me as your woman does.'

'Cymbellea is not my woman. I have no woman.'

'No, you do not.' Wornu sighed as if filled with regret. 'A pack-leader with no woman is half a man.' He spat on the ground at Zaqri's feet. 'Emasculated.'

Zaqri stared at the blob of spittle as the rest of the pack sucked in their breath and backed away. 'Do you challenge me, Brother?'

'You are my brother no longer,' Wornu said in his deepest bass. 'I do challenge. My mate and I, Hessaz of Gorsh, give formal challenge.'

Zaqri's face fell and he said sadly, 'Wornu, you and I have fought shoulder to shoulder for decades. This is not worthy of you.'

Wornu wrinkled his nose as if from a bad smell. 'Are you afraid? It is not fitting for a pack leader to seek to avoid a challenge.'

Zaqri growled. 'I'm not afraid of you, Wornu.'

'Then you're a fool.' Wornu tapped Zaqri in the middle of the chest. 'Let us resolve this, Brother. Step into the Noose and we will make a swift end.'

The pack inhaled as one, eyes flickering from one man to the other. Then Hessaz stepped behind Wornu and gripped his shoulder. 'I stand with my mate in the Noose and stake my life,' she cried.

'My mate and I against you and yours,' Wornu said to Zaqri.

Hessaz sneered. 'Except he has none. Or so he says.'

What's a Noose? Cym wondered as she looked from man to man. Wornu was bulkier, heavier, and more thickly muscled, but Zaqri was taller and faster. But there was also Hessaz, probably as dangerous as Wornu in her own way. Two against one.

And if Zaqri dies, I'm next.

Cym swallowed then, as if in slow motion, she reached out and gripped Zaqri's thick bicep in her right hand, mirroring Hessaz's posture. 'I stand with Zaqri in the Noose,' she said as loudly and firmly as she could. 'I stake my life.'

11

A Tightening Noose

Social Organisation Among the Dokken

There is little information to work with, but it appears that the Dokken live largely solitary lives, except those with an affinity to animagery, who gather in large clans in the wild. These seem to share some bond, as herd beasts do.

ORDO COSTRUO COLLEGIATE, PONTUS 761

Southern Dhassa, on the continent of Antiopia
Awwal (Martrois) 929
9th month of the Moontide

Whatever reaction Cym might have expected from her sudden pronouncement, derisive laughter wasn't it. Even as Zaqri threw a startled look over his shoulder at her, Huriya's harsh cackle filled the circle of close-pressed Souldrinkers.

'No, girl.' Huriya swayed into the space between the combatants, her sheer presence enough to make even Wornu and Zaqri take a step back. 'The word is *mate*: to us this means married in the eyes of the pack. There has been no such ceremony. Even mated at all would be a start, but you've not even done that.' A malicious titter ran through the gathered pack.

Zaqri looked at her, fully aware of what she was doing. <*You would do better to run whilst I fight.*>

<*I'd never get away.*> She read in his face that he knew this too. <*Help me,*> she pleaded silently.

Zaqri looked at her in silence, then away. Finally he looked around until he spotted the nearest elder. 'Tomacz,' he said, 'a couple have the right to wed at any time, is that not so, Eldest?'

Tomacz frowned, his eyes flickering from Zaqri to Wornu to Huriya. 'It is so,' he admitted.

'Pah!' Wornu exclaimed. 'This weakling desperately seeks a woman to die with him. Craven bastard, seeking skirts to hide behind! To think we ever supported you!'

The pack hissed in agreement, and Cym felt the antipathy of the pack towards them rise to new levels. She could feel it: Zaqri's reign was over, whether he defeated Wornu's challenge or not. He'd lost their respect, because of her.

Zaqri raised his head. 'Nevertheless, if she wishes it, I would wed her.'

More hissing, more anger. 'You pollute us!' someone shouted. 'She's a damned mage-blood!'

'Forbid this, Eldest!' another called. 'It is a mockery! Let the coward die alone.'

Tomacz roared for silence. 'They have the right to wed! Nothing forbids it!' He looked like he wished there was. 'Though it brings us all shame, they do so!'

This brought howls of derision. 'Zaqri is soul-kin to you, Tomacz!' Wornu bellowed. 'You favour his cause!'

Hessaz stepped in front of her man. 'No, no! Let the girl pretend to be his. Let her fight!' Her eyes narrowed. 'She's nothing! I'll tear her apart.' Her eyes burned into Cym's. 'I can smell her fear.'

Tomacz looked at Zaqri, then at Huriya. 'Seeress?' he said hesitantly.

Silence fell. Huriya preened, looking from Wornu to Zaqri to Cym. 'Well, why not ... ? One night of love before they die together. It sounds perfectly poetic to me.' She looked at Cym with malicious eyes. 'Do you claim the craven who slew your mother as your *beloved* husband?'

With her gnostic sight, Cym could see the aura-tendrils of the pack withdraw from Zaqri. He looked about him, his eyes bereft.

She nodded slowly.

'Then, packmaster, you may claim her,' Huriya pronounced mockingly.

Zaqri swallowed, still struggling at the withdrawal of the pack from his mind. It must have felt like an amputation. He swayed slightly, then turned and in a faint voice said, 'I claim this woman, Cymbellea di Regia-Meiros of Rimoni, as my mate before the pack.' His voice was disbelieving, as if his ears did not credit what his mouth was saying. Then, before she could react, he stepped forward and scooped her into his arms. She tried to wriggle free, but his arms were like vices, clamping him to her as the men and women of the pack gathered about, lust and hunger filling the air. No one asked her whether she was willing or not. 'Tonight we will spend alone, as is traditional,' he said, a jibe at Wornu and Hessaz for their ostentatious exhibitionism. 'Tomorrow,' he added, staring at Wornu, 'we fight to the death.'

The pack yowled as he swung about and shouldered his way through them and out into the night. Cym felt like a child in his grip as he strode through the gathering. Hands reached out and touched her, some with pity, most with malice. Someone left four bloody lines down her thigh, then darted out of reach. A flicker of healing gnosis cleansed the wound, but there would be a scar. She winced, and glared into the shadows.

At the fringes, some pack-members shifted into animal form and began to howl.

'Put me down!' Cym said, kicking and twisting to get him to release her once they were alone. He did so: he opened his arms and simply dropped her to the sand. She hit the ground with a grunt, then bounced to her feet. 'Who do you think you are, carrying me off like a bloody prize?'

He gave a hollow laugh. 'Your mate, apparently.' He looked more leonine than ever, his golden hair cast in silver by the giant moon above. The cooling air made her shiver, as did his luminescent aura, tendrils reaching out to her then coiling away.

She jabbed a finger at him. 'You're nothing to me but a shield from that poisonous bitch Huriya. I'll help keep you alive for my own good, but after that, you're going to help me find Alaron before Huriya does. She's *evil*.'

He raised an eyebrow. 'Evil? Really? Viciously ambitious, cold-hearted and childishly promiscuous, yes, but evil? What does "evil" even mean? Under most definitions all my brethren are evil.'

'But she embraces it. You . . .'

'Yes?'

She shut her mouth and faced him, wondering what to do.

All the nights lying near him pounded through her brain. Animal attraction, that's what the other Rimoni girls of her father's caravan would have called it, and they'd have been laughing at the little joke. She felt it, certainly; she knew it went both ways. But she finally had to admit the truth: it was more than that. She admired his demeanour, his strength, his fortitude, his bearing. He was a leader, for all his political naïvety. He reminded her of her father, the epitome of men in her eyes. *But he killed my mother*. 'At least you fight your worst impulses,' she conceded.

'A fine epitaph. Would that all folk did the same.' He sat, pointedly waiting until she joined him, defusing some of the anger crackling between them. When he spoke again his voice was softer, sadder. 'I had the choice, when I found out what I was: to live with it, at the cost of the lives of others, or to kill myself. I chose to live. Do not underestimate the gravity of that decision. Some of our kind find it easy, others do not. Some of us like to think we're part of Kore's plan, others, that we're Kore's biggest mistake. I choose to regard myself as a predator, like a lion. I do not question the right or wrong of it. I was born as I am. Philosophers can chew that over until their teeth fall out, but I can't be bothered. I am a lion and I choose to eat. If human life is so precious, why do I exist?'

It might have sounded arrogant, except that his voice was so humble and full of regrets. She had no doubt that he meant it – or that he suffered, despite it. She'd observed that he appeared to be judicious in his hunting and sparing in his use of the gnosis. He was both piti-able and fearsome, and almost impossible to hate, though she was still trying.

'If we find the Scytale, maybe it can cure you all?' she suggested, trying to placate him.

'That can happen with or without me.'

'I don't want Huriya and Wornu to find Alaron – they'll just kill him. He's my friend, and I led him into this. It was my stupidity that led Huriya to the island. I have to stay alive to help him, and for now that means helping you.'

'Very well.' He looked her up and down. 'Girl, tomorrow they will check you again, and if we are not mated, then you will not be eli-gible to fight.'

She flinched, nervous again. 'I don't understand you. You were married to Ghila for so long, and now, after just a few months, you're ready to move on – and don't tell me you're only doing this because you must: you've been giving me hot eyes from the day we met. Are you really so fickle?'

'I am not fickle,' he said forcibly. 'Ghila meant much to me, but we were not truly a love match. I resolved to defeat the previous packleader, a vicious brute, and I needed a strong woman to fight alongside me. Ghila was that woman. We learned to be mates, as best as two people thrown together by circumstance can.' He looked at her intently. 'I will not speak ill of her, but she and Hessaz were twins, in body and in soul: loyal if placated, cruel if thwarted. But Ghila is dead now and life continues.'

'So I'm just the next convenient woman?'

'No! You are the most inconvenient woman there has ever been! Beautiful, fiery, stubborn, clever, determined – all that I might have wanted, yet I meet you on the wrong side of a war and find you are magi. And then there is the blood-matter between us. If there was ever a woman I should not lose my heart to, it is you. But hearts do not listen to reason.' He reached out, touched her arm. 'There is something about you I need, and even if Ghila still lived, I would crave it. I don't even fully known what it is, but I've risked everything for it.'

It felt as if the night had suddenly drawn breath. She tore her eyes away, heart pounding, and sought the face of the moon for guidance. *Mater Luna, patron of lovers . . . What do you want of me?*

The moonlight revealed nothing except the land around her: a desert, but teeming with secretive life: birds and insects and snakes and lizards and all manner of creatures, fighting and mating, a quiet and desperate dance of survival. *Live*, it said. *Create life. Fight to go on.*

Thank you, Great Goddess. She clasped his hand. It was big and warm. 'Do we have to do it in front of everyone?'

'No. Hessaz and Wornu were showing off, making a point.' He stood and pulled her to her feet. 'Come.'

He led her to the tent where she normally slept alone, but this time he entered as well, immense in the tiny space. He knotted the flap closed and all at once they were lying alongside each other, inhaling each other's breath, thighs and shoulders touching through their thin cotton clothing.

'I know what happens,' she whispered. 'I lived in a travelling cara-van. No one has secrets. Not like your pack, obviously, but . . .'

He put a hand on her cheek, stroked it, went to kiss her.

'No kissing,' she said firmly in a low voice. 'This is not about love.'

He stopped, pulled away, gave her room to tug off her tunic. He did the same, and immediately he thickened and became erect. She rolled onto her back on the rough blanket and he followed her and gripped her shoulders as he propped on his elbows above her. Her mouth forbidden, he kissed her left breast, above her fluttering heart, his hot mouth enfolding her nipple. A flush of heat swelled through her, as if her soul were being drawn into his mouth. It felt too good to ignore, but the sensation frightened her too. 'Is this how Nasette was changed?' she whispered, scared now and unable to con-ceal it.

He raised his head from the engorged nipple. 'No. That is a matter of the gnosis, not of mating.' He bent to her other nipple, brought it to the same bursting wonder as the first. His right hand slid over her thigh, stroked her mound.

'No – don't touch me.'

He frowned. 'It will be easier for you if I stimulate your passage.'

'I don't want it to be easy. I don't want to enjoy this.'

Zaqri looked stung, but he lowered his hips to her, engulfing her as she opened her thighs to receive him. He was twice her bulk and his weight pushed the air from her lungs, and as the tip of his member found her folds and pushed inside, her body stiffened. He worked himself slowly inwards, grunting softly, trying to ease his passage, and she gritted her teeth at the painful intrusion.

'You are wet inside,' he whispered in her ear, then went all the way in. Something tore painfully and she jerked beneath him and shook until the ripping sensation passed. He began to thrust, his member immense inside her, like a spear stabbing her slowly towards a kind of death. For a few moments they moved as one groaning, sighing thing, getting louder as his movements became more vigorous. She had to fight to breathe, but an animal heat was rising inside her that she fought to conceal. His face went wild and he gripped her harder, as he started thrusting faster and faster until he gave a soft, almost gentle moan and she felt him expend in her. His body quivered, the uncontrolled convulsion almost teasing a response in her, then he sagged, crushing her as she gasped for breath.

The thought came unbidden: *This should have been more than it was.*

He lifted himself on his arms, though he stayed inside her, and stared down at her face. He looked like a demi-god. His heat and thickness inside her was filling her with a spreading warmth. Her hands involuntarily stroked his sides.

'You are not hurt?' he asked in a formal voice. She shook her head mutely and he pulled out of her and rolled to her side. Their bodies filled the small tent and the air was warm and close. He looked concerned for her, hesitant; oddly, that annoyed her. She liked him more when he was certain – she needed him to be so on the eve of a death-match.

'Well, is that enough to satisfy the pack?' she asked, her voice more bitter than she'd intended, and he flinched. *He wanted this to be perfect and I've ruined it for him.* There was no pride in the realisation. *And tomorrow we'll most likely die together . . .*

'Yes.' He looked down at her, his face hardening. 'Do you know how the ritual challenge works?'

She shook her head. 'No.'

He nodded towards the flap. 'Follow me.' He crawled outside, unconcerned at his nudity.

She glowered at his brusque tone, but reluctantly followed, wrapped in her blanket. 'Tell me,' she said, keeping her tone businesslike as she joined him before the fire, which he kindled with a gesture.

'Tonight the pack will mark out a large territory, roughly square-shaped and at least a mile wide. Each participant starts in a corner, diagonally opposite their partner. At dawn, when the sun rises, you are free to move anywhere inside the square. Any who leave it while an enemy lives forfeits the challenge and is killed. The objective is to kill your enemies. You get no weapons, but can use anything you find that was not forged by men. Tooth and claw, the gnosis, and perhaps a rock or stick: these are the only permissible weapons. It is as much a hunt as a fight. The deadliest strikes are those you do not see.'

Cym sucked in her breath. She'd barely begun to learn the gnosis, and Wornu and Hessaz had years of experience. She'd never really hunted in her life, except on the road through Sydia and that had been a disaster. 'Why is it called the Noose?'

'Because an hour after it begins, the pack will begin walking inwards, constricting the arena until the combatants are forced together. Tightening like a noose.'

Sol et Lune . . . 'Can't you just resign, if he wants the job so badly?'

'No,' he said shortly. 'To take the leadership is for life. "Until death I will serve": that is the oath. And I never said that I don't want the leadership: I do. Huriya is taking this pack into disaster and Wornu will only speed that.' He set his jaw, his voice intent. 'Wornu and I are both the equivalent of a pure-blood mage. Hessaz is the equivalent of a half-blood, like you. But both are experienced fighters, and you are not. Your gnosis is no more than I would expect from a yearling.'

'My father was rich by Rimoni standards, but not enough to afford an Arcanum education for me.'

'That's irrelevant. Wornu and Hessaz will show no mercy. But think on this: Souldrinkers group together, like with like, birds of a feather. It is how we teach each other, as we have no colleges. But you're an outsider, with an outsider's affinities. Neither Wornu or Hessaz have wide experience in fighting the likes of you. I am a match for Wornu or Hessaz alone, but not them both. We must find a way to use your skills to surprise them. You are the key to our survival.'

Cym felt goosebumps rise at the thought. 'I'm mostly Hermetic and Air . . . but my training was secondhand, and erratic at best so I'm mostly self-taught. Morphic-gnosis, healing, illusion . . . And I can fly in human form, but that's incredibly tiring. I once crossed forty miles of sea, but it nearly killed me.' She paused. 'And I can manage a little spiritualism.'

'Spiritualism?' Zaqri looked interested. 'I have heard of it, but never seen it. How does it work?'

'You separate soul from body: it's the strangest sensation, really creepy. You can use the gnosis while in spirit form, but your body is vulnerable, and so are you. It's really dangerous and I'm not good at it.'

'But it's something our opponents cannot do – I doubt they even know about it, let alone have ever seen it. It may give us an opportunity.' He looked at her thoughtfully. 'Let us explore that.'

Cym did not think she would sleep, not with all she'd been through and what was to come. She wanted to flee, but she knew she wouldn't get far. Flying with Air-gnosis was no match to shapeshifters in bird form. In the end it came down to winning or dying, and with that simple thought came resignation and, after that, sleep.

Zaqri shook her awake, his heavy hand warm on her shoulder. It was dark, and the silence of the night was oppressive, but there was a faint, pale glow in the east. 'It's time,' was all he said.

She came awake immediately and stretched awkwardly. Her loins felt uncomfortably tender, and she smelled of him. She wrinkled her nose as she rose, then found water and washed before shrugging on her thin shift. Zaqri put a bowl in front of her filled with meat and rice in a wet curry gravy and using her fingers, she wolfed it down. She pulled her tangled hair into a ponytail and tried to slow her breathing. To her faint surprise she wasn't trembling, though she was very much afraid – not of death, but of the bits before, the *losing*. There would be pain, of course, and the looks of gloating triumph on her enemies' faces, and she dreaded those most of all.

Around her, the land and sky seemed to bloom into vivid life, from the glow of impending dawn to the kiss of the cool air. Then her stomach churned and her bowels clenched and she had to blink back sudden tears at the terror that these were among her last minutes when there was so much more she wanted from life.

'Purge yourself,' Zaqri urged. 'Do it before the contest, so you do not have to in the Noose. You don't wish to leave spore. And as you purge the waste, purge your fear – they are both just shit you don't need.'

Feeling like there was a python wriggling in her guts, she fled for the dung hole beyond the camp, squatted and shat while tears stung her eyes. When she returned on shaky legs, Zaqri gave her a calm look. 'Good. You will be fine now.' His hand felt strong and solid on her arm. For a second she wished she could just cling to him and hide from the world. He was as solid as the stone beneath her feet as he led her to the middle of the camp. A few of the pack murmured encouragement to him, but no one said a word to her at all.

Wornu and Hessaz waited in the midst of their followers, wearing nothing but loinclothes. They were caked in wet mud from head to foot and were limbering up, breathing deeply, their faces taut but expressionless. Hessaz's face flared into momentary malice when her eyes met Cym's, but apart from that she gave little sign that she or Zaqri even existed. But Wornu strode over to Zaqri. Though Zaqri was over six foot and well-built, Wornu, massive and thickly muscled, dwarfed him.

'My time has come,' he proclaimed loudly.

Zaqri met him head-on and the two giants started squaring off, eyeball to eyeball.

Cym glanced at Hessaz, who spat in her direction. Cym poked her tongue back at her, then turned away, keenly aware of the eyes on her. A rat-faced woman called Fasha scuttled towards her, dropped to her haunches and sniffed her groin, smirking. 'They have mated,' she told the pack. A few whooped, but most sneered.

'Hope your first and last time was good for you, honey,' big Darice rumbled.

Huriya appeared, looking smugly pleased with life as she surveyed the four rivals. 'Are we all ready then? I look forward to seeing this resolved so that we can resume our hunt.'

'I am ready,' Wornu rumbled. He reached out as if to touch Zaqri's chest with his finger, but Zaqri smacked his hand away and they scuffled until all four combatants were suddenly being pulled away in different directions. There was no chance for final words.

Cym stared at Zaqri as she was hauled off. <*Buona fortuna,*> he sent before he was lost in the pre-dawn darkness. A hand wrapped about her forearm and she looked around to see the greybeard, Tomacz. She straightened and tossed her head.

Tomacz nodded approvingly. 'That's the way, lass. Show no fear.' He led her through the darkness, heading southeast towards the line of hills. It was undulating ground, filled with steep hillocks and gullies, where visibility would be short. Fine stalking territory.

'Where are we going?'

'Not far.' He gestured about him and those of the pack trailing them fell away. 'Each of the four in the contest gets a second, to guide them to their starting point. Zaqri drew the furthest station, two miles away, which means you have the nearest, opposite him in the square.' He looked her up and down. 'You're no warrior, girl. Have you killed before?'

She thought of lying, then admitted, 'No. Never.'

'I thought not. But you're a survivor, I can sense that. Here's my advice: don't try to flee the contest. That is suicide. Don't try to hide – Hessaz could track a bird, let alone a babe in the woods like you. Get to Zaqri's side as quickly as you can and help him. He's a match for Wornu.'

She and Zaqri had discussed and discarded this option during the night. 'How do Wornu and Hessaz fight?' she asked, to see whether he echoed Zaqri's views.

Tomacz glanced sideways at her. 'Wornu is as powerful as a pure-blood mage, but he is not skilled or refined in his gnosis. He uses shapechanging and Earth. He likes to burrow deep and ambush from close range from below. He's also fond of hurling boulders. He's almost blind to illusion.'

'Zaqri thought the same.'

'Hessaz is primarily a shapechanger, animal or human form, but she has a brain and she is strong in illusion. Zaqri has hinted that you also have skill in that area, but you'll struggle to beguile her. Her weakness is in Sorcery – anything you know in that field has the best odds.'

She nodded gloomily. It pained her to be the weak link, but she gritted her teeth. *I will get through this. Zaqri will keep – for now I need to keep him alive and myself too.* 'How long have we got?'

'The pack will walk inwards at a slow gait after an hour, shrinking the Noose. By midday, you'll be contained in a circle one hundred yards in diameter. Few of these contests last long after that.' Tomacz looked at her hard. 'Don't let Zaqri down, girl.'

'He killed my mother.'

'You cannot fight well together when you are not in harmony. You should have made peace with him. You should have demanded a Weyrgild, like the Schlessen do. Life is too short to wallow in vendetta.'

'Barbarians might sell their honour for gifts, but I'm Rimoni. It's blood for blood, that's all there is to it.'

'Foolishness. We're not meant to deal in absolutes. Even the Kore preach forgiveness over revenge.'

'The Kore have been exacting punishment on my people for centuries,' she retorted. 'If you can't tell me anything that might help me win, then shut up.'

Tomacz sniffed. 'He should have married Hessaz and fed you to a youngling.'

Rukka te, old man.

They went on in silence until they reached a small dale. A pile of three stones marked her starting point. 'This is the place.' Tomacz turned to her and made one last exhortation. 'Girl, we are not monsters. We have only ever desired the right to live free. But *that one* is pulling us into a conflict that will destroy us all. Wornu is her cat's-paw. Be victorious and you will break us free of her hold on us. Wornu's followers will be forced to bend the knee to Zaqri anew, and Huriya will have to go on alone. Fail, and she will drag us all to destruction.' He glanced towards the east again. 'You have ten minutes. Make yourself ready.' He withdrew to watch from a nearby hillock.

She let her night sight fade to adjust for the coming dawn. The faint wind kissed her cheeks as she pulled her gnosis to the surface, warded herself from scrying and primed her shields. Her hand trembled despite anything she did, and the thought that she was going to die very soon overwhelmed her and wouldn't go away.

Then the glow in the east became a light that stabbed across the plains and shadows sprang aside like night spirits afraid of the sun's fire. For a few more seconds she was in shadow herself, then as the first rays of light struck her, she leaped into movement, streaming towards her right – towards where Wornu would also be in motion, a mile away across the broken ground.

The sun rose, driving the darkness west with swift strokes, and the shafts of light glittered on the raised blades of the Inquisitors in their morning prayer. Adamus Crozier led the *Invocation for Battle* in his clear voice:

> '*Kore be in my eye that I may see*
> *Kore be in my heart that I might judge*
> *Kore be in my blade that I may strike true*
> *Kore be in my holy gnosis that I may be invincible this day.*'

Each line was echoed by the kneeling Acolytes of the Fist, some mumbling, others speaking clearly, according to their nature.

Malevorn mouthed the prayers silently, his mind on the carnage to come. *Is Mercer here? Or the Scytale? How strong are these Dokken?* He looked sideways at Raine. Her eyes were closed as she prayed aloud. She was a true believer, or she faked it well. Religion was their profession so it paid to look devout. He copied her and raised his voice. *Who knows who is listening?*

When he opened his eyes again, Adamus Crozier was looking straight at him. He nodded once and turned away. What it meant, Malevorn couldn't tell.

One of Quintius' men had scouted the camp and reported maybe a hundred of the creatures, a formidable number – but many were women, or children not blooded into the gnosis. For fifteen Inquisitors, it was no easy fight, but they would be fine provided they held together and fought as a unit. At Meiros' island they had discovered that the Dokken were sometimes powerful, but they were poorly armed and barely trained.

They finished their prayers and stood, kissed their blades and sheathed them, then mounted up. 'Walk silently until I signal,' Malevorn told his mount as he slid into the saddle. It whickered softly, its 'assent' sound. *These things could probably speak if they had a human tongue.* Khurnes were clearly a huge advance on ordinary horses, but they were somewhat unnerving too. But as they wound along what looked like a long-dry riverbed he forgot the matter and let the mission take over.

They were expecting to have to take down perimeter guards, but encountered none: apparently the Dokken thought themselves safe. *No one's beyond our reach.* He glanced about him, taking stock of his fellows, the remnants of the Eighteenth Fist. Elath Dranid was a shadow ahead. Beside him Raine's sallow face puckered as she chewed on beef jerky. Most men Malevorn knew didn't eat before battle, but she was nerveless. Beyond her was Dominic, lost in his own misery, just as he had been since the Isle of Glass. Malevorn felt nothing but contempt for his former closest friend – Dominic was weak, his innocence broken by defeat and death. *And being rogered up the arse by Adamus, of course . . .*

The crozier brought up the rear, his feminine face a mask of calm, his eyes constantly calculating, no doubt plotting to ensure that it was he, not Quintius, who got the Scytale – and the glory.

Where do we stand in his plans? Adamus seldom confided in him or Dranid. It looked like he had reached some kind of accommodation with Quintius. *Men like him don't spread favours beyond those loyal to them personally.* He wished he'd got closer to the crozier. *But not as close as Dom . . .*

Another ridge, another pause, and the Inquisitors bunched up, waiting. Malevorn looked around and spotted Artus Leblanc in the pallid gloom. The Acolyte glanced back, scratching his cheek as if the scar there had suddenly itched. Their eyes met blandly and Leblanc looked away. Somehow that troubled Malevorn more than a confrontational glare. *It's as if I don't matter any more.*

Adamus Crozier waved them all into a loose circle. 'The Dokken are over the ridge and down a long slope, about three hundred yards away. Beyond is a watering hole and after that the terrain becomes uneven. There are no guards, and the camp is half-empty. Most of the men are away.'

'Do they know we're here?' asked Dominic in a worried voice.

Quintius looked down his nose at the young Acolyte. 'They do not. In fact, this is opportune: a divided enemy is more easily destroyed. We will attack as planned. If this Alaron Mercer is their prisoner, he will be held in the camp, and easily seized. If not, we will put the survivors to the question, and see what there is to learn.'

The Acolytes stirred, eager to fight. Malevorn was of the same mind, and so were Raine and Dranid: longing to strike back at these creatures that had humiliated them at the island.

Adamus Crozier took over the briefing. 'This is what we will do: once we top this final rise, we will see the camp, and they us. We will gallop straight over the top of them, wheel and recharge, except for Brother Dranid's men, who will guard the perimeter facing the broken lands on the far side while the rest of us seek Mercer.'

Dranid's eyes narrowed; he was clearly disappointed. Nevertheless he saluted. 'Understood, Holiness.'

'Excellent, Brother Dranid. Once through, establish a perimeter point every fifty yards. The rest, wheel on my command. Take a few adults alive and kill the rest.'

The Acolytes struck fists against their left breasts in salute.

Malevorn glanced at Raine. <*They think to keep us from the prize. Watch your back.*>

She picked her teeth, and belched. <*Always do: when I'm not watching yours.*>

<*Mind on the job.*>

<*My mind is on you.*>

<*Ha! I told you: all women fall for me in the end.*>

<*Don't get above yourself, arsehole.*>

They grinned knowingly at each other.

'Let's move,' Quintius said in his crisp voice.

They spurred to the ridge-line, the khurnes as silent as their riders. For a few seconds, everything went still, with just the snorting of the khurnes and the creak and clank of leather and metal providing the backdrop for the thudding of his heart. The camp was a squalling mess of children running about; a few adults were hunched over pots and cooking fires. The sky was empty and no beasts roamed the tents. Quintius was right: most of the Dokken were gone.

Then the Commandant's mental voice echoed in all of their skulls and the lead khurne leapt forward. The rest followed, and Malevorn focused his attention on guiding his steed. Dust spewed up from the hooves, and the thunder of their advance was like a storm breaking.

Somewhere in the camp, a child cried out.

Huriya Makani watched impatiently from the edge of the small gully that marked the edge of the Noose. If Zaqri was victorious, her growing control of the pack might be snatched away; if it had not been for that she might not have overly cared who won this pissing contest.

Only she and Zaqri knew at this stage that they were pursuing more than just Ramita Ankesharan and Alaron Mercer. *If Wornu fails me, I'm sure there will still be dissidents against Zaqri's leadership, especially once I reveal that the Scytale is at stake . . .*

Zaqri's fascination with this Cymbellea was aggravating and self-destructive, but her Sabele-memories told her that Zaqri had always had a strongly moralistic streak, and a desire to appear noble and heroic and generous that bordered on narcissism in her eyes.

Tomacz trudged up the slope towards her, his face hostile. Sabele had been a rarity among Souldrinkers: a specialist in the more arcane aspects of the gnosis, when most were hunter-gatherers on the fringes of a more sophisticated world. They resented her as much as they revered her.

'You could have stopped this,' the Eldest said accusingly.

She arched an eyebrow. 'Neither would thank me.'

'What game are you playing, Seeress?'

'No games, Tomacz. This is serious business. There is much at stake.'

Tomacz looked sceptical. 'Really? Why are we chasing a girl across Dhassa for you?'

She put her finger to her lips. 'I can't tell you, Tomacz. It's a secret. Zaqri knows, and the Rimoni – that's all.'

'Why? Why not tell us all?'

'It's too dangerous. I'll tell Wornu if he wins, and maybe Hessaz.'

'Lady, by Brethren law, this pack may not leave our ancestral territory. We are near those borders.'

'I know. Zaqri told me he would refuse to leave them even if I gave my blessing. Wornu has promised otherwise. This is a war: laws do not exist in such times.'

'Laws always matter, Seeress. They are what preserve who we are.'

'No, they are just silly little rules we break when it suits us to do so.'

He scowled at that. 'You are leading us on a trail of death, Lady.'

'I have a lot of deaths on my hands, Tomacz.' She met his eye as something surfaced inside her. 'I remember your father: blue eyes and long dark hair. Two bodies ago, for Sabele.' She smiled reflectively. 'He had a fine voice; he sang beautifully.'

She blinked away memories of people she'd never met with a shudder.

Tomacz peered at her, his face a little pale. 'How many lives are within you, girl?'

Too many. Right now, Huriya could pull them out at will, but she could always sense that other presence inside: Sabele, waiting like an old spider. She hadn't known what she was taking on when she'd consumed Sabele's soul on the Isle of Glass – it had just been opportunism. But now her greatest fear was not of enemies but of the crone inside her own head.

This is my body. My brain. I own it, not her.

Inside her, that spider-presence laughed patiently.

Thunder rolled from the south, where a low ridge flanked the camp site. In the campsite, a child screamed for his mother.

They both turned their heads and as she did so, she saw, beyond the tents and campfires, sunlight strike a line of steel-clad riders rumbling down the slope with lowered lances.

12

The Glory of War

Religion: Kore

And thus it was that Corineus ascended unto Heaven, and through his sacrifice, Mankind were gifted the gnosis, and thus their freedom. For this reason Corineus is marked as the holiest of men, and his worship has spread far and wide, in Yuros and even unto Antiopia. In time the praise of Kore and his chosen son Corineus will rise unto the heavens and they will be worshipped in every corner of Urte, and then will Mankind be truly redeemed.

BOOK OF KORE

Johan Corin led the group who found the gnosis, and thus has been made a god, but he was just a man, and did not even survive the Ritual of Ascendancy. Do I hate him? No, though I hate what has been done in his name.

ANTONIN MEIROS, HEBUSALIM, 783

Southern Dhassa, on the continent of Antiopia
Awwal (Martrois) 929
9ᵗʰ month of the Moontide

Keeping a lance steady on a galloping khurne was damned hard, especially when it was careering over undulating ground. But the beasts seemed to flow, as if their senses had somehow been enhanced so they could read the ground so perfectly that Malevorn barely had to concentrate. A ragged boy-child ran across his path, chased by a woman. His khurne's horn tossed the boy aside, momentarily

240

skewered then gone before he had registered the sight, then his lance took the woman in her side as she turned towards him. With a torn shriek she was gone and so was the lance, stuck in her body and wrenched from his grasp. Beside him Raine rode down another woman as she was halfway through transforming: her body was a hideous bone- and flesh-popping mess that burst apart as the khurne's hooves slammed down on her. Malevorn's steed leaped a tent and its fore-hooves crushed the skull of a girl cowering behind the canvas without breaking stride. He felt an exultant energy rise inside him: the exhilaration of combat, when your fate depended upon luck and skill in equal measure. His blood sang.

<Wheel right,> crackled Dranid's voice through his head, sounding more alive than he'd been for months. *<Malevorn, first point, Dominic second!>*

He drew his sword and obeyed, and within seconds they were smashing through a small cluster of half-beasts and their whelps, cutting them down ruthlessly. Behind them, Quintius' riders had slowed and were hacking at the shrieking women they'd herded into the middle of the camp. In a haze of dust and blood, Malevorn followed Dranid as they peeled off, slowed to a trot and rode towards the edge of the camp, facing the broken land beyond.

When the rest of the Dokken come, it'll be from here. He wondered how many were out there, and how far away. He glanced right, and signalled for Dominic to close up. The young Acolyte's sword was bloody and his eyes wide, but he slowed his khurne and moved parallel to Malevorn, fifty yards away, Raine and Dranid pounded onwards to their allotted positions.

In the broken lands before him, the rising sun blasted into his retinas. He twisted a little to avoid the worst of it, and extended his senses. There were only two figures visible: a grey-haired man in a short tunic and a diminutive young Keshi woman. He'd glimpsed her at the Isle of Glass. *If she knows where Mercer is, we'll want a word with her.*

He spurred forward as somewhere in the broken lands, a jackal yowled.

For a long moment there was no sound, then what sounded like a hundred voices answered its cry.

Cymbellea di Regia sped along a narrow defile, seeking a hiding place. Sunlight punched through the gaps in the land. Every second exposed her more to these hunters with decades of experience in stalking and killing.

There must be somewhere . . .

A mile wasn't far: 1760 yards, and easily traversed. She searched frantically, terrified that Wornu might appear before she'd found the refuge she needed.

Hessaz's skill-set was too much like her own, but Wornu's was not and that gave her a chance. She and Zaqri had agreed that she had to find Wornu's blind spot or die. Of course, it also meant she was going up against someone who could crush her with a single blow – but the plan was to not give him the chance, instead, to disorient him with unfamiliar gnosis until Zaqri arrived to finish him off.

My life's in the hands of the man who killed my mother. Sol et Lune, how did I get into this?

She scrambled over a small rise and couldn't stop herself from glancing back when she heard a jackal yowl from the north, where Hessaz had started. It sounded horribly near. Then she spotted what she'd been seeking: a crevice just wide enough to slide into. She used Air-gnosis and glided over to it so there would be no tracks, landed at the edge and lowered herself inside. This crack in the land was barely two feet wide and it smelled of dead animal, but she wriggled inside until she was out of the light and lying flat.

The next step was harder. She crossed her arms over her chest and closed her eyes, trying to slow her frantically beating heart. She needed to be calm for this exacting task. It took far too long, minutes when it should take seconds, but she was entirely self-taught in spiritualism, the art of travelling outside the body – she'd only unlocked it by accident, when she'd awakened from a deep sleep to find herself looking down on her own body, lying with the other girls asleep in the maiden's wagon. Her body had looked so lifeless beneath her she'd thought herself dead and she'd panicked, screaming as her insubstantial astral body flickered about the confined space – but none of the other girls woke; no one else heard a sound she made. She raged and wept and pleaded; she shook them and found their bodies as immovable as stone, her hardest blow unfelt. Only the rising sun had driven her back into her body.

She'd learned a lot since then, all by trial and error, and if she concentrated, she could now leave her body at will. She was too scared this morning to achieve it easily, but finally there came that *tearing* and she pulled free like a seabird rising from the water. Her spiratus flowed upwards, leaving her body behind, unmoving, barely breathing, but alive. She flashed out of the crevice and into the shadow of a rock-fall. Normally she avoided sunlight when doing this – it *burned*, a dreadful searing pain – but this time she had no choice.

By now she could feel Wornu's approach: he was like a rolling boulder to her gnostic senses, loudly trundling closer and closer. He was making no effort to conceal himself – she guessed he was doing it on purpose to show her how little he feared her. She flitted from shadow to shadow until she was in his path, and prepared to face him.

He came out of the east with the sun behind him, casting him into silhouette. He bore a huge hunting spear, just as Zaqri had predicted, fashioned in a few minutes from stone and wood and the gnosis. No doubt Hessaz and Zaqri had done the same, but she didn't have the Earth- or sylvanic-gnosis to do the same.

But I have other skills . . .

She willed a small rock-fall with telekinesis to draw his attention, then stepped into the light as if blundering about helplessly and pulled her spiratus half into the world of substance, allowing him to see her.

The dark shape went still. 'Cymbellea?'

She froze in surprise. It wasn't Wornu.

It was Zaqri.

The plan wasn't ideal, but it was the best Zaqri could come up with under the circumstances. In a stand-up fight Cym would be useless, and he was not certain he would prevail one-on-one with Wornu, let alone if Hessaz was involved. They needed an edge: something that would enable them to take down one of their enemies fast. Despite being the stronger, Zaqri believed Wornu was the more vulnerable, especially to the surprising ability Cymbellea had revealed last night.

Cymbellea. Her name shivered through his spine; her restless face and windblown hair tangled up his thoughts. An unbroken colt with brilliant eyes and a piercing mind. He refused to believe that beneath the armour of her blood vendetta she did not feel for him what he felt. He'd wanted her so badly that he had almost disgraced himself, not once but many times these past few months. And yet the moment of consummation had been spoiled by its necessity, and her coldness to him.

I'll not lie with her again until she is willing – or until we are together in the grave.

He scooped up a handful of twigs and stones and hurriedly forged them into javelins using sylvan- and Earth-gnosis. No doubt Wornu would have created a war-spear and Hessaz a bow. Once armed, he began to trot southwest in long, loping strides, aiming to intercept Hessaz. It pained him to face her: Hessaz and Ghila had been so alike that she could as easily have been his mate as Ghila. In the end Ghila's more impish nature had appealed more than her fiery, tenacious sister, and he'd never regretted the choice, for all Ghila's faults.

I didn't pick this fight, Hessaz.

He had run less than half a mile when suddenly there came a rumble like thunder from the southeast. He frowned at the heavens. Thunder usually presaged a dust-storm, which would make this Noose messy indeed. But there was no wind, and the sky was clear all the way to the southern coastal ranges.

If it isn't thunder, what is it? He paused as the very earth seemed to go still, opened all his gnostic and natural senses and *listened*. If he really, really concentrated, he could hear a pin drop. Or the cry of a young child, more than two miles away . . .

No—!

As he realised what was happening he dropped his javelins and fell into lion-shape without breaking stride, pelting back towards camp. The Noose was forgotten in his desperation to protect his people.

The blow was like a punch to his side: an arrow hammered into his flanks, through his ribcage and into his lungs. For about two seconds he barely felt it, then the force of the blow made him stagger sideways. His legs went from under him and his forward momentum threw him into a face-grazing slide. Dust filled his mouth and nostrils and eyes, and all his gasping couldn't inflate his lungs. Blood bubbled up into his throat and his ribs started grinding in agony against the wooden shaft, each movement sending the jagged stone point ripping deeper inside.

He blinked his eyes clear and tried to stand.

He couldn't.

Hessaz appeared, another arrow nocked and her face pitiless.

'Cymbellea?'

She waited as Zaqri jogged towards her, his face splitting into a satisfied smile. 'Wornu didn't see me coming. I flew low in eagle form and took him from behind unawares.' He hefted the war-spear, kissed the shaft in his right hand. 'The big bastard wasn't the man he thought he was.'

Could it really be so easy? She sagged in relief, her arms opening as she forgot in the relief of the moment that she hated him, even as some nagging part wondered at his uncharacteristic gloating, and how his voice sounded strange ...

He bent back his arm and hurled the spear right at her chest.

She gaped at him, fatally frozen by the sudden violence. The spear took her between the breasts with full force ...

... and passed right through her spiratus.

It still hurt like Hel: the spear had substance and she did not, so its passing tore a hole right through her aetheric form and out the other side. She clutched the hole in her spiritus like a death wound.

Then it closed, she staggered, flickered and was whole again.

Wornu! How could I ever have been so stupid? His true face emerged as he lost concentration and stared at her, baffled.

She silently berated herself. *He can* shape-change, *stupido!* She darted into the shadows again and tried to regain her composure, to keep herself *here*. Thunder rolled in the distance, but neither Cym nor Wornu noticed. Ten feet apart, they locked eyes, and Wornu's big brutal face went slack as he struggled to reconcile what he had just seen.

Cym threw a burst of light at his face and made herself vanish.

Hessaz stared down at Zaqri, a single tear running down her left cheek. 'You were the only one I wanted,' she whispered. 'Did you even know?'

The camp ... He tried to forge the thought into something she could hear, mind to mind, then tried to speak, but all that came was a gurgle and his mouth filled with blood.

'You made me envy my sister. My own sister.' She drew the bow to full power, took aim. 'Then when she died, I thought ... *But no*. You'd seen that damned gypsy and it was all her-her-her. You bastard. You're not worthy of my love.'

He tried again. <*The camp ... the Inquisitors ... Your daughter—!*>

This time she heard him. She looked around wildly, then focused. 'No,' she whispered, as the realisation struck her. She lost her grip on the arrow and it fell into the sand. '*Pernara!*' she screamed, and in an instant she was gone and a giant raven was tearing out of the dell and across the sky.

Zaqri tried to move again, tried to change, but no matter what he did the shaft remained imbedded in him. His roar of agony came out as a whimper. For a few moments the world was touched with brilliance: a vivid, unbelievable colour. Then as swiftly it turned grey, then black.

Cym pressed her spiratus behind a boulder in a deadly game of hide and seek: keep Wornu occupied until Zaqri came, that was the plan. He couldn't kill her, not unless he caught her full on with a mage-bolt, but Wornu hadn't figured that out yet. Then an awful howl rose from all about her: a cry of terrible, awful fear and rage.

It was the sound of sixty Souldrinker warriors howling as one.

Wornu heard it too and backed away, his eyes round as saucers. 'The camp, gypsy! The camp! We have to go!'

You might, but I rukking well don't.

'Peace, girl! Pax!' He threw his hands up, searching for her wildly. 'I must go!'

<*Then go,*> she urged him.

She wasn't sure if he had heard, but either way, he turned and ran. *Thank you, Mater Luna! Thank you thank you thank you.*

She cancelled the spiratus and her form dissolved into a streak of unseen mist that tore across the desert. All she could see was light, all she could feel was pain as her spiratus started fraying and burning as she sought the faint call of her own heartbeat. *Closer, closer . . .*

There!

She fell into her body and it jerked upright, almost hitting her head on the rock ceiling above. Her heart thudding, she wriggled out of the crevice and crawled into the open. Far above, giant ravens were streaking across the sky, flying southeast. If any of them saw her, they didn't care.

Not a single part of her wanted to follow them. She turned her face to the north and ran for her life.

The greybeard and the Keshi girl had vanished by the time Malevorn was in position. The birdsong was gone and the air was deathly still. He twirled his longsword in his hand idly, facing the badlands and the risen sun. The terrain looked like the aftermath of giants having a pottery-smashing competition; the low sun turned his vision into a dazzling smear. *Brilliant tactics, Quintius. Are you trying to get us killed?*

Probably, was the chilling answer. *They don't want us – probably don't need us. And Adamus can always find a new arse to fuck.* He turned to Dominic, on his right. The young Acolyte looked jittery. <*Close up, Dom,*> he sent. <*They're out there.*>

He saw Dominic blanch and urge his khurne closer. Beyond him, Raine and Dranid were holding steady, surveying the mess before them. There were any number of breaks in the rubble from where an attack might come. He glanced behind him to where Quintius' men were slaughtering babes and pregnant women and no doubt calling it glorious.

Is Mercer in there? Is the Scytale?

He muttered instructions to his steed and edged closer to Dominic, wishing it was Raine at his flank. She would hold her nerve, but something had cracked inside Dom and it made him vulnerable to predators like Adamus Crozier.

<Steady, Dom. The first sign of trouble, you head for Dranid and Raine.> He widened his call. <Dranid, Raine, we should close up. If they come in force we're screwed.> He saw Raine wave in acknowledgment and spur her khurne towards him, Dranid following at a canter.

He began to wonder if the flogging they'd get for disobeying their orders might be better than what was to come. *What's a few scars on my back if that's the price for getting out alive?* From out of sight came a chorus of howls and shrieks and deep-throated roars: a cacophony of bestial throats venting all at once. He readied his wards and kindled fire in his left hand. Somehow he felt calmer as the moment approached.

Maybe there're just a dozen or so of them out there. Maybe I'm worrying about nothing.

Then with a yowl, a leopard came bounding between two immense smashed boulders and hurtled towards him, eating up the hundred yards separating them in huge strides. More creatures followed, most on all fours, but some were bipedal: immense, ape-like forms who bounded semi-upright. Massive birds zipped along above them, their cries rending the air as they came.

He raised his sword.

I am an Andevarion. I refuse to die here.

'Mal, what do we do?' Dominic called in a shaky voice.

'It's too late to run – they're faster than us. Close up, Dom. We hold on until Quintius comes.' He glanced beyond him and saw that Dranid and Raine were coming towards him at full-pelt now. He felt a surge of gratitude and loyalty. They were a Fist of the Kore: bloodied, depleted, but still strong. Still the elite.

'Let's give these animals Hell!' he shouted.

He set sights on the leopard and hurled the ball of flame in his hand.

Huriya sucked in her breath as the Dokken flowed towards the four Inquisitors and their horned beasts. Beside her, perched on top of a great pile of boulders, Tomacz growled, his jaw reshaping into something more primitive. He hunched over as blood and drool began to run from his mouth. Above and behind were their kindred, swarming towards the enemy. Huriya recognised two of the Acolytes, the handsome young dark-haired male and the ugly woman: they'd been in the group which had assailed them at the Isle of Glass – so they were obviously still trailing them.

She bared her teeth at the effrontery. <Rip them apart!> she urged her Brethren.

Beyond them, the camp was in flames and Inquisitors were milling about in the middle of it, hacking into the women and pounding the children beneath their hooves. Only these four guarded the perimeter. The shapeshifters flowed towards them, an incoming tide – then fire and lightning blossomed from the hands of the riders and struck the oncoming beasts in a torrent of coruscating blasts.

She blinked, faintly dazed, even at that distance, as the front ranks of the attackers were engulfed. Amidst the fires she saw blue cones of light, the gnostic shields of her Dokken, winking out as the combined fury of the four Inquisitors burned through them. The heat and choking smoke rolled over the ground, blinding them all, and the attack faltered. Chasander, the leopard who'd led the charge, was a crisped husk, all those near him likewise burned to skeletons. The whole pack felt their agony, linked as they were in mind and soul, and they screamed together.

But the fallen had absorbed the first fires of the Inquisitors, allowing the second rank to leap over their fallen kin and into battle. And more were arriving all the time, coming in threes and fours from the other sides of the Noose, desperate to join battle. Some she recognised, like big Darice, goat-headed Kraderz, and Elando with his fanciful bat-form, but most were just bestial shapes, hurtling into the fray.

She saw a giant bear launch himself at the dark-haired Inquisitor, who cut the bear in half with one savage blow. A jackal flew at the woman and was skewered on a lance then hurled away. The older Inquisitor on the left spurred his steed into the press and as she watched, hooves and horn and blade were all dealing death. More fire bloomed about the fourth one; he might look like a stringy weakling but there was nothing weak about his gnosis. Close-up images of the dead and dying, shadow-bursts of pain and all the psychic debris of wounds and deathblows resounded through the pack-link. She willed the link away and gripped the rock beside her for support. *How do they endure it?*

She saw other pack-members staggering as she was, overwhelmed by what was happening to their family. Beside her, Tomacz was completing his change. Great canines had sprouted from his mouth as his lips retracted and now he was dropping to his haunches as the wolf within him fully emerged.

Huriya concentrated her mind and prepared to take part. She focused her gnosis on the slender young knight, the vulnerable-looking one, who was preparing to face big Darice. She gathered her mental forces. 'You're first,' she whispered.

Malevorn's khurne reared up and drove its front hooves into the skull of a jackal. He clung on, as much with telekinesis and instinct as training, and hacked blindly at a dark shape looming up on his right. His gnostically enhanced blade crunched into the shifter's skull and a black bear fell to the ground. He hauled on the reins, gathered more gnosis and blazed fire at a massive raven that raked at his head. The bird's bones appeared, a shadow in the flare of red-orange, and he blinked and spun round in time to see Dominic go down.

Raine had just beheaded a ram-headed man wielding a battle-axe and Dranid was pressing back a whole snarling group of creatures. Dominic had been fighting confidently, taking heart from the feats of those with him, when suddenly he gasped and clutched his skull and his shields fell apart.

'*Dom!*' Malevorn spurred towards him, but the damage was done: he'd been rendered momentarily helpless and in that instant the Dokken surged forward, yowling like nothing he had ever heard. Jaws clamped on Dominic's legs and those of his khurne. The construct went down, screaming like a human as jagged teeth ripped it open and its entrails spewed onto the ground. Malevorn bellowed, hurling beasts aside with his gnosis as he tried to reach Dominic, but he was already too late. Dominic's boyish face had vanished in a spray of blood and fur as a giant she-bear ripped him apart.

<Mal!>

Raine's voice tore him back to sanity. He yanked on the reins and shouted at his khurne to get clear. The steed thrashed about, seeking an opening, and Malevorn rained down more fire and lightning, trying to drive the shifters away, to get a few seconds' respite, though exhaustion was crowding in and he felt breathless, drained.

The Dokken fell back from Dominic's corpse, snarling triumphantly. But more were arriving every minute, and now they'd started circling around to cut off the three surviving Inquisitors. He reached Dranid and Raine and threw a look back at the camp, but it was lost in a haze of smoke.

<WHERE THE FUCK ARE YOU, QUINTIUS?> he bellowed into the aether.

Instead it was only Artus Leblanc's mental voice he heard. *<Hold your position, Andevarion.>* Then in a more intimate sending, *<Enjoy Hel, Shithead.>*

Rukk you! If I get out this . . .

Dranid reached him, his breath gusting but his face a mask of calm. Blue gnosis-fire licked along his blade, but his khurne was visibly wobbling. He cast Malevorn an ashen look. 'Quintius isn't coming, is he? It's up to us.'

Raine swore, and blasted fire at a jackal venturing too close. The Dokken still circled, catching their breath. Many had flowed past them, heading for the camp, but enough remained to cut them off from help, and they were circling closer.

<As one, we break for the camp,> Malevorn told the other two. *<It's our only chance. On my call!>*

Malevorn felt something frighteningly powerful touch his mind, then retreat. His wards against mental attack flared into life and he followed the point of attack back to an outlined figure on the boulders above. The Keshi girl, he realised, as much from instinct as anything. *Kore's Blood, how strong is she?*

He opened his mouth to call for the retreat.

But the little Keshi witch struck first.

Dranid suddenly yowled and wrenched at his reins, first left and then right, sending his khurne into a mad dance as his defences collapsed, and even as he did, an arrow slammed into his khurne's neck. The steed wobbled and fell, and Malevorn could hear Dranid's leg audibly crunching as he struck the rocky ground. The Inquisitor bellowed in pain as another wave of Dokken launched themselves at him. Raine and Malevorn tried to reach their captain, but the press was immense and all they could do was block and shield and fight for their own lives, using whatever came to hand – telekinesis, magefire, thrusting swords into mouths and throats.

The whole world *lurched*.

Malevorn's khurne lashed out as something gripped its back legs and he glimpsed a massive python just before it wrapped itself about the khurne's hindquarters and dragged it down. He beheaded the snake as he rolled clear, fell onto the body of a wolf and used it to clamber to his feet. He saw another arrow puncture the ribs of Raine's khurne and she too flew free. He ran to her side, beheading another snake as he went, then cutting a raven in two as he reached her and stood back to back.

Dranid was gone, a shapeless, gory mess beneath a pile of ravaging beasts.

And still there was no sign of rescue from the other Fist.

< Adamus!> he demanded, pleaded, begged, *<ADAMUS!>*

Raine's shields blocked an arrow from the right as they circled, seeking a weak point, something to attack, but they were confronted by an unbroken wall of beasts, slavering and growling. More giant birds shrieked above, eagles and vultures and ravens, all man-sized.

<Raine, I'm going to fly us out. When I signal, grab my belt.>

<Got it.> Her mental voice was like his, terse and calm.

Kore's Blood, she's wonderful.

A big grey wolf arrived at the fringes, followed by a bipedal bull with a massive war-spear. Then he spotted the archer, a scrawny crop-haired bitch with a hatchet face. They began to close in.

<Don't let them take us alive,> Raine whispered into his brain.

<They won't. Grab me!> He reached for his Air-gnosis as she gripped his belt. *< Let's g—>*

He began to lift her as the Dokken lunged. The grey wolf leaped and he cleaved its skull, saw it fall back into the maelstrom of beasts, heard Raine shouting in fury as she hacked a raven apart, and then—

—*absolute, overpowering agony.*

There was a torture device used by the Inquisition called an Iron Maiden: a metal casket, lined inside with spikes which were screwed deeper, slowly, bit by bit, so that the prisoner was pierced all over, and eventually bled to death – those few who didn't break and spill every secret they'd ever had first.

The Keshi girl's gnosis struck Malevorn like an Iron Maiden slamming closed on his soul. It was as if his mental shields did not exist. Her power dwarfed his and she rammed fresh bloody pain into every part of his body. Beneath him, he heard Raine scream and he could feel that same agony engulfing her. Her hand lost grip of his belt and before his telekinesis could catch her, she'd plunged to the ground. Bullhead caught her wrist in his hand and snapped it as easily as snapping a twig.

Malevorn tried to reach her, but his whole body was shutting down. The Keshi girl's telekinesis held him in the air and he watched helplessly as the beasts engulfed his lover. Her mail came apart like tin, and her body like a gutted rabbit. Her mouth spewed a wordless bloody spray, her face bulged and her eyes flew wide, staring up at him as he rotated helplessly in the air.

<I love you,> she said into his mind.

She vanished beneath the press of fur and blood.

He tried to do something, anything, screaming his loss and hatred in grief and fury, but the Keshi girl's face flashed in the sky, and then all creation winked out.

Cym ran north, keeping a wary eye on the skies above. Oversized birds no longer streaked across the skies and there was smoke rising from the direction of the camp. If she tuned in her gnosis she could make out cries of fury and distress; she had no idea what had happened but she hoped it would keep them busy for a long time. She needed to get outside the Noose arena and then find a deep hole and crawl into it. Even the best scryer struggled to penetrate stone. If she could evade capture for a few days, maybe they would give up and move on.

Then she saw the vultures, circling somewhere to the left of her path, and she stopped and peered at them. *I've got no food*, she reminded herself, as if justifying her subconscious urging, which was pushing her to go that way for other reasons. She gave in and scurried through a narrow defile. The palate of scents and colours deepened as the sun rose higher and started to warm the earth. She climbed another slope and stopped dead, staring in horror.

A lion lay on its right side, an arrow jutting into the air. Blood was caked about the shaft and running down its flank. A dozen vultures were already on the ground, screeching and milling as they squabbled for the right to feed first, working up the courage to dart in and tear at the still-warm flesh. Another three dozen were still in the air.

Even from forty yards away, she could tell it was Zaqri, and a range of emotions hit her. At first she felt cheated, that someone else had killed the man she'd pledged to end. Then surprise, that a single arrow had killed him when he'd seemed so competent as a mage. *Unless Hessaz caught him with his guard down.* And with that, a tableau formed in her mind: Zaqri, like Wornu, overcome with grief and rage, abandoning the contest and running for the camp ... with ruthless Hessaz lying in wait ...

Anger. Loss.

All those nights, lying beside him for warmth, knowing he wanted her but wouldn't take what wasn't offered. Teaching her, sharing his life with her, offering all he was, though she threw it at his feet, over and again. The lion watching over her at night, protecting her. His golden smile and confident manner; his majesty in any shape.

Why I can see these things clearly only now he's dead?

She stood up and strode forward, blazing mage-fire into the nearest vulture and killing it instantly. The rest took to the air in a storm of indignant screeches and beating wings, but she ignored them. She reached the fallen lion's side and stared down at him. He wasn't moving. The crude arrow in his side was buried deep.

She found herself blinking back tears, choking on wet breaths of air that clogged her throat, grieving for what could have been. *If another had slain my mother, what then?*

She fell to her knees and put her hand on his side, remembering his face above her in the tent, and the heat of his body. That heat was fading fast.

You wanted him dead, the vultures seemed to be calling. *Enjoy the moment . . . and leave us the carcase.*

Breath wheezed faintly from his open jaws, and his ribcage quivered.

Rukka mio, he's alive!

Malevorn Andevarion woke from a nightmare of bodies piled on top him and creatures tearing at him with bestial faces and huge teeth, pulling him down no matter how many he hacked away with his sword . . . and then . . . all he saw was Her. The Keshi girl. She'd reached through the tangled bodies to where he lay pinned, her angel-whore face smiling beatifically. She reached out, touched his temple.

She was a goddess – an eastern goddess, arisen to destroy all that he was. She was terrifying, all-powerful.

His fears increased as he looked about him, his pupils dilating as he sought to make sense of the darkness. An animal reek filled the air, and the stench of bodily waste and blood. His chainmail was torn like paper, the boiled leather ripped apart and a steel helmet beside him crushed like clay. A wave of pain struck him and he flinched. Dimly he sensed amber eyes all about him, shimmering in the darkness.

He cringed fearfully.

Then the goddess spoke, in a voice forged from miracles that vibrated through him like a perfectly formed note. His tangled bewilderment settled into something like order. A thousand bars of light flashed across his vision, then vanished, and his intellect plunged into the void. 'Get up, Malevorn Andevarion. Come here.'

He looked about him blankly as his body rose without his volition. Yellow eyes sent their hatred at him, but no one moved as he pulled himself to his feet, his ruined armour clinging awkwardly to him as he stood. A mailed sleeve gave way and fell to the ground. He could barely move for the fresh scabs that pulled and tore as he moved.

He'd been lying on the battlefield, a valley floor of sun-blasted sand and rocks, dotted with spindly brown bushes. The ground was covered in bodies and soaked in blood. Perhaps red bushes would grow here now. It was sunset, he thought, and all about him, men and women were labouring, digging holes and carrying rocks – and bodies, too, mostly of animals and half-animals with limbs and heads lopped off, or smashed or broken, with torsos pierced and covered in blood. There were four horses too … no, not horses; khurnes, their bodies partially gorged upon. Beyond, he could see tents and other belongings smouldering.

The goddess waited patiently for him. She motioned for him to kneel before her and his body did so without consulting his mind. A small independent part of him babbled away, repeating, *She did something to me! She's been inside my mind!* He knew the sensation – he had been trained to recognise it, and how to fight it. But the bindings he sensed inside him were stronger than any he could have imagined. This was Ascendant-level gnosis, far beyond him; for now at least, he belonged utterly to her.

'Do you know what has happened to you?' she asked.

He shook his head slowly as his eyes fell on three headless, dismembered human bodies, white-skinned and blood-drenched. Inquisitors. He looked at her, a question in his mouth he flinched from asking. She smiled and pointed languidly to a place over his shoulder.

Three lances had been buried in the ground, point up. On them were skewered three heads, the steel tips piercing right through the crowns. Flesh and blood had dried to gore and tendrils of rotting meat in the sun.

Dranid, shredded until he was barely recognisable.

Dominic, his naïve face caught in final bewilderment that such a thing could ever happen.

And Raine, her ugly-loveliness frozen in a moment of softness.

He dropped his face to the dirt and howled his grief.

The Keshi girl laid a hand on his shoulder. 'Yes. We slew your woman, and one of the pack took her soul. These others also.' She reached down, lifted his chin and met his tear-wracked eyes. 'Do you remember what else happened?'

He tried to recall. Nothing came.

She smiled her radiant smile. 'You and I had a chat, remember? I needed one of you alive, to understand how you found us and what you know. Your commander would have been more suitable, or perhaps the . . . what is the word . . . crozier? But they fled. The only one I could preserve was you.'

He remembered how to speak. 'Kill me,' he croaked.

She shook her head. 'Not yet, pretty boy. You're now my personal slave – my bodyguard. You really are a formidable fighter. My . . . *memories* . . . go back five hundred years, and I do not believe I have never seen anyone as skilled as you. You slew dozens of my kindred. If I had not been present, it is likely the four of you would have defeated us, or at the least, slain many, many more.' She stroked his cheek, making his skin tingle. 'So you belong to me now, until I have no more use for you. Then you will be consumed.' Her voice was entirely matter of fact.

He stared at her feet and tried to reach for his gnosis, but of course there was nothing there. He tried to leap at her, but his body wouldn't respond.

She felt his struggle, though, and laughed. 'I cannot let you use your gnosis: that has been chained.' She bent over him, peered into his eyes. 'I've been inside your mind, Slave. It's a vile place. You are a self-centred, arrogant, bullying piece of dung, aren't you?'

He bowed his head. Her criticism wounded him on some profound level; that this goddess might not esteem him. He retreated into that small scrap of independent thought and tried to rally himself, to think or to plan, even to mourn, but she pulled him back with a shimmering thread of gnosis and forced him to attend her again.

'So, Slave: tell me everything you know about your comrades and how you found us.' She smiled brightly, and added, directly into his head, *<Then you and I will have a private chat about the Scytale of Corineus.>*

13

Taking the Long Way Home

The Rimoni Empire: Military Organisation

*Despite their defeat, we found much to admire in the discipline and profession-
alism of the Rimoni legions. Each was one being, five thousand swords and
hearts, but one mind. We have therefore left the basic model intact. Modern
developments such as more efficient missile weapons and, of course, the gnosis
have made the Rondian legion even more effective.*

ANNALS OF PALLAS

*Southern Keshi, southwest of Shaliyah, on the continent of Antiopia
Thani (Aprafor) 929
10th month of the Moontide*

From a low rise, Ramon watched the lines of men and wagons as they
snaked through the shallow valley below. They were making slow
progress – what had from a distance looked like a dead flat plain
turned out to be a rubble-strewn nightmare of wheel-breaking holes
and ruts. Even on the poor road running through it they were making barely ten miles a day. That wasn't enough. A Keshi skiff had been
seen by one of the scouts, searching the valley to the west of them; it
wouldn't be long before enemy cavalry showed up. The Efratis River
was still at least a week's journey to the south.

About him were the twenty men of his new cohort. They'd been
sticking close to him, though they were all on foot and he was
mounted. The terrain made keeping up with him pretty easy. He'd
offered them horses if they could get some, but they'd declined.

'Cavalry are soft bastards,' they all responded. He suspected they thought the same of magi.

He waved a hand at the tall, deeply tanned officer, Pilus Lukaz. He was Vereloni, from one of the towns lining the Imperial Road; his people were kin to the Rimoni and Silacian, with similarly dark skin and hair. Fourteen years ago Lukaz had run away and joined the legions marching past, en route for the Second Crusade. Now he was a Pilus, the leader of a twenty-man cohort. Lukaz was tall and athletic, with a natural air of command. Ramon was beginning to like him a lot.

He swung down off Lu and slapped the horse's rump, sending her trotting off seeking forage. Food for the horses was only one of a thousand logistical problems they were having. 'How are the men, Pilus Lukaz?'

Lukaz chewed over his reply. 'They are unsettled, sir. Defeat was an unknown to us, and we appear to be fleeing deeper into enemy territory, are we not?' His deadpan tone never changed, whatever he was discussing.

'I prefer to think of it as taking the long way home,' Ramon replied easily. 'Tell me about your cohort, Pilus.'

Lukaz eyed him cautiously. 'What would you like to know, sir?'

'Let's start with how you array in combat, so I can understand how we will be able to work together.'

Lukaz took his time to reply; there was never anything hasty about him, nothing unconsidered, though he wasn't even thirty yet. It was part of what made him a leader, Ramon decided, and something he himself might do well to emulate.

'Well, sir, when we face the enemy, the strongest and most solid go to the front.' He pointed to a clump of big Rondians. 'Serjant Manius, with Dolmin, Ferdi, Trefeld.' He then jabbed a thumb at a pair of blond Hollenians. 'And Hedman and Gannoval. They anchor us, use their bulk to keep us solid. Once you start going backwards, you're rukked.'

'So six in front.'

'Then another six behind them,' he went on, 'smaller men, but reliable. It was the Rimoni who worked out that a man can fight for only a few minutes at a time before he needs a breather. The second rank rotate with the front line as frequently as they can.' The second-rank men were also clustered together, around a big, genial-looking man with somewhat swarthy features. 'That's Serjant Vidran: he keeps them together: the rest of his line are Bowe, Ilwyn and Holdyne, Gal Herde and his brother Jan.'

'This Vidran looks big enough to be a front-ranker?'

'Aye, but he's a little too fond of living – he thinks too much.' Lukaz clicked his tongue. 'The front-rankers take the brunt of the fighting, sir, and too much thinking isn't a good thing. You just shove and stab and rely on the man behind you to pull you out before you run out of steam. But Vid's smart; he knows exactly when to switch the front and second ranks, so he makes that call, mostly. He's best exactly where he is.'

'And the rest?'

'Eight others, sir: Me and Baden with the standard, then six flankmen, three on either side. The flankmen have to be smarter, because when the enemy can't break your middle, they'll try and get round you. The flankmen are our best swordsmen, but they're usually lighter and faster, not the sort to anchor a line. They'll look to flank the enemy if we're going forward, or keep us from being flanked if we're defending. They've got to be good at reading the fight, and reacting.' He pointed out the third cluster of men. 'They tend to stick together too, but they're more rivals than mates. We've got Ollyd, Neubeau and Tolomon on the right, Harmon, Briggan and Kent on the left. Stroppy types, mostly, think they know everything.'

'They give you trouble?'

Lukaz looked a little uncomfortable. 'They're all good men, sir.'

'You've got them well-organised: like pieces on a tabula board, all positioned to best advantage,' Ramon commented.

'You have to know what you're working with, sir. The old pilus taught me that. Armies are big, but they're made up of men: you put them where they understand their role and they'll do it, most times at least.'

'I'd understood the Crusades didn't involve much fighting?'

'The magi might think that, sir, but with only fifteen magi to a legion, there are a lot of places where we rankers have to act alone, usually against a Hel of a lot more Noories than us. Especially on garrison duty. When a legion gets left to garrison a town, the magi either ask for transfers or down tools and go drinking. They tend to leave the actual soldiering to us.' He coughed a little self-consciously. 'No disrespect meant, sir.'

'None taken. I'm not like that, Pilus.'

'We've noticed, sir. Right from the start, you took an interest – the men like that.'

'What did you make of Shaliyah?'

Lukaz paused again, considering his words, then said frankly, 'You magi let us down. Why did you not see the storm coming?'

'A storm like that takes days to create, and considerable maintenance to hold it together, and you're right: energy like that should have been detected. But if you know where and when it must strike, you could prepare it out of our "gnostic hearing".'

'So the sultan really did know we were coming?'

'To the day, and for at least a month, I'd say.'

Lukaz blinked at that, then returned to his subject. 'Also sir, when the fighting started and the enemy magi appeared, all ours went haring off, looking to duel them, leaving the rankers unprotected. If they'd concentrated on protecting us instead, we could have held the line and backed out of the path of the storm.'

That was pretty much what Ramon had been thinking. 'How should rankers and magi fight together, in your view?'

Lukaz took a while to answer, but Ramon waited patiently. He was getting used to the man's way. 'Everything I've heard you magi say is that defensive gnosis is stronger than offensive, so those magi who fling spells over half the battlefield are just showing off, wasting energy. Seems to me a mage's place is not glory-hunting upfront or in the air above, but right in the middle of a cohort, defending the men, sir. Let the soldiers win the battle for you.'

'That is the opposite of what we're taught,' Ramon said.

Lukaz grunted. 'Apart from a few one-sided scraps in Argundy, the only battles between mage-led legions were back in Noros, during the Revolt. The way I heard it, the Noromen magi did like I'm saying and were the stronger for it. But those big-knob Pallacian magi don't want to fight as a team with mere rankers: they want to be riding a flying horse out in front of everyone. It's all duels and glory with them. That might be fine when you're fighting weaker enemies, but in a close fight, teamwork is what wins the day.'

He fell silent, and Ramon gave him a wry smile. 'That's a lot to think on. Thank you, Pilus.'

'Sir.' Lukaz went to leave, then stopped. 'May I speak frankly, sir?'

I thought you were. 'Of course.'

'The opium – you saved us with it, but I don't believe you brought it with us to burn on a battlefield.' He didn't wait for Ramon's response. 'Four men have died in this legion alone from the stuff, and more than thirty that I know of in others. It is a blight, sir, and I am ashamed that this legion has been associated with it.'

Ramon hung his head. Any number of lies occurred, but they were a long way behind enemy lines and he wanted this man's respect. Time for the truth. 'My mother . . . is a prisoner of a familioso chief, what we call a Pater Nostra, a Father of the Night. I serve him so that one day I can free her, and her daughter to him, my half-sister. He sent me into the legions to arrange and sell the poppy.'

'Is your family worth the lives of all those men?'

'It is when I bring down his whole familioso and free my home-land from him for ever.'

'You can do this by selling poppy?'

'If I do it right, I can collapse the world around him. More than ten thousand people live in the villages of my home. Are their lives worth less than thirty addicts in a Rondian army?'

Lukaz said slowly, 'You are a dangerous man, Magister.'

'To some, maybe – but not to everyone.' He looked up as a movement in the skies caught his eye, then gave a sudden joyous shout as a square-sailed windskiff came hurtling over the ridge, barely ten feet above the ground. About it were three giant ravens, cawing hoarsely as they darted in to attack, then recoiling from bursts of blue fire.

'Baltus! Here!' Ramon shouted, aloud and with the gnosis, and the skiff swerved towards him as the cohort jumped to their feet. A javelin flew, gouging a line of sparks from a gnostic shield encasing one raven, enough to cause it to bank away. The other two rose higher, calling disappointedly, then soared over the column of men. They circled for a minute, then shot away to the north.

'I guess that means they've found us,' Ramon muttered.

Baltus Prenton guided his skiff towards a flat space nearby and Ramon ran to meet him. The windcraft jolted to a rough, sliding landing, and Baltus sagged in his seat, looking half-dazed.

'Are you all right?' Ramon called.

The Brevian Windmaster looked up with exhausted eyes. His face was drawn, his normal jollity almost eclipsed. 'Sensini! Thank Kore!'

'I don't think anyone's ever used that precise phrase before.' He'd not seen Baltus since a few hours before Shaliyah, when he'd been ordered to find and lead in a caravan of supply-wagons. Ramon had supposed he'd simply kept flying west after learning the army's fate, as the wagons certainly hadn't arrived.

'I've been hunting for you for weeks,' the Windmaster panted, 'and I've had those Kore-bedamned Souldrinkers after me most of that time.'

Ramon felt a quiver in his spine. 'Souldrinkers?'

Baltus said grimly, 'You can tell, if you look at them carefully. There were lots of them, in bird and jackal shape, mostly, on the back trail. They slaughtered the baggage train. I went back to report and found the army gone and the mother of all storms.' He shook his head. 'Why didn't we know the Keshi had magical help?'

'Who knows? How did you find us?'

'You can see a lot from the air. I went high as I dared, to avoid the shifters.' He slapped the side of his craft. 'My *Birdy* did well, but they've got skiffs too – and not all their magi are Dokken, either. They've got both, working together.'

'All the emperor's enemies are banding together,' Ramon observed.

'If they'd caught me—' He drew a finger across his throat. 'They're quick, these Keshi craft with those triangular sails, but their magi are weak, mostly quarter-blood at best. I could out-climb them, and if I called the winds, I could outrun them – and I've got a few tricks up my sleeve too, thank Kore.' He clambered to his feet and stretched wearily. 'So here I am. What's the news? Where's the rest of the army? Where's Echor?'

'Well, if I told you that Seth Korion is in control of what's left of the army, does that give you a measure of how rukked-up this whole expedition is?'

Over the next five days, the remnants of Echor's southern expeditionary force wound out of the broken lands north of the Efratis and onto the floodplain, a vast expanse of silt. During the Moontide the Efratis and its hundreds of tributary rivers usually ran low, though it never fully dried up.

That was the theory, at least. Instead, Seth Korion was staring at the brown torrent raging across the entire floodplain and trying to reconcile it with the crude map in his hands. Around him magi and officers made up their own minds about the best route forward.

'Why is there so much water?' he wondered aloud.

'It's the aftermath of the gnostic storm at Shaliyah,' Ramon Sensini suggested, and that harridan Jelaska immediately nodded her agreement, as did Sigurd Vaas. Renn Bondeau agreed too, and he almost never supported the little Silacian. *I guess he must be right, then.*

'So what do we do?' he said, worried that he sounded weak for asking.

'We stick to the plan,' Ramon replied. 'Fill up the water-wagons, then take the river-road to Ardijah. There's a bridge there, remember.' He glanced at his own copy of the map, which had a lot of extra lines and dots on it. 'Baltus has scouted the way ahead and it's still clear.'

Seth frowned. 'I thought I sent Baltus to scout our rear.'

'Waste of time,' Ramon replied. 'He can't be two places at once, and we need to know what's in front more.'

'But we need to know where the enemy are!'

'We do: twenty miles back. I set some Trip-wards on our back trail and they're being slowly triggered.'

Seth wasn't appeased. 'You changed my order.'

'I *adjusted* it. You were in prayer with the chaplain and Baltus needed fresh orders after he'd confirmed what my Trip-wards had already revealed.' Ramon grinned and waved a hand towards the flowing torrents below. 'At least we've got plenty of water now.'

I should reprimand him. But the proximity of Jelaska Lyndrethuse and Sigurd Vaas, both tough and competent magi, was intimidating. And he'd probably done the right thing. 'Very well,' he said grudgingly.

'Once the Keshi horsemen reach this road, they'll be able to ride us down in a few hours,' Vaas said gruffly. 'We'll need a rearguard.'

'I'll take that, with my maniple,' Renn Bondeau piped up instantly. *Still glory-hunting, even here.* But Bondeau probably was the best man for the job.

Seth was about to agree, when Ramon said, 'I've got a better idea. Let's all do it.'

Renn Bondeau scowled. The rest just looked perplexed.

'The whole army?' Seth asked.

'No, us – we magi, and a few cohorts to deal with any who get through our initial defences. If we can teach them a lesson about following us too close, they'll be slower to pursue, and our rankers will see that they still have magi fighting alongside them. It'll give them something to hang some hope on.'

'An easy victory would boost morale, and maybe buy us the time to reach Ardijah first,' Jelaska agreed, patting him on the shoulder. Seth noticed Severine Tiseme glaring indignantly at this familiarity.

For Kore's sake, now they're fighting over the little villain! 'All right. Let's do that,' Seth said, so that it might look to at least a few people that he was actually in control.

They set up their ambush on the road behind them, with all the magi involved, except for him, Tyron and the healers. Apparently they were 'too valuable' – or maybe it was to maintain the illusion that the commanders were with the main body of the army, or something.

I think they just want to be heroes, Seth thought grumpily, but he left them behind, laying their elaborate plans, and with Tyron, rode west along the road to Ardijah with the footmen. The healers, Lanna Jureigh of the Thirteenth and a greying Estellan woman named Carmina, sole mage survivor of her Brician legion, had two dozen wagons laden with wounded from Shaliyah. The two healers looked exhausted.

'So much for the glory of command,' he commented gloomily to Tyron. His friend looked away; he was no fighter anyway. The chaplain had more worthwhile skills, in Seth's opinion: poetry and theology.

'The credit always goes to the commander in the end,' Tyron told him, which was a comforting thought.

The midday sun might be cooler than during the march across Kesh last year, but it was still bad enough for men raised in the cold climates of Yuros. It wasn't the only problem either: flux had been running through the soldiers, leading Seth to the conclusion that armies were little more than giant defecating machines.

'Sir!' A mounted scout trotted to meet him. 'There is a junction ahead.'

'And?'

'Well, there's a track that leads north, sir, and we don't know what's up there.' He looked over his shoulder uncertainly. 'Sir, do we proceed across the junction, or scout the way north first?'

Seth looked at Tyron. *<I don't know? What should we do?>*

<I'm a chaplain,> Tyron replied, unhelpfully. He might be full of good advice about philosophy and salvation, but had little to say about practical soldiering.

What would Ramon do? Seth found himself wondering. *Halt every-thing and play safe? Or laugh at such a trivial problem? Or maybe . . .*

'Send a cohort of mounted Estellan to scout the track, but keep the column moving,' he ordered, and the scout saluted, and galloped off.

A few minutes later a party of swarthy, dark-haired Estellan – *who don't look very different from the enemy*, now Seth thought about it – thundered past with lances high, dipping the points in salute then wheeling away down the northwards path that vanished into the low hills bordering the floodplain. He and Tyron decided they'd best wait for them to report back, so the column proceeded westwards whilst they chatted about the poet Marcel, who had been commissioned to capture the glory of the Second Crusade. They agreed that his fam-ous line, *pounding hearts resplendent in the intoxication of victory*, seemed to have nothing at all to do with what they were going through, and what's more, made little sense anyway. The poet Guilnes' line, *Gritty eyes bleeding tears of homesickness*, was much closer to reality, they decided.

As the healers' wagons were passing, Seth heard the pounding of hooves on the northern road.

'That will be the Estellan cavalry,' Tyron commented. 'About time.'

'What are they doing?' Seth squinted at a dozen riders who had careered into sight and were thrashing at their horses like madmen. Their hooves shook the earth, far more than he could have believed from so few men. 'Are they racing?'

Then an avalanche of Keshi appeared, screaming to Ahm and bear-ing down on the Estellan riders like the Ghost Hunt of Schlessen myth.

'Kore's Blood!' Seth jerked into motion, glancing swiftly from side to side as he tried to see who or what might be deployed, but there were only wagons full of the wounded in sight, except for the guard cohort that followed him about.

Unbelievably, in the midst of the onset of panic, some rational part of him noted that what he *should* have done was deploy a mani-ple right *there*, where the track narrowed between higher ground, and sent more than just twenty men along the road. But then dread set in, and a kind of paralysis, and all he could do was open and close his mouth like a goldfish, leaving Tyron, beside him, to shriek orders at the pilus.

'Form up, form up,' the chaplain cried. He singled out a runner and ordered, 'Bring men! Any men! Run!'

The young soldier shot away along the eastern road like a startled rabbit.

As the cohort formed a ragged line, two deep, one of the rankers grabbed the reins of Seth's horse and pulled him in behind the line. Tyron came with him, struggling to control his spooked beast, and Seth's mount caught the fear and began to jerk about. Both men had to cling on and rein in hard, and Seth barely registered the Estellan riders go down, caught from behind and stabbed in the back. The dead men's horses ran on, thundering wildly past the cohort and straight towards the hospital wagons.

The tide of Keshi riders kept coming, scimitars waving as they ululated triumphantly. He tried to count them – forty, sixty? – but his brain could barely engage. The pilus was bellowing orders and the rankers were locking their shields together, but they were covering only half the open space. The Keshi poured closer, a tide of men and horses.

'Sir! The gnosis!' the pilus shouted in his face.

Huh?

Tyron shouted, and blue fire billowed from his hands into the onrushing enemy. One rider reared up and fell as the one behind him collided with him and the two went down in a billow of dust and thrashing limbs, but the rest flowed around them. They slammed into the cohort's front line and the space in front of Seth became a mass of men and beasts, the riders' horses rearing up and crashing their hooves against the cohort's shields like a wave breaking, battering on steel, wood and bone. Scimitars slashed downwards. The noise was deafening.

The line of Rondians buckled, but the second rank shoved forward, plugging gaps and stabbing up into the chests and necks of the horses, shouting to Kore as they kept driving forward. The Keshi recoiled, the horses flailing backwards and the riders lashing about frantically to avoid being dragged from their saddles. But a glance left and right told Seth that the rest of the Keshi were simply going around them.

He jabbed a finger at a Keshi who seemed to be breaking through, more in panic than aggression, and mage-fire flashed. The man convulsed in shock as the narrow burst of energy blasted into his face, and he collapsed. Seth shouted in triumph and started doing it again and again, blazing away in a haze of anger and fear, barely thinking.

Half his bolts went astray, but his attacks took toll. Then the arrows began to fly, the first one flickering past his nose and hitting someone behind him. He realised he'd completely forgotten to shield – the most basic of mistakes – and rectified that in a frightened frenzy. He couldn't see Tyron, only a swirling mass of Keshi pouring around the sides of his cohort and aiming arrows. Some had already reached the wagons, and he could feel the throb of the gnosis – the healer-magi were protecting their patients. He whipped his horse about again, blasted fire into the face of another Keshi, swatted away a maddening swarm of arrows. He cast about . . .

. . . and saw Tyron lying on his back with an arrow through his left eye.

Something inside him snapped, and a torrent of rage poured out. First came the rational spells, like the sylvan-gnosis he used to wreck the bows of the Keshi, then wind and lightning burst from him like a scream. Even then, it wasn't hugely effective, but it did blast over a few of the enemy, and it forced the rest to recoil as dust blasted up into their faces. Then he started to think, and let his more natural affinities take over: he was primarily a Hermetic mage. It wasn't as effective in combat as other Studies, but he was a pure-blood and facing only *mounted* men . . .

The Keshi dimly felt the blast of pure terror and despair that throbbed from him, but their horses – targeted through his animagery – went into a frenzy. They panicked, first thrashing about, then tearing away, their riders clinging on desperately. Those who tumbled off were speared before they could rise as Rondian reinforcements poured into the junction. In seconds the attack had completely fallen apart and the brief engagement was over.

The junction flooded with soldiers, but Seth barely noticed. He was huddled over the cooling body of Tyron Frand, crying so hard his eyes felt like they were burning away. He felt like he was floating alone in a cloud of grief, but suddenly Lanna Jureigh was standing over him, her usually gentle face hard and angry. 'Get up. You're our commander.'

'They killed him – he forgot to shield – I forgot. We should have shielded—'

She slapped him, not with her hand, but with her mind, and he reeled, but she pulled him upright, using telekinetic gnosis to augment her strength. She looked nothing like a healer right now. 'Stand *up*. We've lost more than just one man and the soldiers need to see their general.'

'No, they don't. I failed them, I let them down—'

She mind-slapped him again, so hard he staggered, but again she held him upright and berated him in a low voice, pitched for his ears alone. 'Yes, you did: you set no outriders and you led us through a junction you didn't scout. You let the rest of the magi gallivant off on some meaningless mission half their number could have achieved. Then you fought like a barely-blooded child.'

He stared at her, trying not to fall to his knees again, not with so many watching. *I deserve this*, he told himself.

Her face softened, just a fraction. 'You also saved us.'

He swallowed, nodded.

She gripped his shoulder steadily. 'Learn from this, General Korion.'

He looked around, finally registered all the other dead: as many Keshi as Rondian. No doubt the rest of the Estellan cavalry were dead too. 'Someone else should be in command,' he whispered.

'Ideally,' she agreed, 'but for now, it's you.' She stepped away and, very showily, went down on one knee. 'Hail to General Korion, who saved the day,' she shouted.

The gathered men responded, crying, 'Hail! Hail!', all acclaiming their general who had saved the day. It was a myth in the making, but he had to pretend it was real for their sakes, while his only friend in the whole army lay dead in the dust at his feet.

14

News of Victory

Noors

The term 'Noor' comes from an Old Rondian word for dark. It was initially used for the darker-skinned peoples of south Yuros, but more recently it has become a blanket term for the people of Antiopia. Though not originally intended as such, it is a term of derision, not used in polite circles. Perversely, some Antiopians themselves use the term when dealing with Rondians, muddying the waters over the correctness of the term.

ORDO COSTRUO COLLEGIATE, PONTUS

Northern Javon, on the continent of Antiopia
Thani (Aprafor) 929
10th month of the Moontide

With a despairing wail, the young Rondian legionary came at Elena, his sword a blur. About them were the twitching bodies of his comrades – but the movement was their nervous systems failing from the mage-bolts that had taken them from behind. The rest had been cut open and blood was still pumping from fresh wounds.

Elena had raised her hand to fire off another bolt when Kazim ghosted in and buried his blade in the soldier's back, punching through his boiled leather breastplate as if it were silk and skewering his heart. As the dying man sagged into Kazim's waiting arms, Elena looked away, not because there were more foes, but so she did not see what Kazim did next.

Instead she surveyed the tangled bodies about them. *They should have run. Their mage was already dead.* But that didn't unnerve her; what left her shaken still was the reminder that her lover garnered his power from killing, then denying another soul whatever afterlife existed. *If Kore exists, he surely can't have intended such a thing . . .*

The look on Kazim's face as he rose from his 'feeding' told her that he didn't think Ahm approved either.

The six men protecting the dead mage were strewn before her; the rest of the Dorobon cohort lay dead or close to it around the pool she'd poisoned; they'd been delirious already before Kazim had launched lightning into the water and caught almost all of them in the blast. The mage hadn't been able to protect them, he might be a pure-blood, but he'd been a Fire-mage, with the wrong skill-set to combat the poison.

She walked over to the pool, immersed a hand, extended her awareness and began to purify it. It took a long time, but she owed it to the Jhafi who relied on it for water for themselves, their livestock and their crops.

The sun was dropping towards the west and the waxing moon was rising in the east when she finally looked up. Kazim was stalking among the corpses, looking for valuables, anything they could trade for food and equipment. His pupils were dilated: the aftermath of taking another soul. This butchery offended him, she knew. *That's war, my love. At least we're safe.* This was the fifth patrol they'd destroyed since that first way-station, and the third dead mage. Magi were precious – these losses would be hurting the Dorobon badly.

Kazim came and knelt beside her at the water's edge. 'Is it clean yet?'

She sent a final pulse of cleansing gnosis through the pool and took its measure. 'Yes.'

Kazim splashed water onto his face, scrubbing fiercely at his whiskery, blood-spattered visage. 'You're all right?' he asked afterwards.

'Not a touch.'

The mage they'd slain was a well-dressed youth with a fashionable beard and moustache. His handsome features had been contorted by the agony of having poison dissolving his insides while another mage blasted him with water-borne lightning. He'd apparently been a diviner, but he hadn't seen death coming. She plucked a sapphire periapt from his neck and took his gold ring, a griffin signet bearing the word *Fidelus*.

Loyal. I suppose he was.

'It's just slaughter,' Kazim said in a low, dead voice. 'They can't touch us, not if we're careful. They don't stand a chance. This is not war.'

'Oh yes it is: this is precisely what war is. It's the stories that get it wrong, all that talk about stupid things like glory and honour.'

They looted two flasks of brandy and a hard cheese from the pilus, together with what few coins they could find, so at least they could pay for supplies next time they were in need. They picked up a couple of uniforms that looked like they might fit them, then headed for the dell where they'd left the *Greyhawk*.

They were halfway back, with Elena trying to calculate how long they had until sunset, when she glanced back and cursed. 'Shit! Get down!'

Kazim obeyed instantly and she cloaked them both in a haze she hoped would blend into the mirages all round them. A sleek, dun-sailed windskiff had appeared from the south, with illusion rendering it all but invisible to a non-mage. *Kore! That's Gurvon's skiff!* She could make out three shapes in the hull.

Kazim growled throatily. 'Him?'

'Mask yourself and stay close. Don't look at it, or try to scry. Use the gnosis sparingly. We've got twenty minutes before the sun goes down, and an hour after that before full dark.'

'We can take them,' Kazim said in a low voice.

She shook her head. 'We don't know who is with him, or how many others are here.' She glanced around and picked out a sheltered route towards the next outcropping. 'Stay low. Crawl.'

He wanted to argue, but she slipped from his grasp and began to shimmy forward on her belly, chafing knees and elbows. The dust soaked into their bloody clothes, but they reached the boulders undetected. She looked back and saw the skiff circling the oasis, only a few hundred yards away. She slipped into the lee of the nearest boulder and pulled Kazim to her. 'We'll wait here until they land, then move.'

He put his lips to her ear. 'Let's attack! There's only three of them—'

'No! It would be just like Gurvon to sacrifice a few low-bloods to lure us out. There could be a dozen more magi hidden and waiting. We've got to get out of here as soon as darkness falls.'

I knew it was too easy . . .

'You're afraid,' he growled, not willing to let it go.

Her eyes narrowed, not in anger but consideration. Then she thought, *Yes, and that's no bad thing. Gurvon always has something up his sleeve, a way to attack your blind side,* she admitted to herself. *Yes, I'm afraid.* If you could, you should always be the one to choose the battleground. You didn't let the enemy do it. She glanced sideways at Kazim's young, hard face, with its rakish beard and golden skin and amended herself: *No, I'm not afraid of Gurvon. I'm afraid of losing you.*

'We're not ready,' she said instead.

'How can we not be ready? We've trained for months – we've wiped out six patrols now. We can destroy him.'

'No,' she whispered firmly. 'Follow me.' She slid from his side and began to crawl away. She heard him exhale angrily, but he came after her and she released her own pent-up breath. He was like the young Rondians Gurvon used to recruit, full of their own invincibility. It could take years to knock it out of them – if they lasted that long.

Kazim hadn't yet taken on a mage in a fight; so far Elena had dealt with those. There hadn't been time to teach him the finer points of gnostic duelling, so his role was to blast from a distance, then close in fast. A clever mage like Gurvon would take him down in a heartbeat, despite all the months she'd spent training him. Some things only the real world taught.

They reached the *Greyhawk* undetected as the sun went down and the landscape fell into gloom. The skiff was covered in its dun sails and hidden beneath the lee of a rock. Full dark was still some time away, however, and she knew Gurvon would be watching the skies: the bodies had still been warm when they left, so clearly fresh. 'We must wait now,' she told Kazim, and pulled him into the lee of a different boulder, where the shade was thickest. They huddled together as the shadows deepened, quivering at the slightest sound, while the quarter-moon climbed the sky.

Finally twilight became full night and at last she felt safe enough to move. 'Let's go,' she whispered, and they dragged the *Greyhawk* into the open and re-set the mast and sail. In minutes they were rising just above the ground and turning into the wind. It was too dark to navigate normally, but if they could just get away from here, she could open up her senses and begin to feel their path home. 'Steer southeast,' she whispered, almost the opposite direction to where their base lay. 'I want to make sure we're clear.'

Kazim looked at her quizzically, then followed her instructions. She set the sails and tied them down, then wriggled around the mast, nestled herself against Kazim's thigh and peered behind them. She opened up her senses, listening hard. She might be only a half-blood, but few people could operate near her undetected, even pure-bloods. After a time, she began to relax. 'I think we might have got away,' she breathed.

Kazim bared his teeth, luminescent in the moonlight. 'Next time we fight, yes?' he asked hopefully.

'When we fight Gurvon, it will be well-planned, and at a time and place we choose.'

He kept one hand on the tiller and stroked her head with the other. 'It is hard to run away.'

'We won't always,' she promised him. She reached wider, feeling relaxed enough to begin finding landmarks to navigate by, eager to be home and get washed. That was when she sensed something. She cast about: an owl, above and behind, following them. *<Kaz, keep flying straight, and don't look up. We've got company.'*

He started, almost looked. 'What is it?'

'An owl, about two hundred yards back. It's unlikely to be a shapeshifter, not given its size, but it could be controlled by an ani-magus or possessed by a daemon.'

She felt him shudder slightly. To him such things were still crea-tures of darkness, not the tools of the mage's trade. He was learning, but not fast enough.

'Either way, the mage controlling it can see through its eyes, and that means we're in trouble,' she whispered. She moved back to the mast to give herself a clear line of sight.

Kazim looked at her worriedly. 'What do I do?'

'Bear to the right. Keep heading away from home.'

She peered. *Now, let's see . . .*

She had no affinity at all for beast-magic, but Gurvon did, and if he was controlling that damned bird, he could potentially track them wherever they went. And it mightn't be the only one he had in the sky.

I don't have the affinities to deal with this . . . but Kazim does. She turned his way. 'If I showed you how to do something, could you? I warn you, it won't be pleasant.'

He nodded warily. 'Of course.'

'Okay, listen with your mind.' She opened up to him and con-nected with his aura. Every mage's aura had a 'feel' unique to them; his was a pleasant soft leather. She had been told hers was like cool water. *<Here's what I want you to do . . .>*

She took over at the tiller so that he could prepare, and shielded her own mind, because what he was about to do could affect more than birds, and he'd never done anything like it before. She took one last glance upwards with her gnostic sight to check where the owl was, then told him: *<Now.>*

He looked at her uncertainly, clearly not proud of what he was about to attempt, then he set his shoulders and released his gnosis. A pulse of psychic energy washed out from him and she blanched at its force. She felt the owl go down, like a flickering candle winking out.

At the same time around a thousand other candles went out around them.

Gurvon Gyle shuddered as the birds he was linked to died in an abrupt flare of agony. For a second he was dazed and helpless, clutching onto the rock. The world was a black yawning hole and he was falling into it. Then he pulled his mind clear, shaking. *Great Kore . . .*

'Boss?' Mara Secordin didn't really do concern, but she did do curiosity. Her slab-like jowls quivered and her eyes widened momentarily. 'I felt that,' she said with an air of disbelief.

He pushed himself upright. *Kore's Blood, they probably felt it in Pallas . . .* He reached out with animagery, seeking his linked birds. He drew a complete blank.

'My birds are dead, and so's pretty much everything else within what I'd guess is a mile's radius,' he reported, scarcely believing it. He reached out, looking for other animal minds, and found a gaping void. 'There's *nothing* left.'

Rutt Sordell was beside the skiff, scrying. He looked up and said warily, 'Elena doesn't do animagery.'

'Someone with her does.' Gurvon rubbed his temples as he straightened. He trusted Mara, as much as he trusted anyone, but it didn't do to look surprised in front of her. She was a predator, and weakness excited her in all the wrong ways. 'The eyewitnesses at that waystation said there was a Noorie with her.'

'I like Noorie men,' Mara commented distantly. 'Spicy and lean. A little small, though.'

He winced at the various mental images her words conjured, and changed the subject. 'That killing pulse was of Ascendant strength.' He pushed away from the boulder and steadied himself, then lurched towards the skiff. 'Who the Hel has she got with her?' he muttered.

Sordell bent over his scrying bowl again. 'She's well-shielded,' he complained. 'I can't get anything.' Abruptly he tipped the bowl over, spewing liquid light over the sand, where it drained away as it faded. 'The bitch is too slippery.'

Gurvon cursed silently. 'Make contact with the Dorobon. Tell them to collect their corpses. And double the reward. There must be a Jhafi somewhere prepared to break ranks.'

It would be to no avail, of course. The sky was empty, above them and all the way south. In the morning the natives would find dead birds and lizards by the hundreds, the last remaining trace of their skirmish. It was easier to be a ghost than to catch one, and Elena knew that as well as he did.

We're going to have to try something else . . .

Brochena, Javon, on the continent of Antiopia
Awwal (Martrois) 929
9th month of the Moontide

'He's angry,' Staria Canestos remarked softly. 'The hunt goes poorly.'

Cera looked sideways at the mercenary commander, who had joined her at the women's table in the Great Hall. Usually the Estellan sat with the men, but tonight she was piqued at Francis Dorobon for something and avoiding him.

'Good,' Cera muttered. 'Viva Elena.'

'Elena Anborn is a nasty little snake. I'd hate to have to track down the squinny bitch myself.'

'Elena is a good person,' Cera retorted. 'You didn't know her as I did.'

'The Hel I didn't! I offered her a maniple command once – thought she'd fit right in. One of my girls thought so too: took her for a saffy and tried to win her over. Got her fingers burned – literally.'

'You have female soldiers?' Cera asked, mostly to change the subject.

'Thought that'd get your attention,' Staria said dryly.

'What do you mean?'

'Oh, please.' The Estellan woman scanned the room, then dropped her voice. 'Just a few dozen girls, cooks mostly, but some can use crossbows and knives pretty well. Plus I've a couple of women magi with a taste for cunni juice. I'm not one, in case you're wondering, but I'm around 'em enough to spot them.'

Cera flushed. 'You don't know me either.'

Staria gave her a faintly sympathetic look. 'I know the way of it, girl: you've got to pretend like most of your sort do. Men still rule the world, and it's damnation for anyone who doesn't want to spread for 'em. I sometimes wonder how Kore or whoever could be so cruel as to make mooners and saffies.'

Cera swallowed. 'But I'm not—'

'The signs are there, if you know what to look for. Most don't see 'em, though, luckily for you. Even Gyle doesn't have you worked out. He can sniff out a plot in a trice, but he's emotionally blind: that's why he thinks he can seduce a girl whose parents he murdered. That's his weak spot.' She smiled grimly. 'There, see: I've given you a gift, little Queen: your enemy's weakness.'

Cera tried to back out of the conversation. 'Really, I don't . . .'

Staria silenced her with a gesture. 'It's in the way you make eye-contact. You are guarded with everyone – naturally shy, I'd say. But with men, your barriers stay up, whereas a part of you wants to open up to another woman. You don't trust men; they scare you to be around, but you believe in your heart that another woman wouldn't hurt you.' She slurped her ale. 'That's *your* weakness. Another gift: I am generosity itself tonight.'

Cera thought about that. 'Thank you, I suppose.'

'I feel for you, little Queen. If you weren't so obviously imprisoned here, I would offer to take you away and surround you with people who understand. It's a hard life, but not without rewards. I have many children like you, mooners and saffies from all over: lost souls who honestly believe that they are cursed, who would give all their hearts to be normal but who cannot change their own nature. Some are angry, some belligerent; some try to hide their difference and others flaunt it, but all share the fundamental sadness of the outcast.'

The mercenary's voice had taken on a reflective lilt, but then she leaned back with a grim smile. Symone, Gyle's effeminate red-headed mage-agent, had stolen into the hall and taken a seat at the end of the lower table. 'Now that one I'm sure even you have worked out.'

'He's new.'

'Mmm. "Symone Fontaine", or so he calls himself. But see, I know the only magi Fontaines, and he's not one of them.' Staria glanced sideways at Cera. 'The magi are a small community, and while the Dorobon are insular, I've been all over and I know who's who. That kid is using a made-up identity.'

Cera peered at the young mage with renewed interest. *Symone showed up after Octa's strike against Gyle. And yes, he is strange . . .*

'Mightn't he be a bastard? Someone's well-kept secret 'til now?'

'It's possible.' Staria scratched her nose, then chuckled. 'With that one, I'd be more inclined to believe it's really a woman under those robes, one who got pregnant to a mage and is now pretending to be male.' She snickered.

Cera had to think about that. 'Pregnancy manifestation? Gyle told me of it – he said if I got pregnant by Francis, I might gain mage-powers for a time.'

'Often it's permanent, especially if you're bred by a pure-blood,' Staria replied. 'But no one ever trains pregnant women so they seldom amount to much.' Her eyes went back to Symone. 'Like that wet fish of a maybe-male.'

But Cera's mind had gone racing on. *Mater Lune, why hadn't I thought of it before . . . Portia!*

Hytel, Northern Javon, on the continent of Antiopia
Jumada (Maicin) 929
11th month of the Moontide

Portia Tolidi staggered from the privy, moaning softly with each step. It wasn't just the physical discomfort, though that was bad enough. Her stomach was so taut that she thought the skin might split at any minute. Everything itched and ached. Her hips were stiff and her lower back throbbed and her breasts were a torment of stretched skin. Her belly and breasts were marred with silvery marks despite the creams the women applied several times a day, and when she looked in mirrors, her face was far from the porcelain perfection demanded by her uncle and her king.

What will my fate be when I'm just another used-up woman, surrounded by younger, fresher girls busy thrusting their way up?

As if the torments of her body weren't bad enough, her other senses were a torture. Her eyes were fizzing, blurring her vision, scents she was certain she shouldn't have been able to smell assaulted her from across rooms and down corridors: intimate and imperceptible smells that revealed a person's identity before they entered the room, as well as what they'd eaten, who and what they'd touched, and what they'd been doing. And her hearing was filled with painful sounds, as if her eardrums had been tightened past enduring.

I can't stand this. I can't take it, not any more . . .

She was six months gone and entering the final phase – the third trimester, the midwives called it. She stumbled to her bed, missed and fell to the floor. She got to her knees, groaning, and tried to summon the energy to haul herself up. Her maids were nowhere to be seen, as usual, but she didn't care because she hated them seeing her like this.

They're spies for him *anyway, the vicious little leeches.*

She fought for purchase on the rug, got her right leg under herself and pushed, managing to crawl forward and get her stomach onto the mattress. She stayed there, just propped there, panting.

Someone touched her hips and she gave a small shriek and threw a panicked look back over her shoulder. She met her uncle's leering, beady eyes. His unhealthy skin was flushed and he exuded alcohol from every pore as he gripped her hips and ground his crotch against her bottom.

'Uncle, please,' she begged. 'I'm not—'

His face was uncaring as he fumbled with her skirts, trying to hike them up and bare her to him. She let herself fall forward and rolled over, tears blurring her stinging eyes. *Not this again. I can't take it any more.* 'Uncle, I'm sick!' she cried.

He glowered down at her. 'Would you refuse the king, eh? Would you refuse your mighty husband?'

Alfredo got like this sometimes, overcome with a raging jealousy of Francis, or of whomever he'd sent her to. But she'd had no one but him inside her since she'd returned to Hytel. 'He wouldn't want me like this,' she snapped back, her disgust for once overcoming the terror her uncle held over her. 'Please – I just vomited.'

He responded by unbuckling his breeches and letting them drop. 'Come here!'

'Uncle! I'm begging . . .'

'I'll teach you to beg! Come here!' She tried to crawl away, but everything hurt, then he shouted, 'COME HERE!' and suddenly something snapped inside her.

She lashed out, her vision swimming as brilliant light smeared across her eyes. Something uncoiled from the fug of colours, a vivid emerald, then dirty browns, and something like a tentacle or maybe an arm with splayed fingers reached out while she howled her hatred at him. The limb of dark light seemed to take root in his groin and it felt like she was gripping his erect tool, and, more than that, it felt as if she was remembering every single time it had been inside her, every penetration, and she hated it, wanted it gone, wanted it to shrivel and wither and die, like a branch, ripped off of a tree. A vast rush of energy seemed to flow between her and her uncle, almost as if they shared one body, though her mind remained free of his, to her vast relief, because all of a sudden she could dimly sense a wave of twisted urges and desires and she knew it would engulf her if she let it.

Then her mind cleared, as if the impossibility of what she was experiencing had caught up with her, and she collapsed and fell to the ground, completely spent, utterly exhausted . . .

. . . until she turned, as if subconsciously drawn to look, and she stared, aghast, at what she'd done.

Alfredo Gorgio was no longer a man. He was a eunuch.

He was yowling wordlessly as he stared at his bared groin where his cock had withered to an inch-long twisted stick of dried skin and his scrotum had shrunk almost to nothing. He had clearly endured agony, but there was no blood, nothing that was going to immediately kill him. His face was trying to deny the evidence of his eyes.

'Portia . . .' His voice trailed off. 'You . . . You . . .' He tried to speak, failed.

One of Rykjard's magi had tried to tell her something about gnosis in the wives of magi: *Pregnancy Manifestation,* he'd called it, but she'd not listened – she hadn't seen any reason to. But now . . .

Portia felt an incredible surge of potentiality.

Sweet Mater Lune! I've become a mage!

Alfredo reached down to his belt, hanging around his ankles, fumbling until he'd unsheathed his dagger. He brandished it at her and screamed, 'You have to fix me! You have to *fix* me!'

She swiped her hand across the space between them and without even touching it sent the knife spinning away. It was as if she had extra limbs, strong, puissant limbs that only she could see. Her vision was clearing now, and her other over-extended senses too. She felt like this discharge of power had lanced a boil of energy. She was filled with the sudden desire to see her torturer choking, and instantly her power – her *gnosis* – gripped him like a ragdoll and slammed him against the wall. She pinned him there while she squeezed, watching as his eyes bulged and he squeaked and wept for mercy.

She dropped him. *I owe you one thousand, nine hundred and fifty-eight deaths, one for every time . . .*

One death wasn't enough.

'You will never touch me again.'

He lay there weeping and looking at his ruined body. Then he looked up at her incandescent face and started pleading, 'Please, Niece – *please.*'

How sweet his helpless desperation sounded.

'You will never touch *anyone* ever again.'

He tried to rally, and threatened, 'I'll have you burned as a witch! I'll have you hanged, drawn and quartered! I'll have you stoned! I'll—'

'When revealing your state would see you laughed from the city?' She stalked towards him and started down at him. 'You would become an object of scorn and ridicule – for the rest of eternity! I think not, *Uncle.*' She kicked him, flexing this wonderful power. The impact bent him in two. 'Do you recall, *Uncle,* how you laid claim to me from the moment I was old enough to be used? Well, now I lay claim to you, you perverted *pezzi di merda*! You belong to me now, and so does everything you own!'

Every indiginity she had ever endured was the price she'd paid for this moment, and suddenly anything at all was possible. She trembled with the fear and pleasure of the moment, as exquisite as any she'd ever experienced. It filled her with a longing to share it.

'I want paper, Uncle. I need to write to my Sister-Queen.'

Brochena, Javon, on the continent of Antiopia
Jumada (Maicin) 929
11ᵗʰ month of the Moontide

Cera Nesti had to blink furiously to keep her eyes dry as she clung to her little brother, though he wasn't so little any more – though Timori was only nine, he was almost her height now. But there were unfriendly eyes here and she didn't want to show them how desperately afraid she was for him.

'Darling, where have they been keeping you?' she whispered, one eye on Gurvon Gyle, openly watching from the balcony above. She looked around the old nursery garden, where she, Solinde and Timori had used to play all day, and stroked his straw-coloured hair.

Timori nestled against her. 'I don't know – not far. I can hear the market criers. They're funny, I like them.' He imitated their calls, giggling, and she filed away the information: that was the water-sellers' call.

'They're going to let me see you more often,' she whispered. 'Magister Gyle has promised.'

As much as one can trust anything that snake might say.

Timori looked doubtfully up at the grey-clad mage. 'He visits once a week but he doesn't say much. He treats me like a child.'

Cera smiled at that. Timori Nesti was rightful king of Javon and knew his station. He looked underfed, though; he was too skinny, and there was a fragility about him that she didn't like. He'd had to deal with the murder of his father and mother and one of his older sisters; the violence might not have touched him physically, but she could almost see the emotional wounds.

'Look, I've brought you a new doublet,' she said brightly, to cheer him up.

But it was blue. 'I want a violet one, like your dress,' he admonished her. 'We are La Viola, Sissy – we always have to remember that.'

'Sometimes we have to pretend,' she whispered. 'Like I do.'

'You *married* him,' Timori said, his voice accusatory, his big eyes upset.

Oh dear. 'I did it so they wouldn't hurt you, my dearest – only for that. I know you understand.'

Timori looked away. 'Maddy and Symone say that you marrying him only proves that you're—' He bit his lip. 'You shouldn't have married him, Cera. It wasn't worth it.'

She seized his head in her hands and turned it up so she was looking straight into his eyes. 'Timi, I would marry Shaitan himself if it kept you alive. Everything I have done and everything I will ever do will be for you. *You* are the real king – the one the people are longing for.'

'Symone says they're going to elect a new king, then they'll cut off my head.' He was just a little boy again, and his voice was tremulous.

Cera squeezed him close. 'You shouldn't believe what they tell you, Timi. They are all liars.' When she was sure he'd taken that in, she glanced around surreptitiously. 'Tell me about Maddy and Symone.'

'Maddy looks after me. She's nice. She gives me sweets.' He giggled. 'Though she eats more of them than I do.'

'And Symone?' she asked.

Timi's nose wrinkled. 'He's mean to me. That's him there.'

Cera turned and saw the slender mage in the middle distance, leaning against a wall, examining his fingernails. When he looked up, she could almost feel the malevolence in his pale eyes. She looked past him, feigning nonchalance, though her heart was racing. She remembered what Staria had said and added her own suspicions.

'I'll tell Magister Gyle that you don't want Symone near you,' she told Timi.

The little boy nodded dutifully, clearly not believing she had any sway with Gyle. She couldn't blame him for that.

The grey-clad mage must have got bored, for he chose that moment to descend the stairs and join them. 'I think that's enough,' he said impatiently. 'Time's up.'

'It's only been five minutes!' Cera protested indignantly. 'You promised me ten!' Timi clung to her waist as if he was prepared to fight rather than be prised away from her.

'You misheard me,' Gyle replied flatly. He clicked his fingers and Symone came forward.

Timori stayed glued to Cera's side as the slender young man approached, then his cheeks went white and he wriggled around behind her. Cera studied Symone's strangely androgynous gait and her mind raced.

The young mage extended a hand. 'Come with me, little King,' he said in an oily voice, the sort of voice an adult who loathed children might put on.

'I don't think I know you,' Cera said, looking straight at him, taking in his details. He had wavy hair, thin whiskers and a narrow visage. His stance was odd: thighs pressed together, back arched and shoulders back, the way a woman of breeding might stand.

Then she had a flash of intuition too powerful to be wrong: a year ago Elena had unmasked a shapeshifter, a legend among magi, named Coin, who could take anyone's form, of either gender. Cera had briefly seen the shifter, chained in the tower above – but she'd thought Coin dead. She had been told so by Gurvon Gyle. *Why did I ever believe anything he said?* she wondered. This 'Symone' was Coin, of that she had no doubt. The androgynous face was a clue, but the eyes were confirmation.

She averted her face, suddenly terribly frightened, and for a moment she couldn't speak. Then she gripped Timori's hand and found the courage to breathe again. Letting him go would feel like an awful betrayal, but what choice was there?

'Timi, I'm sorry,' she said, 'but they say you have to go now.'

'I don't want to! I want to stay with you!'

'You must, darling.' She bent and whispered in his ear, 'Be brave, Timi. One day this will be over and we'll be together again.'

He wavered, then blurted a farewell and darted past Symone like a sparrow evading a cat. He went pelting through the garden and Symone's face contorted in annoyance. Once again his eyes met Cera's, but this time Cera was ready and her mask was in place. The mage scowled warily, then hurried after Timori.

Gyle looked at Cera. 'I want a word, Cera.'

'As if I have a choice,' Cera said, trying to sound indifferent. 'You promised me ten minutes.'

'To be brother and sister, not king and queen-regent,' Gyle retorted. 'Timori lives on my sufferance: the sooner you both forget the Nesti ever held the throne, the safer you will be.'

She lifted her head defiantly. 'Our people still regard Timori as our rightful king. You forget your own arguments that persuaded Francis to marry me: that you Rondians are too few to rule this land, that only the continued clemency towards Timi and me is preventing the uprising you all dread.'

'That is a temporary problem, Cera. The game is changing all the time – when the Dorobon settlers arrive next month, we will have enough men to subdue this land, and after that, you and Timori will be living on my sufferance alone. Consider that, and be grateful for what you have.' He fished inside his pocket and handed her a slip of paper. 'Your Sister-Queen is at least grateful for what life has given her. Perhaps you should follow her example and concentrate on pleasing the king, instead of fermenting trouble in your Beggars' Court.'

Portia's written to me! Her hand shot out, but he jerked the envelope out of reach.

'Let's talk about that court of yours first, shall we?'

Bastido! She lowered her hand and glowered at him. 'What?'

'Last night I received a letter jointly signed by the Maula of Fayeed-har Dom-al'Ahm, the Sollan High Drui Josip Yannos and Grandmaster

Tullesque of the Kirkegarde, exhorting me to stop the Beggars' Court. This venture was supposed to divide my enemies, not unite them, so I am shutting you down.'

'No!' she exclaimed before she could control her reaction. 'No, you can't!'

'Can't I?'

But yes, he could – of course he could.

She swallowed and instead sought to reason it out. 'Why should you, when it's doing exactly what you wanted? You've got half the clergy locked up, the bureaucrats are paralysed and the Dorobon constitution can't go ahead. The whole city is in turmoil – and none of it is aimed at you. Meanwhile it's helping so many people. Please, we're achieving so much!'

'You're encouraging vigilante justice.'

She caught her breath, because she knew he was right. People were administering the punishments she couldn't – that was the ugly side of what she was doing. 'If you gave me the right to hand out legally enforced sentences, then people wouldn't take matters into their own hands,' she started, but Gyle gave her a withering look.

'No, Cera, I'm certainly not giving you that.'

'Then make Francis hold court instead.'

'If I could I would,' he said briskly. 'No, Cera, you will stay out of the Beggars' Court.' He looked at the letter in his hand, then pocketed it and walked away.

Rukka te, Gurvon Gyle. See if you can stop me.

'Let me kill her.'

Gurvon turned to 'Olivia Dorobon', conscious of the eyes on them both. 'You will stay away from Cera Nesti.' He doubted it was coincidence, bumping into Coin at the bottom of the stairs to his suite in the west tower. She'd probably been waiting here for hours. 'I'm busy, Coin.'

A sulky pout crawled over Olivia's face. 'You're always too busy for me. Why am I even here?'

Gurvon pursed his lips. *Because it'd be too difficult to explain Olivia's sudden disappearance.* 'Francis needs stability, and you're part of that,' he said, trying to make his voice sound conciliatory.

'I'm the best shapechanger there has ever been, yet you've got me doing *nothing*.'

'You can't always be killing people.'

'I'm not a killer.' Olivia's plump face contorted angrily, then she added, 'I think Cera knows who I am.'

That gave Gurvon pause. If Cera knew, her revealing the shapeshifter to the wrong people could be damaging. 'How?'

'She met my eyes and I think she might have recognised me.'

'You *think* she recognised you? When was this?'

'A few days ago.'

'Then why only tell me now?'

'I've tried, but you won't see me!' Her expression grew stony. 'I can't let anyone live who knows. I never have.'

Gurvon bit his lip. 'No – you're not sure, and she's useful to me. Stay away from her.'

The shapeshifter scowled. 'Have you spoken to my mother?'

'Yes.'

Coin's face changed – not physically, but emotionally, from sullen defensiveness to childlike hope. *The body and gnosis of a deadly mage, and the maturity of a twelve-year-old.* 'Mother knows I'm alive?'

'Of course – she was most relieved,' he answered, not quite honestly. Mater-Imperia hadn't been at all pleased to learn that her problem child still lived. Yvette Sacrecour had always been an embarrassment to her sacred dynasty. Lucia had demanded that Gyle send her home immediately, but he wasn't one to waste an asset, especially one as uniquely skilled as Coin. And he still felt in control of her, despite this difficult phase.

'Could I . . . *speak* to Mother?' she asked diffidently.

'Relay staves are difficult to make and they burn out swiftly – right now I have too few even for matters of state.' He overrode her protests. 'Yvette, I know your mother loves you, even if she doesn't always remember that. The time will come – but it's not yet.' He tapped her shoulder. 'And Yvette? You will stay away from Cera Nesti.'

'You don't understand the risks I face,' she whined. 'If she tells Francis Dorobon—'

Then I'd be well rid of you, and perhaps I could blame Lucia. Aloud, he put on his most reassuring voice. 'Yvette, I will tell Cera Nesti that your identity remaining secret is a condition of Timori's safety.'

'And are you going to continue to shut down her stupid law court?'

That was another question altogether. He'd been thinking that the Beggars' Court had outlived its usefulness, but perhaps not. This combined clerical outrage might be used to wring concessions from them. When it came down to it, the clergy held far more power than a mob of Noorie women, so keeping them under pressure was useful.

'Perhaps.' He tapped her sternum. 'But you will stay away from her, you hear me?'

Coin's false face was envious. 'You're still fascinated with her, aren't you?'

'That,' he replied coldly, 'is not your concern.'

15

Strange Alliances

Diversity Amongst the Blessed Three Hundred

The dominance of Pallas and the Rondian pure-blood magi can blind historians to the fact that the followers of Corineus hailed from more than a dozen different racial groupings. The original Blessed Three Hundred included Rondians, Bricians, Brevians, Hollenians, Argundians, Estellans, Noromen, Andresseans, Ventians, Midreans, and even some Lantric poets, and there are pure-blood enclaves in all these lands, descended from the original followers. So though 'Rondian' has become the blanket term, the reality is far more diverse, and divided.

ORDO COSTRUO COLLEGIATE, PONTUS, 689

Brochena, Javon, on the continent of Antiopia
Akhira (Junesse) 929
12th month of the Moontide

The wall of noise that hit Cera as she entered the zenana gardens was like being struck by a sand-storm. There were young women clambering on the iron gates; they'd been there for the last three days, hammering rocks against the metal and rhythmically chanting her name. They were calling now, leading a crowd that had grown to be thousands strong, the chanting loud as thunder: 'CERA! CERA! *CERA!*'

She'd tried to enter the zenana each day after her talk with Gurvon, but she'd found the doors bolted and guards standing ready. There was no other way to get to the gardens, so she'd stood on her balcony instead, and shouted greetings down into the packed plaza below. Francis had come to her room, pulled her inside and struck her, leaving her dazed and humiliated as she pleaded for him to stop, but afterwards she staggered out to the balcony again and showed those gathered below her bruised face. The blows made her feel stronger, not weaker. This was *her* holy Crusade, and it was righteous and true.

The next morning, the doors to the rear courtyard were unlocked again.

See, Gurvon Gyle: you have loosed this djinn from her cage.

She spoke to the crowd about being strong, her bruised and swollen eye socket her own battle-scar. The first person to speak that day was a man, Hazmani, the husband of Mukla, the first woman she had heard. He had relented and publically agreed to take back his wife and acid-marred daughter, and he was cheered on by the hoarse-voiced women. Tarita whispered in her ear that he'd been threatened with death if he didn't. 'The acid-thrower was found dead last night,' the maid added, her button eyes glinting righteously.

In the middle of the afternoon, after hours of listening to wrangling women, there was a sudden uproar and a knot of men pushed their way into the square. They were not armed, as far as Cera could see. They were surrounding Godspeaker Ilmaz, the same clergyman who'd invaded the Beggars' Court before. He strode towards the gate surrounded by a knot of his ruffians, one of whom was leading a frightened young woman. Her bekira-shroud had been torn, baring her face.

'A judgement!' Ilmaz shouted. 'I demand a judgement!'

Cera understood immediately that this was a test. A quick glance around showed soldiers filing onto the walls above: men of Staria Canestos' legion, prettily plumed and coiffed and oiled, but no less fearsome for that. The women in the courtyard pressed forward, howling insults at the Godspeaker and demanding that he release the girl. Such open hostility to a holy man would have been unheard of even two months ago, but the Beggars' Court was undermining so much.

'What, does the Godspeaker acknowledge our right to sit in judgement?' Cera asked, feigning astonishment, and the crowd laughed along. 'Remarkable!'

'The Maula of Fayeedhar Dom-al'Ahm wishes to see whether your concept of justice extends beyond alleged crimes against women,' Ilmaz shouted back. 'It does not mean he finds you competent! But he wishes to explore your mind on this matter.'

'What matter?'

He displayed the girl-prisoner like a trophy. 'The matter of this girl's perversion.'

That silenced the crowd momentarily and Cera sat back, suddenly wary. The girl looked utterly petrified, and Cera knew full well that witnesses could be made to say anything if the fear or the reward were enough.

Ilmaz's mouth twisted. 'This girl is accused of unnatural relations with another female.'

There was a sharp intake of breath through the courtyard, and it went rippling back into the plaza beyond. This was an offence, no matter who sat in judgement. If proven, al-Shaar demanded a stoning; in Sollan law it was a flogging offence, and in the civil court, the woman would be disowned and placed in a religious house. Each punishment was equally fatal in its own way.

Cera felt her own skin prickle with a flush of wet heat, and not only for the seriousness of the charge. *Sol et Lune, do they know about me?*

She felt like every eye that turned her way was boring into her, seeing through the veil of flesh to her very soul. She felt sweat beading on her scalp, and was acutely conscious that Staria Canestos was on the balcony above, with a dozen of her battle-magi, male and female.

Mater Luna, watch over me . . .

She managed to speak. 'What does the girl have to say? I wish to hear from her!'

Ilmaz thrust the girl forward, right to the iron gate. 'Speak, girl!'

The young woman, small-built with a round face and wide eyes, looked utterly cowed as she clutched the iron bars. Her expression was completely miserable. Her mouth started moving, but no sounds coming out.

'What's your name?' Cera asked quietly, forcing the whole crowd to stop talking if they wanted to hear.

'Kiraz, Ma-majesty,' the girl babbled. 'Please, I—'

She broke off as Ilmaz tightened his grip on her arm and muttered something in her ear, no doubt reminding her of just what he could do to her and those she cared about. 'I am . . . I mean . . . I have . . . I'm sosorrysosorryIcouldn't . . . she *made* me do it!'

Cera felt a tingle inside, rising anger. *How dare you drag this poor girl in here?* But she was equally aware that her credibility was on the line here. The women in the crowd might be grateful that she was exposing crimes against them, but few would be sympathetic to the girl privately, and none publically. However she might sympathise, she could not fail to condemn.

If it's true.

She swallowed and looked at Tarita, who was clenching her fists so tightly that her knuckles were white. Tarita knew everything about her secret relationship with Portia. She looked rigid with fear, but she made a small nod, which Cera had no idea how to interpret. She took it as encouragement.

'Godspeaker,' she said, re-finding her voice, 'the girl is clearly scared out of her wits! How can I believe any admission of guilt under such circumstances?'

'She confessed!' Ilmaz shouted. 'Why would she speak a lie that condemns her?'

This time the crowd's reaction was muted, a confused babble, and Cera had to shout to be heard. She had no plan yet, only a vague intention of being seen to be fair. 'I would hear her speak, free of intimidation! I would hear both sides of the case, as I hear them all!' She stood up. 'Open the gates! Admit the girl!'

Ilmaz glared up at her. 'What surety do we have that you will not give her sanctuary?' Again the crowd appeared confused, as if unable to decide who they should be supporting.

Mobs like simple truths, Gurvon had once told her.

'I do not give sanctuary to the guilty!' she shouted back. 'How do we know you are not holding her family hostage right now, to force her to condemn herself?'

'I am a Godspeaker of the Amteh! I do not stoop to such things!'

'But some do – we have heard enough tales of crimes perpetrated by clergy in this court over the past weeks to fill a book! So do not presume your title elevates you from suspicion! If you want my judgement, you must release the girl to me!'

Ilmaz's eyes blazed and the crowd of women turned on him again, jabbing accusing fingers at him and screeching. Cera reluctantly admired his courage – or perhaps it was just sheer pig-headed arrogance that made him stand unflinching before such a seething throng. Finally he shoved the girl at the gate, where she clung desperately to the railings, her eyes darting left and right.

The clerks at the gate hurriedly pulled the gates open and hauled the girl through. Someone gave her water and tried to calm her while Cera stood and gestured to Tarita. 'What is going on here? Do you know anything of this case?' she whispered urgently.

'No, Lady,' Tarita responded, still fearful. 'I've never heard of this.'

'Why this crime?'

'I don't know. Coincidence, Lady. Your secret—'

Cera put a finger to the girl's lips. 'Don't even say it. There are magi here.' Her eyes went up to Staria Canestos' crooked face, peering down at her expressionlessly. 'Why are they here?'

Tarita again shook her head. 'I'm sorry, Lady, I don't know, I'm sorry.'

Cera wiped perspiration from her brow with her veil and took a few deep breaths. 'Go and ask the mercenary commander what is happening, please.'

Tarita bobbed her head then ran, while Cera returned to her throne. The girl was being helped to her feet. She looked ready to faint, and who could blame her? Cera wished she could lie down herself. She glanced up, saw Staria Canestos leaning over Tarita, whispering in her ear, her face grim.

I'm right: this won't be good at all.

'So,' she started when the girl had positioned herself, kneeling below the throne. 'Kiraz, yes? Tell me, who is your family? Where are they? Are they here?'

The girl shook her head. 'I have dishonoured my family. My father

297

is here.' She pointed to a man protected by Ilmaz's group of body-guards. 'My mother and brothers are at home.'

Cera gestured and a copy of the *Kalistham* was produced. 'Place your hand here,' she said gently, pointing, then started, 'Do you understand that by touching the holy book, you have drawn the eyes of Ahm Himself upon you, Kiraz?' she asked. Inwardly she was rolling her eyes at such superstitious nonsense, but she knew the people believed in such things, and that included this girl. 'Now, tell me what happened.'

Kiraz spoke quietly, and the crowd fell silent, straining to hear. 'I am seventeen, and the eldest child of my family. My father is a water-seller, and I labour as a bearer for him. Every day, I carry water from the river in bucket-yokes, and deliver to whomever my father says.'

Cera studied the girl: she was slight, but her shoulders were broad and her hands callused. It was not unusual for girls to have such heavy tasks, though it was generally for only a short time in their lives, before they were married and vanished into their husband's home. They were normally chaperoned by their brothers while work-ing. Seventeen was late to be unmarried, however.

'Go on.'

'My father has recently began sending my brother and me to deliver water to the new camps on the edge of the city, because the soldiers do not have access to the best wells. We did good business.'

Cera's eyes flashed upwards to Staria Canestos. Her camp was on the edge of town. She looked back at the girl and asked, 'Where is your brother? How old is he?'

'At home.' The girl's eyelashes fluttered anxiously. 'He is sixteen, and soon to marry.'

'You are not married yourself, Kiraz?'

The girl shook her head. 'I was late to bleed,' she admitted, hang-ing her head.

Cera sighed – there were all manner of superstitions about girls who bled late; amongst the poorer classes anything out of the ordin-ary could so easily turn into a major problem – even such a simple thing as this could make a girl unmarriageable. To these people late bleeding could mean the girl was just unfeminine, or, worse, potentially infertile, or even a witch – or, worst of all, a safian.

'I have had no suitors since my second engagement was terminated,' Kiraz muttered.

A hiss ran through the crowd. There was little sympathy there.

Cera let out her breath in frustration, then glanced up as Tarita hurried back down the stairs towards her, her face taut with worry. Cera waved a hand for Kiraz to wait, then signalled for Tarita to come forward. 'Well?' she whispered.

'The mercenary woman says there was a misunderstanding this morning, involving this girl and one of her women.' Tarita bent even closer. 'She also says that if you ask too many questions, there will be blood spilled, and not just the girl's.'

Cera glared up at Staria, her skin chilling as if from a hidden breeze. 'What does she mean?' The Estellan's face was impassive, but her deep-set eyes were intense.

'She said that you cannot protect this girl today and that you must not ask about the brother.'

Pater Sol, what do I do?

'Very well. Thank you, Tarita.' She waved the maid away and turned back to Kiraz. 'This camp – it is of the Sacro Arcoyris Estellan legion, si?' When the girl nodded, she asked, 'What happened there?'

Kiraz glanced at Ilmaz and her father and hung her head. 'When my brother and I delivered water to this post, we were met always by four soldiers: three men and one woman. One of the men was a jadugara.'

A hiss ran through the crowd at the word and eyes rose to the balcony where Staria and her retinue were stationed. Cera raised a hand for quiet and indicated that Kiraz should continue her story.

'The woman helped me with the yoke, so that I could deliver water to the women's tents. She asked me about my life, and she told me that I was strong and pretty, that I would make a good soldier. She said it was sad that no one would marry me, but that it was not the end of the world. I thought she was very kind to me – kinder than my friends were.'

The women listening in the crowd scowled, while Ilmaz looked on smugly. The father's face was more complex, Cera noted: shame and anger mingled on his face. *Of course, his honour will suffer if this sin is proven. To have perversion in one's genes would be socially crippling. It might destroy his whole family's prospects. And yet he refuses to defend her . . .*

Of course, the Amteh teach that only men have real honour. So do the Sollan and the Kore faiths. We women only have shame . . .

'On the third time I visited,' Kiraz said, 'she gave me a sweet-cake, and touched my shoulders. She said I had good muscles. Then she asked me to take water into her tent. It was very small, and I had to crawl in to place the bucket at the far end. She followed me and grabbed me and turned me onto my back and she lay on top of me.'

The girl looked so utterly mortified that Cera was filled with deep sympathy for her. She wished with all her heart she'd never started this and a bitter taste filled her mouth as she gestured for Kiraz to continue.

'She kissed me, all over my face, and told me that I should run away from home and stay with her.'

Cera kept her face and voice as nonjudgemental as possible. 'What did you do?'

'I told her to stop. I told her I had to go home. I tried to push her away.' Kiraz hung her head. 'But then she offered me money if I did what she wanted.' She gave a small sob. 'So I did. It was a lot of money.'

Cera closed her eyes. *Damned with her own words.* 'And then?' she asked, resigned to the worst.

'She gave me silver, and I gave it to my brother and I went home. But on the way, we met my father and some other people, and my brother accidentally spilled the silver. It was more money than we see in a month, so questions were asked, and his . . . my . . . dishonour came out.' Tears were spilling down her face now. 'I only wanted the money. I am not . . . I am not what you think.'

His . . . My . . .

Don't ask about the brother.

Cera felt a sick feeling grow in the pit of her stomach. *I see now.* She looked up at Staria Canestos. 'Can this tale be verified?'

Ilmaz banged his staff upon the iron gate. 'The father has given his testimony,' he shouted. 'So has the brother.'

'I'm talking to the mercenary commander,' Cera said coldly, looking up at Staria.

The mercenary woman was fingering her periapt idly. 'Your court has no jurisdiction over my people,' she called, her voice cutting through the babble of the crowd.

The reply drew an angry snarl from the listeners.

'But is the tale true?' Cera insisted.

Staria shrugged. 'I don't know.' Or care, her demeanour clearly said.

'Who was the mage present?'

Staria narrowed her eyes warningly. Beside her, a younger man with a certain family resemblance to Staria leaned over the balcony. He had a beauty to him few women could match, from perfectly manicured from toenail to forelock, but it was an entirely male beauty. 'It was me. I am Leopollo Canestos, Primus Battle-magus of the Arcoyris Estellan. I saw nothing of what this girl describes.'

Leopollo Canestos . . . Staria's adopted son . . . merda! No doubt you saw nothing because you were in another tent with the brother, who then spilled the silver and blamed his poor, hapless sister, who was probably entirely blameless. His father would have had little choice other than to play along, because the sins of a son are so much worse than those of an unwanted daughter. Then Ilmaz got involved, and Staria won't help her because she's got enough shit to worry about, establishing her people here without her brother buggering young men for money.

She rubbed her brow tiredly.

Condemn a girl wrongly, or condemn a whole family and stir up street warfare against Staria's people?

She didn't need to be a diviner to see what would happen if she exposed the truth: it was the sort of tragedy that played itself out regularly in Javon: a dishonoured family could not marry off their children; they lost patronage from above and clientele for whatever business they had, not to mention suitors and friends falling aside as they slid down the community pecking order. So the father would protect his honour above all, because without it, his line would be extinct inside a generation. And if that failed he would strangle his children, one by one, then his wife, then drown himself in the river, hoping the holy waters would wash away all of their sins.

She met Kiraz's red-rimmed eyes and they shared a moment of understanding: both knew the truth of the matter, and regardless of that, she would die for her family. *And she'll die even if I exonerate her, because her father will destroy the whole family before admitting his line is tainted.*

Cera raised a hand for silence. 'The girl has pleaded her guilt,' she said sadly, fixing the triumphant Ilmaz with a cold eye. 'Let her be returned to her family, to determine whether any punishment is merited. Let them consider that under Sollan law, the girl would be removed from society and placed in solitary confinement within a convent. A stoning is not the only acceptable punishment before the laws of this land.' She doubted the family would take this chance for a lesser sentence, but she felt compelled to at least raise the possibility. The father had already shown he would clutch at any straw to keep his son's name from being besmirched.

Kiraz was led back outside, her shoulders heaving and her face buried in her veil, and was bundled away through a near-silent crowd.

Cera raised a hand, her appetite for justice thoroughly curdled.

'I think that is enough for today.' She stormed away, amidst murmurs of disappointment.

Poor blameless Kiraz will be a corpse by dusk.

'You earned our respect today,' Staria Canestos said grudgingly.

Cera stared out the window. Letting the mercenary leader into her suite was no way to deal with any taint that might attach to her own name, but there was nowhere else they could talk in private. At least Staria had raised wards to prevent Gyle from listening in.

'Will it happen again?' Cera asked eventually.

'With my son? Who knows? He is indiscriminately lusty.'

'And was there truly a woman trying to seduce the girl as she said?'

'Not really. One of my people did flirt with her, but the girl wasn't offered coin, and it all stopped when she said no.' Staria tapped her fingers impatiently on the railing. 'Her tale was a fiction to protect her brother. Leopollo should have known better, but . . .' Staria paused and looked at Cera with an expression that was half apologetic, half truculent, then said, 'My children take love where they can find it, little Queen. They cannot marry, even though most are as devout as anyone else. Society doesn't know how to deal with us, here or in Yuros. That's why we keep moving.'

'But you're here to stay now, aren't you?'

Staria smiled grimly. 'Perhaps. Come winter we'll be marching west, for Forensa and Kestria.'

'Forensa is my home,' Cera told her coolly.

'I'll bear that in mind.' The mercenary looked her up and down, focusing on her still-blackened left eye. 'Does Francis Dorobon mistreat you often?' Her voice had a subtle touch of menace.

Cera rubbed her eye socket gingerly. 'This was the first time.' *If you don't count the rukking.*

'Do you have a bodyguard?'

'Not since Elena.'

'Hmm. Do you want one? A woman – she is a mage, and skilled at arms.'

'Why would you offer her?'

'I said: I owe you.'

Cera turned half away. 'And would she be . . . you know?'

Staria chuckled. 'The young woman I have in mind is . . . adventurous.'

'Then she's the last thing I need.'

'You think? From my vantage, I saw armed men in that crowd today, hovering near the gates. When you opened them to admit the girl, several came forward, and they were held back only by the God-speaker's word. Your life is in danger every time you hold court, my young queen, and the segregation in your society means that a male bodyguard could not properly protect you. You need a female bodyguard.'

'Elena's presence caused enough gossip. Thank you for the offer, but association with your legion is damaging enough. I will not taint my name further.'

Staria looked about to say something waspish, then she just grunted and spat over the railing. 'Yet there you are, just as *tainted* as the least of my children.'

'Why do you say they are your children?'

'Because most have been disowned and have no parents. I am as much a mother to them as anyone.'

'And are you?'

'Safian?' Staria rolled her eyes. 'In all honesty, I'm as chaste as a nun these days. I have been from the day my father died and I assumed control of the company. Before that I liked a man inside me, but the thing is, men think they own you if they can climb inside your bed. As a commander I can't afford that, so I resist any temptation these days.' She cocked her head and looked Cera up and down. 'What do you make of that?'

Cera licked her lips. Her time with Portia had been so fleeting, yet such an awakening ... she yearned for more. She could not imagine anyone but Portia in her arms, though – not now, when their love still felt alive, though her heart was beginning to murmur that Portia had been grateful to get away from Brochena. 'I like being in charge too,' she admitted. 'Too much to risk it for ... fleeting things.'

'Like having a warm body in your bed?' Staria asked sympathetically.

Cera closed her eyes, remembering Portia nibbling at her lips while her fingers slid over her most intimate places with languid urgency, those moments of transcendent bliss, and the most delicious loss of control. 'Perhaps. I don't know.'

'You're still young; you should explore. But I'm past that now. I get more satisfaction from seeing my children grow.' She pulled a tart face. 'And I still have ten fingers.' She cackled aloud when Cera blushed. 'Don't try and tell me you don't know what I mean.'

Cera looked away, flustered.

'Anyway, consider my offer of a bodyguard: I suspect you'll need one. And I will repay you for what you did today. It mightn't have felt like it, but you saved many lives at the cost of one.'

'I can't be proud of it.'

Staria shrugged. 'Blame men. Blame honour. Blame my brother, or me, if you really want. Just don't blame yourself.' Then she turned and was gone.

When Cera bled a few days later, to her intense relief, she retreated alone to the Blood-tower, as demanded by al-Shaar.

'Good evening!' Tarita said cheerily as she bobbed her head. She seldom remembered to use titles, and usually spoke to Cera as if they were sisters. Having lost Solinde and Elena, Cera liked the little illusion of family between them. 'Is all well?'

'All is well,' Cera responded, though her courses were still in heavy flow and she was in some discomfort. She looked at Tarita, wondering again precisely how old she was: she couldn't be more than fifteen years old, despite her maturity – but she was growing older, if not taller, and increasingly furtive, so many secrets did she bear. She was Cera's eyes and ears in the city, and her contact between Cera and the underground too, men like the criminal lord Mustaq al'Mahdi, the so-called Sultan of the Souk. She had every right to be wary.

'I went to market today,' Tarita said chattily. 'Most of the stalls were only half-stocked. Some districts of the city are almost empty, but the traders say the Forensa Road is full of refugees, leaving here. The Nesti Council have guaranteed shelter and food for all.'

Cera thought back to when she was running the Nesti Council. At the time it had been stressful, but looking back, they seemed like the best days of her life, being listened to by those worldly, experienced men, making decisions that shaped lives. With Elena at her side . . .

'They also say the Dorobon settlers have arrived at the Krak di Condotiori. Thirty thousand people! They are mostly coming here, they say, to fill the empty houses the local people have left behind.'

This will be their stronghold: their island in a hostile sea.

Tarita's voice dropped. 'Kiraz – the safian – she drowned herself last night.'

Cera clenched her hands. 'They say drowning is a better death than many,' she said, though the words felt empty. *I wonder if she had help?* She hung her head, feeling horribly guilty, though this had been the girl's choice.

'They are saying on the streets that the Godspeakers are going to declare a ninda against you, my lady,' Tarita went on in an angry voice, offended that anyone dared censure her queen. 'There are youths who harass and beat young women if they come to the Beggars' Court. Husbands and wives are fighting.' Her voice dropped. 'Perhaps it would be best to stop?'

Cera shook her head. *If I do that, I am nothing but a traitor who married a foreigner and did nothing with what that sacrifice purchased. I can't stop.* She said only, 'We must be brave. I'm not afraid of their ninda: their censure means nothing.'

Tarita didn't look at all happy, but she bobbed dutifully. Her voice dropped further. 'I heard today that another Dorobon patrol was wiped out on the Hytel Road. Another mage is dead. They say it was *her* again.' Elena was Tarita's personal hero.

Cera felt her throat go dry. *One day she'll come for me.*

Then a cold voice cut across the room. 'So you've heard,' Symone remarked from the door.

Tarita jerked away and curtseyed awkwardly to the Rondian mage.

He flicked his sleek reddish hair back from a face too thin to be truly masculine. His demeanour was taut with suppressed menace as he blocked the exit.

'This is the Blood-tower,' Cera said sternly. 'No men are allowed in the blood-rooms.'

'Or what?' Symone looked at Tarita with narrowed eyes. 'You're rather well-informed for a menial.'

Cera went to put a protective arm around Tarita, but she moved away and addressing Symone, said brightly, 'Sir, I must be about my duties. May I pass?'

Symone glowered, then stepped aside. 'Of course.' But when Tarita came within reach he seized her forearm roughly and growled, 'Know your place, maid.'

Tarita squirmed, making a distressed noise, and Cera snapped, 'Don't hurt her!'

'Get out of here, bint,' Symone snapped, shoving Tarita on her way.

'You are blood-cursed!' the maid shouted. 'Ahm will strike you down!' She slammed the door as she left.

Cera swallowed. *I wish she'd left the door open . . .*

Symone turned to face her. 'She forgets her place and if you don't remind her, I will.'

Cera said nothing. *Am I right? Is this the creature who killed my sister? What is he – she? –doing here?*

Symone went to the balcony's edge as a commotion arose outside: a band of young Jhafi men who had entered the plaza and were shouting at the walls, 'Shaliyah! Shaliyah! Shaliyah! Death to the infidel!' Rondian legionaries on the walls ran about doing nothing as more poured into the square. 'Long live the Sultan! Death to the infidel!' It had become a nightly ritual, with more joining in each evening.

'So,' Symone said, turning to face Cera. 'I know you know.'

'Know what?' she answered timorously.

'This.' Symone's face shifted, flesh and bone moving, hair writhing like snakes, growing shorter then longer, changing colour – white-blond, brunette, auburn, ebony, ginger, grey – as she tried on a myriad faces in a few heartbeats. The one he finished on was like raw flesh, with fang-like teeth and scaly skin, a fright-mask to intimidate her.

Cera kept her face averted during the sickening display, wondering what would happen if she screamed. She'd seen this being naked and exposed when Elena had chained it to the walls of the tower. She'd seen its true form, when it had looked almost pitiful. But there was nothing pathetic about the creature before her now. 'You're Coin,' she blurted at last.

'Correct,' the shapeshifter said bitterly. It stalked closer, and Cera found herself powerless to move, even when it laid hands on her forearms and pinned them to her side. A snake tongue slithered from its mouth and tasted her skin. 'I could rip your heart out, like I did

Olivia's.' Coin's eyes bored into hers. 'I could take your place – no one would know.'

Cera couldn't help picturing a scaled hand plunging into her chest, ripping through flesh and bone and emerging with her madly pumping heart grasped in its talons. She almost fainted.

Then a rock struck the wall below and the moment was broken. Voices floated up, screaming, 'SHALIYAH! SHALIYAH!' The shape-changer's eyes flickered from her to the gathering mob below and Cera wondered if that rock had saved her life.

When Coin spoke again, the menace had abated subtly. 'Shaliyah was part of our plan. The southern army was led by an enemy of the emperor. His demise was carefully orchestrated, the sacrifice of a piece on the tabula board.'

Despite her terror, Cera was stunned. 'You're saying that your emperor sent his own army into a trap?'

'Duke Echor was a threat to the emperor. I killed his brother when he tried to seize the Imperial throne and now he's dead too.'

Sol a mio . . . 'How many men were in the duke's army?' she asked carefully. Below, the square continued to fill, and songs of celebration rose from the burgeoning crowd.

'Probably fifteen legions, at least.' Coin sounded inordinately proud, as if he'd orchestrated it all himself.

Cera did the calculations. 'Sixty thousand men – two hundred magi – how could such a force be defeated?'

'They found a way.'

She kept talking, not just to distract the shapeshifter, but because she genuinely wanted to know. 'What sort of emperor sends his own people into a trap?'

'Our one.' Coin's voice became disdainful. 'It wasn't his idea, of course. He's dumber than Francis Dorobon.'

Cera took that in even as her knees shook and sweat stuck her cotton kameez to her skin. 'How would you know whose idea it was?'

'Because it was Gurvon's.' The words hung in the air like a boast, as if they were meant to impress her. 'That's who you're up against, Cera Nesti. He rules the rulers. And he belongs to *me*.' Coin's voice had gone up an octave in the space of the sentence. The fervour was disturbing, and his body shifted, becoming more female. 'He brought me back from death, and he's *mine*.'

He . . . or she . . . is in love with Gyle – or maybe it's only lust, but it's eating him up. 'Mater Lune,' she breathed.

'We are the power behind thrones, he and I, and we're going to win.' Coin's voice had a belligerence that suggested she was more than a little drunk, but the threat in her voice was plain. 'And you? You're in our way, you Noorie bint.'

Cera's back was pressed to the balcony rail and she was increasingly conscious of the gulf behind her, and how simple it would be for the mage to send her over the edge.

She lifted her chin. 'Does Gyle know you're here?' she asked, desperate to make Coin reconsider the path she was on, because the air between them was charged with impending violence.

Coin blinked, and that was enough for Cera to know that Gyle wasn't aware, and nor would he approve of her actions. It gave her the courage to stand her ground and not look away.

Coin's voice rose again. 'If I were to hurl you from this balcony, the world would call it suicide and move on. Even Francis would barely notice.' She reached out and gripped Cera's forearm painfully. Her breath reeked of sour wine. 'You think you're a queen, but you're only a pawn.' Suddenly the shapeshifter was Symone again, horribly *male* and pressing her back against the rail. 'We can be rid of you whenever we want, you mudskinned slut.'

But Cera could see through this bluster now to Coin's dread of losing Gurvon Gyle. 'Get out before I scream,' she said firmly.

Coin hesitated, then tried to regain control. 'The original plan was that I replace you. Perhaps I still will?' He grabbed Cera's salwar and pushed her until she was curved backwards over the balcony rail.

She felt her knees begin to go and locked them even as she lifted her chin defiantly. *I survived the early months of Francis and I'll survive you too, Coin. You cannot break me.*

'Did you kill my sister Solinde?' she asked suddenly.

She didn't know where the question came from – it certainly

wasn't self-preservation. But as she stared into the shapechanger's eyes, her sister's face suddenly flashed in front of her – and then she realised it was because Coin's mind was *bleeding*, sending out involuntary thoughts, and that Coin was remembering Solinde right now . . .

Coin recoiled, his whole expression changing from fury to guilt and self-loathing. He'd raised a hand to strike her, but the blow never fell and instead his hand hung in the air between them, before falling to his side.

His face changed back to the person she'd seen unmasked by Elena: an androgynous face with thin ginger hair and fragile bone structure, and big wet eyes. 'I never. I swear—'

Cera swallowed. 'Then who did?' she demanded.

'I *liked* her. She was my *friend*.'

'Your friend?' Cera stared, disbelieving. 'When?'

'In the cell – when I learned her shape – we *talked*. Gurvon told me he wouldn't hurt her, he said he'd keep her safely out of the way. *He swore!* But then Mara . . .' Coin swallowed, almost physically dragging her mind from the memory. 'It wasn't Gurvon's fault . . .'

'The Hel it wasn't,' Cera snapped.

'You *must* stop obstructing us.' This time Coin's words came out as more plea than threat. 'Or we – *he* – will hang your brother. *Please.*'

She tried to imagine what it would be like to be this person, for ever caught between genders, forever a freak. *Coin is fixated on Gyle, but I don't think those feelings are reciprocated.*

'Coin, Gurvon Gyle doesn't care about anyone but himself. He's using you.'

'No, he *loves* me.' Coin's denial stank of desperation. 'If you were dead, he'd realise . . .'

Cera felt his urge to violence returning, but she had a weapon now. 'He lied to you about Solinde.'

Coin started to deny it, but her anger collapsed and her face shifted again, back to Symone. A paroxysm of anguish contorted his visage and he whirled and fled.

Only when Cera was sure Coin was well gone did she sink to the floor, trembling in shock.

Below her, a riot had started, but she was barely aware.

'SHALIYAH! SHALIYAH!'

It was months since the great triumph at Shaliyah, but still the Jhafi weren't tiring of the chant. Hundreds of young men continued to publically celebrate the victory, screaming taunts and insults, and wrecking and burning whatever was to hand. Gurvon had finally given up turning a blind eye and tonight he'd ordered a Kirkegarde cavalry unit to subdue them; the Church soldiers had gone charging into the people, belabouring whoever came within reach with maces and trampling many more with their horses, killing dozens and injuring hundreds, while Gyle watched from the walls, sipping coffee and trying to control his irritation.

Mara Secordin and Rutt Sordell knew better than to come near him in this mood, instead hovering nearby in case he needed them, but Coin wasn't so wise. The shapeshifter, wearing her 'Symone' guise, stormed up, clearly distressed.

Rutt had just reported seeing Symone leaving the Blood-tower in tears.

I can guess why . . .

He whirled on her angrily. 'Yvette, you went to see Cera, despite my order not to.'

'How do you know?' Coin blurted stupidly.

'Because I know *everything*.' He jabbed a finger into her chest. 'Why?'

'I . . . I told her that if she didn't stop obstructing us, I'd kill her . . .'

'Is that why you went to her? To *kill* her?'

'No! I just threatened her – she knows about Olivia.'

'You *revealed* yourself to her?'

'She had guessed already,' Coin whined. 'I wanted to scare her into silence.'

'So how did that go?' he demanded sarcastically.

311

Coin bowed his head. 'She was very frightened.'

'So scared that she made you cry, or so I hear,' he said scornfully. 'Get out of my sight! Go back to Olivia's rooms and don't come out! Play with her dolls – it's all you're rukking well good for!'

Coin's face crumpled.

And I've lost her. Coin had always been damaged goods, but now she was broken. He could see it clearly; the shapeshifter's whole demeanour had altered. He was on the verge of raising a hand to signal to Mara, but there were soldiers on the parapets above; they might be out of earshot, but they could see him clearly. This was too public.

'You told me that Solinde would only be imprisoned, not killed,' Coin said miserably.

Not that again.

During the time she'd spent with Solinde Nesti, right at the beginning of this mission, Coin had begun to sympathise with with the Nesti princess. So he'd lied to her, the only way he could persuade her to get the job done – and then she'd walked in on Mara's 'royal meal', and that had caused Coin's breakdown while she was with Fernando Tolidi. That in turn had allowed Elena to discover Coin's involvement.

I should have let the wretch die.

'I'm not like you,' Coin whispered. 'I can't do all these things and not think about them.'

'Then go home – run back to Mummy and see if she'll give you a cuddle.'

'But you said—' The shapeshifter wavered, bewildered. 'My mother—'

'Lucia doesn't give a shit about you, Yvette,' he gritted, his control completely lost, for once telling her the truth, no matter how she might react. 'She wished I'd let you rukking well die – *now get out of my sight!*'

Her face went white and Mara began to glide closer, and damn, but it was tempting . . .

Coin backed up, her face mottled, her gnosis glimmering, and

Gurvon belatedly remembered that this emotionally broken thing was a pure-blood mage who'd killed a dozen men or more.

He raised his own shields and stepped back. *Rukking Hel! I've messed this up badly.* He waved Mara away and reached out a hand, tried to retrieve the situation. 'I'm sorry, Yvette. I lost my temper – I didn't mean any of that. I'm stressed – we all are, aren't we? Please, go back to your room. We'll talk later, once we're all calmer.'

He wasn't sure she would go. For a few seconds, the lost child in her warred with the shapeshifting monster and a dozen subtle changes rippled through her face and body, moving at blinding speed, before she settled into Symone's form again.

When the shapeshifter spoke, his voice was plaintive. 'I might be a freak, but I have a heart and a soul.' His chin wobbled. 'I'm so scared – every night I dream that Kore will cast me into the Eternal Pit when I die.'

Good grief! After the kind of life she's had, she's still a Believer? Incredible . . .

But she wasn't coming at him with tooth and talon, and that was good . . .

'Damn it, Yvette,' he murmured in what he hoped was a placatory voice, 'you must believe me when I tell you that Cera Nesti is nothing to me but a conduit to Elena.'

'And what am I?'

'A comrade-in-arms,' he said quickly. 'More – you're someone whose welfare I care about.'

'Care about,' she echoed, then, 'What does that mean?'

'It means I am concerned for you, Yvette: that's a lot. I look after my own. You know this. I rebuilt you, Yvette – never doubt that I care.'

She looked utterly confused now, but she clung to those words, as he'd hoped she would. She stammered apologies as she left.

When she was gone he sagged against the wall then glanced at Mara. 'You're right, she'll have to go. But not yet. We're still too thinly spread.'

'Coin is a weak link,' Mara replied in her flat, hungry voice. 'You notice them more when the chain is short.'

'I know – but right now there's just you, me, Rutt and Madeline.' He grimaced. 'I'm going to pull more of the team out of Yuros and bring them here – we need to get our numbers up again. For now, we'll just have to keep an eye on her.'

Mara looked utterly unimpressed. 'We don't have enough eyes to do that, Gurv. Let me kill her – I promise you'll not even find her bones.'

It was tempting . . . But he shook his head.

Perhaps I'll regret it later, but for now I can still use her.

16

Deciphering the Runes

Sorcery: Clairvoyance

There are a number of ways an ordinary person can thwart a Seer. They can conduct their business in closed rooms with stone walls and no windows, or beside a large fountain. Better yet, be underground, or underwater, or both. Meet in darkness, and at irregular times. But the only really foolproof way is to hire another mage to set wards for you – if you can find one you trust more than the one you suspect is spying on you.

JULIANO DI TRATO, SILACIA 555

*Mandira Khojana, Lokistan, on the continent of Antiopia
Akhira (Junesse) 929
12th month of the Moontide*

Summer came to the valley below the Mandira Khojana monastery in a profusion of wild poppies that covered the high slopes. People brought food and other supplies, and the monks went down to the mountain villages to tend the sick and dispense their knowledge and wisdom, doing everything from repairing houses and bridges to acting as notaries, recording wills and contracts.

The days rolled by, warm beneath serene blue skies, even here among the peaks, but for Alaron and Ramita they passed in a blur of fresh accomplishments and body-bruising failures. Alaron could clearly feel the benefits of Master Puravai's training regimen now, and not just in his body, but in his mind as well. He could exercise harder, and concentrate longer. And at last he was feeling at home among the novices.

Few of them spoke fluent Rondian, but they all had some words, and were eager to use Alaron to practise upon. He had learned their names early, and as the days went on, he made a few tentative friendships: young men he could laugh with during the physical rough-and- tumble of the morning training in the yards. Yash was still his closest companion; the novice in turn gained kudos for his friendship with a Rondian mage.

Like any group, there were conflicts at times, but they were swiftly dealt with by the masters. Sometimes their justice was harsh, often humiliating, but it was always fair.

Each afternoon, after a hurried lunch of soup and flatbread, he would leave the novices to their academic lessons while he went to the library, to wrestle with the Scytale and its secrets, trying to track down the complex chemical symbols by studying the medical scrolls that had been gifted to the monastery over the years by passing Ordo Costruo magi. Most days he made little to no progress, but by Junesse he had identified another seven symbols, and had narrowed down another thirty.

Late afternoon was the best part of the day, when he and Ramita studied the gnosis. They had both mastered all four of the elements now, and that alone felt utterly incredible. At the Arcanum he'd been taught such a thing was impossible. He wished Ramon was there to see him purify water, or make it dance, even breathe it now. He could call the wind and recharge the skiff's keel all by himself – he had never even dared to dream of doing such things! He imagined himself going back to Turm Zauberin one day and amazing those tutors who'd called him a numbskull, and worse.

But best of all was just being with Ramita. The more he got to know her, the more he appreciated her pert wit and surprising sophistication. She might not have had his education, but she was intuitive and logical and dogged. He treasured their time together.

As they started on the other parts of the gnosis, the more cerebral parts – Hermetic, Theurgy and Sorcery – so the amount of mental work increased. He'd always been a fair mystic, able to link minds for better sharing of information, and he engaged that now so he could demonstrate and share the skill with her, as he and Ramon had once done with Cym. This time he had a much better idea of what he was doing and it speeded their progress markedly, but it came with additional facets: he caught glimpses of her feelings, her memories, her moods – never much, and they both shut it down as soon as they were aware – but it still happened, breaking down barriers they'd scarcely even been aware of. He saw nothing he didn't like. Even the things he didn't understand, like her religious devotion, and her self-effacing sense of duty, he began to find charming rather than annoying – but at times it felt too personal, on both sides.

Some days he could feel her pain, like when she remembered too vividly all she'd lost to be here, and there were times when he revealed too much, like his old feelings for Cym, or his moon-dreams about Anise in Silacia, but even those were receding as time passed. If they'd been at home in Norostein and Ramita was any other girl, he'd be giving her flowers and maybe asking to walk with her, but Ramita was Lady Meiros, a Lakh widow to whom truly terrible things had happened, and he had no idea how to deal with that.

Ramon would've called him a wimp. Perhaps he was, but he just tried to enjoy what they had.

Those rare evenings when he wasn't so exhausted he collapsed, he relaxed with Yash, who taught him to play a board game called Goha which involved black and white stones placed in specific sequences or patterns. It wasn't long before Alaron realised that the young novice fled whenever Ramita appeared.

'I think you have an admirer,' he teased her one evening.

'Who? Your friend with the big stick?' Ramita then blushed furiously and started giggling. 'No! That is not what I meant to say! I'm sure his stick is the normal size! No – I mean–!' She dissolved, and Alaron enjoyed the sound of her laughter.

'Anyway,' Ramita said when she regained her composure, 'Zain monks are celibate.'

'They're still men.'

'I'm a new mother – I have never been less attractive, of that I am sure.'

Alaron shook his head. 'I think you're very pretty.'

He'd spoken without thinking and at first he thought he'd offended her, but she took the compliment composedly. 'Thank you, Al'Rhon – but I am a widow also, and it is not my concern to be pretty. I still mourn my husband.'

'I know.' She was still wearing widow's whites, though Meiros was dead more than a year now. 'Mourning periods in Yuros are usually a year,' he said, trying to sneak up on that question, but her response took him aback.

'In southern Lakh the widow is sometimes burned on her husband's pyre – if not, she goes into a widows' refuge. She may not marry again.'

He blinked, aghast. 'That's horrible!'

'I think so too – but that is in the south, where people are strange. In the north of Lakh, where I am from, mourning is one year, and then the woman must be cleansed and purified by a priest, after which she may remarry.'

'Your husband died just over a year ago.' Then he bit his lip. 'I'm just saying . . . I'm sorry if I've given offence.'

Her face clouded. 'I know. But I am not ready for another man. I may never be.'

'Why not?' he asked, his tongue darting ahead of his brain. 'I mean, it is right to mourn, of course, but—'

She interrupted. 'There was a young man to whom I was promised. I loved him all my life, but he followed me north, and he murdered my husband. I loved them both, but one killed the other. Most days I think I will never love again.'

He looked away, remembering memories he'd inadvertently seen of hers, of a younger man holding her. *Sweet Kore . . . did she cuckold Meiros?* He couldn't imagine it of her. *It must've happened before she was married . . .*

'I'm sorry,' he said lamely, at last. He stared into space, trying to think of Cym or Anise, but that did no good at all.

She took his hand and pulled it to her. 'Hold still,' she said.

He looked at her curiously as she fished into a pocket and drew out a piece of orange string. She carefully knotted it about his right wrist.

'What's this?' His voice took on a panicky tone. 'Did you—? Are we—? Are we *married* now?'

She snorted. 'Married! Of course not! You really are a barbarian! That might be how things are done in your homeland, but marriages in *proper* places take days of preparation and ritual, not a piece of string!' She reached out and tweaked his chin. 'It means that you are now my brother, Al'Rhon Mercer.'

'*Your brother?*'

'Yes. I just adopted you. This is a rakhi string. It signifies that you are my brother.'

He flushed painfully. 'Oh . . . So what does that mean?'

'Your duties are to protect me and guide me, and to find me a new husband.'

'Oh.' *How did I get myself into this?* 'Um, what's in it for me?'

She put on an affronted face, but her voice was amused. 'It is a great honour, and a serious obligation, Goat! You get the privilege of calling me sister! And I have to give you a new string once a year, at the Raksha Bandan festival in Shaban – your Augeite. And I will cook you sweets.' She beamed at him, though her eyes were serious. 'I make very fine sweets.'

'I see.' He thought he did, too: *Brothers can't marry sisters.* 'And what do I call my sister?'

'Didi. And you are my bhaiya.'

'Didi. Okay, I accept. When do you want me to start looking for a husband for you?'

'I'll let you know.' She waggled her head in a 'right then' manner, and dropped her voice. 'Have you learned all you can here? Is it time for us to go on?'

'Not yet: there're still hundreds of scrolls I've not got to. And I feel like I'm missing half the clues this place could offer. I wish Ramon and Cym were here.' Then something struck him and his voice trailed off . . .

'You have an idea?' Ramita asked. 'Please, tell me.'

He pulled out the Scytale and laid it on the table. He pointed first to the runes, then picked up one of the leather straps. 'In ancient time, the legions used scytales to encode messages. It had one strap that you wrapped around it in a certain way, like this, to make a link between certain symbols, so if you got an encoded message and you knew the right configuration, you could decrypt the message – so it looks like gibberish, until you work out what the correct symbols are.' He unwrapped the strap to show her.

'But the Scytale of Corineus has *four* straps, see? And there are these domes all along the length where the straps can be attached. That means there are *thousands* of combinations – and I don't know even know what all the runes mean yet, just some of them.'

She waggled her head: *I think I understand*. 'But you have an idea, bhaiya?'

'Well, what I think is that there is a specific combination for any given person, based on things like their birthday, their affinities if they are a mage, and other things like that. The runes seem to be a code for unravelling what kind of person should be given what particular mix of the potion. I understand most of the gnostic runes, but the chemical ones are outside my knowledge – and I can't find them anywhere in the archives here.'

Ramita looked thoughtful. 'My husband didn't speak of this.'

'The Scytale wasn't devised until well after the first Ritual – I doubt Meiros ever saw it. They say Baramitius tested different drugs on Corineus' followers for years before the Ascension.'

'Then he sounds despicable.' Ramita tapped her fingers on the table. 'To determine my affinities, Justina tested me: she asked me lots of questions, and made me use gnosis on different elements. Do you think this Scytale might do the same?'

'Kind of: I think it helps you make a better, safer potion for that particular person.' Alaron showed her the four elemental runes at the top of the Scytale, and the other four, symbolising the theoretical Studies at the other end. 'Look, did Lady Justina show you these?'

Ramita cast her mind back. 'Yes! They were the symbols on her board: Earth is my prime affinity. Well . . . it was! Do these even apply to us any more?'

'I don't know . . . but let's just go with it for now. Look, if I twist both ends, like so, new symbols appear in each of the sixty-four holes, see? And if I clip the straps to these domes, these others are concealed . . . So if I was assessing you . . . the first layer of symbols include a feminine one, so if I take this strap and clip it to this dome . . . and these could represent age . . . you're still young, so this one . . . but look, there are still six more things to determine, like this next one, which just seem to be colours, see: blue, brown, green and grey.'

'Eyes,' she said instantly. 'Eyes are those colours.'

He slapped his forehead. 'Eyes! You're right . . .' He looked at her. 'Brown eyes. So . . .' He felt a little surge of excitement as he went to move the strap and tried to click the next dome, but the brown symbol was too far around and the previous one popped out as he tugged. He let out a another frustrated grunt. 'Damn! I thought we were onto something there.'

Ramita reached for the Scytale and he found himself about to snatch it out of reach. *I didn't come half way round the world for her to break it* . . . Then he realised how ridiculous that was: the artefact was wrapped in so many spells it was practically indestructible.

He let go and she turned it over in her hard little hands, frowning as she poked and prodded it.

'See, it won't go,' he said. 'And I don't know where the other straps go. It makes no sense.'

Ramita looked up. 'You think that matching the characteristics of a person to these symbols will reveal a recipe, yes? In this recipe is it best to have lots of ingredients, or few?'

He screwed up his nose. 'Well . . . it depends. I think it's more likely that there's a core recipe that's got variants, than the other way around . . .' He thought about that for a moment, then finished, 'Yes, I think that's most probably the case.'

'Well, in that case I would think you would pin all the straps, yes? Then you will cover more of the red runes on the body of the cylinder and leave fewer variants?' She clipped the domes down, this time leaving the panels representing Earth, female, young and brown-eyed uncovered. 'See? That way I can cover them all and leave uncovered just the ones that are important, yes?'

He stared at the Scytale, and then at her. 'You know, you might actually be onto something.' Then he stammered, because he'd not meant to sound so condescending, 'I don't mean *actually*, I mean—'

'Al'Rhon. *Goat*. Shut your mouth, like so.' She made a closing gesture with her finger.

'Yeah. Sorry. Thinking before I speak isn't my strongest point.'

'Don't feel bad. All men are brought up to think women are lesser. Then you fail to educate us, just to make sure. That you even know you are doing it makes you one of the most promising men I have met.'

He grinned at that, but instead of smiling in return her eyes suddenly misted over, as if something in his face had triggered a memory too sad to contain, and she began to cry.

He floundered uncertainly, then reached out and enfolded her, half-expecting to be pushed away, but she didn't. It was an awkward embrace: she was so short she only reached his ribs, but she clung to him and sobbed until her tears had soaked his shirt. He murmured some stream-of-consciousness babble about looking after her, stroking her head, and all the time wishing he was manly enough to tip her head upwards and kiss her.

'What's wrong?' he asked eventually, as her weeping subsided.

'For a moment, I saw my husband,' she whispered, completely killing his ardour. She stepped away and he let her go.

She looked at me and saw her husband ... He had no idea what to make of that.

'Life's drum never stops beating,' she said softly. 'It is an old Lakh saying: I think I understand it now ... *bhaiya*.'

17

Ardijah

Hermetic: Sylvan-gnosis

Sylvanic Gnosis is a neglected aspect of the Gnostic Arts, in our view. But you are best to respect the Woodcrafter, whose gnosis can wreck a windship or a building, whose potions can restore you or poison you, whose arrows fly true, and whose will can send a tree striding across the battlefield.

ORDO COSTRUO COLLEGIATE, PONTUS

Ardijah, Emirate of Khotriawal, on the continent of Antiopia
Akhira (Junesse) 929
12th month of the Moontide

Ramon helped Severine Tiseme down from her wagon. The Pallacian girl was holding her belly and grimacing in pain. In the past month it had swollen up like the inflated pig-bladders the children kicked about his village in Silacia. She clutched at him as her legs wobbled. *She's not built for suffering and discomfort*, he thought guiltily; Sevvie was many things, but not robust. She wasn't exactly a survivor, and that worried him – one of many things troubling his sleep.

Death in labour was common enough in the masses, but it happened at times to magi too, despite healing-gnosis and the best of care. He tried to put that fear from his mind and smile for her, even though she had become incredibly tetchy of late. The romance between them was souring: most nights she wouldn't even share a tent with him, let alone anything more – she had conceived this mad idea that he and Jelaska had some kind of affair going on. *Jelaska!*

Apart from anything else, Jelaska was with Sigurd Vaas and Ramon had no desire to fall foul of the big Argundian. And paranoia was far from Severine's only unattractive quality, he was finding out. But things hadn't come to a head, and anyway, she was carrying his child.

'Where are we?' she asked breathily, clinging to his arm.

He pointed down from the hill-top to the vista below: there were twin islands in the middle of the floodplain, linked to this bank and the far one by giant causeways. Water boiled through arches beneath both roads. 'Ardijah.'

She squinted diffidently, and wrinkled her nose. 'It's not very big, is it?'

'It is too small for any of the maps we have,' Ramon agreed. 'But it's a key point on a major trading route, linking Khotriawal Emirate to southern Kesh. It's really just a place where the two ends of a bridge could be anchored and a causeway built.'

'So what it's generals call "strategic", hmm?'

'Very.' He studied the water flowing past them, which looked like it was running lower than even a few days ago, well within the normal floodplain boundaries. The freakish conditions caused by the Shaliyah storm were finally fading as nature reasserted itself. But crossing anywhere but here was still out of the question.

Severine looked at the town longingly. 'Can we go straight in, or do we have to kill someone first? I'd murder for a feather bed.'

'You might have to.' He glanced towards the command group. 'I'll go and talk to the Lesser Son.'

'You should be nicer to Seth,' she said. 'They're saying he drove off the Keshi at the crossroads all by himself.'

Ramon pursed his lips. That wasn't how he'd heard it from Lanna Jureigh: a panicked reaction and a fluky spell after messing up the basics big-time. *I should have been there – or left Sigurd with him, or Bondeau, even Kip.* Any one of them would have handled it better than Korion had. And they'd lost the chaplain; he might've been useless, but he was still a mage. *What mage forgets to rukking shield?*

'If you can find us a bed, you can join me in it tonight,' she said, her voice diffident. 'If you still want to.'

'Of course I still want to,' he replied, unsure if that was entirely the case. He pecked Sevvie's cheek dutifully and went to see what the plan was. Or rather, to make sure it was *his plan*.

The magi were gathered about Seth, staring down at the causeway and the two fortress-islands in the middle. Heads turned as he entered the gathering. Kip grinned, and Jelaska and Sigurd nodded a greeting. Bondeau looked at him sourly, the others had neutral expressions on their faces.

Ramon's ambush for the Keshi had been a mild success: a few dozen of the enemy's advance guard had been caught in a maelstrom of fire and lightning and burned to a crisp: death en masse, with no losses. As a result, the Keshi had certainly become more cautious. *But some of us should have been with Seth . . .* It'd been Ramon's idea, and so it was his fault. He needed to rebuild credibility.

Seth looked hollow, as if the marrow from his spine had been bled away. He clearly would rather be alone, but generals had to be visible, *touchable* – and in obvious control of what was happening. There were subtle signs of a kind of grim determination forming as well, though, as if the soft, prevaricating part of Seth Korion was being pared away, revealing something brittle but harder beneath.

Right now, the young general was pointing towards the town across the causeway, where pennants were flying, and armoured men patrolling the walls. 'There are two halves to this town,' he started, 'linked by a bridge – the northern causeway is too long to cross before they can close the gates. So how do we get in?'

'If we had a couple more days,' Bondeau said, 'we could wait for the storm-water to drain away, which would leave us a plain we could cross, apart from the middle channel. Then we could attack the nearer keep on three sides.'

'It's no use talking about what we *wished* we faced,' Jelaska sniffed.

'At least it's only Khotri men. They've got no magi,' Seth commented.

'We didn't think they had magi at Shaliyah either,' Sigurd observed dourly.

'What did you see when you flew over the bridge-towers, Windmaster Prenton?' Jelaska asked the Brevian.

Baltus gestured flamboyantly. 'Just a bridge and a pair of close-packed walled towns at either end. There're a lot of soldiers in a big camp on the other side of the river too.'

'So even if we could take Ardijah, there's an army on the other side?' Seth asked anxiously.

'If the Khotri don't want to just let us march through, yes,' Ramon replied, trying hard to keep from sounding sarcastic. There'd been an unspoken truce since the incident at the junction: both he and Seth knew they'd not performed well, but attacking each other would see Renn Bondeau pushing for leadership again, and neither wanted that. 'We should talk to them,' he said calmly. 'I'm told that the Khotri don't like the Keshi much.'

'The Keshi aren't "afreets" to them,' Jelaska remarked, 'but we are.'

'What would we say anyway?' Bondeau sneered. 'Please may we move our army into your territory?'

'Why not?' Ramon replied. 'We're not invading – we're just manoeuvring.'

'It doesn't work like that,' Sigurd said. 'Soldiers rape and pillage and kill people. It's what they do. No one lets even their own army into their towns in peacetime if they don't have to.'

'All right, so let's bribe them,' Ramon suggested.

Seth looked exasperated. 'With what, exactly? We've got nothing they'd want. We should attack.'

Wins one fight and thinks he's his Daddy ...

'That causeway is wide enough for about ten men riding abreast,' Baltus commented, 'and it's open to the entire gate-tower and surrounding walls. I don't know about you chaps, but I don't think I could shield a dozen arrows at once, or even one ballista – did I mention they have at least four of those positioned over the gate?'

'How far behind us are the Keshi?' Sigurd Vaas asked.

'A day at most.'

'Any bright ideas?' Jelaska asked. 'Because otherwise it's a frontal assault down the causeway.'

As if drawn by a magnet, everyone turned to Ramon, even Bondeau, who looked ready to pounce on whatever he said.

Ramon rubbed his chin. 'Let me talk to them. At least I might get an idea of what we're up against – anything they say or don't say will be instructive.'

'Waste of Kore-bedamned time,' Renn Bondeau swore.

'We'll see. I'll need Storn; he can speak their language.' Then he turned to Seth, as an afterthought, 'Well, great leader?'

'Very well. There's nothing to lose, is there?' Seth sounded tired.

Ramon frowned: the loss of Tyron Frand had clearly hurt Seth badly. He looked in desperate need of a new confidante.

Sevvie? he wondered. *She's a nob too . . . No, Seth doesn't really talk to women. Lots of men can't – we live such different lives.*

He put the thought aside for now; there was too much else to do.

Arranging the parley took an hour, with lots of waving white pennants and Storn shouting in Keshi from a point on the causeway about one hundred yards from the gatehouse. Initially they were dealing with guardsmen, then an immense and luridly dressed man arrived, surrounded by men in dark cloaks. Ramon fed Storn his lines and the tribune dutifully translated – which turned out to be not as easy as he'd hoped, for the Khotri dialect differed somewhat from Keshi.

'Who's the big guy?' Ramon asked Storn as they awaited a reply to their last request.

'He says he's Vizier to the Caliph of Ardijah.'

'Caliph?'

'The ruling nobleman.' Storn frowned. 'I don't think they mean to make a deal, sir. I think they know the Keshi are coming too; I reckon they're planning to just delay us.'

'Offer them gold.'

Storn's eyebrow's shot up. 'Gold? *Our* gold?'

'Indeed. We've got rather a lot of it.'

'But—'

'Seriously, Storn! We've got most of the Southern Expedition's gold in our wagons, have we not? But we won't have it for long if the Keshi catch us outside those walls.' He considered for a moment, then said decisively, 'Offer them fifty thousand.'

Storn's eyes bulged. 'That's more than the annual wages of the army! You can't give that away, not just for a talk!'

'Of course not – but I can dangle it, can't I? At worst it'll make them want to extract it from us so the Keshi don't get it.' He pointed to the vizier in the distance. 'Ask.'

Storn muttered and looked rebellious, but after a moment he shouted out a few phrases, all the while waving his arms about in expansive gestures – presumably to convey the magnitude of the offer, Ramon thought.

There was a startled yelp from the vizier, then he and the cloaked men went into a huddle. It took them a full minute to reply, but even in an unknown tongue, Ramon could hear the studied eagerness of the conman who thought he'd found an easy mark.

'They say they'll talk,' Storn told him sulkily. 'Four on each side, no weapons, and no more than one mage in our group. They propose sunset.'

'And waste another half a day? Not rukking likely! Tell them we'll parlay right now . . . and tell them I want to speak to the caliph himself as well as his vizier.'

There was a further rapid exchange, and this time Ramon could see when the Khotri agreement was reached. He looked over his shoulder to where the other magi were watching from the small rise above the beginning of the causeway. He closed his eyes, clutched his periapt and sent a mental greeting to Seth. <They'll talk.>

The general's son sounded startled at the contact. <You can reach me from there?> There was some four hundred yards between them; it was a reasonable feat for a low-blood.

<Evidently,> Ramon replied. <Now listen up.> He rattled through the proposal as quickly as he could, but he didn't mention the gold, nor why the vizier had agreed to the parley. <So, do you agree?>

<I suppose you wish to be the negotiator?> Seth replied snottily.

<Obviously.>

A sigh, then, <Very well.>

He closed down the link and turned to the tribune. 'It's on, Storn. Ten minutes.'

Time passed quickly as they brought up the men he'd chosen for the task: big, bluff Vidran, and the flankman Kel Harmon, a lean young man with fashionably long flaxen hair and a very high opinion of himself. He'd picked them specifically; they were Pilus Lukaz's men, the best fighters in the cohort.

Ramon looked at Vidran. 'Where are you from, Legionary?'

'Midrea, sir, but I'm part Schlessen.' Vidran took off his helmet and ran his fingers through his lank black hair. 'That's where the muscle comes from,' he added with a grin.

'Half-barbarian,' Harmon sniffed.

'And you are—?' Ramon asked.

'Pallas born and bred, sir,' the flankman replied. 'Tockburn District – best people anywhere.'

Vidran grunted, 'Thieves and cut-throats!'

But as Ramon turned to scan the gate for activity he could see Vidran and Harmon exchanging wry smiles and hear the low banter.

'When's the enemy going to reach here, sir?' Vidran asked, his voice relaxed.

'Probably the day after tomorrow.'

Harmon grunted. 'I'd have thought they'd all be back in Shallywotsit, getting lammy.'

Ramon raised an eyebrow. 'Lammy?'

'Y'know. Lammy – pissed.'

'Drunk?'

'Aye, that. Lammy.' Harmon laughed drily. 'That's if the Noories drink. Do they, Vid?'

'The ones that ain't Amteh fanatics do,' Vidran replied, his eyes darting about. The big ranker was constantly watchful, Ramon noticed. 'That's most of them, I guess. Man's gotta drink, yar?'

Harmon chuckled. 'Too bloody right.' Then the set of his muscles altered and the slightly nonchalant look on his face was replaced by something altogether grimmer. 'Here they come, sir.'

Ramon whispered a silent prayer to Papa Sol as trumpets blared and the gates rumbled open to allow out an open palanquin bearing a man and woman, he in colourful Khotri robes, she in a black bekira-shroud, borne on the shoulders of four big men, naked to the waist and impressively muscled. They were trailed by the waddling vizier and one of the dark-cloaked advisors.

Ramon warily watched them approaching, his eyes constantly scanning them for signs of threat while Harmon and Vidran studied the walls. He got the impression that the vizier was sick with fear, but the caliph and his woman looked composed, almost smugly at ease.

Which one's the mage? Ramon wondered. He glanced at Storn. 'Tell them that the bearers can come no further.'

Storn relayed the message, and to his relief the palanquin was gently lowered and the caliph rose to his feet. He was a big, lean man with dark, tanned skin and a face that might have been chiselled from granite. His head was shaven, apart from a black topknot, and he had an almost barbarous vitality to him, not at all what Ramon was expecting of the ruler of a small town.

The woman with him cast back the hood of her bekira-shroud, revealing a stunning face, wide-mouthed and red-lipped, with big bewitching eyes and a sultry, almost mocking expression on her face. Her copper hair rippled in the faint breeze. She didn't look right either: all the Antiopian women Ramon had seen were meek and shrouded things, seldom seen in public. He began to feel his apprehension rise.

The third man kept his hood up, and just the hint of a vulturine nose distinguished him. Ramon stared at them, his unease turning to alarm. Their skin was surprising: none of them had the the natural darkness of an Easterner but the burnished hue of a tanned Yurosian. But it was their auras that made him catch his breath: every one of the three was all oily film and roiling tentacles.

These people weren't just magi: they were Souldrinkers. *The enemy's beaten us here.*

The stone-faced man spoke first. 'I am Yorj Arkanus, Leader of the Brethren. This is my wife, Hecatta, and my colleague, Zsdryk.' He indicated the hooded man with the hatchet-nose, then waved a loose hand towards the vizier. 'And ... whoever he is.'

The vizier cringed. His eyes met Ramon's, pleading for help so plainly he could have been shrieking it from the rooftops. His clothing was absolutely sodden with sweat, with huge wet stains under his armpits, around his belly and down his back as well: not too much sun, but too much fear.

So this parley was a sham, a delaying tactic to keep them busy while Salim's army came up behind them. It was a traditional hammer-and-anvil scenario – and they were caught in the middle. And here they had three gnosis-users against just him.

Ramon gave a half-bow, as if all if this were totally expected, trying to appear unflappably cool, though his heart was thudding painfully hard. He made his own introductions, then turned to the vizier. 'I trust the real caliph and calipha are well?'

'He and his wife are completely irrelevant,' Arkanus interjected. 'This whole emirate will soon belong to me.' He chuckled. 'We've been watching you from afar, magus – I arrived in Ardijah a week ago. The caliph and his family are my prisoners.' He sneered. 'Perhaps you'd like to join them and sit out the coming battle?'

'I don't think so.'

'I am as strong as one of your pure-bloods,' Arkanus boasted, 'and so is my wife and so is Zsdryk. I have thirty Fire-magi with me and a dozen Earth-magi, all of our Brethren. A thirty-strong pack of animagi accompany the army – more than enough to deal with you and yours.'

Ramon filed the numbers away. *Sol et Lune, we are in trouble.* 'Is there a point to this parley?' he asked calmly.

'You asked for it,' Arkanus growled. 'I believe there was a question of gold?'

'That seems irrelevant now.'

Arkanus smirked. 'It does rather, seeing as we'll be taking it off you anyway.'

'Then I think we are finished.'

'Perhaps we will simply kill you, right here, to send a message to your commander?' Arkanus suggested mildly.

'Your honour is justly renowned,' Ramon replied sarcastically, while his pulse throbbed.

331

'Do not speak to me of honour, mage,' he spat. 'In the name of your god you have murdered and tortured my kindred for centuries. There has been no tool you have not employed to entrap and destroy us.' Arkanus stalked towards him, tapped him on the chest. 'But I will allow you to return to your commander. I wish him to know who awaits him in Ardijah. Get you gone, and pray for an easy death tomorrow.'

The hooded man, Zsdryk, snarled something in a guttural voice; the intonations were Sydian. His mouth was full of long yellowed teeth, like an old wolf.

Harmon and Vidran took an involuntary step back; Storn took three.

Ramon motioned to them to back away whil he kept his eyes locked on the three Dokken. Arkanus watched him every step of the way, while Hecatta whispered in his ear and Zsdryk just stared. The vizier looked like his knees were wobbling so hard beneath his robes that standing was almost beyond him.

Ramon murmured a command and they turned and walked away, all the while their backs tingling in fear of a ballista shot or arrow from the wall.

Now what do we do?

Vidran put a hand on his shoulder. 'Sir?' His voice was calm as his eyes.

His hand steadied Ramon somehow. 'Thank you, Vidran.'

'What's the plan, sir?'

Seth Korion waited on the hill as Ramon Sensini climbed towards him. He'd never seen the little Silacian look so angry. 'What happened? Can we enter?'

'The Dokken are already here. The parley was a sham.'

The magi all groaned aloud.

'I told you it was stupid,' Renn Bondeau said.

Ramon glared at the Pallacian until Jelaska put a restraining hand on his shoulder and whispered something in his ear.

Seth felt like breaking down. They had fled across the desert, exhausting themselves to get here, and all the time they had just been running into the enemy's arms. 'What . . . what do we do?' he asked, trying to keep his voice firm. 'Move on?'

Ramon looked at him contemptuously. 'Well, *General*, we've almost run out of stores and I rather suspect that if we travel a few miles further west, we may well run into another army.' The Silacian ran his fingers through his hair. It looked like he was thinking furiously. 'No,' he said distractedly, 'we need to think this through.'

Renn Bondeau slapped his thigh impatiently. 'Think, think! Thinking gets us nowhere! We must attack, now!'

'We should emblazon that on your gravestone,' Jelaska drawled.

Sigurd Vaas stepped in front of Bondeau and tapped his breastplate. 'You will be silent now.'

Bondeau straightened and for a moment it looked like he was about to start a brawl. But Vaas had a hard reputation . . . They settled for glaring at each other until one of Bondeau's Brevian friends pulled him away.

Seth watched helplessly, wishing he could come up with a plan, but his brain refused to suggest anything. The Silacian huddled with his confederates, Jelaska, Vaas, Baltus and Kippenegger, as if only their opinions mattered. It was humiliating, having to wait like this, but he could think of nothing useful to contribute.

Finally Ramon Sensini turned back to the group. He looked like he'd recovered a little of his usual obnoxious spirit – his grin wasn't as forced this time. 'Listen, thanks to their boasting leader, we know that there are forty Souldrinkers inside Ardijah – but the soldiers are all Khotri, and I don't think they're happy. Remember, these are Dokken: *everyone* hates them, even here. What if that Khotri army on the far side aren't here to block us, but to keep the Souldrinkers penned inside?'

Bondeau went to say something, then shut his mouth when Vaas met his eye.

Ramon pointed at the sun. 'It's almost midday. I think we do need to attack, but not in the way we're expected to.' He jabbed a finger at the Windmaster. 'Ready your skiff to take Storn and me across the river: I want to talk to the Khotri on the far side. We'll need to circle out of sight so Arkanus doesn't work out what we're up to. Jelaska, these Dokken are all Thaumaturges and animagi. Sorcery is their weakness, and you're our best. You need to prepare something to support our assault. Bondeau, take all our cavalry and go find some enemy to kill on our back trail. We need you to slow Salim down and buy us time – but you need to get out alive.' He looked about the group. 'Who's our best sylvanic mage?'

Wilbrecht, one of Bondeau's Brevian friends, put up a hand.

'How many wagons do you think you can convert into boats in the space of an afternoon?'

Wilbrecht blinked. 'To seal the timbers so that they are watertight? That is simple, at least to hold for a short time. But they will barely be able to be steered.'

'We have Water-mages for that,' Ramon replied. 'Get onto it.' He looked at Sigurd. 'There are three pure-blood equivalents among the Dokken, but they don't use periapts and I'm guessing they don't have anything like our Arcanum-style training. Can we take them down?'

'If we know their weaknesses.'

'You've heard them. We'll need to use Sorcery and Theurgy, attack their minds.' He clapped his hands. 'Anyone else got something to contribute?' He looked at Bondeau as if expecting an objection.

'I'm fine with my role,' the Pallacian muttered. 'At last, some actual fighting.'

'Who will lead the frontal attack?' Kip asked.

'I will,' Seth replied quickly, firmly, though he felt like he'd just declared an intention to slit his own wrists.

Everyone looked at him sceptically.

'It's my duty,' he said firmly, as his face drained of colour.

18

Unmasked

The Death of Emperor Magnus

909 saw the most recent transition of power in Pallas, from Emperor Magnus to Constant, his son-in-law. Though Constant was legally the heir, it was nevertheless a bloody transition. Some doubts remain about whether Magnus died naturally, and a large number of supporters of the older sister, Natia, died amidst violent unrest, including her husband. Natia herself has been imprisoned. Much of the violence was was directed towards Constant's mother, Lucia Fasterius, seen as a malign influence by most of those who died.

ORDO COSTRUO, HEBUSALIM CHAPTER

Northern Javon, on the continent of Antiopia
Jumada (Maicin) 929
11ᵗʰ month of the Moontide

Elena Anborn slipped into the opium den, anonymous beneath a bekira-shroud. The town was called Mentazi, near the city of Riban, the Aranio family's stronghold. It had taken her three nights to fly there. Kazim had taken the skiff off on another errand elsewhere, which meant she had no way to get out fast, but the Dorobon presence here was weak, and she was pretty sure Gurvon was still hunting her along the Hytel Road, not here.

The rich, smoky haze of the den was barely filtered by the gauze over her face. Only her hands and the bridge of her nose were uncovered, but she was sunburned brown enough that it would take a discerning eye to pick her out from a similarly attired Jhafi woman.

Any woman in here would be taken for a whore, but most of the hashish addicts were too far gone for lust, so she passed untroubled. Elena had never been tempted, not even in her lowest moments, to use the drug: opium and hashish were for fools or the hopeless, and she'd never had a moment in which hope did not offer solace far greater than the poppy-milk.

Though most lower-class Jhafi condemned the drug-traders, too many of the wealthy – both Rimoni and Jhafi – were ensnared by the stuff. As well as the measure of protection given by wealthy users, the trade was far too lucrative to stamp out, so those who needed the drug had no problem finding a den in most larger towns and cities. The rooms here were dimly lit, and figures sprawled on divans, either puffing from hookahs or bone pipes, or already comatose. They were all men, though some had naked Jhafi girls draped over them.

She found the man she sought in a room upstairs. The window had been flung wide and the fresh air was a welcome relief. He rose and bowed formally, smiling politely though his eyes were wary. 'Sal'Ahm, Elena.'

'Sal'Ahm, Harshal.' She unmasked, glancing about her. 'This is secure?'

'The Dorobon do not come here.' Harshal ali Assam kissed her cheeks formally and she returned the gesture, catching a whiff of expensive scent. His shaven skull gleamed in the lamplight as he sat and smoothed his expensive robes. He was the younger brother of the Emir of Forensa, with many ties to the Nesti – but he was much more than a pampered Jhafi princeling. He was the most well-informed man in Javon, in many ways the Jhafi equivalent to Gurvon, except that his loyalty to his people was unswerving and complete – and he was neither a mage nor an assassin.

'I hate these places,' she told him. 'Mind, the taverns in some parts of Yuros are just as bad. We all need our drugs, I suppose.'

Harshal waved an arm. 'Then I apologise for choosing this venue, but such dens remain the most private of public places. Please, be seated.'

Elena looked about her, using her gnostic senses to detect any listeners, and when she found none she sat opposite Harshal. He lifted the silver-chased flagon from the low table between them and poured the clear fluid, then added iced water, turning the arak cloudy. He made a show of drinking first, to demonstrate that it was safe, and ate a few nuts and a date from the small platter of dried fruits and nuts, for the same reason. They waited in silence until it was clear there was no poison in either.

'It is sad that it has come to this, my friend,' she said at last.

'You must forgive me, Elena, but first we heard the rumour that you had betrayed us to your former lover, and now you are hunting Dorobon magi and the price on your head doubles every week. We have been confused. And you have not made contact until now.'

'I never betrayed the Nesti.' She fixed him with a firm stare. 'The tale is hard to believe, for a non-mage, but I think you are one who will understand it.' She proceeded to tell him as much as she dared of her capture and possession by Gurvon and his minion, that night almost a year ago, just before the Moontide began. She left out Cera's part in her capture; she did not wish that story to circulate among the Jhafi, not at this stage, at least.

'My purpose now is to harry the Dorobon,' she concluded. 'I wish to make travel outside Brochena untenable for them, unless they move in force. Ultimately, I would see them thrown out of Javon and the country returned to self-rule.'

Harshal listened in silence. His expression had become strained when she was describing her possession by Rutt Sordell, but she knew that he'd spoken to Lorenzo di Kestria, who had seen Sordell's scarab first-hand. And his religion included the possibility of dae-monic possession too, by spirits they called 'afreet'.

When she finished, Harshal asked a few probing questions, then fell silent, contemplating her words.

'Donna Elena, I believe you,' he said finally. He touched his fore-head and then his heart in a flowing gesture. 'I am not a mage, but I can recognise truth when I hear it. But why would you – a foreigner – care about Javon?'

'All kinds of reasons,' she said honestly. 'I like it here – or at least,

I did when Olfuss ruled. I swore to protect the Nesti family, and I meant it. Just before he died, Olfuss offered to buy me from Gurvon's service, and I intended to accept. I like the warmth here, and I like the people. Also, there's nowhere else that would have me! And Gurvon Gyle is here and I very much want to see his head on a spike. So it's a mixture of the personal and the pragmatic.'

He accepted that with a wry smile, then asked, 'How may we aid you? Do you require sanctuary amongst us? Will you return with me to Forensa? They say the Dorobon will move against us soon.'

'It's best I stay in the shadows for now, Harshal. If Gurvon knows where I am, he can contain me. I can do more damage operating independently, for now at least.'

Harshal nodded regretfully. 'You are undoubtedly right, Donna Elena, but I had to ask. Is it true that you have an ally, a mage of Jhafi blood?'

'Best I say nothing of that.'

'Then I ask again: how can we help you?'

'With information. It's hard to stay abreast of events while hiding in the wild. Tell me about the Royal Convocation. I've heard nothing. Do you have a new king yet?'

'We do not,' he replied, sighing heavily. 'Elena, it was not a good meeting. The Rimoni houses cannot rally behind a single candidate. Each house promotes itself – or doesn't even attend. And many Jhafi with the requisite blood have withdrawn, claiming that the Nesti soldiers stood by at Fishil Wadi and watched the massacre. The Convocation was a disaster, and no candidate gained the required majority.' He hung his head. 'Anyone who opened his mouth was cut down to size, me included, and I do not even have the blood to be a candidate. I despair for Javon.'

It's worse than I thought . . . but at least Timori still has value to Gurvon. 'So they still hope for Timori's release?'

'For now.' Harshal dropped his voice. 'They also noted that Cera is causing great disruption and division by taking civil cases in her Beggars' Court. It has divided the clergy, and many speak against her.'

Elena felt a surge of tangled emotions rise in her: unexpected pride in her princessa's courage and resourcefulness warred with the bitter memory of her betrayal. It was several moments before she trusted herself to speak. 'Is this Beggars' Court so divisive?'

Harshal leaned forwards. 'For the most part she is supporting those who would otherwise be condemned by the clergy – usually women. The clergy feel threatened – they claim she is Gyle's pawn – and many Godsingers have been arrested for rabble-rousing against her. Gyle has arrested many clergy, which fuels the rumours that the two collude. Brochena is a very dangerous place these days, filled with Rondian settlers and many more soldiers.'

'Then it is good that the Convocation chose not to elect a new king,' Elena said slowly, still working through the ramifications of Harshal's news.

'Perhaps so,' he said. 'Portia Tolidi is pregnant and has been sent to Hytel. She will give birth in a few months. But Cera's womb remains empty. They say the king loathes her and no longer beds her.'

Elena scratched her nose. 'All the better,' she decided. 'I think that if she fell pregnant, the people would turn against her.'

'I think that also. Tell me, is it really true that Staria Canestos' legion are all frocio – what is your Rondian expression? Ah yes, *mooners*?'

'Most of them – but don't think that makes them soft, Harshal. They fight like demons.'

Harshal said slowly, 'We will be wary. Very well: I will report to the Regency Council, such as it is.' He looked up, then voiced something that had clearly been preying on his mind. 'Donna Elena, can you tell me what happened that night when Solinde died in the tower?' Harshal had been a suitor for Solinde's hand.

'One day, perhaps, I can tell you,' she said, 'but not yet.' *Especially as it wasn't Solinde anyway*. She sought a more comfortable subject: 'How do the Nesti feel about Cera now?'

'They still revere her, Elena. They forgive her marriage, for they see it as a selfless act to protect her brother. All believe that she remains true to her family. Her maid Tarita is an important source of information for us.' He stroked his goatee. 'All speak fondly of the days when she sat as Regent with you at her side. Were she to somehow be spirited back to us and you to reappear once again at her side, I believe all would rejoice.'

She could hear the hope in his voice. *Could I ever work with her again? I don't know* ... 'The queens are very heavily guarded, Harshal. I'm not so keen to die attempting a rescue.'

'I understand, Elena,' he said regretfully.

'Our heads must rule our hearts,' she told him.

'That would be sensible.' After a moment he asked, 'And how is your heart, Donna Elena? Does your mystery man care for you?'

Elena felt a smile spread across her face, enough of an answer to a sharp man like Harshal. 'He looks after all my needs.'

'I am pleased for you, truly. You have a glow to you, Ella. War and love clearly suit you.'

'That's a very backhanded compliment!' They laughed, regarding each other with a certain understanding. In another time and place, Harshal ali Assam might have been closer to her than most. 'What about you? Isn't it well past time you married?'

He pulled a face. 'I'd as soon not be tied to one alliance at this moment. The political situation is shifting constantly and my marriage is a tabula move I must play carefully.'

'You old romantic, you!' She chuckled, then leaned forward. 'What else can you tell me of the situation in Brochena, and the Dorobon troop movements?' The Hytel Road was becoming dangerous now, and she needed to know where else she might best operate.

He raised a finger. 'We do have some news: King Francis is moving men toward Lybis. It is an isolated place, and Emir Mekmud is fiercely independent, as you may recall. He is reputedly on the brink of open rebellion, something none of the other lords dare at this point.'

Elena pictured Mekmud, Emir of Lybis: not someone to relax around. 'Perhaps I should shift my activities as well, to shake things up. The caravans on the Hytel Road are well-guarded now.' She looked up, smiled warily at Harshal. 'Have we gained anything from this meeting, Harshal?'

'Greater understanding of what moves us. Some news. The joy of seeing your face. All these things are worthwhile, Donna Ella.'

'Flatterer.' She touched her forehead. 'Sal'Ahm, Harshal. Please, convey my greetings to the Regency Council.'

'I shall. Sal'Ahm, Ella. May He watch over you.'

Kazim Makani hauled in the sails and let the skiff drift groundwards as energy bled from the keel. He guided it to the ground beside another, this one with the distinctive Keshi triangular sails.

While Elena was in Brochena, meeting with a political contact, he had a different mission. Someone had triggered the wards Elena had set at the monastery on the slopes of Mount Tigrat. He'd been under orders only to observe, and he'd had no intention of disobeying – until he had recognised the skiff below.

It was night-time, but his gnostic sight needed no light. There was no one on watch and the only signs of life were on the far side of the deserted monastery, where a fire burned.

He slipped along the familiar corridors, feeling the place take shape around him. This was where his life had changed, where he'd been pulled back from the abyss of fanaticism and turned into someone new: he'd awakened in the hands of an enemy and come to learn that she was something far different to everything he'd ever believed.

And this was also the place where he'd killed his blood-brothers to save her – from them.

As he stole down the hall leading to the stone gardens where the fire burned, he heard a man's voice chanting funerary prayers. Then he saw him, kneeling beside the pyre, his arms raised to heaven while the bones cracked in the heat of the dancing flames.

'Ahm who is mercy, take these unto you. Ahm who is healing, restore them to life.'

Kazim scanned the garden, but it was otherwise empty. He waited respectfully until the prayers were finished before standing up and calling out, 'Sal'Ahm, Molmar!'

The man whirled, his sword flashing into his right hand and his left bunching as if holding unseen forces. The Dhassan mage peered about him, his eyes still dazzled by the firelight. He was an older man, grizzled and grey, but a dangerous warrior nevertheless. 'Who is there?' he called, as shields kindled about him.

'It is Kazim Makani. I come in peace,' he added, because he knew the skiff-pilot would fear the worst.

'Kazim?' Molmar replied hoarsely. 'What are you doing here?'

'I came to see you.' *Actually, Elena told me to observe only, and if it had been anyone else but you, that's what I'd still be doing . . .*

Molmar took a deep breath. 'They say in Halli'kut that Kazim Makani has sipped from forbidden cups and is no longer our brother.'

Molmar had not been among those who had been here in Decore, when Gatoz had beaten and attempted to rape Elena. Kazim had killed Gatoz, and many others with whom he'd sworn brotherhood, including, most painfully, his friend Jamil. But the skiff-pilots present that day had escaped to carry the tale of his sin to the rest of the Hadishah.

'Will you let me explain?' he asked, afraid Molmar would refuse.

Molmar considered for a long time, while the fire spat and crackled behind him. At last he said, 'Very well, Kazim Makani, explain to me. Why did you kill your sworn commander Gatoz, your blood-brother Jamil, the Scriptualist Haroun, who was your close friend, and all these others? Those who escaped said you betrayed us for a woman – and not just a woman, but an infidel mage accursed by Ahm? So yes, by all means, explain!'

Kazim exhaled in relief. He sat, to reduce the threat he posed, while Molmar leaned watchfully against a pillar. 'Please, Molmar, for the sake of what we have shared, believe me: I swear on Ahm Himself that all I say is true.' He paused to collect himself, then related how he'd awakened as the captive of Elena Anborn – how he'd seen her disgorge from her mouth an insect-creature that had apparently been possessing her; how he had gradually come to understand that far from being an enemy of the shihad, she too wished to fight against the Dorobon. He told Molmar of the understanding she and he had reached – it helped that Molmar himself was also a mage; he understood how the gnosis could be used. 'Then Gatoz came, and he thought only of humiliating her, then sending her to the breeding pits.'

Molmar himself had been born in a secret Hadishah breeding house, a place where captured magi were bred to serve the shihad. 'Were you fornicating with this infidel woman?' he asked bluntly.

'No,' Kazim insisted, 'though Gatoz and Jamil and everyone else thought I was. They thought I was a stupid boy being led around by my balls – but I swear to you it was not true.'

' "Was not". So you are with her now?'

'Yes.' He lifted his chin. 'As a man, having made an adult's choice.'

Molmar said slowly, 'There are rumours, that she and another are plaguing the Dorobon.'

'We are. She and I, together.'

'Is one of her worth more than Gatoz, Jamil and all the others?'

'Such equations did not enter my head; what Gatoz was going to do was evil.'

'If you still measure a matter of such import in such a way, then you are still a boy.'

'No,' Kazim said simply, 'I am not. I use different scales to judge such matters, that is all.'

'The loss of so many has been a catastrophe for the Brotherhood,' Molmar told him. 'Our ability to operate in Javon has been severely compromised.'

'Then blame Gatoz. He could have embraced Elena Anborn as a comrade in arms; instead he chose abuse and subjugation. The world is better without him.'

'Gatoz was a hard man, and—'

'Call him what he was!' Kazim said angrily. 'Gatoz was a sadistic bully allowed to run amok!'

'War makes heroes of such men,' Molmar admitted. 'That is our world. I am not proud of everything I have done.' His face became reflective. 'But we do what we must in service of a higher cause.'

'And I have not betrayed that cause, Molmar – what I have done has helped that cause, that I swear. The Javonesi want the Dorobon gone, and Elena Anborn has become Javonesi. She speaks their tongue, and ours. She understands the shihad; she has shed blood in its service.'

'So you say – but can I believe it?' Molmar looked at Kazim sadly. 'What would your father say if he knew?'

'I believe that he would be proud of my choices and my actions,' Kazim told him firmly.

'I don't know, Kazim . . . I want to believe you, but you have caused so much damage. The survivors who fled said you were burning like an afreet, that you slaughtered our brothers without pity.'

'I did *nothing* without pity,' Kazim countered. He raised both hands, palms outwards, and stood. 'Molmar, I want to be able to talk with you freely, to fly together, as we once did. I want to be able to work with the Brotherhood in future, to fight side by side. But there is one factor that prevents Elena and me from moving more openly among the Jhafi, and that is the fear of reprisals. I am here tonight to ask you, please, to tell your captains that we wish to work together.'

Molmar stood too. 'Kazim, I will report everything you have said. That is all I can promise.'

There was no brotherly farewell, no hearty embrace. Wariness hung in the air between them. But there was hope, Kazim thought, and for now, that had to be enough.

'May I contact you again?' he asked just before he walked away.

Molmar paused, then nodded.

Two days later he and Elena trapped and killed another cohort of Dorobon soldiers on the Hytel Road, hoping to mislead their hunters into believing that they were staying in that area. Then they flew southwest, towards Lybis.

Cera Nesti wasn't sure why the idea hadn't occurred to her before. *Probably some hope I'd be able to use them again myself one day*, she admitted to herself. But telling Francis about the secret passages that riddled the palace had worked: he had been appalled, and his clever friend Craith Margham had immediately resolved to use them himself, but Roland Heale had stepped in and curtailed that idea, instead insisting they were all blocked up.

Gurvon Gyle had first denied all knowledge of them, and then been forced to admit that he'd known all along. All in all, it had been quite amusing. More importantly, it now meant Cera could enjoy the solitude of her room without fearing she was being directly spied upon – though a mage could still scry her.

The Kore had a rite called Confiterium: any sin confessed to a priest by a true believer could be absolved after some form of penance. Confiterium was said to bring closure and release. Revealing the secret passages to Francis had felt that way to her.

I spent too much of my life sneaking around, she reflected. *Perhaps I should confess that to a Kore priest.*

Apparently her act of cooperation had started a train of thought in the king's mind, because a week later, shortly before she was to leave for the Beggars' Court, Francis entered her chambers unannounced, not something he did often. Cera, dressed in violet, was perched on a stool ready for Tarita to pin up her hair and do her make-up. She regarded him in the mirror with some surprise. He had lost a little weight he didn't need anyway, and his brow was becoming lined and his eyes dark from lack of sleep. He was clearly worried, perhaps even frightened, but he sought to conceal it behind his usual bluster.

'What exactly can an Imperial Legate do?' he asked, trying to act as if he really didn't care about the answer, but was vaguely curious.

Her eyebrows shot up. *He's asking me for advice?* She answered quickly, before he changed his mind. 'It's an advisory role, with the ability to step in on "high matters" – things affecting the security of the empire.'

'That's what Craith says – but Gyle seems to think *everything* is a high matter.' He struck a pose, looking out the window. 'I suppose he would, when he's up from the gutters.'

'Get the statutes out,' she replied. *I doubt Gyle has made his way up from any gutters – he's a half-blood mage.*

'I'm not a Kore-bedamned clerk,' Francis sniffed. 'I want to know the answer, not look for it.' He *tsked* vexedly, and made as if to leave.

345

It was the first time he'd ever asked her about policy and she wasn't about to let that pass, especially when there might be some reciprocal gain for herself. '"High matters" is a term describing Imperial jurisdiction, and it was left deliberately loose,' she said hurriedly. 'It's only ever been invoked in cases involving matters of war or trade directly relating to the empire or its allies.' *Ha, I am still la Scrittoretta!* 'He can't use it to dictate your policy domestically, or your relations with, say, the Harkun nomads. He can't dictate your appointments, nor can he overturn your legal judgements.' *If you ever made any.* 'You're still the king.'

He nodded peremptorily. 'Of course I am.' But he was hovering now, torn between need and pride. 'He's proposing sending *my* legion to the Rift forts. He says they need field experience.'

She raised an eyebrow. 'They're getting plenty of that on the Hytel Road. Tell him to send Canestos: her people are causing trouble, so sending them somewhere isolated would be better for all.'

There had been more incidents regarding Canestos' 'children'. Though she couldn't help but sympathise with them, they were a big problem in a country as traditional and conservative as Javon.

'But Sir Roland agrees.'

'Roland Heale,' she interjected contemptuously, 'has gone from being a Dorobon warhorse to Gyle's trick pony. You've lost his loyalty.'

'Heale? But he's been with the family all his life!' Francis sounded shocked.

'And he's been overlooked and taken for granted, and then shunted aside for your friend Craith, whom you love so much.'

Francis looked stung. 'What do you mean?'

'*Sol et Lune*, open your eyes, Francis! Margham distracts you with hunts and Heale kowtows to Gyle on every matter. They see what's happening: they tried to warn you, but now they're just trying to preserve themselves.'

'No – they are my loyal friends!'

'Francis, a king doesn't have *friends*: he has *dependents*! He has *adherents*! Loyalty is bought. And they've seen how you reward it: you cut off the heads of the men who supported your own mother against Gyle! That's the lesson you taught them: that loyalty to the Dorobon ends in death. So they're toadying frantically to Gyle instead.'

'So are you,' Francis snapped. 'Gyle made me marry you, and he saved you from my mother ... You are as much his creature as anyone.'

'In saving himself, he had no choice but to save me. Of course I was relieved, but I didn't mistake that for anything but circumstance. I owe him no gratitude. And as for marrying you ... do you think I *wanted* that? Wake up, Francis! He's flooded Javon with his friends and stolen yours! He's ruling without a crown, but sooner or later he'll want the whole thing: crown, title, the lot.'

'But Mater-Imperia Lucia is my friend! She—'

'Your *friend*? Your *mother* was her friend, and Lucia did nothing to support her. Meanwhile Gyle's men are ransacking *your kingdom* and sending everything of value to Kaltus Korion. That tells me Lucia doesn't care who's in charge, so long as the Crusade is well-supplied.' She met his eyes and said bluntly, 'By the end of the Moontide, your soldiers won't even remember your name. They'll all be mercenaries in Gyle's pay.'

His stricken face told her that her words had sunk in. His cheeks flushed and sweat broke out. 'I am a Dorobon,' he muttered to himself. 'I am a pure-blood, born of the Blessed. I am *invincible*.'

You pathetic little boy. She struggled to contain the thought that maybe the time had come to follow the examples set by Heale and Margham and the rest and make peace with Gyle. *At least Gyle understands my usefulness.* But her whole soul rebelled at the thought of putting herself in the service of – *in thrall to* – the man who'd wrought so much evil on those she loved.

Abruptly Francis' face changed again as he remembered who he was and who she was. He looked down at her disdainfully, then, with the faintest gratitude, announced, 'You will present yourself in my chamber tonight.' He spoke as if he was bestowing alms on the desperate.

Sheer loathing of his arrogant contempt drew her words out before caution could check them. 'My lord, I'd rather not,' she said angrily, then caught her breath.

Tarita, watching silently, sucked in her breath and went still.

Francis had started turning away; now he swung back to her, his expression puzzled. 'What did you say?'

She stood. *He heard me. He just wants me to back down.* 'I said that I'd rather not.'

They'd not had physical contact for weeks now, but that had been on the pretext of being his choice. This was different: she'd outright refused him. Men could beat a wife for that and few would look askance. For a few seconds she feared the worst as he raised a fist, then he blinked and lowered it. 'But . . . Are you ill? Are you bleeding?'

This was her opportunity to plead an excuse, but she found she could not. 'No. I simply do not wish to go to your room.'

'You're my wife and you will do as I say.' His priggish face was torn between anger and dislike. 'You swore on the *Book of Kore* to obey me and you will, you fat . . . ugly . . . *mudskin*.'

She flinched at each word, then stuck her chin out. 'You promised to "honour" me. I've seen no sign of that.'

She heard Tarita gasp and felt her own heart thundering. Her whole body was sweating as if she were standing before a furnace, soaking into her dress so that it felt as if it had doubled in weight. Her knees shook, but she stuck out her chin defiantly, feeling oddly strong amidst all this weakness.

He raised his hand again. She offered her cheek. *I dare you.*

'I have every right to you,' he snapped. 'I am a pure-blood mage of the—'

'I don't care about all that. I don't want to lay with you.'

His jaw dropped and his hand quivered, fingers still open, the muscles twitching.

She put her hands on her hips, feeling recklessly brave. 'So unless you want to add rape to your sins, go away and leave me alone.' Her voice shook while she said it, but she could feel her spine stiffen inside. She lifted her eyes back to his, and locked on. *Blink first, you weak, weak, weak bastido.*

His hand dropped and he looked away. 'I don't understand,' he said plaintively. 'I don't strike you. I don't mistreat you or make you do impure things. I don't use other women; I have been faithful to my wives. I admit you're not my favourite, but you're descended of Rimoni and Noories, for Kore's sake! I am so far above you that only in such a time of madness could we ever meet. *Lessers do not reject their betters!* So tell me, how have I earned this . . . disobedience?'

She just looked at him, momentarily lost for words. *Sol et Lune, if that is what you think, how is mere reason ever going to change your mind?* She floundered for a few seconds – Rondian was only her third tongue, though she had some fluency, but the words she needed weren't ones she'd used often, and when they did come, they tumbled out in a helpless, passionate rush. 'Francis – I can't *stand* you. You repulse me in ways I can't articulate. I find you odious, loathsome . . . Frankly, I would rather lick the privy clean than be with you. I would rather die than have your baby.'

He stared, his mouth working slowly, like a child trying to read. His hand went up and down three times as his urge to slap her warred with whatever passed for honour in his self-image. Then his eyes narrowed as he grasped for some explanation he could accept. 'Gyle . . . you and Gyle are—'

'Oh, please! I hate Gurvon Gyle even more than I despise you! I would throw myself from my balcony before I let him so much as touch me.' She dropped her arms to her sides, fighting for composure. 'Francis, there is no one else and there's no one to blame! Our marriage is a fraud – it always has been. Its sole function was to tie the kingdom together. We don't need to see each other to do that, and we'd both be happier if we didn't.'

He took that in with the most perplexed expression she'd ever seen. 'But . . . my honour . . . I have needs . . .'

She sighed. 'Francis, your court is full of settler women.' She'd observed them from a distance, this invasion of pale-skinned, pale-haired men and women, crowding into the streets of *her* city, their thick foreign accents almost indecipherable, even though she knew the words. Every single one of them displayed a bizarre arrogance, as if the lowliest of them were somehow better than Javonesi of any class. 'I'm sure you won't want for company.'

He drew himself upright. 'I am a Dorobon, descendant of the—'

'Yes, yes,' she interrupted tiredly. *I'm so sick of his 'I am this, I am that'*, she thought. 'Francis, I don't care. I have needs too, but I'd rather they went untended than be with you. Your needs aren't my problem. Please, just leave.'

'I'll close your Beggars' Court.'

She was well ahead of him. 'Gyle sanctioned it. Talk to him.'

He looked at her slyly. 'But it's a domestic matter. He hasn't the right, you've said so yourself.'

Well, at least he took that on board. 'I will continue to go to my gardens and listen through the gate. Men have no right to enter the zenana uninvited, but I may do as I please there. What happens in the streets outside I cannot control.' *But good luck clearing them without a riot.*

He lifted his finger to make a point, seemed to lose his thread, then abruptly stiffened and backed away. 'I will have you put aside. I will send you home.'

'Excellent. I've been longing to see Forensa again.'

'Your brother is my prisoner!'

'He's Gyle's prisoner. Was there anything else?'

His face, which had gradually been returning to its normal pallor, went puce again. He stammered for a moment, then he whirled round and stormed away. The doors shook as he slammed them with a gesture, and then at last he was gone.

Cera sank to her knees in the middle of the floor and dropped her head. She was shaking so hard she could barely feel the stone beneath her.

Tarita edged forward. 'My lady?'

She'd never felt so drained, so weak and so powerful all at once. She lifted her hands, and when Tarita took them, she pulled her into a kneeling embrace, hugging her as if she were her sister Solinde come back to life, all the while shaking and crying and laughing.

'I told him! I told him! I really did it!'

Tarita's whisper was fearful. 'What will he do? My lady, we must leave! He'll kill you!'

A Jhafi man would, if his wife spoke to him like that, and a Rimoni man too – or some would, the very worst of them. She'd heard too many such cases in the Beggars' Court these last weeks. But everyone knew married couples who co-existed like strangers sharing the same house. Some were perfectly amicable, like that of Lord Theodyne and Lady Brita in Forensa; and there were others whose hostility was public knowledge, like Lord Jacop di Oseria of Riban; everyone knew how much he and his wife Veirana loathed each other. And yet these were not valid grounds for putting a wife aside: state marriages were made for more important reasons; mere likes and dislikes were no reason for annulment.

'He won't,' she said, regaining her confidence. 'He may be a stupid ass, but he's an honourable ass. You'll see.'

The next months proved her right: Francis did not press her, nor did he seek to end the marriage. He still had her sit with him at state occasions, though he never showed her public affection either. She picked up second-hand news of Portia, how she fared, how her pregnancy was progressing, but no letters came. And she watched the city change as the settlers clustered into the area they renamed 'Oldchurch', fanning out around a Sollan shrine they'd re-consecrated to Kore – the shrine where she and Francis and Portia had been married. But Oldchurch did not deal easily with the rest of the city; it quickly became a gated enclave, guarded at all times. Tarita told her the Jhafi described it as 'a boil filling with white pus'.

And still the crowds came to her Beggars' Court, their numbers unchecked.

The most wonderful thing was the sense of freedom she'd gained by her outburst. Though she'd lain with Francis only one week a month, whilst she was fertile, the sense of emancipation, of not having to put herself through that ordeal, was liberating. Knowing she no longer had to put up with the physical indignity, or run the risk of having to bear his child, made her feel like she was master of her own body and soul. She might still be a prisoner in a cage surrounded by enemies on every side, but she was at least free to follow her own pursuits.

I just wish Portia were here . . . or someone . . .

She'd always prized intellectual pursuits above physical ones, but that didn't mean she didn't have needs too. *Just like Francis . . .* But she would never have admitted that to him. To have finally sampled love's fruit only to have it snatched away was cruel, a form of torture, but she was becoming resigned to losing Portia. The silence between them spoke volumes. She imagined the Dorobon baby inside Portia colonising her, driving her steadily away. *How could I ever compete with the miracle of motherhood?*

At her worst she took to sly glances at Tarita, who was pretty and sweet and unashamedly worldly, but even had she been that way inclined, she was only a maid and the gulf between them was too great. They had more familiarity than most mistress-and-servant relationships, but to go so far would be out of the question. She too had her pride. *Just like Francis . . .* Anyway, Tarita had a lover now, a man of Mustaq al'Madhi's gang; from time to time, if pressed, she would mention him, coyly. He sounded raffish and dangerous, not someone Cera would have liked, but he'd clearly turned Tarita's head.

So she set her heart aside and buried herself in her self-appointed tasks, taking pleasure in good verdicts and sound decisions, enjoying the increasing rapture of the crowds outside the zenana gates. She was relieved that Francis and Gyle stayed away, and Staria's legion had indeed marched east to the Rift Forts; the only one Rondian she saw regularly was 'Olivia Dorobon'. who had taken to watching the Beggars' Court from her balcony. 'Olivia' had apparently been confined to her rooms – by Francis or by Gyle, no one could say whom – and what little Cera glimpsed of her was a shattered face, wet with tears, eyes fixed on her. Some days the shapeshifter's presence felt like a dagger poised over her heart; other times she pitied the wretch.

If I told Francis who his sister really was, what would he do?

In the end she decided to say nothing. But the threat of Coin's presence made her increasingly uneasy as the days and weeks passed.

Akhira, the onset of midsummer, began with a series of storms that came rolling out of the northwest, bringing stinging sands and swirling winds and leaving a coating of brown grit on every surface. The heat rose steadily after that, as did the human stench of the city. Cera began each morning on her balcony, sipping coffee. This was a rare day in which she had nothing special to do. The Royal Court was in recess, and Francis was off riding with his court, Gyle included. The Legate seemed to be trying to charm his way back into Francis' affections, which worried Cera; Francis was stupidity itself when it came to flattery and fun.

There was no Beggars' Court today, and she had to admit to being relieved. She felt too emotionally battered to deal with another long, harrowing day of hearing about the horrific things that people could do to others.

Then she heard a sound from above, of someone beginning to cry, and glancing up, she saw a strand of rope briefly drop from the balcony above before being hauled back up. A table shifted, something making it creak. The sobbing was heavy, starting deep in the abdomen and discharging in big wet gulps. A voice begged Kore for release; the tone was strange, but she knew at once who it was and what was going on.

She ran, and within half a minute she was pushing her way into Olivia's suite. The room was untidy, strewn with clothes for both genders, including outfits she recognised, some Olivia's and some Symone's.

The weeping came from behind the curtains that concealed the balcony. She called out, 'Coin!' and heard a strangled cry in response as she wrenched the curtains aside to find a rope tied to a lamp-hook in the roof and a noose looped about the neck of the androgynous being standing on a small table, poised to spring over the rail.

'No!' she shouted, 'Coin – *stop!*'

The shapeshifter turned her head. Her true face, boyish with thin ginger hair, was streaked in tears. 'Go away!'

Cera stopped, scared into motionlessness. *If she's set it right she'll break her neck . . . If not she'll take two or three minutes to asphyxiate . . . Unless survival instincts take over and she uses the gnosis to save herself.*

The coolly rational part of her brain asked, *Do I care?*

But the anguish on the face of the strange being tore into her and she put aside their last conversation and focused on trying to calm the stricken shapechanger. *She didn't kill Solinde. She's not entirely evil – and now she needs help.* 'Please, Coin – you don't have to do this,' she said urgently.

'I heard them talk,' Coin whispered.

'Heard who?'

'Gyle and my mother – they talk once a week, and he never told me.'

Her mother? Who's she in all this? 'What about?' she asked, then instantly regretted it, as Coin's mind was clearly taken back to the anguish that had driven her to this.

'Everything.' Coin choked on the words. 'You . . . Me.'

If I get this wrong she'll jump. 'What people say about you doesn't matter, Coin.'

The shapeshifter ignored her. 'Gyle told her that I was becoming a liability.'

'Gyle lies all the time.'

'And my mother . . .' Coin started sobbing again, a heart-wrenching sound. 'She s-s-said, "*S-s-she's always been a l-l-liability*."'

Cera winced. *Sol et Lune.* Just when she thought Gyle and his cronies had reached the bottom of their heartlessness, they revealed new depths. 'Coin, your mother might have been trying to hide her true feelings from Gyle – if they move in the same circles, personal ties are dangerous.'

'N-n-no one moves in the same circles as m-m-my m-m-m-mother.'

Cera blinked. *Who in Hel is her mother?* It was becoming more and more imperative that she get the shapeshifter down. She was only a lunge away, but she doubted she could hold on if Coin did decide to jump. It was going to have to be Coin's decision.

'She still might not have meant what she said.'

Coin glanced back miserably. 'I s-s-suppose.'

With that acknowledgment, a tiny amount of immediate peril drained from the tableau.

Cera stared at the shapeshifter, unable to not do so. Coin's body-shape was all wrong, even obscured as it was by the nightshirt. The shoulders were too wide and the legs too muscular for womanhood, but the shape was still more feminine than masculine. Her forehead was long, her chin weak and her hair thin, and her expression was utterly miserable.

'If you do this, Gyle wins, not you.'

Coin sagged a little. 'Do you want to see how repulsive I am in my real form?'

'We are what we are,' Cera replied, unable to think of anything more profound.

'You have no idea what you're saying.'

Cera forced herself to be dispassionate. 'As I understand it, you can look like anyone.'

'Yes, for a while – but I'm still me, underneath.' The self-loathing rose again in her voice. 'A monster not even my mother can love.'

'If your mother cannot see through the body to what is inside, then she is the one who is the monster.'

'My soul is as warped as my body,' Coin went on. 'I'm a *murderer*. I've *killed* people, just to please Mother. Or Gurvon.'

I know – including Portia's brother . . . The temptation to walk away returned, but Cera stayed. 'You thought you were doing the right thing. Now you know better.' She reached out slowly. 'Killing yourself won't make it right, you know.'

'Only one person has ever treated me as a human and not been repulsed by what I am.' Coin looked at Cera with anguished eyes. 'Your sister.'

Oh, Solinde. You really did love all the world. Cera blinked back tears.

'Solinde was an angel. But killing yourself won't bring her back, or make it right.'

'Nothing can.' Coin looked away, out over the city. 'My life is worthless.'

'Never! Coin – Symone – whatever your name is, don't do this! My father used to say that we all have some great act in us, a moment when we can make a difference to the world. If you jump now, you'll miss that moment.'

'I've had mine,' Coin said flatly. 'I killed a good person, and then another and another, and I've never stopped.'

'Then perhaps your moment is still to come.' Cera dared to step closer. 'Please?'

The shapeshifter looked down at her, then at the ground below, and her resolution drained away. 'My name is Yvette,' she sobbed, and collapsed into Cera's arms.

Cera led the trembling hermaphrodite back inside to a sofa, wrapped her in a cloak, poured some brandy from a decanter and forced Coin – *no, Yvette* – to drink it, holding her in her arms. When the first glass was gone, she gulped one down herself, then poured another. All the while she was conscious of the loathing and pity she felt.

She can't help what she is, but she's used it to kill innocent people . . . including Portia's brother . . .

'Yvette, you can tell me whatever you want, or nothing at all,' she said at last. 'It's up to you.'

Cera wasn't sure what tale she expected, it was certainly wasn't the harrowing litany of parental rejection and emotional torture she heard – or the jaw-dropping revelation that Yvette was Mater-Imperia Lucia Fasterius' disowned child.

Sol et Lune, she's in line for the Imperial throne . . . if such a one could ever claim it.

'Officially, I don't exist,' Coin mumbled, 'but to those few who knew that she'd given birth to a monster, she and her husband put it about that I was the child of incest, and that was why I was deformed.' Yvette started crying again. 'She would rather have people think that

356

she fucked her brother than that her *imperial cunt* could ever produce a freak like me.'

'I sure no one believed that.'

'Oh yes, they did! It's exactly the sort of thing people love to believe! Even your friend Elena thought it; I could see it on her face when she stripped me in that tower room last year.'

'Sometimes when a lie is spoken often enough, even good people can believe it.'

'Your Elena wasn't a good person. She almost killed me. Gurvon brought me back from death.' Tears welled up in her eyes. 'He put me back together again from almost nothing. I fell utterly in love with him for that.' Her shoulders heaved. 'But he knows what I am and he can't stand being near me either.'

Cera gritted her teeth. 'Yvette, Gurvon Gyle is a *pezzi di merda* who would sell his own children for a copper.'

'But he *understood* me . . .'

'I thought that too, once.' *And he twisted everything so that black was white.* 'Then I realised what sort of man he is – and now you do too. He's leading everyone here around by the nose, and something has to be done to stop him.'

Their eyes met. Yvette's lips were still trembling, but she tried desperately to force the faintest of smile of recognition. 'He really is a piece of shit, isn't he?' she whispered timidly.

The shapeshifter was like a child, like her little brother. *I can make a game of this, make her laugh . . .*

'Gurvon Gyle is a camel's turd,' Cera told her.

'A donkey's pizzle.'

'A puddle of toad's piss.'

Coin giggled childishly. 'A pus-drinking dung-beetle.'

'A cock-sucking gullet-worm.'

Yvette wrinkled her nose. 'Eewww.' Then she burst into semi-hysterical laughter, and Cera laughed too, in sheer relief. *She's not going to kill herself. Thank you, Mater Luna!* She found herself trembling as much as the shapechanger.

There were more tears, and then a slow, awkward peeling apart.

There was something desperately needy about Yvette Sacrecour, a yearning for affection that was so palpable it was almost more repellent than anything in her appearance. Her whole being was wrapped up in the need for someone to cling to. Cera moved away a little on the sofa, trying to re-establish some kind of distance, because she could see exactly what was going to happen next: all of the shapeshifter's obsessive yearning was going to be redirected at her.

'Yvette, there is something I need to say. Are you listening?'

Yvette's eyes were already far too bright and intense as she looked at her. 'Of course.'

'I want us to be friends.'

'Yes, yes, so do I.' Yvette's whole body was bent towards her.

'But *only* friends. My heart is already claimed by another.'

She watched her words wound, and could see the next downwards cycle forming. She moved to cut it off. 'A true friend does not lead the other on with false promises.'

'You think I'm ugly too.'

'In all honesty . . . your body is hard to get used to, but that's not what is important. What's important is that despite everything you've been through, you want to be a better person. And because of that, I truly believe you will find happiness, if you give life a chance to provide. Maybe even love: why not? That person won't be me: because my heart is already given. But I wish us to be true friends.'

Yvette's face vacillated back into uncertainty. 'Truly? I've done awful things—'

'But you won't from now on. I'm sure of that.' Cera held out her hands. 'Friends?'

For a long time her words hung there, until the shapechanger took a forced breath, and wiped her face. 'All right. Friends.'

They hugged, the blanket between them, for a long, long time, then Cera took Yvette's hands in hers and asked the question that had been burning inside her brain for ever. 'Do you know where they're holding my brother?'

Yvette nodded.

Now that she knew where Timori was, Cera could finally made plans to run. There would be four of them: Cera, Timori, Tarita and Yvette. Her plan required two things: first, simultaneously extricating herself, Tarita, Yvette and Timori; then they had to get to Mustaq al'Madhi and hope the crime-lord could get them to Forensa. Just one slip would see a formidable band of magi come down on them; death after that would be a kindness.

In the two weeks after Cera had saved Yvette's life, the shapeshifter was fawning in her devotion, to the point that Cera had to keep reminding her to remain hostile in public. More than that, she'd had to persuade Yvette to make peace with Gyle. Though for the shape-changer it was a humiliating back-down, it was necessary so that Yvette could play her part. It appeared to have worked, as she was restored to her duties, most importantly she was again permitted a part in guarding Timori.

They set a date: they would make their run in the last week of Jumada – Maicin – during the Darkmoon. The week before, they met in Cera's suite, ostensibly for tea. Yvette, disguised as Symone, warded the room against scrying. Cera had told Tarita that Symone was allied to Elena – she could think of no other story that might persuade Tarita to trust the shapeshifter. She was painfully aware that Coin had killed Fernando Tolidi – Portia's brother, Tarita's lover – a secret that would destroy their fragile conspiracy. *How I'll unravel all this in the end I don't know.*

'What word from Mustaq?' Cera asked now, at their final preparatory meeting. She didn't like dealing with the crime-lord, but he was a vital part of the resistance to Dorobon rule.

Tarita was proud to be the centre of attention. 'Mustaq has scouted the building where the prince is being held and confirmed that there are Rondians there.' She turned to 'Symone'. 'You were right.'

'Of course,' 'Symone' said impatiently. 'Madeline Parlow looks after him; I'm only sent there occasionally. There's no pattern to it. There are three other guards, but none are magi. Maddy is sweet on one of them.'

'Can you defeat her?' Cera asked.

'Of course – Maddy's nothing. She used to be a nun.'

Cera was genuinely surprised. 'Really? How did she end up in Gyle's group?'

'She's from Noros – during the Noros Revolt she left her nunnery and joined the Grey Foxes, out of patriotism. After the war she couldn't settle back into the convent. She'd never enjoyed it; she likes comfort and good things too much.' Coin's face twisted disdainfully. 'She is greedy and weak.'

Cera would have liked to form her own opinions, as she doubted Coin's maturity was sufficient to read an older person, but she had never met Parlow. 'Will you be able to kill her quickly?'

'Easily. Trust me in this.'

The more confident she sounds, the less I like it. Cera frowned, but they were in Coin's hands in this matter. 'Well, while you free Timori, Tarita and I must get out of the palace.' She turned to Tarita. 'You know a way?'

'Yes, Majesty. The secret passages were all closed when you told King Francis about them, but they did not find them all. There is still a tunnel to the outside from the old female servants' quarters.'

'How does no one know of this one?' Cera asked doubtfully.

'The early Rimoni kings wouldn't allow Amteh Scripturalists to bless the servants,' Tarita replied. 'So the men dug a tunnel and smuggled in someone to bless us on holy days. The cellar where the tunnel begins is now just a storage area.'

'Who else knows?'

'Since the servants were murdered last year it's just me – and I have told no one.' Tarita now lived in a tiny cell outside Cera's quarters. 'The only difficulty is reaching it unseen, because you've got to go through the scullery. But that's empty during the middle part of the night.'

'Is it easily passable?'

Tarita nodded vigorously. 'It is. I tested it just last week, when I went to speak to Mustaq al'Madhi. It emerges in a disused part of the stables behind the Sollan Church in the square outside. There are spiders and rats, though.'

Cera shuddered. 'I hate rats.'

'No one likes rats,' Symone said, taking the opportunity to put her hand over Cera's. 'But they won't hurt you.'

Extricating her hand without upsetting the fragile balance of Coin's mind was a delicate operation, so she let it stay, despite the warning look Tarita gave her. They moved to the timings, and she went to get writing paper from her desk, using the opportunity to free herself. As Coin couldn't predict when next she'd be asked to relieve Madeline Parlow, they had to set a date and time in advance and work to that. They decided on ten days' time, when Cera would be bleeding again, so she wouldn't be expected to appear in public. After midnight they would slip out through the tunnel, while Symone and some of Mustaq's men snatched Timori, and they would rendezvous at one of Mustaq's safe houses.

'Can we trust Mustaq?' Symone asked nervously.

'Mustaq is a bad man,' Tarita said, 'but he hates the Rondians even more than he loves money.'

'I hope so,' Cera said, 'because we're going to be entirely in his hands.'

19

Leading the Attack

The Emirate of Khotri

The Emirate of Khotri, based around the city of Khotriawal, has long been a thorn in the side of both Kesh and Lakh. It is strong enough to act independently and shrewd enough to play off the two nations against each other. Their greatest coup was the seizure of the Lakh throne in the ninth century.

ORDO COSTRUO, HEBUSALIM

Small kingdoms are the grit in the sandals of larger ones.

AMISAL BHANGULI, OMALI PANDIT, DILI 862

Ardijah, Emirate of Khotri, on the continent of Antiopia
Akhira (Junesse) 929
12th month of the Moontide

Leading an army into battle was the stuff boyhood dreams were made of, especially for the sons of magi, caught up in their invincible youth. For most of his life it was what Seth Korion had aspired to, but this moment had arrived too late: he had seen too much and felt his own mortality too keenly to be anything other than petrified.

'Fearlessness is an illusion,' Ramon Sensini had told him. 'Real courage is being afraid and acting anyway.'

Well, I'm going to do it . . . but I'm so scared I could vomit.

Arranging the joint assault on the city hadn't been as quick as they'd hoped. It had taken Sensini time to convince the Khotri commander that there was something to be gained by reaching an accommodation with an enemy, and while the aggravating little Sila-cian was away, Seth had stewed in his own fear, his hands trembling and his mind fixated on the morbid conviction that he was going to die, here in this Hel-hole. He'd doubted any deal could be done – but it was, and ironically the groundwork had been laid by Antonin Mei-ros and the Ordo Costruo. They'd apparently taken a keen interest in Khotri, and that included building the causeway and bridge here at Ardijah, among several other engineering feats within Khotriawal, the capital city itself. It helped that the Khotri were Ja'arathi Amteh, the less extreme variant of the faith, who didn't automatically hold all magi to be demons.

It also helped that they had mutual enemies: Yorj Arkanus was intent on seizing the emir's kingdom, and he was backed by dozens of Dokken and had hundreds of Keshi soldiers already inside Ardijah. Ramon was offering Rondian help in getting rid of Arkanus, then leaving Khotri as soon as they'd resupplied – for which he was offer-ing to pay. Seth had to take the skiff across the river and shake the Khotri general's hand personally to seal the deal, but by then it was a formality.

After that it was all logistics and planning: the attack had to hap-pen fast, before Salim's forces arrived. Seth needed to prepare the attack while not appearing to, which was harder than it sounded, while his magi readied the wagons for the floating attack. Little things kept cropping up, tiny delays that set the attack back, until finally he was able to give the go-ahead for the fourth night-bell.

Which should be soon . . .

Right on cue, the distant time-bells of Ardijah rang out, loud and clear – *Clang!, Clang!, Clang!, Clang!* – and before the echoes of the fourth chime had even faded away the signal lights flashed from upstream and across the river and with a massive roll on the drums and to the blaring of bugles, the foot-soldiers of the Sixth Maniple of Pallacios Thirteen started slowly onto the causeway. They were illu-minated by a trail of torches that sprang to light all along the bridge, leading them into the teeth of the enemy archers and ballistae crews. Seth joined Sigurd Vaas at the head of the column, trying hard to believe that this was in some way as heroic as it might sound at a banquet, years from now.

His head was pounding and his senses overloading with the mundane: the clip-clopping hooves and marching boots; the rumbling drums. The clangour of alarms inside the fortress carried clearly over the rush of the waters surrounding and beneath them.

Seth trotted forward, keeping his head up, trying to conceal his absolute terror.

This is only a feint. We just have to keep enemy eyes forward.

It might be nothing but a ruse, but it promised to be deadly for all that.

While they were providing a slow and deliberate assault to draw Arkanus' attention, the wagons would be floating downstream, bearing the best of the battle-magi and their guard cohorts. But even that wasn't the real surprise: that would be the attack from the rear by thousands of Khotri hidden on the southern isle – which would also be the signal for the Khotri inside, stationed on both islands, to turn on the Souldrinkers.

Too many moving parts, his father would have said: *too many unreliable allies, too many things that could go wrong*. And he could see they were indeed placing too much reliance on uncoordinated units turning up at exactly the right time, with too many unknowns. *Too bad, Father. We have no choice.*

He kept his eyes forward. To look back was bad luck or bad for morale or something; he couldn't remember exactly. Behind him were the archers, mostly Estellan, each bearing a spiked shield that could be driven into the ground to provide cover. Then came the laddermen, chosen from the biggest rankers, who would storm forward and climb up to the battlements once the defence had been distracted by the other attacks. If they got that far.

His heartbeat was louder than the drums.

O mighty joy! Breathless we surge, Kore in our hearts and death in our hands! Seth was beginning to think that the composer of the famous battle hymn had never set foot outside his monastery. *Fucking poets!*

Someone shouted – a command – and enemy arrows erupted

upwards and then hissed through the night as they rained down. Seth and Vaas had their shields ready. Seth set his as wide as he could manage. A gnostic shield was effectively an extension of his own aura, an unconscious telekinetic blocking of incoming missiles and blows, but it was imperfect and where there were lots of blows, one or more might slip through. And the wider he extended, the more draining it was to hold, and the flimsier the coverage.

Most of the first volley were deflected, falling off sideways into the river, but he could hear cries: some at least had met their mark. But not many. *So far, so good.*

Some blows were too powerful for almost any shield, though: he heard a vicious *crack!* as the first of the ballistae released an instant before the ten-foot shaft of the giant crossbow quarrel ripped through the air. It struck his shield just off-centre, momentarily shredded the warding, and he felt the breeze as it whipped past his left shoulder and into two men behind him, impaling them through chest and belly and hurling them against the parapet.

Then the other three ballistae fired: two shafts sailed over his head and into the marching men behind, ripping holes in the ranks and making the whole column recoil. The third struck Vaas' horse, just below the neck and went all the way through and out the other end, skewering it as if for roasting. The beast was thrown backwards, shrieking as it died, and Vaas was thrown clear, his shields striking the causeway walls in a burst of blue sparks.

Seth shouted in terror and involuntarily spurred his horse forward, and the Estellan archers bellowed their fiery war-cries and came after him. From then it was a nightmare as arrows shafted out of the darkness all round them. They pushed onwards and reached the wider landing before the gates, where they were finally beneath the line of fire of the four ballistae, only for searing flames to start washing down from a dozen cloaked figures above. The gnostic force was so strong he could barely protect himself, let alone anyone else. The stink of burned meat filled his nostrils and all around him the Estellan were charred to ash and blasted into oblivion.

Then boulders began to rain down.

Shields! He tried to hold them strong, to keep the men behind him alive, as more and more of his archers rushed forward to assail the fortress, but the Dokken could shield too, and few Estellan shafts found their target.

Seth caught sight of one of the men Ramon had told him about: the Sydian Zsdryk. His hood was cast back and his vulturine face was alive with glee as he blazed flame down from above. He saw Vaas engage him, sending mage-blasts upwards, and all of a sudden dazzling, chilling light was coruscating between the two magi.

Through the press came the Argundian laddermen, giant spade-bearded men with their distinctive conical helms gleaming in the light of the flames, howling their guttural battle-songs as they pushed their way into the maelstrom. Around Vaas stone and fire were being thrown continually, making his shields blaze a myriad colours. Those not warded were smashed by rock, or consumed by fire, and Seth watched aghast as skulls and limbs were crushed like eggshells, as faces were burned off, as horrifically injured lumps of malformed flesh not even identifiable as men were left in tangled, writhing heaps.

And still his men charged onwards, and now their ladders were rising against the walls.

Sigurd Vaas staggered onwards too, blasting more gnosis-fire upwards as he bawled, 'Attack!' and again, '*Attack!*', and something in the man's iron will had Seth urging his terrified mount forward as well. He glimpsed a boar-faced Dokken above, directing incandescent flames down on one of the ladders, and sent a mage-bolt at the beast-man. Fuelled by terror and outrage, the mage-bolt – easily the most powerful he'd ever cast – blazed through the man's shields as if they were paper and he disappeared from view.

Seth found himself yelling triumphantly, and took aim again.

The nearest ballista rolled right to the edge of the platform above and swung in his direction and he panicked and sent the first spell he could think of, but the warping spell aimed at the timbers wasn't well-cast: Zsdryk batted it away almost effortlessly – and then the ballista bucked and Seth threw himself sideways out of the saddle. The shaft carved the air where he had been, hammered through the planted shield of an Estellan archer and ripped the man's leg off in a spray of blood. More arrows fell around Seth as he struggled to reset his shields, and one pierced his thigh and pinned him to the dirt. Blinding pain shocked through him and he rolled, trying to unpin himself, and – *Thank Kore!* – it came free and healing-gnosis instinctively flooded the wound. He snapped off most of the shaft and left the rest where it was – he could deal with it later; right now he had work to do. Someone held out a hand and he grabbed it and lurched to his feet. His horse reared and vanished over the parapet: a whinny and a splash and it was gone.

'Sir, sir!' the men about him clamoured. 'Get to the rear!'

'No!' he shouted. *I'll show you, Father!* 'I'm fine!' He poured more healing-gnosis into his leg, sealing the torn flesh and blood vessels, while all around him boulders and arrows still fell. *Were we supposed to get this close yet?* he wondered. He couldn't remember what the plan was any more. It didn't matter: the Argundians continued to press forward, now all mixed up with Pallacians from the Thirteenth, Coulder's old maniple, tramping over the ruined bodies of those who'd gone in first.

He raised his shields again to protect those around him as another ladder disintegrated in a withering blast. The attack wavered, and a Pallacian, the pilus from his personal cohort – *what is the man's name?* – seized his shoulder and pulled him back to the edge of the killing ground. Looking back, he could see the rest of the causeway was still filled with torches and men, all awaiting their turn at the impregnable walls: a snake of light, waiting to strike.

Sigurd Vaas hurried towards him through the red smoky haze. 'I think we've got their attention!' he cried, then looked down and saw the broken arrow sticking out of Seth's thigh and shouted, 'Get to the rear, boy!'

An instant later Vaas was ripped in half by two ballista bolts at once, his body jerked away in a blur. The after-image seared Seth's retinas as two pieces of shredded meat and bone swathed in scarlet – all that remained of the Argundian mage – came rolling to a stop twenty yards away.

Seth gripped the parapet as around him the Argundians wailed in despair and the tide of men began to ebb. For a second he was frightened that he was going to be left alone here, and that dread overpowered all other thought. He staggered toward the nearest standard-bearer and grabbed the flag from his startled grasp. 'Next wave!' he bellowed, his father's face floating before his eyes. 'Kore is with us!'

Then he turned and lurched forward once more, screaming, '*FORWARD!*'

Behind him someone started chanting his father's name: '*KOR-I-ON! KOR-I-ON!*'

Fridryk Kippenegger sang of his fatherland, the deep-forested expanse at the heart of Yuros; he sang songs of heroes and Stormriders, of mystic swords and glory. Nonsense, of course, he'd been fighting all his life and he knew full well that war was butchery and madness, but you couldn't come through it victorious, let alone sane, unless you pretended it was something else.

So as the fast-moving current pushed the wagons closer and closer to the walls protecting the northern gatehouse, he moved onto the next stanza, the one about the dragon-slayer and a sword of fire and gold.

'Shut the Hel up,' Jelaska snapped. 'This is a secret mission, you idiot!'

He ignored her and sang louder, and the men hidden in the base of the wagon grinned as they held on grimly: their armour was so heavy, they knew they'd drown in seconds if they went in.

The Brevian, Wilbrecht, laughed. 'They'll never be able to hear him above that.' He indicated the cacophony at the gates.

Their wagon came apart as they struck the rocks at the base of the tower and the men gritted their teeth and swallowed their alarm as they thrashed about until they found their footing and managed to clamber up the slippery weed-encrusted boulders to the base of the walls.

The next 'boat' struck and they helped the newcomers up, then the next and the next. There were eight men to each wagon-base, and seven wagons deployed for the purpose. Wilbrecht deployed his sylvanic gnosis to shore up the wagons while Hulbert, the Hollenian Water-mage, guided the craft. Jelaska was here to do – well, whatever it was she did; something nasty and sorcerous, Kip supposed.

He met Wilbrecht's eye. The wagons fixed, the Brevian had a bow nocked and gnosis ready-kindled on the arrowheads. A cheating way to kill, Kip had always thought. *Typical of a race who wear skirts . . .*

'Ready?' Wilbrecht rasped.

'Yar! Always, little man. Don't point that thing near me.' He rotated his right shoulder, flexed his biceps and glanced at Jelaska. 'How do we get in?'

The haggard Argundian woman jabbed a thumb towards a bridge that crossed the central channel and joined the two island-forts. 'Weren't you listening to the briefing?' she said scornfully. 'That way, up onto the bridge and in. I'll follow when I'm ready.'

'Yar, yar, I was listening,' Kip lied. *Details are for small people. I'm here to fight.* He bowed his head and muttered a prayer – though not in any hope of having it answered. The Schlessen gods were vindictive bastards who didn't answer prayers, but they were sure to punish those who *didn't* pray. Mostly they wanted blood, and it was always best to offer someone – or some*thing* – else's. *Minaus Bullhead, hear me! A calf, burned for you when I return home. This I swear.* He reckoned he currently owed the god about seventy beasts, more than he could hope to own in a lifetime.

'Kore will protect us,' Wilbrecht said, smugly sure that *his* god *did* answer prayers.

'Kore? Neyn, Kore has no power here. In battle there is only the Bullhead.' Kip drew his sword, kissed the blade. 'Let us go and find some of these Dokken, yar? See if they can fight.' Schlessen legends were full of them, snatching babies and killing the unwary: fairy tales, he'd always thought. 'Let's see how they like cold steel.'

They clambered around the base of the walls, their movement masked by the clamour at the gates, though they could see people moving above them. Perhaps Jelaska was concealing them, because no one called out or raised an alarm. In a few moments they were beneath the central span. A wagon rolled past as Wilbrecht joined him. 'We move as the gates are opened for the wagon,' he breathed, his voice calm. 'Save us the trouble of knocking on the door.'

Kip grinned. *Good man, this, for a skirted Kore-kisser.*

The signal came seconds later, a mental command from Jelaska. Kip soared upwards with a kinetically enhanced leap and landed square on the bridge, the stone solid beneath his feet and a dark shape before him. He glimpsed a swarthy face and thrust, the blade of his sword going into the man's mouth and out the back of his head.

He kicked the corpse away. *For you, Bullhead.*

There was more shouting, and a mage-bolt seared past his shoulder, missing everyone. It came from somewhere above, but there was no time to look; he was already storming into the loosely spread enemy soldiers, a two-handed sweeping blow hacking down a Keshi archer partway through drawing his bow.

'Minaus!' he bellowed, surging onwards. Wilbrecht had gone the other side, his bow-string thrumming, and he felt more gnosis-blasts shaking the air. Another Keshi, this one armed with a curved sword, erupted from a doorway, but he blocked, took a slash on his mailed arm that barely tore the skin, battered down the man's guard and thrust six foot of straight steel into his guts. The Keshi looked down with panicked eyes that rolled back up into his skull as he slid to the ground.

'MINAUS! THE BULLHEAD IS HERE! VORWAERTS!' he bellowed at the Pallacians swarming onto the bridge behind him as he made for the gates. Wilbrecht appeared from the far side of the wagon, arrows flying as he cut down the fleeing enemy. *Yar, in the back,* he thought. *Typical Brevian!* They pounded forward together, through the gates, one hacking, the other shooting down the remaining gatemen, and found themselves in a small square from which narrow streets wound away in all directions. Wilbrecht lit an arrow with gnostic fire and sent it blazing into the air. It burst into flame: the signal that they were inside the northern keep.

A few seconds later another rose from the south side of the river in answer, and hundreds of torches sprang into light as the Khotri army surged along the southern causeway.

As the signal-arrows arced gracefully through the sky, Baltus Prenton laughed aloud and sent his windskiff slewing gracelessly past the southern island. He was struggling to guide it, for the little vessel had twenty legionaries clinging to ropes and hanging from the sides. Ramon Sensini, in the prow of the skiff, peered down anxiously, but although an array of terrified faces turned his way as the craft staggered through the air, no one had yet fallen off.

'Hold on boys, nearly there!' Ramon called, his eyes on the southern fort's outer gate-towers. He could see a strong force there, with ten or more robed figures wrapped in faintly visible gnosis shields, and dozens of archers, but the ballistae platforms had been emptied and the deadly apparatus dismantled and moved to the northern gate for the assault the Dokken were anticipating there.

They were certain the Khotri wouldn't get involved: chalk up one for the plan. He selected a robed shape, presumably a Dokken, who was clearly in view and oblivious to the cloaked skiff passing right by him in the darkness. His mage-bolt streaked across the sky, a narrow thrust of pure destructive energy, ripped through the unfocused shield and punched a coin-sized hole in the Dokken's chest before burning out the other side. The Dokken collapsed with a grunt as his colleagues around him shouted in alarm, and the sky lit up.

Baltus laughed again, and banked away, leaving the counter-strikes ripping harmlessly at his rear shields: the Dokken, too concerned with protecting themselves, failed to factor in the windskiff's speed, so the vessel lumbered past untouched. Not that Baltus' manoeuvring was much appreciated by the men clinging to the ropes below the hull.

'Fuck! Fly straight, can't you?' someone wailed.

'Enjoy the view,' Ramon shouted back unsympathetically and grinned at Baltus at the chorus of cursing that arose in response.

He scanned the way ahead, using his gnostic sight to penetrate the darkness. The wagon-boats were clustered around the northern island, beneath the bridge just as planned. He grinned. *Phase two, right on schedule!* Buona fortuna, *Kip!*

Beyond the northern keep he could see the causeway was filled with torchlight, and now the noise reached him: the crescendo of battle that had haunted his dreams since Shaliyah. Baltus sent the skiff climbing ponderously towards the highest tower, and Ramon reached down with his left hand and fed his own gnosis into the keel to help the overloaded skiff. Even with the two of them working to keep it on course it was wobbling badly and they careened over the battlements with just inches to spare. There was a great flash of flames from the northern gatehouse and Ramon suddenly caught sight of thousands of men fighting on the causeway. *Come on, Vaas!* he cried to himself, *keep them pinned!*

Baltus brought the skiff about and hovered it about ten feet above a roof-top garden. They could all see that there were several Keshi archers stationed there, but the cloaking spell had worked and they were only just starting to look up. 'Go-go-go!' Baltus called urgently, and Ramon leaped out, using Air-gnosis to steady his fall.

Behind him Lukaz's cohort released their grips on hull and ropes and dropped, yelling in fear and exhilaration. The skiff, suddenly unburdened and filled with energy, shot upwards, while twenty-one bodies struck the roof-garden's grass and flowerbeds and twisted and rolled to their feet. Ramon heard at least two men cry out in pain as they landed, but he had other things to focus on as he struck the ground between two Keshi archers who were just spinning around to deal with this new threat.

'*Arrivederci!*' he shouted, and flipped his hands. Using telekinetic force he hurled the hapless guards over the parapets, then fired off a mage-bolt at another. The blue fire made the man's ribs glow as his chest burst apart. Then Kel Harmon landed beside him, the flank-man all grace and power as he slashed his shortsword through another man's bow and into his shoulder. The archer staggered and Harmon flipped him over the edge.

The rest of the cohort had found their feet except for Holdyne, who was rolling around, clutching his right ankle and yowling in agony, and Hedman, who was silently cradling his arm to relieve a dislocated shoulder. The few remaining Keshi on the rooftop tried to make a run for the stairs, but Lukaz gestured and the cohort ranged forward. Harmon's blade was a flickering blur as it tore out the first Keshi's throat in an eye-blink, while young Trefeld and big Manius combined to cut down another. Vidran launched a javelin that took another man through the back and pinned him to the wooden door until rat-faced Bowe wrenched the Keshi off the door and threw him to the ground, then punched his sword through his breastplate, just to make sure. The last man, seeing the cohort closing in, chose instead to jump, wailing, from the parapet. Ramon went to the edge and peered down. They were about five flights up. Even in the dark he could see the man, an ungainly heap in a narrow street below.

He turned back, and shouted to Lukaz, 'Find a way inside!'

While the flankers dragged Holdyne and Hedman to cover, Lukaz got the front ranks into formation facing the corner doorway. An arrow whistled past Ramon's face and glanced off Lukaz's shoulder as someone shouted in Keshi from a neighbouring building. Ramon threw up his wards just in time to block another flight of arrows and the cohort hit the ground in tortoise formation, their shields interlocked and covering them all. More arrows flew, but their tortoise shell held as the wickedly barbed points slammed into the wood and bossing. Ramon, in the middle of the huddle, kept his head down, feeling the the tension as the enemy kept hammering the shield-wall. Then an arrow pierced it, eliciting an agonised hiss from Kent, who stared at the shaft in his thigh, then slowly sagged to the ground.

'Dolmin, Ferdi, see to Kent,' Lukaz shouted. 'Vid, find me a way out of here!'

'Boss, there's stairs to a lower terrace,' Vidran called laconically. 'The archers will lose their line of sight.'

'But there's a door this side too!' Bowe shouted back.

'Hold positions!' Lukaz shouted, grabbing Bowe's arm to keep him inside the formation. 'We'll take the stairs on Vid's side.'

'Then make it soon,' Manius shouted as more arrows struck. 'Someone farted back here.' A chorus of jeers and denials rose from that side and Ramon smiled to himself.

Lukaz's voice remained calm. 'Vid, call the steps! Lads, keep the shields locked! Ferdi, bring Kent!'

The next minute felt like hours as more arrows found the gaps between shields, but the men were armoured as well as shielded and apart from a graze on Trefeld's forearm and a scratch on Briggan's cheek, they got to the staircase unscathed and clattered down into another garden area a level down. Away from the rain of arrows, Ramon could hear muffled shouting and the rattle of latches on doors, then on the far side of the garden a crowd of armoured men burst through the doors Bowe had pointed out and pounded towards them.

'Fuckin' Noories!' Bowe screamed as the cohort wheeled and the front rank presented shields and spears. Years of drilling had made their responses automatic; they fell into position effortlessly and the ranks were formed and flankers ready seconds before the Keshi charge reached them.

Ramon stood up, his shields bursting into light about him, and slammed a mage-bolt into the lead man an instant before the rest of the Keshi men struck their line. For the next few moments he was totally unnecessary. Every man in the cohort knew exactly what he was doing; moving almost as one they slammed their shields and spears into the faces of the enemy with brutal force, and though more and more Keshi were piling in behind the first-comers, the cohort took one step forward, then another, each one called by Lukaz and echoed by Baden the bannerman. They stepped and thrust, stepped and thrust, and the powerful rhythm helped to power them forwards. The Keshi with their slashing swords and small shields could not contain them and were soon giving ground as sheer muscle and bodyweight turned the tide: the front rankers, led by Manius and Dolmin, were simply too big and strong for the smaller foe.

In a few moments Ramon, at the heart of the formation, was stumbling over the dead and maimed bodies of the fallen. The second rank were stabbing down into the corpses with brutal efficiency to ensure there'd be no nasty surprises left behind them. The flankmen were cutting down any Keshi that came at them from the side, as they swept forward. Then Vidran called the switch and the second rank stepped through, their momentum making the change deadly effective. The few Keshi still managing to hold their ground were cut down as those behind gave way in a sudden despairing wail. At Lukaz's signal the flankers pushed out and forward, forming a pincer movement, and with Harmon and dark-skinned Ollyd cutting a swathe, the Keshi were forced back into the stairwell from where they'd emerged.

Then the Keshi broke and blood sprayed everywhere as those who tried to run were savagely cut down from behind. Vidran reached the doors just as they were slammed in his face by those Keshi who had got below. Lightning crackled along the frame and the rankers stepped away and looked at Ramon.

'It's just a warding,' he panted. He extended his gnostic senses. 'It's not overly strong – you could break it down just by bashing at it, though it'll take a little time.'

'Can't you—?' Bowe waved his hands in a mystic way.

'Waste of energy.' Ramon turned to Lukaz. 'Smash it. I'm going to use that back stair. Who can you spare?'

'Harmon, Ollyd, Tolomon.' Lukaz pointed. 'Follow the boss. Keep together, stay alive.'

Ramon sprinted back into the courtyard above while the men began to batter at the double-doors with axes. The archers on the neighbouring rooftops had to be busy elsewhere, as they traversed the garden without a shaft coming their way. Ramon dealt with the lock and the door flew open to reveal a circular stone stairwell.

'I'll take the lead, Magister,' Harmon said instantly, his usually bland expression animated as he darted past, followed by Ollyd and then Ramon, with Tolomon bringing up the rear. At the first landing the door opened onto a long corridor. There was noise from both directions and the legionaries looked at Ramon questioningly.

He probed in both directions, seeking the mental touch of the mage who had warded the doors holding back Lukaz's men. After a moment he had him: somewhere below. *This house belongs to someone important*, he thought to himself. *It was the biggest building inside the walls and it's got a well-tended roof garden.* He thought for a moment, then ordered, 'You three: find the doors the others are trying to break through and join them. I'm going below to find the mage who set those wards.'

'What if they're still there by the doors?' young Tolomon asked nervously.

'Don't worry, he's underneath us.' He looked at Harmon. 'Take the lead, hit them hard – and shout if you need me.' The legionaries saluted with varying degrees of formality, then ghosted away down the corridor.

Ramon took a deep breath and headed down the tower staircase into the darkness.

Kaltus Korion always said that timing was paramount. Seth remembered everything his father had ever said to him – every slight and condemnation as well as every opinion or fragment of advice – and those words popped into his mind now because at the moment he staggered forward, clutching the battle-standard like a crutch, a windskiff flashed over the top of the gate-tower and a burst of fire engulfed one of the four ballistae. The craft was almost instantly peppered with mage-bolts, but it burst through unscathed, with the counter-fire doing nothing more than illuminating the night sky behind it. He was sure he heard Baltus Prenton whooping joyously, even as half a dozen Dokken became giant rooks and launched themselves in his wake.

The skiff's attack was enough to disrupt the fire from above – *timing!* – and Seth found himself running towards the gates, hurdling dead bodies under virtually no fire. The next wave, mostly Pallacians of his own maniple, swarmed after him, roaring his name as they slammed their ladders against the walls and swarmed upwards like beetles. He blasted the first archer he saw with mage-fire, then another, and another, trying to make the defenders keep their heads down. He dimly recalled that this attack was supposed to be a feint, but he wasn't really sure what that actually meant when it came to it and Sigurd Vaas was gone so there was no one to ask. The rankers themselves were pushing the action forward and he was so astounded and impressed by their reckless courage that he wouldn't have called them off even if he'd known how.

It was almost frightening how skilled the rankers were at dealing with magi. The Dokken Fire- and Earth-magi were hurling flame and boulders, doing awful damage, but the legionaries locked their big shields together, braced against the ground and hurled their spears and javelins and arrows, forcing the magi to defend themselves from physical missiles and trying to wear down their shields, all the while having to deal with direct gnostic attack. It was attritional: to fight like this took took real, *knowing* sacrifice: the men went into this accepting that the first two or three waves would almost certainly die to create the chance for those behind to get close enough to kill.

But it was working. He saw one Fire-mage spitted on javelins, then an animage with a jackal head fell, pierced simultaneously by three arrows.

As the first men began to pour up the ladders, Seth engaged his Air-gnosis and soared to the top of the battlements. He landed awkwardly, the arrow in his thigh jarring agonisingly as he hit the ground, but that discomfort was overridden by a surge of adrenalin and terror as he found himself confronting the vulture-faced Zsdryk, fresh from pulverising three legionaries with a hail of bricks snatched from a pile of broken masonry.

Zsdryk saw Seth and his face contorted ferociously. Purple light swirled in his hands and something like mist swirled towards Seth. At its 'head' was a skull-like white face with crystalline teeth.

Necromancy! Seth's eyes widened and his brain completely failed to deal with this unexpected manifestation. That an Earth-mage might also know some necromancy was really not that hard to predict, but he'd seen nothing to suggest these Dokken had such arcane knowledge or experience.

He would have died instantly had not the legionary behind him, a homely, middle-aged man who looked like a farmer, thrown himself in the way. Through his gnostic sight Seth saw the ghostly mist-creature shred the man's soul, though his body, when it fell, was unmarked other than the scream of agony and dread on the soldier's face.

That image was imprinted on Seth's brain too as he was flung aside.

Then the ghost-creature came straight at him. The soldier's sacrifice had bought him about two seconds.

Progress in the streets of Ardijah's northern keep slowed to a crawl as the trapped Keshi archers realised the trap closing around them and began to pour back from the walls, seeking some way to safety. Fridryk Kippenegger's shield-wards were just about stretched to the limit – he was only a sixteenth-blood, the weakest gnosis possible, and his meagre powers were almost exhausted. But he was young and strong, and he had all the native ferocity of his people, so he stormed onwards, only using his gnosis to shield for those vital seconds that it took to get him within striking range – and from there, his big zweihandle did the rest. The Keshi all used light weapons: their scimitars broke on his massive blade as if they were made of clay.

Fighting with concentrated ferocity, he drove one cluster of Keshi into an alley, turning away their clumsy parries and hacking straight through their poor armour into flesh and bone. The last group of enemy soldiers at the end of the alley wailed their off-key ululations and fled. Alone for a moment he leaned against the wall and caught his breath, winded from the intensity of the fighting.

He straightened and turned, zweihandle raised and ready as booted feet ran up behind him, but it was only Wilbrecht, who waved as he passed and said, 'Bruda,' grinning savagely. *Brother*. There was nothing like fighting together to make brothers of men. Kip gripped his sword and went to follow, but as Wilbrecht rounded the corner, an unseen force hammered into him, lifting him from his feet and slamming him into the wall so hard it partially caved in. Kip caught the edge of the force and found himself spinning round like a top before being dumped in the mud. Through blurred eyes he saw Wilbrecht's bloody form unpeel bonelessly from the dented wall and flop to the ground. A shadow cast by the torches stretched longer as someone approached.

Kip tried to find his feet as *something* behind him hissed with a chilling eagerness that sent a shiver through his heart. He threw a look back over his shoulder and blanched.

Minaus, save us!

He pressed himself against the wall as a glowing thing with too many teeth and claws swooped along the alley from the direction he'd come. He half-raised his blade, but the thing ignored him, flowing straight past him and vanishing around the corner. A second later light exploded from there, followed by the concussive blasts of powerful gnosis-discharges at close range.

He dimly sensed another of the things stalking closer, and heard it calling softly, '*Hecatta! Hecatta!*' as it passed. It had reptile eyes and oily skin that constantly changed hue, and he was too frightened to breathe lest it notice him. It too went around the corner, shrieking triumphantly as if it had found its life's true purpose.

He would not have followed it for all the beer in Schlessen.

Another figure entered the alley as he managed to clamber to his feet. 'Kippenegger,' Jelaska greeted him amiably, her eyes glowing purple. 'How do you fare?'

'Alive,' he panted. He looked at poor Wilbrecht. *Poor bastard, chose the wrong god.*

'Good for you.' She reached up and patted his cheek affectionately, then continued past. 'Keep it that way: don't follow me.' Her hands suddenly sprouted a mesh of violet skeins of light like puppet-strings that extended into the darkness around the corner. 'Find another way.'

He gratefully took her advice.

The moments bought by the legionary's death saved Seth's life: those two seconds were long enough to pull him out of the paralysis of terror. He felt his limbs and his brain unlock with an almost audible click, and then he was able to retrieve the information: it was an eidolon, a spectral being of the aether, like Magister Fyrell used to summon in his classes. They weren't hard to deal with, as long as you didn't let sheer terror freeze you. They were insubstantial and they preyed on the spirit, but they were 'only as deadly as you allow them to be' – now he remembered the magister's very words. Malevorn had always dealt with them easily in class, but then, he was a sorcerer and good at *everything*. For non-sorcerers, banishing this sort of monster required a combination of the gnosis and combat . . .

Seth gripped his periapt and conjured white fire along the blade of his sword. As the eidolon closed on him, it fixed its ice-like gaze on him, seeking to paralyse him with fear. But he was well past terror now and as he stabbed his glowing blade into the spectral flesh, he started pouring energy into it – and the thing fell apart almost instantly, flailing about impotently, then vanishing with a tortured howl. *Life-energy . . . not so useless as my classmates thought . . .*

Zsdryk swore in his own tongue and Seth braced himself for a gnostic duel – but the Souldrinker just turned and dived from the walls. A black winged shape emerged from his cloak and vanished into the darkness. Seth tried to blast it with mage-fire, but it was too quick for him; before he'd readied his hands it had flashed away into the dark and was gone.

And then the shock of the arrow protruding from the scabbed-over hole in his thigh hit him. He wobbled and nearly fell over, but the legionaries clambering over the walls spotted his wavering body and a couple of them grabbed him. This time he let them. The immediate peril was gone – and anyway, there was suddenly nothing left in his legs. He slumped between the two men and darkness hit him between the eyes like a giant black pillow.

Ramon plummeted down the tower stairs and at the next landing he blasted open the door – there was no time for subtlety – and braced himself for a retaliation that didn't come. The spiral stairs continued downwards, but this was the level he needed, he was sure of it. He took the corridor into the heart of the building. It wasn't that huge – no bigger than a well-to-do merchant's house in Norostein – but it was well-lit with oil-lamps, and when he peered through the first door his guess that someone important lived here was confirmed. The dining room might be small, but judging by the table set with silver goblets and platters, an intimate meal had been interrupted. He passed on, slipping silently through the shadows to the next room.

There was a large painting on the wall of the bedroom, of a massively obese man with huge moustaches, like a walrus in silks. Sitting at his knees was a richly dressed, serious-looking young woman, thin as a spear-shaft, with a round, practical face and a small mouth. *The caliph and his wife?* The four-poster bed was unmade, and the lingering scent of a woman's perfume wafted past his nose. The clothing in the closets had been strewn across the room, as if someone had tried on and discarded everything in some frivolous inspection.

These are the calipha's rooms, he guessed, *but someone's been playing in here.*

None of this was helping the assault. He turned, and hurried back to the corridor, stepping through the door . . .

. . . and then freezing.

There was a woman in a bekira-shroud with her back to him, creeping cautiously towards the door he'd smashed open. She must have heard the noise and come to investigate. Her greying hair was tied in a ponytail, and her earrings suggested she was Lantric. His gnostic sight revealed her nature instantly: she was Dokken, and just as appallingly, pregnant.

He glanced back to ensure no one was coming at him from behind, but all he could hear was a loud hammering: that, no doubt, was Lukaz and the cohort smashing their way into the level above. Several floors below, he could make out the bustle and noise of household staff scurrying to obey a male voice bellowing instructions.

At Turm Zauberin, the ethics tutor – sweet old Agnes Yune – had given them all manner of scenarios which were designed to reveal character and guide them in behaviour to ensure that they all emerged as Kore-fearing Emperor Constant-loving true servants of the Rondian Empire. Not that that had ever been Ramon's goal . . .

Aggy, you'd have loved this – you might even have posed this exact question! As I recall, the pure-bloods knocked her out, then delivered her to the Inquisition to do their murdering for them. Alaron – bless him – let her go. But me . . .

He'd come last in ethics – not just last, he'd actually scored zero. It had become a game: to always chose the most reprehensible course of action, to wilfully destroy Aggy Yune's prissy little passion plays.

He drew his stiletto. *Just below the left shoulder, level with the armpit. The blade punctures the heart, it stops, and she has about three seconds before everything stops. When my time comes, I hope it's that easy . . .*

She wasn't much of a mage, because she didn't sense him as he glided in behind her, then hesitated.

I'm about to kill a pregnant woman . . .

But she's a Dokken.

He punched in the thin blade while putting his hand over her mouth to keep her silent. She sagged against him and dropped to the floor and died less than a minute later. The foetus lasted another minute. He felt it die, because he'd linked part of his awareness to its heartbeat. He felt he kind of owed it that, although he couldn't have said why.

Agnes Yune had some strange ideas about when a child became human. So did the Kore. Whatever they thought, this felt like murder . . . but there was a war on.

From above, he heard the sound of sudden violence – the cohort had obviously broken in – and that distraction nearly cost him his life.

Someone bellowed behind him and he spun to see an immense shape waving a huge scimitar coming at him. Instantly he fired off his most powerful mage-bolt, even as the man emerged into the light. The searing burst of energy punched into the man's huge chest, charring his clothes and sending him lurching backwards, screeching in his own tongue. As a lamp lit his face, Ramon recognised him from the oil painting.

Merda! It's the rukking caliph!

'Sir,' he cried, 'I'm sorry!' *Damn it, I'm supposed to be rescuing the poor bastido!*

He ran towards the caliph as he staggered away, following him to what turned out to be the top of the central staircase. Below, people were milling about, both servants and soldiers, and all obviously terrified. They were trying to block off the doors and windows with whatever they could find – he could see planking, chairs, tables, even a metal bath.

When they saw their lord at the head of the stairs, clutching a bloody and burned hole in his chest, they cried out in shock and outrage, and as Ramon stared in horror, the caliph tumbled backwards down the staircase, smashing his head as he went, and landed at the foot in a bloody heap.

Rukking Hel, I've just killed the Caliph of Ardijah . . .

A woman stood staring at the massive corpse that slid to a halt at her feet.

He recognised the calipha from the painting as well. In the flesh she was even thinner, as skinny as a stick, and about half as pretty, but she had a vivid, birdlike presence. She was clad in a glittering, heavily embroidered gown encrusted with gems – he was quite certain they were real – more befitting a ball than a battle.

Ramon watched as her face changed emotion five times in two seconds: *fear-anger-worry-hope* – then something that looked a lot like *triumph*. She looked up at Ramon, pushed out her small bust and cast him an enquiring look. 'Magus?'

Sol et Lune! That was the shortest mourning period in history.

'Calipha. How may I help?'

383

As she looked up at him, her head held proudly high and her eyes appraising, there was a clatter behind him and his cohort poured down the stairs and took up formation about him. Lukaz glanced at him. 'Sir, what is your command?'

'Just wait,' Ramon told him quietly, his eyes on the calipha. Her servants were still shouting in alarm and the braver ones, mostly the soldiers, threw themselves into a cordon about the young woman, who hadn't flinched.

Moving as if she had been born for this moment, she drew herself to her full height – which was not even as tall as Ramon – and replied in Rondian, the tongue he'd addressed her in, 'That rather depends. Are you here to rescue me or ravish me?'

He shouldn't have had to think about that. 'Ahhh. Rescue . . . ?'

The young woman raised her eyebrows and looked at him in the way that only someone born to rule could truly manage. 'You say this, who have slain the caliph, my husband?'

'Errr . . .'

She looked down at her expired husband with the most virulent look of hatred and contempt he had ever seen. 'The caliph is dead,' she announced, in tones of the utmost satisfaction. 'Long live the calipha.'

She turned and looked at her people, who were looking in confusion from the dead man to his living wife. '*Uzyn kranli Calipha Amiza!*' she shouted, jabbing a finger to the floor. Ramon saw half of the people kneel immediately, but the other half were wavering, and they were the armed ones.

'*Uzyn kranli Calipha Amiza!*' she repeated.

Time for the rescue bit . . .

He stepped to the head of the stairs and shouted, 'Long live the calipha!' and when they looked blank, he did his best to mimic her words: 'Oozun . . . cranley . . . calipha amiza!' He kindled mage-fire in one hand and jabbed a finger at them. '*Kneel!*'

Thankfully, the calipha's people caught on fast; they fell to their knees before their mistress and the new ruler of Ardijah smiled triumphantly up at him before ascending the stairs to stand at his side.

She shouted orders to the men and women below and they burst into action, sealing off the entrance and dragging away the body of the caliph. It took eight men to do it. Then she looked at Ramon, her eyes hot. 'Thank you, Magus. You have freed me.'

'You're most welcome.' He eyed her up and down. She wasn't a beauty, but she had a kind of intense conviction that could freeze limbs. 'I am Ramon Sensini, Pallacios Thirteen. We're liberating Ardijah.'

'Wonderful! I am Amiza. Welcome to my home.' She grabbed his arm and as she dragged him towards the nearest room, an office with a massive divan against one wall, he caught a glimpse of Pilus Lukaz and his men, gazing at him in bemusement.

Then the door slammed shut and the Calipha of Ardijah was all over him. His conscience began to jabber at him, but relief at his survival and the exhilaration of victory were telling him something far different and he found himself helpless as she thrust him towards the divan, shedding layers and revealing skin the colour of the crema of a Silacian coffee and as smooth as the costliest silk.

'Now,' she said in a decisive voice, 'you ravish.'

Sorry, Aggy, ethics were never my thing . . .

And then, some time later . . .

Sorry, Sevvie . . .

Dawn, appropriately red, shimmered on the waters of the floodplain. The vivid palette of oranges and pinks swirled at the fringes of the bloody sun as the light chased the night from the sky and lit the moon in marbled cream and grey. Ramon thought how strange it was that the most beautiful sunrises came after those nights filled with the most horror.

He sat on the battlements by the cupola at the northeastern corner of the northern gatehouse. Last night archers had fired a torrent of arrows down upon Seth Korion and Sigurd Vaas' men from here; this morning there was little to show that such a battle had taken place. The last few wagons trundled across the causeway into the keep, leaving the space before the gates almost empty now. But the air was thick with smoke and the acrid smell of blood. Corpses were being hauled away to the funeral pyres, and the captured Keshi were being marched south to be handed over to the Khotri commander. He didn't like to think what would happen to them, but right now he had more immediate problems.

Sevvie was sitting beside his knee, watching the sun with a strained look on her face – not because she was in pain, but because she didn't care for the calipha, who had been openly flirting with her man – in fact, they had just had quite a spat about it and things were still tense between them. His own sense of guilt didn't help.

At least she doesn't know how far it went.

Jelaska had captured both Yorj Arkanus and Hecatta with her conjured necromantic spirits, but unfortunately Zsdryk had got away. Even so, they had control of both the northern and southern island fortresses, and the calipha's men had turned on the Keshi garrison with glee once Ramon had secured her aid.

Their own losses hadn't been bad, despite the carnage at the gates, but they could ill afford the death of Sigurd Vaas. Jelaska had taken the news with fatalistic fortitude, like someone who expected bad news as a given, though Ramon was sure he'd heard her muttering something about a curse.

Now Kip ambled over and stood beside him, the sunlight bronzing his massive shoulders. He looked as cheery as a man who'd enjoyed a really good night out. Regret and sorrow didn't appear to be part of the Schlessen tribesman's nature. He was pleased to see Baltus Prenton here too; the Windmaster had outmanoeuvred the Dokken shifters pursuing his skiff and now he and Kip were sharing some potent spirit they'd unearthed from somewhere and chuckling over the more grotesque deaths they'd witnessed. They paused every now and then to toast one of the fallen.

An irregular thumping sounded on the stairs and Seth Korion hobbled towards them. The arrow in his thigh had been removed with much swearing and the expenditure of a great deal of healing-gnosis, but he was already moving as if the wound were days old. It obviously still hurt though, and he looked relieved to throw himself down on a bench someone had dragged over.

'General,' Baltus greeted him, passing his flask.

Seth took a rash mouthful, spluttered and choked. Then he had some more.

So Baby Korion fought like a hero! Wonders will never cease. Ramon tried to spot visible signs of this new and heroic Seth, but he still looked as uncertain and intimidated by life as usual.

'Any news of Bondeau?' Seth asked, but everyone shook their heads. There had been no news of any of the force they'd sent off to slow down Salim's main army.

After a moment, Baltus said, 'While I was trying to shake off those animagi I glimpsed a few flashes away to the east – maybe ten miles away? It could have been them . . .'

'They should be back by now.' Seth sounded anxious. 'We should send scouts, or try to scry them.'

'I have tried,' Jelaska admitted, 'but I got nothing – although he could be warding. That would affect me as much as an enemy.'

Seth swallowed and peered across the river.

Rukka mio, he actually cares. Ramon allotted him a few credits. 'I'll send Coll,' he said at once.

'Safer if I fly out for a look,' Baltus replied. 'Just let me rest up for a few hours.'

'What does that Noorie woman want?' Severine put in, her face still tetchy. 'That calipha. Skinny little bint has been strutting about the streets, making everyone she meets kiss her feet. Is she on our side?' She glowered up at Ramon, furious that the calipha had insisted – in a very proprietary way – that Ramon escort her while her subjects swore allegiance to her.

Luckily, Sevvie didn't know that she'd thanked him again in private afterwards too, and *very* passionately. He was feeling a bit bad about that, but he had considered the consequences of refusal.

Damn those ethics!

Jelaska interrupted his train of thought. 'The calipha has

generously given us rooms in the second tower, and she has allowed us to bring our army across – the bridge-keeps are too small to house more than a quarter of our men. She could have made things very awkward for us, but instead she has persuaded the emir's soldiers to pull back and allow us to set up on both islands.'

'Well, I don't trust her,' Severine said, fixing Ramon with a stare. 'Why is she helping us? And why does she have to speak to Ramon all the time?'

'I rescued her – of course she's grateful,' Ramon explained, not looking at her.

'Too bloody grateful,' Severine said sullenly, crossing her arms.

The other magi all looked at each other awkwardly, except Baltus, who winked ostentatiously at Seth. 'I'm rather impressed with her,' the Brevian said. 'Apparently she's already packed off the caliph's other two wives: sent them back to their families with nothing but their clothes. She is clearly a woman who knows how to deal with rivals.'

'So am I,' Severine said tersely.

'She's not a rival,' Ramon said, equally curtly. 'She was in need of a protector and I happened to find her first. But,' he said, looking firmly at Sevvie, 'I am *not* interested in the calipha, except for how she can help us get home.'

'I know what you men are like,' the Pallacian girl said, holding her belly as if to emphasise her vulnerable state. 'Any opportunity and you'll take it, then blame the woman.'

Sevvie's words were uncomfortably close to the truth, but lies were contagious: once you started, you had to keep telling new ones to cover up the old ones. He fell back on a half-truth. 'Sol et Lune, woman, she scares me! I'm not going near her.'

'I'll talk to her.' Kip smirked. 'I'm not scared of women.'

'You should be,' Jelaska growled.

Seth raised a hand. 'Enough. She's been useful to us. Let's talk about what to do next.'

Ramon gave him a grateful look. 'Thank you! Some leadership!

Who'd have thought.' He met Seth's eyes, and for possibly the first time there was humour on both their faces.

'We need to rest, and reorganise,' Jelaska said. 'The soldiers are exhausted, we have a lot of fresh wounded, a lot of men to mourn ...' Her voice dropped away for a moment, then she continued, 'and we've got to get ready for Salim.'

'We need food,' Ramon added. 'Cloth for bandages. Ointments and purifying spirits. Leather. Wagons, to replace those we used for the river attack. Steel, timber. Horses. Whatever we can purchase from the calipha.'

Seth snorted resignedly. 'What do we bargain with? Won't the Emir of Khotri cut her adrift if she starts demanding such things for us? She's not our hostage.'

'She should be.' Severine glowered.

'We can't afford to antagonise the Emir of Khotriawal,' Ramon replied, 'not with Salim a day away. But if we can keep the calipha onside, she will give us a way to talk to the emir. So we must keep her happy.'

'Well, we all know what'll make her happy,' Sevvie replied snarkily. 'More parading with her favourite mage.'

Baltus and Kip sniggered behind their hands like schoolboys and Ramon sighed. *Remind me ... oh yes, she's having my child ... and ethically, I'm a bad person ...*

'Look, I'll never talk to her again, all right? Someone else can – send Bondeau when he gets back!'

'That doesn't answer my question,' Seth reminded him. 'What can we bargain with?'

Ramon exhaled. It had to come out some time. 'Well, how about gold?' He'd managed to hide the quantity of gold they had, but the time had come .... They needed to be aware of what they had ... well, some of it. 'Most people seem to be fond of it.'

'Gold? What gold?' Seth scoffed. 'We don't have any gold.'

Jelaska gave Ramon a sceptical look. 'Have you raided the calipha's treasury?'

'No.' He motioned for them to lean in, then gave them the acceptable version of what he'd been doing since he got to Antiopia. 'While we were still marching east, Storn and I took the opportunity to reorganise the stores. Instead of moving actual gold around, we extended the informal promissory note system and combined that with bringing the Southern Army's bullion under our care. It's a system the familioso use to move stolen goods,' he added, truthfully.

'So?' Seth asked blankly.

Baltus understood first. 'You're saying you've got the Southern Army's bullion in your wagons?'

Most of the Northern Army's too, actually . . .

'Of course, not all of it . . .' he scoffed cheerily.

Everyone in the circle blinked.

'And we still have it?' Seth asked in a puzzled voice.

'We do,' Ramon replied. 'I got it out of Shaliyah and we've been hauling it around ever since. It's been hidden in the bottom of the stores wagons.'

Sevvie smiled at him at last. 'He's fiendishly clever sometimes, *my* man.'

He really hoped that meant their argument was over. 'I've managed to keep it together since, though it's slowed us down a little.'

'I can see why you'd keep it secret,' Jelaska commented after a moment's silence. 'After all, legionaries aren't famous for restraint over certain things.'

'Gold, women and drink,' Baltus put in, clicking flasks with Kip. 'My favourite things.' The two men took a swig together.

'But what did you plan to do with it all?' Jelaska enquired, fixing him with her grim stare.

'Oh, just make sure the troops get paid. And since Shaliyah . . . well, when you're trapped behind the lines, having something to open doors with is important. How do you think we got a parley yesterday?'

'Why wasn't I told?' Seth demanded.

'You've quite enough to worry about.' Ramon raised a placating hand. 'It's just logistics – a tenth maniple matter. My maniple are here to make sure you all get fed and clothed, remember?'

'Why do I get the feeling that if this matter hadn't come up, we'd have never known?' Jelaska enquired acerbically. 'It seems to me that you've been stringing us all along. Who even knows where the gold is? Did Echor know? Did his Logisticalus know?'

'Of course,' Ramon lied blithely. 'If you'd asked me before Shaliyah, I could have shown you the orders.' *And you just try proving otherwise!* 'So unless anyone else wants to sulk about not being put in charge of the baggage train, can we please get on with the many more practical concerns we face?'

He leaned back and watched Jelaska give up, and that triggered the capitulation of the rest.

Heh! And I didn't even have to mention the opium.

Seth Korion sighed heavily and rubbed at his wounded thigh. 'Very well. Status report?'

'We lost more than two hundred men in front of the gates, but few elsewhere,' Jelaska replied, glancing down at a sheet of paper in her lap. 'Sigurd and Wilbrecht are dead,' she added sadly. 'I tell you, I'm cursed. Any man I touch dies.'

'I'd risk it,' Kip said blithely, and when they all gave him withering looks he just shrugged. 'What?'

'I don't play with children,' Jelaska sniffed, glaring at him.

'Bondeau isn't back yet,' Ramon reminded them, changing the subject before Kip got shredded.

'But on the bright side,' Jelaska resumed, her voice husky, 'we killed more than twenty Dokken, and my summoned spirits captured the infamous Yorj Arkanus and Hecatta.' Her voice warmed a little. 'They like to think of themselves as pure-bloods, but it's only through stolen souls. Neither could deal with *real* power.' Her eyes met Ramon's, as if to emphasise that he couldn't either if push came to shove.

'What do we do with them?' he asked, then added, 'They'd make good bargaining chips.'

'Do you see *everything* in terms of bargaining value?' Jelaska asked. 'This pair have been wanted for *centuries*. Kore knows how many they have killed. I say we execute them,' Jelaska went on, directing her words at Seth. 'Without these two, the Dokken will fall apart. Hang their heads from the battlements and let's see how much control Salim can exert over the rest.'

Ramon thought about the seething, raging pair in the cells below. Jelaska had Chain-runed them while they were still unconscious. Execution was too good for them, there was no doubt about that – but would they be more valuable still alive?

His train of thought was interrupted by cries from the men on the causeway below, who were shouting and pointing. They all turned their heads, and then slowly rose to their feet. On the east road, a line of dark shapes had appeared, marching steadily towards them. As they stared, the sound of Amteh hymns flowed across the water. Salim's army had arrived.

A Meeting of Minds

Gnostic communication

A case can be made for the supremacy of any of the sixteen Studies of the Gnosis, but to me, the most important is one that is not tied to any study: the ability to communicate mind to mind, often at great distance. Most magi use this simple but necessary spell without really appreciating how vital the ability to exchange ideas and information over vast distances is to our empire.

ALVARA BENYS, GRADUATION THESIS, BRES ARCANUM 891

Brochena, Javon, on the continent of Antiopia
Rajab (Julsep) 929
13ᵗʰ month of the Moontide

Gurvon Gyle gripped the relay stave and closed his eyes to remove the distractions of the far-off city sounds and the slow crawl of sunlight across the floor of the tower room. The room was empty, but for the burned-out wreckage of Elena's training machine, 'Bastido'. He wasn't quite sure why he kept the debris, but it pleased him to do so. He exhaled, and focused on a symbol – a secret Imperial Seal – which he conjured in his mind, then sent his mind questing, seeking another such symbol burning in the aether, that place that was neither of this world nor quite beyond it. Other presences hovered there, waiting.

<My lords,> he greeted them.

<Magister Gyle, welcome.> Mater-Imperia Lucia Fasterius was politeness itself. Grand Prelate Dominius Wurther gave a bland but distant

smile, but the other presences were less welcoming: Tomas Betillon and Kaltus Korion merely grunted and Calan Dubrayle glanced sideways, distracted.

There was another presence, one Gurvon didn't recognise: a rakish and self-satisfied face with luxuriant dark hair and a full moustache peppered with grey. <*Magister Gyle?*> the stranger enquired. <*We've not met: I'm Jean Benoit.*>

Gurvon had to work to keep his expression impassive. <*Guildmaster Benoit! This is a surprise.*> He looked at Lucia. <*I had not thought the Guild of Merchants part of this group?*>

<*It's a one-off,*> Tomas Betillon grumped. <*I see enough of this slimy prick in Hebusalim.*>

<*Tomas,*> Lucia chided mildly. <*Behave.*>

Gurvon cast his mind back to the initial meeting, when he had put to this group a plan for the Third Crusade. One of their stated goals had been the destruction of the power of the merchant-magi – led by Jean Benoit. He recalled Lucia's virulent contempt for the traders, particularly those who had been using their economic power to buy magi children to breed with. He could not have been more surprised if he'd found Elena Anborn present. <*Mater-Imperia, you called this meeting at short notice: Is there a problem?*>

I hope it's not something I've done.

He quickly ran over his own position in Javon, but all felt secure: King Francis Dorobon had been largely pacified and unaware of his political emasculation. The mercenary legions he'd acquired were settling in, and supplies were flowing south to Kaltus Korion's army as she'd demanded. The Javonesi nobility were divided and unwilling to elect a new king of their own knowing that would condemn young Timori Nesti to death. And Cera Nesti's Beggars' Court was doing an excellent job of dividing and distracting the Jhafi clergy. Even Elena Anborn's guerrilla attacks had subsided. He felt cautiously optimistic that Javon was on the brink of becoming secure.

Mater-Imperia cleared her throat. <*About this time in the Crusade, an issue often arises that requires the Guildmaster's input. I will hand over now to the Lord Treasurer, as this matter is his particular concern.*>

The circle of faces hovering in the aether turned to Dubrayle.

<*Well?*> Kaltus Korion asked tiredly. The general looked strained. Since Shaliyah, his Northern Army had been dealing with bushfire uprisings in every town and city. Of course this had been anticipated, but it was still presenting enormous difficulties. It had forced him to abandon the frontier edges of his conquests and pull back from Hall'ikut, instead concentrating on a largely defensive battle as the Moontide entered its second year.

It probably didn't help him that I stole three of Korion's legions, Gurvon thought. Adi Paavus, Hans Frikter and Staria Canestos' mercenary legions had been bribed to leave Korion's service and join Gyle in Javon, something Kaltus had been furious about, but Lucia had been cornered into ratifying the transfer after the fact.

<*The problem that has arisen is about the flow of money,*> Dubrayle began.

<*Isn't everything with you?*> Betillon muttered.

Dubrayle ignored him and launched into a lengthy presentation filled with numbers and percentages and trends in currency and bullion, the scale of which was eye-poppingly large. Gurvon prided himself on having a head for figures, but Dubrayle's monologue left him floundering. What he did understand, however, was that the Lord Treasurer clearly had thousands of informants throughout the empire – not spies, but counters and clerks and record-keepers, creating a web of mundane information that made Gyle's own network – his magi-spies and some hundred ordinary people in a few key cities – look hopelessly inadequate.

<*Stop, stop!*> Wurther interrupted. <*I am just a devout man of Kore, so perhaps I'm not so worldly as the rest of you – but am I the only one here who has no idea what you've just said, Calan?*>

<*I don't even know what language he's speaking,*> Betillon growled.

Lucia smiled tolerantly. <*It is a little involved, Calan. Perhaps the summarised version?*>

Dubrayle looked pained. <*All right. Very simply, here it is: Moontides are always crazy. Goods can appreciate in value by a factor of ten and then collapse on the same day. But this Moontide has been the worst ever.*

Investment in the Crusade has risen to insane levels, sucking bullion from Imperial coffers. The worth of a Rondian gilden has trebled inside a year, note issuance has reached untenable levels and money is pouring into Pontus and the East. Prices are rising in unprecedented ways.>

Betillon frowned. <*Er . . . so our coins are worth more, trade and investment is up and the Crusade is being fully supplied this time – and you think that's bad in some way?>*

<*As I said earlier,>* Dubrayle said in a martyred voice, <*speculative investment in promissory notes has reached almost epidemic levels. As you know – no, let me rephrase that: as you should know – all banks, including the Royal Treasury, issue promissory notes far in excess of their actual gold reserves. Money is worth what the markets dictates, and to ensure commerce continues; one must have confidence in the institutions issuing promissories. As long as that confidence and trust exists, traders will treat promissories as real money, exchanging them for real goods. That's how the system works. We typically issue promissory notes at a ratio of ten times the value of bullion held – the private banks and some of the guilds do the same – and then we let the gold price handle the slack. But unauthorised Imperial Notes have shown up, bearing our seal but originating in the armies themselves. I'm trying to trace the origin of these 'Crusader notes', but the trail is tangled. Conservative estimates place the value of notes in circulation at nearly eighty times our bullion reserves.>*

Gurvon whistled softly. *Okay. That, I get.* He glanced across at Benoit, wondering, *But should we be telling him?*

The Guildmaster looked fairly concerned, but he noticed Gurvon's sideways look and addressed him. <*Magister Gyle, this happens every Crusade about this time. But in the past we've been concerned about issued notes reaching double the normal issuance – twenty times the bullion reserves – not eighty times the bullion levels.>* He turned back to Dubrayle. <*My guild is highly exposed here: we are the biggest users of Royal Notes in preference to bullion, because paper is far safer to move in potentially hostile areas. Essentially these Crusader notes amount to counterfeiting, for all that the seal is apparently genuine.>*

Dubrayle resumed the narrative. <*The army has often issued notes while on campaign, but what is different here is the scale: it is utterly beyond precedent – and of course, there is the fact that someone has dared to issue notes bearing my own seal as Treasurer.>*

<It's none of my doing,> Kaltus Korion sniffed. <I've not got your seal, but I daresay it's easy enough to forge.>

<I will get to the bottom of it,> Dubrayle vowed with the intensity of a knight pledging his honour in a duel. *<But the reason I wanted the Guildmaster here is to signal quite clearly that we're aware of the problem, and to ask for cooperation in unravelling the truth and managing its resolution.>*

Benoit preened unselfconsciously. *<Of course we will help to track down the culprits, provided the Crown will pledge to cover all such issuance nonetheless.>* He looked enquiringly at Dubrayle and then at Lucia. *<Bluntly: we need to know that all Crusader notes will be honoured by the Treasury. Otherwise how can we continue to trade, and therefore supply the army?>*

Lucia considered the question for a moment, and then said firmly, *<Legitimate issuance, as Calan says, will be underwritten. Forged or illegitimately issued notes will not. Let the risk fall on the bearer.>*

<With respect, Holiness,> Benoit replied, *<it seems to me that both legitimate and questionable notes are now deeply embedded into the system. Some unlucky investors might be badly hit, including investment banks like Jusst & Holsen, who will not simply accept the losses – they will spread them around, especially to their depositors. This will destroy confidence in every marketplace. It could lead to insurrection on a scale not seen since the collapse of the Rimoni Empire.>*

Gurvon caught his breath. *Could it truly go so far? I thought just our saving were at stake?*

Dubrayle looked grave. *<As the Guildmaster says, the key is confidence. The crusade is going well from a Rondian perspective, notwithstanding the demise of the Second Army at Shaliyah. Holders of Imperial Notes will not panic unless anyone reveals there are problems. Although I should stress that notes on issuance far outweigh even the wildest overestimates of the plunder we've taken.>*

<Are you saying the market is going to take a hit regardless?> Gurvon asked.

Dubrayle pulled a face. <No. The gold price may be volatile for a time, however.>

In other words, yes: we're all going to take a hit.

Lucia looked around the circle. <Gentlemen. I would suggest that you ensure that your own holdings are adjusted slowly and discreetly to take this matter into account. Do not move in bulk, and do not tell anyone what you're doing: if they're not your nearest and most beloved, they do not matter. If the market panics, you will lose badly. It is as Calan says: confidence must be sustained. Do you all understand?>

Dubrayle looked at Gurvon and smiled wryly. <You look surprised, Magister Gyle. Don't be; we had similar problems in the First and Second Crusades as well. This time the stakes are much higher, but the pattern is clear. Over-exuberant speculation as the Crusade begins, crushed by reality at the end. Ride the updraft, then cut loose.>

And bugger everyone else . . .

He nodded to show he understood.

<And Guildmaster Benoit knows that whatever our political differences, his people and ours are in the same boat where this matter is concerned. He can't ride it out without us, nor we without him.>

Presumably Benoit had threatened to go public if he wasn't given a role in managing the situation, Gurvon guessed. *Thank Kore my imperial contract for the plan stipulated that I'm to be paid in bullion. His gold was due to be shipped to Javon by Jusst & Holsen in a few weeks, after numerous delays.*

<I believe we're finished here,> Lucia said lightly.

<One thing, Holiness, if I may?> Jean Benoit put in. <It has been brought to my attention that the Inquisition are searching for one of my guild members, a Noroman by the name of Vannaton Mercer. There have been caravans intercepted and searched, people detained and questioned, and some heavy-handed Inquisition thuggery, but they refuse to tell me reason why.>

Gurvon watched in fascination, as Lucia and Wurther struggled to contain a sick look that crawled over their faces. Then Lucia's matronly mask descended and her voice was steely as she replied, *<Mercer is wanted for crimes against the empire, and the Inquisition have been ordered to find him. If you know of his whereabouts, you are obligated to Kore Himself to surrender him, Guildmaster.>*

Benoit pursed his lips, then smiled ruefully. *<I'm sorry, your Holiness, but I don't understand. There are no public orders for his arrest, nor crimes listed against his name.>*

<That is normal in cases of espionage and imperial security, Guildmaster,> Lucia replied in a voice that suggested that she had no wish to discuss this further.

Benoit understood. *<Ah, the old 'we say he's a spy so we don't have to explain' story.>* He tsked irritably. *<Well, Mater-Imperia, I have no idea at all where Mercer is. But if he shows up, I will be certain to contact the Inquisition immediately.>*

Gurvon considered the Guildmaster's bland expression. *He has Vannaton Mercer, I'd stake money on it. But why is this trader suddenly so important?*

Wurther had regained his jovial poise. *<Your promise is noted, Guildmaster. Be assured that the Inquisition do Kore's work in this matter.>*

<I was under the impression that the Inquisition do Kore's work in all matters,> Benoit said dryly. *<Thank you for including me today, Mater-Imperia. I will work closely with the Lord Treasurer's people to trace these illegitimate promissory notes and contain the problem.>* His face vanished from the aether.

It was the question of Vannaton Mercer that stayed with Gurvon afterwards as he sat gazing out the tower window at the city below. There were hordes of people in the plaza and alleys behind the zenana, where Cera Nesti was hearing civil disputes in the Beggars' Court. Horses were being saddled in the southern courtyard, for the king to go riding. And somewhere out there in the wide plains of Javon, Elena Anborn was planning her next move.

Elena Anborn was Vannaton Mercer's brother-in-law. Could this be coincidence?

He remembered that look on Lucia's face when the mask had slipped. And Wurther's too. *But not the others*. There had been only one other time when he'd caught a glimpse of the fear behind Lucia's public certainty: earlier this year when she'd inadvertently let slip that there was 'a major card she did not hold'.

Could it somehow be linked to Vann Mercer . . . or Elena Anborn?

400

20

Red Rivers

Bloodlines

We are each a part of those who came before us. Their blood flows in us, a red river that runs through time, linking men and women to their children and their parents. It is a miracle, a gift that life can beget life. The red rivers will flow until the end of time and the coming of Ahm.

KALISTHAM

Mandira Khojana, Lokistan, on the continent of Antiopia
Rajab (Julsep) to Shaban (Augeite) 929
13th and 14th months of the Moontide

The moment Alaron had developed the gnosis, after a hideous migraine that flushed his skin scarlet and left him feeling like his head would burst into flame, his father had taken him to the Arcanum. Vannaton's trading business was profitable and they were backed by the Anborn family money, so they could afford to send him to Turm Zauberin, the most prestigious Arcanum in Norostein. But Alaron was a quarter-blood, a figure of contempt for his classmates and tutors alike. Merely a trader's son, with neither breeding nor connections, he'd had no defence from the mental and physical bullying from the likes of Malevorn Andevarion, Francis Dorobon and Seth Korion. Nor had the tutors protected him. Instead, his confidence had been completely crushed and by the time he left Turm Zauberin, he still could not use many of the powers he should have mastered. He'd been competent enough at the basics and passed the final exams – until a trumped-up excuse had deprived him of even that. He'd been publically failed and denied use of his gnosis as punishment.

Now, free of the bullying and corruption, Alaron felt that he was finally becoming the mage he should have been. Even before he had arrived at the Zain monastery he'd been blossoming as he faced and dealt with crises he could never have imagined at the Arcanum. Now even he could sense the change: he *believed* in himself now, and that belief was permeating *everything*. With the gnosis, confidence that impossible things would happen when you willed it was crucial.

And now this . . .

It wouldn't have looked like much to someone who did not know the gnosis: it was, after all, just four things floating in a circle above his hand: a stone, a drop of water, a tongue of flame and a swirl of air like a mini-tornado.

Earth, Fire, Water and Air.

Sitting cross-legged across the room from him, also dressed like a Zain novice, Ramita mirrored his moves, juggling the four elements at once. According to Arcanum tutors, what they were doing was impossible, yet here they were.

The first thing all magi were taught was that they had affinities and blind spots: things they could do, and things they couldn't. That went for *all* magi, from the Ascendants to the lowliest sixteenth-blood mage. There were a few relative generalists: because their affinities were weak, they had a slightly wider range of skills at the price of weaker usage. To some extent his Auntie Elena was like that. But he'd never, *ever*, heard of a mage doing what he and Ramita were doing now.

Their minds were linked by a thread of Mysticism. He attuned it to her as he let the flame wink out, the wind die and the stone and water-drop fall into his palm. But with his gnostic sight, he could see tendrils – *like the four arms of the Sivraman statue* – holding the essence of each element, awaiting his need for them. At his core, his gnosis was pure energy, not filtered through any affinity at all. He saw the same in Ramita's aura: a pure core upon which lesser powers danced attendance.

Master Puravai clapped his hands gently. 'Well done, Brother Long-legs, Sister Ramita. Very well done indeed. Now show me the Hermetic.'

The mystic link pulsed as he and Ramita reached for different powers. Her aura was so strong, it felt like he was playing catch with a giant, but for now they both still needed that link, for she had the raw power and he the Arcanum-ingrained knowledge. Together they fed energy into the tiny motes of gnostic light circling them: different shades of emerald and brown light in the aether mixed with crimson and flesh tones, separating into nodes of energy. He reached for the deep emerald and kindled it to light, then used it persuade the twig before him to sprout leaves. Sylvan-gnosis. Ramita did the same, more awkwardly, but when she channelled her gnosis, the twig before her grew to a branch. Then they both called birds to their hands then sent them away, changed their left hands to wolf-claws and back, then made and healed cuts on their own arms.

Alaron released the connection, sagging a little.

'Magnificent!' Puravai applauded. 'Well done indeed.'

Alaron looked at Ramita, breathing heavily. It was more tiring and much slower than when his core was Fire-infused, but the variety of things he could do was unprecedented ... except no doubt for Antonin Meiros, of course.

Ramita's late husband was like a ghost, haunting them both. Alaron could feel the bond between him and Ramita growing, but always he was conscious that she was the widow of the greatest mage the world had ever known. It gnawed at him, to be so close to her but unable to get closer. He'd spent years fixated upon Cym and minutes infatuated with Anise, but this felt deeper and more real, despite their many differences.

'I suppose Lord Meiros did it better,' he said, consciously being humble because otherwise he might run around screaming for joy.

Master Puravai smiled a little. 'Actually, no. He acknowledged that the theory was good, and he most certainly gained a wider access to the gnosis, but he was too old to reach his full potential. The centuries had calcified his gnosis so that he was never able to fully expand his palette as you two have. Some things in life are only possible for the young and malleable.'

'Kore's Blood—! You mean this has never been done before?' Alaron closed his eyes. *Let me just bask in that for a while . . .*

When he opened them again, he saw that Ramita was staring at his face while tears rolled down her cheeks and he knew, with a level of intuition he'd never before attained in his life, that she felt exactly for him what he felt for her, but for reasons of duty nothing would ever come of it. And that it was breaking her heart too.

His good mood crumbled.

'I think we both have to start learning how to do this alone now,' he said aloud, while he severed their Mysticism-link. It felt like taking a knife to his heart-strings. 'Otherwise we won't be able to function on our own.'

Puravai said gravely, 'I think you are right.'

Ramita stared glassily into space while he got up and walked away.

Ramita put her hands behind the back of her head, gritted her teeth and slowly peeled her back from the floor and curled up to touch her elbows to her knees. Sweat beaded her forehead and soaked her tunic in ugly patches under her arms and between her breasts. She gasped for air, wincing as her tortured stomach muscles clenched unwillingly.

What made this harder was that the 'floor' was actually halfway up the wall of the training room, and her feet were touching the ceiling. She was pinned to the wall by Earth-gnosis, and just to make it harder, Master Puravai had been making her juggle oranges with telekinetic gnosis while she exercised.

Her belly was now as flat as if she'd never given birth, and she had never felt so strong or supple. The vain part of her enjoyed looking in mirrors when no one was around, admiring the changes. Puravai had been suggesting she should learn to fight with a Zain kon-staff, but she'd been resisting that; her mother would have been horrified at the thought of any daughter of hers learning how to fight.

Training alone was nowhere near as fun as with Alaron, but it was necessary, she agreed. *Before my stupid heart leads me into something foolish.* She crossly banished Alaron from her thoughts, flipped and landed on the floor. She visualised an open eye in the middle of her forehead, with a mutable iris; this time she imagined it as a skull and used it to kindle purple light in her hand and hurl it at a plant in the corner of the room.

It crumpled to a withered husk in three seconds.

It was a hideous power, but one of many she'd been learning. She still needed Alaron to tell her what was possible in Sorcery and Theurgy, so that she knew what to attempt, but once she was on the right path, he would step away and let her work on it alone. That was fine, because she'd been his guide in Hermetic gnosis. But being with him was getting so hard to endure; he looked very fine now, handsome and strong, and with an air of confidence about him, of mastery, as if he now felt himself capable of dealing with everything in the world – except her. Perhaps because Lord Meiros had been white she didn't mind Alaron's pallid skin colour – it had become no more significant to her than his eye colour. He was a good person, and fun to be with, but there was too much at stake for dalliance. It was still his hands she imagined on her body on sleepless nights. If self-pleasure was a sin, she suspected she would be going straight to Shaitan's pit. And she knew – the mystic links were a little too intimate at times – that he was similarly afflicted.

Both threw themselves into other matters to stay busy: she added yogic exercise when she wasn't caring for her infants; Alaron pushed his weapons training. And they both continued investigating the Scytale.

It was Ramita who made the next breakthrough on that project.

She had readied the twins for sleep, before eating and resting herself, and after a great deal of thought, she decided it was time to remove her widow's whites: she could not go to the mughal's court dressed as a widow, after all.

Alaron noticed instantly when he came in to join her for dinner. He didn't mention it, but his smile was a little more solemn.

She cocked her head towards the twins. 'I need to feed them before I put them down to sleep.'

Alaron coloured and got up to leave – he was always shy when she fed her babies – but she wanted his company, because she'd had an idea about the Scytale and it was pressing on her mind. As she began to unbutton her smock, she asked, 'How does your research come along?' She put Nasatya to her nipple, wincing at the pleasure-pain of the infant's mouth.

Alaron was trapped: still blushing furiously, but too polite to leave a lady in mid-conversation, he reluctantly sat down again, carefully looking the other way.

The Scytale project had also been progressing steadily. Of the eight variables, they had they identified five: age, eye colour, elemental affinity, gnostic affinity and gender – though, oddly, the gender options were four, two male and two female. They had puzzled over that, until Ramita suggested that it might have something to do with the gender one was attracted to as well as one's own: she knew several *heejara* – men who lived as women – in Aruna Nagar, so the concept was known and seemed to fit. The last three variables took longer, until eventually Alaron realised the sixth was related to the cycles of the moon, in particular the position of the moon on a person's birthday – most people knew theirs, as it was recorded for birth-auguries. And that very morning he had solved another bit of the mystery, thanks to a treatise left at the monastery by the Ordo Costruo on examining types of blood.

'The book was the most boring thing I've ever read,' he told her, 'but I recognised the four runes on the Scytale in it. I've no idea how I'm supposed to determine a person's blood-type, though. Who even knew that blood could be different?'

Ramita hadn't known either. 'And the last one?' she asked.

'I've not seen those runes before either. There are twelve of them in a kind of descending spiral at the bottom of the Scytale, just above the gnostic affinity symbols on the base. So I don't know if it is even one set or three, and—'

'Birth month,' Ramita said absently.

He stopped talking and knocked his head against the wall. 'Why can't I see these things? Of course!'

Feeling extremely pleased with herself, she removed Nas and put Das to her other breast, aware that Alaron was trying very hard not to peek. *I know I'm teasing him unfairly, but it's nice to feel desired, even if I know it cannot become anything more.* 'So, that must be it, yes? All eight variables identified!'

His face lit up. 'I think so, yes. Those twelve month-runes must be Lantric – the month names we used are derived from Lantric.' He looked like he wanted to gallop about like a colt that has just learned to run. 'We've done it! We've solved the Scytale. Except,' he added, sobering up, 'that we don't know what any of the chemical compounds are. We just know what type of person gets which set of symbols.'

She stroked Das' head as he suckled, blissfully unaware of the matters of huge import being discussed over his head. 'Then that is the next step. How many are unknown?'

'Too many of them,' he admitted ruefully. 'But I recognise aspects of at least half. What I don't know is whether the Scytale contains the whole recipe or just additives to a base mixture.'

'You will work it out,' she said confidently. 'But I have an idea. When my mother is cooking something new, she tests her recipes on friends and family, to make sure the food tastes good. Why don't you do the same here?'

Alaron frowned. 'But I don't know the ingredients— Oh! You mean using the eight characteristics?' He looked excitedly at her. 'Why not? We need to test our theories somehow. I'll ask Puravai's permission to interview all the young monks so I can practise using the Scytale on real people. If I can get an idea of the variables in a normal group of people, it will help in interpreting the results when we do it for real.'

'I think you will learn a lot from doing so,' she said. 'Real people are complex.'

He smiled sadly. 'Yeah. If there's one thing I know for certain, it's that.'

Now that they had begun to think of leaving, Julsep rushed by. Alaron had been given permission to interview the monks, which was an interesting and unique experience. After morning training, he would talk to the novices – it was entirely voluntary, but there was always a stream of young men queuing in the courtyard he was using. Most of the questions were obvious, but the one about gender and sexuality was awkward. They couldn't very well ask a young monk if he preferred boys or girls, so they needed to sneak up on the subject obliquely. Ramita had suggested: 'If you could choose again, would you still become a monk, or would you rather marry?' But as most of the young men claimed they still wanted to be monks, that suggested this wasn't the right question to determine sexuality. And they still had no idea how to determine blood-type. He had tracked down one scroll on the subject that linked blood-type to personality types, but someone had annotated it with such scathing criticism that he doubted its usefulness.

By the end of the second week Alaron had catalogued most of the novices, and a few of the initiated monks, who had approached him out of curiosity. He even used the information of people he knew, like Cym, Ramon and even his father. It didn't provide any great revelations, but it helped with creating hypotheses.

All the while, his own gnostic reach was increasing. He began to feel like he was inhabiting that statue of Sivraman, with four 'ghost arms' holding his conjured Fire, Earth, Water and Air; his aura had a sorcerous eye on his brow and a lion's cloak slung over his shoulder representing Hermetic gnosis. He struggled with his Theurgy symbolism until settling on the four women who meant the most to him to represent each study. Ramita was Mysticism, because he felt so linked to her. Cym he chose for Illusion, because he never felt like he'd known the real her. His mother Tesla was Spiritualism, because she was now a spirit; and Anise's lovely eyes made him think of Mesmerism. At the Arcanum they'd had to learn about all the studies, even those they couldn't use, so they could protect themselves. Now, as he explored, those lessons came back to him and he made new gains every day ... which meant that by the end of Julsep they had no more excuses to delay their departure. The time had come to leave this haven and seek Vizier Hanook.

'So, Alaron Mercer, you are leaving us,' said Puravai in his gravely melodic voice. Alaron and Ramita had gone to the master's office together to tell him of their intentions. The master showed not a whit of surprise. 'I had hopes that you might join us and become "Brother Longlegs" in truth.'

Alaron wasn't sure if the master was serious or just being polite. 'We have to go to the mughal's court.'

'Indeed, and I fully support that plan. I knew the vizier, as I told you: man is a social being and Hanook always was destined for the outside world. That is why we have city-based monasteries as well as sanctuaries far from the hustle and bustle of the world.' He clapped his hands and Yash walked in. His steps were light and eager, but his face worried. 'Brother Yash has asked to accompany you to Teshwallabad, en route to his new life in a monastery there.'

'I know Teshwallabad,' Yash said eagerly. 'I've lived there before, and I have asked to be transferred.'

'We would welcome the company,' Ramita said, after some consideration. 'Provided the windskiff can carry three.'

Alaron smiled. 'It'll be cosy, but we should manage. Only ... the babies?' They'd discussed that matter over the previous evenings, inconclusively.

Ramita lifted her chin. 'Master Puravai, Al'Rhon and I have talked much about this. Al'Rhon would have me leave the children here with a wet-nurse, but I cannot be without them. *I cannot.* And so they will come with us.' She looked at Alaron defiantly. 'That is my decision.'

'The court is a perilous place, Lady,' Puravai said.

'I will not be separated from my children,' Ramita said firmly. 'This is not to be debated.'

*

The new moon signalled the beginning of Augeite. In the outside world there would great celebrations among Amteh-worshippers, for Julsep – Rajab in Ahmedhassa –was the Amteh holy month, a time of austerity and prayer. The new moon of Augeite heralded the end of thirty days of privation, in the festival of Eyeed. But the day was barely marked at the monastery and Alaron and Ramita spent their final days there preparing the windskiff, provisioning it with dried lentils and other stores and poring over maps. They intended flying at night, to avoid alarming the local people; the journey would take about a week.

Leaving was surprisingly hard. Alaron was touched to be given a new kon-staff, decorated with gaudy friendship cords from each of the three dozen novices with whom he'd been training. He knew them all well now, from their mannerisms and the way they fought to the raw data from his Scytale research: ages and birthdates, the colours of eyes, and all the other categorisations. *I'm going to miss them*, he realised. *The monastery itself too. It's like a second home.*

They left without ceremony the day after Eyeed. Luna's brilliant face lit the mountains in silver, set the snowy peaks aglow and carved the valley and slopes into light and shadow. Their breath frosted as they took to the air. Only Puravai had come to watch their departure. Ramita was wrapped in blankets, the children asleep in her lap. Yash was anxious to be away quickly, as if he feared Puravai might change his mind and make him stay.

Puravai slipped an envelope into Alaron's hands. 'Give this to Hanook in greeting,' he murmured. 'Do not open it, or damage the seal.'

Alaron slipped the envelope into his coat. He was wearing his Rondian clothes again, and his swordbelt. He laid his kon-staff against the keel of the skiff, alongside Yash's, then he and Ramita fed an extra burst of gnosis energy into the keel and he called the wind as they rose. In seconds the monastery was a dark huddle below. Puravai shrank to a saffron dot, and then the folds of the land blocked everything out.

Alaron set their course through the upper valley, heading for a pass into the east.

'Praise be to all the gods,' Yash breathed. 'I am flying!'

It wasn't a homecoming, but crossing northern Lakh stirred Ramita's heart. Most nights they flew for five to six hours, averaging thirty miles each hour, or so Alaron estimated as he compared the country-side below to landmarks on the map. They began covering up to a hundred and fifty miles in a night, and still the land below crawled past, as they crossed the featureless Sithardha Desert, its dunes like the waves of the ocean rendered in sand.

They slept the sweltering days away beside the hull, Ramita and the children on one side, the two young men on the other. There was little privacy, and Yash was even more embarrassed about breastfeeding women than Alaron, who helped Ramita where he could, passing her each child in turn, and cleaning them for her. Such women's work appeared to beneath the young novice, which irritated Ramita, but by and large they got on. Yash proved to be an eager flier; he was keen to understand how the sails and tiller worked, and how to use the wind. Alaron or Ramita had to power the keel, but they were soon able to let Yash fly the craft alone.

The distances would have been unthinkable on foot. Flying made the journey a simpler thing altogether: a week put the desert behind them and the land took on greener hues as they neared the vast basin of the great Imuna River. It was more than five miles wide, a sluggish brown snake basking beneath the sun and moon. Ramita stared at it avidly, her lips moving in prayer.

This is the holiest of rivers, she told her children silently. *Imuna, daughter of Baraman the Creator, will look after us.* She looked back at Alaron as he turned the tiller and swung the craft southwards, taking advantage of a warm wind from the north. His hair was thick and unruly – he'd not cut it for months – and she found herself idly fantasising about taming his shaggy locks. *He shouldn't go before the vizier looking like a barbarian.*

They wound down the river, past settlements they tried to identify on Puravai's map. Ramita discovered she knew many of the names from her life in Aruna Nagar, where goods came to market from everywhere: this town made good chillies, and that one was famed for its pomegranates.

'Look at the size of these places,' Alaron exclaimed at one point. 'Most of them are bigger than Norostein!'

'Clearly your Norostein is not a very large town,' she replied.

'It's the capital of the whole kingdom of Noros,' he replied, gazing down at the expanse of houses they'd identified as Ghanasheed, a minor town on the river.

'But that's only Yuros,' she reminded him. 'Everything is larger here.'

'Except the people.' Alaron chuckled. 'In all ways,' he added with a sly wink.

Yash looked affronted, but Ramita found herself giggling. White men were certainly bigger, and her husband had been . . . *ahem!* . . . a *tall* man.

Kazim, of course, had been the biggest boy in the neighbourhood; he was much taller and heavier even than Alaron, or most of the white men she'd ever seen. For the first time for many weeks she wondered where he was. She had not forgiven him – she doubted she ever would. *You are part of my past now*, she told his memory. *I do not need to think of you ever again. Or you, Huriya. I do not know you any more.*

A few days later, some three hours before dawn, they made out the night-lamps of a huge settlement, and the glowing white domes of many Dom-al'Ahms glowing in the dark expanse. Largest of all were the golden sandstone walls of what had to be the mughal's palace, crouched above the city like a slumbering lion. The dome of the palace not only reflected the moonlight, but appeared to be giving out its own faint light.

'Teshwallabad,' Ramita said, savouring the word on her tongue. 'We've arrived!'

Alaron pulled the skiff into a banking descent and tried to pick out a place where they could hide their craft. He settled on a low hill well inland from the river and steered for the far side of it, concentrating on the tricky task of landing in darkness. As they drew close to the ground he threw a flare of light ahead of them, revealing a rocky expanse with a flat area that looked sandy to one side. He took them in while Ramita held the children to her and shielded them all. Before they touched down, Yash leaped out, holding the hitching rope in what was now a practised manoeuvre. He landed agilely, planted his heels and hauled, and Alaron pulled in the sails and doused the energy in the keel. The skiff sank smoothly and easily to the ground.

Alaron looked at Ramita as one of the twins spluttered awake and began to wail. She silenced him with a wish, clutching them both tight to her bosom. 'All okay?'

'Theeka,' she responded softly, 'hush, darlings.' She let all the calmness she could muster brush gently against the two tight little bundles of energy. 'Sleep on, all is well.' *I hope.* She thanked Parvasi-ji for their safe arrival.

There was work to be done, but first they climbed to the top of the rise, partly to ensure they were not in sight of any farm buildings, but mostly just to look on Teshwallabad in the distance. The dome of the mughal still glowed in the pre-dawn light: an eerie pale gold that spoke of wealth and splendour.

Ramita held Nasatya to her breast while Alaron carried Dasra. *He looks good, holding my child*, she thought fondly, then bit her lip. *Will my next husband be so gentle and kind?*

She had made harnesses for the twins, with shoulder straps that allowed them to be held against the back or the chest, leaving hands free. Alaron wore his so the child was in front, but she usually had the child behind her, not pressed against her swollen breasts. The thought reminded her that it would soon be time to wean them.

'What a place!' Alaron breathed, staring at the distant dome and palace.

'Do you know how the mughal came to rule Lakh?' Yash asked. Ramita knew, but Alaron shook his head, so Yash went on, 'Kesh and

Khotri were having another war, and the Emir of Khotri sent messengers to the Maharajah of Lakh, pleading for aid – this despite frequent war between Lakh and Khotri also. The Maharajah of all Lakh was the great Raj-Prithan, and he had ambitions to be Lord of all Ahmedhassa. So he sent a great army north, to aid Khotri and perhaps gain a foothold there.'

Despite knowing the tale, Ramita still felt a stir of anger. The fall of Raj-Prithan was the great nightmare of her people.

'It was a trap,' the monk said grimly. 'Kesh and Khotri had secretly forged a peace and were conspiring together to draw out Raj-Prithan and destroy his armies. There is a place northwest of Ullakesh where they say the valley is white with the bones of Lakh dead. They captured and executed Raj-Prithan, then the Khotri invaded and seized Teshwallabad. The son of the emir became Mughal of Lakh, and he and his descendants have been pushing south ever since. Everywhere they go they persecute those of the Omali faith and put their own people in lordship over the local rajas.'

'When did this happen?' Alaron asked.

'1288,' Yash replied. 'That date is carved upon our souls at birth.'

'There are 454 years between the Yuros and Antiopian calendars,' Alaron noted, doing the arithmetic, 'so that's 834 in our time – ninety-five years, not so long ago.'

'Long enough,' Yash muttered.

Alaron looked at Ramita. 'Why would your husband send us to an Amteh ruler?'

'He is not,' Ramita replied. 'He's sending us to Hanook, the vizier.'

'What's a vizier?'

'The head counsellor,' Yash replied sullenly. 'He helps the Amteh oppress our people.'

'My father always said Hanook often prevented the Amteh from doing far worse,' Ramita replied, remembering dinner-table conversations, all the good-natured shouting between her parents and their friends about such things.

'How does the mughal keep control of such a huge land?' Alaron asked.

'Fear,' Yash replied. 'At the merest hint of rebellion, they come with soldiers and slaughter all who resist – innocent people. They reward those who spy on their fellow Lakh.' He was breathing heavily. 'They killed my parents.'

Ramita frowned. 'You are not here to take revenge,' she reminded the monk. 'You are a Zain.'

Yash made a holy sign. 'I am a child of Zain,' he agreed. 'The wind passes through me. I feel neither heat nor cold.' They were lines from the morning prayer.

'My husband trusted Hanook. We must also.'

They returned to the skiff and unloaded it, then removed the mast and covered the hull with the sail. Alaron looked at her with a smile and waggled his fingers. 'Shall we hide the skiff?'

Together they engaged Earth-gnosis and then telekinesis, swiftly excavating a hole and lowering the hull into it. As a final touch Ramita added some vegetation to make the ground look undisturbed, then Alaron dusted it with Air-gnosis so that no one could see the disturbance. Yash watched with awe, though even he didn't appreciate what he'd seen: their first in-earnest use of multiple forms of the gnosis.

Ramita nursed the twins and laid them in the shade to sleep, after which the three travellers went to the low ridge to watch the dawn. The domes of the city appeared above the river mist and smoke, and the wailing of the Godsingers rang out, a comfort to her ears. Alaron hadn't heard it before – they had travelled through the wilds as they crossed Dhassa. 'It is the call to dawn worship,' she explained. 'The faithful pray six times a day.'

'Even the Kore isn't that demanding!' he exclaimed.

'It's only the really, *really* faithful who pray so often,' she said with a laugh. 'We knew some Amteh in Baranasi who just shut the curtains for ten minutes and had a cup of chai.'

Alaron grinned. 'That sounds like home. The Kore have services every day, at dawn, midday and evening, but hardly anyone goes except once a week on Sabbadai. "Only the saints go to heaven", that's what we say.' He peered towards the gleaming Mughal Dome, the main dome of the mughal's palace, now revealed in all its glory. 'Look at the size of it!'

'The mughal's palace is the greatest in the entire world,' Yash announced, both proud and bitter. 'Master Puravai says it took a century to build, and contains a massive Dom-al'Ahm, an armoury and barracks, state rooms, and the private residence of the Mughal of Lakh and all his household.' His voice was a mix of awe and disgust. 'Mughal Tariq has fourteen wives, one for every year he has been on Urte. He is due soon to take a fifteenth, on his next birthday.'

Alaron winced. 'Hel, isn't one woman enough trouble?'

Ramita fixed him with a stare. 'What are you trying to say, *bhaiya*?'

'Nothing, *didi*. Just a joke,' he said swiftly.

'Mmm.' She looked at Yash. 'How will we make contact with the vizier?'

Yash pulled a baked clay token from his pouch. He showed it to them: a disc bearing a circle of intricate Dhassan script. 'This is the monastery's token. I will take it to the vizier's officials with a letter from Master Puravai and ask for audience. Beyond that, I cannot say. I do know it is not safe for either of you to enter the city openly.'

That sounded sensible, so she and Alaron let the young monk stride purposefully away. They quickly lost him in the haze, well before he had entered the maze of half-finished stone buildings and rough lean-tos that fringed the city. 'We should sleep,' Alaron said at last.

Ramita was tempted to lean against him as they once did in the hull of the skiff on their flight south, pressed close together, his heartbeat against her ear. That was entirely the wrong thing to do. She went to the far side of the skiff, wrapped herself in a thin shawl, lay on her side and shut her eyes.

They dozed the day away, taking turns on watch, but dusk came without incident. While Alaron cooked, Ramita played with the twins, who were crawling now, and filled with curiosity. After discovering that sand wasn't edible, they were determined to find a lizard who wanted to stay and play with them. Both had thick black hair, but their skin was paler than their mother's. They could now stomach a little solid food, when it was washed down with breast milk. She enjoyed the way they seemed to always know where the other was. They would not gain access to the gnosis until their early teens, but it was easy to imagine that somehow the twins were inside each other's heads, communicating wordlessly. There was a togetherness about them that was both beautiful and eerie.

At last Ramita lay the twins aside and draped her blanket over herself, surreptitiously studying her breasts. They were swollen and tender; the only time they were comfortable now was after feeding. She had seen her mother go through weaning and knew that once she stopped feeding the twins, she would face a few weeks of discomfort as her body learned to cease making more milk. *I'll miss it, though*, she thought, *that feeling that I am so needed by my little ones*.

Alaron coughed discreetly, reminding her that he might just be getting an inadvertent eye-full. She covered up, and he waggled his head in a 'that's okay' kind of way, a grin on his face. 'See, I now speak Lakh,' he laughed. 'I can do the head-wag.'

'Yes,' she said with a smile, 'but you do it with a strange accent.'

They'd just finished their tiny portions of lentil curry and Alaron was reflecting ruefully on how long ago it was since he'd had a nice big juicy steak when he saw a line of torches emerge in the middle distance, a trail of glowing orange lights that flickered their way towards them. He took a deep breath and tapped Ramita on the shoulder. 'They're coming.'

They cleaned up hurriedly, and repacked their belongings. Then they gently lifted the sleeping infants and bundled them into their harnesses. The twins stirred as if sensing the tension in the air, forcing Alaron and Ramita to send soothing impulses urging them back into sleep. With Ramita holding Nasatya and Alaron with Dasra, they turned to face the oncoming column. Alaron thoughtfully twirled his quarterstaff, subtly limbering up in case he had to act suddenly.

Ramita noticed. 'Will they attempt to seize us?' she asked anxiously.

'They can try,' Alaron replied, feeling uncharacteristically eager to try out his new skills, both gnostic and martial. 'We shouldn't just assume they're friendly.'

The cooling air was prickling his skin as his sweat-soaked robes turned cold. Beside him Ramita shifted uneasily and it occurred to him that though she'd been in danger before, she'd never seen that danger coming. The attack that had slain her husband and the fight at the Isle of Glass had both come out of the blue.

He touched her shoulder. 'We're magi. We can handle this.'

She stuck her chin out. 'I am frightened for the children, not myself.'

'I know, but your husband said we could trust this Hanook character, didn't he?'

'What if Yash didn't even reach him?'

Alaron rolled his shoulders. 'Then we'll soon find out.'

There were a dozen men, and all armed but for the central pair, who walked on ahead, palms empty to show peacable intent. One was a tall figure with lordly robes and a pale turban wrapped about a long, narrow face. His skin was as dark as the turban was light, and he had a grey goatee that tapered to a point. His skin was smooth and youthful; he looked too young to be so grey.

Yash was with him, and his face was awed. Alaron tried to convey a million questions with a single glance. *I should have taught him how to receive mental communication while we had the chance.*

'Are you all right?' he asked in Rondian, and Yash nodded.

The man in the turban fixed his eye on Ramita, then surprised them by speaking Rondian as well. 'Do I have the honour of addressing Lady Ramita?'

'I am she,' Ramita responded firmly. Alaron could sense her gnosis gathered and ready; the slightest misstep by this man would see him thrown halfway back to the city.

'I am Dareem, son of Vizier Hanook. I bid you welcome to Teshwallabad.' Dareem touched his fingertips to his forehead with a reverent gesture. 'Sal'Ahm, Lady. Peace be upon you.'

'Namaste, Lord Dareem,' Ramita replied, then indicated Alaron. 'This is Al'Rhon Mercer.'

'You speak Rondian very well,' Alaron said as he and Dareem exchanged bows. *Better than most folk back in Norostein.* 'But my name is Al-a-ron: I'm not a goat.'

Dareem smiled faintly, and turned back to Ramita. 'Will you come with me, Lady, and accept my father's hospitality?'

Of course they wouldn't attack us openly. They'd try to gain our trust, and separate us, and then . . . Alaron looked at Ramita and saw that she was ready to accept, but she was awaiting his approval.

What choice do we have anyway? He nodded.

Dareem bowed again. 'I am sorry, but we do not have transport back to the city. My father is under close surveillance, so we must be discreet. But I will get you into our palace unnoticed, I promise.'

'Who's watching him?' Alaron asked uneasily.

'My father is an important man,' Dareem replied. 'Everyone is watching him.'

'But who in particular?'

Dareem waggled his head. 'My father has many enemies, Al-a-ron. And you have a whole city of them.'

That's true! I'm probably the only Rondian 'afreet' to ever come here. Alaron bowed his head. 'We're in your hands.' He stroked Dasra's hair, hoping they were doing the right thing.

Dareem's men had brought a small palanquin. As Alaron helped Ramita climb into it, he noticed how tired she looked. It was good that she could rest. For his part, he was happy to walk with Yash and the soldiers back across the stony plain and into the ramshackle maze that was the outskirts of Teshwallabad. Once in the crowded streets he raised his hood; there were countless rough-clad people all crowded together in tiny dwellings and coughing and snuffling around smoking fires. Cooking smells filled the air. Dareem's armoured and armed escort kept passersby at arm's length, but Alaron noticed many a resentful glare at the armed men.

'This is not a good area,' Dareem muttered apologetically, 'but the main roads are constantly watched.'

Alaron was tired, but he used the gnosis to imbue himself with a little extra strength and managed to keep his feet from faltering. Eventually they came to a small square where a covered wagon waited, half-filled with supplies. Nothing seemed untoward, so they accepted Dareem's invitation and climbed into it. Alaron settled beside Ramita on a narrow bench and whispered, 'So far, so good.'

Her teeth flashed white in the darkness. 'I believe this is the right thing: it is Destiny.'

If her crazy belief in 'destiny' is what's getting her through, I can live with it. He bent forward and kissed her on the forehead, although he had no idea if that would be considered improper or not. 'I'll protect you, didi, no matter what.'

'And I you, bhaiya. But Al'Rhon, men and women do not touch in public here.'

He pulled away and bowed his head. 'I'm sorry.'

Dareem and Yash joined them. The young Zain seemed to trust Dareem, which reassured Alaron. 'We'll take this wagon to the back of my father's palace, where supplies are delivered,' Dareem told them. 'Hopefully the watchers will attach no importance to such a conveyance.'

In the front, a driver flicked a whip, and the wagon lurched forward. Initially Alaron was on edge, but the journey through Teshwallabad proved uneventful, sometimes forcing a path through presses of people, at other times traversing almost empty back-alleys, until finally they crossed a large square and passed through a pair of great cast-iron gates. A guardsman poked his head inside, saw Dareem and put his knuckles to his forehead.

'Keep your hoods raised,' Dareem reminded them as they disembarked. There were soldiers everywhere, but no-one made a hostile move. Dareem took them up wide marble stairs to a massive marble edifice that dwarfed even the Governor's Residence in Norostein.

Another man was waiting inside the door, bowing as they stepped inside. 'Welcome,' he said in fluent Rondian. 'I am Hanook.'

The vizier was an older replica of his son; one could trace his lineage in the shape of the skull, the smooth skin, the wise but intense eyes. Instead of a turban, he wore a small flat-topped cap, delicately embroidered and sporting gold tassels, and a full-length robe of deep blue. He walked with the aid of a long stick, which Alaron recognised as a kon-staff: so a weapon, not just a prop for age.

As the doors started to close behind them, lamps revealed an inner courtyard garden overlooked on all sides by balconies. The marble glowed in the flickering torchlight. There were statues everywhere, brightly coloured renderings of Omali gods, some serene and others fierce. Ramita made an approving noise. Alaron stopped before one of Sivraman, similar to the statue at Mandira Khojana. He smiled in recognition.

'It is wonderful to finally meet you, Lady Meiros,' Hanook said, going to Ramita. 'I am sorry that I cannot greet you more publically, but most Lakh believed your husband to be evil incarnate.'

'They did not know him,' Ramita replied, lifting her head.

'Indeed not.' Hanook gestured to a man standing as still as the statuary. 'Ishad will show you to your rooms, and then I pray you will join me for supper.' He vanished through a door, taking Dareem with him.

Alaron looked at Yash. 'Well?'

Yash looked about uncomfortably. 'What a place! It makes the monastery look like a jhuggi.'

'I mean, can we trust them?'

The monk met his eyes uncertainly. 'They have received me politely and listened to my words. They have promised that Lady Meiros will be safe.' He dropped his voice. 'This is an Amteh city, my friend. Your powers are considered evil here. It is a great risk for them to even receive you and the lady.'

'My husband would not have sent me here unknowingly,' Ramita said firmly. 'We knew the risks.'

'In many ways, the greater danger is to you, Al'Rhon,' Yash pointed out. 'People here know a Lakh girl married Lord Meiros, but no one imagines she had any choice and so most forgave the union. But you are a Rondian mage: a living blasphemy.'

Alaron swallowed. 'I know.'

'But Vizier Hanook has been welcoming to me, and he still practises the Yogic Way.' Yash dropped his voice. 'My friend, I am a street-boy who became a monk. Truly, I do not know how to judge the mighty.'

'None of us do,' Ramita whispered. 'I am a market-girl, and Alaron is a trader's son. But this is where we are destined to be, so we must find wisdom.'

Alaron glanced at the waiting servant, Ishad. 'Okay, let's check our rooms, then get some food. I'm starving.'

Ishad led them up two storeys and along a winding corridor to a foyer which led to three suites of rooms. Alaron insisted on scanning each with the gnosis before allowing them in. The rooms were huge, with marble floors and wide balconies, and big windows covered by carved wooden shutters that were painted with mythic scenes. The bed looked strange to Alaron's Yuros eyes: the mattress was barely off the floor and covered not by blankets but a very thin cotton cover, intensely patterned. It was too hot for blankets, anyway. There was no sign of anything dangerous, and when he knocked on the walls they sounded solid enough. By then his stomach was rumbling. 'I could eat a horse,' he exclaimed. 'Can we be ready in five minutes?'

Ramita looked astounded. 'I will be at least an hour,' she announced, and vanished into her room.

What could take an hour? He threw a pained look at Yash, then re-entered his room, sat on the low bed and pulled off his boots. Sitting so low to the ground was disorienting. Floral scents rose from a basin of heated water and he pulled off his shirt and rinsed himself quickly, then changed into his one clean shirt. The thought of a hot bath was enticing, but more pressing was the thought of food and drink.

An hour . . .

He went to the door and set wards that flared and then vanished in a mesh of pale-blue light, then did the same at the windows before using Earth-gnosis to lift a tile, scoop a hollow space and lay the Scytale and his notes within. He set a hidden ward over it, invisible even to gnostic sight. It was exacting work, and by the time he was done he was absolutely starving. It still felt like another hour before finally Ramita knocked on their doors and declared herself ready.

All Alaron and Yash could do was gape.

The girl Alaron had spent months with, rough clad for travelling or wearing Zain robes, had been transfigured. Her small form was wrapped in a pale-blue saree, with fold upon fold of the most delicately patterned lace embroidery he'd ever seen. Her belly was bare, a minor scandal in his eyes but apparently that was fine here, and there was no doubt she had recovered from pregnancy: her midriff was a gentle curve of toned brown skin. Her hair was tied back severely, and jewellery hung from the most unlikely places – gold rings on her ear lobes were linked to her nose-rings by delicate chains. Bangles and rings clinked and clanked as she shifted under his scrutiny, glittering in the lamplight.

'You look incredible!' he exclaimed, while Yash just continued to gape. He assumed the finery was Hanook's gift.

Ramita waggled her head ironically. 'Good. That is the effect I was hoping for.' She looked extremely pleased with herself as she posed. 'Do I look worthy of my husband?'

Alaron could only nod mutely.

She brushed his hand with her fingers. 'I am glad you approve, bhaiya, because I am leaving the twins asleep in my room. I have cast wards. Are they sufficient?'

Alaron checked her wards and found them to be startlingly strong. 'I don't think I could break in there,' he admitted, and Ramita looked even more pleased.

Smiling radiantly, she said, 'Then shall we go?' and offered her arm.

'You bet,' he said fervently. 'Before I die of hunger on the stairs.' He closed his hand around her forearm, as carefully as if she were made of porcelain, and together the three of them went to dine with the vizier.

'You are, if I might venture to say, an unusual trio,' Vizier Hanook observed.

Alaron could only agree with that. They were seated cross-legged around a low table: his long legs were seizing up, but everyone seemed to find it perfectly comfortable. Didn't these people know about chairs? Though in truth he'd only just noticed his own discomfort, so busy was he filling his stomach.

The food was odd by Rondian standards, but he had to admit it was far more varied and interesting. Best of all, there was actual *meat*, spiced and served fried with no sauces except for a yoghurt-based cooling dip. He was already addicted. There were lots of vegetables, too – he couldn't identify them all, but thanks to Ramita's cooking he could at least handle the strange flavours. They ate with fingers, as they had at the monastery, but Vizier Hanook did it in such a fastidious manner that it came across as the height of good manners. It was all served with a very pleasant chilled lemon drink, a good alternative to wine, as he was cautious about having his wits dulled by alcohol in this house of strangers.

They had given Hanook and Dareem a largely fictitious version of how they came to be here: in it Alaron had been an auxiliary to the legions who had become detached from his unit and found Ramita hiding in the Dhassan countryside west of Hebusalim. He had taken pity on her, and they had journeyed here, via the monastery, following the advice of her late husband to seek Hanook's protection. The children were self-evident, but they didn't mention the Scytale and nor would they, not until they were certain that was wise. They spoke in Rondian, the only language they had in common, though that meant Yash was somewhat excluded.

'What is a vizier?' Alaron asked curiously, after they had eaten.

'A scapegoat,' Dareem suggested drily.

Hanook laughed. 'A juggler.'

'Or a nursemaid.'

Hanook rolled his eyes. 'Thankfully our mughal is well past that stage. I am Chief Minister and Advisor to his Sacred Majesty, the Mughal Tariq Srinarayan Kishan-ji, whose name is sung in Paradise.' He pronounced the mughal's name with such serious reverence that it suggested a subtle jest. 'I was vizier to his father before him, and advised his father's elder brother before that, whilst also tutoring his son.'

'We don't understand the politics of Lakh,' Alaron said carefully. 'Are you able to explain the situation here?'

Dareem chuckled. 'We don't have all night.'

Hanook smiled fondly at his son. 'Dareem is right. It is a short question but the answers are many and complex, as these things often are. I take it you know a little? Then let me be brief. Lakh has never been one kingdom: it was hundreds, sundered by language and customs and bitter, intense rivalries. But all – nominally, at least – paid homage to the Maharajah, the King of Kings. The history of their struggles for supremacy fill a thousand books. But in 834, as your Rondian calendar dates it, the Amteh-worshipping Khotri tricked and killed Maharajah Raj-Prithan and invaded. The Khotri Emir's son became 'mughal', an Amteh title signifying one who is both king and Godspeaker: a dangerous thing, because they claim to both speak and act for God. Usually there is separation of the two titles, carefully preserved to prevent tyranny. But Mughal Turig, our present Mughal's great-great-uncle, was a powerful and remarkable man. Though Raj-Prithan's army numbered a million souls, they were vanquished by a tenth as many.'

'How?' Alaron wondered aloud. 'Even magi would struggle with those odds.'

'Turig of Khotri had two things the Lakh armies lacked: horse-archers, trained with composite bows that could puncture armour, and the Amteh faith. Amteh is a warrior religion, and their holy book, the *Kalistham*, exhorts its followers to conquest. Turig used his rank as a Godspeaker to inspire fervent belief in his invincibility. Strengthened by this, his soldiers were indomitable, and they destroyed a generation of Teshwallabad manhood. This city has barely recovered.'

'It is an offence to the gods,' Yash declared.

'I had thought a monk put aside such concerns,' Dareem observed mildly.

Yash lowered his gaze and muttered, 'I am still a Lakh.'

Hanook ignored the byplay and continued, 'Mughal Turig took Teshwallabad and proceeded to defeat the remaining northern Lakh rajahs, until the whole of the north acknowledged his rule. Since then the Mughals of Lakh have been gradually extending their influence into the south. The rajahs of southern Lakh have never united, and fear of the mughal's ruthlessness deters them from open war. The mughal was also shrewd enough not to try and suppress the Omali faith, knowing this would be both impossible and highly inflammatory. He does discriminate against it, but in small ways only, seeking to weaken allegiance to the Omali gods over the long term; for the short term he wanted normal life to carry on. Of course his men get involved in incidents of cruelty and stupidity, but probably no more than the Lakh nobility inflicted on their own people. Lakh is tamed – for now, at least, like an elephant that has grown used to the whip-hand.'

'Why isn't the mughal fighting alongside the Keshi in the shihad?' Alaron asked.

'A good question. For one thing, the mughal is afraid to leave his own lands for fear of an uprising. For another, he is Khotri, not Keshi: the people who live around Khotriawal see themselves as a separate kingdom, hostile to the Sultan of Kesh. They believe – quite rightly! – that Salim would love any excuse to avenge himself for any number of past conflicts. And relations between the Emir of Khotri and the Mughal of Lakh are strained. While Turig was setting himself up in Teshwallabad, one of his younger brothers seized power back in Khotriawal. With vast deserts between and a new kingdom to pacify, Turig could do little but protest, but the feud simmers on down the generations, with neither able to put an end to it. There is now open hostility between the mughal and his forebears in Khotri, and neither have great interest in aiding the shihad.'

Alaron glanced at Ramita. They didn't sound like people who would want to intervene in the Crusade. And he couldn't yet tell where Hanook's sympathies lay, let alone whether he was someone who would make good use of the Scytale.

'I believe that my late husband spoke to you of me?' Ramita said to the vizier after a long pause.

Hanook said solemnly, 'He did indeed, just a few days before to his marriage to you. He wrote a follow-up letter some months later.'

'What did he say?' she asked eagerly.

'Lady, he asked two things: first, that I move to protect your family, who were newly enriched and might fall prey to the unscrupulous. And second, should aught happen to him and you came to me, that I protect you and yours.'

Alaron looked at the two nobles warily. 'And you agreed?'

'Of course.'

'Why?'

Hanook blinked slowly. 'You are clearly a direct young man, Master Mercer. The Court of the Mughal is a place of subtlety and obliqueness. Such a straightforward question is highly unusual. So in reply I would remind you first that Antonin Meiros is the most hated man in Antiopia, and one does not acknowledge connections to him lightly. The very fact that you and Lady Meiros are under my roof right now could see me arrested.'

'Your soldiers saw us.'

'Their loyalty has been carefully nurtured from birth.' Hanook stroked his goatee. 'Let me explain a little: There are four major groups at court: Khotri Amteh tend to be either Ja'arathi moderates or fanatical shihadi. There are opportunists of all races and faiths, drawn to money and power. And least of all, there are the Lakh patriots. And they all hate and fear the magi and the Ordo Costruo: it is the one thing they all agree upon. They pull at the mughal from all directions, and he is only fourteen.'

'Which group do you fit into?' Alaron asked.

'None of them. I stand in the middle and steer a path of survival for the mughal.'

'Whose interests will you serve? The mughal's, or Ramita's?' Alaron asked.

Hanook frowned. 'I am sure I can serve both.'

Alaron didn't much like that answer. 'I'm here to protect Lady Meiros. If I don't like what I hear, I'm taking her straight out of here.' His heart began to thud, but his protectiveness towards Ramita overcame his nervousness. 'Good luck trying to stop me.'

Hanook's eyes hardened. 'There is no need for threats here, young man. Lord Meiros asked me to be guardian of his wife for strong reasons and you must believe that I do have her best interests at heart.

Better than you can imagine. And as for our ability to restrict your coming and going ...' He flicked his fingers and a tongue of blue flame flared above his palm. 'I am not helpless before a battle-mage.'

He's a mage! And therefore Dareem is too ... Alaron sucked in his breath. 'Who are you?'

'I am Lady Meiros' nephew.'

Alaron felt his mouth drop open, and saw Ramita's do the same. They looked at each other until the little Lakh girl squeaked, 'How is this possible?'

'Lord Meiros had a son, Adric, who was murdered a few years ago, prompting his hunt for a new wife – a hunt that led to you, Lady. But when Adric was young he had an affair with a woman whilst on a clandestine mission in Khotriawal, eighty years ago, during Turig's invasion of Lakh. I was the result. Despite Adric's formidable powers, my mother died in childbirth, so Adric had me raised me in secret, away from the rest of the Ordo Costruo. I grew up at that very Zain monastery you visited. When I reached adulthood I travelled to Khotriawal, where I attracted attention as a scholar. At my father and Lord Antonin's urging, I used my skills to gain a posting to the court of the mughal, as tutor to Turig's sons.'

Alaron puffed out his cheeks. 'So you've been operating as a spy under the nose of the whole court?'

'Not a spy. I serve peace, as Lord Antonin did. It hasn't been easy,' Hanook admitted. 'It takes much restraint to not use powers that come as easily as breathing – especially when assassins are trying to kill you, as many have.'

'So you're a half-blood?' Alaron asked.

'Indeed. And Dareem is three-quarter-blooded, thanks to a relationship in my youth with a pure-blood woman of the Ordo Costruo.'

And there was me trying to threaten them. Kore's Balls! 'I'm sorry,' he said. 'I didn't mean to be rude.'

'No offence is taken. We are reassured at your loyalty to Lady

Ramita.' Hanook sipped his drink calmly. 'I've been here forty years without being unmasked.'

'So what is your objective?'

'To preserve the mughal. My mother, Adric's secret woman, was a princess of Turig's harem. The mughal does not know this, but I am also his great-great-uncle by marriage.'

Alaron looked again at Ramita. He badly wanted to take her aside and speak privately; he feared Hanook and Dareem would overhear any attempt at mental communication. 'Lord Vizier, this is a very difficult situation,' he started.

Hanook grinned boyishly. 'It is, isn't it? Especially as Lady Meiros here is now also a mage in her own right, I presume? Due to the pregnancy manifestation?'

Ramita coloured. 'Er, yes.'

'The Godspeakers would lynch us all if they knew we were here – but with great risks come great opportunities. This is a chance to introduce the gnosis into the royal family of Lakh; to allow our people to stand as a Great Power alongside Rondelmar and Kesh.' He fixed Ramita with a steely eye. 'Lady Meiros, how would you like to become the senior wife of the Mughal of Lakh?'

21

Tending the Lion

Religion: Sollan

The religion of the Rimoni Empire was centred upon the cycles of the sun and the moon. The Sollan faith is now prevalent only in Rimoni, Silacia and Verelon, and amongst the Rimoni of Javon. It is illegal everywhere the Rondians dominate, as they have imposed worship of Kore upon their dominions.

ORDO COSTRUO COLLEGIATE, PONTUS

*They try to say that Pater Sol and Mater Luna are false gods ... **false**, when they impose this lie upon us, that Corineus was the Son of God! Johan Corin, son of Tavius the Senator? Him a god? The notion defies belief!*

ANONYMOUS, RYM, 386

Southern Dhassa and Kesh, on the continent of Antiopia
Thani (Aprafor) to Rajab (Julsep) 929
10ᵗʰ to 13ᵗʰ months of the Moontide

Waking at all was a surprise, Malevorn thought dimly, as a jolting rhythm bumped him from the darkness. He immediately wished it hadn't. Everything hurt, ached, itched, stung or simply blazed with pain. And his face – no, his whole body – was being buffeted. He forced open his eyes and found his face was pressed against a bony, grey-furred back. The tuft of a tail sprouted from right beside his right eye, and the noxious stench of animal and shit filled his nostrils. His arms and legs were lashed tightly together around a living cylinder of bone and muscle. Below, packed dirt – a *path* – bobbed past.

After a few moments he worked out that he was naked and chained to the back of a donkey; his skin was raw and blistering in the fierce sunlight and he had a host of minor wounds, all chafing or bleeding. Whoever had done this to him had positioned him facing backwards for extra humiliation. The creature's arse stank to high heaven.

Gagging, he twisted, and managed to make out that the donkey was being led behind a horse. A Keshi girl – the one who had crushed his mind after capture – was riding it as if born to the saddle, which dimly surprised him. But he had more urgent facts to ascertain: whether his bonds were secure, and where the Hel he was.

There were other creatures alongside; some were beasts and others walked on two legs, though many of those had animal features. For a few minutes all he felt was the sickness of dread: *The Souldrinkers have me . . .* It was every mage's worst nightmare. He closed his eyes and fought for composure. His gnosis was locked away, of course. He could feel the strength of the Chain-rune like a python coiled about his heart. He was helpless, utterly and entirely.

She said I must serve her . . . Never! That led him to think of the consequences: *They will torture me, for information and pleasure. Then they will kill me and consume my soul. Kore will never welcome me to Paradise, and my family will never be restored to honour.*

His eyes stung with the bitter unfairness of it all.

I was destined for greatness!

His waking brought no outcry, but they noted it all the same, those beasts trotting alongside with their jaws curved as if laughing at him. A few of those in human form raked claws down his back as if branding him, the fresh wounds stinging and bleeding, instantly drawing the flies that clustered maddeningly all over his body, the touch of them a horror all in itself.

They left him on the donkey for three more days, or maybe even longer; he'd lost all sense of the passage of time. He was left to shit and piss down the beast's flanks. The flies in his wounds drove him insane; the chafing got worse and his humiliation was unbearable. He screamed at them, raged, begged, wept, but they ignored him, just laughing as his pride dissolved. His joints tortured him mercilessly, and every wretched step the donkey took was a fresh torment. Delusions mingled with reality: he saw his father, plunging a knife into his own heart, over and over; the Arcanum masters mocking him; Alaron Mercer and Ramon Sensini, merchant-magi in fine robes, selling him at a slave market; Francis Dorobon and Seth Korion turning away in disgust; Adamus Crozier forcing him to suck his cock; and Raine Caladryn being torn to ribbons by a pack of rats, only her face visible as she screamed for him. Consciousness came and went, and only the darkness soothed him, though it brought little respite.

Then water splashed down his throat, making him splutter as he choked, and he realised he was on the ground at last, his limbs so feeble he could only writhe in the dust. A jackal barked in his face, leering at him with laughter in its eyes. Then the Keshi girl appeared, swaying towards him like a temptress in diaphanous silk, her dark heart-shaped face splitting into a vivid smile. Thankfully, though the compulsion to do her bidding lingered, he was able to restrain himself from grovelling before her this time: that spell had run its course. But she didn't need to bespell him to fill him with fear as she approached.

'Well, well,' she said in accented Rondian. 'Our guest has awakened.'

More beasts, jackals, wolves and leopards, padded closer, and human and semi-human forms as well, all snapping and growling at him. He spat blood and phlegm and tried to find something approaching dignity. 'Call your animals off, witch,' he said. It was supposed to come out resonant with Imperial might, but instead it sounded like begging.

'I don't think you're in a position to make demands, Inquisitor.'

I was the star pupil.

I am my family's last hope.

I'm so sorry, Father.

'Get it over with,' he said despairingly.

She tinkled with laughter. 'Get what over with?'

'Killing me. Just do it.' He swallowed. 'Please . . .'

She waggled her head from side to side in a weird way. 'When I'm ready. But we need to talk first.'

'No. Please.' He closed his eyes and willed his heart to stop, but the damned thing kept pumping.

'My name is Huriya Makani,' she said amiably. 'Malevorn, isn't it? I got that from your mind when I chained your gnosis. Listen, what have you got to lose? Words are just words. If you don't speak them voluntarily, I will have to pull them out of your head. Think of the damage that will cause.'

'You're going to kill me anyway. What difference does it make?'

'We both know that if I enter your mind unwillingly, I risk destroying your intellect and most of what I seek to learn will be lost.' She walked around him, her nose wrinkling. 'I will do that, if I must. But civilised people find other ways to relate.'

'Civilised?' He spat derisively. 'Animal! Do you prefer to lie with your vermin in beast or human form?'

The pack snarled, almost as one, and behind him, jaws snapped and slathered. Some lunged closer and a vision of Raine being torn apart filled his head. To his shame, he cringed.

'Enough!' Huriya snapped at them.

The beasts backed off and began to change: a ghastly display of bodies twisting and warping, skin bulging as bones mutated, features melting and remoulding. The agony and ecstasy on their faces was obscene. He had thought himself immune to any sight after his initiations into the Inquisition, which had included assisting in the torture of heretics, but this was truly a vision of Hel. He averted his eyes and closed them tight before they imprinted on his brain.

Kore has abandoned me.

As did Adamus Crozier and Commandant Quintius . . .

'Do you want to know what happened to your comrades?' she asked lightly.

He grimaced and opened his eyes again. Her expression was all mock-sympathy and he hated her for it. But when he thought of how Raine had died, he hated Adamus and Quintius as much, or even more.

'When your *friends* saw you were hard-pressed, they could have

433

come to your aid. Instead they left, in no great hurry. You were sacrificed like pawns in a tabula game.'

He looked down, hid his face.

'Did they not esteem you, friend Malevorn?'

My heroic brethren slaughtered the women and children while Dranid, Dom, Raine and I fought the warriors. Then they ran away.

Presumably Quintius would only help Adamus if we weren't involved.

Huriya's pack had by now regained what humanity they retained. There were some forty of them, mostly male, just a handful of women remaining, and no children at all. They were bloodied and filthy, and had a uniform look of thirst in their eyes. 'When do we kill him?' someone asked.

A massive man with a tattooed scalp stomped forward, holding a spear. 'Tonight!' he roared, and the pack bellowed its exultation at his pronouncement.

'No, Wornu!' Huriya snapped in reply. 'He is *my* prisoner.'

'He is a prisoner of the pack!' This Wornu was massive beyond anyone Malevorn had seen. He spoke Rondian – they all did, apparently – but the tattoos were Sydian; the curse of the Souldrinkers had apparently spread to many races.

'He has knowledge we will need for the mission we spoke of,' Huriya responded in a reasonable voice.

'How so?' Wornu answered cautiously. A woman joined him, a lean creature with dark skin and silver-black hair cropped short, definitely Antiopian. She held a bow and had a quiver over her shoulder. Malevorn recalled the arrows that had slain Dranid.

'Let the one who consumes him gain his knowledge and share it,' the archer rasped.

'That won't work: unless the soul passing is willing, memories are lost.' Huriya spread her hands apologetically. 'Believe me, I too want nothing more than to kill him, but we need what he knows first.'

The pack growled as one, their frustration clear.

'Seeress Huriya, I am Eldest, now that Tomacz is dead,' an older male said. 'What are you seeking? Why do Inquisitors also seek it? Why have we left our packlands?'

A chorus of growled agreement greeted this small speech and Malevorn looked about him, interested despite himself. *There is dissent here. Not that it's going to matter to me in the end . . .*

Huriya stood over him possessively. She had a sultry charisma combined with a steely certainty, as if she were so convinced of her own magnificence that those about her could not help but agree. She spread her arms if she were their mother, drawing them to her bosom. 'Federi speaks rightly. It is time you all understood. You have suffered so much loss and you deserve to know why.'

'More than half of us died, Seeress: almost all the women, and every child,' Federi said plaintively. 'There are only forty of us left. Our pack has almost ceased to exist.'

'What could justify this, Seeress?' a woman called. 'There are only eight wombs left among us.'

'You have the right to know,' Huriya agreed. 'What we seek is a great treasure, an artefact called the Scytale of Corineus. Wornu and Hessaz know this already, but it is time you all did. Brethren, let it suffice that this artefact is one that could cure our condition and transform us into magi without the need to kill and feed.'

The pack fell silent, stunned.

Federi reacted first. 'Salvation, Lady?' he whispered. 'Salvation in the eyes of the Kore?'

'Yes: we would become as them, pure magi, untainted by our curse.'

The reaction of the pack members ranged from blank disbelief to holy revelation. Some babbled questions while others fell to their knees and raised prayers to everyone from Minaus, the Schlessen god of war, to Ahm, Sol and Luna, and even to Kore.

'But why do you protect this Inquisitor scum?' Federi asked, and every eye turned back to Malevorn. Their gaze beat down on him, but by now he had regained something of his pride and he looked around him defiantly.

'The Inquisition are hunting this same artefact,' Huriya told them, 'which is why they keep crossing our path. And they know far more about it than I do – *that* is why I kept this one alive, to help us unlock its secrets.'

'Ah.' Federi bowed his head. 'I understand now, Seeress. Finally.' He shook his head. 'Why could we not have known this before? Would we not still have Zaqri among us? Would we not all have been at the camp when the Inquisitors struck?'

Huriya's eyes narrowed. 'It was Zaqri who refused to share this information with you,' she claimed. 'He was under the spell of the Rimoni girl.'

There was something in her face when she said this that rang false to Malevorn; all Inquisitors were trained to recognise falsehood. *She's playing games with them. She's of them, but she serves herself first.* He then considered what she'd said: *this Rimoni girl must be Mercer's bint . . . I wonder where she is?*

The pack clearly took Huriya's words at face-value, though. 'Zaqri should have killed her,' Federi agreed, voicing the mood of the gathering. 'He failed us all in that. But where is this Scytale now?'

'In the hands of the two fugitives we seek. You know their descriptions already – a Rondian mage and a Lakh woman. I now believe they are going to Lakh, and so shall we.' Huriya paused, and added, 'If you will join me?'

The pack roared their agreement, and Huriya used that approval to dismiss them, telling them to set up camp, then she bade Wornu to bring Malevorn and follow her. 'Let us – you, Hessaz and me – have a *chat* with him,' she said, preening.

Malevorn felt his heart sink. This was it. He'd fought for advancement every day of his life, fed by the burning need to restore his family's honour, and it was going to end in an anonymous death far from home. His family would never learn what had happened to him: that he'd been betrayed to death by the plots of a Crozier and a fellow Inquisitor, then torn apart and consumed by God's Rejects, his soul denied the afterlife. The injustice of it left him sickened and despairing.

The pack dispersed, clothing themselves from the satchels most bore on their backs, then setting up camp. Wornu dragged Malevorn with him to an open bit of ground surrounded by scrub and rock formations and cast him on his back in the dirt. The archer –

Hessaz – glared down at him, the beast inside her clear. Huriya sat on a boulder and studied him.

Malevorn glared up at Wornu, seeking some pride to cling to. 'Do your worst, scum.'

The butt of Wornu's spear hammered into his belly and left him gasping and retching, almost blacking out from the pain. It was a while before he could even think again.

'Pretty thing,' Hessaz remarked coldly. 'Like a girl.'

'How white his skin is!' Huriya commented. 'Pale as a nightworm.'

'Slugskin,' Wornu sniffed. 'Look, you can see his blue veins. Revolting.'

'Better a slugskin than a shitskin,' Malevorn retorted defiantly.

Wornu raised his spear-butt over his face. 'Better whole than a cripple,' he growled. He spun the spear until its wide leaf-head was poised over Malevorn's genitals. 'Or a eunuch.'

'Peace, Wornu,' Huriya said quickly. 'First, we talk with him and give him the chance to save his pallid skin. If he refuses, then you may do as you will.'

Wornu scowled but subsided as Huriya stepped into the middle of the clearing, subtly taking control. Malevorn stared up at her, feeling his fears rise again. She might be tiny, but he found he feared her far more than the bullish, brutal Wornu.

Holy Kore, please make this swift . . .

'So, here we are all seeking the same thing,' Huriya mused in a sing-song voice. 'The Scytale of Corineus, holiest of holies. Are you going to talk to us, Malevorn?' When he didn't react she didn't look surprised. 'You know, it seems to me that he needs a change of motivation. Something we should have done to that damned gypsy . . .'

'No,' Hessaz protested. 'No, Seeress, you can't! He's a damned Inquisitor!'

'He doesn't deserve it,' Wornu spat. 'The pack will not accept him.'

What are they babbling about? I'd never join them . . .

Huriya stepped closer. 'I do not ask you to accept him. He will be my responsibility. But we need his loyalty if we are to unlock his mind.' She nudged him casually with her foot, as if he were a dog. 'He's an ideal case. His loyalties are broken, and—'

'My loyalties are not—' He collapsed, choking, his lips sealed shut by a peremptory gesture from the tiny Keshi girl.

'Don't interrupt me,' she snapped, her face momentarily vicious. 'As I was saying, his loyalties are broken. I have seen a little of what's inside his head. He's a vain, bigoted bully with a streak of moral cowardice he's entirely blind to. He would justify any crime in the name of self-advancement and think it noble. His only loyalties are to himself and any soul as twisted as his own.'

Malevorn was still gasping for air; her slander barely registered – and anyway, it was easily ignored. *Her opinions are beneath me.*

Wornu frowned and looked at Hessaz, who stared at Malevorn with a highly displeased expression on her severe face. 'He would be strong if unrestrained.'

'I don't intend to set him free, not until the artefact is in our hands and he has demonstrated his utter loyalty.' She looked down at him. 'At any rate, we can't trust a word he says until after we've changed him.' She gestured to Wornu. 'If you hold him down I'll do the rest.'

The massive Sydian frowned. 'I'm still against this, Seeress, but so long as his powers remain Chained, let it be so.' He gestured, and a kinesis-blow threw Malevorn once again onto his back in the dust and grit.

'Piss off, big man. You're not my type,' Malevorn snapped dazedly, with a bravado he didn't feel.

What are they going to do to me?

He tried to struggle, but Wornu pinned him like a child. Huriya knelt beside his head and stroked his cheek. 'Play nicely,' she said brightly, waggling a finger. 'Now, do you know the tale of Nasette?'

He woke again. At least he wasn't attached to the arse-end of a stinking donkey this time. He still felt battered and raw; he'd struggled against Wornu until Hessaz had produced a cold blade and held it against his jugular vein, then cut his throat. After that it all got blurry, though he could recall the feel of Huriya's lips against the cut, and her mouth brimming with blood. She'd swallowed it, infused it with her gnosis as he lay dying, then at the last second vomited the glowing scarlet fluid into his mouth. A convulsive gulp had sealed his fate: a simple, disgusting process, so basic he wondered more people didn't know of it. Here was Nasette's secret laid bare: not pregnancy, nor being wounded, nor fucking ... she'd ingested gnostically-infused blood.

After that, he didn't want to die. He wanted to live.

I'm not a coward. Cowards are like Seth Korion, who blubs in the face of hostility and aggression. I'm just rational: what would be the sense of dying? It's just what Kore-bedamned Adamus Crozier or Fronck Quintius would want. I can still restore my family. I can still stand before Emperor Constant, Scytale in hand, purified anew and Saviour of the Empire ...

After he'd thought that through, it wasn't so hard to swear loyalty to the little mudskin harlot and her devil brood. It was the practical choice. Death achieved nothing. Survivors won. Winners survived. And he didn't doubt that it had worked – he could feel it to the depths of his bones. *I'm a Souldrinker now ...*

'How do you feel?' Huriya purred from beside his ear. He opened his eyes and looked about him. He was in a tiny little hut, a mud hovel with a straw roof and a single cot laid against one wall. The stink of a slop bucket assaulted his nostrils, and the spice-laden smell of something glooping towards the boil on the tiny fire.

He was lying on his back, naked, but wrapped in a blanket. He felt ... *well enough*, he decided tentatively. Alive. Functional, though his gnosis was still chained up. No, more than that, it was also empty, like a stomach awaiting a meal. He craved ... not food, but *something*. The Chain-rune dulled that hunger, though.

He faced the little Keshi witch. 'It worked?'

Huriya's face was full of self-satisfied cleverness. 'Yes. You are now one of us. "God's Rejects" is the term you use, I believe. You have no gnosis unless you kill and drain another's soul ... but you're Chained anyway. Your former brethren would kill you on sight – if you were lucky. If they take you alive, I understand the "correct" punishment is to be hanged, drawn, quartered, and then roasted over a slow fire to expunge your body of evil. Your living kin will then be put to death and your possessions will revert to the Church. Am I correct?'

He nodded mutely.

'Excellent. There is no way to cure this affliction, except with the Scytale of Corineus: an artefact thought to be beyond hope of extraction in a vault somewhere in Pallas. Except that now it turns up in the hands of a Rondian mage and a Lakh market-girl. Incredible, yes?'

'You'd never let me use it, even if I placed it in your hands.'

'Why should I not? Once we are all equal in the eyes of the Kore, what reason remains for persecution? We would bring all our brethren into the light, and believe me, there are a lot of us – not as many as the magi, but with the Scytale, we would not be short of new friends. A new Ritual of Ascension, to found a new empire.'

'That's a fantasy.' But as he considered, the more he thought, *Why not?*

'See,' Huriya said warmly. 'You're coming around.'

'I've sworn vows—'

'To faithless men who threw your life away. And the life of your lover, too, yes?'

He blinked. *Raine . . .* It had been weeks since he'd thought of her. A vision of his last sight of her face as the Dokken buried her and began to rip her apart swam across his eyes. 'I love you', she said, who'd sworn she was incapable of 'that emotion'. *Did I love her too? How does one even tell? And what does it matter anyway?*

Love doesn't exist. Just lust and hunger.

'You don't owe your former masters anything, Malevorn Andevarion. But you owe me your life.'

He closed his eyes and churned through various scenarios of escape, of somehow gaining the Scytale on his own and restoring it, despite being a stranger lost in a hostile land without access to the gnosis. Then he abandoned such notions for the foolishness they were.

The bitch is right. I have no choice.

He exhaled heavily and met her gaze. He gave her his most meaningful melt-your-heart look and said, 'You are right, my Queen. I do reject them. I pledge my true loyalty to you alone.'

Was there a flash of girlish coyness in the satisfied look on her face?

They travelled on, riding captured wild horses, bareback and primitive, fringing the coastal ranges as they left Dhassa and entered southern Kesh. A few towns were set about a giant bay Huriya called the Rakasarphal. There was some story about it that the Dokken told each other, something about a Creator-God and a serpent. Malevorn was amused to hear these primitives and their ignorance, but he was careful to hide it now. The Rakasarphal was a spectacular place, regardless, the delta a maelstrom of constricted seas, the cliffs dwarfing even those on the Dhassan and Pontic coastlines. The damp air kept this land relatively green, though the salt had seeped deep into the soil, which prevented extensive agriculture. It was, however, mercifully cool.

They still hated him, of course: they still kicked him and slyly raked him with claws and teeth. But they found him clothing and they fed him and gave him water, and they let him ride alone – unarmed, but controlling his own steed.

To put them off guard, he devoted himself to his new queen, tended her horse at day's end, gathered wood for her fire and learned how to boil and spice the vegetables and grains they bartered for in the villages. His skin turned pink and peeled, his wounds scabbed over and turned to a morass of scars, then darkened as if he were turning Noorie. But he was alive. He began to lay plans again.

Where are you, Alaron Mercer? And how will it feel to drink your soul?

Southern Dhassa and Kesh, on the continent of Antiopia
Jumada (Maicin) to Rajab (Julsep) 929
11th to 13th months of the Moontide

Cym perched on a wide rock at the lip of a narrow gully, a dead hare lying beside her, its fur charred by her mage-bolt. The rock warmed her pleasantly after another day spent in the close and foetid darkness below. She went naked, to preserve the useful life of her tattered tunic and boots. Her feet were now hard as leather anyway, and her skin browner than the sand.

Luna rose, and sent the usual shiver through her: she'd always found the moon's vast weight in the skies above unnerving. Hungry now, she slid across the rock and down into the cavern below.

A rumbling sound rose from beside the cavern's small pool: the loud snoring of a lion. She barely noticed it as she walked to the smoothest rock wall and gouged another mark in the surface. There were fifty-seven strokes carved there, one for every night she'd spent here with her patient. Two months that felt like an eternity. She lit the fire she'd prepared earlier then skinned and gutted the hare, skewering chunks of flesh on green twigs to roast.

The lion woke and rumbled, a plea for water. There wasn't a noise or movement of his that she didn't understand. She'd washed his wounds and sealed them with the gnosis, and spent weeks cleaning away his shit and piss. She'd fed him and watered him, kept him warm through the cold nights; devoted her days to him.

She still wasn't sure why. It was too complicated.

When she'd bent over him that day, with freedom beckoning and time precious, it would have been so easy. She tried to walk away – but she couldn't. Instead she'd beaten off the vultures and used the gnosis to lift him and take him north out of the Noose, questing ahead with her Water-gnosis until she found the hidden cavern and its treasure: the promise of life in this arid land. A pair of foxes were using it as a den, but she'd killed them and fed him the meat. She'd worked the arrow out of his body with excruciating slowness, using the gnosis, where she could. There were always broken bones to set and wounds and illnesses to treat in her father's caravan, so she'd been healing ever since she gained the gnosis. She had a talent for it – though she was almost entirely self-taught as neither Alaron nor Ramon had ever paid much attention in those classes – but Zaqri's wound was the deadliest she'd ever worked on, and it had taken all her patience and concentration. When she'd finally eased the shaft from his flank, she'd never felt such pride.

After that, letting him die would have been a waste.

Since then it had been long, slow days of close care, interspersed with hunting, something she still struggled with. But being a mage had its advantages, and she persevered. Sometimes she sensed scrying, which sent her scuttling for the cave, but there hadn't been many attempts, and the last one was weeks ago.

After three weeks, she worked up the courage to return to the Dokken camp. She found nothing but three lances topped with eyeless, desiccated skulls. There was nothing left to identify them but a few clumps of hair clinging to the scalp. The nearby ground had been dug up, hinting at mass graves beneath. There was nothing to scavenge: the camp itself was nothing but churned sand and ash, her flying carpet was charred beyond repair and the gem was gone.

At night she lay against the lion to share warmth. He slumbered uneasily, moaning softly, but his wound remained uninfected and gradually his breathing became easier. She didn't think too closely about what she was doing, or why. It just felt right: payment for his protection, perhaps, when she'd been his prisoner.

It means I can kill him in good conscience, she told herself.

She was aware that he was unconsciously drawing on the gnosis to survive, and that his reservoir of magical strength was running low. For two months he had been little more than a beast, but thirst for the gnosis was drawing him back to awareness. She could see his eyes clearing and tonight, for the first time since this ordeal began, she could feel the presence of the man within the beast.

'Buonasera,' she said. 'Water?'

A throaty growl. *Yes.* She scooped a handful and fed it to him gently, feeling a jitteriness in her stomach. He was returning to himself and she was going to have to deal with that. Now the danger was over the urge for flight returned; the need to move on and leave him. Alaron was on the run from the Dokken and the Inquisition and doubtless in trouble. And he had the Scytale, the prize of nations.

But when the lion fixed her with his big eyes, she couldn't move. His throat moved awkwardly and inarticulate sounds came out. He was trying to speak, human words, with a mouth that was incapable.

443

He growled, a frightening sound in the close cavern, but she recognised it for nothing more than frustration.

He tried to rise, straining his limbs, but his whole body refused. He'd been on his side for so long, the muscles had atrophied and seized up. He mewled and whimpered, then snarled in helpless anger.

She rolled out of reach and left him to it. There was nothing she could do now. The rest would be up to him.

They slept apart for the first time since they'd come here. She stayed above, clothed and armed, waking in the faint light of dawn to hear the lion prowling below, growling at his inability to scrabble from the cavern.

'Zaqri,' she called, and used telekinetic gnosis to boost him up the slope, onto the rock face at the base of the crevice. He snorted, peering upwards with longing eyes at the seam of light above. Then he scrambled towards her on shaky legs, his paws cascading dust and sand behind him, and he clambered into the daylight.

Now what?

He looked about him, blinking dazedly in the light, tried to roar. It was a strained, weak sound compared to his normal earth-shaking bellow, but it still made her chest swell and her eyes moist. She'd saved him. She no longer owed him anything. Except vengeance.

She'd intended to move on then, but two days later she was still there. She found she couldn't abandon him, not when she realised his plight; he was too weak to hunt, and he hadn't changed back from lion to human because he couldn't. His subconscious had forgotten the way back.

Let that be my vengeance, part of her thought.

But she couldn't leave it there. She needed him if she was to find Alaron and the Scytale. The problem stole her sleep and sent her pacing the night, beseeching Mater Luna for answers.

Mater Luna sent a hunter.

He was a scrawny man from a nearby village, clad in a loincloth, holding a throwing spear. She saw him coming a mile off, heading for this very outcrop, the highest local vantage point. She wriggled into the crevice, masked Zaqri's snoring with illusion, and waited.

The hunter came closer, moving quietly from rock to rock, using the contours of the land to conceal himself, until he surprised her with how close he was. He clambered up the rock to survey the wide lands, searching for prey.

She slipped out behind him, kindling her gnosis, painfully aware that she was crossing a line. She had stolen before, from dear friends as well as strangers, but to kill a man – that was different.

I have to find Alaron. I have no choice.

Some instinct warned him, a moment before her mage-bolt exploded into his chest and he was thrown backwards. He struck his head and went still.

Pater Sol, forgive me.

I must watch, as penance for my sin. First she lowered the unconscious man down into the cavern, which woke the lion. Zaqri quickly realised what was on offer. He looked up at her with an unreadable expression in his lion eyes, then his jaws salivated, and he struck. The first bite broke the man's neck, and as he died, Zaqri moved his head to above the man's mouth and sucked. She saw the lion's aura change and climbed out of the pit, praying to Mater Lune for forgiveness.

When she returned, Zaqri was asleep again. In human form. She used her telekinesis to remove and bury the hunter's remains, then watched the night march past, feeling like the most evil woman alive.

Next morning she was cooking a bird when he emerged from the hole. He had a blanket wrapped around his waist. 'You came back for me,' he said, his voice rusty. 'You healed me.'

His voice thrilled through her, the first words spoken to her in more than two months. The way her pulse quickened and her skin went moist was disturbing. 'I did,' she acknowledged warily.

'Why?'

Because I had to. 'I found you. You were still alive.' She looked away. 'You would have done the same for me.'

To her relief, he didn't press the question. Instead, his eyes flew out into the middle distance, and he asked in a haunted, horrified voice, 'The pack? There was an attack . . .'

'They've gone.'

'Then . . . did they—? Were many killed . . . ?'

'I don't know. I went to the campsite. There were no bodies, but the earth had been dug over, and the stink of death was everywhere. There were three heads spiked on lances, like trophies.'

'The Inquisitors would have buried their own,' Zaqri noted. 'As we would have.' He closed his eyes. 'There must have been many losses.'

She felt for him, to her surprise. How many had survived? Faces and names she'd not thought of for days returned: *Wornu, Hessaz, Tomacz the Eldest, Fasha, the Brician woman Darice, Kenner the cock-waver, Kraderz, Elando . . . Huriya – no, hopefully not her . . .*

'I heard the women call for aid,' he told her. 'It drove the Noose completely from my mind. I forgot all caution. Hessaz shot me – she would have finished me off, but I managed to convey to her what was happening. She left then, to try and save her daughter. She left me to die.'

'I guessed as much,' she told him. 'Wornu was like you: he stopped hunting the moment the first call came.'

Zaqri looked affected by that. 'He loved the pack too, in his way.' He looked at Cym. 'And you?'

'I ran . . . But then I saw the vultures and found you.'

'If the pack had come back, they would have renewed the Noose. You did well to hide us.' He moved finally, sat on his haunches, hugged his knees. 'But now we are without a pack. Outcasts.'

We. A little word that loomed large when he spoke it.

'How long have we been hiding?' he asked. His voice was throaty with disuse.

'Two months,' she told him miserably. *Two months, while Alaron gets further and further away . . .*

'*Sol et Lune!*' he swore. 'I've never been so long in animal form. I don't think I would have found my own way back without you.' He glanced up at the moon, pale in the dusky sky. 'I wonder where your friend is now?'

'Dead, I'm sure. Or so far away he may as well be.' She blinked away tears. 'If Huriya didn't get him, the Inquisition would. He doesn't stand a chance.'

'He evaded us for long enough. You shouldn't give up hope.'

'Maybe.' She looked him over. His lean, pale face was shrouded in a golden beard and shaggy hair, and he was markedly thinner, his body whittled away by the battle for survival. But his chest was still massive, the corded muscles in his arms and legs still taut: male perfection, despite all that he'd been through. He was enough to make her breathe faster. He got up, and she stood too, letting him come to her and enveloping her in his arms. She breathed in the sun-baked smell of him, the animal scents and the blood. Slowly, she returned his embrace, let him sniff her hair, stroke her back, savouring her first human contact for longer than she could recall.

'Thank you,' he whispered into her hair. 'I owe you everything.'

She put her hand on his chest, pushed him away. 'Yesterday, you . . . *we* . . . killed a man. We should move before his kin come looking.'

He nodded heavily. 'For what I put you through, I'm sorry. I should be able to care for myself.'

'It was my choice.' She pushed him away. 'So, you're the one who can put a value on these things: what is a life worth in these lands? What is the . . . *weyrgild*?' she asked, sarcastically.

He sighed heavily, as if her tone had reminded him that things between them were far from resolved. 'A horse. Or a camel. Two asses, or six goats.'

'Well then, we must get busy.'

They found the hunter's village. They had hoped to be able to slip in and out unnoticed, but with a man missing the villagers were watchful, and as they led in the beasts they'd caught, torches flared.

Cym glanced at Zaqri but kept walking, shielding them both against arrows. The beasts – four desert asses snorting their discontent – jogged between them, confused by their odd-smelling captors: humans that smelled of lion. Cym slapped the lead one when he tried to jink sideways and strode after it. She was clad in her ragged tunic, her hair tied back and her face now dark as a native, but she was still an alien in this land.

The body of the dead hunter was slung over the back of one of the asses. As they stepped into the cluster of torches, a wailing cry arose and a woman in a bekira-shroud, the hood pulled back exposing a round, dark face of middling years, staggered forward, dropped to her knees and immediately began to pull out clumps of her hair by the roots. More woman poured out of the houses and clustered about her, trying to restrain her as she wailed. Then the men closed in.

Cym kindled fire in her left hand to warn them. It illuminated her face, which though dark, was foreign-featured, and lit Zaqri's golden hair and skin, and his pale eyes.

The men froze, choking back cries of fear. 'Afreet,' they hissed.

They think we are demons. Fair enough.

The villagers waited fearfully for them to act. Eventually one of them, clad in the white robes of a Scriptualist, stepped in front and began to babble prayers while casting salt in front of them.

<*He believes salt repels afreet,*> Zaqri said softly in her mind. <*I am content that he keeps that illusion.*> He refrained from crossing the line of salt, instead facing the villagers and addressing them in their tongue.

Cym could feel the anger and fear in them, and the hatred, absolute and utter loathing. *To them we're the most vile beings imaginable.* But it was fear that won out. None of them dared to move.

Making sure not to cross the line of salt, she dropped the tether of one pair of the desert asses before the wailing woman. The other pair they used for bargaining. The Scriptualist, who'd probably been assigned to this place in the middle of nowhere as a punishment, was clearly petrified, but Zaqri haggled fairly. Their bounty was a sack of lentils and a bag of curry powder, two water bottles, three thick blankets and two sets of tunics and leggings, and two steel knives. He passed one to Cym gravely.

They left walking backwards, still warded against arrows, but none came. No doubt the villagers had noticed that they'd needed no torches to walk the night. Afreet indeed.

Once clear of the village they retrieved the ass they'd kept to be their own beast of burden and Zaqri loaded their goods. When they reached their den they unpacked the beast and Cym set an imperative in its mind to stay close before setting wards to alert her if any predators came. By the time she got back, Zaqri had set mage-lights into the ceiling and was cooking curried daal and hare-meat.

They ate in silence, watching the way the still water of the pool caught and reflected the light.

'See,' he said, at last. 'A life can be recompensed.'

'This Rimoni woman thinks it inadequate.' She set her jaw, unwilling to admit to the double standard. He didn't press the point.

'We need to move on, find Alaron and Ramita,' she said firmly.

Zaqri considered. 'Huriya thought this Ramita would go into Lakh. It's a vast land, and very populous. They won't be easy to find: a needle in a haystack – though from what you've told me, he would be a very distinctive needle.'

'He'll be hiding. The trail is cold, but we've got to try. I've got nothing else left' – she looked at him – 'except the right and obligation to seek revenge.'

He dropped down in front of her so they were face to face, kneeling in the sand. 'Cymbellea, in Rimoni and Silacia I have seen whole communities destroyed by escalating cycles of vendetta. There are better ways. The Zains will forgive their own killer. The Ja'arathi say that a man who exacts revenge upon another will never enter Paradise. The Omali say that a man consumed with vengeance cannot gain release from the cycle of life.'

'I am none of those.' She drew her knife and pressed it right above his heart. It was razor-sharp. 'You think I wouldn't do it?'

'Not at all.'

'An eye for an eye, the drui preach,' she went on, gouging a shallow cut over his heart.

'Then take my eye, and forgive me afterwards.'

'You took a life.' Her eyes hardened. 'I'd do it, if I didn't need your help.'

'I know.' He suddenly looked tired. 'Cymbellea, the fact is, I have nothing left either. My pack is now closed to me, the only family I've known for half a century. No other Dokken group will accept an outcast. My kindred in Rimoni are long dead. Human society rejects me. For me, there is now only you.'

She stared into his eyes, then at the blood trickling through his chest hair. He'd never seemed more terrifying.

I could do it, Mother Luna, I swear! But it would be so pointless . . .

She sheathed the knife. *Damn you.* 'I'm going to Lakh. I don't care how far it is, but I'll find Alaron and Ramita, or Huriya, or the Inquisitors. I'm not giving up! Will you come?'

He nodded acquiescence. 'As you wish.' He looked into her eyes and dropped his voice to a gentle murmur. 'Cymbellea, I know what is really hurting you. I've been inside your head, remember: you stole the Scytale from your friends and it has brought disaster upon everyone you care for. That is your true pain, and no amount of hurting others will salve it.'

She went numb, the knife dropping from lifeless fingers into her lap, gashing her thigh. She barely felt it. The sharper blade was through her soul.

22

Parleys and Exchanges

Ardijah

My dear Lord Meiros, the Emir of Khotri thanks you for the gift of the bridge at Ardijah. But we regret that due to the disquiet of the local populace when confronted by the gnostic powers of your brethren, we are unable to openly welcome you to our city.

LETTER FROM EMIR FAISAL AL
BURNAK TO ANTONIN MEIROS, 898

The work proceeds, though the caliph's demands are ridiculous, and I suspect the public rallies are designed as much to avoid payment as any expression of genuine sentiment. Even the goatherders of the outlying deserts are desirous of this bridge.

LETTER FROM ADRIC MEIROS TO HIS FATHER,
LORD ANTONIN, 898

Ardijah, Khotriawal Emirate, on the continent of Antiopia
Akhira (Junesse) and Rajab (Julsep) 929
12th and 13th months of the Moontide

Seth Korion wiped his sweating brow, replaced his helmet and nudged his horse with his heels. The beast snorted phlegmatically and trotted to the front of their small group. The gatehouse felt a long way behind him. He peered along the causeway, at half a dozen approaching people, some riding, some walking.

Stay calm. Nothing is going to go wrong.

He tried to reassure himself by recounting the approaching party, but it was still six, the agreed number, including prisoners. He glanced sideways at his own prisoners, the tall man with the top-knot and the voluptuous redhead. Both looked somewhat the worse for wear. Each was tied to a horse, the ropes securing their wrists, then attached to the pommel, and unseen runes confined their powers.

The rest of his group included Jelaska for gnostic support, and two soldiers Ramon Sensini had suggested: a tall part-Schlessen named Vidran, who appeared to be the most relaxed man in the army, and a handsome and somewhat arrogant-looking pretty-boy named Kel Harmon, who apparently had a reputation for sword-play.

Won't do him any good if this turns into a gnostic duel.

The first parley had taken place at dawn: he'd sent Sensini to do the talking, and Jelaska to keep an eye on Sensini. They'd returned to report that Renn Bondeau and a Noroman mage, Lysart, were prisoners of the Keshi. A third mage, Kyrcen, was dead. The herald proposed a straight exchange of high-ranking prisoners.

A good thing I didn't behead Arkanus and Hecatta after all.

The exchange was to be at midday. Each side was allowed two magi and two humans to escort two prisoners. The actual exchange would take place halfway along the causeway, out of range of the archers of either side. 'Let it be an honourable exchange,' the Keshi herald had declared.

Which is why I didn't involve Sensini any further . . .

'Are you ready?' Jelaska asked him tersely.

'As I'll ever be.'

'You're aware it probably won't be the real Salim?'

He nodded. The Keshi sultan was believed to use impersonators, a vital role when you had enemies capable of penetrating every defence. Rumour had it there'd been at least three imposters murdered during the previous two Crusades by Rondian Imperial mage-assassins. There was even one story going round that had the real Salim dead and his continued rule a fiction perpetuated by the imposters.

'Can we tell?' he asked.

'Not without a mental scan, and the real Salim is supposed to have been trained in shielding his mind.' Jelaska looked thoughtful. 'I presume they also train his impersonators.'

The river was dropping daily and the floodplain was now just a swathe of rivulets on either side of the main channel, though the exposed riverbed itself was a quagmire of quicksand. The heat and humidity were so intense Seth felt certain he would melt before they reached the middle, but he told himself crossly to *buck up and look like a commander*. He mopped his brow, straightened his back and fixed his eyes on the approaching party. He recognised Zsdryk, the Dokken necromancer, and shivered slightly. He'd been lucky during the attack. Although it was midday, and the height of the sun and brightness of the day inhibited necromancy, Zsdryk would be far from helpless.

The other Dokken, a woman in her seventies with sun-blackened skin and thick, tangled grey-black hair hanging in ropes to her waist, was almost as cadaverous as Zsdryk. She wore a widow's white bekira-shroud, and looked seventy.

Probably means she's about two hundred . . .

A Keshi soldier led Bondeau and Lysart, both bound and roped to his saddle. The two Yurosian magi looked bruised and downcast, but otherwise unwounded. They were apparently the only survivors of their force, and Seth wanted badly to know how – and why. Then his eyes went to the resplendent figure of the Sultan of Kesh and stayed there.

Salim of Kesh looked every inch of the legend: noble, dignified, educated, fearless. And he had the most perfectly formed face Seth had ever seen, with a neatly trimmed dark beard and the calmest of green eyes. His silk robes were embroidered with gold and silver thread and set with gemstones; his chainmail vest gleamed like diamonds. Steel plates were shaped to his shoulders and chest, but instead of a helmet he wore a white turban so bright it hurt the eyes, with peacock tail feathers affixed with a gold brooch.

It made Seth feel unworthy to even look at him. *Well, if he's the imposter . . . that'd make two of us.*

The Keshi ruler – or his decoy – raised his right hand and halted. He studied the Rondians, then fixed upon the Imperial sigil on Seth's chest. When he spoke it was in perfect Rondian, with only the faintest trace of an accent. 'General Korion? I am Salim.'

Salim: no string of grandiose titles, though I bet he has lots of them. No pompous display like one of Father's friends would insist upon. He doesn't need to . . .

'Seth Korion,' he replied, his throat dry.

'I trust we will deal with each other honourably in this exchange?' Salim said evenly. 'The polite terms of address for me are Exalted One, Great Sultan, or Holy Lord, General.'

'I will leave that for your own people, Sultan.'

Salim smiled faintly. 'Please identify the two magi in your group, General.'

Seth gestured to himself and then Jelaska. 'And yours?'

'I believe you have met Zsdryk? And this is Kadimarah. I was surprised to hear that a Korion commanded here, General. But my prisoners tell me you are the son of the famous *Kaltus* Korion?'

'I'm surprised they told you anything at all, Sultan.' Prisoners were supposed to hold their tongues. 'I take it no torture was required to extract this admission?'

'Just wine, General,' Salim – or his imposter – said with the faintest trace of irony. At least Bondeau and Lysart had the grace to squirm at that. Sensini had made it clear that he thought no prisoner exchange was worth getting Bondeau back.

'And their gnosis is bound?'

'They are under a Rune of the Chain, of course,' Salim said, obviously conversant with the term.

'Of course.' Seth looked at Bondeau and Lysart, who were staring up at him in sullen resentment. 'I presume the same applies?'

'Indeed. Kadimarah Chained them herself.'

The woman's dark visage creased into a yellow-toothed smile.

Both Kadimarah and Zsdryk had that strange aura that instantly identified the Dokken, and in her case it was particularly strong, almost nauseating to look upon with gnostic sight.

Salim glanced at Yorj Arkanus and Hecatta with an ambiguous expression, then faced Seth. 'So, General Korion. Your army is trapped in hostile ground between us and the Khotri. You are blockaded, with no hope of rescue or escape. This might be an opportunity for us to discuss the terms of your surrender.'

'On the contrary, Sultan, our friends of the Khotri have provided for us very well, and our relations with the Calipha of Ardijah are very amiable.' *A little too amiable, possibly.*

Salim looked somewhat put out. 'Really? We have been in contact with the Emir of Khotri over this matter.'

'Then perhaps we have your Sultanhood to thank for the Khotri men who stormed the southern island?' Seth replied, pleased with his own drollness. It was especially rewarding to see Salim's silken façade a little ruffled.

'Well,' the sultan said, his face falling a little flat, 'in that case, let us be about our business.'

'Of course.' Seth glanced at Jelaska, who slid down from her saddle. Zsdryk did likewise. They walked around each other carefully, the Dokken necromancer going to Arkanus and his consort while Jelaska went to Bondeau and Lysart to verify their identities. The task was made slower by the Chain-runes, which blocked all their gnostic activity.

Please let this happen without trouble . . .

Jelaska looked Lysart over, then cuffed Bondeau's cheek gently. 'It's him, damn it,' she confirmed dryly. She looked back at Zsdryk, who was staring deeply into Yorj Arkanus' eyes. 'Are you done?'

Zsdryk glanced at Salim and gave a reluctant nod. He spoke in a surprisingly high-pitched voice, which Seth found amusing, like hearing a dog meow. 'The Chain-rune masks their minds, but the appearance is right.' He looked at Jelaska suspiciously. 'I do not see how she can claim to be sure.'

Jelaska gave him a superior smile. 'A well-cast Chain masks the mind completely, but I could drive a bullock cart though this one.'

Kadimarah scowled.

'You can't beat Arcanum training,' Jelaska said airily. 'Shall we go?

It's up to you to release the Chains in your own time. Mine are water-tight, of course, so they'll take you a while.'

Zsdryk's sour face tightened, but he was clearly more than a little intimidated by Jelaska. He looked instead at Seth, seeking to bolster himself. 'Your general can attest to my skill,' he said in his thin voice. He took the ropes from Vidran and pulled Arkanus and Hecatta along behind him. He passed Jelaska coming the other way, but would not meet her eyes as she guided Bondeau and Lysart back to Seth's group.

Possibly-Salim made a flowing gesture with his hand. 'General Korion. I believe this exchange is complete.'

Jelaska stepped between them, flicking her grey tresses from her face. 'Actually, there's just one more thing.'

Something in her voice made Seth, who'd been basking in the relief that things were going off without a hitch, pause apprehensively. *What—?*

Jelaska gripped her periapt, which flashed as gnostic energy discharged in some unseen way. The six Keshi turned towards her and Zsdryk snarled, backing against Arkanus to protect him, raising his shields in a flash as Kadimarah called blue fire to her fingers.

But Seth was watching Salim, whose expression went from disdain to disgust. *So this is your honour*, his eyes said.

The Chain-rune engulfing Ramon's gnosis vanished as Jelaska's spell took hold; the disorienting surge made him stagger against Zsdryk's back as Arkanus' appearance sloughed from him. A Chain-rune normally cancelled any existing gnostic effects, but Jelaska knew an advanced method that locked them in until the Chain was removed or the energy preserving them dissipated, normally less than an hour. They'd put on the finishing touches moments before leaving the gatehouse.

Beside him, Hecatta's face remoulded itself and Severine's appeared, wide-eyed and scared. It had taken a lot of work to take Sevvie's small talent for shapemastery and make her look like Hecatta. She fell to her knees as the change overcame her, but Ramon had a closer affinity for shapemastery and he took it in his stride.

His hand went straight to his stiletto.

As Zsdryk warded the first of Jelaska's mage-bolts, Ramon stabbed the Sydian Dokken in the left side of his back with the expertise imparted to him by Pater Retiari's *familioso* assassins. Zsdryk stiffened as Ramon struck again and then again, hammering the blows into him, leaving Jelaska to go for Kadimarah.

With a deadly howl, Zsdryk wrenched himself free and turned, his eyes and mouth glowing necromantic purple. His face had gone utterly grey and blood was welling from his mouth, but the violet gnosis that flashed from his hands was still virulent. Tendrils latched on to Ramon's skin, semi-visible suckers that fastened onto his aura, and Sevvie's too. Instantly energy flowed from him to the necromancer, whose stance strengthened. He tried to fight it, blasting away with mage-bolts, but Zsdryk straightened and the blood started flowing back into his mouth.

Beside him Severine screamed and fell forward, face-down.

No—! Sevvie! He tried to rally, to fight back but he had no idea how to fight Necromancy. Seconds ticked by and all he could do was try to keep on his feet as his life poured out of him.

Then Zsdryk's head came off in a sweep of steel and Vidran was towering over him, the big Schlessen's genial face uncharacteristically savage as he shouted in defiance. The hairless skull flew, struck the parapet in a wet thud and lay there, open-mouthed and stunned. The torso collapsed in a flap of robes and a spurting gush of blood, to quiver and jerk to stillness.

Behind Vidran, Ramon dimly saw Harmon cutting down Salim's bodyguard in a flurry of steel. The man was shielding – obviously an extra mage the Keshi had slipped into the group – but Harmon's skill with the blade left the other man no chance to attack gnostically, and the few telekinetic pushes and mage-bolts the man fired were evaded with almost preternatural grace, before a stunning coup-degrâce that saw a dagger appear in Harmon's left hand and go lancing under the Keshi's guard and into his groin. The Keshi hunched forward, then fell on his face.

Beside them, Kadimarah and Jelaska were fighting – or rather, hauling spectral beings into the light and sending them at each other. The torrent of half-seen spirits was contained within a globe of warped air that engulfed the two women, the ghostly shapes ripping and biting and raking and slashing at each other. As Ramon climbed unsteadily to his feet, Jelaska flung another creature into the maelstrom of spectral flesh, a bat-winged fish with giant jaws that swallowed all in its path. Kadimarah saw it coming and howled before throwing more half-seen creatures at it, but the fish-demon swelled in size and engulfed them all. The Lakh witch wailed in despair, backing away and blazing at the spiratus-creature with a torrent of energy. It turned blue and then violet and finally went bright scarlet before exploding, but by then Kadimarah was on her knees, utterly spent, her shields frayed. She cast about for a moment, then began to crawl towards Sevvie, who was lying on her side, unconscious, her arms cradling her belly.

Ramon gave a panicked cry and tried to intercept her, but he was too weak and could barely move. Kadimarah reached Sevvie and her hand grew a spur of horn. She raised it over Sevvie's heart.

If she feeds, she'll be strong again . . .

His mage-bolt took the Lakh woman in the side of her head. She rolled sideways, and Vidran's axe swept through her neck. Another severed head rolled on the bloodied stones.

For a few seconds, everything was still. Then Harmon spun his sword and turned. The tip rested against Salim's neck. 'Stay right there, Exalted One.'

'Two in one day,' Vidran commented. 'These Dokken are easy, yar.' He reached down and offered Ramon a hand, his expression becoming concerned. 'You all right, boss?'

Ramon ignored the hand and crawled to the pregnant girl. He rolled her over. Her face was withered, her skin blotched with age-spots, and her hair was turning grey. 'Sevvie?' he cried urgently, 'Sevvie—!'

Jelaska strode to his side, blazed gnosis-fire at a big bug crawling onto the parapet beside Zsdryk's fallen head, then looked down at Severine. Her face changed from grim satisfaction to alarm and she shouted, aloud and with her mind, 'Get Lanna Jureigh out here! Now!'

Ramon tried to stand, staggered again and would have fallen if Vidran hadn't grabbed him. The big man felt like a tree, an immense oak that could hold up the sky. 'Help her,' Ramon tried to shout, but it came out as a whisper as the sky spun above him and the marrow ran from his bones.

'Boss, you don't look so good yourself.'

It was the last thing he heard.

Seth Korion shifted uncomfortably in his chair, panting softly as he trickled more gnosis into the patient, unsure if he had more to give. It was like trying to piss when your bladder was almost empty. Though what he was doing here was nobler than that, because he was saving a life. Two, in fact.

Severine Tiseme moaned softly. She still held her hands tightly over her stomach, as if the baby's life were more important than her own. He couldn't imagine ever being that selfless.

Maybe if I fell in love, that person's life would matter so much that I would give mine for theirs?

Sevvie's colour was recovering, and so was Sensini's, in the next bed. Lanna Jureigh was asleep in the corner, snoring softly. She was a fine healer, much better trained than he was, but he had the raw talent and the strength of a pure-blood. Healing had always been what he was best at in college, despite his friend's derision about 'women's magic'. His father had been contemptuous too: just another way in which he was unworthy of the Korion name.

How dare they mock me for having this skill?

He now realised that it really was a gift, and a vital one, especially in time of war. He could sense what a body needed, what distressed it and how to repair it. He could visualise the interconnectedness of all the different parts: how the heart pumped the blood and the lungs and stomach enriched it, empowering the sinew and flesh and bones, and how the nerves connected to the spine and up to the brain. It was beautiful. Every human body was a little masterpiece.

The hostage drama had felt like an epic encounter, but in truth, it had been over in seconds. Following the fight they had made a frantic retreat back to the gatehouse, dragging the furious Salim – or his imposter – with them, leaving the bodies of the three dead enemy magi on the causeway. He'd been furious with Sensini and his cronies for pulling the stunt, but it was done, and the men on the walls were still crowing about it.

Damned sneak!

The Keshi had launched a furious assault minutes later, but Seth left the defence in the hands of Bondeau and Jelaska while he concentrated on saving Severine Tiseme and her unborn child. Apparently the Keshi attack had been brief, uncoordinated and easily repelled.

They attacked, even though we hold their ruler. Apparently Salim's banner still flew over his army and scrying the Keshi commanders revealed someone who looked just like Salim. *So do we have an imposter, or the real thing?*

He started at a touch on his hand, and realised that Lanna Jureigh had awakened and was sitting beside him, holding his hand. In the middle of his thoughts, he'd fallen asleep. 'Rest now,' Lanna said tenderly, her business-like expression softened for once. 'She's going to be fine. Baby too.' She kissed his cheek. 'Well done.'

He was suddenly aware that if he kissed her back, some kind of connection would be made. And that she hoped he would. But he felt curiously distant, his mind and brain foggy, and nothing responded. He smiled weakly and pulled himself upright. 'Thank you, Lanna.' He teetered away to seek a proper bed, somewhere he could be alone.

Ramon woke first and immediately looked across to the other bed. Lanna Jureigh was there, bending over Severine. Sevvie's nightdress had been hiked up, exposing her stomach, and the healer had her ear pressed to the bulge and was listening intently.

'Is everything all right?'

'Getting there. The child's heartbeat is weak, but it's regular.' Lanna scowled. 'What were you thinking?'

Ramon felt his face colour. 'Sevvie was the only one of us who could disguise herself as Hecatta. I had no other option ...' He thought back on those terrible seconds on the causeway when it looked like Zsdryk was going to kill them both, and shuddered. 'But you're right, it wasn't a good idea.'

Lanna stood over him, examining his colour, taking his pulse and checking the colouring of his eyes with cool dispassion. 'And likely for nothing too. It won't be the real sultan.'

He grinned. 'We'll find out.'

'Where are the real Arkanus and Hecatta?' Lanna asked.

'Alive.' He smiled grimly. 'Never waste an asset.'

'I wish you would kill them. They're evil beings.'

'I suppose so, by most definitions.'

'No, I mean it. I examined them ... there's something about those two in particular. I've seen a Souldrinker before, you see – we caught one in Dhassa, during the last Crusade. His aura was tainted and he was feral. He was like an animal, but he wasn't evil, any more than a wolf is evil. But those two ...' She shuddered.

'What happened to this Souldrinker you caught?'

'The legate hanged him. It was more merciful than handing him over to the Church. We felt sorry for him.'

'No one feels sorry for that pair below.' He looked down at himself, tried to gauge his own strength. 'How long do I have to stay in bed?'

'A few more days. That necromancer took more than you probably think.'

'And has Baby Korion got over our little trick?'

'You shouldn't call him that,' she said stiffly. 'He saved Sevvie and your baby, not me.'

Ramon looked away, ashamed of his flippancy. 'I should thank him.'

'At the very least.' Lanna passed him a cup of water. 'Drink. You need to keep your fluids up.' She pulled a disapproving face. 'General Korion wants his chief advisor on his feet as soon as possible, even if he does have the honour of a sewer rat.' She turned and stalked out.

Seth gestured to the guardsman, who unlocked the guest suite. They had bricked the windows up so that there were no views in or out, to disrupt scrying. It was that or keep the Sultan of Kesh – imposter or not – in a dungeon cell, and he didn't think that would be proper. The rooms were in the Calipha's central palace; that ambitious young woman had moved to her larger palace on the southern island, which was a great relief to Seth – and to Sensini as well, it appeared. She had quickly found a new protector, though: Renn Bondeau was spending his nights with her.

Seth found the man who might or might not be Salim of Kesh sitting in an armchair, reading from a book. He looked up and his face became a mask of disdain.

'My Lord Sultan, I trust you are comfortable?' Seth asked, looking about at the sumptuous rooms. They were far better than his own, with tapestry-lined walls and deep rugs on the stone floors. The bed was larger than a stores-wagon, and there was a brass bath with elaborate clawed feet against the wall.

How did our prisoner get the best rooms?

'You broke the rules of the parley,' Salim said coldly. 'You have no honour. No man will ever take you at your word again.'

I know – thanks to Kore-bedamned Ramon Sensini! But he knew better than to reveal the internal disputes of his army to an enemy. 'War is war,' he said simply. 'Arkanus and Hecatta gave a false parley before you arrived, so what confidence could we have that they would not try the same·again? If we both truly believed in honour, you would have sent Bondeau and Lysart over the causeway unescorted and I would have done the same with Arkanus and Hecatta.' He tapped his sword-hilt impatiently. 'And your bodyguard had the gnosis.'

The sultan looked away. 'I never knew that, I swear.'

'So you say.' Seth lowered himself into the opposite armchair. 'Interesting, don't you think? You were being protected by a hidden mage. That says to me that you are valued. So perhaps you are the real Salim.'

'I am just an impersonator,' the man who might not be Salim replied. 'You now know we have magi, and that Rashid Mubarak has defected to us from the Ordo Costruo with many followers. The man was probably a secret protector deployed by Rashid.'

'Does this Rashid have many spies in your court?'

'No doubt, just as we have many in his. This is normal.'

'You're well-informed for an impersonator.'

'What use is a look-alike who knows nothing? We live with Salim; we know all he knows.'

Seth sat back, tried to imagine that. 'It sounds bizarre.'

'Salim' shrugged. 'It is the life Ahm gave me.'

'What is your real name?' *Though I doubt I can believe your answer.*

'Latif. I was a jeweller's son, spotted for my resemblance to our sultan. I have been taught to dress, to speak, to behave as he does – I am one of several, each close enough in appearance and aptitude to be used publically.'

'What a strange life!' He looked at 'Latif'. 'I could get Jelaska to look inside your head and see if any of this is true, you understand.'

'We have been trained by Rashid's people to protect our minds. We both know a forced reading would damage me – and for what purpose? I am telling the truth.'

'The presence of that secret mage argues otherwise. And since that initial assault, no doubt an instant reaction by a junior officer, your army has not attacked. That suggests to me that you really are Salim.'

'I am of value, even if I am not Salim. It has taken years to train me, and much expense. Salim would pay for my release, possibly more readily than for those two Souldrinkers.'

Seth thought about that while continuing to study the other man. Even if he was only an imposter, he was still remarkable: clearly intelligent and cultured, and courageous too, to have such composure when in the hands of the enemy. He wondered how he himself would behave if in the same situation.

And the imposter had wonderfully piercing eyes of deep emerald, and they were studying him just as intently.

'So, *Latif*, let's talk about the Souldrinkers,' Seth said eventually, aware that the mood between them was less frosty now. 'The Kore hunts them down without mercy. I understood that your church does so too?'

'The Amteh is a Faith, not a Church,' Latif responded.

'What's the difference?'

'One is an edifice, the other' – he touched his left breast – 'is in the heart.'

'So your heart allows you to align with renegade magi and Souldrinkers?'

Latif frowned. 'I too have misgivings, but this was not my decision; it was the sultan's. Rashid of Halli'kut proposed the alliance, and it was agreed that victory was not possible without such allies.'

'The Kore would never make such an alliance,' Seth announced.

'It is very easy to make noble declarations about what one would or would not do when one has thousands of battle-magi. When you are watching your cities fall and your people's enslavement, perhaps you will discover the limits of your scruples. Then talk to me of this again.'

'These are God's Rejects! They're a perversion of Kore's gift to humankind!'

'So you say. Their version of the tale is somewhat different.'

'They feed on the living soul, man! To defend them does you no honour.'

'You call your gnosis a gift, but is a "gift" that has enabled the conquest of millions truly the gift of a righteous god? You have the power to rule, but does it also give you the right? The *Kalistham* states that the gnosis comes from Shaitan and was made to bring about the end of time. It is no gift, but a curse.'

Seth stood up, affronted. 'I am a pure-blood of the Blessed. How dare you call my gift into question?' he shouted, his temper flaring into tongues of blue gnosis-fire on his fingertips.

Latif did not move but continued staring up at Seth with those unreadable, soul-penetrating eyes.

Seth snapped his mouth shut, feeling like a fool to be goaded into losing his temper by an *imposter*.

He spun and stormed out.

*

Ramon and Kip rubbed their chins thoughtfully. 'What do you think?' Ramon asked the young Schlessen.

'I think we kill them,' Kip replied, shrugging his massive shoulders. 'Chop, chop, done, yar?'

They were in the dungeon the caliph had maintained beneath the gatehouse. It was far enough underground that seepage from the river had rendered it dank, mossy and noxious, and it had all the torture equipment a practical and ruthless ruler like the caliph might need. Right now, it housed the two Dokken leaders. Seth Korion wasn't sure what to do with them. The Kore demanded execution for such creatures, and there weren't any more hostages to exchange.

'That Brician chaplain Gerdhart wants to administer something called the Sacrament of Exorcism,' Ramon commented. 'When I asked him what that was, he described some kind of slow dismemberment.'

Kip flexed his arms absently. 'In Schlessen, we encase them in a wicker cage and burn them alive. We believe that if they are buried intact they rise again, twice as strong.'

'In Silacia they are also burned, in firepits, except if they are Firemagi, in which case we drop them in acid and dissolve their bodies. We fear that if the dogs eat them, they will take over the body of that dog and return for vengeance.'

'Yar? I guess you can't be too careful.'

They turned to study their captives, not really expecting that such tales would have any effect on their demeanour, but you never knew. *This pair have done worse, I expect, but giving and receiving are quite different things.*

Yorj Arkanus and Hecatta looked up at them with unfocused eyes. Their auras were masked by the Chain-runes, which concealed even their nature, but both exuded hatred for the world. They had been imprisoned for almost a week, their gnosis bound and their wrists tied above their heads, forced to pee and shit down their own legs. The stench in the room was vile, the conditions inhumane – but it was nowhere near as bad as what the Kore chaplain from the Argundian legion would do if given custody.

Ramon though torture was vile . . . but so were the prisoners.

He had always felt that any enemy of the Rondians was probably in the right. As a Sollan he'd been raised to regard the Kore as nothing more than a giant lie, fermented to combat the Sollan gods and their hold over the people. But the notion that an enemy of Pallas was a friend of Silacia had never extended to the Dokken – not because they were supposedly rejected by Kore, but because of what they did: devouring souls to gain access to the gnosis. The gnosis wasn't enough to justify taking even one life, in his view, let alone the hundreds this pair boasted of having slain.

Arkanus and Hecatta had not been silent prisoners; indeed, they had held nothing back. Fastened to the walls, powerless, they had crowed like fighting cocks about their successful 'hunts', telling him willingly about the magi they had trapped to empower other Dokken, from Schlessen through Sydia and into Dhassa. They revelled in the details of kidnapping mage-children and raising them until they attained the gnosis, then butchering them to strengthen their own brood. There was not one iota of regret: they expected to die, and wanted the tale of their infamy to be told. They wanted to die as *legends*.

'Hand us over to the priest,' Arkanus had exhorted him. 'Let him hear our confessions! I want my deeds known!'

That was not to say they had not offered him gold and treasure beyond compare to free them, and other delights, should he wish to avail himself of Hecatta's lush, willing body.

After all she claimed to have done, Ramon would rather have cut his own manhood off than sink it into her.

'So what do we tell little Korion?' Kip asked him.

Ramon had been sent by Seth to make a recommendation as to whether clemency might be extended, or he should bend to Kore Law and hand them over for execution. He hadn't yet made up his mind. 'I don't know.'

They lapsed into silence until Arkanus whispered, 'Silacian. Come here.'

Ramon knew he shouldn't. But he did. 'What?'

'Closer,' the Dokken lord whispered hoarsely. 'I have something to say, for your ears alone.'

Ramon looked at the man, sickened to be so close. Warily, he used the gnosis to pin the man's head to the wall, lest this was some ruse to try and bite him, as he'd attempted before. Up close, the stink of faeces and sweat was overpowering.

Arkanus tilted his head sideways and spoke softly in Rimoni, a dialect he knew Ramon understood and Kip didn't. *'We can make you one of us.'*

Ramon recoiled, stared. 'What, like Nasette?' he said doubtfully.

'Nasette's tale was real. It can be done.'

Ramon stared, trying to determine if this was a lie or the truth. But the man sounded as if he truly believed what he was saying. 'Why would I ever want to be one of you?'

'Because for us, there are no limits, Silacian. You are – what? A quarter-blood at best? Would you like to have the power of a pure-blood? To live for centuries, beyond the power of all laws? If you were one of us you could just reach out and take it all. Like we have.'

Ramon met the man's eyes. 'How?'

'Tempted, are you? Clean us, feed us, and I will tell you more.'

Ramon stepped back. 'No. I have no desire to be like you, not ever.'

Yorj Arkanus glowered at him. 'Then you are a fool. What hope is there for you? You will never be anything other than low-bred scum in their eyes. You will never be what they are, those shining pure-bloods! They keep the real power for themselves – they always have.'

Ramon stayed silent.

'You know I'm not lying. Free me, and I will transform you – I will give you Hecatta's soul: she's as strong as a pure-blood. Instant power, boy! With your Arcanum training, you could be great amongst us. What loyalty do you owe these Rondian churchmen and generals? After what they've done to your people, how can you even wear their badge?'

Ramon swallowed, overcome suddenly by childhood memories of being bullied and picked on for his size and foreign blood and bastardry. Then the gnosis came – his mother had not even realised his blood, because she'd been had by every Rondian in the valley. Suddenly, their lives were transformed: the familioso stepped in and Pater Retiari himself made him his ward and dared to petition his real father, the only mage his mother had rukked. His mage-father had bought her silence with money and funded his education: all for Pater Retiari's benefit.

He tried to picture himself as a mighty, pure-blood-fuelled Dokken. Of course he would be forced to hide from *real* magi, to leave this life for ever. But he would be doing that anyway once he returned to Silacia.

To be like a pure-blood . . . To take Arkanus' place in their society. To live in a Keshi palace . . . Who gives a rukk about the damned Crusade anyway?

He looked at Arkanus, and then at Hecatta.

Arkanus would sell his wife's soul for his own safety . . .

That's what made up his mind, in the end: that this monster would bargain away his own mate, and he had no doubt she would have done the same.

Sevvie has my child inside her. Whatever else could I need?

Apart from getting Mother free of Pater Retiari, of course . . .

He wondered whether Chaplain Gerdhart would turn down such an offer. He wasn't impressed with the man. Would Bondeau refuse? Even Baltus? He turned to Kip, sent a silent opinion.

Kip's bluff, good-natured face hardened. 'What did he say to you?'

'Enough to convince me that a quick death would be the right course.'

Arkanus' face widened in shock and he threw a look of utter hatred at Ramon, then looked at Kip. 'Neyn, Kamerad! Neyn!' Guttural Schlessen tumbled from his mouth in pleading tones, clearly the same offer.

'Like you?' Kip spat. 'Unheilich Ungeheuer!' He looked at Ramon. 'He offered you this also, yar?'

Ramon nodded disgustedly.

Kip's blade flashed in a silver arc that almost severed Arkanus' neck. The man's final panicked look remained as his head fell sideways, blood fountaining up like an overflowing sewer to pour down his body. His face went slack, his eyes wide and staring. His choked cry roused Hecatta, who gave a wailing, bereft cry and turned to Ramon, her eyes suddenly frantic, as she babbled words in every tongue at once, offering herself in any way he wanted her, pleading, begging.

Ramon pushed his stiletto through her ribs and into her heart and made himself watch her die.

Then he turned around and vomited.

Kip laid a hand on his shoulder when he straightened, his face pale. 'These Ungeheuer are better dead and gone! Better than someone believing their lies, yar?'

'They might not have been lies,' Ramon panted.

Kip snorted softly. 'Now you tell me.'

Ramon looked at him, somewhat aghast. The Schlessen laughed. 'Ha! Got you!' He roared with laughter and slapped Ramon on the shoulder. 'Come on, mein freund, let's go get drunk.'

First I've got to explain this to Baby Korion.

He thought about that. *No, I'll tell him later.*

'Si, amici, let's do exactly that.'

23

Escape

The Greatest of Sins

To deny the husband his rights to her womb is one of the greatest sins a wife can commit. She kills his heirs and the future of his line. There is no place for such women in society.

GMARDIUS SIXTUS, PONTIFEX, RYM, 278

I fear I love thee too greatly, but I cannot stay away. What is life without the solace of love?

SISTER INGRETTA, IN A LETTER TO LADY FELICE
GANTARIUS OF BRES, 823

Brochena, Javon, on the continent of Antiopia
Rajab (Julsep) 929
13ᵗʰ month of the Moontide

Nothing ever goes entirely to plan. Elena had repeated that many times. *There are always variables,* she'd said: *it's how you adapt to them that makes the difference. It's how you improvise.* Cera tried to keep that in mind as she huddled in the sitting room of the Blood-tower, listening to Francis Dorobon prattle.

The night of our escape and he chooses it to visit me for the first time since we argued! What are the odds?

Francis would have interupted her in the act of packing had Tarita not been vigilant; as it was, the maid had diverted him to a waiting room until Cera had changed back into her blood-purdah robes and gone to join him.

'I need to talk to you,' Francis had said, sidling into the women's suite. It might be forbidden to all men, but no one was going to try and tell their king that. As she rose to her feet to remonstrate, he'd hung his head and mumbled, 'I need your advice. I can't think straight.'

You can't think at all. I bet Gyle is dancing rings around you. But it was almost touching. 'My lord, I am on blood-purdah. Men aren't supposed to come here.'

'I lose more blood if I get cut while practising with my sword,' he whined. 'Women in Yuros don't hide away; they carry on as normal.'

Yeurch. She wrinkled her nose. 'We're not in Yuros, my lord. "A moon-soiled woman must stay aloof, lest their pollution spread",' she quoted. 'That's in the *Kalistham*.'

He waved a hand dismissively. 'I've just had four days of being pulled every which way by Gyle. Perdonello is presenting the new constitution and Gyle keeps objecting to it all. I can't think on my feet . . .' He looked at her plaintively. 'I need you there, in the room. You know about these things.'

Yes, I do . . . but I'm getting out of here! Tonight! Please, just go away! But Francis was clearly not going to be put off. 'Just summon me into the council, if you want to. You have the right, Francis: you're the king!'

'But you're not allowed in councils: you're only a woman.'

'Mater-Imperia Lucia is in your emperor's council. I'm told she virtually runs it.'

'That's just rumour,' he said sullenly. 'But you do run the Beggars' Court . . .'

I know, and leaving it behind is the only thing I regret. But please, just rukk off!

She tried again, 'Francis, I'm on blood-purdah! I've got a headache. My stomach is bloated and my bowels are loose. *Need I go on?* All I want to do is sleep.'

He all but put his hands over his ears as he rose and backed away. 'I can summon you, you say?'

'Next week, when I'm out of the Blood-tower.' She forced a yawn. 'Francis, it's late. We can talk again tomorrow.'

She supposed he must be truly desperate to come to her like this – desperate enough to swallow all that pride. 'I'm sorry, you are right,' he said meekly. 'But ... we must seek reconciliation, wife. This charade isn't right.'

'No couple should have to pretend like this,' she agreed. *That's why this kingdom should permit marriages to be dissolved, across all classes. Something for Timori when he's king.* 'Goodnight, my lord.'

She let him kiss her hand, something which awakened a puppy-dog expression on his face as he left.

Then she forgot him the moment he was gone.

'Tarita, are we ready?'

The maid slipped into the room, her impish face caught up with the excitement of the conspiracy. 'The midnight bell will ring in half an hour or so, Madam.'

Cera, who had always been a serious girl, responded with a matching grin as the excitement of the escape finally hit her.

'Then go, Tarita. I'll meet you in the kitchens just after it rings.' She kissed the girl's cheeks, squeezed her hands as if they were sisters or dear friends, not lady and servant. *If she was a warrior I would knight her.* There was no such custom for women, but perhaps she could arrange an advantageous marriage once they were all safe in Forensa.

She returned to her packing and changed into her travelling attire: male salwar and plain long-shirt, then a hooded robe over the top. She put a knife into her belt, then stuffed into her pack a change of clothing and her most precious possessions: a few items of jewellery from her parents and her small ceremonial circlet. Finally she put on her Nesti signet.

Then all there was to do was to wait. And pray.

Gurvon Gyle was sipping imported red wine, a fine Brician merlo, savouring a lingering plum finish and trying to decide where to hide his money. His long-awaited bullion from Jusst and Holsen, payment for his part in the emperor's plot, was arriving in two weeks' time. But Calan Dubrayle's warnings about the Crusader notes had made him nervous of putting the money into any local bank, because the Dorobon financiers were holding so many such notes it scared him. The Rimoni bankers had been more cautious, but he wasn't going to go to deposit money with likely enemies. *I'd be safer to bury it all than hand it to them.*

Apart from that, everything appeared to be going well. Francis Dorobon had been sidelined and was ineffectually stewing over some joust he'd lost with Cera Nesti. The whole court knew he'd been banished from her bedchamber, and the streets knew too. *We'll move on him soon . . . it'll appear to be a tragic accident.* He'd not yet decided Cera's eventual fate. Six months ago he'd have thought her irrelevant, but the Beggars' Court had made her an important hostage again, perhaps more useful than the boy-king Timori. Even if the Javonesi elected a new king, Cera would continue to matter. So he was happy to let her continue to play her parlour games.

Which just leaves the question of Yvette . . . There had been signs that she was coming to her senses. She'd come to him and begged forgiveness, after which she'd performed adequately in her duties, including a convincing performance as Olivia Dorobon at the last state function. Lucia Sacrecour still wanted her dead, but Mater-Imperia's agents – there were at least two amongst the Oldchurch settlers – had not yet worked out that Olivia was Coin, at least as far as he could see. *I can still use her. I'm too short-handed to just toss her aside.*

A ward prickled at his mind, one set in the corridor outside, then a second later someone knocked at his door. 'My Lord Gyle? Are you there?'

'Wait!' Frowning, he rose and went to the door and scryed the far side using the brass plate as a conduit. It showed him the evening's guard commander, a Dorobon soldier called Elissen. There was no sign of anything untoward and he opened the door. 'What is it, Elissen?'

The guardsman bowed apologetically. 'It may be nothing, my lord, but an urgent courier came for the king from Hebusalim, but we can't rouse him.'

Gurvon wavered. It could just be that Francis had passed out drunk, but there were worse explanations. 'I'll come.'

He followed Elissen to the top levels, where Francis was housed in the old king's suite and Olivia in the queen's. Cera Nesti and Portia Tolidi had been kept on the lower level, in the former nursery. The only other suite, Octa Dorobon's old one, was empty.

There were two doormen stationed outside the king's rooms at all times, and they were waiting anxiously when he and Elissen arrived. 'Has anyone been in or out this evening apart from the king?' Gurvon asked them.

'Just the Noorie Queen,' one of the doormen sniggered. 'We get to pat the bint down before she goes in and gets herself nailed.' He finally noticed the coldness in Gurvon's eyes and blanched. 'Sorry, my lord. I meant no disrespect.'

'Give me the keys to this level,' Gurvon said coldly. *Isn't Cera in the Blood-tower this week?* 'Is the queen still within?'

'No, my lord,' the other doorman replied.

Gurvon extended his senses, but came up against wards . . . Francis' own. The king should have been aware of such a probe, but there was no reaction.

There could be a simple and entirely non-threatening reason for all this, but he'd not survived so long assuming the best of people. A skilled mage could slip past a human guard easily enough, one way or the other. *It might not even have been the queen they admitted.* The thought drew his eyes to the opposite door, to Olivia's suite.

'Wait here.' He took the keys and went to Olivia's door, knocked softly, but there was no response, and when he looked, he realised that there were no wards either. Magi did not leave wards in places they did not intend to return to. Increasingly apprehensive, he unlocked the door and entered.

It was not immediately clear whether Coin had ever occupied the room. The shapechanger owned little of a personal nature. She didn't use weaponry or armour and wore only whatever clothes suited her current form. The cushion on the sofa was cold, but the dregs at the bottom of the sole wine glass were still liquid. But something, instinct perhaps, told him she was gone.

To scry her would be to alert her that her absence had been noted. So he stopped, sat, and tried to work out exactly how much shit he was in.

Why would she leave? Who would she go to – or with?

He returned to the king's door. The wards and locks were of pure-blood strength, so he was forced to summon Rutt Sordell, in the body of Guy Lassaigne. The diviner scurried up the stairs minutes later, his pasty face anxious. 'Hello? Is something going on here? I was just calling on the king for a nightcap,' he added quickly, maintaining the fiction of his assumed identity with commendable presence of mind.

'Ah, Sir Guy,' Gurvon replied, playing along. 'We're a little worried for the king.'

Sordell looked at him anxiously, then went forward and examined the wards. Thanks to his efforts to master his new pure-blood form, he broke them in a minute. By then a small crowd was gathering: curious servants, a mix of the Dorobon and mercenary magi, and courtiers. Craith Margham arrived, puffing, his beady eyes everywhere as he questioned the doormen.

Damn this. Whatever we find is going to be common knowledge by dawn . . .

Sordell drew his sword. 'Please wait here, my lord.' He entered the room cautiously, while Margham joined Gyle.

'What's happening, Gurvon?' he drawled. Margham liked to treat everyone with familiarity.

'A disturbance, and no response from the king. He might just be drunk, but . . .'

Margham's mouth twitched apprehensively. 'Franny?' he called aloud. He pushed past, following 'Lassaigne' into the king's rooms.

Gurvon paused and sent his mind questing outwards. He checked his office, in case Coin was in there, but there was no sign of her, or anyone else, and no disturbance of his wards. Then he tried Cera Nesti's suite, recalling Coin's threats to kill the girl – *the last thing I need right now* – and again got nothing, before remembering that Cera was in the Blood-tower, where he'd never been, so could not easily scry. So he re-focused his search onto the queen herself.

He almost missed her, his gnostic eyes hampered by the stonework and the unexpected position of the target. Because Cera Nesti was not in the Blood-tower: she was clad in travelling clothes and descending into the depths of the keep . . . He stopped, his mind racing: *She'd only run if Timori was safe* . . . Then it all fell into place, just as Rutt Sordell burst out of the king's suite, his jaded face preternaturally pale.

'Gurvon,' he breathed, 'we've got a fucking big problem.'

Madeline Parlow was hungry, or more exactly, she had a particular craving: for rose lokum. So after peering in on Timori Nesti, who was sprawled in blissful innocence across his bed, toy soldiers scattered on the floor, she went to the kitchen.

Lokum was a Jhafi delicacy, a delicately flavoured sugary gel, the most luscious sweet Maddy had ever tasted. Rose was her favourite, but cherry or apple or mint were also divine. She had come across it last year, when she'd first arrived in Brochena. One day she'd gone to the market with Serjant Rhinus, a food lover like her, and an expert on the various native delicacies. There might not be much particularly eye-catching about Rhinus, a bluff mercenary, but he shared her tastes, and that was a joy.

The rose lokum had sealed the deal: with one small cube, her taste buds had gone into ecstasy and she would happily have surrendered whatever virtue she had left for just the promise of more. But Rhinus hadn't been so crass as to take advantage of her exuberant reaction; he'd let her choose the moment and she adored him for that too. Too many of her spontaneous lovers had become regretted indiscretions, but Rhinus was a treasure.

Maddy was a quarter-blood mage, a decent catch. A little dumpy these days, perhaps, and she couldn't run twenty yards without losing her breath, but she wasn't as soft as her mousy looks and mild face might suggest. She'd seen combat, and killed. She was a clairvoyant and a farseer; Gurvon had always said she was vital to his Grey Foxes, that she was 'the grease on the axle' keeping the wheels turning, an image that made her giggle.

She was well aware that not all of Gurvon's associates were nice people. If they weren't hard like Rutt or Mara, they were vicious like the unlamented Samir and Vedya. Sometimes they were both, like Elena. She was also aware that most of what Gurvon did was illegal, but she didn't care about any of that. Her humble family had been bypassed on the road to riches and if she wanted to enjoy the best things in life – the sweets and wines and cheeses, the loveliest perfumes and art and jewellery – then she had to earn them somehow. She wasn't pretty enough to marry well, and wedding one of Benoit's merchants would see her completely disinherited. For a time she'd thought to be a nun of Kore, but they ate *muck*. Gurvon provided what she needed; that was more than enough justification for her.

Over the past year in Brochena, an understanding had grown between her and Rhinus. Though she would eventually marry another mage, to preserve her bloodline undiluted; she and Rhinus would share their lives somehow. He joked about being butler of Parlow Manor, a mythic estate they built in their imaginations.

Parlow Manor came crashing down at midnight.

She entered the kitchen, calling merrily, 'Rhinus darling, I was just wondering if we had any more of that rose lokum?' She was already savouring the sweetmeat.

Rhinus looked up, a smile lighting his crooked face. Beside him, Jacquo rolled his eyes, opened his mouth to tease the two of them: the Epicures, he called them. He was a sweetie, Jacquo, if you looked past the one eye and the scars. Not many could, sadly.

Young Tholum was outside, she presumed. But there was an unexpected third person in the kitchen. 'What are you doing here?' she asked.

'Gurvon sent me,' Symone replied.

Maddy didn't like Symone. There was something not right about him, something that made her skin crawl. It wasn't that he was quite obviously a male *frocio* – a 'mooner', as the rankers called them. It was the way that he didn't seem to fit his own skin, like an irritable snake trying to rub a layer of dead scales away.

'Gurvon said nothing,' she replied worriedly.

Symone primped in that feminine way he had. 'He's worried Elena is about.'

'Elena?' Maddy looked worriedly at Rhinus, just as the sixth bell began to chime: midnight. Each hour had its own key and sound-pattern, so that you always knew by the second chime what hour it was. They all paused, because the church was close and the sound drowned any chance of conversation.

Symone laid a hand on Rhinus' shoulder. 'Elena could be any-where,' he said, not very reassuringly.

For a heartbeat, they were all perfectly still.

Then Symone's hand sprouted talons and he ripped sideways through flesh and gristle. Blood sprayed, Rhinus' smile fading as his eyes went wide, the gaping slash below his chin opening as air gushed horribly, then he fell sideways.

Maddy heard a shrill scream fill the room as Jacquo's hand went for his dagger and something hammered into the back door. The scream was hers. She was vaguely aware that she should be doing something, but all of her mind went to drinking in her last sight of dear Rhinus' face as he fell in slow motion to the floor.

A cloaked shape burst through the back door, levelled a crossbow and fired. Jacquo crashed over backwards, the bolt jutting from his right breast. Maddy tried to react, but all she could feel was her dream future disintegrating.

Symone flowed across the space towards her, ripping through her shields contemptuously. The last thing she saw, lying shredded on the floor in a pool of spreading numbness, was Rhinus' empty face.

You've gone on ahead, my darling . . . to Parlow Manor.

She rushed to join him.

The royal palace of Brochena, even after the sealing of the secret pas-sages, was a hive of corridors, halls, ante-rooms and twisty little stairs. Someone unaccustomed to them could get lost in seconds, but

Cera, drawn all her life to secrets and hidden passages, knew exactly where to go.

As the sixth bell chimed, she lit her candle and slid through the door to the Blood-tower. The half dozen others on blood-purdah in the lower rooms, women of bureaucratic families whose cycle coincided with hers, muttered and dreamed as she crept down the stairs and out into the labyrinthine ways that the servants used to access and clean the tower while remaining out of sight of the well-to-do. Spiralling down the backstairs, she followed the narrow passage past the bowri where she and Portia had first made love. She moved unseen through the men's quarters, where the castle labourers snored, and down the tiny wooden steps to the storeroom Tarita had described.

It looked like she had arrived first. The food store was dark and silent, the shadows jumping as the candle she held trembled. The darkest recesses remained steadily unlit, and the room stank of blood and raw meat. There were rows of butchered carcasses stretching on into the dark. The tunnel was in the cupboard at the far end, Tarita had told her.

She lingered a little at the front of the room, waiting for the sound of Tarita's footsteps.

Thank heavens for her courage and wit, especially after Portia went north. I couldn't have done this alone.

Then she stopped as boots sounded behind her, too heavy to be feminine.

'Stop right there.' Gurvon Gyle's voice cut across the space coldly. 'Not another step.'

What is a man? It was a question that had occupied the greatest minds of the empire, and before them the philosophers of Lantris and Rym, for millennia. *One thing he's not is a bug lodged in someone's brain.* But that was what Rutt Sordell now was. It was far from ideal, but he liked it better than being dead.

Lessons had been learned from his time spent in the body of Elena Anborn. As Guy Lassaigne, he spent every second he could adapting to the body and practising his use of the gnosis. The other Dorobon magi had complained; 'Guy, you've changed!' they said, oblivious to just how much. He'd never been a good actor, so he compensated by slowly changing Lassaigne's persona to his own.

There were issues, of course: controlling the body from within a Revenant-scarab was awkward, but he was fully nested there now, and well-attuned to the central cortex through his gnostic links. His physical responses might still be a little lacking, but he had never been a warrior; it was the mental responses that mattered, and they were now almost perfect.

He floated above the squalid lanes of Brochena, borne by Air-gnosis and kinesis, as around him the night came to life. Someone had been blocking all his attempts to warn Maddy Parlow, and that required proximity to the subject. Gurvon doubted Coin was acting alone, and Sordell concurred. This was confirmed as he approached the safe-house. His inner eye began to make out human auras in the shadows: Jhafi thugs with drawn weapons, and no one had raised the alarm.

In his left hand he conjured gnostic light, purple-hued, from his favoured necromantic links, while with his right he gripped a sword. Gurvon had stayed to reel in Cera Nesti, thinking that Coin would be with the escaping queen, but it was now clear that the shifter had other prey in mind. As Sordell swooped into spell-reach, the shadows erupted and men began to pound into the alley and smash in the door of the safe-house.

He darted through the air, selected the man giving orders and blasted necromantic light at him. Violet light engulfed the Jhafi; his clothing crumbled to dust and so did half his chest. His death cry was a ghostly wail. Those around him looked up, saw Sordell and raised crossbows. Missiles began to fly.

A bolt slammed into his shields and bent them almost to his chest, punching him backwards even as the missile disintegrated. Sordell retaliated furiously, sending a stab of light into the darkness, and the man shrieked and clattered to the stones. Another bolt sang, glancing off his shields, and he blasted again, thin shafts of light that were faster to fire. Already half the Jhafi were running away. He soared to the wide-open door of the safe-house and conjured up an eidolon-spirit. He sent it inside, where it tore the souls from three men before a silver blade sent it wailing to oblivion. He gasped as the gnostic bond through which he controlled it snapped, but recovered swiftly, rejoicing at his acquired pure-blood energy. Necromantic sight showed him wispy shapes rising from the men he'd slain and he snared them and held them as he readied his next spell, seeking his prey.

Then a window shattered outwards and Symone – Coin – burst out. The hermaphrodite had a frightened young boy – Timori Nesti – thrashing in his blood-smeared hands. Coin saw Sordell and froze.

'Give up the boy,' Sordell rasped. Around them, Coin's Jhafi helpers were scattering, terrified by the open use of gnosis. The bells were clanging from a nearby Dorobon watch-house and Rondian voices could be heard, drawing closer.

Coin responded by raising one hand; the mage-fire she kindled with pure-blood gnosis was bright as a little sun. Sordell responded, but his greater fear was that Coin would take to the air. Shapeshifting – morphic-gnosis, as they'd called it in college – was a study based upon Hermetic- and Air-gnosis; most Morphic-magi could fly.

'Come on,' Sordell drawled. 'You don't give a shit about the boy. You're only doing this for Cera, and we already have her.' He sneered and added provocatively, 'Gurvon's probably fucking her up the arse as we speak.'

'You're lying,' Coin replied, her voice thin and scared.

'Nice try, traitor, but your little plan has failed.'

Coin's eyes burned a little brighter. 'Not all of it,' he – she – *it* – responded. 'Have you visited Francis Dorobon's room tonight?'

Sordell paused. He certainly had. Seeing a man's genitals ripped from his groin and stuffed down his own throat wasn't something he'd forget quickly, even jaded as he was.

She did that to a pure-blood! Though he supposed that when Francis had lost his genitals, he'd been so traumatised that fighting back was impossible. 'Live by the cock, die by the cock,' he retorted, pleased at the drollness of his response. 'We've got your little Noorie queen, Yvette. That's who you're doing this for, isn't it?'

'No ...' Coin began shaking her head, scanning the darkness, limbs poised.

Here we go.

With a scream, the shapeshifter erupted into the air, the boy-king clutched in one hand, while molten energy blazed towards Sordell.

He was ready, of course, and as the shapeshifter shot skywards, so did he.

Try to take anyone you find alive, Gurvon had told him.

Rutt shouted aloud, summoning the spirits he'd spent the past minute binding, and Coin's head twisted from side to side as the violet-limned ghosts of the freshly dead flashed out of the darkness. The hermaphrodite blazed gnostic fire about her as she shifted about, the boy in her arms thrown about like an oversized rag doll. The nebulous forms shrieked and wailed as they were carved apart, but that was fine: they'd achieved their aim: distracting Coin while Sordell got closer. He alighted on a rooftop thirty yards from his target, gripped his periapt tight and struck.

Knowing one's enemy was a tremendous advantage in gnostic combat. Coin was a specialist, ultra-strong, but in a narrow field. Getting close could see him ripped apart, and trading mage-bolts risked the boy-king. His foe's weakness lay in non-tangible attacks, and that was where he now focused.

He tore open a glowing hole in the air, and from it slithered a summoned spirit, what the ignorant might call a daemon. Unlike the recent dead, Coin's gnostic fire barely touched this conjured spirit. A skilled wizard like Sordell could summon such a being and hold it in the aether, just out of reach until needed. Now, with a pure-blood's body, he could summon spirits of far greater power. As it materialised, he felt dust and dirt, filth and muck from the streets, water from a stagnant pond and all manner of loose debris flow into it, giving it substance. Coin sprayed it with mage-bolts, but it had sufficient native tenacity to endure as it swarmed through the air towards the shapeshifter.

A skilled wizard would have banished the spirit, but Coin had no such affinity. The summoning flowed *through* Coin's attacks in a flash, and then tentacles sprouted, latching onto the shifter's face and covering mouth and nose. Coin's shriek was muffled and in a desperate attempt to fling it off, she lost her grip of Timori. The young king fell to the ground, landing in a heap, and was sensible or scared enough to freeze in place.

Coin finally succeeded in blasting the summoning away and it splattered against a stone wall. It tried to reform, then fell apart, but by then Sordell had locked onto Coin's mind with a mesmeric grip. For a few seconds they fought silently, and Sordell got flashes of a life spent in confused and abject misery: an irresolute, needy being with no core identity, desperate to be wanted, and a collection of lurid fantasies about making love to Cera Nesti. But before that it was Gurvon Gyle, and before that Solinde Nesti, and before her a stream of others, each ending in crushing rejection. It was a simple matter to summon those scenes, one after the other, right back to Lucia Fasterius telling her deformed child that she'd been fortunate not to have been drowned at birth.

Coin collapsed, eyes emptying as the worst moments of her life knocked her into a stupor. Sordell caught the falling mage and wrapped her in gnostic bindings, then he turned to Timori Nesti and extended his hand.

'Come with me, boy. Your sister wants to see you.'

For Cera, the following days were a numbness, as if she had been drugged and never quite thrown off the sluggishness. Locked in a dungeon, all she could feel was the axe, slowly descending. She had prayed they would kill her immediately, but instead they left her in a bare cell, with just a blanket and a bucket for slops. There was no sign of anyone, not Tarita or Coin or Timori, not even a guard.

The blanket was too thick to knot and hang herself with, and there was nothing to hang from anyway. Trying to strangle herself didn't work: she managed to pass out but not fatally, and then they took the blanket away. She tried starving herself, but Mara Secordin force-fed her, her dead eyes pitiless.

Finally, they came for her, led by Sir Roland Heale. 'Get up,' he said gruffly, his deep-set piggy eyes glinting in his jowly face. Someone threw cold water over her and she was wrenched to her feet.

They took her, still dripping, to the bureaucratic chambers adjoining the palace, a court room for dispensing justice in capital cases. Gurvon Gyle sat in the senior seat, presiding. Three men sat with him on the judicial bench, two of whom she knew: Josip Yannos, the head of the Sollan Church in Javon, and Acmed al-Istan, the senior Godspeaker of the Amteh, had been part of her Regency Council. The third was the Kirkegarde Grandmaster, Etain Tullesque, clad sumptuously in black, white and gold. She wondered where the king was and if he knew what was being done to her.

The Kore Grandmaster spoke first. 'Cera Nesti, you are accused of murdering your husband, the king. How do you plead? And before you respond, know this: you were seen entering his chambers prior to his body being discovered.'

Her jaw dropped. 'But . . . No! He was alive when he left me! I never left the Blood-tower, except to . . .' Her eyes went to Gyle's face. 'Tell them! Tell them!'

His grey eyes were cold and remote. 'You are also charged with having unnatural relations with your maidservant, Tarita. You will also answer that charge.'

'No! No! You *know* that's not true!'

Even as she spoke her denial, she knew that whatever she said didn't matter.

I was seen leaving Francis' rooms, and he's dead. That must already be widely known, too credible to be denied. Francis is dead: the streets must be in uproar! I'd be seen as a heroine . . . so they need to break my reputation . . . With so many clergy locked up, deals could be cut around the one thing they can all agree on: that I need to die horribly, with my reputation destroyed.

Josip Yannos leaned forward. 'How do you plead, child?' His voice held just a trace of sympathy, as if he suspected this might be some ruse of Gyle's. But he was still obviously intent on self-preservation, and likely to do whatever Gyle had told him to.

Godspeaker Acmed just stared at her, a look of pure loathing on his face. He'd been a hard man to deal with at the council table, pricklish at being forced to deal with a woman, but she'd thought she had won him round – but it was his clergy Gyle was locking up, because of her Beggars' Court. If he was convinced she was safian, then any respect he might once have had for her would be gone, even without her apparent murder of Francis.

Francis is dead? Truly?

'I deny all of your trumped-up lies. I didn't kill the king! I'm not a safian! Sol et Lune, I've bedded the king more times than I can count!'

Gyle's mental voice filled her mind. *<Of course you are. I know it now: not Tarita, of course, but Portia Tolidi. Would you like to see her dragged into this?>* He sounded disgusted, personally offended.

She felt her heart hammering madly, thought it would burst. *How could he know . . . ?*

'Confess, Cera,' Gyle said aloud. 'Tarita has.'

The clergymen glowered at her, their faces filled with disgust.

No no no no. 'These are lies! If Tarita has confessed, then it is for fear of torture, not because it's true! What is it you really want? Tell me what concession you want and I'll give it. Just let her alone.'

Gyle turned to the three clerics. 'See how she thinks, my lords? It is as I told you: she is a devious, calculating creature. An unnatural being, barely female at all. What manner of true woman dares to sit upon a throne and call men to heel? Recall also that she consorted with Elena Anborn, a known safian.'

'Elena was no— And I'm not! You're lying! She was *your* lover, for years!'

Gyle curled his lip. 'I don't deny she had me fooled. But she revealed her true colours when she got her fingers into you.' He turned to the clergyman. 'You gentlemen will know what serpents women can be.'

'We know you lie, girl,' Tullesque purred. 'Your denials mean nothing at all. We have signed confessions from your maid herself. The trial will be but a formality. Confess, and speed the process.'

The three clerics nodded in unison, their eyes as condemning as Gyle's. 'Cera Nesti once claimed before her council to have the nature of a man,' Acmed noted. Cera remembered that meeting: she had humiliated the Godspeaker, forced him to back down on some issue. She'd thought the slight forgiven.

'Is this how you serve the shihad?' she asked him bitterly.

'Beings like you cannot serve the greater good, Cera Nesti,' the Godspeaker retorted, his iron face unflinching. 'A snake is only ever a snake.'

'On this we three are all agreed,' Josip Yannos added. 'A woman's place is in the home. A man's place is at the centre of affairs. The other proofs merely complete the picture.'

Mater Lune, spare me! 'That's the heart of it, isn't it? You can't stand the fact that I had the guts to stand up and fight for my family, and you're going to put me in my place. From daring to claim the Regency, to daring to hold court: I got above myself! All your lies and accusations boil down to that.'

The three clergymen regarded her with narrowed eyes. 'Perverse and wicked creatures cannot be permitted to live,' the Grandmaster declared. 'So says the *Book of Kore*, words echoed in every holy text.'

Acmed nodded in agreement. 'The *Kalistham* condemns such women utterly. "Let the woman who closes her womb to her husband and debauches in wickedness be returned to the earth",' he quoted.

'Confess, Cera,' Gyle advised. 'Or we will hand you over to the torturers to prove your guilt.'

Mater Lune, please! No— She felt her legs began to shake. Her father had waged a long struggle to have torture removed as a weapon of the judiciary, something she'd been immensely proud of. 'You're barbarians,' she spat. 'Torture is illegal here.'

'The Church of Kore is above your petty laws,' Tullesque said. 'We use whatever means we require.'

Tears were streaming down her face. She wiped at them furiously, ashamed at the terror and the weakness. 'Please, mercy. People will confess to anything under duress,' she babbled, then she began to scream, '*Tarita! TARITA!*'

'She calls to her lover,' Tullesque smirked.

'The death of King Francis has cast a pall over the city,' Gyle said, 'but the new Regent's Council, in the name of Francis Dorobon's unborn heir and headed by the Imperial Legate – as is my right in such a time of crisis – has regained control. Your fate is the last important impediment to peace in Brochena.'

She wanted only to curl up and die, but she needed to know. 'Where's Timori? He's just a boy—'

'The young king is well. Your attempt to kidnap him failed and your associates are dead. He will remain as our guest, a deterrent to hostilities being raised by his family.'

'Timi knew nothing of this. He's an innocent.'

'Of course he is,' Gyle said condescendingly. 'We don't make war on children, Cera.'

She blinked away tears, tried one last plea. 'Please, I have done nothing wrong. The country will rise if you kill me.'

'No, not for a perverted safian. Every judgement you decreed in the Beggars' Court is suspect. Civil law will be restored to a new Civil Justice authority, blending the clergy and the bureaucracy.'

Godspeaker Acmed nodded vindictively. 'When your crimes were made known, the population rose to condemn you. Your name is cursed in every Dom-al'Ahm.'

Her heart sank as his words sunk in. *Sweet Mater Luna . . . he's probably right . . .*

Gyle added, 'Rondian rule of Javon is here to stay, Cera. These clergymen recognise this. What is needed is a demonstration that most of our beliefs are akin: that Kore and Amteh and Sollan faiths alike recognise some truths as universal. One of those truths is that *frocio*, both male and female, are subhuman and must be exterminated.'

'What does Staria Canestos think of that?' Cera asked bitterly. *Where is my 'friend' now, anyway?*

'Staria knows which way the wind is blowing. Anyway, she is far away, at the Rift forts. So, I ask you again: how do you plead?'

She forced her eyes open, made herself look at him. 'Guilty. Guilty, and I would not change a single moment.'

487

24

Casting Stones

The 'Grave Matter' of Lineage

The matter of lineage is of great moment in theological debate in Rondelmar. The gnosis is irrefutably carried in the bloodlines, and dilution weakens the gift. This highlights the question of what else is passed down from father to son, mother to daughter. While skin colour, hair colour, build and facial stamp are all obviously linked, what of behaviours? The 'Grave Matter', as the Arch-Prelate terms it, is whether the child of a sinner is stained by their parent's guilt, and therefore doomed to the same sin?

SOURCE: ANNALS OF PALLAS

Brochena, Javon, on the continent of Antiopia
Rajab (Julsep) 929
13th month of the Moontide

Gurvon Gyle grasped the relay stave and readied himself for what was almost certainly not going to be a pleasant experience. Clearing his mind, he awaited the tickling touch of other minds. Coordinating the timing of such contacts when the participants were spread over different continents could be problematic. For a long time he was left waiting.

He was in Elena's training room in her tower, as high places were best for such Air-related gnosis as Clairvoyance. From it he could hear the incessant Jhafi chanting, through which the name of Cera Nesti ran through unmistakably, like a recurring note on a harp glissando. The level of devotion was unexpected, mostly by women, but not entirely. When soldiers drove them from the street, or even their own menfolk, many went to rooftops and continued their wailing. Not beatings, not even deaths had stopped them.

The clergy had lied to Cera Nesti when they told her she was universally condemned: in fact few believed the safian charges – even though they were true, and that was mortifying when Gurvon recalled how he'd once lusted for her himself. And now she was seen as a martyr-in-waiting. He'd lied to her about the maid too: Tarita had eluded capture and vanished.

For the first time in his life, he, Gurvon Gyle, Imperial Legate, was feeling out of his depth.

Until this mission in Javon, his forte had been small-scale plots, where the personalities of the key players were known and the variables relatively few. But here, cultural differences made the reactions of the people difficult to judge, and the scale of the operation meant that he didn't even know the names of potential key players. Mobs were mobs, but he was beginning to discover – a little late – that Jhafi crowds behaved differently to Yuros ones; they had different touchpoints and fault-lines. The clergy were self-deluded in their claims that the populace would follow them blindly. For every demonstration that burned the queen and her maid in effigy, there were a dozen singing hymns for her freedom. The energies that had been building through her Beggars' Court were turning into something even more dangerous.

Once she's been stoned, the fervour will die. She'll be forgotten.

<Magister Gyle?> Tomas Betillon's mental touch was like being slapped by a studded leather gauntlet. Simultaneously an image of the man's coarse face appeared in the smoke above the brazier in front of him. The echoing effect of using the staves reverberated around the chamber with a strange timbre.

<Governor Betillon, I am here,> he replied tersely.

<What the fuck is going on, Gyle?> the Governor of Hebusalim growled. *<You were told to keep Javon stable. Now you've killed bloody Francis Dorobon as well? What in Hel are you doing?>*

<I did not kill Francis and nor did I order his death.>

<You're in charge, Gyle, and that makes it your fault. We all knew that you'd move on Dorobon some time, but you were told not to jeopardise the situation until after the Moontide. If I had my way you'd be flayed.>

<I did not do this, and Francis Dorobon has no one to blame but himself. If he'd—>

He fell silent as the icy touch of Lucia Fasterius joined the link from the Summer Palace in Bres. Treasurer Calan Dubrayle and Arch-Prelate Wurther Dominius joined from Pallas, and then Kaltus Korion, from Kesh. Images of their faces formed in the air around him.

Terse greetings were exchanged, then Lucia turned to him and demanded, <Explain, Magister. Why is the person whose personal safety you guaranteed until after the Moontide now dead?>

<Make it good, Magister,> Dominius Wurther put in, <or I'll send a Fist of Inquisitors to ask you in person.> The Dorobon family were also his best friends now, it appeared.

Gurvon put on his most humble mental voice. <My lords, I swear upon my honour ... > He broke off as several of the listeners snorted openly. <I do have honour, although it may not be how you would define the term, and it may be more flexible than most, but it is real to me. I swore to keep the supply line open and I will. I swore to keep Javon secure and I will. But I am not responsible for Francis Dorobon's self-destructive stupidity.>

<He was murdered by the wife you arranged for him, Magister,> Mater-Imperia Lucia observed in her icy mental voice. <A mere human. How could that happen?>

He paused. This was the point where he had to make a decision on what to reveal. Should he maintain the fiction that was being presented as fact for the Javon court? Or should he reveal the true killer: one of his own agents (bad enough) – and Lucia's estranged and freakish daughter (even worse)?

The trail of questions over how he could have lost control of an agent and the circumstances of the killing were likely enough to have his title of Imperial Legate revoked. But there were ways out of this, if he had the nerve ...

<My lords, Cera Nesti has been put on trial and sentenced to die for the death of Francis Dorobon. But the truth is >– he took a deep breath – *<the real killer was Elena Anborn.>*

Silence greeted this announcement, but not derision. He took heart at that.

<We cannot permit the populace to believe that Elena Anborn could penetrate the palace, so we needed a scapegoat. Fortunately, Elena disguised herself as Cera to enter the king's chambers, and the guardsmen saw her come and go: this tale got out before it could be contained, giving us little choice: we either acknowledged Elena's success, or blamed the only credible option: Cera Nesti. It's a shame, because her marriage to Francis helped stabilise the transition, but now we have more troops, that need was less urgent anyway. We're still holding her younger brother as hostage.>

He got a few more seconds' respite as they took this in, then all the men spoke at once.

Kaltus Korion's voice rose above the rest. *<Elena Anborn? A year ago you told us she was possessed. Then suddenly she was raiding in north Javon! You told us she would be captured – how could you permit her to kill the Korebedamned King?>*

Gurvon quelled his temper, but let it inflect his reply. *<Elena is a trained assassin who has had four years to adjust to Javon. It took the empire twelve years to find the Kaden Rats. Elena is just as elusive.>*

Lucia's voice cut across the angry babble that rose at his defiance. *<How did she penetrate the palace?>*

He faced her image squarely. *<I believe Coin changed hands,>* he replied, with the slightest emphasis on the third word. Her eyes widened faintly. *Yes, your freak-child was involved, Mother of the Empire.*

<Has the problem been dealt with?> Lucia asked after a second in which she struggled to maintain her judgmental mask.

<Firmly and finally.>

Silence fell over the link and Gurvon could feel the confusion of the four men, who'd clearly been expecting Lucia to eviscerate him. He could sense them going back over the brief conversation, trying to work out what had changed, but he doubted any would understand.

While all knew she had a disowned child, most thought Yvette Sacrecour to be either confined or dead. He was pretty sure the codename 'Coin' had never been associated with Lucia, either publically or even in private circles. He only knew because he'd hired Yvette. *And I curse that day.*

Calan Dubrayle read Lucia's mood-change faster than the others, whether he understood exactly what was going on here or not. <*An embedded mage-assassin is a nightmare to deal with, Mater-Imperia,*> he said evenly, going for the voice of reason. <*Perhaps Magister Gyle has handled this situation as well as could be expected?*>

Tomas Betillon made a disgruntled sound. <*No, you can't let him off! He's fucked up once too often!*>

<*He's the one who let Anborn slip,*> Kaltus Korion reminded them all in a tight, angry voice. <*It's still his fault!*> He turned to face Mater-Imperia. <*You cannot let Gyle off the hook this time, Lucia. How many last chances are you going to give this worm?*>

Mater-Imperia did not look best pleased to be addressed on such familiar terms. Her eyes hardened to chips of ice. <*It is my prerogative to decide this, Kaltus. Not yours. Just as it is my prerogative to decide what roles any of you play.*> With that reminder of her authority hanging in the aether, she turned back to Gurvon. <*But I am far from pleased, Magister Gyle. You have manoeuvred yourself into a position of authority, then let us all down with your unique blend of chicanery and incompetence. You told us Elena Anborn was not a threat, when palpably she is. You claim that keeping Timori and Cera Nesti alive has prevented war, but I see no evidence of that. I've not used the words 'last chance' before, but I will now: you will find and kill Elena Anborn and bring convincing proof of her death by the end of Septinon, or you will be removed as Legate and arrested for treason. Am I understood?*>

He swallowed and hung his head. *Only the hint I gave of Coin's role in this débâcle has given me this small chance . . .*

He wondered for a moment what would happen if he simply told them all to go to Hel. After all, he controlled four legions and had a strong hold over the Dorobon one as well, now that Heale and Margham were onside. They'd barely reacted when Francis was found dead – they'd clearly thought him responsible, regardless of the blame shovelled onto Cera Nesti. Lucia would need to despatch at least eight legions to be sure of retaking Javon, and frankly, the Crusade couldn't afford that.

But there were other ways she could get to him: her own assassins, or trade sanctions, or simply outbidding him for the loyalty of Rykjard, Canestos, Frikter and the rest. *There will come a time for me to declare my autonomy, but that time is not yet . . .*

<*I understand perfectly, Mater-Imperia.*>

Betillon and Korion snarled disgustedly, while Wurther *tsked* softly.

For a few seconds silence reigned, then Dubrayle spoke again. <*Are we done on that matter? Well, while we are all gathered, I need to raise a matter concerning the supply of the Crusade. The Treasury has recently become aware of . . . fresh difficulties . . . resulting from price-inflation and speculative investment in the Crusade. The problem I mentioned last time we all spoke? It's worsened. Inflationary issuance is debasing the Rondian gilden and related currencies, resulting in—*>

<*Does anyone actually know what he is saying?*> Betillon complained.

<*I'll be damned if I know,*> Arch-Prelate Wurther remarked amiably. <*Which is of course theologically impossible, in case any of you were wondering.*>

<*Shut your fat face, priest,*> Korion snapped. <*He's talking about supplying my army. Say on, Treasurer.*>

<*Thank you,*> Dubrayle said tersely. <*As I was saying, there has been incredible use of illicitly authorised promissory notes issued in Dhassa and distributed in Dhassa, Kesh and Pontus. Benoit's merchant banks are technically insolvent to the power of eleven! My investigators have traced the source to Echor's army, Kore rest their souls.*>

<*Meaning?*> Betillon asked in a pointedly bored voice.

<*Meaning someone in Echor's army managed to raise credit on a fake Treasury seal?*> Gurvon asked. He'd done some counterfeiting in his time, but only coinage. <*That could only have begun if someone was convinced that the issuer was genuinely backed by you, Treasurer.*>

Dubrayle looked ready to spit. <*Yes indeed, something like that, Magister Gyle. It appears some military logisticalus tribunes produced the original*>

false promissories, crowing of incredible returns to be made from opium trading. They paid massive initial returns, and triggered the avalanche of money flowing into Pontus from the West. We've been forced to issue further promissory notes to stay afloat.>

<Opium, Calan?> Wurther tutted. <In the Treasury's name? My, my!>

Kaltus Korion pulled a face. <I still don't see what this matters. Imaginary money buys nothing.>

<That's where you're wrong,> Dubrayle replied. <Promissory notes aren't imaginary because they're issued with a value that the Rondian Treasury has pledged to support, and right now there are far more promissories in circulation than there is gold. We are one crisis of confidence away from the whole market collapsing.>

<So what? Pay in gold. Holy Kore, you make simple things complicated, Calan,> Betillon grumbled.

Dubrayle's gnostic image rolled its eyes. <Don't you get it yet? The empire could be bankrupted by this!>

That stunned them all into silence.

<Stop!> Lucia Fasterius said sharply. <Stop this discussion, right now! Calan, I'll not have you making statements like that without having given me the background information in detail first. Until then, this is just alarmist gossip that is serving no purpose.>

<But with all due respect, Mater-Imperia, I can't afford to pay for the next wagon caravan to leave Pontus,> Dubrayle replied, his normally calm voice beginning to fray. <There is not enough gold in Pontus to pay the suppliers, and I do not have enough bullion to cover the issuance of even a tenth of the promissory notes in circulation!>

They all fell silent again while Gurvon stared at his hands. *My gold ... my payment for securing Javon ... it's still in Pontus, with Jusst and Holsen Banking ...*

Lucia's face remained icily calm. <Calan, I want you to take a windship to Bres and join me at the Winter Court before the week is out. I want a briefing, in person. Meanwhile, the Royal Treasury will stop issuing gold and issue only promissory notes.> She held up a hand. <Yes, I know that means we're adding to the problem, but I will not see us part with gold in exchange for a

promise that someone may have no intention or even capability of honouring. I want us to have this problem under control by the time we all next talk ... in Septinon. Agreed?>

Dubrayle nodded shortly, the others grudgingly.

Lucia fixed her eye on Gurvon. *<And Magister, I'm well aware that you were expecting gold from us this month. You'll have to wait until you've captured Elena Anborn for us and thus secured your position. Though perhaps I could issue you with a promissory note instead?>* she added archly.

When the meeting was over, Gurvon sat for a long time in the tower room, barely able to think.

The clergy demanded a spectacle, and Gurvon was forced to give them one. The venue was a former gladiatorial arena set up by the early Rimoni settlers before they were forced to abandon the barbaric practice. It was now used for large-scale public entertainments like concerts, plays, and executions.

For two weeks the streets of Brochena had been awash in protest, factions of Jhafi clashing as they championed either Cera Nesti's innocence and heroism or her guilt and damnation. The city was exhausted after ceaseless chanting and marching, vigils, beatings, fighting, fires lit, rocks thrown at soldiers trying to keep the factions apart; it felt like the entire populace had been left gaunt and hollow-eyed.

Especially its Imperial Legate.

The Regency Council was presiding: Gurvon himself, plus Sir Roland Heale and Sir Craith Margham for the Dorobon, Grandmaster Etain Tullesque for the Church of Kore, and Endus Rykjard and Hans Frikter for the mercenaries. Gurvon found himself sitting beside Craith Margham, who displayed all the foppish airs of a Pallas courtier as he clutched a scented handkerchief to his nose and surveyed the crowd.

'Don't these wretches ever wash?' Margham complained. He was a pure-blood, and his line had adjacent lands in Rondelmar and a long alliance with the Dorobon. The young man clearly saw himself as the eventual new king, though they were all taking care to pretend they were acting for Francis' unborn child in Hytel.

The arena was filled past capacity, with more than a thousand Jhafi men, the most deeply fanatic Amteh worshippers, answering the Godspeaker's call for believers to come and hurl the stones that would batter their former queen to death. Commoners, Gurvon guessed: illiterate labourers and peasants. The mass of them together was overpowering, and there were thousands more in the streets outside. The Jhafi were at least six to one in favour of Cera, but the most violent were those here to kill the queen.

This event had split the Jhafi community body and soul, he knew that. Tens of thousands of them, more than half of them women, were holding vigil and prayer, led by moderate Ja'arathi clerics who were preaching in open defiance of Godspeaker Acmed al-Istan. If Gurvon strained, he could hear their chants even in here. One of the moderates, a Godspeaker named Talfayeed al'Marech, had even called for a Convocation of the Amteh, seeking to depose Acmed as head of the Jhafi faithful.

Far away, a bell tolled, and an expectant hush fell over the arena. The time had come.

Gurvon Gyle rose to his feet and called for silence. His words would be translated by the Scriptualist beside him, hopefully accurately. He'd been studying the language recently, using Mysticism to accelerate the learning, so he'd know if the man misquoted him.

He took a deep breath. 'People of Javon! Today heralds a new era of justice! Today, the Crown and the Amteh join with the Kore and the Sollan faith to bring down righteous punishment on the wicked!'

The men of the crowd crowed and shouted and waved the rocks in their fists. The noise was a wave that shook his throne. It made him wonder what it would be like to have that hatred turned on him, how it would feel to be the woman below, waiting to be led out. Rykjard's cordon of magi looked very few, compared to the bloodthirsty crowd.

In a box on the other side of the arena, Acmed al-Istan watched and waited, surrounded by grey- and white-bearded clerics. The Godspeaker looked unperturbed. Gurvon had found the man quite reasonable to negotiate with, despite his stiff-necked reputation. Acmed claimed to deplore the zeal of some in his flock. Gurvon wasn't fooled: he'd dealt with fanatics of the Kore many times and some of them were the blandest, most serene souls he'd ever met: they spoke in hushed voices and made the worst and most depraved deeds seem utterly reasonable.

Let's get this damned charade over with.

'Bring out the prisoner!' he shouted, screwing up his notes.

The call was taken up and below, the doors to the tunnel leading from the pits beneath were thrown open and a squad of armoured legionaries hauled out one small Jhafi woman. They had to raise shields as the first stones began to fly, hurled by men impatient for the killing to begin. It reminded him of hangings in Norostein, during the worst days after the Revolt.

Where's that damned maid? He'd wanted to have two prisoners to parade today, but Tarita had still not been found. He suspected Mustaq al'Madhi had her well-hidden. He'd have to deal with the crime-lord soon, but the man was increasingly hard to find.

He forced his eyes back to the young woman walking barefooted into the middle of the small circular arena. It was barely forty yards across, but the feverish heat of bloodlust filled the space. All of a sudden he didn't really want to watch – but he had no choice.

The queen was clad only in a rough shift. Her arms were bruised, her hair matted and tangled, her eyes buried in swelling and welts. She could barely stand, though she looked as if she was fighting for dignity. She was trying to speak but no sound came out. Her mouth was rimmed with blood from the removal of her tongue: he'd insisted upon that, to prevent any final words that might trigger chaos.

Beside him, Craith Margham turned suddenly and vomited. Roland Heale looked just as ill. These were noblemen who punished their subjects second-hand; they seldom had to deal personally with such things. He trusted this would be a lesson they wouldn't forget: *See? This is what I'm prepared to do to control Javon.*

To his left, Rykjard, Frikter and Tullesque appeared unmoved, as he'd expected. He nodded to them, then spoke again. First he announced that the maid Tarita had been strangled, as her station did not warrant death in this place. The crowd grumbled, but it was Cera they wanted anyway.

He addressed her next. 'Queen Cera Nesti! You are charged with regicide of the rightful king of Javon, Francis Dorobon, and you are jointly charged with the perversion of Safia. You have corrupted the royal marriage bed and brought dishonour on your house!'

He paused while the Scriptualist repeated his words in Jhafi. *I bet he didn't translate the word 'rightful'.*

The girl below stared up at him with blank eyes, swaying slightly. She was drugged to the point she could barely stand: the most mercy he could afford. 'You have confessed these sins,' he shouted. 'Let judgement begin.'

He picked up a rock.

He was a mage: he could ensure this stone killed her with one smashing blow to the skull, but then the crowd would be cheated of their part in the death and would look for other targets. There would be a riot.

The mob is thirsty, and their appetite must be met. Didn't I tell Cera something like that?

His rock struck the girl's belly, doubling her over. He heard one wordless cry from her ruined mouth, then the air filled with flying stones that thudded into the ground with hard cracking noises, or struck flesh and bone with a wet crunch. In the space of half a minute, the girl was reduced to unidentifiable pulp beneath a bloodied pile of stones.

25

Kirkegarde

The Inquisition and the Kirkegarde

*The Kirkegarde are the original defenders of the Church of Kore, a military arm
dedicated to protecting what is arguably the most powerful institution in Yuros.
The Inquisition came later, when Arch-Prelate Acronius won the right to hunt
down heresy within the empire. On one side the protectors, on the other the
hounds. The relationship between the two has been fractious, to say the least.*

ANTONIN MEIROS, ORDO COSTRUO, HEBUSALIM 742

Emirate of Lybis, Javon, on the continent of Antiopia
Rajab (Julsep) 929
13th month of the Moontide

Rutt Sordell was, true to his nature, a worried man. It was a default
emotion for him, and though he'd enjoyed the thrill of victory when
he'd brought down Coin, it was almost with relief that he lapsed
back into anxiety.

He was on the Lybis Road, still in Guy Lassaigne's usurped body.
Beside him Mara Secordin was sitting gracelessly on her mount,
sweating like a pig, while they waited with their escort for a band of
riders to reach them. He had been warned to expect the newcomers.

They swept up, the cohort of white-cloaked Kirkegarde riding
smooth-galloping mounts with the preternatural speed and intelligence of constructs. Each bore a single horn on their forehead:
khurnes, the new steed of choice. The Kirkegarde unit was a hundred

men, a fifth of the maniple, and it was led by Grandmaster Etain Tullesque himself.

He and Mara both knew the bargain Mater-Imperia had forced on Gurvon: find Elena Anborn or face arrest. Unexpectedly, Tullesque had volunteered his services in the hunt. Gurvon suspected Tullesque just wanted to claim the glory and negotiate for his own reward at their expense, but Rutt had to admit they needed the help.

Stay close to Tullesque, Gurvon had told him, *and don't trust him an inch.*

So as Tullesque reined in this khurne, he gave a grudging smile and bowed. 'I am at your command, Grandmaster.'

'Magister Lassaigne,' the Grandmaster replied condescendingly. 'Your mission remains the same: find and execute Elena Anborn. But now we do it my way.' A Grandmaster of the Kirkegarde might be effectively only a maniple commander, equivalent in military rank to a legion battle-mage, but Tullesque had a pair of junior Church-magi reporting to him, which regular battle-magi didn't, and he wielded all the authority of the senior clergy. He was tall and strongly built, though he had a dandy's air about him, with his shoulder-length curling hair and fashionably styled beard and his richly accoutred clothing, from the kidskin gloves to the non-standard silk cloak and tabard. But the Kirkegarde were among the best-trained and equipped soldiers in the empire, and in addition, he was also a pure-blood mage of some repute.

Tullesque nudged his horse closer and stared into Rutt's eyes as if trying to see the scarab within. 'Magister Sordell – although I understand that publicly I must address you as "Guy Lassaigne"?' he asked softly. His eyes held both the contempt of the soldier for men who wore disguises and the contempt of a mage for a man reduced to what Rutt now was. He raised his voice again: 'Well, Magister *Lassaigne*, I now control your mission and you will serve me. I have been briefed by Gyle himself.'

'Is Gurvon contactable?'

'Of course. But all communication is now to be through me.'

'But Gurvon knows the target intimately—'

'I know exactly how intimately he knew the target, Magister. I myself hunted you "Grey Foxes" in the Noros Revolt. We had some successes.'

Rutt's eyes narrowed. *Oh, did you just?* He recalled comrades who had been captured by the Kirkegarde and tortured to death, the desecrated bodies left to be found. *You're one of those, are you? Well, you didn't catch Gurvon, you didn't catch me and you didn't catch Elena.* Aloud he said, 'Elena Anborn is especially elusive, Grandmaster.'

'Well, we had best be on our mettle then,' Tullesque replied briskly, 'for my orders are that if she is not brought to justice, her former colleagues will be.'

'I have an Imperial Pardon,' Rutt replied stiffly. *They cannot . . .* He closed his eyes. *Of course they can. They can do whatever they damned well like.*

'What the emperor gives, he can take away,' Tullesque responded offhandedly. 'Come, show me your plans.' He eyed up Mara, then added, 'Just you, Lassaigne.'

Rutt was immediately uneasy. Big, ugly Mara was solid as the stones; her presence centred him. But he bowed and dismounted. 'At once, Grandmaster.' He strode towards his pavilion. 'This way.'

Inside, he poured arak. He couldn't go without the stuff these days; its bitter-sweet sting restored some equilibrium. Tullesque turned it down, muttering about 'foreign piss', which merely reflected his insular crassness as far as Rutt was concerned.

He pointed at the maps. 'There is a pattern to the way Elena operates,' he told the Grandmaster. 'She likes to pick off the weak and isolated, so we've created such a target for her. It's a typical caravan of goods and mail going to Lybis. We've loosed some whispers that a royal courier is travelling with it carrying letters for the Emir of Lybis – nothing that out of the ordinary, but unusual enough that it should gain her attention. We're tracking this courier, very loosely. It should be enough to draw her in. If she strikes, we close the net over her.'

'How is she travelling? Is she alone?'

'We believe she has an accomplice: a Keshi mage. They travel by windskiff, and only at night.'

'A Keshi mage ... Ordo Costruo?' Tullesque asked. 'I've heard the sultan had Dokken in his army at Shaliyah.'

'I've heard that too. Either, perhaps. Elena has no pride: she'll use anyone she can.'

Tullesque grunted, studying him. 'You absolutely hate her, don't you? I can read it in your face.'

'She destroyed my body, betrayed our cause ...' *Cast me out of her body. Killed half the team. Fucked us all over.* 'She deserves to die.'

'And this courier you're dangling as bait?'

'He's genuine: a sacrifice to bring Elena in. We expect to lose him.'

'I heard you were a cold fish, Sordell,' Grandmaster Etain sniffed. 'What are your own resources?'

'Me, Mara and a cohort of soldiers, plus we have some of Rykjard's men nearby, under Rhumberg.'

'That's not a large force.'

'Too many men will make Elena suspicious and scare her away.' He tapped his skull. 'I have divined the possibilities. This plan offers the best chance of success.'

'I have heard that you have some repute as a diviner. Have no fear, Magister: if we get even a sniff of Anborn's position, I'll get her. Our khurnes can outrun a windskiff over a short distance in all but gale conditions.'

Perhaps on a training ground, but on this terrain? 'Might I ask your affinities, Grandmaster?'

'Sorcery, Magister Sordell, with Fire and then Earth as my preferred channels.'

'So you are primarily a Wizard and Necromancer, Grandmaster?'

'Indeed, Magister Sordell. No need for me to ask your skills: I've been told all about you.' He suddenly kindled purple light in his right fist that flared into Rutt's eyes while he uttered a series of alien clicking, whirring sounds. Abruptly, Rutt felt as if the roof of his mouth was being torn open and purple light started gushing forth as he lost control of his limbs and fell to his knees. For a panic-filled few seconds he lost all sight and smell, then touch was the final sense to fail him. His last sensation was something hard scrabbling inside his blood-filled mouth. Then he *was* that thing, the scarab that contained his soul, pushing through flabby lips into the light.

Something vast reached down and grasped him and he was lifted and held in a gauntlet, dripping blood and the protective slime he secreted inside the cavity he'd burrowed in Lassaigne's head. 'Ah, Magister Sordell, there you are,' boomed Tullesque. The sound was deafening. Rutt rolled up his many legs, cringing, his feelers bending inwards, his mandibles clicking frantically.

'You see, Magister,' Tullesque said, 'when you lost your original body, you became a lesser being, and as such, vulnerable to other Necromancers. Do you understand me? I could crush you in my hand and you would become nothing more than pulped shell and scum. For that is all you are now, Rutt Sordell: *scum*.'

Tullesque dropped the scarab and he fell and landed on Guy Lassaigne's vacant face. The young man was still breathing and he crawled back inside the mouth as quickly as he could, burrowing back into the roof of the mouth with desperately flailing legs.

As he reconnected to the gnosis channels he had established normal human vision returned, then, slowly, his control of the body. It hadn't been quite perfect, and now it would take days to recover full control.

Iwillkillyou Iwillkillyou Iwillkillyou . . .

'No, you won't, Magister Sordell,' Tullesque replied with smug condescension. 'You will do nothing of the sort. Instead, you will serve me as fervently as you have ever served Gyle, and you will be grateful to do so. Understood?'

Rutt could barely focus his eyes as he crawled to his knees. In the moments of unconsciousness Lassaigne's bladder had relaxed and the smell of piss filled the tent. 'I understand,' he croaked, biting his tongue over the last syllable and convulsing in pain.

'Excellent,' the Grandmaster purred. 'It's good to have a clear understanding over the pecking order, don't you think?' He turned back to the charts. 'So, how shall we set this trap?'

Elena Anborn crept to the ridgeline, hidden deep in the shadow, then edged through a gap so she could see the road below. Heat radiated from the rocks, through her leathers and into her flesh, though evening was coming. She was sweating uncomfortably with the exertion of maintaining a shield and the stress of remaining unseen. Below, the wagons under the Dorobon flag moved slowly. They were well-guarded, but most were these days. Security was tightening along all the roads, even here, where she'd not yet struck. Word from Mustaq al'Madhi suggested that this caravan included a royal courier.

Kazim ghosted into place beside her. 'What do you think, Ella?'

'It's well guarded. Two magi this time – so perhaps there really is a courier in that carriage.'

'There are two of us as well.'

'I don't like this one, Kaz. It's the first one we've been told about, rather than finding on our own. That's enough to make it smell bad.'

Kazim nodded slowly, and she was reminded that one of the many things she liked about him was his growing maturity and patience, the way he no longer rushed in thoughtlessly. 'So we let it go?'

'Perhaps. Just because it might be a trap doesn't mean there's nothing to learn. Let's keep watching.'

They were probably halfway to Lybis, in a broken landscape of fractured hills and gritty flatlands. Spindly trees and tough, reedy grass tried to find purchase in the sun-baked soil, and roaming herds of small antelope and deer were stalked by lions and jackals. A string of tiny settlements lined the roads, tending plots of grain and small herds of hump-backed cattle. The lack of water kept the gatherings small and poor, among the poorest in Javon.

The shadows lengthened and the sun dived towards the horizon, and when nothing had come past their vantage in the half-hour since the wagon-train had gone, Kazim touched her shoulder. 'I do not think there is any trap.'

'Do you not?' She placed her ear to the rock. 'Listen.'

He followed her example, pressing his own ear to the cooling stone. After a moment he discerned a faint rhythmic thud reverberated distantly through the earth which resolved itself into the sound of horses, appearing through the haze on the road two hundred yards below: a dozen white-clad riders, their lance-pennants and shields bearing the red heart and silver dagger of the Kore. There were two non-knights with them, clad in Dorobon blue.

'Kirkegarde,' she whispered. 'Soldiers of the Church of Kore.' And that confirmed the rumour Mustaq had passed down, that the Dorobon's Church knights had been sent this way. 'Those are Dorobon magi with them.'

'What are they riding?'

She squinted – his eyesight was better than hers, she had to admit – and just made out that the Kirkegarde had what looked like some kind of ceremonial head-mounting on their horses' heads. 'Just horses, I think, with an armour spike?'

He shook his head. 'No, it's a horn. Are horned horses native to Yuros?'

'No – I've never seen them before. Perhaps it's some new kind of construct.'

'Are there no ends to the perversions of you magi?'

She smiled grimly. 'Probably not. So let's keep our heads down.'

They pressed further into the shadows as the sun fell and the Kirkegarde moved onwards and out of sight. Light leached away, turning the brown earth and the blue skies to pale grey, and Luna rose in a waxing crescent, her pitted face spilling silver light across the ground, enough to just see by. This time they really were about to leave when she heard the second force rumble past. This time they had wagons of their own, and a cohort of plain red-cloaked mounted legionaries as well as many more of the Kirkegarde. And jolting along awkwardly among them, she could just make out a huge cloaked shape riding a cart-horse.

Mara Secordin . . . what's she doing out here?

Beside her rode a man with blond hair, and though he wasn't close enough to recognise, she knew that hair-style. Habits die hard, and she was willing to bet that one of the first things Rutt Sordell did when he took a new body would be to tailor that host to his own ways. *So at least we know who we're up against . . .*

They slipped below the ridge and away, winding back through the empty land as the night fell around them. The only sounds were the distant, mournful yowls of the jackals. The skiff was hidden a mile away, their camp already set up. They lit a sheltered fire, boiled spiced lentils and then ate. They made love, then lay a little apart, letting the night air cool their sweat.

'So, what will we do?' Kazim whispered.

'Spring the trap – but not the way they think.'

He caressed her forehead, ran fingers through her hair. 'You knew some of them, didn't you? I could tell by the way your breathing changed.'

He sees so much now. It was part of how their auras were beginning to blend. She'd given up trying to stop it; it just kept happening, faster than could be prevented. They were turning into something new: two bodies, one aura. Perhaps only physical separation could stop that? That was the last thing she wanted.

'Rutt Sordell was there. He nearly killed me, back in Brochena. He stole my youth, for a time, using necromancy. I went grey – it took me months to recover. He's a body-thief now, a little beetle.'

His eyes narrowed. 'The one that crawled from your mouth?'

'Yes, exactly. And Mara Secordin's here too. She's a monster, nothing more or less.' She looked up at Luna's silver arc. 'I'd like to kill them both, if I can. It's long overdue.'

'You keep telling me not to let emotion colour my thinking,' he chided her.

'I know, but this is why we fight: to rid the world of people like Rutt and Mara.'

'I understand. But how will we do it?'

She kissed his cheek and whispered, 'As it happens, I've got a plan.'

26

The Sacred Lake

Hermetic Magic

Hermetic Magic, first codified by the Ascendant Bravius, is the application of the gnosis to manipulating living things, and was the second branch of the gnosis defined, after Thaumaturgy. Bravius identified four facets, based upon whether it was applied to plants or to living creatures, and whether that was used for healing or for altering or dominating those creatures. Thus a Hermetic Mage can be as diverse as a Healer, a Woodworker, a Beast-tamer or a Shapeshifter.

SOURCE: ORDO COSTRUO COLLEGIATE, PONTUS

Lybis, Javon, on the continent of Antiopia
Shaban (Augeite) 929
14th month of the Moontide

Elena peered through the stone lattice at the crowds, mostly women, marching past below. There were thousands of them and the air was throbbing with their chanting and wailing. Many had lowered their bekira-shrouds, apparently so that they could rip clumps of their hair from their bleeding scalps as they wept. There was an air of mass hysteria about the whole procession as they displayed their sorrow and fury, baring and then pummelling or even lacerating their breasts, all the while wailing louder and louder. She'd seen such sights before when prominent Jhafi had died, but nothing had ever come near this. The sounds and sights etched themselves into her brain, made her skin tighten like drum skins and her ears throb. Every women marched with her left hand in the air, the Nesti crest etched in henna on the palm, or freshly carved in with a knife. 'CERA! CERA!' they shouted, and her name came echoing back from the surrounding mountains.

'It's been like this for days,' Emir Mekmud bin al'Azhir told them. 'Ever since the news came of the death of the Dorobon. We do not believe the lies they say, that she was a perversion. She has slain the Dorobon king. She is a hero-queen, like the legends tell: a martyr of the shihad. So they march: women mostly, but many men also. It has not abated, even though word has come that Cera Nesti is dead.'

Cera is dead. Elena could barely believe it, though all along she'd feared Gurvon would turn on her former charge. 'Has there been rioting?'

'No, except for a few hotheads and criminals who sought to use this situation to their own advantage. The people know that my sympathy lies with the queen as well, and I have not sought to hinder their demonstrations. They march round the lake seven times daily, as a sign of bonding themselves to Queen Cera. They burn effigies of Gurvon Gyle and call on me to rise against the Dorobon.' He chuckled. 'All quite peaceful, really.'

The emir was not a man from whom laughter was ever expected, but he had a subtle sense of humour. He was almost as large as Kazim, though his waist was thickening as his life became less about riding and raiding and more about ruling and judging. He was a man entirely composed of rough edges: he had a rugged, weatherbeaten face, stern eyebrows and a thick, unkempt beard. Elena had met Mekmud once before, when Olfuss still reigned, when he'd come to Brochena for some state occasion. She'd been impressed then by his zeal and intelligence, and his ability to hold a grudge. He wasn't an immediately likable man, but he was a fearsome presence.

Lybis was one of the most isolated of the cities of Javon, not so much by distance as by the terrain. It lay high in the mountains of the western coastal range, around a sacred lake, and the road there was difficult, especially the latter stretches. Elena and Kazim had flown over it the previous day, and realised it would take Sordell's party more than a week to get here: so plenty of time to arrange a welcome.

Lybis had a long history, mostly of banditry and cattle-raiding onto the plains. The castle had been considered impregnable until the Rimoni and Jhafi had combined forces and brought modern siege equipment to pummel the walls. The emir of the time had sued for peace; his mighty outer defences had been torn down and he had pledged never to rebuild them. No emir since then had broken that promise – but they had vastly strengthened the inner walls, the palace-keep where Elena now stood. Mekmud's ancestry informed the way he viewed the world: as a hunting ground, where status, safety and security were won by the strong, the fierce and the cunning.

'CERA! CERA! CERA!'

The rhythmic chant intruded again, drawing her attention back to the masses below as they continued to flow past. There were dozens of young women, bare to the waist and smeared in animal blood, being carried on the shoulders of their men-folk while they howled in grief and outrage. None of them would have ever even seen Cera Nesti, let alone met her.

I knew her better than anyone, and all I feel is . . . what?

'Lady Elena, about your plans—' the emir began.

She raised a hand to stop him, too overcome to deal with the practical just now. 'Please, I wish . . . I need to be alone.'

Mekmud had probably never been spoken to so abruptly by a woman in his life – but this was not just a woman: this was the legendary Elena Anborn. The White Shadow, the Jhafi were apparently calling her. He closed his mouth and left. Kazim looked at him, then her, and followed.

She turned back to the lattice, letting the sounds from below wash over her.

Cera – oh Cera, what have they done to you?

They had not expected to find the city of Lybis in ferment, but a windskiff had flown in, part of the Dorobon courier network, with news that King Francis Dorobon was dead, murdered in his bed by

Cera Nesti. There was a sordid story being circulated of Cera and her maid Tarita being safian lovers, but the Jhafi had simply refused to believe that: Cera was a heroine and a martyr and it didn't matter what lie the Rondians used to justify their murder of her. Apparently a Regency Council had been formed in the name of the baby growing in Portia Tolidi's belly. They'd condemned Cera and Tarita to death and carried out the sentence before Elena even heard the news.

The awful thing was, Elena did not know how to grieve. Cera had been like a younger sister during her time as bodyguard to the Nesti children, her favourite: smart, diligent, and passionate about statecraft and politics. When Olfuss had been murdered, Cera had become her younger brother's regent and Elena her closest confidante. For a time it had seemed that nothing could stop them. They had won over Olfuss' officials and advisors, defeated the Gorgio and driven Gurvon's magi into hiding.

But then Gurvon did what Gurvon did: he *polluted* things, twisted and confused people until they acted against their nature, all the while believing they were doing the right thing. Cera was just an immature girl, besieged and tricked into doubting her closest counsellors and falling under the spell of her enemy.

When Cera betrayed Elena, handing her over in exchange for Gurvon's pledge to protect her family from the Crusaders, she doubtless thought she was preserving her line. It was the kind of cold-hearted decision that Elena herself had coached her in, feeding her political books on statecraft written by some of the most ruthless minds in history, filling her head with the need to separate heart and head. The irony was that at that time, Elena herself had been losing her faith in such methods; she had been relearning love and compassion.

So how can I hate you, though I once said I'd kill you myself?

And how can I grieve, after what you did to me?

But she did grieve, here where she was alone. She slid to the ground, and let the tears flow. Her shoulders heaved as she tried to breathe through the horrible pain of visualising a faraway arena and *her girl*, alone in a crowd of hate, as the stones began to fly.

Whether Cera had been safian or not, she didn't care. She'd known men who loved men and women who loved women and she wasn't about to judge. The fringes of society, where she'd lived most of her life, attracted such people. They had their passions and cares, the same as anyone else's, but different too, because they were always wary of exposure, judgement and condemnation. Living as a spy wasn't so different: you concealed who you really were, took fleeting consolation when you could, and tried to maintain the façade of normality.

To Gurvon it's just a move in the game. He doesn't give a shit that two beautiful young women died horribly because of it. And the Sollan and Kore priests and Amteh Godspeakers who put their name to supporting it, damn them too. Who is their imaginary god to condemn love of any kind?

When at last she looked up again, the sounds had dimmed as the marchers had passed by and were heading out around the lake again. The streets below fell into the never-quite silence of city life. She wiped her eyes.

Kazim was leaning against the doorway to the small chamber, watching her. When she saw him he hurried to her. 'Are you all right?' he asked, bending over her, offering a hand up.

She slapped his hand away, not sure why except she was angry, now the sorrow had been wept away. 'I'm fine,' she snapped, clambering to her feet. 'I said I wanted to be alone.'

'I thought you wanted to kill her yourself?' he said, his face puzzled.

'Well I can't now, can I?'

'Is that why you're upset?'

She whirled on him. 'Of course it rukking isn't! Imbecile!'

'But if she did . . . *that* . . . then she deserves to die. It is the law.'

Her temper snapped. 'Oh, is that right? Those dirty girls deserved to die, did they? Too bad she was sold into marriage to a fucking idiot and made to do whatever he wanted! Too bad she was surrounded by poisonous bastards like Gurvon until she don't know what wall to put her back against!'

'But it's the law . . . If every woman—'

'Oh shut up! Tarita wasn't safian! I know that for a fact! And I very much doubt Cera is either. And even if they were, why should they be killed?'

'But the *Kalistham* says—'

'The *Kalistham* says,' she echoed with dripping sarcasm. 'The *Book of Kore* does too: books written by poisonous old men who hate women and hate love because they'll never know it and don't want anyone else to put something ahead of their god. Everything pleasurable in life is anathema to them, because the only happiness they acknowledge is some paradise you can only reach by dying!'

Kazim's mouth dropped open.

She had to fight not to slap him. 'Do you love me?' she rasped.

'Huh?'

'I said, do you love me? Simple question: you say you do all the damned time! Say it now!'

He blinked, wavered. 'I . . . yes, I love you . . .'

'Good, now take a stone and throw it at me.'

'What?'

'Go on!' she looked around, spied a small pile of stones left over from a recent repair, flicked her hand and made one sail into Kazim's hand. He caught it, staring.

'Ella, what are you doing?'

'Go on, killer! Throw the rukking stone at me. I've lain with women, two of them. Once when I was a stupid college girl wondering who I was, because my sister told me I was a safian because I liked sword-fighting and archery: so when a girl who really was safian made advances, I tried it. It wasn't my thing. But still, when a mission called for me to seduce a target's wife, I did it. She was good, too: she wet my purse.' She glared furiously at him. '*Now, throw the fucking stone!*'

He dropped it, backed away and fled.

And she collapsed to her knees again, and those Kore-damned tears flooded out, more of them than she'd ever imagined, and she couldn't make them stop.

Rutt Sordell stared at the back of Etain Tullesque's head as the column wound its way into Lybis, another clay-coloured semi-ruined maze of stone and shadows, but this one was the end of the road, a hill-town built around a so-called sacred lake. There had been some trouble at the gates with Jhafi mourners for the queen. The towns-folk were still chanting Cera Nesti's name, as if her calumny meant nothing. *Kore's Blood, the histrionics of mourning here are incredible!* The Kirkegarde had needed lances to drive the crowds back.

Of course, it could have been handled better, with some show of respect perhaps, but Tullesque had allowed blood to be spilled and the crowds had grown and started hurling abuse and stones at them. *Kirkegarde: they never change.*

In the Noros Revolt, Rutt had attached himself to Gurvon Gyle's Grey Foxes, even though he was an Argundian, and the Revolt wasn't his fight. War meant easy access to dead bodies. Necromancy had many uses, and a lot of those were not sanctioned by the Gnostic Code – the most interesting parts, in his view. Not all the Foxes had wanted him, but Gurvon needed a Diviner and Necromancer in his unit and he'd soon proved himself. Gurvon didn't care *how* he got information as long as he got it, and Rutt could wring secrets not just from the living and the dead, but from the spirits too. *If you'd fallen into my hands, Etain Tullesque, I'd have had you begging for mercy through your toothless gums ...*

A pleasant fantasy, when Tullesque could crush him like a cockroach.

The journey to Lybis had taken two weeks and still Elena Anborn had not shown her face. Every passing day mocked them. *She's no fool. She's seen through this foolish trap – and who wouldn't?* He hung his head, clenched his teeth. *We're failing Gurvon.* He glanced back at Mara, who had two pythons draped about her torso and shoulders. Her massive horse was wobbling from her weight and its eyeballs were almost popping out with terror, despite her gnostic control. The crowd were terrified of her.

<Still no Elena,> he sent to the ogress.

<She's near,> Mara returned, grimacing at every jolt of her horse. <I feel her eyes on us.>

<She won't try anything, not with all these damned Kirkegarde around.>

<If it was just us, she would try to kill us. I can feel her hate.> No one knew about the hunger of enmity like Mara Secordin. It was pretty much all there was to her.

The column clattered into a plaza where a Dom-al'Ahm faced the buttress of a keep built from pinkish sandstone blocks. The Kirkegarde's unearthly steeds reared in unison, driving the press of people to the fringes, allowing Grandmaster Tullesque to canter over the flagstones unimpeded, right to the gates. Wisely, they were open, and the local lord stood waiting humbly, without even a bodyguard. Emir Mekmud bin al'Azhir, head of the ruling house, was a barrel-chested man with a tough reputation, but he offered no threat.

The crowd were *that* close to rioting, but the Kirkegarde were used to hostile mobs. Some rocks were thrown, but when gnosis-fire was kindled, the people drew back.

Rutt rode through the swirl of horsemen at Tullesque's back, Mara just behind. The Grandmaster remained mounted, peering down at the emir with condescension all over his face. Mekmud bin al'Azhir remained impassive as Tullesque motioned Rutt forward. 'You speak the language? Tell them I require his palace. We will make it our base while searching for the Anborn woman.'

Rutt did as he was bid, awkwardly but apparently effectively. He'd used the gnosis to learn the Jhafi tongue, though he seldom practised.

'The slayer of King Olfuss,' Emir Mekmud welcomed Rutt sarcastically. They'd met once before, when Gurvon's new bodyguards had been welcomed to Brochena, more than six years ago now. 'My house is yours.' He turned on his heel and marched away contemptuously. His soldiers watched stony-faced from the walls.

It took almost an hour to get everyone inside and to ensure all of the emir's men were out. Only servants were permitted to remain; the women among them were relatively safe as the Kirkegarde would not rape Noorie women – not out of pity, but to protect their own sanctity. The servants still looked terrified; they probably had no idea they were not pure enough for the holy soldiers.

I don't like this, Rutt thought as they entered the palace. *It's too much like putting one's head into a lion's mouth.* But Gurvon had put Tullesque in charge and he didn't have to like it, he just had to obey.

Elena watched the Kirkegarde enter Lybis from a balcony on a large house on the far side of the lake. The famed Gulabi Zenana, the Pink Palace, housed the emir's many wives. It had one hundred windows, all facing the lake, and each had a tiny room behind where the emir's wives had roughly ten square metres each to themselves. It was usually abuzz with music and singing and the babble of female voices. The top level was a pleasure suite, where the emir consorted with his wives; that was where she and Kazim had been housed.

She was still staring out over the lake when the emir arrived. Kazim was off somewhere, sulking over their argument. *I guess I'm sulking too,* she admitted to herself. Being apart from him hurt; their auras were straining for each other.

'Lady Alhana?' Mekmud's hard face regarded her evenly, but there were flickers of doubt in his eyes.

He knows I've been crying. He thinks I'm weak. She rose, bowed like a man. 'Emir, we are ready.'

'You are resolved to make your strike here, Lady?'

'Yes, Emir. But are you ready also? This is a big step: open rebellion against the Dorobon. Even the Nesti have not done so. There will be repercussions.'

Mekmud made a dismissive gesture. 'They think they can come here, to my city, and demand my house. They take my rooms and eat off my plates. One hundred and twenty men, in a city of thirty thousand souls. The arrogance steals my breath. The insult to the honour of my fathers stuns me. Had you not counselled me to do otherwise, the gates of the city would have been closed to them and we would have fought. My people demand it, for the honour of Cera Nesti. They believe she will reach down from Paradise to aid us. So it is time to teach these Rondians that the Jhafi are not craven and the men of Lybis least of all.'

'They have seven magi: three Kirkegarde, two Dorobon and two mercenary. The magi alone could bring your palace down around your ears if this goes badly.'

'I would rather be a lord of rubble than allow them another night of peace, Lady Alhana,' the emir growled. 'I do not count the cost. A man cannot, when honour is at stake.'

I won't debate that point with you right now.

'Your young man reminds me of my younger self,' Mekmud noted. He looked away, coughing a little, as he did when discussing something personal. 'You and he are lovers, yes?'

'We are,' she replied, hoping that was still the case.

'I have Hadishah contacts, Lady. They say Kazim Makani is a renegade, not to be trusted.'

'I trust him with my life.' *And my heart.*

Mekmud looked at her appraisingly. 'You argued, earlier.'

The whole city probably heard us. 'A small matter.' She sipped some rose sharbat, and sought a new topic. 'How do you view the execution of the queen, Emir?'

He shrugged. 'She is a martyr.'

'And the charges against her?'

Mekmud scowled. 'Lies, probably.' He glanced about him. 'Lady Alhana, I have many wives and they dwell here in this palace, the Gulabi Zenana. When I wish to see one, she is summoned to this upper suite, for me to enjoy her yoni. I have favourites, but few of my wives have any great wit or conversation; most were selected to pacify certain key allies and rivals. Some I see perhaps once a year. They live their entire lives in this place, forbidden to see anyone but each other. They have their own hierarchy and politics, I do not doubt. They have no understanding of my world, and I have no understanding of theirs. If I were to learn that some *entertain* each other in private, I might be concerned, but I do not go out of my way to know. So long as the only lingam that enters their yoni is mine, and no one's honour is called into question, little else matters.'

Elena nodded slowly. *That's probably as liberal and open an attitude as any male has in this age and place*, she reflected. *Any male at all, actually, regardless of his faith.*

He raised a finger. 'This does not mean that I condone such debaucheries, Lady Alhana. But if a ruler is to avoid falling overly under the influence of the clergy, they *must* retain a healthy sense of scepticism. Otherwise a holy man will twist you around his fingers, because he has the ultimate argument at his disposal: that he speaks for his god. A ruler *must* view clerics as *fallible humans*, not a mouthpiece for the divine. Otherwise the ruler will become a tool of that cleric.'

Mekmud picked up his own sharbat and took a sip. 'So when I hear that a woman is to be tried and condemned by clerics, I perceive weakness on the part of her family. Her guilt is for the family to decide, and the punishment also. Cera Nesti killed an infidel usurper: her name should be being trumpeted to the throne of Ahm, not decried by Acmed's brood! Acmed is bargaining with Shaitan himself – that is what is clear to me.'

'All three faiths united to condemn her,' Elena noted.

'But the people on the street see more clearly than the clergy,' Mekmud replied. 'It is as I say: the holy men are fallible. But rest assured,' he added dryly, 'I am not.'

She smiled. 'Then how can we fail?'

Mekmud raised his cup. 'To our success, Lady Alhana. The struggle for freedom starts here.'

Rutt Sordell and Mara Secordin were given small suites next to each other and overlooking the lake, with stairs down to private bathing ghats. Bathing in this particular lake was supposed to wash away sin – a ridiculous notion, in Rutt's view: the water was thick with mud and floating offerings of flowers rotting in the water. He wouldn't bathe in it even if he was caked in shit.

The lake was fed by trickling snow-fed streams but warmed by the summer sun. Bathing was part of Javon's religious culture, and on the far side he could see masses of locals, dark-skinned people of all ages, mingling on the public ghats, their colourful clothing laid out on the stone to dry in the sun. The communal nature of it stirred something unexpected in him. He'd been a solitary man all his life, living for the gnosis: the thrill of a successful divination, or the prising of knowledge from a trapped soul, these were his pleasures. He was an explorer at the edges of awareness and consciousness, a pioneer of the mind. These weeks on the road had cost him much research time and he resented every second, especially as he knew he needed to read the spirit world if he was to find a way to free Gurvon.

As he stared out of the barred window he saw Mara emerging below. She waddled down the stairs, one of her pythons still wrapped about her. He had no desire to see her disrobe, and no real interest in the commotion that would ensue soon on the far side when a swimmer on the edge of the crowd was pulled under and never emerged again, not when there was finally time to light his brazier and enter the unknown.

With a slightly martyred sigh he turned his back on the light and life outside and began to set up his tripod. To the heated bowl he added special powders that eased contact with the spirit world while he chanted a repetitive mantra, a form of self-hypnosis to get himself into the right frame of mind. He inhaled the smoky air and closed his eyes.

'Elena Anborn,' he said, dropping the name into the void, where it was heard by the hundreds of prickling intellects that listened in the aether, some of the millions of tiny nodes of awareness that formed the web of souls. 'Where is Elena Anborn?'

The spirits began their whispered replies, sibilant hisses and half-heard sighs that bypassed his ears and bedded in his mind. Minutes crawled by like hours. Then his eyes flew open.

She's here!

Elena drifted about in the water, wrapped in a bekira-shroud to mask her colouring. She had on only a thin shift over her undergarments so as not to hamper her movement. There were Jhafi all around her, washing, praying, playing, but none took notice of her, repelled by a subtle gnostic working that made her uninteresting, not worth looking at. Her eyes were fixed on the far bank.

<There's Mara,> she sent to Kazim, who responded sullenly. Things were still awkward, and had been for the past two nights. Her furious outburst had clearly troubled him. *I should've kept my mouth shut. He didn't need to know that shit.* It was their first real argument since

they'd become lovers, and it was as if the magical bubble around them had been pricked. Suddenly everything about their relationship felt like it was built on flimsy foundations. Lying in the pleasure suite of the Gulabi Zenana, on the same bed but not touching, was worse than going into battle. She desperately wanted his arms about her, but they were both too angry to try and make up. And the threads linking their auras, which had been becoming so entwined, had severed as if a knife had passed between them.

We're too different. Our love can't last. Losing him terrified her, but she didn't know how to go about making up, so instead she swallowed her bile and focused on the task at hand. She was about to take a huge gamble, taking on Mara Secordin in her primary habitat.

Mara's favoured aquatic shape was that of a huge water-beast, a thing the coastal villagers of Yuros called a shark. It was a shape she had taken so often and for so long that she had lost most of what made her human. Some days she could barely talk, and even the faintest trace of blood could drive her mad. She was also one of the deadliest beings Elena had ever met. Mara was purpose made flesh; her combination of Hermetic and Water-gnosis gave her access to Animagery, Healing and Shaping – so her body could take huge punishment and still recover. That combined with her ability to rip a man or even a horse to pieces in an eye-blink meant that even purebloods who had tried to stop her had invariably died. If she was trouble on land, in the water she was even worse, where the elegantly brutal body of the shark allowed her an attack speed of more than forty-five feet per second. Elena had seen the effects for herself several times.

I must be insane.

But water was also where Mara would be least wary, for she regarded herself as invulnerable there. Elena's theory was that it would be in her natural element that Mara might be vulnerable, for in water she lost all reason and humanity and reverted completely to the beast inside.

So as the mountain of flesh on the far side of the lake descended the stairs, peeled off her snakes and her clothing and lowered herself into the water, Elena pushed off from the ghat and slid from her bekira-shroud as she went under, away from the shore to the deeper waters where the silt and muck below was undisturbed. Her Water-gnosis supplied breathable air and her fingers and toes webbed a little, to speed her passage. The Jhafi bathers fell behind her and within moments she was quite alone. Gnostic sight allowed her a kind of vision, based on the aura of living things, or their absence. She groped through the filthy depths, seeking what she'd planted there the previous night.

She found it quickly: a small, distended body, a Jhafi boy of maybe eight years old, a hole in the aura of life. It was emptied of blood and spells had been laid on the flesh so that the eels and fish would leave it untouched. A chain ran from out of his mouth towards the shore. Mekmud had obtained his body for her; he'd been an orphan, doomed for an unmarked grave. To use him this way was repugnant, but necessary.

Carefully, she unsheathed her dagger and put it between her teeth, then pulled a small vial from her bodice and unstoppered it. Red fluid radiated out into the water and dissipated: *blood – her own blood*. They said that in the ocean, a shark could sense blood in the water over very great distances.

About half a minute later, from over a hundred yards away, a giant water-beast quivered at the taste of the fluid and its eyes went from black to red.

Lybis reminded Kazim of Baranasi, though this was only a lake, not a river, and the lake was only four hundred yards across and apparently only twenty feet at its deepest. Sacred bathing in this land where water was life and death was primarily a Lakh custom, but here in Lybis the tradition had been translated into a peculiarly Amteh variant, with bathers strictly segregated, and only the men permitted to disrobe at all. Even so, it had become imbedded in Lybis culture.

Beside Kazim was a white-clad young man. He was a Scriptualist, a spindly boy with a fluffy beard, who reminded Kazim of Haroun. He was of the same ilk, too: serious and self-righteous. He'd been mesmerised by Elena to think Kazim was his superior and now he was waiting to do whatever Kazim told him.

He peered across the water and focused on a shape in a distinctive bekira-shroud, black with a triangle pattern on the edging of the robe. Elena. As she moved out into the depths and then dropped from sight, he turned and tapped the boy on the arm, and he responded as instructed by ringing his bell.

As the bell rang, men and women began to leave the water, climbing the wet stairs to the many Dom-al'Ahms that faced the water, some large and some tiny. The water emptied of everyone except Elena and Mara, both unseen below the surface. *Be safe, Ella*, he prayed silently. *Ahm watch over you.* He looked up at the sky. *I mean it! You look out for her, or you'll answer to me.*

Ahm doesn't care about half-safian white women, the dark voice at the back of his brain told him. It spoke in the tones of all the Godspeakers and Scripturalists he'd ever met, but mostly it spoke in Haroun's voice.

He hung his head, heartsick at his confusion. He'd never been able to deal with ambiguity. He wasn't simple, but he craved simplicity, black and white answers to life's questions. But the woman he loved was too complex, too strange for him to know. She was slipping away and he didn't know how to try and win her back.

At least action was better than waiting and thinking. At least he *understood* action.

While almost every other man present headed for the Dom-al'Ahms, Kazim hurried around the shore towards the keep, close to where Mara Secordin had entered the water. There were Rondian soldiers on the walls above, but no one was taking any interest as he passed beneath them and dropped below their line of sight. In less than a minute he had reached the curtain wall which extended right into the lake. Above him was a tower, but the watchman was staring out over the water, not looking down. Kazim slipped into the water, went under and paddled quickly to Mara's private bathing ghat, where he emerged unseen; an inner wall shielded him from the sight of the men in the tower. He clambered out with as little splash as possible and moved up the steps on his hands and knees, hoping no one was peering down from above.

So far so good.

He topped the steps and peered forward, just in time to register a glimpse of jaws opened wider than his head, and fangs like fingers flashing towards him.

The thing that had been Mara Secordin glided carefully through the water, tasting blood and knowing it.

Elena!

She's here! How dare *she be here!*

Mara's tail wove smooth patterns as she circled closer and saw her quarry. She was swimming beneath the surface, beside another darker-skinned, indistinct being that barely moved. The taste of death was in the water, along with the blood, but it was definitely Elena, the blood told her that. No two persons' blood tasted alike; blood was a never-ending, always changing feast on which Mara could happily gorge for ever.

Human life was so stultifying compared to the endless teeming waters and the mindless, life-affirming hunt, and here was prey she had sought for a very long time.

Elena clearly couldn't see her; her movements were the awkward jerking of non-fish that set the senses of every water-predator on alert. She was blind and helpless in the dark waters, and the taste of her blood was maddening. Mara's native caution began to dissipate, the urge to dart in and *bite-rip-killkillkill* was becoming overpowering. But she was an experienced hunter, as a human as well as in beast form, so she continued to circle, getting closer, closer, closer.

Elena swivelled, turning sluggishly, to face her.

This is my domain, Elena. You're going to die here . . .

With a massive thrust of the tail Mara propelled herself through the water, her shields extended, the gnosis shimmering through her body, her jaws opening and snapping shut on human flesh. The taste of flesh and blood filled her mouth.

Only Kazim's reflexes saved him. As the python struck, he twisted and his hand flashed upwards, battering the snake's head aside just enough to avoid having his skull crushed and fangs as thick and sharp as nails hammered into his brain. Instead, the reptile's bite snapped on empty air, but its thick body lashed around him, and though he tried to roll clear, a coil wrapped around his hips and the head flashed around. For a split-second the snake's eye locked on his, then it rolled its head backwards, its jaws snapped open again and it *lunged*.

Kazim caught its head, top jaw in his left hand, bottom in his right, howling silently as its fangs speared his left palm. He almost lost control; if he had loosed his gnosis, he would have brought every competent mage within a few hundred yards running to see what the attack was ... but Elena had trained him well and he held on though the pain was excruciating. The python threw another coil about him while the first slipped up from his hips to his waist and started to squeeze. His stomach muscles clenched to protect his guts, though his gorge rose in a sudden flood. The snake pinned his legs and began to crush him, but still he held on desperately, even as the python wrenched its head from his grip and positioned itself, ready to bite again. His hands suddenly free, he snatched at the dagger at his waist – then dropped it as the snake's steely coils tightened, seeking to pin his arm to his side. He reached for the blade despairingly, beginning to doubt he would survive this encounter, but it remained stubbornly out of reach. His lungs were beginning to empty and his throat to fill with the contents of his stomach.

The python's head bobbed above him, seeking an opening. It was at least three times the length of his body, and unimaginably strong. Any ordinary man would have been dead by now ...

But he was a mage, and though he could not strike back with his full power without rousing the garrison, if he got a second to compose himself, he might just be able to ...

Elena had laid out his affinities for him months ago, and one was Animagery. She'd made him practise back in the monastery on Mount Tigrat by luring lizards. This mighty beast was not so different.

This time when he caught its eye again, he reached out with his awareness and fell into its mind . . .

Must kill must squeeze must please mistress must protect nest must feed and consume. Must crush!

<Release . . . gently . . . gently release . . . Be still be quiet . . .>

For an instant the python's head stopped moving and the coils of its upper trunk loosened, just a fraction – then it hissed and spat and its jaws flew open and its head lunged forward and clamped down on his left shoulder. He jerked in utter agony as the fangs buried themselves to the bone and the last of his air was forced from his lungs. But in that same instant, his right hand had swooped and gripped the hilt of his knife. Even as his vision wavered, he found just enough awareness to stab the snake through the eye, straight into the brain cavity.

He must have blacked out for some time, because when he came to, he was still wrapped in the snake coils, but they were flaccid. The beast was dead. And someone was standing above him, a dark silhouette holding a glittering knife.

The plan was simple, relying heavily on the probability that in the water, Mara's judgement was impaired; her normal immunity to illusion clouded by the blood-frenzy once she got her prey in sight. Gurvon Gyle's mantra about always having a plan to deal with every enemy had been playing on Elena's mind one evening in Brochena when she had noticed that the fishermen who plied the tidal salt lake used a very spiky, heavy anchor to grip the lakebed. The anchor was like a spiked mace; the weight and the spikes kept the fishing boat in place. It was when she'd seen the fishermen hauling them out of the water that the idea had begun to form.

Swapping her image with that of the dead boy with the anchor sewn into his torso was simple enough. It would never have stood up to measured scrutiny, but that was precisely what Mara was incapable of when caught up in a blood-frenzy. When the shark engulfed the boy in her massive jaws, multiple spikes of steel punched through her body from the one place her shields could not protect her.

From within her.

Mara might have thought, if she was thinking at all, that she was biting Elena in half. Instead, she slew herself. Most of the spikes tore through Mara's mouth and jaws, but two were driven up into her cranium and the healing-gnosis that might have saved Mara did not even engage. She thrashed about on reflex, but it was too late: her brain was already dead.

Blood filled the water as Elena kicked away towards the southern shore and the keep. She breached the surface once, to check what was lying ahead, and her heart started pounding in fear. She kicked back into the depths to move more quickly, trying to process what she had seen: *Kazim, lying unmoving, bound in a python's coils*. She surfaced again and flowed up Mara's private ghat, dagger in hand, oblivious to the dirty lake water dripping off her. She darted to Kazim's side, all arguments and anger forgotten in her fear for him. Of course she recognised the huge snake, Mara's favourite pet, but as she got closer she realised it had a dagger stuck through its left eye socket and was obviously dead. Kazim, though deathly still and pallid, was alive, thankfully. The python's younger counterpart was nowhere to be seen – just as well, or Kazim might well be lifeless too. *Stupid!* she upbraided herself; she'd never even considered the pythons might be a real threat – but it must have taken Kazim by surprise. Something to blame herself for later.

<Kazim? Wake up!>

He opened his eyes, flashed his beautiful smile and she felt a debilitating wave of relief. She forgot she had ever been angry with him, kissing him fervently.

'Any damage?' she whispered, pulling a heavy coil of snake away from him. For the first time since she'd seen him she glanced anxiously about her. On the far shore, the Dom-al'Ahms were full, and a dark stain had risen in the middle of the lake. But this little garden was overlooked only by two barred windows above, and in neither was there any movement or sign that they'd been seen. A flight of stairs led to a door above.

'Damned thing got me good,' Kazim admitted sheepishly. 'Surprised me as I came out of the water.' He winced as he tried to move. His shoulder was bloody, and so were his hands.

'Here, let me look.' She peered at his wounds, then used healing-gnosis to disinfect them. Python weren't venomous, but without proper treatment the puncture wounds might heal badly and go septic, especially those on his shoulder. 'Can you go on?'

'Of course,' he growled, staggering to his feet. 'I'll manage.'

She looked around again, considering. It was possible they wouldn't be disturbed in Mara's rooms for some time, and the blood was already diffusing in the middle of the lake. If they were lucky, no one would even notice it before it had gone. 'Okay,' she murmured, 'let's get inside.'

They dragged the dead python to a spot beneath the stairs where it wouldn't be seen and recovered the satchel filled with clothing and weapons they'd buried the previous night. They climbed the stairs unchallenged and found the door at the top unlocked. Once inside a mage-bolt dealt with the second, much smaller python, which was coiled on the bed, dozing. It died before it could do more than lift its head.

Kazim's wounds were not too hard to deal with. She used Mara's jug of drinking water to clean them, then sealed them with healing-gnosis in a few minutes. She had barely finished before he grasped her face and kissed her: the first proper affection they'd shared in too long. She held him close, then wrinkled her nose and whispered, 'We both stink of lake water.'

'Shall I ring for hot water?' He grinned. 'I could soap you clean if you do the same for me?'

'No!' She laughed and wriggled from his lap. 'Keep your mind on the job. It's about an hour until the evening meal – Mara would not usually attend, so there is every chance we'll be left in peace for a while.'

She sealed the main door to the suite, then peered back at the lake again. The prayers continued, and the bloody patch was almost gone. 'Goodbye, Mara,' she whispered. 'I can safely say that you won't be missed.'

Kazim peered out the window. 'So the eels in the lake will feast well tonight.'

'It all went perfectly, just as I hoped. She was dead before she knew it.' She was surprised to feel a small tremor at the thought. 'I hope I go the same way.'

Kazim hugged her from behind. 'No, you will die at a great age, surrounded by dozens of children.'

'Really? Whose?'

'Yours and mine.'

'Kaz, I don't know if I'll be able to have children by the time the Moontide is over.' She twisted in his grip, looked up at him. 'I'm an old woman.'

'No, you are eternal.' His smile lit her heart to the core. 'You will see.'

He really means it – he wants children. She had never wanted to bring a child into a world like this. But he'd forgiven her, and that sang loudest in her soul. She fell against him, held on tight.

'There is a large and comfortable bed, just over there,' he murmured in her ear, 'if you wished to make a start.' He sounded like he was only half-joking.

She shoved him away, a lump of pure relief in her throat. 'Get away with you! I'm not going to be caught with my pants around my ankles!' She wagged her finger at him. 'Especially not with a dead snake on the damned bed!'

'There is a bigger snake here,' Kazim laughed, gesturing at his crotch, 'and it's very much alive.'

'No,' she said firmly. 'I'm still angry with you.'

He hung his head, which made her heart wrench. Then he looked up, his face ashamed. 'Alhana, I was wrong. You know so much more than me. I should always listen to you.'

She looked at him, felt the wall of anger inside her shudder. 'Kaz, we can talk later—'

'No, we talk now, before we go into danger again.' He touched his heart. 'I love you: I know this in here. I do not care what you did before you met me, only what you do now. If you tell me that it is right that two who love should be allowed to, then you have seen more than I have and I hear you. I have been brought up knowing only one way, the path of Ahm. But the men who taught me to love Ahm also manipulated me into killing Antonin Meiros and his followers. So I have learned to differentiate between the pure love of Ahm and the words of those who claim to speak for Him. I still believe in Ahm, the All-God, but I also believe in my love for you.'

She stood and stared at him, awestruck. It was the longest speech she had ever heard him make, and it was obviously from his heart. She suddenly felt horribly unworthy as she realised that to Kazim, love was a celestial state, a state of permanent ecstasy, the sort of love invented by poets and singers.

Kore's Blood, I'm only a woman, not a goddess. How can anyone live up to such dreams?

He dropped to one knee. 'Please, take me back into your heart.'

She swallowed, blinking away stinging eyes. *Kore's Blood, must he make such a scene?* But how could she resist such fervour? It made her feel that maybe some kind of goddess really was inside her. 'You never left it, you fool.' She went to him, cradled his head against her stomach, then drew him to his feet and kissed him hard. She wondered at herself, to let herself be transported by such a swell of emotion.

But the mission intruded. They were in a room of a palace full of enemies and they'd spent too much time with their guard down already. She put a finger to his lips. 'Later, when we're safe, I'll let you make it up to me,' she whispered.

He let her wriggle free. 'You are right, my love. We need to be ready for anything. Pleasure can wait.'

'Good grief, you're growing up.' She went to the door, listened for sounds. 'All clear. Listen, we need to rest and prepare for the next stage. If Mekmud's spies are correct, Sordell is just next door, practising his divining, but he'll be locked and warded in, and those wards will be too strong to break without bringing all of the keep down on us. We need to wait until the emir's man arrives to summon Rutt to dinner, then we'll jump him as he comes out.'

'Are you sure he'll eat with these Church knights?'

'No,' she replied frankly. 'They may well hate each other: Rutt is a pain in the arse, and so was every Kirkegarde knight I've ever met.'

' "The angels sing in harmony, but in Shaitan's realm all is discord",' Kazim quoted. He looked impressed with himself, and exhilarated now that the shadow between them had passed. 'That is from the *Kalistham*: My tutor would be astounded that I can recall it! I will make a Scriptualist yet.'

'I very much doubt that,' Elena scoffed. 'Aren't they supposed to be celibate?' She drew her sword from the leather bag and took up her station beside the door. Kazim took an armchair and cradled his scimitar. Time passed, the dusk-bell chimed, then came a distinctive knock at the next door to theirs.

That should be the servant, summoning Rutt to dinner.

She waved Kazim closer and, taking a deep breath, started running over the spells that she would bring out first, the initial shielding tuned against Necromancy and the first mage-bolt to engage Rutt's shields while she cleared the door and let Kazim and his blade through . . .

She heard a second knock on Rutt's door – *he'll be deep in concentration* – and a muffled reply. A few footfalls sounded outside her door, then another knock. 'Dinner, Lady Mara?' a man called hesitantly in Rondian with a Jhafi accent.

She waited, for a count of three, then made a shuffling noise and dropped into a low tone to mimic Mara's voice. 'I am coming.'

The servant walked away quickly while she looked at Kazim and strained her ears to hear Sordell's door open.

Right . . . here goes . . .

She burst from the door, the gnosis flaring about her, shields and wards coming to life at once.

They saved her life.

Three crossbow bolts hammered into her shields. One stopped

dead, fusing the spell, and the other two were deflected just enough to miss, though one tore her tunic at the shoulder. Ahead of her she glimpsed four white-clad Kirkegarde soldiers, three crossbowmen and one knight, almost filling the small chamber. Rutt Sordell was pressed against the far wall, and beside him something in a ragged grave-shroud floated above the tiles.

She froze in shock, criminally slow to react as the knight looked straight at her and necromantic-gnosis flashed. Memories of what Sordell had almost done to her in Brochena paralysed her mind, the dread of death-magic almost enough to overturn her all her training and experience. She stood like a deer surprised at a watering-hole.

Behind her, the windows and door to the lake blasted open in a hail of splinters and glass.

Kazim had moved when Elena did, scimitar in hand and shields lighting up around him – then she stopped and went into a fighting crouch while crossbow bolts flew around her. Two zipped into the room, one striking the wall, the other splintering on his own shields. Over her shoulder he glimpsed a man with curly grey hair, then he saw a shrouded shape that his brain refused to engage with. Elena had gone stock-still, but he could see the crossbowmen drawing their swords and sensed the gnostic forces rise even as the lake-side door behind him crashed open.

Ahm on High! He grabbed Elena's shoulder and jerked her backwards, out of the path of a withering blast of purple gnosis-light. It flew across the room and caught the chest of the first Kirkegarde knights to burst into the room from the lake-door. The knight screamed and fell backwards onto the man behind him. Kazim hurled kinetic gnosis and slammed the main door shut, as Elena clung to his left arm, uncharacteristically shocked. Kazim threw a hasty ward over the door-frame, sealing it shut, and shoved her from him. *'Alhana! Move!'*

The second Kirkegarde from the lake-side threw off his dead comrade and charged. He was a mage and his shields flared about him as he launched himself at Elena, but Kazim intercepted him, blocking his blade and forcibly hurling the man backwards before spinning to face the main door as it rattled and his wards were assailed with a flurry of blows.

'Kazim, the lights!' Elena pulled herself together and her straight sword flashed out, blocking an overhand blow from the mage-knight. She parried again and again, giving ground.

Kazim gestured at the oil-lamp and hurled it at the next man in, but the newcomer threw up his buckler and slapped the lamp to the corner of the room. It shattered and flaming oil caught the edge of the wall-tapestry and blazed up as the rest of the room went dark. Steel on steel belled through the suite as he called on his gnostic sight and darted past Elena. Fire flickered on his blade as he thrust it through the breastplate of the man with the buckler, who crashed sideways, bellowing in pain.

Behind him the door shivered again as Kazim cut down the next man and was trying to angle in on Elena's foe when the mage-knight picked her up in a telekinetic grip and hurled her across the room, battering her against the wall beside the main door. Elena's shields protected her enough that she bounced off the cracked plaster, but she fell heavily and lay gasping. *He's a pure-blood*, Kazim guessed as he roared and hurled himself at the man's back, Ascendant-power gnosis empowering his blade as the man spun to face him.

The Kirkegarde knight met his blow with both a gnostic-shield and his physical buckler, the energy crashing together, but Kazim's scimitar crunched through leather and brass and left a chunk of the shield on the floor. The man's eyes widened at the unexpected power of the blow, but Kazim didn't give him any chance to centre himself; he flew at him, flowing into a series of movements ingrained by months of training: jab, slash high, feint another, then low, cutting through his weakening shielding, then slashing open his thigh to the bone.

Blood gushed as the man grunted and staggered. Another Kirkegarde burst in from the lake door, but Elena had recovered her breath and rolled from her prone position, driving her blade straight-armed up into his groin. Her foe stiffened, dropped his sword and clutched her blade, eyes and mouth agape, then she twisted and let him fall away as she came upright.

Kazim was still battering at the mage-knight, keeping his mental shields fixed and strong, giving the man no time to seek the gaps in his gnostic defences. A complex combination Elena had taught him opened up the man's defences and he pierced first his shield arm, then his shoulder, before he beat the mage's blade aside and drove his own through the breastplate and into his chest. As the man's face went slack and his legs began to give, Kazim kissed him, inhaling his soul. At some level the intimacy shocked him – flashes of a life seared into him, then evaporated – but what he felt most was the blazing energy that coursed through him, turning the world momentarily scarlet and gloriously vivid. He was dimly aware of Elena behind him, thrusting through the shattered window into the chest of a man waiting to enter via the door. He was crackling with puissance as he turned back to the main door just as it shattered.

Rutt Sordell knew enough to let Etain Tullesque go ahead; you never went first into a fight involving Elena Anborn. You skirted it, and awaited your chance. But Tullesque was no fool either. He turned to the shrouded figure beside him, something hidden in a bekira-shroud that stank of Necromancy.

The thing unhooded itself, revealing a visage of desiccated flesh clinging to bones and the hands of a week-old corpse. It was possibly female, probably Jhafi, with empty sockets lit with sparks of violet light. The stump of a tongue waggled as it gurgled its hunger, a trail of dark sparks glittering in the air as it lunged through the door, gnosis-light streaming from its hands. A thin cord of light trailed back to Tullesque's hands.

Impressive . . . A Spectral mage. His throat tightened, as it always did in the presence of someone whose skills outweighed his. The corpse had been re-enervated and then used to house an eidolon, but one with its own gnostic powers. It was the kind of Wizardry and Necromancy combination that few could manage. His fear of Tullesque went up another notch.

Tullesque didn't follow it in; all his concentration was required to control his summoning, for the slightest break in his concentration would see the thing's hold on this reality lost and in its last few seconds before collapsing it would flash back along that gnostic thread and attempt to take its summoner with it back to whatever Hel it had been plucked from. It was tempting to stab the Grandmaster in the back and provide just such a distraction, but Gurvon needed Elena's head and Tullesque might just be the man to provide it.

So Rutt waited dutifully as the spectre flew straight at Elena Anborn.

Sweet Kore, an eidolon! Elena recognised the thing that came through the door by the feel of its icy aura before she even turned. Her heart almost froze, but she threw up a warding of healing-gnosis, the only thing she knew that could counter such a death-summoning. She would have to trust that Kazim could deal with the three Kirkegarde pounding up the stairs at her back.

The spectral shape came at her in a rush of cold air, its aura sucking at the living and the dying. Motes of energy were flowing towards it like snowflakes swirling in a storm, and only her shielding protected her, and Kazim behind her, as he hacked at the newcomers one by one. She dimly felt the Kirkegarde men succumb to the spectre's life-sucking aura and die, but all her concentration was focused forward as she fought the life-sucking spectre trying to absorb all the energy sources in the room. The burning tapestry went out, and the water in the basin dried up. The dead python crumbled to dust on the bedclothes.

But she could still fight, just. Staggering towards it, she gripped her periapt in her left hand and fuelled her blade with all the life-energy she could dredge up. She raised her sword and swung – but she was too close; the spectre's hand flashed out and grabbed her sword-arm by the wrist. For a single second, life warred with death, then the thing's eyes froze her, caught in the terror of crumbling to dust in its hands.

Flesh began to quicken on its arm where it gripped her and she saw the skin on her own arm begin to flake and turn purple. She felt the most incredible weakness flow through her and her legs started to wobble.

Then steel flashed and the eidolon's hand was severed from its arm. The appendage dropped and crumbled while the spectre yowled. Then Kazim used telekinesis to hurl the spectre away from him and back through the door, then slammed it shut. Elena dimly heard three muffled screams, but all her effort was going into just standing, staring at her wrist where the shape of the death-summoning's hand was burned into the flesh. She swayed and fell . . .

. . . into Kazim's arms.

'Alhana!' he cried.

She looked at him dazedly. 'Let's get the fuck out of here . . .'

Then everything went dark.

Rutt Sordell staggered aside as the shrouded spectre was hurled backwards, through the doorway, shrieking with rage. It struck Etain Tullesque and knocked him over, then turned on him. The Grandmaster grunted in shock as the spectre twisted and hung above him, its visage filled with hate for its summoner. Rutt could clearly see the spiderweb-thin thread of violet light that tied the Kirkegarde knight to his creation: the link that would allow it to pierce Tullesque's wards and rip his soul out.

The spectre's right hand had been severed and it was still yowling in anguish; that agony was all that kept it from striking instantly. But the hand was reforming, fuelled by spirit-energy it was pulling from everyone around it. As Rutt watched with appalled eyes, its joints popped and its sinews wept yellowish fluid, and fresh blood dried on its fingers. The energy came from the three crossbowmen, whose auras were snuffed out in the same instant that they collapsed soundlessly. He'd have died the same way had he not been well-warded. Thankfully, its eyes were fixed on Tullesque, not him.

Rutt would have dearly loved to have let it have the Grandmaster, but that would mean Elena got away. Instead, he raised his hands and committed a rare act of selfless courage. Reaching with his own necromantic powers, he sought to snare the spectre.

He cast a web of violet light about it, protecting Tullesque but drawing its attention on himself. Seconds turned to years as it turned on him, following a new path of control, leading to him, not Tullesque – then, with pure terror, he realised that he was not strong enough to master the spectre, not with the handicap of his imperfect control over Guy Lassaigne's body. And it was too late to vacate the body and run. His scarab would wither in seconds the moment it was exposed.

The spectre took another step, and another. It reached out.

Suddenly he was bathed in purple light and Etain Tullesque's voice crackled around him. Renewed gnostic-light lit the spectre, trapped it and enfolded it, and Rutt fell backwards against the wall and sagged to the ground as the Kirkegarde mage-knight reasserted control over his summoning.

The shrouded thing went still. Its arms fell to its side and its head dropped.

Rutt looked up at Tullesque. For an instant, there might have been gratitude in the Grandmaster's eyes, then he turned back to the spectre and commanded: 'Bring me Elena Anborn, dead or alive.'

With a flurry that dropped the temperature of the room even further, the death-summoning turned and smashed straight through the door – only to find Elena and her Noorie gone.

With a howl of rage, the spectre took to the air and flashed out into the night.

Within the room was carnage. One of Tullesque's mage-knights was a dead husk, as were half a dozen of his knights. The Grandmaster's face was thunderous as he whirled to scream at the further soldiers pouring down the stairs into the lobby area. 'Rouse the garrison, and scour the city! *Find them!*'

The officer leading the reinforcements saluted, barking orders as he hurried away. But he was back a few minutes later. 'Grandmaster, a windskiff just lifted off from the other side of the lake.'

Tullesque spat a curse. 'Damn it, how—? All right, we must make new plans. Mobilise the men! Alert Gyle! We must flood this region with windcraft. The hunt does not end here, it begins!'

Tullesque turned finally to Rutt Sordell, who had regained his feet. 'Well, Magister. I thank you and I commend you. I owe you my life. A Tullesque does not forget his debts.'

Rutt bowed, his heart still thudding. 'Nor do I,' he panted. *Nor my humiliations*.

Tullesque went to the lake-door, staring out into the night. The cord of light still ran from his fingers out into the skies. 'Find her, my lovely,' he whispered, just loud enough for Rutt to hear. 'Find her and kill her.'

27

The Bakhtak

Combining Gnostic Effects

The more accomplished of our magi have found ways to blend their disciplines to greater effect – for example, Earth- and Fire-gnosis together can be used to hurl flaming lava at a target, harder to shield and harder to negate. Opportunities to explore even more destructive techniques are precious – thank Kore for this war!

GENERAL BRENDIS RANTHORN, BREVIS,
DURING THE THIRD SCHLESSEN WAR, 634

Emirate of Lybis, on the continent of Antiopia
Rajab (Julsep) 929
13th month of the Moontide

Elena came to her senses with the wind whipping through her short hair and the crack of canvas sails above. She jerked awake, the image of the spectral creature leaping to her mind and looked about. Everything was dark except for the faint glow around Kazim's right hand as he poured Air-gnosis into the keel of the *Greyhawk*. He must have been doing it for hours, because he looked drawn; his teeth were pulled back in a snarl and his eyes were bloodshot. To her gnostic sight, he looked even worse: his aura was a swirl of crimson and black, a tentacled void that boiled about him. A terrifying number of those tentacles were buried in her own aura, like worms burrowing into her soul, pulsing as they fed.

'Kaz?'

He looked across at her, and a look of utter relief filled his face. 'Alhana! Ahm be praised! I thought you were lost!'

She pulled herself up, though that only told her how frighteningly weak she was. *How much is he taking from me – and how much did that God-awful eidolon take?* She looked around dazedly. 'Where are we? What's happening?'

'We're running, that's what.' Kazim threw a look over his shoulder. 'But that *bakhtak* won't stop coming.'

'Huh?' She looked back and stared behind them. It was Darkmoon, Luna's face hidden, and the star-studded heavens were turning to indigo. They were weaving through narrow mountain clefts, the landscape shadowy except for the occasional blotches of snow still to melt. At first she saw nothing ... and then something dark scudded over the last ridgeline and even half a mile away she knew what it was.

'Holy Kore, how long have I been unconscious?'

'Two hours,' Kazim told her grimly. 'You went out like a candle flame, halfway round the lake. I had to carry you the rest of the way. But I got you out.'

She looked down at herself. Her sword arm was bruised to the elbow and the hand-print of the creature looked burned into the skin – but at least it was living tissue still. Otherwise she felt okay, just incredibly tired. She crawled down the hull and buried her head against his chest. 'You did. I love you.'

His eyes went round with pleasure and wonder. 'You're only saying that because I pulled your arse out of the fire,' he teased. But his eyes never lost that look of joy.

I do love him. I do ... And this is what it feels like ... She immediately tried to rationalise it: they'd fought together, saved each other, their auras were linked ... but that didn't really explain it at all.

Love isn't rational, her sister Tesla had once told her, trying to explain why she was marrying Vann Mercer. *It just is*. She blinked back tears and laid her hand beside his on the keel. She tried to concentrate on the danger, instead of the relief. 'Where are we going?'

'Wherever the wind takes us,' he replied. 'When I got us aloft in

Lybis it was blowing westwards, so that's the way I flew. It's not strong enough, though, and I've been having to try and generate more to stay ahead of that damned bakhtak.'

'What's a bakhtak?'

'It is a ghost of the night.' He glowered. 'So how do you kill it?'

'Lots of ways. I can do it, I think.' She faltered, then admitted, 'No, I'm not sure.' The fact was, the damned thing terrified her. For a moment it had become the embodiment of all she feared and now she doubted she was up to dealing with it. That doubt could be fatal. 'With those things, you've got two options: banish it or kill it. Banishing is easier, but you've got to be a Wizard or a Necromancer and I'm neither.'

He shrugged. 'So we kill it then.'

'We try – but it'll be near impossible, because it can pull energy from all round to keep itself alive. That includes drawing energy from your spells. It takes healing-gnosis to keep it at bay. I can do that, but you can't, so we'd have only a few seconds to kill it before it gets us.'

They looked at each other, let each other see the worry and the fear.

'The bastard who summoned this knows what he's doing,' Elena said. 'He knows who I am and he's tailored this thing specifically to get me. Our best hope is to run. These sort of summonings can't be maintained beyond dawn – sunlight messes with the Necromancy.'

Kazim looked encouraged by that. He returned his attention to the *Greyhawk* as they shot along a gully, then brought the windskiff around a granite outcropping and into another long valley, almost doubling back. They both scanned ahead worriedly: there was no visible exit; they'd flown into a cul-de-sac of stone. There was a small lake at its base, though it was in shadow, a black emptiness beneath the jagged cliffs. Snow clung to the peaks and their breath streamed behind them. Their fingers had gone numb and the chill was cutting through them both, drawing on already plummeting gnosis levels.

Looking at Kazim's aura, twined about her own, was like watching a vine choke the life of a tree. She could feel the linkages, feel her energy flowing out of her. He knew it too; the look on his face told her that. But they both knew he couldn't afford to stop doing it.

Will it kill me before the spectre does?

'I can't see a way out of this valley!' he said suddenly.

'Rukka!' Elena breathed, casting about frantically. She engaged her night sight, but sheer cliffs rose on all sides except back the way they came. The wind was swirling, caught in a funnel by the enclosing cliffs. They were losing speed and had nowhere to go.

The spectre floated lazily around the outcropping, its shriek of gleeful fury audible all the way down the valley.

Kazim gripped the tiller and tried to catch the swirling winds but they were slipping ineffectually past and the sail flapped uselessly against the mast as they hung in the air. They'd lost all momentum. 'What do we do?' he shouted, fear coming out as anger.

'Stay calm, Kaz. It's still minutes away.' She scanned the cliffs, then pointed. 'Look, there!'

He peered upwards, wishing the moonlight was brighter. There was a lighter patch on the rock face, and he turned the skiff towards it, rising sluggishly. The bakhtak howled triumphantly and its ragged death-shroud flapped in the wind as it flew unerringly towards them.

'There! There!' Elena gasped frantically. 'It's a cutting, to another valley!'

He blanched. The cleft she was pointing at ran between two overhanging cliffs, almost a tunnel, and it looked incredibly tight. But the ghoulish thing streaming towards them froze his blood and he was feeling dangerously spent. He could see what he was doing to Elena too, the way her aura was growing fainter, but he couldn't stop his gnosis from draining hers.

One last effort.

No, not 'last'. Never that . . .

Her hand on his lent him strength; more than that, it soothed him, calmed him, helped him think. He called the wind and this time it came and caught the sails, sending them lurching forward with growing momentum. But when he looked back, the bakhtak was almost on them – barely forty yards away, and so close he could see its glowing violet eyes.

'Take the tiller!' he shouted, twisting and rolling into the small aft cavity behind the pilot's bench. The craft bucked as their weight changed, but he kindled a mage-bolt and hurled it at their pursuer, then another, then another, firing wide thrice, before finally one connected. The thing shrieked as the white light blazed at it and drew back, snarling.

'Okay, let's try it,' Elena called breathlessly. There was plenty of power in the keel, and the wind was behind them so all she had to do was steer. Kazim prayed she was up to it, because she looked worn-out, like a preview of old age. The starlight had turned her hair silver and etched lines in her face. And the bakhtak was closing in again.

Rutt Sordell stood guard over Etain Tullesque atop an open-topped tower, the highest in the emir's palace. The height allowed better linkage to his death-summoning. Somewhere to the northwest, the creature was pursuing Elena Anborn and her Keshi ally, whoever he was. From up here Rutt had clear views over the town and lake. The streets were restless, but a line of torches revealed reinforcements: more Rondian soldiery arriving, following a forced march through the night.

Rutt smiled to himself. Actually, 'reinforcements' wasn't precisely the right word.

Tullesque was deep in concentration and oblivious to his surroundings. Controlling a summoning of any sort required some degree of the mage's attention; one this powerful required full concentration, and the longer the chase went on, the harder it was to maintain that. Rutt had guided Tullesque to the tower top himself, helping him every step so he did not slip and lose the link.

Or to put it another way: Tullesque is completely in my power . . .

The column of torches had reached the gates of the emir's fortress now. No doubt their arrival would cause considerable consternation, for these were not Dorobon men, or more Kirkegarde, but Endus Rykjard's mercenaries – officially the Pallacios XX, but known in the army as the Blackthorns. Rykjard's lieutenant, a giant Hollenian mage named Arnulf Rhumberg, had been in mental contact with Rutt for an hour or more now.

Rutt approached Tullesque carefully. 'What is happening, Grand-master?' he asked, as loudly as he dared.

Tullesque's eyes, glazed and bloodshot, continued to stare into the skies. Slowly, awkwardly, his lips moved. 'Trapped . . . I have her . . .'

Excellent.

Rutt looked to the east. Dawn was about to become a factor. 'You must hurry, Grandmaster. The night is passing.'

Tullesque nodded to show his understanding. 'It . . . won't . . . be long . . . now.'

Someone hammered on the door at the foot of the stairs that led to the rooftop and Rutt hurried over and hissed, '*Quiet!* The Grand-master must concentrate!'

'Sir, there are mercenaries at the gates. What are our orders?'

'Who is this?'

'Tribune Brayle, Magister.'

One of Tullesque's officers. 'They are our reinforcements, Brayle. Admit them at once and send their commander to me.'

'Yes, sir.' The man clumped away and Rutt leaned against the door, breathing a little heavily. Deception was not his greatest skill – he was Argundian, and prided himself on his honesty. *I'm not a saint, but lying is not among my sins,* he liked to say. But needs must, sometimes. He hurried back to Tullesque's side, praying that the Kirkegarde Grandmaster was about to solve the Elena problem for them once and for all. He arrived just as Tullkesque burst into a strange dance.

'Now!' Tullesque roared. 'Strike to kill!' He clenched his fists, then crowed in triumph, 'Dead! *The bitch is dead!*'

Elena set the skiff hurtling towards what was little more than a hole in the cliff-face. The winds coalesced behind them, propelling the little vessel at an increasingly terrifying speed. She dared not look back, but she could feel the chill of the spectre's presence right behind them.

Then they hit the cutting, the shale of the slopes whipping past no more than a yard beneath the keel. The right-hand cliff was almost touchable and the left one was getting closer as they soared along the cut – then suddenly the earth fell away and she had to haul the tiller about with all her diminishing strength. The sails flapped and the boom flew across, barely missing her face, as a rock wall loomed ahead.

She felt Kazim's gnosis flaring again as he started firing bolt after bolt behind them, and she heard the spectre yowl each time a bolt connected . . . then it fired back. The purplish bolt of light flashed past her left shoulder, just an inch or so away from her, and hit the rock wall. Kazim's shields flared, such a drain on her that she almost lost control as a dizzying wave washed over her.

'What was *that*?' he shouted.

'It's the ghost of a mage!' she replied. 'It's got its own gnosis! Hold on!'

The cleft veered right, along a ridgeline like a serrated stone knife, then she hauled left again and drew the wind with her, aiming for a lighter patch of darkness dead ahead. They shot out into space again and sideswiped a boulder, cracking timbers and jolting them both. The craft tipped sideways and she frantically threw herself to the right, using her bodyweight to counteract the tilt, hanging half-in and half-out of the skiff. Then the mast struck the left-hand cliff and snapped, halfway down.

The whole craft spun, almost flinging her out, but somehow she managed to cling on as they struck the slope and began to career backwards down the scree. For a few seconds the craft righted itself and she found herself staring past the stump of the mast at darkness above them. 'Kaz!' she screamed, as they shot down a steep slope littered with boulders. Kazim was still with her, hunched over and firing another volley of mage-bolts up the slope as the spectre appeared at the top, howling in fury.

Then the slope vanished beneath them and they were airborne again – but not sustainably. The keel was badly damaged and leaking power and they started tumbling downwards, completely out of control. She had time to glimpse a flat plain, with a river winding towards a glittering expanse: the sea.

Then they struck a lower slope, the hull splintered at the front and the craft lurched sideways in a spray of earth and stone, and then she was falling away, weightless. Her last glimpse was of Kazim flying over the top of her, spinning head over heels. Then something smashed into the back of her head and the world collapsed into blackness.

Kazim used kinetic energy to enfold himself as he spun in the air and turned the uncontrolled fall into a cartwheel and an almost graceful landing on one knee, facing upwards, his scimitar drawn and a mage-bolt ready on his finger-tips. Then he dropped to the ground as the skiff hurtled past him and he heard it hammering into the boulders below. He threw up shields as his eyes sought Elena in the wreckage.

No, no no no—

Had he been anything less than he was, he would have been slain – but as the bakhtak dropped from the sky, he felt it come and turned his readied mage-bolt on it. Finally he caught the thing with his full power, and Ascendant-level energy blasted into it at close range, hurling it down the slope, its flesh so brightly illuminated that he could see its bones. Its rags burned away, what little hair was left on its skull crisped, and it landed with a thud some twenty feet down the slope and lay there, sizzling in the thin snow that crusted the slope.

There was a dark mound on the slope above where the skiff had flipped over.

<Alhana? Ella!>

His eyes penetrated the gloom, making out splayed limbs and an unmoving body. He couldn't feel her mind, for the first time that night, and his heart hammered, his throat went utterly dry and his chest contracted until he could barely breath.

'ELLA!'

Nothing.

Then from below he sensed a presence and turned as the twig-like arms of the bakhtak began to move, like a corpse rising from a grave.

It came upright, its snapped left leg re-straightening, and the snow formed on its bones, becoming a kind of flesh. Violet light rekindled in its eyes

Lord Ahm . . .

He backed towards Elena, but the bakhtak flashed overhead, a blur of darkness and he screamed in sheer terror, more afraid than he had ever been in his life, as it reappeared above Elena's broken form. She didn't even move as it reached for her.

'NOOO!'

Using a combination of his own natural athleticism, Ascendant-power telekinetic force and blind, unthinking desperation, Kazim covered the distance in a second. He grasped the numbing ice-flesh of the dead thing and pulled it from her. It turned on him and opened its mouth of rotting teeth and purple death-light, illuminating the hideous, rotting face as it snarled.

The silver arc of his blade, lit by gnosis, swept through the bakhtak's neck, power flashing and his scimitar almost melting with the energy he was pouring through it, but something snapped; the skull flew, bounced, and rolled into a snowdrift and the corpse dropped.

His left hand, his whole left arm, had gone utterly numb, but he dropped his ruined hilt and poured fire into the corpse, and then the head, and kept burning until only charred nothingness remained. For the first few seconds he felt it struggling to reform and rise, then the dark light in it winked out, the flames turned a clean and healthy red and the snows became water and flooded away.

He dropped to his knees beside Elena and just held on, pouring back all he'd taken from her until there was nothing left to give.

That was how they were found, him wrapped about her, their flesh as cold as the stones.

Rutt gestured and Arnulf Rhumberg's massive blade plunged into Grandmaster Tullesque's back. The Kirkegarde commander gasped once, but anything he might have done to preserve himself was undone by the gnosis-bolt Rutt blasted into his face.

'You were supposed to behead him,' he grumbled as the corpse slid off Rhumberg's sword and fell twitching to the stone.

The massive Hollenian, a towering mountain of blond hair, shaggy furs and layers upon layers of chainmail, grunted unrepentantly. 'He had his arms up, didn't he? Awkward angle, that.' He rectified the matter with another blow, severing the neck and almost breaking his sword on the stones. 'There, got 'im, din't I?'

Sordell could hear the tramp of Rhumberg's men below as they took over the palace, asserting control by sheer numbers. The Kirkegarde wouldn't be happy, and soon they'd be even more suspicious, but . . . *how'll they prove anything?*

A few seconds earlier, right after announcing that Elena was dead, Tullesque had staggered and then stood there, silent and motionless. Some trauma had flashed along his link to the spectral summoning, leaving the Grandmaster stunned for a few heartbeats.

Just long enough to kill the prick, Rutt thought, smiling cheerily. 'Ah, here we go.' A leggy black scarab more than four inches across was forcing its way out of Tullesque's mouth. He let it drop to the marble floor, then stamped on it. The crunch made the giant Rhumberg wince.

'Fuckin' hate insects, I do,' the Hollenian remarked, shuddering. He wiped his sword on Tullesque's white cloak and said blithely, 'Don' mind chopping a fella down, 'specially cunts like 'im, but bugs . . . I bloody hate 'em.' He looked at Rutt admiringly. 'Glad you got that big fucker, sar.'

'So am I.' Rutt wiped off the slime on his boot-sole on Tullesque's gleaming tabard. 'How many men have you brought?'

'Lots, sar. Four maniples. That's two thousand men, that is.'

'I know how many men in a maniple, Rhumberg.' The Hollenian was an Earth mage, simple-minded, but blazingly effective on a good day. 'How have the Kirkegarde taken to your arrival?'

'A bit disgruntled, sar.'

'I expect losing their commander won't help.'

'What'll we tell them?'

'That he lost control of his summoning. Tragic, really. If any of them question it, arrest them for subversion.'

Rhumberg grinned. 'Yes, sar!' He saluted, and hurried off, leaving Rutt alone.

For a while he just stared into space, wondering whether Elena really was dead. And what about her companion? 'Someone killed that damned spectral-mage,' he mused aloud. 'I suppose we'll have to go and find out who.'

'We will indeed,' said a familiar voice behind him.

Rutt spun round, his face lighting up. 'Boss!'

Gurvon Gyle grinned. 'Rutt, well met!' They shook hands, clapped each other on the back.

'What are you doing here, Gurv? I thought you were going to stay in Brochena.'

'Not when you've found Elena. I want her dead, and though I trust you more than anyone to get the job done, I wanted to deal the killing blow myself.' He spat on Tullesque's corpse. 'I've flown all day and night on gnostic winds to be here.' He looked about him. 'Where's Mara?'

Rutt drew back a little. 'She's dead,' he said, faintly regretful. 'Elena killed her.'

Gurvon blinked once. 'By the Kore! I always thought Mara was indestructible.'

'So did I, I suppose.'

There didn't seem much else to say.

Gurvon gripped Rutt's shoulder. 'Samir. Arno. Vedya. Now Mara. They were the heart of us, the core members of the Grey Foxes. Now Elena's killed them all.'

'She might be dead too.'

'Until I see the body . . .' Gurvon sighed. 'In a way, I hope she isn't. I want it to be one of us who finishes her, not some stinking pure-blood like Tullesque.'

'Hey, I'm a pure-blood now,' Rutt protested, an uncharacteristic smile creeping across his face.

'So you are.'

'Who's in charge in Brochena, Gurv, if you're here?'

Gurvon tutted softly. 'The rest of the Regency Council, each watching the other. Hans and Endus know not to cross me, and Heale and Margham don't have the nerve.' He clapped Rutt on the shoulder. 'My friend, can you keep a secret?'

He turned and looked at him. 'Of course, Gurv – it's why you hired me, remember?'

'I have a *guest* with me: politically, *very* dangerous. I want you to find me a secret place to stow them.'

'Of course.' Rutt thought for a second. 'Timori Nesti? Brochena getting too hot?'

'Keep it dark, Rutt.' Gurvon touched a finger to his nose. 'So, where did Tullesque's creature last see Elena?'

'Tullesque kept me appraised, and I tuned in on the chase myself. It was around forty miles northwest of here. Give me a few moments with a map and compass and we'll have the spot, more or less.'

'Do that. I want a mounted detachment ready to leave by midday. I'll lead it personally. Until I see the body, I'll not believe she's dead.'

28

An Audience with the Mughal

The Mughal's Dome at Teshwallabad

The Mughal Dome is a miracle to behold, an immense palace that glitters in the sunlight and can be seen for miles around. It is perhaps the most beautiful of all constructions in Ahmedhassa, and a tribute to the skills of our people and the unnamed foreign engineers who aided us.

PINATH SALKEMISH, ROYAL
ENGINEER OF THE MUGHAL, TESHWALLABAD

Teshwallabad, Lakh, on the continent of Antiopia
Shaban (Augeite) 929
14th month of the Moontide

Ramita Ankesharan held Nasatya against her left breast, and fed him the bottled milk. His brother wailed in protest at having to wait, but she sent him calming thoughts and he quieted. Her breasts were still distended and the skin stretch-marked, but the ache from weaning was beginning to recede. *Six months old*, she thought proudly, though it felt like for ever, being nursemaid and dairy cow for her babies and their insatiable appetites. *But how they are growing!*

It was wonderful to be in her homeland, though Teshwallabad was not Baranasi, where her heart was. In some ways, it felt like being back in Hebusalim: shut away in a marble palace while the wail of Godsingers filled the hours, and all the same restrictions: do not go outside; do not be seen at the windows. Stay safe.

I just want to go out! I want to go down to the markets and haggle for sweets. I'd even settle for just going outside.

It had been three weeks since they'd arrived in Teshwallabad, and being in Lakh made her miss her family more keenly than ever. Vizier Hanook had hidden them in the south, in Dili, hundreds of miles away. He had given her the details, including their new names, and promised a reunion when the danger had passed, but she chafed for that moment. Separation from the bustle and noise of her brothers and sisters was like losing a limb, and being so long without her mother was hollowing out her heart.

I wish I could just leave here and go far away, to somewhere where no one knows who I am. Just me and my sons. And my family. And perhaps my new bhaiya . . .

She smiled fondly at the thought of Alaron Mercer meeting her mad family. How would he cope with Mother and Father and their constant, goodhearted squabbling? Or the twins, stampeding about? And what about Jai and Keita and their child – though Hanook had not seen them, so who knew where they might be?

Alaron would go grey within a day of meeting us all.

The young Rondian was away in the library, where he had been spending most of his time; Hanook was more than happy that Alaron was content to scribble away in the semi-shadows. Alaron had been genuinely excited by the old vizier's library, though Ramita struggled to understand; she had learned to read only last year and she still couldn't match the way Alaron could scan a page in seconds and understand it; a skill as magical as the gnosis itself. She tried to imagine a world in which all young children were taught such skills, but her mind baulked.

Nas gurgled and pulled his mouth from the bottle, so she laid him on a towel on the floor to roll about while she fed Das. Both had thick black hair, which they surely got from her, but their skin was pale gold, the colour the noble women of Lakh all craved. Dark skin like hers betrayed a low birth-caste or a life in poverty, the legacy of her forebears who spent their lives labouring outdoors in the punishing sunlight. Her sons would be envied, that was for sure.

And they will be handsome too, like Jai – and like the statues of my husband when he was young.

She smiled at these thoughts and tried not to think about the other thing hanging over her life like a shadow: possible marriage to the mughal. It seemed ridiculous to even contemplate such a union: she was just a market-girl, after all! But she was also this other thing: Lady Meiros, a mage of unmeasured strength. What might her children be? Could she and the mughal establish a dynasty that enriched the realm? It was a powerful thought, that her offspring could mean so much to so many. But it was demeaning too, to be regarded as nothing more than a particularly fruitful womb.

But when have women been anything other than that? Even my father, who loved me, sold me to a man for the best price he could get. And am I not supposed to find a way to end these wars? Will selling myself into another marriage truly aid that?

She felt her contentment curdle as other doubts surfaced, like what would happen to her sons should the mughal wish to take her to wife? Would he adopt them, or would they need to be hidden away?

No. I refuse to believe that. The mughal will take me to wife and adopt my children as his own. We will pretend they are his. My family will come here, and we will live happily for ever after. That is how it will be.

She finished feeding Das and after playing with the twins for a while to tire them, she put them into their cots. Then she had to focus on the next task, a secret assignation she could not miss. She pulled on the drab and dirty clothing they had given her to wear and went down to the foyer. Today she would finally be allowed outside, to observe the mughal.

Dareem was waiting for her, as always, faultlessly patient and polite, but she could not shake the feeling that he saw her as nothing but a game piece. His clothing was as rough as hers, but he still looked like a lord to her.

'Lady Meiros, are you ready?'

'I think so,' she murmured uncertainly.

'No one will know you out there. I'm the one who risks attention.'

He smiled in that self-satisfied way he had, then his face rippled into another, coarser visage. 'It is the day of open court today, when the mughal publically hears plaintiffs before whoever can squeeze into the courtyard.'

Her first steps into the open air and sunshine were dizzying, but then she had to concentrate on the crowds, ebbing and flowing through the tangled streets, the stench and perfume of humanity and beasts flowing together into a fug that hung in the steaming air. Camels and donkeys hauled carts through the choked arteries of the city, all ludicrously overburdened with goods. Men and women with baskets on their heads pushed and shoved, their faces set and grim. Tiny shops presided over by family owners filled every conceivable cranny, clamouring to the passersby to stop and look. *Looking is free!* She'd used the phrase herself in Aruna Nagar.

Dareem looked at ease despite the deafening press; he was pushing as hard as he was pushed and swearing like a street-denizen, while Ramita kept her head down and followed him like the dutiful daughter she was pretending to be. Finally they came up against a cordon of soldiers and gaudily clad officials who had blocked off half the square before the massive crystal-domed palace.

Dareem pulled out a clay disc and showed it to the officials, whilst slipping one a handful of copper coins, and they were waved through.

The vizier's son leaned and spoke in her ear. 'If anyone asks, we are kin of a plaintiff,' he reminded her. As they found a space for themselves, Ramita noticed that beyond another cordon there were some men in very fine apparel, with thick sheaves of paper and haughty airs, who all seemed to know each other. 'Avukati,' Dareem told her. 'Experts on the law. If you want to gain a favourable outcome, it is best to hire one – though they'll charge you nigh as much as you might gain from a successful plea.'

Ramita had heard her father make the same comment many times; in trade one occasionally needed to take a case against a cheating rival. But her attention was fixed on the awning-covered raised plinth at the end of the square, next to the gates to the palace. She struggled to get a view as trumpets blared and marching feet echoed all about. Everyone around her was much taller, but she caught glimpses as the mughal himself mounted the dais, flanked by a cloud of soldiers and his advisors. Apart from Vizier Hanook, all the other advisors were Godspeakers, robed in white with bushy beards and stern faces. Dareem pointed out the chief one. 'That is Vahraz, my father's greatest rival.'

The whole crowd bowed thrice for their ruler, who then raised a hand for silence and declared court open in a thin but carrying voice. Everyone before the dais sat on the ground, which at least meant that her view was clear. It was a routine morning, according to Dareem, starting with a string of disputes from the lower courts where the decision had been appealed. Ramita quickly saw a pattern emerging: the man with the best-dressed avukati invariably won, and that told her that the mughal's court was a kind of market: money spoke. Some cases were vigorously debated, but most had a perfunctory air. The better dressed avukati spoke well, the poorer dressed ones with desperation or resignation. Hanook occasionally whispered in the mughal's ear, but just as often it was Vahraz who gave advice.

Most of the time her eyes remained fixed on the young ruler. Tariq Srinarayan Kishan-ji was almost fifteen, two years younger than her, and had a plump face, a small mouth and pale, creamy skin. He wore a crowned turban that looked heavy and uncomfortable, and his long black hair, oiled and curling, fell about his shoulder. He had the beginnings of a paunch already, and narrow, watchful eyes. His every word was hung on, but he said little beyond giving his decision with a wave of the hand towards either a white or red banner – white for innocent, red for guilty. She thought he was nervous of the powerful men who flanked him and sought to hide it with a puffed-up manner.

'Has your father spoken of me to his Majesty?' she whispered to Dareem.

'He has. The story Father used is that you are in hiding, seeking sanctuary in Teshwallabad,' Dareem replied softly. 'He is nervous that a Lakh mage-woman is loose in the world, and worried that a southern rival might accept you if he does not. He is also – quite rightly – frightened of the unrest that marrying a mage would provoke.'

She listened to this with mixed feelings. Though the haven the mughal represented was desirable, she did not think after seeing him in the flesh that marriage to him was something she would enjoy. He was a raja and she was from the market. He would see her as a lesser being, no matter who her first husband had been.

Dareem read her easily. 'You are not pleased, Lady. You think him someone from another world to you entirely. You are having doubts.'

She nodded hesitantly.

'You need to understand that Tariq has been given whatever he wanted from birth, but he also has had to deal with the threat of having all of it snatched away at any moment. The court has been one of intrigue from the beginning. There are spies here from Kesh and Khotri and all the kingdoms of Southern Lakh. There are different sects of the Amteh seeking pre-eminence. There are plots everywhere. And Father and I are not the only secret magi here.'

Ramita blinked fearfully. 'Really?'

'Salim of Kesh has planted low-blooded magi here too, using similar tactics to our own. I myself have eliminated two in the past four years. There are Hadishah here too, aiding the cause of the shihadis. This is a house of knives, Lady Meiros: a multi-sided concealed conflict that every so often turns bloody.'

'You are not a good negotiator, Dareem of Teshwallabad. You are not selling this venture to me.'

'We would not send you into this blind, Lady Meiros. I seek only to inform your choices. But know this: Tariq does not beat his wives, though he does have favourites, those who use their looks and feminine arts to influence him. He enjoys the pleasures of life far more than either Father or the Godspeakers think proper.'

'Does he have brothers?'

'Not any more,' Dareem replied grimly. 'His elder brothers fell under the sway of a shihadi fanatic and attempted to seize power from their father while Tariq was still a child. They failed, and paid the price.'

'Who is his heir?'

'One of his two newborn sons,' Dareem responded, 'born one each to his favoured wives. There are also two daughters.'

'He's been busy,' she noted drily. *Fourteen and he's sired four children! Darikha-ji, what kind of life is this?*

'Traditionally, attrition is high in royal households,' Dareem replied. 'Plenty of heirs are required to secure the succession. So long as the throne keeps a tight grip on its powerbases, the stability of the realm is enhanced. A palace coup seldom touches the people.'

'The rajas of Baranasi were always knifing each other,' Ramita agreed. 'We barely noticed.' She pursed her lips, thinking hard. 'Given that he is young and his heirs younger, who would rule if he died?'

'A good question. Technically, a Regency Council chaired by Father would preside. That is what happened when Tariq's father died, leaving him as mughal-elect. Vahraz claimed that Father would seek to seize power, but he proved the Godspeaker wrong by handing the throne to Tariq when he came of age at twelve years old.'

'How old are his wives?'

'The eldest is twenty-two, the youngest is eleven. They are political alliances, mostly. Many are Lakh and Omali by birth. But his favoured wives are Khotri princesses. And all his wives must convert to the Amteh,' he added.

Ramita put a hand to her heart. *No . . . I could not . . .*

Their conversation was suddenly disturbed by a loud wail from a woman from a place near the stage. Everyone craned their necks and everyone around them stood. Dareem took her hand and pulled her to her feet. 'Lady, this is now the time for clemency appeals, on behalf of those condemned to die.'

'What will happen?'

'A final plea is made before the people. Those who have been condemned and await sentence are brought forth, and the mughal may give a pardon, or lessen their sentence if he finds cause.'

'And if not?'

Dareem made a chopping motion with his hand. 'Death. Usually at sunset.'

Ramita looked at the plinth. Mughal Tariq was leaning forward, licking his lips, his stance subtly eager. He was leaning slightly to one side, towards his right, where Vahraz and his Godspeakers stood. All afternoon he had leaned more towards his left, towards Hanook. She realised that this was the part of the afternoon the young man had been waiting for.

'Does he ever give clemency?'

'In some cases,' Dareem said carefully. 'Lady, a ruler must be feared as well as loved. He must never be seen as indecisive or weak. That is why these open sessions are held, so the ruler's hand is visible to his people.'

'I understand,' Ramita replied. She did, too. In the market, people had to understand that you weren't a soft touch. But her sons would be waking soon. 'I don't need to see this. May we go?'

Dareem looked reluctant to leave, but he took her arm and steered her through the crowd and back past the cordon and into the masses beyond who were all pressing forward, no doubt eager to see blood at sunset. It was a struggle to break through into the quieter backstreets.

'A queen does not need to see the workings of the court, Lady. The wives are confined to the zenana from marriage until death. Only if the mughal goes on a processional are favoured wives permitted to travel.'

The same four walls until death, locked behind them in a permanent war with the other wives. I would be nothing but a pampered broodmare – is this what I want? Is it truly what my husband intended, after going to such lengths to make me into a mage? Is this my duty now?

She had always been a dutiful daughter. *Though I was not a faithful wife.* She felt tears brimming behind her eyes at the thought of the life laid out before her.

'My Lady?'

She straightened, met his eye. 'Sorry. I am ready to go on now.'

'We will look after you, Lady,' Dareem said, understanding in his eyes.

By which you mean that you will install me in that boy's harem and reap what benefits you can.

An old Lakh scholar with a hacking cough tugged at the stack of scrolls, making the whole bank of shelves rattle alarmingly. Alaron considered using telekinetic-gnosis to ensure it stayed upright, then decided the shelves had probably survived such treatment for centuries and went back to his transcribing. Hanook's library was cool, but not damp – the vizier had gone to considerable lengths to ventilate the long room with dry air. The scrolls contained centuries of mostly Lakh writing; they were completely undecipherable to Alaron, but the Hanook had added to the library during his own tenure, and that included texts from Yuros. It was one of those that Alaron was copying now with increasing excitement.

The sheath of parchment he'd found stacked in a pile labelled 'Yuros' was old, but not ancient: a copy of an original document given by Antonin Meiros himself to Hanook forty years ago, during one of the vizier's clandestine visits to Hebusalim. Hanook himself had told Alaron about it when he had first asked to do some research; the vizier had appeared to be mildly unsettled by the request, and Alaron wondered if he had said the wrong thing.

'No – it is just something that Antonin Meiros said when he gave me these papers: he told me that researchers might come here, and that I should be sure of them before I allowed them access.' Then Hanook had looked at Alaron intensely. 'My father and my uncle kept me as a family secret all my years. Even my Aunt Justina didn't know of me. They did not trust even their own people in the Ordo Costruo with the knowledge of my existence. This was in part because Antonin had declared that no magi should operate in Lakh and I was a violation of his own edict.'

Alaron shifted uncomfortably at this. Ramita worshipped her dead husband and it didn't sit well that the old mage might have been a hypocrite in certain matters.

This must have showed on his face, because Hanook had gone on, 'The very fact that Adric Meiros came to Khotriawal tells you that the

Ordo Costruo took a keen interest in matters beyond Hebusalim. My father told me that even then they were becoming aware that other groups with the gnosis were abroad in the lands, trying to win status in kingdoms all over Ahmedhassa. Most were weak, low-blooded, but from time to time they came across powerful magi – sometimes renegades of his own order, but also Souldrinkers, the so-called Rejects of Kore. I myself have faced these beings at times, trying to inveigle their way into court. We kill them, or expose them to the Godspeakers anonymously and let them deal with them. So Antonin Meiros' vigilance in this matter was right and necessary.'

For a fleeting moment Alaron feared that Hanook took him for such a thing, but the old vizier had fixed him in the eye and asked, 'Do I need to know what it is you study, young man?'

'Sir,' he'd replied, 'if you are at all unsure of me, I withdraw my request.'

Hanook had studied him silently for a few seconds, then said slowly, 'I have gone over these papers many times and found nothing but matters of scholarly interest. They are mostly botanic in nature. Antonin Meiros was a Sylvanic mage of great skill, as you may be aware. Is that your interest?'

Alaron had shrugged, though his heart was pounding a little faster. Botany might have been the dullest topic of them all at college, but it was possibly also the key to unravelling the remainder of the Scytale's mysteries. 'I'm just looking for something to do,' he'd said as nonchalantly as he could.

Apparently spending his Arcanum years alongside Ramon Sensini had turned him into a proficient liar, because the vizier had given permission.

And he had found the *exact* text he needed.

The title inscribed on the scroll-case was perfectly innocuous: *Herbal Compounds and Associated Materials*. Inside were sheaths of notes in a spidery hand that Alaron recognised as Meiros' own. He didn't understand the words, except for a sentence at the top: *Final compound variants, from memory*. It was dated 1183LCii, which meant nothing to him. The characters beneath it were foreign to him, line upon line written in an alphabet he didn't know, but as he stared, he realised it did look vaguely familiar. He almost put it aside, but something made him leaf through the next few pages. And he stared.

From the third page on, a list of symbols were placed in a column on the left, with adjacent blocks of text, still in the unknown script, but what made him stop and start quivering in excitement was that he recognised those symbols: They were the exact symbols he'd been staring at for months, inscribed on the inner cylinder of the Scytale.

He'd almost shouted aloud, but at the last minute he'd managed to turn his whoop of joy into a coughing fit like those of the old scholar at the next table. The old man said something conciliatory in Lakh. 'Yeah, the dust,' Alaron replied, trying to stop his hand from trembling.

Now he was copying out the scrolls words for word, as exactly as he could. He might not know the symbols of the alphabet Meiros used, but this was a language, and languages could be translated – how or when or where, he had no idea, but he'd find out.

It was the same thrill he'd felt when he, Ramon and Cym had unravelled the trail of clues that led to the Scytale in the first place. He found himself missing them both hugely, and hoping that somehow they were both alive and well.

He finished writing and waved the copies about to thoroughly dry the ink, while wondering if he really did now hold the secret of the Scytale; that he had the ingredients to the ambrosia that turned men into magi. It seemed unbelievable – but then, so had finding the Scytale in the first place. He carefully rolled his copies up, found another unused scroll case and slid them in. *I'll conceal this with the Scytale* . . .

'Alaron?'

He started guiltily, but it was only Ramita. The old Lakh scholar in the corner looked at her like she was an intruder and barked a warning. They eyeballed each other, but Ramita was clearly agitated, so Alaron stepped between them. 'I'm done here,' he said softly, trying to convey some of his excitement.

She caught his look, and her eyes lit up faintly.

'How was court?'

Her nose wrinkled. 'My behind is sore from sitting all day. And the children were squalling when I got back. These servants of the vizier know nothing about how to care for babies.'

Alaron grinned. 'Let's go and feed them.' For the last week they'd been trying to get the twins to eat more solids, to help the weaning. It was messy, but kind of fun. His latest trick was to distract them with one hand while slipping food into their mouths with the other. The results had been mixed.

Ramita smiled warmly. 'You are good with them, bhaiya.'

So they adjourned to the upper level, wrapped the twins in their heavily stained feeding blankets and spooned a stodgy mess of pump-kin and soft rice into demanding mouths, all the while making silly noises and pulling faces to entertain their charges. The food going in triggered waste coming out, and Alaron changed Nasatya's wraps, then handed him to Ramita.

'You know, I do not think my father ever helped my mother with these things, for any of us children,' Ramita remarked, looking up at him with a fond look on her face. 'It is not considered manly.'

Alaron shrugged. 'My father cared for me. He was plenty manly.'

'So are you,' Ramita replied, unlacing the front of her smock. She allowed the twins only two feeds a day now, but it helped to ease the discomfort she was feeling. 'You are a very good man.'

Something in her voice resonated with recognition, of something inside him or herself – he couldn't tell which, but he found himself looking back at her, a sudden lump in his throat.

She'd been breastfeeding in front of him by necessity for so long he'd stopped noticing. it was like being with the lamiae women, who went topless all the time. But the mood was different tonight and he found himself consciously averting his eyes. They'd played out this scene so often, but this time his eyes kept sliding sideways, back to her. The evening light was glowing softly through the windows and onto her face, making her skin radiate and turning her eyes into luminous orbs that glowed. And she was looking at him differently too, not with her normal businesslike sheen, but more vulnerable.

She knew it too, because she abruptly shook herself and snapped, 'Bhaiya, are you just going to stand there and stare, or are you going to change Dasra's wraps?'

He changed Das silently, his back to her while she put Nas to her nipple. Her soft groan as the infant latched on was perhaps the most erotic thing he'd ever heard. His hands shook as he cleaned up and he had to swallow before he could speak.

'So,' he managed at last, 'how was court, truly?'

She didn't reply immediately, and as the silence drew out, he looked back at her and saw that she was silently crying, tears flowing in rivulets from the inside corners of her eyes. She cooed something to Nas and shifted him from the breast, looking down at him and stroking his head.

'Tariq is just a boy,' she said eventually. 'He is fourteen and surrounded by old men who tell him what to do. He is suspicious of everyone and lives in fear. He overeats and he drinks more than he should for a boy of his age. He is turning to fat already. He plays favourites and lives for pleasure. But what he enjoys most is holding the power of life and death in his hands.'

'He told you this?'

'I could tell this by looking at him. He reminded me of those rich men who used to come to the markets, buying and selling what they pleased, careless of the cost. We traders would bow and scrape to them, do whatever they wanted, but we fleeced them and despised them.'

'So you didn't like him then?'

'No, I did not.'

'Will you marry him?' he asked, his voice faint.

'I don't know. Hanook and Dareem think it's for the best, but I am not so sure.'

Alaron swallowed. He wasn't sure that his advice on this matter was entirely neutral any more. He enjoyed her odd mix of pragmatism and spirituality, and despite the growing feeling that Hanook was as good a person as any to hand over the Scytale to, doubts remained. He knew that the moment he surrendered it, his role in this drama, and in Ramita's life, was effectively over, and that was scaring him too. What was he without the Scytale? Just an outlaw in his own lands.

If I give up the Scytale to them, I may as well become a monk after all ... But I don't want that ... I want a family, and my friends around me. I want a life, not a hermitage ...

He swallowed and concentrated on pinning Das' wrap, then went to Ramita and bent to take the snuffling and contented Nas, while she fastened the front of her smock. Before he could move away, she seized his right hand and pointedly examined his rakhi-string. It had lost its decorations, and the orange colouring had been all but leeched out from months of bathing, sweat and travel. 'I need to get you a new rakhi, bhaiya. Tomorrow is the feast of Raksha Bandan, the celebration of brother and sister. You must bring me a gift.'

'I don't have anything to give you,' he said, his voice husky. 'Only my loyalty.'

She smiled sadly. 'That is more than enough, bhaiya.'

He pulled his hand away. 'Ramita, Hanook told you where your family is. You could live with them, safely hidden. You don't have to submit to what he wants. It isn't Destiny or Duty.'

'You don't understand, bhaiya,' she whispered. 'After I returned with Dareem, Hanook told me that the mughal has agreed that my sons will be adopted if I wed him. They will be princes, perhaps even mughal one day! That is the essence of my Duty: to do well for my children. That is what my father did for me, and now I can do the same for my children.'

'But—'

'Bhaiya, I need to be alone now. I have heard your advice, but I do not need to take it.'

'Ramita, we've got the Kore-bedamned Scytale—'

Her eyes flared. '*OUT!*'

The twins burst into tears at the sudden shout, and the cacophony drove him from the room.

Baranasi, Lakh, on the continent of Antiopia
Shaban (Augeite) 929
14th month of the Moontide

Huriya Makani stalked the backstreets of her old hometown, seeking an elusive scent. Males of the pack flanked her, now and then uttering low growls to drive off the stray dogs that haunted the streets. They'd left their horses at the fringes of the city with Kenner guarding them. Huriya was wrapped in a thick cloak to conceal her gauzy red silks. Night had long fallen, and away from the market stalls that sold food and drink to the passersby, the city was silent. Families had retreated to their tiny homes, packed together cheek and jowl in hovels like badly stacked crates, oblivious to the passing shapeshifters.

The scent she sought could not be found anywhere from Aruna Nagar to the river. It didn't linger in the former home of the Ankesharan family – they were long gone, and a new family roosted there. Huriya snapped a command to her escort and they padded onward. Ramita's family might have left, but surely others remained who knew where they'd gone? And she knew exactly the right place to start looking.

The house she sought was just as she recalled it, grimy on the outside but solid – but that was normal here, where the close-packed life made exteriors public property. She used her gnosis to float to the first-floor balcony. The doors were open to the night air and oil lamps shone inside, making the polished slate floor glow and the sequins in the wall-tapestries shimmer. It was only the home of a trader, but he was a prince among merchants: Vikash Nooradin – Ispal Ankesharan's friend.

Laughter, the clink of goblets and the low buzz of conversation reached her from the dining room. She shed her cloak and slipped into the lounge, her hands trailing over fine fabric furniture coverings and decorative artefacts. Rose and poppy candles scented the air. A gauzy veil was draped over the back of a seat and she wound herself in it for the sheer pleasure of feeling the texture against her skin. Then she extended her senses and listened in on the conversation in the next room.

Vikash Nooradin and his wife had guests, but it wasn't Ispal Ankesharan and his family, or anyone else she could recognise by their voices. *But perhaps they'll know where Ispal is if Vikash doesn't?*

She stepped out of the shadows and into the dining room whilst pulling her gnosis into readiness about her. The voice of Sabele whispered in her ear, as it had ever since that day on the Isle of Glass when she had swallowed the old woman's soul. It still had the power to chill her: Sabele was inside her, intact and waiting. Sometimes she found it very hard to work out where she ended and where the hag whose powers she'd stolen began.

I am me. You are just a ghost.

Sabele laughed. *You think you're my first, girlie? I've had more lives than you dare dream. Shall I show you?*

Shut up, old hag. You're nothing but a piece of my memory.

No, girlie. That's what you're on the way to becoming.

Her sudden rage made her power flare and every head in the dining room turned towards her.

To them it looked like a beautiful and near-naked young woman simply appeared out of thin air – an Apsara or a Rakas – then Vikash Nooradin's eyes bulged with recognition. '*Huriya Makani?*'

'Hello, Uncle Vikash. It's lovely to see you again.'

Her pack filled the house. Jackal-headed men and women humped on the sofas and rugs. Giant wolves and cats lolled around, tearing at the remains of the servants and dinner guests. Once stripped of the flesh, the bloodied bones were chewed over: their gnostic hunger might be satisfied, but their bellies wanted more.

Only Vikash Nooradin was still alive, and that would not be for much longer.

Vikash didn't know where Ispal Ankesharan and his family were, and neither did his fat, pretentious wife. It had given Huriya enormous pleasure to cut *that* cow's throat. There remained the question of whether there was anything at all she could learn from Vikash before she let her followers loose on him for the last time.

He was past words now. The past four hours had reduced the clever, urbane merchant into a piteous ruin. But she didn't need words from him; not now her mind was buried deep inside his and she was turning over his memories of his last moments with Ispal Ankesharan. What she was doing would have left Vikash a drooling vegetable for the rest of his life, but he was fatally harmed anyway.

The Ankesharans had left Baranasi three months after Ramita, telling no one their destination. Soldiers had loaded the wagons, unmarked with any kind of symbols or sigils; they left nothing behind except a parting gift of two lak – years of income for a small trader – as a thank-you to Vikash. They were missed, but no word came.

Huriya scowled, sulking as the trader's consciousness slipped away fruitlessly. *Where are you, Ispal?*

'You're going to need a Necromancer if he doesn't talk soon,' Malevorn said in a flat, dispassionate voice. He'd taken in the torture without emotion; indeed, he'd offered suggestions. He was clad in the garb of a Keshi mercenary, and with his face now tanned and his black hair and whiskers grown out, he looked almost Dhassan.

'He knows nothing,' she replied, certain of it. 'Kill him.' She pulled out her small eating knife, honed the edge with a waft of the gnosis and handed it handle-first to the Inquisitor. He met her eyes, knew she was testing him.

Try to turn that knife on me and I'll crush you.

The Inquisitor, his gnosis still Chained, was not so stupid: with slow precision, Malevorn showed Vikash the blade, then pushed it slowly through his eye and into his brain. The trader cried out wordlessly, disbelieving until the very last that his life would end this way. Then he deflated and was gone.

Huriya studied Malevorn, oddly excited by his ruthlessness.

We of the Brethren are a broad church. I think there is room for a former Inquisitor . . .

Malevorn wiped the blade clean on a tablecloth and returned it.

She smiled approvingly. 'Did you learn where the Ankesharan family went?' he asked.

She had indeed seen something: the glimpse of a face. Vikash had seen it at a distance only, and it wasn't much, but Sabele had recognised the stamp of the features because she had seen an older version of it. 'I saw a face, I think, of the son of someone known to me. Do you know the name Hanook?'

He shook his head.

'Hanook is the Vizier of Lakh. I think perhaps he has whisked Ramita's family away somewhere, which means we must go to Teshwallabad and have a serious word with him.'

29

Slaves

The Slave Trade

Man has enslaved man since time immemorial. So how can anyone claim it to be unnatural?

BAYL TAVOISSON, TREASURER, PALLAS, 811

The city produces a surfeit of useless men and women. The slavers do us a kindness in paying to take them away.

RASAIYAH, CALIPHA OF BASSAZ, 840

What saddens us most is the hideous complicity of the elites of all nations in this demeaning trade.

ANTONIN MEIROS, 843

Southern Kesh, on the continent of Antiopia
Shaban (Augeite) 929
14th month of the Moontide

Cymbellea lay on the rock beside the lion, thankful to take the weight off her legs, and gazed out over the valley below. They'd been trailing a column of men, women and children trudging northwards with heads bowed, since they'd stumbled across them the previous day, after three weeks of travelling eastwards through southern Kesh. Red-cloaked legionaries flanked the column, the lowering sun glinting off their steel helms. More menacing yet were the riders alongside:

the Sacred Heart was emblazoned on their tabards and they were borne by horned steeds. *Inquisitors.*

Beside her the lion's hackles rose again and a low rumble escaped his throat. The great cat was shaggy and rough-looking from weeks on the road. He was lying on his belly, head raised as he scanned, whiskers twitching. *<Cymbellea, is it the same Inquisitors who attacked the Isle of Glass?>* he asked, his warm, rough presence touching her mind.

She shook her head. 'I don't think so, but it's hard to be certain.'

Zaqri snarled, *<Slave-takers, then.>*

'Usually it's ordinary legions who collect slaves, not Inquisitors.'

<That is also my recollection.> Zaqri's brow furrowed *<We need to question one of them. They may know where the other group is.>*

It felt like a long shot to Cym, but what other options did they have? 'How?'

<We'll think of something. Come.>

They trailed the column north to a new campsite a mile on, and as the sun set and the air cooled, they crept closer and found a perch from which to observe. The Inquisitors were in hostile territory and they knew it, judging by the wards set about the camp. The people they were herding were a mixture of Dhassan and Keshi from the borderlands, men and women, old and young, even children and infants at the breast. They had been allowed to bring food and bedrolls – presumably to make the march easier for the Inquisitors to manage. There was little use of whips or chains; it was obvious fear was quite enough to cow the people.

Then they noticed the eleventh rider.

He wasn't an Inquisitor, yet he rode a khurne. He was wearing a bekira-shroud, and yet Cym and Zaqri were both sure he was a man. And when they looked at him using gnostic sight, there was something that pricked Zaqri's interest. It was too far away to tell for sure, but Zaqri thought he might be of his kind. *<We should try to free him – he might be one of my Brethren.>* He surveyed the landscape, then scanned the skies. *<But not tonight. They are wary, and I wish to see where they are going.>*

They backed away into the gloom. Once line of sight was broken,

Zaqri rose onto two legs, changing shape fluidly, and they jogged through the twilight, back to the place where they had left their possessions, then set up camp for the night. Zaqri had caught a desert hare that afternoon and they had stripped a clump of berry bushes they had passed earlier, wolfing handfuls of the fruit, relishing the rich red juices filling their mouths. Partway through, Cym realised that he was surreptitiously watching her, but she was used to his regard by now; she found it oddly flattering. They'd been living so intimately for so long that desire was an unspoken facet of their complex dance.

They hadn't mated again, though – and she really disliked the word: 'mated' had implications of animal coupling driven by monthly cycles. Despite her antipathy for the notion, however, she felt incredibly in touch with the rhythms of her body, from these months of living so close to nature. As her fertile period approached, she could feel a warm heaviness in her loins at nights, eroding her fortitude, her desire to be aloof and hostile. She knew Zaqri sensed it too, but his discipline was iron-hard, as it had been since he met her. It was a strange feeling: she could not forgive, but sustaining hatred was so hard.

Some nights she knew he could not sleep until he'd gone off and purged his own needs. This would be one of those nights; she could feel it in his heat and his eyes. She had nights like that too, but she was careful to control herself, ashamed that she had such urges at all around him.

That night she faced away from him, trying to ignore his eyes on her back, until finally she had to roll over. He was loosely wrapped in a blanket, lying on his back with his head propped on his bundle of spare clothing, his chest and shoulders bare. In the moonlight he looked carved from ivory, a magnificent physical specimen. And his beauty was not merely skin-deep, despite his condition. He carried his hungers with the dignity of an alpha predator.

One of her best friends among the Rimoni had been married off to a man she didn't desire, in a different caravan, and whenever the two caravans happened to meet, she would confide a little of her married life to Cym. Last time they met up, her friend had two children, though there was no pretence of love. 'Don't worry about love,' she'd told Cym once. 'You can make babies with a man you don't like – you can even enjoy the bedding. Love is not necessary.'

Love is not necessary.

She could feel unbearable liquid heat and heaviness between her thighs, right at the core of her, the empty part that wanted to be filled again. She remembered their one time, and how frighteningly complete it had made her, to feel him inside her. She'd tried to pretend it wasn't there, when oh, but it was . . .

Love mightn't be necessary, but I need this . . .

Trembling slightly, she shook herself free of her blanket and crawled towards him. He sucked in his breath, as if scared to exhale the moment away. He just lay there, passive, but not entirely so, because she could see the shape of his erection beneath the blanket. She pulled the fabric away and laid her head on his belly. The stiff member lay against his groin, staring at her one-eyed, and she reached out and gently touched it.

He groaned.

She stroked a finger from root to tip, and he tried not to move, though she could feel him vibrating like an overstrung bow. She gripped his shaft, feeling it thick and heavy in her grasp, and began to massage it. At last his hands moved, stroking her shoulders, combing through her hair. His stomach muscles quivered beneath her head. She moved slowly and tentatively, listening to the rhythms of his body, trying to determine what worked. Tentatively she slid down him a little, then opened her mouth and enclosed him, first licking, then sucking him until his whole body stiffened. It pleased her to administer this torment, so she kept doing it, making him twitch and writhe, felt herself become wetter as she did so, scenting the damp heat that filled her nostrils.

When it became too much to wait, she swung herself astride him and started rocking her hips, sliding her cleft along the underside of his shaft, something she'd spied a married couple of the caravan doing one night when they thought they were alone. The sensation of it made her catch her breath.

She looked down at him, feeling all the longing and all the conflicted emotions resolving. She'd been alone with him too long not to feel this, not to do this. It didn't mean forgiveness. It was just lust. It meant nothing.

He gripped her hips, holding her in just the right place. The contact shivered right through her. She'd been playing with him so far, but now it was about them together. She spread herself a little more, reached down and pulled the head of him to her opening, groaned at the teasing almost-penetration, then gasped as he slid inside, filling her completely. Her arms and hips almost gave way, but she forced herself upright.

His face swam before her, disbelief and studied concentration on his face.

She looked down at him apologetically, whispered, 'That's as far as my experience goes.'

He gave a slight smile. 'I can help. Continue to do this.' He pushed her up slightly so she had to tilt her hips, and as he let her down again she found the rhythm, grinding her pleasure bud against him while enjoying the length of him inside her. For a moment his eyes closed in bliss, then he opened them again and gazed into hers. 'Rub against me; take as long as you like.'

It was different from what she'd expected, more intimate and sweaty and human than her imagination, with more grunting and itchy, uncomfortable bits than other girls had reported. It felt like Zaqri was not doing much, then he would move, a subtle lift of his hips that made his stomach muscles tense and ripple appealingly, then he was moving more and more, until it was him doing all the work, pushing up and into her as she collapsed onto his chest, the sensations in her loins too intense to focus. She held onto him, moaning, as her body climaxed, the sensation sustained by his final vigorous expending of himself inside her.

She buried her head in his nape and shook. *I'm sorry, Mother, but I couldn't resist him any longer.*

He reached for her face, but she turned it away. 'No kisses,' she said, breathing heavily.

He frowned at that, but let her pull herself from him and drape his blanket over them both. Mater Luna stared down at her. Rimoni legend had it that the two largest craters were her eyes. They seemed very focused that night, looking right at her.

'Why now?' His voice was low and content. His arm came around her shoulders, cradling her.

'Why not?' She put on a rational voice. 'It's distracting, to have this *thing* between us and not deal with it.'

'So I am not forgiven, then?'

'No.'

They fell silent, just staring up at the moon as she floated overhead. She'd never felt comfortable before beneath the open night sky, except during Darkmoon when Luna hid her face. The moon always looked too massive to float above. It always felt like it was about to fall. But tonight she felt safe.

'So you were a virgin until me,' he remarked eventually.

'Only just. My father kept coming between me and whichever boy I fancied – sometimes only just in time.'

'It must have been hard for you both.'

'I was a trial.' She took a swig of water from her bottle. 'But he was no saint. He never took a wife, but he seldom slept alone. All the widows used to compete for his attention.' She sighed at the memory. 'Rimoni widows are allowed to court the single men. They have more freedom than anyone else in the caravan. I always wanted to be one of them when I was young – they had the most fun.'

'There is no joy in losing your wife or husband.'

'I know that now.' She twisted her head so that she could see his face. 'How long were you married to Ghila?'

'Twenty-three years.'

'Sol et Lune, that's older than I am!'

'Like the magi, those of us with strong gnosis live longer.'

'You must miss her.'

'I do. But life continues. If we don't move with it, we atrophy and die.' He looked at her meaningfully. 'Life is full of perils, especially this life. I believe in seizing the moment, not in looking back.'

'You don't sound like a real Rimoni when you say that. We are always looking back to when we ruled Yuros.'

He chuckled dryly. 'I know. In my home village we used to spend all our spare time and money on restoring old monuments and artefacts from the Rimoni Empire – villas, mosaics, columns and temples. Families went without meals so that some old idol could be recovered.'

'The Rondians spend all their money on churches and palaces.'

'I certainly wasn't saying they are better than us.' He ran fingers through her hair. 'You are very beautiful, Cymbellea. A classic Rimoni, with a chin and nose like the statues we dug from the ground.'

'Like a horse, you mean.'

He laughed. 'Not a bit. I am not attracted to horses at all.'

'Just lionesses?' she asked archly.

'Ha! I do not mate in animal form. It sheds a layer of humanity I do not wish to lose.'

'I suppose . . . I wouldn't know.'

He shifted abruptly, rolled over and onto her in one movement that stole her breath, his face silhouetted against the moon. 'I think we will find enough pleasure in these bodies to satisfy us.'

She looked up at him, suddenly a little bit afraid. She'd not intended to allow him to initiate anything, but now she found she wanted him again. Tentatively she spread herself, lifting her hips to meet him, all the while careful to avert her mouth from his.

The night passed in a series of long and intense bouts of climbing desire and convulsive release.

They followed the Rondian column north, the trail so clear they didn't need to keep it in sight. Cym had lost all track of time, but Zaqri, studying the stars, told her it was Augeite, under a waning moon: eight months since Alaron and Ramita had vanished; four since the Noose. They'd lost the trail of the Scytale long ago, and sometimes it felt like she only went on because she didn't know what she would do if they stopped.

However, the riddle of the eleventh rider drew them on still.

Though not a prisoner, he was always under the eye of the Inquisitors, as if he were their prized guest. Zaqri was still certain that he was Dokken, but he couldn't say who, as they never saw him without his hood. At night they coupled until exhaustion took them down into dreamless sleep. *Mated.* There was no kissing, though she often wanted to. She didn't bleed during the week she should have. They had rukked throughout the week of her fertility without too much thought for the consequences. She didn't tell him, instead slicing her own skin so that she smelled of blood and praying to Mater Luna for guidance. She didn't think he suspected.

When the column arrived at its destination, the mystery deepened. They watched from a hillside, then used a little gnosis to scry closer. There were fences of wood and wire to pen people – many people, perhaps ten thousand of them. A full maniple of legionaries was camped there, though it was clearly run by the Inquisition. The Dhassan and Keshi refugees they'd been following weren't housed in tents, but simply penned on the open ground. Some were conscripted into the crude open-air kitchens; many more were given shovels to dig latrine trenches. Every day work gangs left for the hills, their escorts returning at dusk without the labourers. Every morning a few more dead were carted from the camp and buried in the grounds outside. These shallow graves drew the jackals and wild dogs, who prowled the fringes of the camp.

'Slavers,' Zaqri continued to maintain. 'They're awaiting windships to transport the prisoners to Southpoint.'

They glimpsed the eleventh rider from time to time, sitting alone, hooded and motionless, always watched, but only loosely. He moved awkwardly, in a lumbering fashion that reminded Cym of a drunk, or a very old man. Intriguingly, his skin colour was of Yuros. It was too far away to read his aura, and with Inquisitors right beside him, scrying was far too great a risk.

'He's one of us,' Zaqri predicted. 'Not our pack, but one of us. But why would they hold him?' He turned to Cym, his eyes intent. 'I say we must free him.'

30

Downstream

Master-General Kaltus Korion

Kaltus Korion, greatest descendant of the line of Evarius, is renowned as the general who brought Leroi Robler to heel in the Noros Revolt. He conducted a ruthless campaign in the latter year of the Revolt, which resulted in the surrender of the Noroman legions. What is often overlooked is that though he vastly outnumbered Robler, still he conducted a war of attrition. Was this prudence, or did he fear to risk his reputation against the master?

The Glorious Revolution,
MAGNUS GRAYNE, 909–910, 915

Ardijah, Emirate of Khotri, on the continent of Antiopia
Shaban (Augeite) 929
14th month of the Moontide

Ramon watched with interest as Lanna Jureigh cradled a Khotri man's broken arm. They were surrounded by men from almost every known land on two continents. *Coming to Ardijah was the right move,* he thought. *Better even than I'd hoped.*

Ardijah, a border town on a well-used trade route, attracted people from far and wide. As well as the local Khotri there were Dhassans and Keshi, tattooed men and women from Gatioch, many Lakh and even a few gaunt, fierce Lokistani. This incredibly diverse place had its own hybrid patois, with words from innumerable languages, so adding a motley collection of legionaries from half a dozen different legions made it a strange brew indeed. At times it boiled over in conflict, but for the most part there was a strange harmony, as if they recognised that foreignness was a condition they all suffered. They were all, in their own way, *strangers*.

The army kept the rankers busy on work detail, trying to repair the buildings and walls damaged during the seizure of the city. As the locals wanted the Dokken gone as much as the legionaries, and they also wished their city to be defensible against the Keshi on the north bank, everyone pitched in, the calipha's men and the legionaries working in unison. Some of the repairs required a variety of expertise, from locals as well as the legion engineers, so cooperation had become essential.

But it was acts like this that had really sealed the bond, Ramon thought as he watched Lanna repairing another broken arm. The minor miracle of a gnostic healing was a big thing to the Ahmedhassans: not just a demonstration that the locals were valued, but also that the gnosis could be used for good. Other uses of the gnosis had helped further that notion: Earth-magi had been deployed to help the rebuilding, Water-magi were purifying the wells, and there were dozens of other tasks where a show of useful solidarity and well-placed gnosis might win hearts and minds.

The crowd cheered and patted each other's backs as the Khotri worker stood shakily and displayed the arm that had been shattered by falling masonry an hour before. A lifetime as a one-armed cripple had averted by the 'afreet magic'. The dazed patient kissed Lanna's hand fervently, though she tried to stop him.

'Please, it's not so hard,' she said tiredly. 'Be more careful, yes?' She looked up at Ramon and gave an exhausted but pleased smile. She'd had marriage proposals by the hundred in the last week, and been gifted so much food she could have fed a maniple.

He gave her a thumbs-up gesture and returned to the square where the accident had happened. Pilus Lukaz was overseeing lines of legionaries and locals as they passed chunks of rubble from a fallen bakery towards a half-built bastion wall. The giant front-rankers towering over the local tradesmen earned admiring calls as they humped the stone to the new site, but some of the Khotri were just as big and it looked like a friendly rivalry was developing.

It hadn't all been plain sailing, of course. There had inevitably been brawls, drunkenness, stones thrown, fist-fights, bottle-fights, knife-fights, coin stolen – in fact, every infraction of the rules he could imagine. They'd even had to hang two rankers for murdering a local behind a tavern to ensure that there'd be no riots. The calipha had been astounded that they would sacrifice two of their own, and some of the legion officers had been downright rebellious, but the reward was this priceless harmony. He was almost regretting that they had to leave.

He found the people he sought atop a tower overlooking the river, near the northern causeway. The four of them – Jelaska, Severine, Baltus and Kip – were sipping wine or ale and looking out at Salim's army massed on the riverbank four hundred yards away. Their cooking fires were streaming smoke into the sky beneath a searing sun.

'I've calculated that we need to move within the month if we're going to reach our lines in time for the big retreat to the Bridge next year,' Ramon told the group. The Lost Legions – as the men had taken to calling themselves – had been inside Ardijah for almost six weeks now and it was already Augeite. 'I've got it arranged. We just need Seth's assent and then we can go.'

'I agree,' Jelaska responded, 'but will Seth? Don't you think he's becoming a little *comfortable* here?'

They all knew what she meant: Korion was spending all his time with the sultan – or Salim's imposter, whichever he was. Whenever anyone walked in on them they'd be usually reciting poetry, or singing, or plucking a strangely strung lute they'd been given by Calipha Amiza.

'Then let's bring Latif with us,' Baltus said. 'Clearly his presence is keeping the Keshi from outright assault, so hanging on to him would be sensible.'

'What do they see in each other?' Severine asked, cradling her alarmingly distended belly and nibbling grapes. 'I mean, Korion is dull as dishwater and the Noorie is . . . well, he's just a Noorie.'

Ramon glanced at her with mildly irritated fondness. That Sevvie could be blind to the colour of his skin but completely scathing of even a hint of colour in anyone else was entirely to do with her upbringing, he'd decided after considerable soul-searching. It made it only marginally less distasteful. 'Latif's rather charming,' he said, 'but you're right about Korion. Poetry and music, Sol et Lune!'

'You're a peasant, Ramon,' Baltus laughed. 'Poetry is the soul of civilisation.'

'Life is a song,' Kip observed, drawing surprised looks from everyone. He coloured slightly. 'That is an old Schlessen saying. My people are very fond of music.'

'They hit sticks and rocks together,' Baltus whispered conspiratorially. 'It's very rhythmic.'

'I'll hit your head with a rock and see how you like it,' Kip growled.

'Anyway,' Ramon interjected, trying to bring the discussion back on course, 'my point is, we need to move, but Korion is ensconced here – and the truth is, he's way too cosy with Latif, almost to the point of fraternisation.'

Jelaska sniffed. 'He says he's getting the imposter off-guard so that he can learn more. Clever, possibly.'

'Korion isn't that clever,' Ramon said. 'I just think that he likes him.'

They all mused on that. 'I suppose Noories are just people in the end,' Severine commented doubtfully.

'Do you think so? What about Silacians?' Ramon enquired acerbically. 'Anyway, the rankers are talking,' he added. 'Not that half of them haven't got a Khotri woman by now – our baggage train will probably have doubled in size when we leave.' He'd taken the decision to pay the troops while they were in Ardijah, not just to restore morale, but also to ensure that they could enjoy the respite the town had provided without resorting to plundering it. Of course, giving the soldiers money had done more than that: it had transformed the twin keeps of Ardijah into a hotbed of gambling houses, whorehouses and opium dens almost overnight as the soldiers did what soldiers always do when they have cash in hand and no one to fight. The calipha's treasurer was a happy man.

During this period of respite, the waters of the floodplain had receded, leaving a treacherous maze of sinkholes and quicksand, and alligators had been spotted moving back into the area in ever-increasing numbers. Despite this, Ramon feared that soon, an assault on the northern island from all sides would soon be practical.

'You know, I sometimes think Silacians are people too,' Severine observed mildly.

Ramon ruffled her hair: things weren't too bad between them just now, partly because everyone knew what Renn Bondeau was doing in the calipha's suite every night. It was no secret that Ardijah's new ruler had decided that a mage-child would be a fine addition to her lineage, and the Amteh Godspeakers could whinge in the Dom-al'Ahm all day and all night for all she cared.

Ramon couldn't decide if Amiza was reckless or courageous, but time would tell, no doubt. He had to admit – if only in the privacy of his own mind – that her decisive lust for life was oddly magnetic.

'I hear the calipha bled as normal last week,' Baltus observed with a smirk. 'She must be disappointed.'

'I imagine sharing a bed with Bondeau is full of disappointments,' Ramon observed.

Severine chuckled. 'It was for me.'

Ramon eyed her disapprovingly. 'I have to say that before you met me, you had no taste in men at all.'

Severine laughed. 'Some would say I still don't. Anyway, I have it on good authority that she retired to the Blood-tower by habit only – she has been heard complaining of an upset stomach,' she added in a gossipy voice. 'So maybe Renn has hit the target after all.'

'I doubt I'll ever have a child,' Jelaska said heavily. 'Every lover I have ever taken is dead. Poor Sigurd is only the latest of a long line of corpses I've left behind.' She swept back her grey mane and shrugged. 'I've come to regard myself as cursed.'

Baltus waved a hand airily. 'Curses are a superstition, Lady. The only real magic is the gnosis.'

Jelaska threw him an appraising look. 'I am willing to test the courage of your convictions, Windmaster.'

'I say, my lady, is that a proposition?'

'I am a plainspoken Argundian, Magister Prenton. My door is open to you.'

Ramon shared a look with Severine. 'Romantic, these Argundians, aren't they?'

'Terribly.'

Kip guffawed and swigged more ale. 'I miss Schlessen girls. Blonde hair in braids and big, soft bodies. The woman here are too small and skinny. They need to be fed better. Beef, that is the answer.'

'A simple man with simple tastes,' Baltus commented.

'A Schlessen, in other words,' said Jelaska, and the two of them laughed, not very surreptitiously looking each other over.

Kip burped and waved them away. 'I care not what you think. I know what's true.'

'He could be right, you know,' Ramon put in. 'Why is it that a whole race of people can be smaller and thinner than another? It can only be what they eat, si? Antiopians eat almost entirely vegetables and spices and very little meat. But their noblemen eat meat – you saw see how fat that damned caliph was? It took eight men to lift his corpse!'

'It's the spices that stunt them,' Jelaska muttered. 'Evil stuff, gives you the shits.'

'No, it's the lack of meat,' Ramon said firmly, 'mark my words.'

'Anyway,' Baltus said, still looking Jelaska over; she was a handsome woman, no doubt, but twice his age, Ramon suspected. Still, how much did that actually matter?

He turned his attention back to the matter at hand. 'The thing is, if we don't move, our position is going to deteriorate. The Emir of Khotri has shifted some forty thousand men to camps south of us and Salim has thirty thousand soldiers on the north bank. In the middle of all this there's us: just twelve thousand men divided over three camps – this northern Bridge-tower, the southern Bridge-tower, and the southern causeway.

'And some mighty women,' Jelaska added, toasting Severine.

'Yes, also stuck in the middle,' Baltus smirked. 'I'm with Ramon on this: Salim and the emir are talking to each other – I've seen skiffs shuttling between them. What if they find common cause?'

Ramon sat up. 'I understand they hate each other, but you're right: that doesn't mean they can't work together at all.' For the past week, he'd also been meeting with the Emir of Khotri's representatives, trying to iron out a deal so the legion could march downstream on the Khotri side of the river to the next fords, then leave the emirate. For it to work they needed two things: to be able to trust the emir, and to give Salim the slip.

'I rather think that convenience can outweigh all manner of normal politics and prejudices,' Severine said, without irony, causing Baltus to wink at Ramon mockingly.

Si, I'm her convenient partner, regardless of normal prejudices. Ramon flicked a rude sign at the Brevian. Aloud, he said, 'You're right. Maintaining an army here is inconvenient to both the emir and the sultan. Salim wants to go north, where the real fighting is, and the emir dearly wants him to go. Moving us on would solve both problems.' He wrinkled his nose. 'The real question is: can we trust the emir and the calipha not to sell us out to Salim?' He stared out over the darkening landscape. Tiny bats were circling the tower like moths around the lamps. The campfires of the Keshi army were a galaxy of yellow stars. 'I don't know that we can.'

'Then we're in trouble,' Jelaska said. 'We're like walnuts between the hammer and the anvil.'

Kip cocked his head. 'Eh?'

'They've got us by the nuts,' Ramon clarified.

Seth Korion lounged in his armchair and gazed admiringly at Latif. The Keshi was picking deftly at the lute, a chord progression that seemed to capture the very essence of the desert: the space, the golden vistas and the heat, brought to vivid life by fifteen strings, played with wonderful mastery. 'All of my brothers play,' Latif said offhandedly as he finished another tune. 'I'm not the best of us.'

'I can't imagine anyone better than you,' Seth told him. 'How can a ruler find time to perfect such technique?'

'I am just an imposter, remember. I'm not real.'

'Don't say that. I only like you because I think you are a sultan.'

Latif smiled slyly. 'I don't believe you. I think you like me because I am a talented and altogether brilliant individual who happens to excel at pretending to be someone else. I could just as easily play you.'

Seth burst out laughing. 'Now you're being ridiculous.'

'No, see! I colour my hair and shave my beard and suddenly I am the great General Korion, conqueror of Kesh.' He leapt to his feet, struck a declamatory pose. 'I order an advance! No, a retreat! Oh, what the Hel, I'll just have another drink!' And he swigged from an imaginary flask.

'No, no! I am never drunk!'

'So you say, but everyone knows the men of Yuros drink too much.'

Seth waved a dismissive hand. 'True enough. It is our greatest vice.' He looked fondly at Latif. 'But really, you could never pretend to be me. Because of this.'

He kindled blue fire on the fingers of his right hand.

Latif stiffened at the sight of it. 'I have some familiarity with your gnosis,' he said, his eyes suddenly hungry. 'Rashid Mubarak frequented the court in secret for many years. We took great precautions to ensure that he did not take control of us.'

'Are you sure he didn't?'

Latif frowned. 'That is the question we always fear to ask ourselves,' he said seriously.

Seth doused his gnosis-fire, regretful that he'd killed the mood. 'The gnosis does set us apart,' he admitted, 'especially us pure-blooded magi. It is a trust, bequeathed to us from Kore Himself. We perpetuate that blessing to our heirs.'

'And what is it like, to bear your god's gift?'

'It is a great responsibility. I mean, as children we are the same as anyone else, with no powers, but we're raised knowing what will be. Then when you're only twelve or thirteen, you suddenly gain the power to crush buildings, burn men alive, fly, summon spirits – whatever your affinities allow. Your slightest tantrum can destroy things or hurt people. So they send us to off to Arcanum – the mage-colleges – where tutors teach us and shape us, and when we emerge we have been taught to fight and kill, to protect others, and to serve the empire.'

'So you are a brotherhood, dedicated to your emperor?'

'Hardly,' he snorted. 'We are brought up to be fiercely competitive – we all know that there's a world of difference between the best and worst, even if we have equal blood-strength. The Arcanum is a place where the best begin their dominance of those around them. We make alliances with those who might be useful to us in the future, but true friendships are rare and rivals are put firmly in their place. In truth, I feared my friends.'

'I am told that your colleague – the devious one, Sensini – was also at your college?'

Seth blinked. 'Who told you that?'

'You are not my only visitor. The healer Lanna comes to check my wellbeing, your chaplain Gerdhart tries to convert me to your church and the old woman, Jelaska, plays tabula with me, formidably well. They speak of this and that.' He waved a hand. 'I am easy to talk to.'

The thought of others spending time here rankled somewhat. 'Sensini is of low blood and low morals,' Seth said crossly. 'He only graduated because he was bonded to the legions.'

'Yet he is clever. They tell me he is your strategist?'

Seth went to argue, then remembered, belatedly, that this charming man was still an enemy, and discussing the politics of the command tent was not a good idea. 'He contributes. But I command.'

Latif inclined his head enigmatically, then gave him a thoughtful look. 'So you magi are a people apart. Superior – God's chosen. You are better than we mere men, yes?'

Seth coloured slightly because he'd expressed that sentiment himself many times, and always with utter sincerity. But when Latif said it, it felt like a slight. Nevertheless, he felt compelled to defend his kind. 'When a person can do what we can, it makes us natural leaders – those with such a gift should control the world.'

'Should they? For whose benefit?'

'I don't see what you are asking. When we magi are strong, the empire is strong and all is well.'

'For whom?'

Seth threw up his hands. 'Why, for the empire, of course! For everyone!'

'Really? What benefit do your common people take from having magi rule them?'

Seth sat up, irritated now. 'Not being conquered. Peace and security. Windships. Incredible buildings. Public works. Animagery-constructs. The list is endless. You don't know what you are asking.'

Latif stroked his goatee. 'Do your Earth-magi build for the poor? Do they create aqueducts to bring water to dry lands? Do your wind-ships transport people for free? Are there gnosis-lamps in every street? Do your Healer-magi cure the illnesses of the poor without charge?'

'The world doesn't work like that,' Seth started, but Latif waved his answer away.

'The Ordo Costruo did as much, and more.'

'They were idealistic fools and they're all dead now – or fighting in your shihad!'

'It appears to me that those who benefit from having magi present in your society are those magi themselves,' Latif said. 'The mighty, enriching themselves further.'

'Don't you talk,' Seth snapped. 'I've seen how your nobility live in their marble palaces, with beggars scrabbling for alms in the dust outside! You're no better than us!'

Latif raised his palm as if to calm him. 'No better, my friend, but no worse, perhaps?'

His words stopped Seth in his tracks and suddenly he felt angry at himself for arguing with his only friend in this whole miserable continent. 'Maybe,' he said, then added, 'I can't help what I am. Let's talk about something else.'

Latif smiled softly, his brilliant eyes shining, but he wouldn't let the matter go. 'We each are given gifts, Seth Korion, to do our best with. For myself, I do not believe that your gnosis comes from Kore or Shaitan. I cannot afford to believe either, when I have both allies and enemies with your gift. I am' – he grinned ruefully – 'by which, of course, I mean "the sultan is" – at loggerheads with the Godspeakers because men and women they condemn as devils are aiding the shihad. Rashid Mubarak tells us that the gnosis comes not from divine beings but from man ourselves, and this gives me hope. Perhaps one day every man will have the gnosis, as naturally as breathing – and where would your Rondian superiority be then? You would have to treat us all as equals.'

Seth looked away. Such a vision of the world sounded positively threatening. Equality was just a dream, a muse for poets. Then he coloured, because all his heroes were poets. 'You give me a lot to think about.' He looked up at Latif slyly. 'You did say "I". Have I caught you out? Are you really Salim after all?'

'All of us brother-impersonators are taught to say "I" so that we do not refer to another man as Salim when impersonating him.'

'You must live closely with the sultan then?'

'We share everything.'

Seth raised his eyebrows. 'Do you even share Salim's wives?'

Latif laughed. 'That, no! That is the one restriction, that the wives must be for the true ruler only.'

'Ha! So tell me about your wives!'

'I cannot, for they are not mine. I do have a woman, though. Her name is Imuz, and she is skinny with buck teeth. We impersonators are always given the least pretty ones,' he laughed.

'Do you love her?'

'Love her? No! What is there to love? She has no interests except in producing children and wearing clothes. She has no conversation, sings like a strangled parrot and eats too much. You can't talk to her, not as we do.'

'Do you have a mistress then?'

Latif shook his head. 'Women do not interest me,' he said airily.

'Noble girls are boring. They have no education; all they learn is how to groom themselves, and how to gossip and plot about trivial things, like who will sit where at banquets. They're dull, dull, dull.'

'They sound like our women. Pure-blood magi girls are brought up to breed, preferably sons. They get enough gnosis-training to prevent them from damaging themselves, then they're farmed out for marriage.'

'Exactly my point. Have you ever had a conversation such as we have every day with a woman?' Latif raised his wine goblet. 'Every day I thank Ahm that I am a man.'

'Ha! So do I.' They drank to that thought, though it made Seth a little sad. 'You know, there are always a few woman-magi who devote themselves to the gnosis, like Jelaska and Lanna. They say they have to work twice as hard as a man to be considered half as good. I sometimes wonder how much talent and skill we miss out on by treating them that way.'

'You think educating women makes the nation stronger?' Latif frowned. 'Now, see, you have given me something to think on also.'

Seth smiled. Then at last he remembered the main reason for today's visit. 'Latif, we are going to move the army.'

'Where to? How? You are trapped here.'

Seth shook his head. 'Sensini has come up with something devious.'

'Ah.'

'Yes, I know, Sensini again. The thing is, do we take you with us?'

Latif's smile drained away. He got up and walked to the little brazier. 'Or what?' He looked back over his shoulder. 'I am told that Arkanus and Hecatta were executed.'

Seth put his cup down, and stood up. 'We are not going to execute you! Kore's Blood, man, you're a hostage! We're not barbarians!'

'The two Dokken were also hostages.'

'They were creatures condemned by Scripture. You're a political hostage – that's completely different. And you're not even you.'

Latif bowed ironically. 'Then of what value am I?'

'We learn from you, just as you learn from us.' He walked to Latif's side, patted his upper arm. 'Since we captured you, your army doesn't attack.'

'The causeway is a slaughterhouse: I am sure that is the reason for the lack of attacks, not me.'

Up close, Latif's eyes were like gems. Seth found the courage to meet his gaze. 'Latif, we're not invaders, not any more. We're just trying to get home. To reach home we must leave here and cross the Tigrates River and march back to Dhassa. If we can, you'll not see us again.'

'What has this to do with me?'

He gripped Latif's left arm. 'My friend, I want you to return to your court and speak to Salim. Explain our goal – tell him we just want to go home. Surely the sooner we are gone, the sooner you can go north and fight the real war against my father's army.

'I could speak for you,' Latif said after a moment. 'Salim would listen.'

'If we set a date by which we pledged to cross the river, then you would know our sincerity. Pursue if you must, attack us if we fail to meet that pledge.'

Latif searched his face. His own right hand was clasping Seth's upper arm as they unconsciously mirrored each other's posture. 'There are bridges over the Tigrates at Vida, about five weeks' march from here.'

'We can make it, as long as we can escape from Ardijah.'

'I doubt Salim could control his men enough to let you leave via the northern causeway,' Latif warned. 'Any troop movement would be seen as an attack.'

'We're planning to leave in the night. We'll travel on the Khotri side of the Efratis – our windskiff pilot found a ford lower down. We could leave you there, with a horse.'

Latif said slowly, 'If you can manage all that, then I will willingly be your ambassador to Salim.'

Ramon stood on a balcony of the inner gatehouse of the northern isle of Ardijah, overlooking the bridge where two columns of men were marching past each other. His rankers were marching out of the keep while a line of Khotri soldiers marched in, and as they passed every Rondian swapped his red cloak for the white cloak the opposite man held as they passed: a crude but effective disguise from a distance. *Sometimes it is the simple plans that work best.*

Beside him stood a slender woman wrapped in a jewel-encrusted bekira-shroud. The Calipha Amiza al'Ardijah's big eyes took in everything, her shrewish mouth pursed as she assessed all she saw. They had just returned from the cellars, where a third of the army's gold had been left in payment for the supplies and equipment the calipha had arranged via the Emir of Khotri.

In the end it all comes down to money.

The cost of doing business with the calipha was not cheap, but she had done well by the army. The gold had been used to purchase vital supplies: not just food, but leather, timber, iron, coal, even complete sets of chainmail and thousands of spears and swords, as well as more than a thousand desert-bred Khotri horses. The calipha's prices were extortionate, but if they were going to get out of Ardijah undetected, it'd be worth it, Ramon was convinced of that.

'You will all be gone by dawn, yes?' Calipha Amiza asked in her thickly accented Rondian.

Ramon glanced sideways at her. He might admire her ruthless avarice but he didn't trust her. *Good thing she thinks that's the last of our gold*, he thought, *or she'd turn on us to claim the rest, of that I'm positive.* But he still kind of liked her. 'Well gone,' he assured her.

'Good. Life can return to normal here.'

'Provided Salim doesn't try and cross anyway.'

'Salim does not need a war with Khotri,' the calipha replied, a faint smile on her face. 'He will pursue you, but he will respect the border. Of this I am confident.'

'I trust you are happy with all of the deal?'

The calipha glanced over her shoulder towards the room inside. 'Renn is precisely the sort of husband I need. Powerful, but easily led.' She smiled smugly. 'Though I enjoyed your comfort in the aftermath of my previous husband's unfortunate demise.'

Ramon flushed. 'Er, about that . . .' The mental image he'd been trying to ignore sprang to his mind: her pulling him into her sitting room with her husband's body still warm, and he'd been powerless to do other than what she wanted. She was a magician too, in her own way. Not conventionally beautiful, but fully aware of her best assets and how to use them – possibly far more than the cloistered wife of a caliph should. Even so, he wasn't proud of that encounter. Sevvie was carrying his child and deserved better. 'I don't—'

Amiza waved a hand dismissively. 'We shared a moment, nothing more. Something we can both fondly remember, yes?' She caressed the back of his hand, smiling secretively. 'You will henceforth be faithful to your wife, yes?'

He shifted awkwardly. 'Si.'

'Anyway, Renn is very nearly the perfect man: he has powerful magic, a large phallus and a small intellect.'

Ramon laughed uneasily. 'How romantic.'

'A woman in my situation must marry with her head, not her heart.' She poked Ramon in the chest. 'You would have been too much trouble, though I think perhaps, you might have pleased both my head and my heart.'

'Severine and I have a child together,' Ramon reminded her. And himself.

'You and I have too,' she murmured.

'*What?*'

Amiza smiled secretively. 'We conceived, that night, you and I. Renn did not enter my bed until after I had already missed my courses.' She touched his hand. 'Congratulations, Magister.'

Ramon glanced anxiously over his shoulder. 'Does Renn—?'

Amiza shook her head. 'He knows I am with child. He believes it to be his.'

Sol et Lune! Ramon exhaled.

'So are you sure you don't want to stay?' she asked slyly.

He blinked, speechless for a moment, and then he sighed regretfully. 'I cannot. The army . . . Sevvie . . .' *Running a kingdom would have been fun, though.* They shared a speculative, slightly regretful look, then she was all business again.

'Perhaps you will leave a little gift for my unborn, Magister? Something worthy of a calipha's child?' She winked. 'Gold is appropriate.'

'I'll see what I can do,' he muttered.

The curtain behind them parted and Renn Bondeau stepped through, resplendent in a richly decorated Keshi coat and a turban. His chin was unshaven and his moustache was growing thickly.

No longer the surly, baby-faced young mage I flew with to Pontus! Ignore the pale skin and he could almost pass for a local nobleman. Which was what Renn Bondeau was about to become.

'Sensini? You're still here?' he observed sullenly.

'Good to see you too, Renn. I guess you'll be out of reach of the bailiffs here.'

Bondeau scowled, then patted his coat, preening. 'It suits me, hmm? Caliph of Ardijah! Once a mage of Pallas, now an Eastern potentate! Who could have foreseen it?'

'No diviners I know,' Ramon replied. He dropped his voice and murmured, 'Watch your back, Renn. You're still an infidel devil to most of the people here.'

'Do not presume to advise me, you sewer rat! Anyway, I am to convert to the Amteh.'

'Really?'

'Why not? Let's see if Kore or Ahm strikes me down at the altar, or whatever they call it here.'

'You do know that they pray six times a day.'

Bondeau's eyes widened. 'Really? Well, that'll change. First law I'll pass, damn it.' He ignored his bride-to-be and turned back to Ramon. 'Oh, and don't try taking refuge here again. This is my town now and we don't need lost soldiers wandering in.'

'There – and I thought I'd come back after the war and bring you some Brician wine, for old time's sake.'

'We had no old times, Silacian. But do send the wine. That's one thing I'm going to miss here.'

'We've left you a cask,' Ramon told him. 'Consider it a wedding gift.' He stepped back, and gave them both a flourishing bow. 'I wish you both health, wealth, happiness and many children.'

'Already started on that,' Renn announced, puffing out his chest.

Let's hope it takes after its mother.

'Sal'Ahm, Magister Ramon,' Calipha Amiza purred. 'I shall not forget you bursting into my house.' Her nose twitched. 'A most propitious and profitable day.'

Ramon took his leave of the calipha and her caliph-to-be and hurried down to the bridge, where Pilus Lukaz and his cohort awaited. They were all mounted now, and had been practising their riding on the southern end of the causeway, out of the sight of the Keshi on the north bank. None of them were particularly confident riders yet, but all of them could trot and even canter at need. Predictably, Vidran, Harmon and Lukaz himself were the best, but Ramon thought a few of the others would soon be equally as accomplished. *They'll get plenty of practise in the next few weeks – we've got twenty-five days to cover two hundred and fifty miles to the bridge over the Tigrates.* It should be a comfortable march, except that they didn't know the roads. Ten miles a day was considered good going for an army in hostile territory.

Pilus Lukaz saluted. 'Are you ready, sir?'

Ramon glanced at the balcony above and the thin woman looking down at him. Renn Bondeau was nowhere in sight. He touched his right fingers to his forehead, then his left chest, and the calipha echoed his actions. *Head and heart.*

Then he turned his mount and they trotted south across the bridge. By dawn they were far away.

That night, after the first day of their trek to Vida and safety, Baltus flew in and reported that the Keshi army had not followed. Their deception appeared to have worked.

Seth Korion watched the tail of the army march away east along the north bank of the Efratis. They were three days out of Ardijah and had forded the river that day. He was now officially back in Kesh. It was evening, and just two horses waited by the river: his and Latif's.

He'd been avoiding Salim's impersonator during the journey, which was easy to do when there were men to supervise, scouts to consult with and orders to write. There was never nothing to do in an army, especially one that had to make ten miles a day or risk attack. And they now had two thousand Khotri women in their baggage train; they'd be a severe drain on food and water, but there would have been mutiny if he'd refused permission for the new legion wives to travel.

But now here he was with Latif, just the two of them, standing beside the Efratis River, and about to part for ever.

'So, my friend,' Latif started. He looked as sad as Seth felt. They were both dressed for travelling and holding the reins of their horses. 'I will speak to Salim, as we have agreed. I am confident that he will agree: you must cross the Tigrates River at Vida by the last day of Rami – your Septinon – or hostilities must resume. Do not let me down, please.'

'Of course! We will not detain your army further. Go and deal with my father, if you can.'

Latif smiled faintly at that. 'We have plans for your father. This is still a war, Seth Korion. A holy war.'

'Can a war ever be holy?'

'When the cause is just.'

'It all seems very unholy to me,' Seth replied. He pulled off his gauntlet and offered his hand. 'Good fortune, Latif. I hope we can meet again, somehow.'

'When this is over, who knows?' Latif took his hand, stepped closer. 'In my land, close friends greet each other with a kiss to the lips. There is no shame or dishonour in the greeting.' He leaned forward and pressed his lips to Seth's. He tasted of cinnamon and cloves.

It left Seth feeling unsettled, scared almost, but he was unsure of what.

'Sal'Ahm,' Latif breathed. 'May He shine His eyes upon you and guide your path.' He stepped away, bowed formally, and swung into the saddle. His little mare pranced, eager to be moving.

Seth raised a hand. 'So tell me, is your name really Latif?'

The impersonator laughed. 'Farewell, Seth Korion!' He loosened the reins and squeezed his thighs gently and the horse leaped into motion. He rode as he did everything, Seth thought: immaculately.

Seth raised a pale hand and stared after him until he was gone from sight.

31

The Vizier's Gambit

The Many Faces of Power

Some say that military might is the pinnacle of power; others that the way to real dominance is the control of minds through religion. Still more claim that social rank or wealth is the key. But I have always held that knowledge is supreme: know more than others and the rest will follow.

ERVYN NAXIUS, ORDO COSTRUO, 904

Teshwallabad, Lakh, on the continent of Antiopia
Shaban (Augeite) 929
14th month of the Moontide

Dareem had introduced Alaron and Ramita to a room beneath the vizier's palace – a place not even the servants knew about – where he and Hanook practised the gnosis, and it was to here Alaron retreated so that he wouldn't have to think about Ramita today. He had his kon-staff with him; he thought it best to start integrating his strangely mutating gnosis with his new weapon.

The room had been dug into the ground to suppress any gnostic echoes, and there was no furniture save for a few wooden targets, frames hung with charred and dented armour. The back wall was similarly blackened and scarred. There was a pool of water at one end, and a big copper brazier filled with coal, and a pile of rocks of varying sizes.

'How do your botany studies progress?' Dareem asked, as he turned to leave.

Alaron said neutrally, 'Well enough,' though it was difficult to act so relaxed about it now that Hanook's library had supplied the last remaining ingredient-runes for the Scytale. He still had questions about the measures of each ingredient required, and a larger problem: was this recipe all that was required, or were they just variants to add to a base compound? He was still chewing on that particular question, but it was not something he wished to discuss with his hosts, not yet at least.

'Lady Ramita is doing what is best,' Dareem said neutrally, though his gaze hinted at sympathy. 'I hope you see that.'

Alaron made a show of examining the gaudy new orange rakhi-string on his wrist, then looked up. 'I need to concentrate,' he said shortly. For a moment Dareem and he locked stares, and all the things they could have said throbbed in the air.

I wonder what he hopes for? Perhaps that it will fall through so he can marry her himself . . .?

He waited impatiently until Dareem had bidden him good morning and left, then sealed the doors. It was a relief to be alone, and he had a burning core of frustrated energy to burn off. He set to work.

First came the kindling of the gnosis, all of it. He closed his eyes, opened his gnostic sight, and spread the 'arms' of his aura, holding the elements. He opened the sigil on his forehead and four 'eyes' of light formed above his head: the Sorcerous studies. He conjured the cloak on his back – four strips for each of the Hermetic Studies – and summoned the four female faces he associated with the Theurgy studies. Whilst none came as easily as just Fire used to, if he held them apart, they were all accessible. He fed them power, waited until they were all solidly in place, then he opened his eyes, twirled the kon-staff and began to move.

Until then, all an ordinary watcher would have seen was a young man standing immobile for a minute, before going into a series of slow but well-balanced staff movements. But now he began to add gnostic blows too, aiming at the wall, first simple mage-bolts, the pure energy strike that was every mage's standard weapon. They set the targets rattling and the air was tinged with the faint whiff of smoke.

So far, so ordinary . . .

He spun, a pirouetting turn, and in quick succession hurled fire, a rock and a blast of air, then finished by trying to douse it all in water. The flame exploded against the target, the rock missed and he fumbled the other two.

He cursed, paused to re-gather his grip on the elements, then tried again.

The second time the Fire and Earth were easier, but he lost Air and Water before he'd even attempted the strikes. *Hel! I'm reverting to old ways. But I can do this . . .*

This time he worked from Water to Air to Earth to Fire. A jet of water erupted from his fingers and missed the target; lightning crackled through the puddle, and the rock and flame were weaker than the previous attempts. He didn't care about that, though: he'd kept hold of all four elements and loosed them on command. He punched the air and shouted in exhilaration.

The next time was better, and the one after that, better again. He began to vary the order, but now he was able to keep control. He upped the energy, then tried different effects: dousing the flames by sucking the Fire-energy away, then manipulating Air and making the pool of water dance, all the while using Earth to make a rock spin in the air. After half an hour he was drenched in sweat and labouring for breath, but brimming with excitement, his earlier bad mood forgotten.

Has anyone else ever *done that? But I need to go further . . .*

He'd not tried the more involved studies before now so he started small, growing a dart of the end of his wooden staff then firing it into the targets. Then he added a raking blow with talons conjured on his left hand. It took time and practise, but at last it came.

He knew enough Necromancy to be able to send a withering blast of purple light into the wall; then he mixed it with banishing spells against an imagined summoning, and illusory images against an imagined foe. Spells he already knew a little about came easiest, of course, but he managed to make a start even on those he'd only been told of.

I can do this, he told himself, trying not to get too excited. *I just need to find experts now, people who can coach me in each Study . . . that's as long as I don't get locked up – there's probably some law against magi who can do every study.*

Finally he stopped, utterly exhausted and almost euphoric. That soured, as for the first time since Dareem had left, he wondered what time it was, and whether Ramita was back.

Today she'd gone to meet the mughal.

'My lady, I promise you that you will be safe, even if this interview does not go as planned.'

Ramita looked up at Hanook. *As you planned*, she thought. Her own plans were not at all clear.

They were walking along a very long, well-lit underground tunnel that ran for half a mile from the vizier's palace to the Mughal's Dome. It had been built to give the vizier secret access to the ruler, and to provide an escape route for the mughal. Right now, it was leading Ramita to her first assignation with the young ruler.

'Vizier, are you an Omali worshipper?'

'I attend an Omali temple every day, to show solidarity with the vast majority of the people of this kingdom.'

'But you are the child of a Rondian and a Khotri Amteh, and you were taught by Zains?'

'That is true, but I have always felt that it is important that some- one at court gives voice to the faith of the people, and as no Omali pandits are permitted to attend upon the king, that role falls to me. As the pandits themselves say, all four winds blow towards God.'

Ramita smiled. Her family's guru said the same. 'I will not give up my faith,' she told him.

Hanook pursed his lips. 'I mentioned earlier that it would be incumbent upon any bride of the mughal to become Amteh. The Ja'arathi sect is milder and—'

'I will not convert,' Ramita interrupted firmly. 'It would be dishon- est and I will not do it.'

Hanook frowned, and sidestepped the argument. 'Of what faith is Alaron Mercer?'

She was a little taken aback. 'Kore, I suppose. Though he only ever speaks his god's name when cursing. I think perhaps that he does not believe in his god at all.'

'And this does not trouble you?'

'Why should it? I don't believe in his god either.'

Hanook smiled wryly. 'Your husband was a noted atheist.'

'He was strange like that,' Ramita agreed. 'But he allowed me to practise my beliefs. Your mughal must do the same if he wishes to marry me.'

'What about this Alaron then? You care for him, do you not?'

Ramita sucked in her lower lip. 'Al'Rhon has been a good and loyal companion. He has never overstepped.'

'You spend much time together. He treats your children as if they were his own.'

'We have shared many dangers in the short time I have known him. I know I can trust him.'

'How does he feel about you?'

She felt a touch of anger at the line of questioning. 'You should ask him, Vizier.'

'Have you slept with him?'

'No!' She stopped and faced him. 'He is my sworn bhaiya and wears my rakhi. We know the boundaries and respect them. Why are you asking these questions?'

'Because, Lady Meiros, you appear increasingly to have taken against this union, despite the great advantages it would bring for you: security and safety for your children, wealth, status and comfort for you. It is a match any girl would dream of, and yet you are baulking. I cannot help but wonder whether the young man at your side has already seduced your heart, leaving you unable to give this marriage opportunity the consideration it deserves?'

She put her hands on her hips and let her temper rise. 'That is completely false! I have *not* fallen in love with Goat! I am thinking *only* of my children! I am thinking *only* of what my husband would have wished! But I am *not* convinced that marriage to a callow boy will achieve what my husband wanted!'

Hanook raised a placating hand. 'Lady, I have tutored Tariq all my life. I admit he is not perfect, but who is? The truth is, you will barely see him. A woman's life is lived in the zenana.'

'Then why meet him at all? Why not do it all by contract and I can meet him in the wedding bed a few seconds before he puts his lingam in me!' She belatedly put a hand over her mouth, not quite believing her own temper, but it was too late; the words were out. So she refused to recall them. 'Well, I want more than that!'

'There is no more!' Hanook threw up his hands. 'To be Queen of the Lakh? You cannot aspire to more! There is nothing higher to aspire to!'

She glared up at him and he down at her.

If thrones were the only currency you might be right, Vizier Hanook of Teshwallabad. But there are other coins I treasure.

For a few long seconds they just looked at each other, both of them panting slightly from the exertion of anger. Finally Hanook took a very deep breath and said, 'What is it that you actually want, Ramita?'

I want my mother. My father. My brothers and sisters. I want to show them my beautiful twins and know they will love them unconditionally as I do. I want to see Kazim and Huriya restored to the people they were. But as she tried to find words to articulate this, it all sounded so selfish, the sorts of things a child would wish for. Her husband had given her the gnosis and told her that she could stop the war. He had not told her to run and hide.

As the mughal's wife, perhaps I can achieve all these things . . .

Her mind was going in circles now, and suddenly she felt increasingly tired resisting her Destiny. She sighed and bowed her head. 'I am sorry. I will meet your mughal. But I have my own conditions for this. He will not dictate all the terms of this marriage.'

Hanook looked less than pleased, but also relieved. 'What terms?'

'I will tell them to him, not you.'

They went on in silence, the vizier contemplative. As she cooled down, Ramita began to feel that her flash of temper had been a good thing. *It showed him that I have my own mind, that I am just not some doormat.*

At the end of the tunnel was a door set in a stone wall, unusual only for its plainness. There were no carvings or fretwork, no painted patterns or gilt embossing, just one symbol, carved on the door. It looked somewhat familiar. They were at least three levels underground, Ramita thought.

Hanook produced a key, but he did not immediately place it into the lock. 'Lady, there is something you need to know,' he said quietly. 'Beyond this door, you may not use your gnosis.'

She raised her eyebrows. 'I suppose it is forbidden, yes.'

'More than this. It is suppressed.'

'What do you mean?'

'When the palace was built, Lord Meiros came secretly with some of his most trusted Ordo Costruo. They assisted with the building, including placing the famous Crystal Dome on top. Does the Dome look at all familiar to you?'

She cast her mind back to something she'd seen just once before, when her husband had shown her ... 'Southpoint. The lights at the top of the tower – just not so bright ... you barely notice it, unless you've seen it before.'

'You are correct, and this dome is made of the same material, special crystals cultivated by the Ordo Costruo. It's making is a carefully guarded secret. The crystals turn the sun's light into gnostic energy – only such a power source could sustain the Leviathan Bridge.'

'Does it strengthen the mughal's palace?' she asked curiously.

'No, that's not its purpose here. What it does is to sustain a spell woven into the very fabric of the palace, akin to the Chain-rune that binds the gnosis, but it is milder, and tied to an area – in this case the main building – rather than a person. Once inside, only an Ascendant can access the gnosis.'

She quietly filed that thought away. She'd not told Hanook just how strong she was.

The vizier patted her shoulder tentatively. 'Please, Lady Meiros, be generous and open-minded. Tariq is still young, but one day he will be a fine ruler.'

We shall see. She nodded dutifully, and covered her face with a silk veil as the vizier unlocked the door. A small bare chamber lay beyond. Hanook knocked on the door in the opposite wall; a slot opened and a dark eye peered through. 'Vizier? You are expected.'

The door was unlocked, and they stepped through into another chamber, larger, with a single throne at the far end. It was tall, and had a high balcony, slotted like battlements with arrow slits. Each one had an arrowhead jutting through. Ramita felt horribly exposed. Tentatively she tried to reach her gnosis, and thought she could sense it, just out of reach.

If there was ever a place to kill a mage, it is here. Why did my husband build such a thing?

She could guess: Antonin Meiros had forbidden his people from meddling in Lakh, but he might not have trusted that others would keep such a prohibition. In giving the mughal a place where no mage could use their power over him, he ensured that the ruler could deal with a mage as he would any man. She wondered if there were other such places dotted about the land.

The double doors at the far end opened and in walked Mughal Tariq. In person he wasn't tall, and his plump face, large eyes and the faintest beginnings of facial hair made him look soft. He had fair skin, for a Lakh. His stiffly brocaded coat fell to his knees, and a scimitar was sheathed in a glittering velvet and gold scabbard. His turban was crowned with a ruby as large as a grape. At his back stalked a large, shaven-headed man holding a giant two-handed curved sword, as tall as the man's own six-foot frame. The weapon was bare and gleaming in his hands. *The bodyguard is called Kindu*, she remembered from Hanook's briefings. His impressive moustaches gleamed with wax.

Hanook and Ramita went to their knees and stared at the floor. She heard one set of boots click on the marble: the young ruler ascending his throne. The heavier tread of Kindu measured a slow circle about her and the vizier, then returned to Tariq's side.

'Vizier Hanook, Lady Ramita.' Tariq spoke in a clear boyish voice.

She and Hanook came up on their knees, then touched their foreheads to the floor. Her skin prickled at the thought that a dozen arrows could be loosed into her back any moment.

'Thank you for seeing us, Great Mughal,' Hanook replied.

'Please rise, both of you.'

Beside her Hanook came smoothly to his feet, and Ramita followed his lead, a little awkwardly, as she was wearing a sari so encrusted in gems and brocade that it had taken four servants to wrap her in it. Rubies were set in her belly button and on her brow. Her arms were covered in gold bangles. Despite the clothing and jewels, she'd never felt more like a market-girl.

'The veil, please.' Mughal Tariq's voice was curious.

Examining his new broodmare. She lowered her veil, simmering, but kept her eyes modestly downcast.

'Hmphf,' the mughal grunted unenthusiastically. 'She is rather diminutive. Very dark. What is her family and caste again?'

'Ankesharan. Trader caste, of Baranasi.'

Tariq looked up at the ceiling, clearly unimpressed. 'And she has the gnostic blood?'

'Very strongly,' Hanook said smoothly.

'A woman can gain this power simply through bearing a child?' Tariq's tone suggested that he found the notion completely inappropriate. 'How can it be so simple?'

Simple? You try bearing a child!

'It is a widely known phenomenon among the high-blooded magi, Great Mughal.'

'So there must be a child?' Tariq sounded even less pleased at this notion.

'There are two. Twin boys.'

Tariq scowled down at her from the throne. 'How old are they?'

'Six months, Great Mughal.' Hanook's voice was apologetic, which annoyed Ramita faintly.

'Younger than mine. And not of my blood.'

'It would be desirable to tie the babies to you by adoption,' Hanook said. 'Familial bonds will give them status here, and help cement their loyalty. Especially as they also will develop the gnosis in time.'

Tariq sniffed, a little disdainfully. 'I would not have them taking precedence over any child of mine in the succession, my friend. I am of the line of Turig. Antonin Meiros was an afreet and this women is only a Lakh.'

Ramita felt her jaw clench.

'Has her womb recovered? Can she bear more children? She has little value if she can't.'

Little value. Ramita smarted at that, and at the memory of her fertility being *proven* by the midwife Hanook had summoned; the scrawny Amteh woman had poked inside her with bony fingers and sniffed them, then declared her still viable. How she knew, Ramita had no idea.

'Examination reveals that Lady Ramita has a normal cycle,' Hanook replied.

Tariq tapped his fingers rhythmically on the arm of his throne. 'I have been offered one of the daughters of the Sultan of Gatioch. She is said to be almost six foot tall, with fair skin and nipples the size of a flower. She is trained in the arts of pleasure, the Godspeaker says, yet still a virgin. And you offer me this used widow of a heretic. Vizier, I am not pleased. This undersized chit with her polluted yoni is not a suitable wife for the Emperor of Kings.'

Ramita glared at him from beneath her eyebrows. *I'm not that pleased with what I see either, oh 'Exalted One'.* But she recognised Tariq's protestations as the bargaining points a trader makes to beat down the price. Hanook clearly understood this too, as he responded with equanimity, 'Exalted One, you know all wives cannot be for pleasure. This girl will strengthen your following in Baranasi, as well as bringing the gnosis into your bloodline.'

'Do I gain the gnosis by ploughing her, Vizier?'

Ramita clenched a fist behind her back. *What a revolting thought! He'd have me on my back for his entire army.*

'I am sorry, Exalted One, that is not the way of it. But your children by her would have a great deal of power. With the Ordo Costruo gone and Rashid of Halli'kut aligning his renegades with Salim of Kesh, you must gain magi if you are to avoid being dominated by the Keshi. Salim's ambitions will know no bounds after his victory at Shaliyah.'

Tariq rubbed his chin as if mimicking an adult. 'This is true. But the Godspeakers will condemn this union.'

'Salim of Kesh has found a way to reconcile his faith with using servants with the gnosis. Presumably his Godspeakers have also found some phrase in the *Kalistham* to justify themselves.'

'Victory in battle wins most arguments. Is that not what my tutor always says?' Tariq observed ironically.

Hanook, that same tutor, bowed in acknowledgement of his ruler's wit. 'Tariq, I do counsel this union. This is a good woman, dutiful and faithful, with a proven womb and the gnosis in her blood. This is a beneficial union, worth even foregoing the dubious pleasures of taking a Gatioch virgin to wife.'

Tariq sighed heavily, no doubt thinking regretfully of virginal beauties with flower-like nipples.

Ramita continued to glower at the floor.

'So she has the gnosis,' Tariq said thoughtfully. 'What danger does this present to me, and those at court?'

Ah, so you're a little scared of me, are you? That cheered her up a little.

'Great One, here within the Dome, where she will live the rest of her days, her powers are constrained.'

She felt a chill at that. She and Alaron had been learning so much – a whole new way of accessing the gnosis – and she'd only just begun to explore what she was capable of. Even that had left her trembling with excitement. She did not want to lose her new powers. And she most definitely did not want to be helpless in a hostile court.

Tariq sounded mollified, however. 'Lift your face, girl,' he said finally, a note of acceptance in his voice.

'Girl'! I'm older than you, you spoilt little brat. She lifted her face and met his eyes, then remembered she wasn't supposed to. His eyes narrowed at the affront, but he didn't say anything.

'Can you sing, girl?'

She shook her head.

'Recite poetry? Perform the *Carnatakam*?'

She shook her head again.

'Speak. I would hear your voice,' Tariq commanded.

She swallowed her temper and said evenly, 'Exalted One, I have no poetry and I do not know the classical royal dances. My songs and dances are of the people.'

'How dull.' He looked at his advisor. 'She's a peasant, Hanook. Do they not teach their daughters anything of value in Baranasi?' He pulled a face. 'I do not like her voice either. It has no music.'

'Exalted One, this is a strategic union. You do not like most of your wives.'

'True enough. I'm bored with all fourteen of them. Are you sure I cannot wed the girl from Gatioch as well?'

'Tradition says one per year, Exalted One. The Gatioch girl will still have nipples like flowers next year.'

Tariq *harumphed*, and went back to studying Ramita. 'Have you anything to say on this?' he asked eventually.

She did. Hanook threw her a warning look, but she ignored him. 'Yes, I have this to say. I am an Omali of Lakh, and I will keep my faith. My children will know their father, and be tutored in the gnosis, with skilled tutors imported from the north, even Yuros if need be. And I will *not* dwell helpless in the zenana. I will have my own annex of the palace, away from the Dome so I may continue to learn the gnosis. If you wish to father children upon me, you will come to my bed, not me to yours.'

Her words echoed about the chamber, and when she stopped speaking, a cold silence enveloped the room. She could almost feel the tautness of the bowstrings above. Hanook's face turned grey, and Tariq was staring at her like she'd grown horns.

He's probably never had anyone dictate terms to him since he was legally a child.

She found she didn't care what he said or thought. It felt good to have stated her position, and if he didn't want her after all, some part of her would be for ever relieved.

Tariq began to drum his fingers again on the arm of his throne, louder and faster, until finally he stopped. He let out his breath. 'She has sharp teeth as well as a sharp voice.' His tones were neutral, with just the hint of fear, as if the enormity of marrying a woman who had the gnosis had only just become apparent. 'Even putting aside the fact that a ruler does not go cap in hand to his wife's chamber hoping to be given entry, we are forced to reconsider the earlier question: if she is not to be constrained beneath the Dome as you said earlier, how am I to protect myself and my court against her?'

Hanook fired a reproachful look at Ramita. 'I am sure some compromise can be reached.' *You need to give ground here, girl*, his expression added.

'I will not have the safety of my children threatened,' she replied stubbornly.

Tariq glanced at the balconies above, and for a heart-in-mouth second she feared he was going to give some signal that would end this debate instantly. Or perhaps he would simply lock her up and give her no choices.

Hanook held up a placatory hand. 'Will you allow me to find a compromise on this matter, Great Mughal?'

Tariq stared down at Ramita, his eyes cold. 'Very well, old friend. You have three days to come up with something, or I shall marry the Gatioch princess.' He looked at Hanook with the ghost of fondness. 'Three days, for your sake.

'And for the sake of your kingdom, Tariq,' Hanook said warmly.

Tariq grunted, got up and strode away.

The underground tunnel was a chillier place as Ramita and Hanook walked back to his palace. *Perhaps that's just the frost coming off Hanook's face.* Finally he turned his head and said, 'I have had to pull upon every heart-string Tariq possesses to get him to even consider you as a bride. You risked it all with your demands.'

'They are not unreasonable.'

'Can you imagine the mobs the Godspeakers could whip up if you posture as if you were ruling Lakh, not Tariq? If you play up your differences, you will attract so much ill will that nothing could protect you. And you will drag me down with you!'

'So instead I should meekly bare my throat?'

'If a mob descends on your annex, you could not defend it, and nor could I! Only by showing submission to Tariq can you gain safety! If the Godspeakers and the people are convinced of our loyalty to Tariq, and your willingness to be nothing but a fruitful yoni, they will be willing to overlook your taint.'

'My *taint*? Is that how you see it too?'

'Of course not! I share that taint – I am *kin* to you! But Ramita, you *must* submit if we are to further our cause!'

She lifted her chin. 'Then think of something that he and I will both find acceptable, or we will leave here and you will never see us again.'

32

Death Camp

Theurgy: Spiritualism

The Ritual of Corineus enabled the powers of the soul, normally triggered at death, to be channelled during life. The Body and the Soul are linked, but they can be separated again. This link defines the art of the Spiritualist: to walk out of his own body, to exist as pure thought and energy, unlimited by physical constraints.

THE HIGHER GNOSTIS
BARAMITIUS, PUBLISHED IN PALLAS, 604

They clearly thought my spirit form some kind of harmless illusion, when they realised that weapons couldn't touch me. I corrected their error emphatically!
JANETTE DE MERE, SPIRITUALIST

Southern Kesh, on the continent of Antiopia
Shaban (Augeite) 929
14ᵗʰ month of the Moontide

'I don't think this is a good idea,' Cym whispered from beneath her cowl.

<We have to get inside if we're to get close enough to break him out,> Zaqri replied. <And no one is looking for people breaking in to a place like this.>

Zaqri turned out to be right: the breaking in was simplicity itself. They simply joined the end of an incoming column, as all was confusion. They had both subtly changed their faces to match the Keshi look: a bigger nose, sharper chin and high cheekbones. Cym's olive

Rimoni skin was sun-darkened enough that she could have been local, especially wrapped in her sleeping blanket, which was as dirty as anyone's and pinned in the Keshi way. Only their height set them apart, so they were both stooping a little.

The guards barely looked up as they shuffled by. They found a place to sit inside the refugee pen and tried not to attract attention, which turned out to be easy enough in a place where the struggle to secure food and water occupied what little energy the refugees had. They were near the latrines, which turned out to be badly dug, overflowing with raw sewerage and infested with sand-rats and crows.

Cym closed her eyes, covered her face and waited for darkness.

They ate from their own small store of dried meat, then Zaqri wrapped his arms about her and cradled her in a chaste embrace that slowly became sleep. The dismal nature of the camp killed any physical desire stone-dead, but his warmth anchored her, kept her here when she wanted so desperately to fly away.

She awakened in the chill of morning, lying on her side, moulded to his body. His hand was over her belly and she worried that he knew that she still hadn't bled. That made her eight weeks gone. It would show soon. She had other fears too: their gnostic auras were apparently binding together. It was worse after sex, and it scared her.

She must have dozed again, because it felt like just a few seconds later when she was startled awake by trumpets and the crunch of hooves in gravel. She fumbled free of Zaqri and knotted her breeches about her waist, which felt tight and swollen. An old woman saw and gave her a hard, knowing look.

The camp came alive with movement and bustle. Fires smoked, pots emitted cooking smells and children squalled. They rose, wrapped in their filthy blankets and joined the hundreds of others pressing their faces through the wire, staring out at the Rondian Inquisitors. Four Acolytes were trailing the man who was obviously their Commandant. One of them was a grey-haired female with a face carved out of bone. The eleventh rider, the one they'd followed all the way into this Helish camp, was readying his horse, moving stiffly. They caught a glimpse of a drawn, pale figure with a shaven skull inside the hood.

'He's definitely one of us,' Zaqri whispered in her ear.

'A Dokken riding with the Inquisition? Impossible.'

'Anything is possible in this world. Don't draw attention to yourself, and cloak your aura, otherwise they may detect us if they look our way.'

She nodded mutely, straining her ears as the Commandant of the Inquisitorial Fist ordered his riders into line, then turned to the legion maniple commander. His voice carried across the stony ground. 'I am Commandant Ullyn Siburnius of the Twenty-Third Fist of the Inquisition. Where is Tribune Gestryn?'

'Commandant Siburnius!' The maniple commander hurried forward, his face anxious and confused. 'You were not expected until the third bell, Commandant ...' The look Siburnius returned withered whatever other protests he might have made. 'Er, we are almost ready, sir.'

'I don't want to hear the word "almost", Tribune. Assemble them, immediately!'

'But I was told—'

'Now, Tribune!'

Gestryn saluted, spun and began to bellow orders, sending his soldiers scattering. Some strode into the pens and began to herd adults towards the gates.

They were shouting something that sounded like *Ishpardi* to Cym. She looked at Zaqri as they retreated into the crowd.

'A work detail,' Zaqri whispered. He was looking around him carefully. He went off to talk to an older man, then returned a few minutes later to whisper, 'Every few days a work group is assembled and taken away. They don't come back. He says they're kept at another place, a labour camp.'

Cym looked at him sceptically. 'A labour camp? Out here?'

'I know. I don't think it's likely either. But these are ordinary people – they don't believe in evil, not truly. They try to rationalise things; they tell themselves that really bad things can't really happen.'

Cym felt a sick lump in her belly. 'Then what's really happening? And why is that Dokken here?'

'I've no idea,' he admitted. 'I have never heard of such a thing – Inquisitors and Brethren are mortal enemies. I don't understand what's going on here.'

After the work detail left there was no excuse to linger near the gates. There was little to do but watch and wait so they returned to their spot and ate furtively, trying not to attract the attention of gangs of Dhassan and Keshi men who prowled the interior of the pen, forcing those who looked vulnerable to surrender their valuables. The scenes when the Rondians brought in the sacks of dried lentils – the only rations they apparently provided – were ugly as the refugees fought tooth and nail over the meagre supplies.

After a while they noticed the remaining five Inquisitors outside the fences were hammering carved wooden rods into the ground. Gnosis surges started to prickle at their awareness.

'What are they doing?' Cym whispered.

'Sealing the camp with wards,' Zaqri replied. 'To alert them if anyone escapes.' He rubbed at his beard. 'Typically, those sort of wards also disrupt scrying and communications – but why would they want to block scrying on a slave camp?'

'We can still disable them and get out . . . can't we?' Cym tried not to sound worried.

'We could . . . but if we fumble it, we'll alert them to our presence.' He sucked in a deep breath of smoky air and coughed. 'We shouldn't have come here,' he admitted. 'You were right after all.'

'Of course I was right. I always am.' She watched the Inquisitors work, wondering what to do. 'If we talked to that Dokken, do you think he might tell us what is going on?'

'I don't know. I thought so at first but every time we see him, he's cooperating so willingly.'

'There's something . . . *stupid* . . . about him though, isn't there?

It's like he can't tie his own bootlaces without help. Perhaps they're controlling him somehow?'

'If that's the case, talking to him might be an even bigger risk.'

'But we have to try something, right? Or just get out and move on?'

They shared another one of *those* moments: when a blank future without purpose loomed ahead, leaving them alone and adrift. 'No,' they said together, then, recognising what was happening, each stammered into silence.

After a moment, Cym ploughed on. 'The spirit-walking ... like I did in the Noose. I could do that to get close to him.'

Zaqri considered that, his face betraying his worry, then he nodded.

So they made a plan – a simple plan, that shouldn't go too wrong. That night she lay on her blanket, Zaqri huddled over her, and she ...

... breathed her soul out of her mouth. It left more easily than before, as if impatient with the bounds of flesh and gravity, and she shot into the air, taking the shape of an owl as she went, just in case anyone with gnostic sight was watching – the spiratus would be visible to such a one, but so long as it looked natural, they'd not realise what it was. She swooped low over the masses of huddled sleepers. Looking upwards, she got a fright when she saw a dome-like canopy of pale blue light covering the camp, then she realised that it was the Inquisitors' wards, a mesh of thin strips of radiance visible only to gnostic sight. It was like a gauzy spiderweb, with lots of gaps, though they were all small – too small for a man-sized creature to go through, but easy enough for a bird-sized spiratus. She picked the biggest hole she could find and darted through.

Outside the dome of light, the vastness of the night called. She was pleased and relieved when no alarm was raised. Turning on a faint breeze, she headed for the barracks. They'd noticed that the eleventh rider didn't mix with the Inquisitors but kept to himself in his own small mudbrick shed. The other cabins were bright with wards and enchantments, but his was quiescent, a dim mound in the darkness. She landed nearby, became a lizard and scuttled forward, unseen by the human guards.

There was no door – probably because the heat was suffocating even at night, especially for these Yurosian soldiers – and she reached the opening unchallenged. Her senses were quivering as she probed ahead, listening and sniffing. She found the Dokken sitting cross-legged on the floor of his hut, hood down, eyes vacant. His aura was a shifting mess of tendrils akin to Zaqri's but his were somehow *raw*-looking. The periapt on his breast was so bright it was painful to look at, and different from any she'd seen. And Dokken did not use periapts anyway. Another mystery.

He turned his head and looked straight at her. 'Who are you?' His voice was a broken scratch, twigs on glass. There was a Lantric rune branded onto his forehead: a triangular shape, a delta.

She squeaked in fright and took a second to recover her poise. 'I'm . . . No, who are you?'

'Who?' His bleak eyes grew larger. 'I am.' He stopped, tried again. 'I am . . . I am . . . I am . . .' His voice began to rise, his tones becoming fearful. 'I am Delta,' he suddenly announced, relief flooding his face. He sagged slightly, the energy in his expression dissipating. 'Delta. I am Delta.' Then his eyes focused again. 'Who are you?' he asked again.

She hesitated, then spoke. 'I've been sent by Zaqri of Metia.' It was a faint hope but not unreasonable, that this Dokken would recognise the name of a Dhassan packleader.

'Zaqri.' The Dokken's face betrayed that he knew the name, then twisted as an internal struggle took place. His eyes became sly. 'I know that name. Zaqri. Yes, I know it.' His fleshy face looked sickly this close, and she could sense there was something wrong with him, like a disease emanating from that horrifically strong periapt. He gripped it tightly and sparks crackled down his arms.

She glanced backwards instinctively and that one look saved her.

A blast of blue fire ripped through the air from the shadow of the next hut. Normal reflexes couldn't have helped, but she was in astral form, quick as thought, and in the instant before the bolt struck she was arrowing upwards, her shape a blur of light. More bolts arced out of the night from three other points while Delta's harsh voice rose to a howl, screeching, 'Master! Beware! Enemies!'

Rukka mia! He must have been alerting the Inquisitors even as he talked to me!

She cast a glance back over her shoulder and was horrified to see three Inquisitors rising into the night, armoured shapes riding the winds, blasting at her with needles of energy. *Hel, they're fast!* But they were flesh-bound, and she was spirit. A naked soul was hyper-vulnerable to the gnosis, but it was also blindingly quick and she flashed away from the camp, leading them into the hills, where she made sure she lost them before heading back towards the dome of light and finding a gap in the web and—

—was suddenly inside her body again, coughing and spluttering as she jerked upright. Zaqri caught her, pinned her to his chest and held her tight. 'Easy, easy, lass, you're back. It's all right.'

After a few moments catching her breath, she looked towards the Inquisitors' huts. Torches were flaring into life and men shouting, an uproar that was waking the camp; they could see armoured figures milling about and hear Siburnius' voice loud in the darkness.

She buried her head against Zaqri's chest, shaken and scared now the immediate danger was gone. Exhaustion filled her, a backlash from so much concentrated use of power, and she stayed there until she stopped trembling.

'What happened?' Zaqri asked, his voice low.

'He betrayed me to them – he pretended to be talking, but all the time he must have been calling them. I tried to lead them away – I'm sure I lost them before I came back.'

He stroked her hair. 'Well done. So you actually spoke to him?'

'Yes! He recognised your name, and said he was called Delta – but that's not his real name. It's just what they've branded him, on his brow.'

Zaqri's eyes narrowed. 'They've *branded* him?'

'Yes. It's barbaric.' She slurped some water. 'I think they're controlling him somehow. He was strange, like he couldn't think properly for himself. He spoke really slowly, almost like he was drugged.' She described the strange periapt he wore. 'I think it was killing him, burning him up.'

Zaqri looked perplexed. 'Our kind don't use them. And I've never heard of such a thing.' Then he looked hard at her, and his hand slid over her stomach. 'We need to talk.'

Cym jerked away. 'What, were you *inspecting* me while I was out there?' she snarled disgustedly.

He patiently ignored her flash of temper. 'Are you with child?'

She flinched. 'That's my business.'

'*Our* business.'

She jabbed a finger at him. 'No! That's where you're wrong. My body, my business.'

His face was blooming with wonder, despite her fury. 'You are, aren't you?'

'Yes,' she admitted, glowering. 'But it means nothing.'

He beamed. 'All those years, Ghila and I couldn't manage it. I blamed myself, blamed her, blamed Pater Sol and Mater Lune. But now this . . .'

She clutched her stomach protectively. 'It means nothing. *You* mean nothing.'

'We were wed before the pack, Cymbellea di Regia. You are my wife, voluntarily, uncoerced, and consummated willingly, and many times over. Don't try to deny it.'

She stared wildly about her at the night. The Inquisitors were still shouting and storming about outside the pen, and the refugees were wondering aloud what was going on. No one was paying her and Zaqri attention. 'I don't deny it,' she whispered. 'But you killed my mother. You don't deserve my child.'

'But it's happening regardless,' he said, taking her hands. 'Look at me, Cymbellea.' He waited until she did. 'I love you. I have loved you from the moment I set eyes on you. Now the gods have gifted us a child. Will you please, *please* set aside this childish vendetta and love me in return?'

'*Rukka te!* The gods haven't gifted us a child – my stupid *body* has! My *weakness* has! And don't you ever tell me that wanting retribution for my mother is childish, ever.'

Something in her blazing eyes made him stop whatever he was

going to snap back at her and instead he drew her closer, so that their noses almost touched. 'But you feel something for me too. Admit it.'

She tore her hands away and clutched them over her breast. 'Yes, I feel something – but that's not what's important! It never has been! Leave me *alone*!'

It was as if he couldn't hear her – as if he didn't *want* to hear her. He clasped her face and kissed her lips until she kissed him back, then he gathered her into the wide expanse of his arms and bore her down onto the blanket.

'I love you, Cymbellea di Regia, and nothing will tear us apart. *Nothing.*'

His eyes drowned whatever it was she might have said, but exhaustion was numbing her mind and body. She twisted away from him and closed her eyes, felt herself sinking into a pool of emptiness. She embraced it, let it engulf her as she wished the world away.

Over the next couple of days Cym and Zaqri kept largely to themselves, though Zaqri was forced to drive off a trio of Dhassan refugees who tried to rob them of their remaining food. One of the self-appointed camp leaders tried to enlist Zaqri in security, which gave them the opportunity to learn a little more about the camp. The Rondians had indiscriminately rounded up people in the southern rural areas, but they had said nothing of where they were going, or what their ultimate fate would be. Attempts to escape were dealt with brutally, and most had become resigned to a life enslaved.

The next work party was assembled three days later with a lot less fanfare, and it caught them unawares. A cluster of legionaries entered the pen and began herding people into a group, and Cym and Zaqri were too close to the action to move suddenly. They kept their heads bowed and hoped to be overlooked. Cym found herself terrified; she had to close her eyes and pray for the armed men tramping past to not notice them. She'd thought the refugees timid and subconsciously scorned them, but suddenly she knew exactly how they felt.

Then the worst happened.

'You! Up! Into line.' Cym felt her heart flutter as the legionary jabbed his sword in Zaqri's direction.

'Me?' asked Zaqri mildly, putting a Keshi inflection into his voice.

'Yes, you,' the ranker replied sarcastically, unsurprised that Zaqri knew a little Rondian – many of the Ahmedhassans here did. He glanced at Cym. 'And her.'

'My wife is pregnant,' Zaqri replied tersely.

The man went to shrug, then he relented. 'Just you then. Join the workers.'

Zaqri threw Cym a concerned look, but stood. <*Perhaps I will learn something,*> he sent.

Fear of separation made her forget her supposed indifference. <*Be careful,*> she sent back worriedly. They were both keenly aware that none of the men sent out on these work gangs had returned here.

Something in his eyes smiled at her obvious fear. <*I've told you, nothing can tear us apart.*> He glared at the legionary, whom he towered over, then trudged away, his aura pulled inwards so that it was invisible to gnostic sight. Inside a minute, an order was bawled out, and they marched away, trailed to the gate by a gaggle of women. Cym joined them, in case they knew what was happening, but they didn't appear to, and anyway, she knew no Keshi. But she had something in common with them; they were scared too.

A few minutes later, half of Siburnius' Fist and the Dokken mage Delta trotted after the work detail without a backwards glance.

Cym returned to her blanket, huddled into it and tried not to envisage what might be happening.

At dusk, she returned to the fence-line, a shawl over her head, where the most forward of the women were begging information. The exact words might be a mystery, but the meaning was clear: *Where are our men?*

The guards ignored them.

Then they all heard and felt the thud of hooves approaching. The woman next to Cym poked at her arm, talking at her. When ignoring her failed to dissuade her, Cym turned to the woman and showed her an illusion: that her tongue had been cut back to a scarred stump, like she'd seen once in Rimoni, the product of rough justice on a farm. The woman blanched at the illusion and backed away, throwing her pitying looks.

Siburnius' Inquisitors trotted into view, their helms facing for-forward, the horns of their mounts aloft. Behind them came the robed man, Delta. They looked unsettled, and their horned horses – khurnes, she heard one of them call the beasts – looked hard-ridden. There were no Keshi workmen with them. No Zaqri.

Food and water were wheeled into the pen and there was the usual stampede. The bereft women still called out questions, their voices increasingly impassioned, the fear in their voices palpable. Cym kept her head down, unwilling to join the mêlée about the wagons, though her stomach was begging to be filled and they had precious little dried meat left in her pouch. The sun fell and Luna rose, a waning sliver of silver. As darkness descended, the cooking fires gradually became the only thing that could be seen. She longed to just fly away, but though her Air-gnosis was sufficient, she knew she couldn't evade the wards about the camp in physical form. In the end she just rolled herself in Zaqri's blanket, breathing in the smell of him, and tried not fight the feeling that the world was falling into Hel.

He didn't return that night, or the next day, and by the end of the week she was out of food and her panic was beginning to overflow. She had to join the scrabbling refugees fighting at the gates of the pen night and morning for a handful of lentils, and now she had no man to protect her, she huddled in the single women's area, pressed against strangers, using her tongue-less illusion to avoid having to speak. Her gnostic sight revealed that the Inquisitors' dome-wardings were still in place, and the Inquisitors, evidently on edge, were now patrolling day and night.

Zaqri must be out there, he must be . . .

Or he's dead.

After another week, by which time she was almost delirious with fear and the bulge in her stomach was clear to all the women around her, she had no choice but to try and find a way to escape.

33

Reunion

Ordo Costruo

Was there ever a more pompous gaggle of cretins than the Ordo Costruo of Pontus? Without even the greed and temerity to go and live off the benighted heathens in Hebusalim, they sit in their freezing marble towers and pontificate about the rest of humanity. But they showed their true colours in 904 when the First Crusade came calling . . . right down to blaming it all on Antonin Meiros.

MEMORIES OF THE FIRST CRUSADE,
GENERAL LARS DE MICHET, ANDRESSEA 916

Southern Kesh, on the continent of Antiopia
Rami (Septinon) 929
15th month of the Moontide

'Scout, sir!' Pilus Lukaz's face wore its usual calm expression, while behind him his cohort shifted and shuffled about. They were still learning the quirks of being mounted, and even as simple a matter as halting sent a few of the riders into dancing circles.

'It's Coll,' announced Harmon, one of the few who'd adapted well to riding.

Kip chuckled amiably. 'He's in a hurry, yar?'

Rat-faced Bowe sniggered, 'He looks like he's got a thorn in his butt.'

The scout was indeed riding awkwardly. They all chuckled as he cantered up, wincing heavily.

'You catch an arrow in the arse?' Ramon asked with a grin.

Coll spat with feeling. 'Boils,' he groaned.

The cohort laughed sympathetically. ' "Man's suffering is endless",' quoted the pious Dolmin.

'So are your damned holy words,' Neubeau replied.

Coll remembered to salute. 'Sir, there's some kind of camp ahead. Thousands of Keshi, and some of our boys.'

Ramon sat up in the saddle. 'Ours?'

A low cheer went up and Ramon could feel his own excitement rising. *Rondians this side of the Tigrates! Have we really reached our own lines again?* After nine months on the march, cut off from any help, were they finally back with the army?

'Well, not *us* as such, sir, but Rondians.' He spat. 'There's a maniple of legionaries, but it look like there are Inquisitors in charge.'

The cohort muttered at that. 'Quizzies' were nobody's favourite people, not even the devout Dolmin. 'Maybe they're lost too?' Vidran chuckled.

'We en't lost, Vid,' Bowe replied. 'We's always knowed where we are – in the wrong fucking place.'

His raw-boned mate Trefeld guffawed.

'In the wrong fuckin' place,' Manius mused. 'Should be our motto, lads.'

'Kore's Word,' Dolmin agreed fervently.

Ramon raised his hand, got silence. 'A legion camp full of Keshi likely means slavers, lads.' He surveyed the faces, which mostly hardened at his words. 'Personally, I don't like slavers. But let's go and find out for ourselves, si?' He turned to Lukaz. 'Send a messenger to General Korion, tell him what we've found. Coll, rest your arse here.' This raised a general snort of amusement. 'The rest of us will push on and see what's going on.' He looked at Kip. 'Coming?'

Kip exhaled through rubbery lips like a camel preparing to spit. Schlessens had once been the most common victims of the Rimoni slavers, and though that was centuries ago, it had never been forgotten. 'Yar, I'd like to meet some slavers, for sure.'

Ramon and Kip spurred forward, moving at a trot so that the cohort could keep up. He listened to the muted rumble behind him.

Ramon knew these men pretty well by now. Most of them had emerged from Khotri with a different view of the people whose lands they were marching through; some even had Khotri wives in the baggage train. The news of a slavers' camp might split opinion, but first and foremost they were soldiers who would follow his orders.

They chewed up the miles quickly and before long they were topping a rise and the sight Coll had described was spread out below. The air was smoky in the bowl, tainted by the ordure of thousands of people penned together. They could see and smell the sewer-pits festering in the sunlight, even from up there. The shrieks of children filled the air, and the fences were lined with desperate-looking Keshi, grimy, dark-skinned people clad in ragged clothes, the washed-out hues of white and orange and blue all fading to dirty grey and dun. As they got closer, he could feel a miasma of resigned despair, doubtless fed by hunger and thirst.

'The legion commander doesn't seem too worried about disease,' he commented to Lukaz. *Or anything else.*

Lukaz adjusted his helmet distractedly, as if contemplating his next words carefully. Finally the Vereloni spoke. 'Magister, this camp is too far south. Unless they have windships coming, it is too far to take these people to the Bridge.'

'Windships are expensive, and rare,' Ramon agreed. 'The empire wouldn't waste them on slave-trading, not unless the price of slaves has gone mad in our absence.' *No, this reminds me of something else entirely.* He felt a sudden sense of oppression.

Rukka mio, isn't it wonderful to be back with the empire . . . ?

'Sir?' Lukaz indicated a small group of riders who had suddenly whirled and were riding hard towards them with the urgency of people who wanted to head them off before they saw too much.

'Inquisition,' Kip growled.

The Church knights pounded towards them, just four of them, but that was comfortably enough to win against two low-blood magi and a cohort of humans.

'Thing with these pricks,' Vidran commented, 'is you never know whether you're on the same side as them.'

'They're on Kore's side and that's it,' Neubeau said.

'That's the same side as all of us,' Dolmin replied dutifully.

Ramon quieted them with a gesture. 'Spread out. Treat them as hostile, but don't do anything unless I tell you to.'

The cohort nudged apart to present no clumped targets, gripped their sword-hilts tight and waited. No one looked like they relished a fight against such foes, especially one on horseback.

'We's all Rondians, ain't we?' Bowe complained.

Harmon put a finger to his lips. 'Shut up, Bowe, you butt-wad. They're the Inquisition. They're a breed apart.' The two of them glared at each other. The cohort mostly got on, but if there was a fracturing it usually involved the generally repugnant Bowe on one hand, and the aloof Harmon on the other.

The Inquisitors galloped in smoothly on their horned steeds and drew to a stop some ten yards away. There were three men and one grey-haired woman. Ramon realised he knew at least two of them.

'So, you again,' the grey-haired woman rasped.

It wasn't the greeting he'd envisaged when they finally made contact with their own lines again. He saluted respectfully, though, while his mind raced. 'Battle-mage Ramon Sensini, Pallacios Thirteen. I bring the greetings of General Korion.'

The woman blinked slowly. '*General Korion?*'

'Indeed. Our main body is east of here, and should arrive very soon.' *Or not. They're probably half a rukking day behind us. Still* . . . 'What is happening here, Acolyte . . . er . . . ?'

'Fist Third Alis Nytrasia,' the woman drawled, looking left and right. The scar-faced young Acolyte who'd been with her last time was at her shoulder, eyeing Kip with cold disdain. 'I understood the Pallacios Thirteen to be . . . *destroyed.*'

'Several units managed to extricate themselves from Shaliyah.'

'Did you run?' the young male Inquisitor drawled mockingly. The cohort bristled, causing Lukaz to raise his hand warningly. The Inquisitors didn't blink, but Ramon could feel how ready they were to unleash havoc.

'We retreated south when the battle turned against us,' Ramon replied levelly. 'We've been marching west since then, avoiding the enemy when we can, fighting when we have to. I ask again, what is happening here, Acolyte Nytrasia?'

She sniffed haughtily. 'This is a slave camp. It's none of your business.'

Ramon remembered the branded mage, and what he and Sevvie had seen in Peroz. *The Hel it is.* He took a breath, and tried to estimate the number of Keshi in the pens. *Sol et Lune! The Inquisition are harvesting souls by the thousand, out here where no one knows.*

Alis Nytrasia was watching him with narrowed eyes. *Trying to gauge how much I know . . . and whether it's worth killing us.* He tried to seem oblivious. 'We are short of food and tired from the march. General Korion will wish us to join your camp.'

'We have no excess stores.' Nytrasia pointed northwest. 'The bridges at Vida are that way, two weeks' march.'

'Nevertheless, we will make camp here. Salim's army is near, and I'm sure the legion commander will be grateful for our presence.' He looked past her pointedly. 'Where is the commander, by the way?'

'Dealing with more important matters,' Nytrasia replied. 'Go away, Sensini.'

Her tone set a bristling noise rippling through the cohort. *Don't do anything stupid, lads,* Ramon prayed.

There was obviously little point in pressing the issue. He pretended to back down, and led the cohort away. The Inquisitors watched them go impassively. He made for a small flat area and extended a veil from scrying over it. He immediately came into conflict with an active spell – the Inquisitors were already scrying him – but he felt them break off – he could almost hear their hiss of annoyance.

'Old friends of yours, boss?' Lukaz enquired dryly.

'You could say that. Kip knows, and so does Severine. These are some of the most evil bastards I've ever come across.' He looked around the dell. 'Those Inquisitors aren't taking slaves: they're on an extermination mission. We need the army here, right now.'

The men looked at one another and he saw everything from loathing to callous disinterest cross their faces.

'They're only Keshi, sir. What can we do?' Bowe asked, his face unsympathetic.

'A Fist has enough power to kick us all the way back to Ardijah,' Trefeld added.

Ramon eyed the pair coolly. 'Maybe. But once the rest of the army gets here, we're going to break this party up.'

The legionaries looked at him doubtfully. 'What's the profit in that?' Ollyd wondered.

'Are they as tough as the tales tell?' Kel Harmon asked, his eyes far away, fixed on the Inquisitors. 'I've often wondered.' The rest of the cohort unconsciously backed away from him.

'The heathen is already damned,' quoted Dolmin.

Kip grunted. 'I'm a heathen. So are half of you pricks.'

'But they're Noories,' Bowe whined. 'That's different.'

Ramon rounded on him. 'Sol et Lune, look at you all! Half of you could pass for Dhassans, you've been under the sun so long. How many of you have a Khotri woman in the baggage train? How many of you shared a pint or a pipe with a "Noorie" back in Ardijah? How many hundred rankers told me, "They're not so different from us, sir" when begging permission to marry a Khotri widow? "Just common muck like us", you kept telling me. Well, that's who're in that camp: common muck like us, getting slaughtered for sport by Siburnius and Nytrasia and their lot. I think we're better than that – but maybe some of you don't?'

The men hung their heads, not meeting his eye. Then Lukaz looked up. 'You're right, boss. If they're just killing for the joy of it, that ain't right. I'm with you.'

Oh, it's so much worse than that.

Vidran nodded, as did Manius and Baden. Then Harmon smiled to himself and tapped his sword-hilt. With the opinion-leaders in agreement, the rest fell into line, even Bowe and Trefeld.

'Good.' Ramon pointed to a nearby rise, which had a view over the camp. 'Lukaz, assign the watch. I'll stay – Kip, I need you to go and find Baby Korion as fast as you can and bring him here.' He wished he had a relay-stave, but they'd not had one since before Shaliyah.

'Yar, no problem.' Kip spurred his horse fiercely and galloped off. In minutes the Schlessen was just a dust-trail in the middle distance and Ramon left the cohort where they were and went to the top of the ridge to view the camp below. The sun beat down and the dry heat was parching. He let his horse graze the stubby brush dotting the slope behind him while, watching Alis Nytrasia and her companions below. He still feared some kind of attack and was keeping his inner eye open for signs of the gnosis.

That was how he spotted a bird, apparently a sparrow, that swooped in from the south and landed in the lee of a low boulder where it could not be seen from the camp. He instinctively warded and was almost set to blast it with a mage-bolt when it spoke into his mind.

<Ramon-amici,> a woman's voice drawled. *<Fancy meeting you here.>*

The bird turned into Cymbellea di Regia – or rather, an image of Cym, for the sun shone through her without casting a shadow. 'Cym!' Ramon squawked. 'Rukka mio, is that you?' He raised his arms as if to hug her then dropped them again. 'Where's your body?'

'Down there,' she said. 'I'll tell you the rest later.'

A million questions leaped into his head as he stared from her to the camp and back again, then back at the men of the cohort. Cym would be invisible to the naked eye, but none of them seemed to have noticed that he was talking to himself. 'You're inside that camp? Sol et Lune! We'd better get you out. There's an Inquisitor Fist down there with a tame Dokken in tow, and they're up to no good.'

'I know.' Her voice cracked a little. 'I think they killed Zaqri.'

'Who's Zaqri?'

She hesitated. 'A friend.' She didn't say it with enough warmth for him to be convinced. 'I've not seen him for weeks, and it's getting desperate in the camp. They keep taking people away and they don't come back. I can't get out because they've warded the fences. I keep hoping . . . The Inquisitors are hunting someone outside the perimeter, so perhaps he got away . . .'

'This Zaqri? Who is he?'

She hung her head. 'Zaqri is a Dokken.'

He blinked. 'You're *friends* with a Dokken? But—'

'Please, Ramon!' She reached out to him, intangible as mist. 'I'm carrying his child.'

He felt his jaw drop. *Sol et Lune*. . . Cym was like a sister to him. 'Did—? Did he—?'

She shook her head. 'No, he didn't take anything. I was willing.'

He stared at her, too stunned for words.

Seth Korion spurred his mount down the slope, followed by the cavalry and every battle-mage he could get his hands on, which wasn't many.

We're up against Inquisitors! But the thought didn't frighten him as much as he thought it should. His motley command had escaped Shaliyah; they'd taken and slipped out of Ardijah, and he'd met Salim. Or whoever he was. He felt oddly capable, and not even the irritating presence of Ramon Sensini could shake that. He had more than ten thousand men at his back, and more than that, he had a sense of moral force that felt like riding a powerful stallion.

Kore sees everything. He knows this is wrong. He will guide me.

Or Sensini will . . .

They do say that Kore finds the strangest mouthpieces to speak his will.

The reunion with their own forces was supposed to be a joyous day, not a confrontation, but here they were, facing a death-camp and a line of Inquisitors. He recalled what Ramon and Severine had told him at Peroz, about the khurnes and how they got their intelligence. The very thought sickened him. He recalled his father boasting at a pre-Crusade banquet of the thousands of khurnes and hulkas that would be accompanying his army . . .

We've slaughtered people to make brighter animals. Is that truly the work of Kore?

Below was the camp, a horde of Keshi crowded in a rectangular pen, with small ranks of legionaries stationed on all sides – not many, but the Keshi looked pacified. As they made their final approach, he concentrated on the Fist arrayed to meet him: eleven khurne riders, all but one in Inquisitor black and white, the Sacred Heart emblazoned on their chests. They were in full armour despite the heat, and mounted, as if ready for the parade-ground. Their lance-pennants were fluttering in the faint breeze.

His eyes dropped to their mounts. *They don't even hide them. They know what they are and they don't care.*

His eyes went to the eleventh rider, no Inquisitor, but so swaddled in his dun robes that no flesh could be seen. He narrowed his senses to focus on that man, and picked up the distorted aura that Ramon had described.

A Souldrinker. He shivered.

The Inquisitor Commandant at the front, a burly, steel-faced man, trotted his big black khurne forward to meet him. He raised a hand in the traditional greeting of equals, which rankled. *We're not equals. I'm a general.* He gave the senior-to-junior salute a little tentatively, but took heart from catching an approving nod from Sensini at the corner of his vision.

The commandant scowled faintly and modified his salute. 'I am Ullyn Siburnius, Commandant of the Twenty-Third Fist.' He looked about him with all the disdain of the mighty Inquisition for lesser beings. 'I was led to understand that I was to meet General Korion?'

'I am Korion.'

'You, sir?'

'General Seth Korion, commander of the Southern Army since the Battle of Shaliyah.'

Siburnius made a show of confusion. 'Despatches reported that no units survived, er . . . General.'

'Fog of war,' Ramon Sensini put in. 'You know how it can be.' He indicated the pens. 'We've come to close down this camp.'

'On what authority?' Siburnius asked coldly.

'On mine,' Seth replied, trying to sound as calm as Ramon. 'I am the senior ranking officer of the Southern Army post-Shaliyah and I have assumed command of all military operations in Southern Kesh and Dhassa.'

'General *Kaltus* Korion assumed full command of the entire theatre of war after Shaliyah,' Siburnius retorted.

'Father assumed we were all dead. He was wrong. Therefore his assumption of authority was premature. I'll talk to *Father* about that when I see him.' *Who will scream at me and spit in my face and humiliate me. But I'll deal with that later.*

'Regardless, the Inquisition have the right to operate how and where we decide, throughout the lands.'

'Duke Echor forbade the Inquisition from operating in areas under his jurisdiction. If I recognise the standards, the maniple aiding you here is one of Echor's, sent specifically to guard the southern flank of his army, not create prison camps. Where is their commander?'

Siburnius looked rebellious, but indicated a cluster of legion officers waiting behind the row of mounted Inquisitors. 'Tribune Gestryn is with his men. I outrank him.'

'Then I will have words with his Legate when I meet him. In the meantime, my forces wish to enter and close this camp. We ask that you go to Vida to ensure the garrison commander there awaits us. My men have marched hundreds of miles in hostile lands and deserve a heroes' reception.'

Siburnius' cold eyes met his, a look designed to freeze him. It did: Siburnius was exactly the sort of man his father surrounded himself with, men of the world who flattened anything in their path. They'd always terrified Seth. He felt himself begin to waver. The Inquisitor drew himself to his tallest height, and began to declaim, 'This is a commercial operation—'

'So where are the traders?' Ramon interrupted.

Siburnius' mouth opened and closed, as if he were incapable of anything except ranting. 'I said, this is a—'

'We all know what it is,' Ramon interjected again, his voice filled with disgust. '*Exactly* what it is.'

Siburnius' eyes bulged and locked onto the little Silacian. 'Sensini, isn't it?'

Ramon grinned impudently. 'With two Ss.' Then his face hardened again. 'How many Keshi have you murdered here, Commandant?'

'Murdered? How dare you—'

'Oh, shut it,' Ramon told him with deliberately aggravating condescension. 'We *know*, Siburnius. We *know*.'

It was oddly pleasant to see someone else trying to deal with Sensini, but Seth could sense that the commandant was about to explode. Time for him to intervene. 'Siburnius, we believe this camp is illegal. You must leave now. For the honour of the empire.'

'We expect you gone within the hour, Commandant,' Sensini added, 'and if we see any move made against the prisoners, we will intervene.'

Siburnius straightened, and his face turned ugly. 'You don't have the authority, *General.* I have a commission signed by Emperor Constant and Arch-Prelate Wurther! I am backed by the laws of Kore himself! We are doing the work of the emperor and the Church and we will not be thwarted. Take your men and leave!'

Their eyes locked, and Seth felt under assault by the absolute rectitude of the Inquisitor. All his doubts returned, because he knew he really didn't have the authority to order this man away. The Inquisition were more or less independent of the army – and he really wasn't legally a general, either. In a court of law, he'd be shredded, mocked and then arrested.

What can I do? I've tried.

He half turned away and looked at Ramon Sensini, whose face fell faintly. It was as if he'd always expected Seth to just give up, right from the start. For some reason it infuriated him.

Then pride and his own sense of fairness took over – but not in a way he'd ever before experienced. For a moment he was about to let loose at Ramon, then he realised that was just stupid; instead, he whirled back to face Siburnius in time for his anger to erupt. 'No, Commandant!' he shouted, '*you* will do exactly as I have told you! I don't care what pieces of paper you think give you the authority to murder thousands of innocents, but I do not recognise them! I'll tell you what I do recognise: I have twelve thousand men and you have ten. Get them out of my way now, or we'll kill the lot of you.'

Holy Kore, did I just say that?

But he had, and as he stood there, struggling to hold his gnosis in check because he *dearly* wanted to *smash* this damned Inquisitor and all his cronies, he resolved to stand by every word. He saw Siburnius' eyes bulge, saw the Inquisitors behind him blink in utter disbelief, saw auras flare and gnosis kindle. He couldn't look away, not in the face of ten Inquisitors; all he could do was pray that the sounds he heard behind him weren't twelve thousand men running away.

Three seconds of utter silence passed as he tried to keep from blinking, then:

'Cohort, present arms!' shouted Pilus Lukaz.

He heard a massive crunching thud as spear butts were thumped into the ground, then raised, the sound taken up rank by rank behind him as the shouts of the officers carried down the lines in either direction. His heart was in his mouth; he felt it hammering, but he kindled wards and put his hand on his sword-hilt.

All the while, his eyes were fixed on Siburnius.

Blink, or die.

The moments crawled by, the suppressed violence almost tangible in the air. The pressure was building at his back and in his face, begging for release.

Siburnius blinked. 'Very well,' he snarled, 'if *right* and *reason* are things you believe yourself to be above, *General*, I will save lives here and withdraw.'

'Save lives ... yeah, about thirty thousand Keshi lives,' Ramon drawled.

Seth glanced sideways: Sensini looked to be the calmest man on the field.

Siburnius threw a barely serviceable salute at Seth and eyed Ramon contemptuously. 'I will see that there is an appropriate welcome for you all at Vida,' he promised, then he turned his khurne and surged away. His Fist wheeled as one to follow.

Siburnius reined in before Tribune Gestryn. 'Prepare your men to march, Gestryn.'

The tribune looked up at him, then at Seth. His whole body seemed to swell slightly. 'I must report to General Korion,' Gestryn said, in a self-disbelieving voice. He saluted Siburnius smartly, then turned away.

The Inquisitor gaped at him, then shot Seth a look of pure hatred.

He raised his hand and his Fist galloped away, the eleventh rider, the Souldrinker, trailing them. They were gone inside a minute and all down the line, Seth could feel the tension dissipating. Cheering broke out spontaneously in some of the ranks, though it was quickly quietened by the officers.

Seth let his breath out slowly. He felt faint, overstretched, dizzy as if he'd just tried to stand up too fast. 'Sweet Mother . . .' he whispered. 'Holy Kore.'

Ramon slapped his upper arm and grinned. 'Well done, Lesser Son. I knew you had it in you.' He trotted his horse forward and raised an arm. 'All right, you lot! Roll forward! Let's take control here!'

Tribune Gestryn maintained he did not know what the Inquisitors were doing; his job was to run the camp and follow orders. For now, at least, Seth had little choice but to believe him. There were more pressing logistical problems to solve: they needed more water, and food too. Their supply situation had been entirely adequate when they left Ardijah, but five thousand extra mouths were going to see them on low rations again by the time they made Vida.

Gestryn's maniple was part of the Vida garrison, he told them. there were two more camps this side of the River Tigrates, and that raised the question of what to do about them.

At a meeting of the magi, Ramon was insistent. 'We have to liberate them all.'

Jelaska, sitting close to Baltus Prenton with her thigh pressed against his, shook her head. 'It would be the right thing to do, but we've got to reach Vida by the end of Septinon – that's less than two weeks away.'

'So you'd leave them all to die?'

'We can't help them,' Hugh Gerant stated. 'We don't even know how many other Fists are here – what if we run up against a hundred Inquisitors? There's only eighteen magi in this army.'

'A hundred Inquisitors? That would be half the Inquisitors in the East,' Severine responded sarcastically, cradling her round belly and fanning herself. 'Don't make them out to be scarier than they are.'

'Even one more Fist and they'd be more than we could handle,' Gerant replied.

Seth looked around him. He'd had to explain why they'd run off a Fist of Church knights, and that truth, that the Church was harvesting souls to create intelligent beasts, had been so vile that it won them all round. Gerdhart, the Brician chaplain, had even quoted verses from a Kore *Scriptorium* that condemned the slaughter of even heathen; apparently it demeaned the slayers. And the laws of the magi concerning construct creatures – laid down by the Church itself – expressly forbade such acts.

'Salim's army is only a week behind us,' Jelaska reminded the group. 'They're tracking us with skiffs and cavalry. If this takes too long, we'll miss our deadline for crossing the Tigrates and they'll come down hard on us.'

'Then what do we do?' Severine asked.

The tent fell silent and all heads turned to Ramon.

Why does everyone always look to him? Seth thought morosely. *I'm a Korion – I'm the general here.* Then he waited with the rest, because he had no idea what to do either.

Ramon sat back in his chair, scratching his nose. Then he looked around the circle. 'You know, I think we need to make this Salim's problem.' He looked at Baltus. 'Do you think you can arrange a parley?'

Cymbellea di Regia huddled beneath a blanket amidst the Keshi and Dhassan refugees. She didn't know what to do. The women around her, many also pregnant, were scared, and the advent of more Rondian soldiers was of no comfort. No one spoke to her – they still believed she'd had her tongue removed. She wasn't alone; apparently it wasn't uncommon here for a rapist to silence his victim that way. Her guts were rebelling from inadequate food and the queasiness of early pregnancy.

The Inquisitors were gone, the gnostic barriers down, but there was still no sign of Zaqri. She had thought of calling to him, but Dokken were anathema to magi and if Ramon's people saw him they'd be obliged to try and kill him.

That's if he's still alive.

Neither her blanket or shift had been washed for days and they reeked – there was no washing water and there hadn't been any food for two days. The number of 'work gangs' taken out into the wilds had increased in the days before Ramon's army arrived and all her escape plans had foundered because of the patrolling Inquisitors' vigilance. She'd been trapped, as helpless as anyone else in here, and that frightened her.

She hung back as the new Rondian legionaries rolled wagons into the pen and began handing out food. She could feel Water-gnosis being expended at the watering hole. Even though she was now supposedly safe, the soul-draining energy of the camp continued to grip her. She felt no volition to move, just cradled her stomach and wondered what on Urte to do.

A mounted man rode past, a slight figure in the robes of a battle-mage, and the Ahmedhassans recoiled from him in fear. *A mage, close up.* She flinched as well, thinking only of hiding, but her face was drawn upwards.

It was Ramon, but his eyes slid blankly over her and belatedly she realised that she was still wearing her illusory disguise. She cancelled it at once, without even checking to make sure no one was looking. As her features remoulded a woman who happened to be glancing her way gasped, made the sign against the Evil Eye and started backing away. But Ramon had felt the expenditure of gnosis and spun in her direction. 'Cym?' he called, 'Cym!'

He dropped from his saddle and flung his arms around her, but she just stood there in a kind of stupor, while the refugees edged away.

'Hey, Sneaky,' she whispered, choking up. 'It's so good to see you.' Then her inner dam shattered and she cried so hard it physically hurt, her eyes stinging and ribcage aching with the force of her sobs.

For an instant Ramon looked shocked – of course, in her spiratus form she'd been so assured – but he must quickly have realised that of course she'd been another person then, out of her body, free to run. Here, she was a captive of flesh and fear, so he hugged her close. 'It's okay, Cym-amica, it's okay. I'm here.'

'Since when has that ever made things okay?' she murmured, try-ing to recapture the strong, spiky person she thought she was. 'It usually means disaster.'

He gave her another squeeze. 'That's my girl. Come on, let me take you away from all this.' His face was full of questions, but she was relieved when he restrained himself, even though she could see it took a visible effort. 'Come with me.'

He drew her over to his horse and with one arm around her shoul-ders, the reins in the other hand, forced a way through the crowds, ignoring the dark faces peering curiously at them. Behind them she could hear raised voice, and one frightened woman – the one who'd seen her change – started shrieking about afreets and Shaitan. But legionaries were stepping in to surround them, rough-looking men encased in leather and metal, their stubbly faces weathered and peel-ing, and then she and Ramon were outside the pen and standing before a heavily pregnant young Rondian woman with a cascade of brown ringlets and a lot of freckles. She waddled forward and took Ramon's hand. 'Who's this, Lovebug?'

Ramon coughed and stepped away, ignoring Cym as she mouthed, '*Lovebug?*' at him. 'Sevvie, this is Cymbellea di Regia. Cym: this is my . . . er . . . Severine.'

Cym eyed the woman cautiously. 'Hello,' she said. Severine looked nothing at all like she'd imagined any lover of Ramon Sensini's. *She's Pallacian! He's Silacian! They're pregnant! Sol et Lune, but war breeds strange bedfellows!*

The two women looked at each other awkwardly, and as her eyes rested on Severine's distended belly, she realised Ramon's lover was doing the same. Apparently Severine saw little she liked. She looked accusingly at Ramon and demanded, 'Who is she to you?'

'Cym's an old friend, from my days in Norostein.' He stepped between them. 'She was caught up in the camp – she needs food and drink. She'll be coming with us.'

Severine's hand went to her mouth, her pretty face twisted and she spat out, 'Then feed the ugly bint yourself!' and stomped away. Behind her, a towering Schlessen and a grey-haired woman failed to conceal their snorts of laughter. After a moment the grey-haired woman hurried after Severine.

Cym watched Ramon as he wavered between pursuing Severine or staying with her. 'That went well,' she observed dryly.

Ramon coughed. 'Si, si – she's, um, well, she's a little highly strung just now,' he tried to explain. 'She's due in a couple of weeks.'

Cym's hand went instinctively to her own belly, but Ramon said nothing – then he stiffened, his eyes going to something behind her, as a big hand fell on her shoulder. Her whole form quivered with utter, absolute relief as she whirled about, then Zaqri pulled her into his arms and engulfed her. She inhaled his sweat, the smell of sun-soaked cloth and hair, the hint of lion fur and blood, and drowned in the heat of him, revelling in the tensile steel of his muscle and the mountain-like solidity of his chest. She clung to him, struggling to breathe, repeating over and over, *Sol et Lune, he's alive.* She didn't know whether to cry with joy or to scream in rage. Part of her had thought that the gods had killed him to solve her vendetta dilemma, but she would still have to deal with it all herself. For now, she was just glad he was alive.

Mater Lune, forgive me, but I don't want him dead. I have to find another way.

Ramon stammered something, then straightened. He was looking Zaqri over with wary eyes, and so were those with him. Magi and Souldrinker, face to face, studying each other, waiting to see what might happen here. Some looked appalled, others, like the giant Schlessen, merely curious.

Then Ramon thrust out a hand to Zaqri. 'Ramon Sensini,' he said, 'of Silacia.'

Zaqri looked ill at ease, more than she had ever seen him, but he too extended his hand. 'I am Zaqri of Metia. Cymbellea's mate.' They gripped hands tentatively: mage and Dokken, but neither typical of their kind.

'Believe it or not, you're not the first of your kind we've encountered,' Ramon observed, removing any doubt Zaqri might have that he knew what he faced. 'Many fought for Salim at Shaliyah.' His words were like the tentative opening jabs of a fencing duel, feeling out the opponent's defences.

'There is an alliance,' Zaqri said carefully, 'but that does not concern me. My only concern is for Cymbellea, and our child.'

Cym quivered at the way he said it, feeling trapped by the gazes of the listening magi who suddenly stared at her with blank, accusatory faces, disgust and horror writ clearly as what he said sank in.

Yes, I've rukked a Dokken. She lifted her head. *Well, what of it?*

Silence clogged the air.

Ramon looked from her to Zaqri and back. 'We're marching west. Cym-amica, you are welcome to come with us.' He didn't need to add that Zaqri wasn't.

She looked up at Zaqri. *I could walk away from him. Is that punishment enough for him, Mother?* But there was also Alaron and the Scytale, unmentioned so far but their existence heavy in the air between her and Ramon. 'Can we talk?' she asked, her voice low. 'Alone?'

Ramon's brow furrowed with worry, but he said, 'Of course.' He looked up at Zaqri. 'If you don't mind?' he said levelly.

Zaqri's hands loosened their grip on her reluctantly, then he turned her, tilted her head and kissed her lips and her heart leaped in her chest as he did so. The taste of him was like a sweet liquor on her tongue. *Claiming me before them all.*

She claimed him also, open-mouthed and coiling her tongue about his.

'I will await your decision here, at sunset,' he said softly. Before she could respond, he turned and walked away.

Sunset. Zaqri waited where he'd said he would, in the no man's land outside the pen. The gates were open, but no refugees had yet left – why would they, where there was food and protection here? The Ahmedhassans were pleasantly puzzled that this new Rondian force was not hostile, and in fact had a baggage train full of willing Khotri women. But those from the same villages or towns were gathering to discuss how they might return home. Zaqri remained aloof, waiting fretfully for his mate.

'So, Zaqri of Metia,' someone greeted him in Rimoni. It was that ferret-faced battle-mage, Cymbellea's friend, Ramon Sensini. Cymbellea was nowhere to be seen.

Zaqri stood, swallowing. 'Magister Sensini.'

'Please, sit again. I'll join you.' Sensini went over to a mound and sat, then pulled out a flask of liquor and offered it to him. 'You can call me Ramon.'

Zaqri looked about. 'Where is Cymbellea?'

'She's gone down into the women's camp. Something to do with her condition.'

Zaqri had to restrain himself from leaping to his feet and running to find her. 'Is she going to stay with your army?'

Ramon sighed, his face rueful. 'She seems to think that she has to go off and save my friend Alaron. You know the name?' When Zaqri nodded, he went on, 'She doesn't know where he is, but ten to one he's in worse shit than we are, knowing him.'

Zaqri felt his heart begin to pound. *She's staying with me ... Thank you, Pater Sol! Thank you thankyouthankyou ...*

'I take it you know what is at stake?' Ramon enquired.

'The Scytale of Corineus. Freedom for my people.'

Ramon looked thoughtful. 'I'd not thought of it in that way, but I suppose you're right: it would be salvation. Perhaps it's even the right thing to do.' He studied Zaqri. 'There were hundreds of Dokken at Shaliyah, led by a man called Yorj Arkanus. Do you know him?'

'Only by reputation.'

'He was an evil cunni who tried to sell me his wife to save his own life.' Ramon looked disgusted at the memory. 'So I killed him.'

Zaqri blinked. Arkanus had been the warleader of the eastern Dokken, the one who'd drawn their whole Brethren into the shihad. *If he's dead, who is leading ... ?*

'I have seen and read and heard nothing but evil about your kind, Souldrinker,' Ramon went on. 'Every holy book, every tale handed down, everything I myself have seen is telling me to lock you up while we decide how to kill you.'

Zaqri straightened. 'I'm not so easy to catch, Magister.'

'Easy there. You see, Cymbellea is like a sister to me. She says that you're a good man, the best of your kind. She begged me not to have you arrested, and I agreed. I've spoken to General Korion and he accepts my word. The proviso is that you'll not harm even the lowliest Ahmedhassan refugee here, and you'll be gone by dawn.'

'With Cymbellea?'

Ramon nodded slowly, painfully. 'With Cymbellea.'

He closed his eyes to hide the sudden sting of tears.

'Where will you go?' Ramon asked.

He thought for a few seconds. 'East – always east. There are Inquisitors hunting your friend, and Dokken too.' *Huriya Makani. Wornu and Hessaz. My own pack – no, mine no longer.* 'We don't even know if he is still alive.'

Ramon looked at him with misgivings writ large on his face. 'I wish I could come with you, but we've got thousands of men here, and now all these refugees. And my lady is about to give birth to my child. I'm honour-bound to see them home.'

'I understand that. I was a packleader once. Leadership is a responsibility.' He added slowly, 'And a child is a precious thing.'

'Si. It is indeed.' Ramon looked as if he'd just confirmed something to himself, something he'd hoped for but hadn't entirely expected. 'I will wish you buona fortuna, Zaqri of Metia. Give Alaron my best when you find him.'

They stood and shook hands, then the little battle-mage strolled away.

Zaqri turned, his heart pounding, and ran back to the camp.

There was an area set aside by common agreement for women only, but he strode unheeding into it, wearing his true face and skin colour, heedless of the looks they gave him as he approached. He wiped his sweating palms on the apron of his kurta, feeling his nerves grow as he walked.

She's going to come with me! She's going to have my child!

He remembered all the years with Ghila, all the still-births, then the final realisation that she was barren. The tears, the blame, the recriminations, the making up, the tentative finding of a new peace between them, despite the emptiness of making love when they both knew there would be no harvest from the sowing. He wondered if it had made her reckless in battle, until she let herself become separated from the others at the Isle of Glass. She had died unavenged as well, although Cym seemed to have overlooked that. He had a strong, uncomfortable feeling that this Alaron they sought might have been the one who took Ghila's life.

How will I feel when I finally meet you, Alaron Mercer? I expect Cym to put her vengeance aside, but can I do the same?

When he reached the middle of the women's camp and the people clustered there saw him, he realised something was wrong. It was in their eyes, the fear and the knowledge. He looked around for her, opened his mind to call. *<Cymbellea?>* There was no reply, but he'd tasted her skin and her soul. She was ... *that way* ... somewhere in the heart of the press and bustle. *<Cymbellea!>*

He ploughed into the mass of women, his mind conjuring images of lynching and murder, of her body torn and ravaged, her heartbeat shuddering to a halt. All around him the dark faces of the Dhassan and Keshi refugees stared at him, their eyes hostile. He shoved them aside, roaring in terror and fury, shouting her name.

He found her right in the middle, lying on her back on a blanket, her shift hiked up to the waist and her legs spread, shrieking in pain and loss. The stink of iron and viscous blood painted the air red. A clutch of old women were gathered about her, some holding her down, others sloshing water. One held a bloody stick.

'NOOOO!' He fell to his knees, blazing gnosis fire into the skies, assaulting Heaven. 'MATER LUNE, NO!'

Perhaps she heard, the goddess of mad acts, for she was certainly present, but her work here was done.

The Keshi skiff skimmed through the air, losing height as it dropped to the earth about a hundred yards from where Seth Korion waited. Its sails fell and it lost momentum swiftly, coming to a stop near the forty Keshi cavalrymen waiting below.

Seth strained his eyes eagerly. A slender, upright figure rose from a seat in the hull and stepped to the ground. Immediately all the Keshi prostrated themselves.

'Never hard to tell who's boss with these Noories,' Baltus remarked, leaning against his skiff. The Brevian looked quite at ease, trimming his nails with his dagger. 'What with all that kneeling and dirt-kissing.'

Seth ignored him and peered at Salim of Kesh as he acknowledged his men, then turned his head to look up the slope towards him. Did he fancy that their eyes met across the distance?

'Shall we grab him again?' Baltus joked. 'Wouldn't that piss them off?'

Seth stiffened. 'We will not. We must re-cultivate our honour, not taint it further.'

'As you say, General. Just making the offer.' He pointed towards the figures below. Two more men had disembarked. 'Anyway, I'm betting that pair are Keshi magi, here to avoid a repeat show.'

Seth tore his eyes from Salim and noted the two. *Souldrinkers? Hadishah?* For a few seconds the old, nervous Seth trembled, then he got a grip on himself. *I am a Korion. I am a pure-blood descendant of the Blessed Three Hundred. I have led the charge and faced down the Inquisition. I refuse to show fear.* It helped, somehow. He took a deep breath and said, 'Let's go.'

It felt oddly unnerving not to have Ramon here, but the Keshi had been very specific about excluding him from the parley and Seth could hardly blame them. And it felt good to be properly in charge for once, not just a mouthpiece. But it also meant he had to get this right on his own.

The Keshi came to meet him: Salim – or an impersonator – and two protectors. As they drew closer, he could sense the wrongness in the aura of the two Keshi flanking Salim. Souldrinkers, then, God's Rejects, and no doubt furious at the fate of their leaders. They'd know, of course: Latif would have told them. He girded himself for trouble.

Salim raised a hand in greeting. 'Sal'Ahm, General Korion.' The sultan looked majestic. His clothing was resplendent, with hundreds of gems glittering in the sun. He was dressed primarily in blue this time, with a white turban. His narrow, intelligent face was just like Latif's, but it had been two weeks; he wasn't sure . . .

'Sal'Ahm,' he replied, his voice catching a little. *I just wanted to see him.* 'It is good to see you, Sultan,' he added. 'Or at least, one of you.' It wasn't Latif, he was almost certain.

'Call me Salim,' the sultan replied.

Who knows who I'm really speaking to? 'Thank you, Sultan.'

'No Master Sensini to spoil our conversation today, I trust?' the Keshi ruler asked wryly. His Rondian was as smooth and cultured as Latif's had been.

'Not today.'

Salim indicated his companions. 'These are Brennan and Tynbrook, of Brevis. But not of your gnostic persuasion, of course.' The two Dokken flipped back hoods to reveal flame-red hair and beards, and pale northern Yuros skin. They exuded wariness and hostility.

'I trust you do not wish to try and turn the tables upon us today?' Seth enquired, not quite keeping the nervousness from his voice.

'I would rather keep my honour intact,' Salim replied evenly. He raised a hand and from the middle distance a servant hurried forward with a tray containing two goblets and a decanter of red wine. 'You are still partial to the Javonesi merlo? It is hard to get currently, but this is seven years old, from a good year.'

It was the same wine he'd had with Latif on their last evening together. Seth's mouth filled with saliva at the memory. He bowed. 'You have an excellent memory, Sultan.'

Salim raised one eyebrow. 'I was briefed fully.' He smiled enigmatically. 'I trust we may speak as friends?'

'Of course,' Seth said, 'though we have not met before.' *I don't think.*

'In many ways, we have met; we know so much of each other.' Salim filled a goblet and passed it to Seth. 'Please – it is not tainted, but I will not be offended should you need to use your powers to verify this.'

Seth looked down at the goblet and then at Salim. He took a sip.

Salim looked pleased at the display of trust. 'Praise be to Ahm, that enemies may drink as friends,' he declared. It sounded like a quote from a holy book. He filled the second goblet and drank as well. 'My friend, let us walk and talk.' He indicated a goat-trail that ran about the base of the rise. 'Shall we?'

Seth looked at Baltus; his eyes were locked on the two Brevian Dokken. 'We can trust Salim,' he said in a low voice. 'We can trust his honour.'

'I'm more worried about this pair.' Baltus glanced at the goblet. 'Do I get any of that merlo?'

Salim waved a hand. 'Help yourself, Magister Prenton.'

Baltus chuckled. 'Knows my name, and we've never been introduced. He's sharp, that one.' He threw Seth a warning look. <*Mind your tongue, lad. He's our enemy, remember.*>

Sadly true. Seth threw what he hoped was a warning look at the Dokken, then hurried to join the sultan. 'How does Latif fare?' he asked, trying to conceal his eagerness.

Salim smiled fondly. 'You are as affable as Latif described. He sends his greetings. But you must understand, it is unlikely he will be allowed to see you again while this war continues. He has been compromised.'

'But he will not be punished?'

'Of course not!' The sultan sounded shocked. 'The problem is that you can now clearly identify him as not being me, and that is valuable information in some circles.'

'I don't move in those circles, Sultan.'

'I suppose not, but nevertheless, we must be mindful. So, what is the need for this parley, Seth Korion? We both have places we must be: you across the Tigrates, and I in the north.'

'We'll be leaving your lands soon – we're going to be crossing the river any day.' Seth took another sip of wine, savouring it this time. It was inky-dark and velvet smooth. *Glorious.*

'The other side of the Tigrates is still my lands, Seth Korion,' Salim reminded him in a somewhat sterner voice. 'You had better not stop there.'

'We won't. We're going all the way to the Bridge and back across it.'

'Then what is it you want? Do you think I can restrain my generals for ever? They are chafing for vengeance, especially after your man Sensini made fools of us all.' He paused, raised a finger. 'Bring him to me and they might be appeased.'

I wouldn't take him up on that, even if I could. How odd. 'I am obliged to protect my own,' Seth replied dryly. 'In fact, I've not come to ask for anything. I'm actually here to warn you of something.' He outlined the situation ahead: two refugee camps, guarded by an Imperial legion and at least one Inquisition Fist. He didn't talk about the khurnes and how they were made; Ramon had insisted on holding back that information in case Salim overreacted. He did report that the camps had been places of brutality and death, though, and that was enough to ensure Salim took the issue seriously.

'What is it you wish us to do, General?'

'Move against the camps, and let us cross the Tigrates safely,' Seth replied.

Salim looked contemplative, and Seth thought he looked like a prophet-king straight out of one of his peoples' tales. And achingly like Latif. 'The Inquisition has an evil reputation among our people,' the sultan said eventually. 'They are the subject of a death-writ by the Godspeakers. Even the Ja'arathi condemn them.'

'If you can take them, they're yours, and good luck in it.'

Salim met Seth's eyes. 'Why do you tell us this? These are knights of your Church.'

'Because I – *we* – believe that what they are doing is evil.'

'Your own people will condemn you when you are back in Yuros.'

'I can handle that,' he said, not believing his own words for a second. *They'll probably hang me.*

'I admire your courage, Seth Korion,' Salim said softly. 'I myself have never been able to confront the Godspeakers as I have wished. They have too much power in my lands. Even I, Sultan of Sultans, must bend my knee to their wishes.'

'Priests are our gateways to paradise,' Seth replied piously.

'Some are.' Salim met Seth's eyes and inclined his head. 'Thank you for this news, my friend. Latif was right about you. "We can trust the younger Korion," he said. I believe that now.'

'Please convey my thanks and greetings,' Seth said.

'I think one day we will all meet again, in better days.'

'I pray so,' Seth replied fervently.

Salim inclined his head again. 'Well, my friend. You have laid a great charge upon me. I will send cavalry north to these other camps and deal with this situation. However, I must warn you that when my soldiers see these camps, they will be enraged. Many will blame you and your men. If you are not across the river by the agreed date, I will not be able to hold them back.'

'We'll be across,' Seth replied, sure on this point at least. 'Before the Crusades the Ordo Costruo built a bridge there, a mile across. It's like a small version of the Leviathan Bridge.'

'I know of it,' Salim replied. 'My father stood beside Antonin Meiros when it was opened; he was the first to ride across. Those were happier times.'

'We can make them come again,' Seth said, at that moment believing it.

'Then we have a deal, my friend.'

Salim kissed both his cheeks formally while the three Brevians watched each other for any late attempts at treachery. There were none.

With Salim's scent lingering in his nostrils, Seth and Baltus flew west.

'So was that the real Salim?' Baltus shouted as they ascended.

'Who would know?' Seth replied, staring back across the rippling mirages to the faraway hills, stark and brown under the desert skies. 'I don't.'

34

The Valley of Nagas

The Tale of Xynos Halfswine

The worst excesses of the Pallas Animagi are revealed in the sad case of Xynos Halfswine, a half-man half-pig created as part of their exploration of human-animal grafting prior to this being declared illegal. His miserable existence as a college exhibit was ended when he was burned alive for the heresy of daring to criticise those who brought him into being.

ANTONIN MEIROS, ORDO COSTRUO, 920

Xynos was, in his way, a hero, and a harbinger of what could be done. The cancellation of the human-grafting programme is a tragedy for gnostic evolution.

ERVYN NAXIUS, ORDO COSTRUO,
IN A LETTER TO MATER-IMPERIA LUCIA, 921

*Coastal Javon, Emirate of Lybis, on the continent of Antiopia
Shaban (Augeite) and Rami (Septinon) 929
14th and 15th months of the Moontide*

The first sense to return was feeling: warmth, around the core of the body, the prickle of a blanket against skin, heat, radiating against cheeks and nose, and itching skin, all over. Then scent: bodily smells, and warm wool, and roasting meat. Hearing next: the spit and crackle of a fire, the bubble of something cooking; distant, merry voices, and someone close by was rasping stone on a steel edge.

Elena opened her eyes.

She saw *him*.

'Kaz,' she croaked. Her heart pounded, quivered, burned.

'Ella!' He dropped his whetstone and scimitar – a new one, she noticed – and flew to her, gathered her in his arms, blankets and all. 'Yes, yes, yes! I knew it would be today.'

For an immeasurable time he just held her, and nothing else mattered.

Sitting up proved too hard and she sagged lower in the blankets, panting slightly as she looked up at him, drinking in the sight. He looked . . . *normal*, his gnosis replete. That hungry look he got when he was low on energy was absent. She tentatively tried her gnostic sight and gave a small gasp.

Their auras were utterly entwined, wound about each other like the roots of two plants that had been potted together. She could see her gnosis pulsing in his; she could feel his in her – she could scarcely tell where she ended and he began. 'Look at it,' she said softly. 'It's like we're the same being.'

He stroked her cheek. 'I know. I don't know how to make it stop.'

'Have you . . . you know . . . fed on someone?'

'No. No one . . . except you. But you keep replenishing yourself.' Guilt coloured his face. 'I think it's why you've been unconscious so long.'

'How long is that?'

'A week.'

'*A week!*' she squawked, trying to sit up, but he caught her. 'Great Kore!' She looked about her. They were in a tent, and it was sunny outside, but that was all she could tell, except that she could hear the sea: the distant thunder of waves crashing against the shore. 'Where are we?'

'I don't know the name. I call it the Valley of Nagas.'

'Nagas? What's that?'

'You will not believe me, I swear. It is best you see.'

He wouldn't tell her more until he'd made her eat some broth. She realised she was naked beneath her blanket, and that he had been tending her. It was a humiliating to think of herself so helpless – she'd always hated being a burden to others – but mostly, she just felt relief and gratitude. When she tried to thank him, he brushed it off. 'You did the same for me, Ella, at the monastery. Twice.'

'But—'

'Say nothing more. And don't leave me in this situation again. I am a warrior, not a nurse.'

She seized his hand, kissed it. 'I don't know any fighting man who would tend someone like that. It is normal for women, but men are not expected to do such things. You have done more than anyone else would have.'

He looked uncomfortable. 'If there had been a maid around, I would have left her to it, believe me. I am glad I was born a man. I thank Ahm daily.'

'Pah! I'm glad I'm a woman.'

'Mmm. I am glad too.' He winked with his usual mischievous lewdness, slid a hand over her left breast.

She swotted it away. 'Hey, you randy beggar! Doesn't take you long, does it?'

'Please, Ella!' He looked aggrieved. 'I have lain beside you every night and had to endure the woman I love being near death. You must excuse my relief that you are better and my hope that our lives will return to normal.'

'I can't wait either, lover. Truly.' She stroked his arm. 'Kaz, do you understand: we are probably the first ever mage and Souldrinker to ever . . .' her voice trailed off, she swallowed, went on, 'to ever fall in love.'

Because that is what it is. I love him. I didn't before, not fully. I mothered him, let him make love to me because I couldn't resist. That was just the beginnings of love. But what I feel now is: real, utter, complete love.

And look what it's done to us . . . Our auras have fused. We've completed each other.

She began to cry.

'Hey, it's not so bad,' he said, wilfully misunderstanding her tears. 'We can always argue again once you're stronger.'

She laughed. 'Yes, of course we can.' She seized his face and let him kiss her tears away. 'This is incredible . . . I can only suppose that once

DAVID HAIR

the last ... barriers between us ... came down, we've been feeding each other gnosis. It's like we're symbiotic. Do you know the word? Two creatures that can only exist together.'

The thought was heart-poundingly frightening – and beautiful.

'And no mage or Souldrinker have ever loved before?'

'Well, who knows about Nasette? Perhaps this was what happened to her?' She shook her head. 'No, this is a first. Not even magi in love experience this. It must be something about the nature of your gnosis and mine together – like the poles of a magnet, the alpha to the omega.'

'I have no idea what you're talking about,' He told her. 'It is simply love.'

'Yes. It is love. You know what else this means? You will never have to kill again to replenish your powers. You just need to be with me.'

'I had been thinking this also,' he said gravely. 'It is a miracle! Thanks be to Ahm most high.'

'I think you are the miracle!' *Love. Real love, after all these years ...*

For a time her mind drifted in a haze, then she recalled his earlier words. 'Kazim, what did you say about "Nagas"?'

'I will show you.' He helped her to dress, supported her as she crawled outside, then pulled her upright. She emerged into the baking sun on a sandy strip of land between a wide riverbed filled with narrow, twisting streams winding around hummocks of stone and gathering in deeper pools. To the left and behind them rose mountains: sheer and white-tipped. To the right she could hear the tumult of the sea crashing against the cliffs, miles away but a constant presence. The earth nearby had been tended and crops were growing, but the farmers were nowhere to be seen. Then she heard laughter like squealing children, above and behind them and she turned, shielding her eyes against the fierce sunlight.

Her jaw dropped.

On the rock face above were dozens of impossible beings: human, from the head to the waist, or nearly so; it was hard to be sure at this distance. But from the waist down, they were snakes, with reptilian tails as wide as their human torsos, extending for a dozen feet, in myriad hues of dun and green.

'What in Hel?' she breathed. 'What are they?'

'Nagas,' Kazim replied confidently. 'There are many tales of Nagas in Lakh. Sivraman creates them when he ejaculates.' He laughed. 'That is one story anyway. They helped the gods to create Urte. They planted the trees, dug the rivers and filled the seas. I never really thought they were real, but look!'

Elena stared, utterly amazed. The creatures climbed the mountainside with ease, flowing up and down the slopes as if immune to gravity. They were all nude, and the males and females were clearly different. The males had one single trunk of snake-body from the waist, while the females had twinned, thinner snake 'legs'. The women's breasts were bare; from what she could see, the males' genitals seemed to be retracted beneath a mound covered by a fleshy hood. Some had growth on their heads like human hair, but on others it was more akin to a turkey's comb.

Kazim cupped hand around his mouth and called, 'Kekro!' and one of the males turned in their direction, waved, then began to slither down the slopes towards them. 'They don't speak Keshi or Lakh,' he told her in a slightly puzzled voice, 'so I've not been able to talk to them. Kekro told me his name, though. He's the boss. He found us and told them to help us.' He dropped his voice to a whisper. 'I think we'd have both died without him.'

She watched, awed by the fluid ease with which the creature descended to them, with easy wide sweeps of his trunk or tail, whichever it was. His torso remained upright throughout. His shoulders were strong, and his chest and belly deep and exquisitely muscled, without an ounce of fat. Unnervingly, his belly skin was scaled, as was his back right to the shoulders.

Elena had grown up begging her parents to tell her 'just one more story': Lantric legends and ghost stories of blood-sucking corpses from the north – tales most thought of as myths. But the magi had made some of those creatures real . . .

'Hello,' she said, in Rondian, sure this being would understand.

The 'Naga' cocked his head and his eyes – little pools of wisdom – blinked slowly. 'Greetings, Lady,' he replied in the same language. 'We are pleased to see you on your feet.'

'You know their tongue?' Kazim confirmed with her in Keshi.

'No, he knows mine.' She tentatively tried out standing unaided and found she could. 'My name is Elena, and I thank you for aiding us.'

'Elena,' the Naga repeated, testing the sound. His alien face was close to human but subtly reptilian. He nodded faintly. His tongue when he licked his lips was human-like but longer, and he used it like a reptile would, in swift flicks. 'Welcome. I am Kekropius, elder of the lamiae.'

Ahhh. The lamia was a creature of Lantric legend. 'You're constructs,' she guessed, then realised how that must sound. To her relief, he didn't take offence.

'We are. An ugly word, but yes, we were made, not born – at least, the first generation were.' He pointed to the younger ones. 'As you can see, we were given the gift of reproduction.' He eyed her steadily and she noticed that others had slithered into earshot and were watching her carefully. 'But you are of the magi. Perhaps you already know all this?'

There was a test in his words. 'I didn't know, I guessed. Animagi are forbidden from making creatures with human intelligence – it is a sacred stricture. To be honest, I am shocked and appalled.'

He looked at her curiously. 'Then perhaps you understand that we are somewhat at a loss over what to do with you. Would you tell the Inquisitors where we are, perhaps?'

'No, not at all! Kore Above, you have the right to live.' That might not be exactly what the ethics teachers at college had said, but she'd never believed those heartless bastards anyway. Life taught many lessons that professors in their protected little environments never learned.

'That is not the view of your Inquisition,' Kekropius said. 'They have hunted us for years.'

I bet they have. 'They're not *my* Inquisition,' she replied. 'They are evil bastards.'

The lamia shrugged expressively. 'Nevertheless.'

'You've let us live so far.'

'So that you might give us your tale. Now that you are on your feet, we will set a date for your trial.'

She glanced at Kazim. 'Have you told my ...' – *uh, what do I say?* – 'man?'

'We have not the words,' Kekropius replied. 'He does not speak our language.'

'What will happen to us if we are guilty of whatever you think we might be guilty of?' she asked, struggling to keep her voice calm.

'That is for the Elder Council to describe,' Kekropius replied. He pointed back towards the coast. 'There are six men of your kind, living beside the sea and fishing the coastal pools. They helped sail us here, but that was under duress. We have not yet decided what to do with them either, but they are not an urgent case, not like a mage.'

She rubbed her face, feeling a little woozy, from standing, and the shock of meeting these creatures. 'Thank you for telling me. I need to lie down.' She clutched at Kazim, who caught her and kept her standing.

'Are you okay, my love?' he asked worriedly.

She nodded as Kekropius bowed from the waist and slithered backwards. The rest of the lamiae drew off.

'What did you say to each other?' Kazim asked softly, waving uncertainly to Kekropius. 'It looked serious.'

She let him take her back into the tent, out of the crippling heat. Then she told him.

'Then we have to run!' he exclaimed. 'I'll get us out, I swear.' He gripped his sword-hilt.

'No, I don't think they want to hurt us. But they might want to keep us here. They're scared of the outside – and who can blame them?' She yawned. 'Let's sleep on it.'

She could not manage much more than to sip a little more soup, then she fell into a deep and heavy sleep. When she woke again, it was still daylight, and she was alone. She managed to dress on her own this time, then, moving slowly and carefully, went to find Kazim, who was sitting on the riverbank, watching the young lamiae playing in the deeper pools. They were darting in and out of the water at alarming speeds, hoisting out fish and eating them whole. As she approached, one of the young males took Kazim a fish, like an offering to a priest. He made a gesture of thanks and the lamia sped away, crowing to his friends.

'Hey, dinner,' she said, sitting beside him, touching his arm and kissing him.

'It's tomorrow,' he said, anticipating her question. 'You look good. Much better.' He stroked her bare thighs, sniffed. 'Smelly, though.'

'Hey!' she cuffed him playfully. 'I've just woken up. And you don't smell so fresh yourself, mister!'

'I washed a couple of days ago,' he protested.

'Yeuwh.' She shoved him away then stood and pulled off her tunic before wading into the water. For a few seconds all the young lamiae stopped and stared and she felt her face flush. She dropped so that only her head was above the water, and as one the serpent-children went back to their play. Then Kazim leaped in beside her and they spent a good hour in the cool water, laughing and splashing as gaily as the children.

'What shall we do?' Kazim asked later, as they lay on the warm rocks in the late afternoon. 'The skiff is wrecked – Kekro's people burned the remains. They burned what was left of that bakhtak too.' He told her about the final few seconds of the chase, when she was out cold. She squeezed his hand afterwards, kissed it.

'You saved me again.'

'It is what lovers do.' He cupped her face, kissed her. 'So, what's the plan?'

'Let's hear them out. You and I are hard to pin down, so if they do find against us, we still have options. But they could be good allies, so let's not anger them before we know where we stand.'

'You are so wise,' he teased. 'Look, your hair is grey with wisdom.'

'*What?*' She was horrified.

'Yes, here, and here.' He touched her temples. 'It went grey that night, when the bakhtak touched you.'

Strangely, it felt like the ground had shifted beneath her. She'd been grey before, after Sordell's necromancy attack, but that had been temporary. Perhaps this would too, but it didn't feel good to be reminded how much older than her lover she was.

'Hey, don't look so down,' he whispered. 'You're still beautiful.'

'I was never beautiful,' she scoffed. 'My sister, maybe, but not me.'

'I think you are beautiful. Like the light of dawn on the mountain snow.'

'Fancy words.'

'My people are great poets. Young men are taught how to improvise verse, to woo their wives.' He sat up, struck a pose. 'My love has eyes of pure moonlight, that pierce me to the heart. Her skin is lustrous pearl, her breasts the smoothest cream that will feed me all my days.'

She blushed furiously. 'Oh, you idiot. Stop it!'

'Her thighs are the cushions that give me repose, her spittle the most luscious honey. I drink of her and am transported to paradise.' He grinned. 'You like? Shall I go on?'

'No!' She laughed, squirming a little, then, lying back, looked up at him. 'I do love you.'

'And I you. If you are wrong about these Nagas, I will kill them before I let them touch a hair on your head.' He winked. 'Even the grey ones.'

The journey would be only forty miles, according to the map, though it was less of a map and more of a sketch, and every mile was either vertical or horizontal, so it was doubly useless. Travelling in a straight line through these mountains was utterly impossible. Gurvon Gyle stilled his khurne at the top of yet another rise and looked back the way they had come down the narrow, treacherous river valley. He could still see the peak they'd woken beneath that morning.

'At least we're moving,' Arnulf Rhumberg muttered, and Gurvon didn't have the heart to tell him they gone further sideways than forward. It was their eighth day on the road, and they were – *maybe* – halfway to their destination. He was relying on Sordell's triangulation to guide him to the required place. In theory, he could scout ahead in spirit form at night, but he wasn't sure he trusted those around him enough to leave his body in their care.

He'd not just brought Rhumberg's maniple along; he'd also commandeered the Kirkegarde's weird steeds for the senior officers once he'd realised just how strong and clever they were. The rankers on ordinary horses were slowing them down, and he was tempted to press on, just him with Rhumberg and a few of his men – but no, that felt rash. Perhaps Elena had bandit friends out here?

By the time I find the site, Elena will either be gnawed bones, or long gone . . . He had almost given up wishing he could find her alive so that he could administer the deathblow. Dead was dead, and he had better things to be doing – better, and more urgent too. *I hope you're being chewed on by jackals, Elena. It's exactly what you deserve.*

The sun was kissing the western peaks and the air was cold and dry. They were still below the summer snowline and the landscape was stark as the face of Luna above, each valley a narrow morass of fallen boulders through which icy streams danced, hurrying onwards as if afraid to linger. At night wolves and jackals bayed, but they never saw them. Once they spied goats, high above, and he found himself wondering what on Urte they found to eat up there.

'We stop here, boss?' Rhumberg rumbled, spurring his horse up the slope.

'It'll do,' he replied.

While Rhumberg oversaw the setting of the camp, he climbed to the ridgeline. Nothing but more mountains greeted his eyes, though according to his map the sea was only ten miles further on from where the spectre had caught Elena. He found a high clear place and sat, opening his mind for gnostic contact. It came almost immediately.

<Boss?>

<Rutt. Greetings from the ends of Urte.>

Rutt chuckled. He'd been unusually cheery since they'd been reunited, but then, he was a born number two and barely functional when left in charge. <*I'm sensing you're west-northwest of me, Gurvon, and only twelve miles in. And you're off-target again.*>

<*That's because it's a bloody maze out here, and this damned map would be better used as an arse-wad.*>

<*My sympathies. You need to move further north more than west.*>

Gurvon looked along the valley ahead: it ran sideways to the way he wanted to go. He sighed. <*I can try. What news?*>

<*Nothing big. Brochena is still in ferment, apparently, but Hans and Endus are keeping a lid on it. Staria says the Harkun tried to take the Rift Forts, but her lot spanked them.*> He sniggered. <*They would.*>

Gurvon nibbled his lower lip. He wasn't sure what to make of the Harkun. The nomads were confined to the lower plateau beneath the Rift forts; he was worried they might throw their lot in with the Javonesi. <*Fine.*> He squinted into the setting sun, a glowing pearl dipping towards the snow-kissed peaks. <*Is Lybis under control?*>

<*Barely. The emir tried to drive us out, but we held on. He's gone to a mountain fortress. Apparently it takes three days to reach it, and even then it's only approachable by one road. It'll be a nightmare to attack.*>

Gurvon tsked irritably. <*Don't bother; he's going to be irrelevant soon. What about my special guest?*>

<*Safely hidden away.*> Rutt hesitated, clearly unhappy about the 'guest'. That was understandable. <*Gurvon, what can I tell Endus about this?*>

<*Nothing. You and I will return to Brochena as soon as I've confirmed Elena's death. That'll ensure my tenure as Imperial Legate continues. Then we can sort out the Dorobon. Timori's imprisonment will keep the locals quiet. Then at last we'll be safe to enjoy the life we've earned.*>

Rutt sent a warm glow down the link. <*Perfect, boss.*> He would be thinking of his interrupted research, the illegal search for knowledge he'd been hankering to continue. <*I look forward to it.*>

<*So do I, Rutt, so do I. Goodnight.*>

He broke the contact, then sat down with his back to a rock to watch the sun go down, a pristine and beautiful reward for another day of toil. Right now everything felt possible. Elena and others had complicated the game, but he could almost taste victory.

Elena and Kazim walked hand in hand into the cavern. They were clad in their heaviest clothes, for it was cold below ground, though the lamiae were immune to the sudden drop in temperature, able to tolerate the depths even after days spent basking in the sun. It felt slightly odd to be dressed again, after the days they'd spent naked – or nearly so – beside the river.

They wore their swords, and no one objected, though the weapons did attract a look from everyone they passed.

The path through the stone was well-lit, and carved as well as any Earth-mage might have managed. Elena had discovered that these beings were all magi, every single one of them: they had shaped the caverns using Earth-gnosis, their most common affinity, and she'd seen some use Water, Fire and Air-gnosis as well. There were about eighty of them, and more were being born every day. The baby lamiae were alarmingly alert, capable and frightening little beings who wriggled and squirmed at an astonishing pace. They were less human, more animal than the adults, and even they had the beginnings of the gnosis, though human magi had to wait until they were twelve or more years before they gained their powers.

The Pallas Animagi made something truly extraordinary when they created these creatures . . .

'My love,' Kazim whispered, 'are you strong enough for this?'

She squeezed his hand in return. 'I'll manage.' *So long as we don't have to fight our way out.* 'I don't know why, but I think everything is going to be all right.' Just being with him made it feel so. He looked so healthy, so *normal*, with his gnosis restored by the simple magic of pulling from hers, energy she recovered naturally just by rest and sleep. *We're almost one being* . . . She had to admit it frightened her a little, being so dependent on another: what would it be like to be apart from him? *What if one of us died?*

She put aside such thoughts and concentrated on the moment.

The path opened into a wide cavern, where they found the entire adult population of the lamiae clan awaiting them. Most, about two-thirds of the clan, were males. Though there was a heavy sense of suspicion in the way the lamiae looked at them, Elena could also sense a clear willingness to give them a chance; that surprised her. *Humans who found a lamia would not be so prepared to listen: Kore's Blood, we'd burn them as demons without even giving them a chance to speak.*

Kekropius awaited them at the centre, with three other Elders: his wife Kessa, a lissom and inhumanly striking being who viewed them with considerable suspicion; Simou, a strongly built, bald-headed creature with a massive belly, and Herotos, a small, timid male with big, alert eyes and a cunning face. As different as humans.

One of the males came forward bearing a large gold goblet filled to the brim with a red fluid: wine, she realised, a little surprised. Perhaps it had been onboard the windship they'd come to Javon aboard? Apparently that vessel was hidden near the coast, its keel powered and ready in case they needed to fly away . . . she would have loved to see it.

Kekropius lifted the goblet. 'We of the lamiae gather, to give judgement. May the gods above hear us.'

'*May they hear us!*' the lamiae responded as one.

I wonder which gods they mean?

Kekropius passed the goblet to his wife, Kessa. Her voice was cool and clear. 'We give thanks that we eldest have been spared thus far, and pledge our wisdom to the clan in gratitude.' She sipped, savouring the taste on her tongue, then passed the goblet to Simou.

'*We give thanks!*' the whole chamber responded, raising their hands, palms forward.

'We give thanks to they who birthed us, both our parents and the Makers, though they rejected us and hunt us still.' Simou held the vessel aloft.

'*We give thanks!*'

Elena exhaled. The Animagi who made these creatures had apparently given them only a twenty-year lifespan. Though the species had been created only fifty years ago, there had already been several generations. When Kekropius had told her why there were so few visibly old lamiae it had put a lump in her throat, despite their alien nature.

Herotos was last to take the goblet. 'Finally, we give thanks to our guide, and pray for his safe return.'

The lamiae raised their hands, palms forward. '*We pray*,' they chorused, '*for Alaron Mercer.*'

Elena almost fell over. Her mouth fell open and a startled yelp escaped it before she could cover it. The cavern fell silent and every eye fixed on her, affronted. She barely noticed.

'*Did you say Alaron Mercer?*' she exclaimed.

Twenty days after he left Lybis, with food and patience running low, Gurvon Gyle found a headless corpse and a pile of ash that still had a trace of Air-gnosis about it. Engaging his gnostic senses confirmed that it was the burned hull of a windskiff. The charred corpse found further up the slope was so leathery and desiccated it was barely recognisable, but the crushed skull had traces of Necromantic-gnosis: this was definitely the remains of Etain Tullesque's eidolon. There was no doubt that this was the last place Elena was known to have been – and there was no sign at all, of her or her pet Noorie.

Who is he? Gurvon wondered for the thousandth time. All the reports were very sketchy. *I'm sure we can take him, whoever he is. I've got more than two hundred men here. If this burnt-out skiff was Elena's, they'll be on foot, so they can't be far away.*

A detailed search took several hours and they began to lose the daylight, but that brought its own rewards: as darkness fell, and his men settled into their latest uncomfortable camp, he climbed up the mountain, and saw a distant prick of orange light.

Kore's Blood, there's someone alive out here! And evidently not wary of pursuit. He smiled grimly to himself, wondering if it was Elena. *She probably thinks she's lost us.*

The next morning, he gathered his magi: Arnulf Rhumberg; a Brician half-blood named Niklyn Vardel, a Fire-mage with a temper to match; and Hetta Descholt, a Hollenian pure-blood, a noblewoman's legitimate daughter who'd run away to join the legions. She was no beauty – her snub nose and flat features reminded him of a Brevian bulldog – but he liked her strut. Her affinities were Air-gnosis and sylvan gnosis, specialising in herb-lore, which she utilised in her main skill: archery using poisoned arrows.

'Last night I saw a light down the valley,' Gurvon told them, 'but the footing is too treacherous for the horses for us to move in the dark. We need to get closer – but not too close.'

'Get me above their camp and I'll feather them for you,' Hetta Descholt said confidently.

'I want Elena alive.'

'So I'll shoot her in the legs for you, no problem,' she replied evenly. Hollenians were not known for harbouring doubts on anything, which was refreshing after years of Rutt's nerves and Elena's second-guessing.

Rhumberg scratched his beard. 'Elena is not the sort to be taken by surprise. I remember her: eyes always open. She might even know we're here.'

'We slept with no fires last night,' Niklyn Vardel whined. 'She won't know we're here, not unless she can see five miles in the dark.' He looked at Gurvon. 'Leave the cavalry behind and let us four take her.'

'That's a variation on what I'm thinking,' Gurvon replied. 'I want three of us to get close and pin her down so she can't move when the cavalry sweeps down the valley.'

'Two hundred soldiers to catch two people?' Hetta wrinkled her little nose. 'I know you say she's good, but aren't we being just a little over-cautious?'

'We don't know she's alone,' Gurvon replied. 'If it were me, I'd have gathered others. That Noorie is probably renegade Ordo Costruo, and they might have a whole band with them by now – not necessarily magi, but whoever she recruits will certainly be handy in a fight.' He looked at Rhumberg. 'Arnulf, you'll lead the cavalry; find a place close as you can get to where we saw that fire, but not visible to it. I'll take you two' – he looked at Vardel and Hetta – 'and we'll pin them in a three-way cross-fire. As soon as the fighting starts, Arnulf will sound the charge. It should be easy, as Niklyn says, but I don't like to take chances around Elena.'

'Do we kill her, or take her alive?' Hetta asked, her button eyes glinting.

'Alive if possible. Mater-Imperia wants her, for what I hope will be a horrible and lingering death.'

'Can we make a start on her here?' Vardel asked. 'We're owed some payback for having to tramp all the way out into this Helish wilderness.'

Rhumberg growled his agreement.

Gurvon looked away for a second. He'd been thinking about this very point half the night. It had been one thing to force Rutt's scarab into her, but could he truly sit back and watch her get carved up for pleasure? Could he hold the knife?

Then he thought of all the suffering her treachery had put him through. 'Sure,' he replied airily. 'Why not?'

The approach down the valley was not easy. The khurnes managed to negotiate the steep scree slopes, but the horses slipped frequently, and one broke its hind leg, which forced a delay as Hetta had to use her healing-gnosis on the animal. There were more delays as they got closer as they had to check ahead constantly to ensure that Elena wasn't sitting on the next ridge with a spyglass and a well-armed welcome party.

Finally they found a staging zone for Rhumberg's cavalrymen, half a mile from where the light had been spotted. Gurvon and Hetta found an excellent vantage point from where they could actually see the remains of the fire – and, better still, a tent. 'A large fire for just two people,' Descholt commented, her face calm, 'but there are no other tents, just that one next to the river.'

Neither of them could see any movement in the tent.

Gurvon stared at the cliffs above, then he drew Hetta aside. 'If you could get up there, you'd have them at your mercy.'

'I've already picked my spot, sir, and the best approach.'

'Thought you might have,' he replied, approvingly. 'Take Vardel to the near end of the cliffs, then press on yourself so you're got two points of fire. I'll come in from across the river to ensure she's got nowhere to run to.'

He glanced back to make sure the column was well out of sight, then gave her his *I find you interesting* look. 'What does Endus pay for a woman of your talents?' he asked, and when she told him, he put a hand on her shoulder. 'Would you like to double it?'

She looked at his hand pointedly, but didn't object. 'I'm told your people tend to wind up dead, Magister Gyle. Leaving a larger purse for my daughter is all very well, but I'm better able to support her if I'm alive.'

'You have a daughter?'

'Uh huh. I was stupid enough to get knocked up in my first week in the legion. That was three years ago and she's grown up half-wild in the baggage train. But I love her.'

'Endus is the father?'

'Nah, he likes 'em prettier than me – and dark-skinned, mostly. It was just some ranker with a nice smile. He's dead now.' Her voice betrayed little regret.

'You must have plenty of suitors, a pretty, wealthy young woman with mage blood?'

She frowned, clearly a little uncomfortable with the turn of the conversation. 'I'm disinherited – and actually, most people think I'm a bitch. And I poison people who do me wrong, like my daughter's father. I didn't kill him, mind, that was some bandits in Verelon. I just made him sick enough to stay away. Most people take a hint from that.'

'Treble the money?'

She laughed. 'I'll think about it.' She rolled on her side and looked him over appraisingly. 'This Elena Anborn was your women, wasn't she? Then she screwed you over?'

'That's about the size of it.'

'But you didn't sound all that excited about carving her up when we talked this morning.'

'I'm not entirely heartless,' he said, because women preferred men who showed a little sensitivity, and he quite liked this Hollenian. He could use someone with a positive attitude. *Who knows, it might rub off on me.* 'But I'm well over her.'

Hetta took that in with a bob of the head. 'Let's talk again once this business is done.' They shared a moment of understanding, then turned back to the distant view of the river valley and the tent.

After a few minutes he saw a distant shape crawl out of the tent and stand. It was too far away for details, but it was clearly a man, stark naked and dark-skinned. A few seconds later a smaller shape with short, sunbleached hair and slightly paler skin joined him. They kissed, then splashed into the river.

He was surprised to note how his temper rose just to see that brief glimpse of affection.

'No sign of anyone else, Magister,' Hetta commented.

'Call me Gurvon, Hetta.' He scanned the cliffs. One of the men had found a discarded snakeskin during the descent, and the cliffs looked to be riddled with dark spots that might be small cave-mouths. 'Be careful when you traverse the cliffs. It looks like snake country to me.'

Hetta acknowledged with a relaxed wave of the hand. 'Look – there are crops growing, far side.' She pointed beyond the tent. 'Perhaps she's been here some time, on and off?'

'She does know how to live off the land.' He looked at her and warned, 'Be careful of Elena, Hetta. She's one of those rare people with no strong affinities – it means she's got a wider palette of skills than most. She's a half-blood, mostly a Water-mage, but a trance-mage too – and the best swordswoman I've ever met.'

Hetta tutted. 'A lot of admiration in that appraisal, Gurvon.'

'It's respect, that's all,' he replied tersely. 'How would you take her down, given that assessment?'

'I have a plan for anyone I might face,' Hetta replied. 'She and I have similar skills, but my blood is purer, while she's arguably the better with a blade. I'd take her down from a distance – that's my normal plan anyway. I like to bind my arrowheads with Contact-runes – it's draining on me, but when they strike they unleash a counter-spell against shielding and wards. The second and third arrows are shot to kill or maim.'

'And the mudskin?'

Hetta peered at the bathing figures. 'He's a big brute, isn't he? We know nothing of him, but he looks physically strong, so again, I'd stay clear. Let Vardel distract him, then hit from the flank, from a distance.'

'What range?'

'I can hit a stationary target or a someone moving predictably from over a hundred yards, but beyond that even the very best can't count on hitting every time.'

Impressive. 'I wish we'd met earlier.'

They shared another silent moment and he wondered what her little mouth would taste like. There was a sense of danger that he liked. *I think she means it about going slow, though.* Well, right now, so did he. He reached out and patted her arm. 'We should get back.'

She smiled appreciatively. 'Sure. When do we go in?'

'They will likely sleep when the sun is at its zenith, so let's move then.'

35

Poisoned Arrows, Poisoned Words

The Creation of the World

Then did Sivraman-ji bring forth the Milk of Creation, in which his children swam: the Naga, snakemen of prodigious strength and skill. The Naga churned the Milk of Creation, and from the raw stuff of Chaos they forged the lands.

THE NIRMANA-SUTRA (OMALI BOOK OF CREATION)

Coastal Javon, on the continent of Antiopia
Rami (Septinon) 929
15th month of the Moontide

Though there was no gnostic scrying, Elena could feel eyes on her as she dried herself. She had weak shielding up, but she was more worried for Kazim than herself. He wasn't capable of the subtlety required, so he had no shields at all and was relying entirely on her warnings.

The lamiae always kept a watch on the various approaches to the river valley, and when one of their scouts had hurried in the previous night and reported a large force of mounted white men on the upper slopes where the remains of the *Greyhawk* lay she'd known at once what they were facing. The description the scout gave of the Yurosian leaders told her exactly who they faced.

The last thing she wanted to deal with now was Gurvon Gyle, not when she was still trying to process the astonishing discoveries of the days before, when the lamiae elders had revealed that Alaron Mercer, her wayward nephew, had somehow managed to help them reach this place – their 'promised land'. The lamiae were refugees, fleeing the Pallas Animagi who'd clearly been breaking all the Gnostic Laws on constructs – and probably doing so with imperial sanction. But even those facts weren't what playing most on her mind, astonishing as they were.

The Scytale of Corineus!

Somehow this fabled artefact had come into Alaron's possession – his, and some gypsy girl who was also the daughter of Justina Meiros, the granddaughter of Antonin Mieros himself! She couldn't imagine how this might have happened, and Kekropius knew little – but he'd held it in his hands: the most valued artefact on all of Urte. It made no sense, that the emperor's most prized possession was abroad in the hands of her nephew and a Rimoni girl, but however unbelievable, that did indeed appear to be the case.

Kekropius told them Alaron and the girl had left almost nine months ago, seeking Justina Meiros, and had never returned, which is why the lamiae – who seemed to regard her nephew as some kind of patron saint! – prayed for his return daily.

Elena loved her nephew, of course, but whilst she'd never have said as much to Tesla or Vann, she'd never been overly impressed by the boy. He'd been vague and naïve, and appeared to have no self-belief at all. *It's hard to believe he could ever amount to anything, let alone become the saviour of a whole new race of beings!*

The next obvious question was: *Should we be going after him?* She'd been turning that question over in her mind, but hadn't reached an answer; both heart and head said he was well beyond her reach.

Anyway, right now we have more urgent issues.

She'd already warned Kekropius of the possibility of pursuit, but the lamiae were not prepared to move, not with crops in the ground and several of the females due to give birth. And they weren't afraid.

She looked at Kazim, who was very self-consciously trying not look like he might be aware of danger. 'Did you see the glint on the spyglasses upstream?'

He shook his head. 'Can we get inside? I feel' – he grinned nervously – 'quite naked out here.'

She jiggled her breasts at him. 'So you don't want to give them a show, then?'

'No!' he said, uncharacteristically prudish. 'You are my woman, not a performer.'

She snickered at him, shifted her hips from side to side. 'Last chance, lover.'

'Just get in the tent,' he growled, lifting the flap and gesturing at her.

Once inside, all trace of levity vanished. The lamiae had excavated a tunnel, leaving them just enough room to dress, which they did, as rapidly as possible. Her sword was hidden by the riverbank so that she would look unarmed to any observer. Kazim squeezed past her and buckled on his scimitar. 'I hate to leave you out there,' he told her as he lowered himself into the tunnel.

'I'll be fine. They'll try and take me alive, but they won't be so fussy with you.'

'I will not be fussy with them either.'

'Take care, my love. These lamiae aren't trained, but there are more than sixty of them ready to fight. That's more firepower than most armies have. Now go: they're already in position.'

He touched his fingers to his forehead then his lips. 'Sal'Ahm, Alhana. May He protect you in the time of trial.'

'His Light on you also, Kazim Makani. See you in the fight.'

He vanished and was replaced by Kessa, who'd been waiting underground. She was the most skilled of the lamiae when it came to mental communication, so she would coordinate between Kekropius' warriors in the caves above and Elena and Kazim below. Elena took a moment to be impressed that the lamiae were far less affected than magi by such things as being underground when it came to gnostic communications and scrying. Perhaps that was because they spent much of their time as cave-dwellers. *Something to explore another day, perhaps.*

'Are they coming? the lamia woman asked. 'We are all ready. I have been speaking to Kekropius in my head. He struggles to keep the young hidden so long.'

'Patience is for older heads,' Elena remarked. Kessa was barely nineteen herself; that was old by lamia standards, though she had not yet began to decline physically. She was entrancingly beautiful, especially in this dim light, with her severe, flawless face, her long, hair-like comb and her high, perfect breasts. But that would have been to ignore the bluish-green hue of her skin, and the pair of snake trunks that served her for legs. Although more or less half-human, she was altogether alien, and she clearly regarded herself as an entirely different species. She'd told Elena only yesterday, 'The Makers made us to be superior to your kind.'

'You are frightened for your mate,' the lamia observed now.

'Terrified,' Elena admitted, wondering, *What happens to the other if one of us dies?*

'How old is he?' Kessa asked curiously.

'Twenty-three.'

'And you?'

'Forty-one.'

'Is it normal for an older human female to mate with a younger male?'

'No, not at all,' she admitted, 'although I am a mage and we generally live longer than humans, and don't show the years so much – but even so, society would be scandalised.'

'It would be a good arrangement though, yes? He has much energy.'

'Ha! He wears me out!'

Kessa grinned wickedly. 'You and he are much in love. We can all see this with the inner sight. Your magical bonds are very strong. Is this normal also?'

'No. I don't really understand it,' Elena admitted. 'He is of a different kind of mage, one who can steal gnosis from others. I think that our falling in love has created a unique bond that two normal magi, or even two of his kind, could not forge.'

Kessa blinked in that reptilian way she had. 'Such creatures as he are spoken of in our tales of the Makers. Our ancestors saw them there.'

'What? The Animagi had Dokken in their breeding camps? Holy

Kore! That's . . . appalling.' *Kore Scripture commands that Dokken must be eradicated, not . . .* 'What were they doing there?'

'Our tales do not remember, only that they walked free among the Makers.'

'Incredible. That goes against everything we're taught.' *But I shouldn't be surprised, not with all the hypocrisy I've seen coming out of Pallas.*

She had more questions, but Kessa stiffened and her eyes became unfocused. Then she looked at Elena. 'Kekropius says that two of the humans have passed the cave-mouths above and another has been seen near the river. It is time to show yourself.'

Elena took a deep breath, then nodded. With an alarmingly swift movement of her snake limps, Kessa swayed close to her and pressed cold lips to her cheeks. 'Good fortune, Aunt of my milkson. Be safe.'

'Milkson?'

Kessa smiled shyly. 'Alaron is my milkson,' she said, her expression complex. 'You and I are sisters, Elena.'

Elena didn't know the term, but she recognised the pride in Kessa's face. *Did she adopt Alaron or something?* She awkwardly hugged her back. Embracing a naked half-human half-snake female was decidedly strange; it left her feeling like she'd stepped into a dream. But she was moved too. 'I am proud to be kin to you and yours,' she replied formally.

She clambered out of the tent and went to the riverbank, feeling very exposed. She sat and worked on looking like she was relaxing and enjoying the view across the river, while with her right hand she located her hidden sword. There was a little nagging blur on the far bank: someone cloaked in illusion. They'd know if she focused too closely on it, so she kept her surveillance light. It was enough to know they were there. The hardest part was leaving her shields light, when anything could be about to loosed at her at any moment.

She fingered the hilt of her blade and tried to imagine all the ways they might take her down.

If I've misread this situation, I'm about to die . . .

Two heartbeats later, the first shaft was loosed.

Her wider shields, the ones that picked up incoming projectiles, screamed a warning and her reflexes took over. She pumped her inner shields as an arrow punched into them low down. The tip exploded in a jagged burst, like lightning-bolts shooting through her shields and cracking them like a pane of glass. Though she had expected the attack, she found herself crying out in alarm – and then real fear as she felt her shields come apart.

She spun and jerked sideways as an arrow and a ball of fire arced down from two points on the mountain above. The fireball struck the tent and exploded with a force that knocked her sideways. The arrow parted the air where she'd been the moment before the force of the fireball struck and slammed into the earth.

Kore's Balls, what's happened to my shields? She leaped off to the water's edge so that the bank would block sight of her from the mountainside, and as she did, a trumpet blared from upstream and riders burst into sight, careering across the flats towards her, barely two hundred yards away. If she'd not already known they were there, it would have been the perfect ambush.

She was still unnerved by the sheer number of riders, but she had to concentrate on trying to remove this damned gnostic effect the arrow had triggered.

For a few seconds she couldn't identify it, then realised it was some kind of static counter-spell. *Clever!* She tried to negate it, but it ate into that spell also, weakened it and then withstood it. She cursed in frustration: not only was this spell new to her, but worse, it'd been cast by a stronger mage.

Time and distance must weaken it . . . She looked around warily, but the archer, who must have had a better vantage than she thought, fired again and this time the shaft tore through her frayed shields and slashed open her left arm as it passed. The pain dissipated what was left of her shields and left her wide open . . .

. . . just as someone erupted from the water, a long, thin blade extended, and punched it through her left thigh.

She yowled, slashing sideways as she fell.

Gurvon!

His face was frozen in an impassive grin that held no humour at all and his eyes were blazing in concentrated fury as he blocked her automatic riposte and stabbed again. She jerked aside, but her leg gave way in a blaze of pain as blood flooded her thigh. The pain was raw and deep.

He thrust again but this time the drag of the river unbalanced him and his blow slid wide. She desperately battered his blade away as the riders pounded closer and closer – but not yet so close that the lamiae would rise.

I have to survive a few more seconds.

She feinted a jab, then slashed at his face. At least the damned arrows had stopped, but she was frightened to back up and expose herself again. The counter-spell was still distorting her ability to reach the gnosis, leaving her with just her blade and her fast-failing footwork. Gurvon emerged from the water and found better footing, and once he'd clambered up he started battering at her guard. With his hair plastered to his skull he looked like some wide-eyed fanatic. A two-handed blow at her side forced her to block and as their hilts locked he rose and slammed his forehead at her face. She jerked away, at the cost of falling half-upright against the bank and he pushed his weight onto her, rammed his knee into her groin, jolting her pubic bone, then ground the same knee into her wounded thigh. It was both excruciating and numbing all at once. Then her leg gave way and she began to slide below him. With what remained of her strength she heaved upwards, then rolled sideways and out from beneath him, but too quickly he regained his own balance.

She struggled upright again in the moment of respite, her thigh throbbing painfully and unable to bear more than a fraction of her weight. They both extended their blades, rasping them together, testing each other's strength. All the while the horses thundered closer, and the smoke of the burned tent filled the air.

'Give up, Elena,' Gurvon told her, his voice coming in gasps.

'Puffed already?' she snarled, then gritted her teeth. The counter-spell planted by that damned first arrow was weakening slowly, allowing her to force a thin stream of healing-gnosis into her thigh, barely enough to matter. 'You should train harder.'

'I don't want to kill you, but I will if I have to.'

'You're such a tease.' She grimaced through the pain in her thigh, which was hurting far more than a clean cut should. Her eyes went to his blade, which she now saw to be coated in a viscous black tar. 'When did you start using rukking poisons?'

'Since I met the new you. She's younger and prettier and she knows all sorts of tricks.'

'True love, huh?' Her voice began to slur. *Rukka, I'm going to faint. It's all I seem to do these days.*

'Who knows? Speaking of which, where's the mudskin you've been dirtying yourself with?'

Just keep talking, you prick. 'He was in the tent,' she replied, trying and failing to slow the spread of the venom. Her left leg was a dead weight. She shifted, trying to work out if she could hop backwards, but Gurvon lunged forward again, seeking to disarm her as the horsemen came streaming into the open space beneath the cliffs, whooping and hollering triumphantly, their lances high, their pennants waving in the breeze. The ground shuddered and the river water was trembling. From high on the bank, someone sent a fireball bursting into the air.

But she couldn't afford to take her eyes off the flashing blade that was coming at her from all sides at once. Her own was increasingly sluggish, and then—

One moment she was trying to block a high cut, the next she was staring down at a thin line of steel embedded in her side. She gripped Gurvon's venom-encrusted blade in her left hand and tried to pull it out, but he twisted it viciously, almost severing her fingers. Her side felt like it was being ripped apart. Pain enveloped her awareness. She didn't so much black out as white out in a sheet of searing agony.

Got you! Finally! Gurvon pulled his blade out of Elena's side as she collapsed, groaning, and kicked her sword into the river. As her eyes rolled back and she went limp he swiftly yanked out her dagger and sent it after her blade. She was alive, which was preferable, but more importantly, she was well and truly out of this fight. *Perfect.* He gripped her legs and dragged her up the bank. Arnulf Rhumberg was standing there, peering down from the back of his khurne with a satisfied smile.

'Where's the Noorie?' he asked nonchalantly.

'In the tent,' Gurvon replied. 'Charred meat.'

Rhumberg grunted. 'She dead?'

'No. The venom isn't fatal. She'll wake soon ... and wish she hadn't.' As he gazed down at Elena, Gurvon realised that unlike the last time he'd had her in his power, this time he really did feel nothing. She was just an impediment now. He'd moved on: he was on the verge of new things, great things, with a kingdom to seize and a new woman who could be everything Elena had been and more.

Rhumberg's horsemen were milling about, some looking for things to break or kill, others just pumping the air with their fists and yelling. On the steep slope above, Niklyn Vardel was shooting celebratory fireballs into the sky. Further along, he could see Hetta Descholt breaking cover, bow in hand. She gave him a firm wave. He could see the flash of white teeth in her smile and warmed to the idea of her even more. He wondered how far he might get over a celebratory cup tonight.

Is this the most perfect moment in my life?

Then came a horrendous ululation, a moaning, shredding sound from the mountainside above. It was as if Hel itself had opened up as a host of massive *things* burst into the daylight from the caves and from the ground at the feet of the riders and from the river behind him, erupting in dust and spray, all flailing talons and blades.

His perfect moment crumbled.

He saw Vardel take a spear in the back that erupted through his chest, saw malformed figures come up beneath the horses and gut them, then butcher the riders as the steeds went down. One came up with a sweep of the blade and beheaded a khurne and he realised the muscular torso was set atop a serpent's body. His brain froze momentarily at the impossibility of it all. *A lamia? Impossible – they're just fairy tales!*

Then a man burst from the burning tent, smeared in dirt and ash but very obviously wholly intact, and came straight at him. *Elena's rukking mudskin!* The youth blurred forward at an impossible speed, slashed a lancer in half from behind, shearing effortlessly through his armour, then threw out a hand at him – Gurvon's shields were up, of course, but a wave of force battered him over as if they weren't there, an *unfair* blast of telekinesis that was far above anything he'd ever endured. He flew head over heels like a thrown toy and struck the ground, skidding to the very edge of the river and lay there for a moment dazed and shaken, his shields sparking crimson. Dimly he recognised his attacker – a Hadishah youth from the group whose attack had freed Elena from Rutt Sordell's scarab a year ago in Brochena – but he looked far more experienced and calm now, and he was bearing down on him with menacing single-mindedness, hacking his way through anyone who got in his way.

There was a roar and a great concussion of gnostic force struck him and echoed across the valley. He tore his eyes away from the mudskin warrior and looked up to the cliffs: boulders the size of catapult stones were raining down onto his remaining riders, who shouted helplessly as they went down, crushed like grapes underfoot. He turned his head to where Hetta had been, but where she had stood and waved at him, there were only serpent-people, tearing bloody strips from something ruined.

No . . . no no no . . . He found his feet somehow, and wobbling, went for Elena, still lying alone on the riverbank. *I need a hostage.* The Keshi youth saw him as he staggered towards her, but Arnulf Rhumberg interposed, quite by chance, as his khurne started bucking away from a serpent-man, then lunged in to skewer the creature on its horn, right through the chest. Blood erupted over the steed's head, painting it scarlet, then it wrenched it free and spun to face the Keshi youth. Gurvon ran, his eyes fixed on Elena's prone form.

How is this happening?

But there were small flashes of hope: as he scanned the ground he saw one of his riders driving his lance into the back of one of the creatures – *they must be constructs* – and further away, a knot of men fighting for their lives had formed up properly and presented a phalanx of steel. Then another wave of boulders crashed down and the phalanx caved in, stamped into the earth like beetles, juices bursting from the broken carapaces.

Another line of creatures emerged from the river now, smaller and mostly female but little less fearsome. They swept past Elena's prone form and into the fray, shrieking like Hel-beasts. One paused, a more mature female, and dropped over Elena, and Gurvon slowed in his headlong rush.

Then a giant male serpent-man detached from the mêlée and came at him, a massive brute brandishing a sword as long as a Schlessen zweihandle. There was no parrying his blow; Gurvon ducked under it and came up punching through its weak gnostic shields; his two-handed thrust carved into the thing's belly and he wrenched his sword upwards. Blood and entrails erupted as the thing screamed and thrashed and its tail swept around. He pulled out the blade, leaped the tail and drove his sword into the thing's back and it went down face-first and jerked into stillness.

Gurvon staggered clear, grunting in satisfaction, and found that the thin line of females had gone past him, leaving Elena just a few yards away, alone, except for the one female who was tending his former lover.

The serpent-woman came erect with shimmering grace. She was almost hypnotically beautiful as she swayed and spread her arms and hissed at him through a mouth filled with thin hooked teeth. The largest were as long as fingers. Her twinned snake legs weaved as she put herself between him and Elena.

He raised his hand and sent a mage-bolt at her – and was stunned when she deftly warded it. But she had no weapon and he kept closing in, still firing. He took a moment to glance sideways, only to see Rhumberg's khurne rearing, then the Keshi youth making a gesture that flipped both beast and rider over backwards. Rhumberg went down with the full weight of the beast on him and his shields flashed to scarlet. He came up again, though, and Gurvon heard his and the Keshi youth's blades hammering together like bells.

He turned back to the serpent-woman protecting Elena and went in fast, leaping over the sweeping snake-leg she unleashed at him, and thrust at the spot between her magnificent blue-green breasts, gnosis-fire springing along his blade, ready to shear through shielding and flesh.

Her narrow eyes went round as he crashed into her, his hands on his hilt as he thrust, but she caught his wrists and twisted as they collided and they both went over. She landed on her back with him on top, and his blade punched through her and into the dirt beneath her body, pinning her to the earth. She still fought on, wrestling for the hilt of his blade to push it out, her fanged mouth snapping at him and her snake-limbs wrapping about his waist as if they were copulating like the Lantric demigod Perios and his lamia lover Calystra. She was strong, but he could feel her weakening by the second. He finished it by hammering his forehead into her face, her nose crunched, her head lolled sideways and her whole body sagged. He scrambled clear, oddly disturbed by the intimacy of the struggle, and staggered on.

Elena lay on her back where he'd left her. He drew his dagger.

An eruption of the gnosis tore his eyes back to Rhumberg's fight just in time to see the Noorie's blade scythe through Rhumberg's waist. For an instant the pair of giants stood facing each other, then with a sound like a sigh, Rhumberg fell in half.

Gurvon gaped and backed away. For a second his eyes locked on the Keshi's, and he read death there. His gnostic sight saw other things too, a complex interlocking of tendrils in the man's aura, skeins of power reaching out, pulling energy from about him, and a thick cord running to the woman on the ground beside him.

He's a fucking Dokken! And he's got his fangs into Elena!

He felt his legs waver in shock and almost superstitious fear, but that didn't stop him from darting to Elena and bending over her. His maniple was being ripped apart and she was now his only way out. He pulled her until she was sitting upright, threw his arm around her neck to use her as a shield and put his dagger to her neck.

<You try it and she's dead,> he said as the Keshi came towards him.

The Keshi looked at him blankly, though he clearly heard his words. *He and Elena must communicate in Keshi,* he realised, and for some reason this stunned him, as if she were an alien being he'd never really known at all. But more importantly, he felt Elena stir as the gnostic link with the Keshi pulsed. He jabbed his knife into her neck, just enough to cut her skin, and shouted out loud in Keshi, 'Stop or she dies!'

The boy froze, and for the first time since this nightmare was unleashed, he felt a thread of a chance of getting out alive, though all around the slaughter of his men went on and he was powerless to intervene.

For Kazim the last few minutes had been a blur of violence. It had been a massive feat of restraint to not leap into the fight the moment Elena was assailed, especially as it quickly became clear that she was in terrible trouble, but they had to wait until the cavalry were beneath the cliffs. To finally attack was a supreme relief, but his terror for Elena sent his sight red. He'd charred men, broken them with telekinetic-gnosis, carved them in half with his blade, neither armour nor shielding anything to him, barely aware of his actions even as he moved through the forms his Hadishah master and then Elena had drilled into him. Enemies barely registered; there was only her, lying beside the river, barely alive, with the man she hated standing over her.

Gurvon Gyle: her former lover. We crossed blades in Brochena. That was the day his and Elena's lives had collided. He remembered the man had been extremely skilled, very economical and precise with his sword – too fast and too clever for him then.

But that was *then*.

Gurvon pulled Elena upright and put her in front of him. He said something with the gnosis in his own tongue; it was gibberish, but the meaning was clear.

The energies flowing between him and her told him she still lived, but the blade at her neck chilled his blood. *He wants to live . . . so he won't harm her if it means he can live . . .*

He stepped forward warily, his blade high, but he stayed out of reach.

'Stop or she dies!' Gurvon shouted in serviceable Keshi. Kazim complied, concentrating on the energy flowing between he and Elena, both ways. He could feel the venom in her, could feel also some kind of spell disrupting her gnosis. It was a complex thing, but its heart was in a little core of light, buried in her latent shield . . . he snuffed it out, and felt her stir.

I need to delay this man, buy us time.

'What do you want?' he asked. All round him those lamiae no longer fighting began to slither closer, swaying menacingly. One was lying motionless in the grass. His heart froze: *Kessa!* Kekropius was weaving closer and Kazim saw his eyes going wide as he took in his stricken mate. The elder reared up, then fell upon Kessa's body, cradling her limp form. Terror and fury filled his face, then he looked up at Gurvon and his mouth flew open, teeth jutting.

Gurvon took a step away, pulling the limp-limbed Elena with him. 'Keep back!' he shouted in Keshi.

Kekropius didn't speak Keshi, but Gurvon didn't know that. He just looked blankly as Kekropius' arm came up and then the lamia roared in Rondian, 'Take him alive!'

Gurvon's jaw dropped as the snake-men swarmed in. If he'd stabbed Elena no one could have stopped him – but then he would have died. Instead he flung away his blade a second before they buried him beneath their writhing bodies.

The sound came in waves, but it was a good sound and she clung to it: Kazim's voice. 'Alhana! *Ella!*' His hands were on her shoulders, shaking her gently. She couldn't see a thing – she had to think carefully before she realised that it was because her eyes were closed. There was something like an ice-shard through her thigh and another in her side, her left hand stung like Hel's fire and a stampede of wild horses had pounded over her body.

Other than that, she was fine.

The last thing she remembered was Gurvon's blade twisting in her side, but her healing-gnosis was holding, re-knitting flesh despite her being out of it, and the venom was finally beginning to recede, combated in ways she couldn't understand but that were clearly to do with her link to Kazim. Somehow he'd fed her enough energy to allow her own healing power to fight the venom, and that disrupting spell too. So she bathed in the sound of his voice, and opened her eyes.

Kazim's face was inches from hers, looking down at her anxiously as he cradled her. A complex wave of emotions crackled between them: love and fear and the sheer need to be in physical contact. Strength flowed into her, from *him*: the Dokken, feeding the mage . . .

The sheer uncharted miracle of their love was encapsulated in that phenomenon. *Kore's Heart, I adore him.* She let that show unreservedly on her face.

Then she looked around, and for the first time she realised the extent of the slaughter. Gurvon had brought two or three hundred mounted men here and they were all dead, and their beasts too. The lamiae had hurled half the mountainside down on the riders, crushing and maiming en masse, before wading in and striking at superhuman speed. Her respect for – and fear of – the Pallas Animagi grew.

The lamiae were all round them, shouting in victory, embracing each other. She looked about for familiar faces. Kekropius was near, cradling a bloodied Kessa just as Kazim was holding her. The symmetry caught her eye. Then Kessa stirred and looked at her mate with love, and then at Elena.

Then she saw the bloody hole in the lamia woman's chest.

No! Sweet Kore, no!

She pushed out of Kazim's arms and crawled to Kessa's side. There was a hole in the lamia woman's chest and she couldn't move. Though Elena tried to seal the wound with healing-gnosis, Kessa died before the spell could take effect full effect.

Kekropius threw back his head and howled.

Elena dropped her head to the ground, blinked away tears of fury, then noticed the one other living human on the battlefield: Gurvon Gyle.

He was pinned down by a pair of burly lamia males, and bleeding badly from dozens of scratches and bites. He looked groggy and his right arm was swelling below the elbow – the flesh visible through his shredded shirt was greenish-purple. Poison. But his face was composed; he was doubtless busy concocting his lies.

Kessa had been supposed to stay out of the fight. She'd sworn she would. Elena looked at the distraught Kekropius and felt the same sort of wail build inside her. Slowly, she stood, and felt Kazim join her and feed her strength, and the whole gathering went silent, even Kekropius. The only sounds were the moans of the few wounded and the growing hum of flies. The sun beat down oppressively. She inhaled the warm breeze and finally found the strength to face her former lover.

'We await your assent to kill him,' Kekropius told her, his voice bereft of emotion.

She inhaled heavily and planted her hands on her hips. She saw the way he was watching her, like a stranger, calculation and cunning all over his face despite his plight and his obvious pain. The thought of actually talking to him nauseated her, and as for really *questioning* him, she didn't have the stomach for such things any more.

I should want to know what you're planning. I should want to know about troop movements and numbers, about strategies and personnel. About why you had Cera and poor Tarita stoned. I should torture you just for the rukking joy of it! But I don't think I can stand to be even a minute in your company.

She turned her back. 'I don't want to hear his lies,' she said. 'Just kill him.'

A ripple of satisfaction went through the lamiae, a hiss like summer winds through grass. She glanced at Kazim, who looked faintly shocked, but he nodded with understanding.

Gurvon's voice broke then: he was – *finally* – truly afraid. 'No! Elena—! You can't!'

Kekropius cocked his head and raised his hand to signal, but he held it up, his eyes searching her face. When they'd laid their plans they'd spoken of capturing him, and he recalled what she'd said then: that it was vital to take him alive. Even in his grief, with his own overwhelming desire for revenge, he had the wisdom to recognise a decision made out of emotion and question it.

'Elena!' Gurvon's voice rose a note. 'Elena, I have her, Elena—! She's alive!'

She turned, her thoughts sluggish. 'Who is alive?'

'Cera Nesti.'

Elena looked dazedly from Kekropius to Gurvon. 'Cera is alive?' *She can't be.* 'A thousand people saw her die.'

Gurvon looked up at her, his face white but his eyes steady. 'I saved her from the stoning and got her out of Brochena.'

Great Kore! She gripped Kazim's arm to hold herself up and shook her head, then realised that she was showing Gurvon just how much he'd shaken her. *I don't even know if it's true.* She swallowed, then made a conscious effort to purge herself of emotion. She had to be cool now, cold and composed, or he would hoodwink them all. 'Why should I care about her?' she asked in a flat voice. 'The little bitch sold me down the river.'

All the while her brain was throbbing. *Rukka mia! He has Cera! Cera's alive!* She didn't even know how she felt about that. She'd once planned to kill her former ward, but now . . . ?

'Elena?' Kekropius asked, his hand still raised to signal Gurvon's death.

Utter mental and physical exhaustion washed over her. 'Wait,' she whispered. 'Gods, I'm sorry, Kekropius. I know what you must be going through . . . but this . . .' *Why is nothing ever simple?* She glared down at Gurvon. 'Come on, tell me, why the Hel should I care about that double-crossing bint? Even if you did somehow pull that off, why should I want her back?'

'Because the people will rise for her,' he replied, his voice stony.

'They will rise in time anyway.'

'But now, if she comes back from the dead? She will be a legend. You could do anything you wanted with a tale like that. The whole of Javon would eat from her hand: a new messiah for you to play with.'

'I notice you're not doing it.'

'I had Olfuss killed, remember? They'd hang me before I got two words out.'

He's holding something back. She was suddenly conscious of the eyes and ears of the lamiae all around. She threw her hands up and cried, 'Enough!' She turned away, trying not to show how confused and at a loss she was. *Rukka!*

'Is he telling the truth?' Kazim whispered.

'No idea.' She bunched her fists, stared at the ground in utter frustration, then decided. 'Kekropius, I'm sorry, but this is too important not to explore at least. I know you wish vengeance for all you've lost today, and you deserve it: but let us at least take that vengeance with a cool head. Let's lock him up somewhere once we've Chained his gnosis.'

Kekropius' fury had gone from hot to cold. 'Very well. Let us deal with the wounded, and the bodies. We must cook what we can to preserve it, and bury the rest.' His eyes burned into Gurvon, then he whirled and slithered away.

The lamiae would butcher both men and horses, Elena realised. She shrugged internally. Was it even cannibalism anyway? Did they eat snakes as well? The ethics of the matter were of no interest to her; she'd stick to fish. 'Thank you, Kekropius.' Then she whispered again, 'I'm so sorry.'

The lamiae clan began to draw away, many visibly unhappy at this perceived leniency. The two who were holding Gurvon lifted him to his feet, keeping his arms pinned, and Kazim stepped past her and went to him. She held her breath as they confronted each other, her former lover and the man she wanted to be with for ever. Both said something, low words meant only for each other.

Then Kazim smashed his fist into Gurvon's belly so hard that he bent in half and crumpled, gasping. The two lamiae holding him aloft grinned fiercely.

'Kazim!' The admonishment was involuntary, and not exactly passionate.

'Someone had to do it,' he replied without a hint of remorse. 'Elena, show me how to do one of your Chain-runes, please. And how to make it *hurt*.'

Elena, Kazim and Kekropius gathered outside the cavern where Gurvon was confined. Elena had wrapped wards around it and Kazim set the Chain-rune under her guidance. The agony Gurvon had endured as they bound him had given her a disturbing amount of satisfaction, although seeing the hatred and humiliation on his face, she had wondered if perhaps they would be better killing him after all.

Not once did he ask after the woman he'd claimed to be his new paramour – but perhaps he'd seen her taken down from behind by half a dozen of the lamiae. She'd put up a fight, Kekropius had reported, but she'd gone under. Elena would have liked to have questioned her about her Contact-rune, but she thought she could probably work it out with a bit of time and practise. It was a useful little spell.

Most of the day was spent healing the injured and tending to the fallen. The most heartbreaking of those losses was Kessa, and Elena was feeling horribly guilty – Kessa had given her life to protect her. Her own condition was improving rapidly, thanks to her healing-gnosis. The venom on Gurvon's sword might have been meant to incapacitate, not kill, but had it not been for her link to Kazim she might never have survived both poison and blood loss.

'So, why should we not kill this man?' Kekropius asked, his voice still raw. 'Who is this Cera Nesti?'

'Cera Nesti was – *is* – the Queen-Regent of Javon; your valley is part of that kingdom.' She gave him a quick recent history of Javon, from King Olfuss' death through Cera's reign as her brother's regent, and young Timori's continued claim to the throne. 'I had thought her dead.'

'But you say she betrayed you – why?' Kekropius looked mystified.

When she thought about it, she supposed that twenty years was a very short time, and the lamiae were a tiny, loyal clan; they were unlikely to have encountered the many faces of treachery.

'I don't really know. I have my suspicions, but really I need to see her, to speak to her, if I am to understand it.'

'Make him bring her to you,' Kazim suggested. 'And her brother the king as well.'

Why not? If you're going to negotiate, you should ask for the world and let the other side feel grateful to get out with anything at all. 'It's worth asking, amori.' She looked at Kekropius. 'Elder, I believe gaining Cera might just about be worth doing, but I am aware that it will rob you of your vengeance and so that decision should not be mine to make. We are in your debt. It must be your decision.'

The Elder looked appreciative of her gesture. 'Speak to him – find out what he will propose, if the exchange is what you think it would be. Then advise me – I will await you here.'

They had sealed Gurvon in the deepest cavern and stationed a lamia guard at the wicker gate; he was waiting in impassive patience. *Such a curious mix, theses snake-people,* she thought, *fierce when roused, stolid when cool.* This one bobbed his head respectfully, then stood aside as Elena removed the wards and walked in.

Gurvon looked up, his face tired and swollen. The cavern was cold and his blanket had been selected for its inadequacy. Having a slop-bucket in the corner wasn't helping his comfort levels much either, she guessed.

'Well?' he said, lifting his head haughtily. 'My life for a queen's? Should be an easy choice.'

'A queen-regent,' she corrected briskly. 'Get up. I'm not talking to you in here. Follow.'

They took him to one of the warmer caverns, where they gave him water and some horsemeat stew. 'You should enjoy it,' Elena said chattily, 'it's your own legion's horses. Rykjard's men, weren't they?'

Gurvon grimaced, but he didn't stop eating. 'I don't suppose you have wine?' he asked, and grunted morosely when she shook her head. 'You've not just gone native, you've gone feral.'

She ignored that and waited until he was done, then pointedly took the spoon from him. She spoke in Keshi so that Kazim could follow the conversation. 'Right,' she said briskly, 'here are my demands. In exchange for your life I want Cera and Timori, and all of my gold, every last fennik you owe me. They are to be delivered to a place of my choosing, somewhere near Lybis.' She smiled coldly. 'That, or I send Rutt your head.'

'I don't have Timori in Lybis, and I certainly don't have your gold.'

She turned to Kazim. 'My love, next time he refuses me, hit him.' Then she turned back and said, 'Gurvon, this isn't a negotiation. This is me giving you one chance to save your life. You will accede to all my demands, or I'll assume you're lying and let the lamiae kill you. You get one opportunity to reconsider your reply.'

His nostrils flared, but his shoulders sagged. 'Kore's Blood, Elena! I'm telling the truth, I swear to you. They told me if I fucked this up, Tomas Betillon would be sent in. I imagine he'll be in Brochena by week's end as soon as word of this gets out. Do you want the Butcher of Knebb let loose here?'

'I welcome the chance to put a knife in his back. You'll promise me Cera, Timori and the gold, or I'll tell Kekropius that you're all his.'

'Damn it, Elena! I had to give Timori to Endus Rykjard to hold because all my people kept dying. He's not just my prisoner any more.'

'And the gold?'

'Impossible. It's in Yuros.'

She turned to Kazim. 'Break his nose.'

Kazim lashed out, a blur of movement; there was a *crunch* and

Gurvon's head snapped back, blood spraying everywhere. He fell back on his rocky seat, crying out and looking dazed. *Kore's Blood, if anyone deserved that, it's him.*

'No games,' she told him. 'You're in Javon, so of course you're getting the gold sent here – this is home now, isn't it? And I know how much you've got, remember? You used to tell me to keep me motivated.'

He wiped his bloody face. His voice now sounded thickly nasal. 'Fifty per cent of my fee has been shipped to Brochena by Jusst and Holsen. I can get it to Lybis in a month.'

'You do not have a month. You have one week.'

He closed his eyes dazedly. 'I'd need to contact Rutt Sordell.'

'I can do that. I have your relay-staves now.' She tapped her palm. 'Do we have a deal?'

He looked at her with utter hatred, but his voice was faint. 'Yes, damn you.'

'Good. I'll contact Rutt tonight. Now, tell me how you faked Cera's death.'

She could almost see his mind working, weighing the variables, trying to see if there was anything he could salvage from this débâcle. But he knew her, as she knew him. 'All right. Do you remember Coin?'

'How could I forget . . . ?' Her voice trailed off as she realised what he was saying. *You bastard!*

He pinched the bridge of his nose, though the blood had already stopped flowing. 'I managed to save her – after you almost killed her – but she was becoming a nuisance. She was always too demanding, and she got these fixations . . .' Catching Elena's impatient look, he focused again. 'She became obsessed with Cera and she agreed to get Cera and Timori out of Brochena. They might have got away with it, too, but Coin decided to kill Francis first, payback for the way he treated Cera, I suppose. Or maybe just to screw me over. That's what alerted us, and we caught them just in time.'

'So it was Coin who was stoned?'

'I offered her death, so that Cera could live. Coin had nothing left to live for by then, so she accepted. She changed form, then I Chain-runed her so she couldn't back out of our deal.'

Elena stared at him, utterly sickened. 'One of the emir's inform-ants told me she had her tongue cut out even before she was stoned.'

He looked down. 'I couldn't risk her trying to speak out in the arena.'

'Kore's Blood, you're a piece of work . . .' She didn't bother trying to hide the disgust in her voice; she could feel Kazim's seething con-tempt, too, even though he didn't know these people like she did. 'But why save Cera anyway?'

Gurvon shrugged. 'I never waste an asset, you know that. She still had some value as a bargaining chip; I thought I might be able to trade her for you, or maybe use her to bring the Nesti under my con-trol, or even threaten the Dorobon with her in case they managed to seize control again. She was always going to have value to someone.' He attempted a wry smile. 'Lucky for me, eh?'

'You're worse than I ever realised. How did I waste half my life on you?'

'She was your pupil, Elena. Perhaps it was you I saw in her.'

The worst thing was, that wasn't so hard to believe: Cera had always been a little cold, and a little too fond of secrets. She was clever, but she was also vulnerable, which made her easy to manipu-late. *Just like me when I was young.*

Finally she asked the one question she was desperate to know the answer to. 'How did you convince her to betray me?'

'That was easy.' She could hear the pride in his voice. 'She was frightened, and looking for reassurance. She was still just a child, for all the crowns and council-room triumphs. I told her that you and Lorenzo di Kestria were plotting together, and when you obligingly started screwing him she thought it was proof of everything I'd told her. I promised safety for her and her precious little brother – I reas-sured her and promised her a way through the maze while you were just feeding her fears and leading her deeper in.'

'And the charges against her?'

'Is she safian?' Gurvon leered. 'Surely you'd know that, about your *darling* protégé?'

'I can do worse than just hit you, Rondian,' Kazim growled.

Gurvon raised a hand, wincing. 'I take it back. But yes, she is – not with Tarita though. She's been bedding Portia Tolidi.'

Elena blinked.

'I know: the most beautiful, most desired woman in the kingdom, the soon-to-be mother of the Prince Royal. A wonderful scandal, isn't it?'

'You're all class, Gurvon. What about Tarita?'

'Gone – still alive, for all I know.'

Elena's hand went to her mouth. 'She is?'

'I think she was probably already in the tunnel when I intercepted Cera – she must've crept away as soon as she realised the jig was up.' He examined the scabs on his right arm and sighed. 'We knew she was spying for Mustaq al'Madhi, but I really thought that had been curtailed when the tunnels were sealed up. After that it didn't seem worth killing her.' He scowled. 'See where mercy gets you?'

'You're alive because of mercy, you pig.'

Gurvon looked at her levelly. 'You know, I could have had Timori killed at any time, but the circumstances were never quite right. He's been a useful little carrot to dangle just out of reach. Both the Dorobon and the Nesti wanted him, but I had him, and that kept this kingdom from degenerating into open war. You'll regret asking for him. It makes open conflict inevitable.'

'I don't think so.'

Gurvon looked at Kazim. 'Listen, Dokken: Elena will use anything and anyone – even a child – to further her own ends. Watch your back; she'll sell you to the Inquisition as soon as she's run out of uses for you.'

Elena felt a little apprehensive; surely this nasty little barb wouldn't take root? But Kazim laughed so unaffectedly that her heart swelled with gratitude. 'My lover dwells in my heart, Gurvon-sahib,' he replied calmly. 'We are one being. Anything you say against her, you say against me'

Something in his simple, calm answer silenced Gurvon completely, as if Kazim's total love and faith in her left nothing to attack.

At last Gurvon sniffed, affecting disdain and boredom, and said, 'I rather think we're done here.'

'You know,' she replied bleakly, 'I think we are.'

36

Power and Precision

Marriage

Marriage is often lauded by poets and playwrights as a manifestation of love, but it is nothing of the sort: it is a legal arrangement for the intergenerational transfer of wealth and influence. Love is nothing but a nuisance, muddying the waters of what should be clear-cut decisions about with whom one should ally oneself; 'love' can endanger the longevity of that alliance. Would that love did not exist!

BAYL TAVOISSON, TREASURER, PALLAS, 816

Teshwallabad, Lakh, on the continent of Antiopia
Rami (Septinon) 929
15th month of the Moontide

Huriya's pack ate their horses and entered Teshwallabad as a pack of wild dogs. They found a wrecked old building near the river and drove off the squatters, except for a couple who were too slow to run away; those they killed and ate too, because the journey had been long. Of course, the hovel did not suit Huriya, who asked Wornu to find her a guest-house more to her taste. Wornu acquiesced, returning with a palanquin; the most eastern-looking of the pack acted as bearers to carry their Seeress into the centre of the city in style. The palanquin was large enough for two and she insisted Malevorn join her, something the shapeshifter men had not expected and visibly resented by, though they didn't refuse.

A carved wooden grille went a little way to lessening the clamour and stink of the city, but it allowed Malevorn only glimpses of Tesh-wallabad as they crept along the close, winding streets and through the wide plazas where wares of all sorts from spices to copper kettles were piled high on stalls set up on carts or laid out on tattered blankets on the ground. They saw crumbling slums and marble domes, cracked clay and crenulated walls, and many, many people, including an old orange-clad Omali pandit being berated by three young Amteh Scripturalists; a beggar with no legs on a wheeled trolley; and a donkey-cart so overladen that the cart had tilted backwards – the poor beast had all four legs off the ground and was staring about itself in obvious bemusement. There were many dark, weathered faces with bushy whiskers and broken teeth, but even more young faces, bright with life. Music and the wailing of Godsingers filled the air: humanity at its most cacophonous.

'I grew up in such a place,' Huriya said, peering out with an expression somewhere between wistful memory and contempt, 'but I always knew I was destined for more. Sabele herself promised me.'

To Malevorn it all looked primitive and degenerate. He put a fold of his scarf over his mouth and nose, trying to mask the smells. 'Revolting.'

'This is the greatest city in all Lakh,' Huriya said coolly.

'I'm from Pallas. This place is a hovel.' Pallas was clean, orderly, and full of greenery and space ... the part his family lived in, anyway. The poor were kept well away from where the good people lived ... where he would one day live again, despite his father's suicide and the family's swift descent to ruin. His name had got him into Turm Zauberin; his wits would get him home ...

'This was ancient when your Pallas was a clutch of mud huts.'

'Compared to Pallas now, this still is.'

'Your city was built on the gnosis. This was built by human hands, centuries before your kind were capable.'

'The past,' he sneered. 'We live in the now.'

'Change is coming,' Huriya replied haughtily. She looked out of the grille, her features uncharacteristically pensive. 'We're going to overturn the entire world, starting here.'

Malevorn scratched his nose. *Yes, we are. But I rather think you and I will have very different views on what happens after that.* 'Where is this vizier?'

'His palace will be easy to find; he is an important man.'

'And when we find him?'

'We will pay him a late-night visit.' Huriya reached out and stroked his cheek. His face had been stained darker, and with his untended hair and beard and the garb of an Antiopian mercenary, his disguise was complete. 'You look tense, Malevorn my sweet.'

He bridled at her condescension, but he had to admit she frightened him too. She was as unpredictable and cruel as anyone he'd met – even at the Inquisitorial Bastion in Pallas. So he met her eyes and gave his most charming smile. 'I've been waiting for a long time to finally catch up with Mercer and that mudskin bint.'

She gave him a languid look. 'Did you know that my first lover was Rondian?' she asked slyly. 'A bull of a man: Jos Klein, his name was. I didn't even know I was a Souldrinker then, and as I had not come into the gnosis, he didn't know either. Then Sabele told me what I needed to do and after we coupled, I killed him and stole his powers.'

'A cautionary tale.'

She laughed throatily. 'I suppose it is, but that was not my point. I was just noting my apparent predilection for white men.' She pushed her foot into his crotch and massaged him through the cloth. She'd been doing a lot of this recently, teasing him, but never quite delivering, and he was becoming sick of the game. When she saw that he wasn't reacting she pouted, then lounged back into the cushioned seat. 'Tonight at midnight we will find this Hanook and see where he has taken Ramita's family. Perhaps she is even here, and the Scytale with her.'

Now there is a hope to cherish.

Finally they came to a place where the crowds were at their thickest, and the palanquin bearers halted and carefully set the box down. Malevorn jumped out and helped Huriya to disembark, and she dismissed Wornu and his men, then pointed towards a street jammed with hundreds of people. Malevorn took the lead and under her guidance bullocked a path down winding alleys between dilapidated buildings until they burst out into open space. In front of them was a wide, sluggish muddy brown river. Huge steps had been built of stone right along the bank on both sides, and to Malevorn it looked like the whole of Antiopia was here, many of them half-immersed, pouring water over their heads in apparent prayer. Bells chimed constantly from temples set all along the riverbanks, and priests chanted endlessly, and so loudly that the faraway sounds of the Godsingers in their towers were barely audible. The city on the other side of the river was as vast as that on the nearside.

Malevorn found himself more than a little awestruck by the sheer number of people, and the size and grandeur of the buildings lining the river.

Huriya flung out a hand theatrically and announced, 'The Imuna River, which also flows through my home city of Baranasi.' She walked down to the river, but Malevorn hung back, intimidated by so many men and women, all dressed in the brightest of colours. The cloth was mostly threadbare and cheap, but here and there he could see richer-garbed families were also making their way through the crowds. It looked like everyone came to the river to immerse themselves in the muddy sludge and chant – prayers, he guessed: Omali-worshippers.

There were more people than he'd seen in his life, except maybe at the great Imperial parades in Pallas, on special days ... but Huriya had claimed earlier that this was just an ordinary day.

He shrank against the wall, feeling strangely small, and watched Huriya go right down to the river, skipping like a child until she got to the final step, then she knelt and wet her brow. He'd thought her agnostic, but it looked like she was praying.

Her face was solemn as she returned to him.

'They say that bathing in Imuna cleans away all of your sins,' she declared.

'Handy. Didn't take long.'

She giggled. 'I didn't even need soap.' She waved a disdainful hand behind her. 'Let's go.'

'Certainly. Anywhere but here.'

'You don't like it?'

'It's barbaric.'

'You really do have no soul at all.'

'I don't know what you mean.' He looked about in bewilderment. 'Where do we go?'

'This way.' She led him back into the press of the alleys and as he followed, he felt more than ever that he was depending utterly on her to survive this maelstrom of alien humanity. *I'm just a toy to her, an extravagance.*

The place she took him was a guesthouse, where she used the gnosis to beguile the host into welcoming them inside without any exchange of names or coin. The place was a monument to opulence, a palace of sandstone and carved cedarwood that must be worth a fortune in this place without forests. Gauzy curtains hung everywhere, and a heady smoke leaked from behind closed doors. The staff, male and female alike, were all young and beautiful, dressed in silk skirts and nothing else. Music and singing filled the air and the main room was decorated with brightly coloured statues perched on plinths, so lifelike he was amazed – until he realised that they really were alive: real people covered in body paint and cloth, each one very slowly moving into a different pose as they passed.

'What is this place?' he asked.

'A whorehouse masquerading as a place where rich pilgrims can stay after immersing themselves in the river.' Huriya looked about her with faint disdain. For someone who had grown up poor, if her tales were to be believed, she looked utterly at home – and by no means impressed. Perhaps the souls within her had seen better.

For himself, Malevorn was fascinated. *Who wouldn't want to be a rich man here? Is this how the emperors lived?* But he was also increasingly on his guard. *What is she trying to prove, by bringing me here? Does she mean to seduce me?* The thought of copulating with any Noorie repelled him, despite her lush sensuality. *She's wasting her time.*

Huriya ordered food and wine to be delivered, then she dismissed the servants and threw herself into the middle of the vast divan, shedding silks as she moved. 'What do you wish for?' she asked over her shoulder. 'Opium? Spirits? Music? Dancing girls? We can have anything we want here.'

'Nothing,' he replied. 'We need to prepare for tonight.'

Huriya laughed. 'Prepare? For what? Bullying an old man?'

He gritted his teeth. 'Let me have my gnosis back. And a sword.'

She shrugged carelessly. 'A sword, perhaps – swords don't frighten me. But I don't think you've been anywhere near well-behaved enough to be trusted with your magic.'

'You should be preparing, scouting, making sure your people know their roles.'

She just giggled and looked about her. 'No, I want to be clean! And perfumed, and fed. And I want a tongue inside my yoni, followed by a long hard lingam.' She laughed lewdly. 'I've gone without for too long.' She struck a whorish pose, beckoning. 'Don't you want to play?'

Not with a mudskin degenerate like you. His lip curled. 'I'll relax when I hold the Scytale in my hands.'

'That will never be, slugskin.' She looked vexed. 'Go away then, sulk in a corner for all I care.' She pulled a bell rope and shouted, 'Bring me wine!'

Hours later Malevorn was still burning with anger as they left the pleasure house. Night had fallen and the long blade of a crescent moon hung like a scimitar above the eastern mountains. He flexed his fist and breathed deeply of the cooling air, but it was still thick with river-mist and the smoke of hundreds of thousands of cooking fires, hanging over the city and reducing visibility to a few yards. He could just make out the forty or so pack-members milling about in the ruined building they had claimed. They all looked replete, having gorged themselves on souls as well as wine and food. He wrinkled his nose in contempt. The stench of their animal mating still hung in the air; Huriya too had wasted the preparatory hours on drunken sex with a pair of male whores while Malevorn waited in another room, trying to clear his mind and prepare for a fight.

At least they'd given him a weapon – a Keshi scimitar – and some ill-fitting mail. He tested the sword's balance again, familiarising himself with the curved blade; it required a different fighting style to the straight swords he'd been brought up with. And all the while he missed Raine Caladryn, who would have been just as iron-willed as he was, just as grimly purposeful. He'd shied away from thinking about her in the months since she'd died because missing someone was weakness. But Kore's Blood, he'd have paid anything to have her standing with him now.

I wonder which of this damned pack drank her soul? He'd never been told, and had never asked.

Huriya gathered the pack, a queen among her subjects. Any pretence that Wornu controlled the pack was long gone; they were all her creatures now.

'My children, tonight we seek two prizes, the Scytale of Corineus and the widow of Meiros and her children – each is equally precious, but there is no guarantee they are here, so that is what we are seeking to determine. You will follow me into the vizier's house and spread out, using caution and silence, at least until the alarm is irrevocably raised. It would be better to accomplish this without attracting any outside notice, but all servants and any guards within must die. If the young mage Mercer is there, kill him. The vizier and Ramita, if she's here, must be brought to me *alive*. Is that understood?'

The pack murmured their assent.

'One final thing.' With her hands on her hips, she glared around the room. 'If any try to claim the prizes I have named as their own, they will be made an example of. This is not a time for seeking personal gain. All will gain equally from these prizes. Is that understood?'

The shifters muttered their obedience, and Malevorn wondered if any would hold to it. Then Huriya clapped her hands and said, 'Let the fun begin!'

A low collective moan of eagerness rose from the Souldrinkers, who then fell into the agonised contortions of shapechanging into their favoured beast or half-beast. Malevorn moved into Huriya's shadow, blanking his mind of everything but the task at hand.

'Good boy,' she approved with a condescending smirk. 'Watch my back.'

I surely will . . . my queen . . . I know exactly where my blade will go in.

They made their way carefully through the sleeping city, past walled buildings with guards who peered at them curiously, and the sleeping homeless, thick as flies around the steps of the temples. The tiny alley-shops were all shuttered and locked. The stray dogs who normally ruled the night streets of Teshwallabad yelped and fled the Dokken pack, and night-watchmen who might have been inclined to investigate found unwitting reasons to turn aside.

At last they came to the edge of a great open plaza, and for the first time saw their destination. Vizier Hanook's home was an impressive construction of stone and latticed windows. A few gleams of light shone from behind shutters on all three floors. Armed men guarded the rooftop battlements and the main doors. It was an inner city fortress, built with an artist's eye.

The pack crept to the edges of the shadows, then fanned out to surround the building. Huriya led Malevorn to a point opposite a side door. Her face was serenely confident.

'What is my role?' he asked.

'Protect me,' she answered simply, and as she spoke he could feel the gnostic threads close about him, ready to enforce her will over him if required. He carefully blanked his mind of all his resentment of her.

They waited, still as statues, until Huriya looked up as if in answer to a silent call. Cut off from his gnosis, Malevorn could not feel the signal that pulsed out, but he could guess at it, for on all sides the Souldrinker pack took to the air or padded softly forward. The first casualty was a guardsman on the rooftop, shot by Wornu's mate Hessaz. Instantly birds became people who dragged him from sight before spreading across the roof.

Huriya turned to him and offered her hand. 'Come.'

He clasped her tiny hand, and with effortless Air-gnosis she bore them both up into the air. The wind rushed past his face for a moment, then they were landing on the shadowy rooftop, which turned out to be a beautifully tended and ornate garden, with cupolas sheltering fountains and pools with golden fish. More bodies were being dragged aside, and he could hear the wet ripping sound of teeth in flesh. They found two doors leading downwards, one beneath a graceful cupola covering a staircase to a closed double-door, the other less grand, so perhaps meant for the servants.

Wornu flowed from bird to human form and descended to the double doors. The packleader paused at the closed portal and looked back in confusion. 'Seeress, it is warded.'

Malevorn saw uncertainty cloud Huriya's face. 'You are certain? How strongly?'

'Strong enough,' Wornu growled, displeased. 'I thought there were no magi here.'

'The Rondian boy – Mercer?' Huriya asked, looking at Malevorn.

'Perhaps,' Malevorn answered, adding, 'but he's only a quarter-blood.' *Perhaps he's here, and the Scytale too . . .*

The Dokken hadn't expected any gnostic resistance, and this small reminder of their centuries of persecution at magi hands was enough to cow some and enrage others. 'What do we do?' Wornu asked, his brutish face contorting with suppressed rage.

Huriya nibbled her lip, then announced, 'We will strike swiftly as planned. Break down both doors at once, and kill any who resist, except our targets.'

Malevorn eyed the group disdainfully. *Stupid bitch, sending her fighters into the unknown.* But he didn't care enough to warn them. He could see that Wornu at least understood the risks.

What if Quintius and his Fist are here? he thought suddenly, and wondered how he felt about that possibility. *They'd treat me like any other Dokken, no doubt. Or maybe worse . . .*

The pack did as Huriya commanded, bunching around the two staircases. With the gnosis, barring clever use of the strengths and weaknesses of different Studies, defence beat an equal attack in the short term, but long term, a weaker attack could undermine permanent wards. Huriya was the equivalent of an Ascendant and Wornu a pure-blood, and thanks to the deaths of Dranid and Raine, there were at least two more in the pack with pure-blood strength, Kraderz and Medelos. So they had enough power to destroy most wards swiftly – but the gnostic reverberations would instantly warn those within.

We'll have to be swift once we've broken through. And somehow I've got to get free of this Chain-rune and get my hands on the Scytale. He eyed Huriya's back as she gave the signal and the Dokken leaders hit the doors with all their force.

The counter-blow was staggering: the doors exploded, not inwards, but outwards, the defensive spells set into the doors smiting Wornu's shielding in coruscating red and blue light while fire and splinters like spears erupted in all directions. The massive Souldrinker roared in fury, unharmed but furious. Malevorn glanced at the other doorway and saw that Medelos had not been so fortunate: the half-trained fool had not thought to shield and he was so badly burned and broken that he was all but unrecognisable. Those behind him staggered way, except for one quick thinker, a bat-headed man named Elando who knelt over Medelos' ruined face and inhaled the mist rolling out.

Without thinking Malevorn stepped in their direction and shouted, 'Get moving, you rabble!' One or two shot him looks of hate, but they began to pour down the staircase as the first shouts of alarm rose from below.

Ramita stood in yet another sari so stiff with gemstones that if she fell asleep standing up, she would probably remain upright. Her next encounter with the mughal would be a formal dinner, involving some of his courtiers: another attempt to make her compromise her position and remove the final impediments to the marriage.

Around her a crowd of tailors fussed like chickens. There was no gaiety or levity as there would have been at home, just a group of immaculately dressed middle-aged men making sober observations about the size of her bust and hips as they took precise measurements. They had been at it for hours and she was about ready to scream.

'Just a few more minutes,' Jindas-sahib, the royal tailor, said without a touch of sympathy, or indeed irony, considering this was the eighth time he'd used the phrase that evening. The other six tailors were variously too absorbed or too tired to react at all.

The twins were in the nursery, playing with a maidservant before their final feed for the day, and her breasts felt full and uncomfortable. She longed for these fussy old men to relent and let her go.

Hanook was sitting on a stool, watching the scene with a look of anxiety leavened with amusement. Their eyes met briefly. It was two days since the audience with Mughal Tariq and their blazing argument in the tunnel afterwards. He'd been at court most of that time, trying to find a solution to the impasse over her powers. Dareem had been busy too, working away in his own suite upstairs, writing letters to courtiers, pulling strings and setting the groundwork for the revelation of Lady Meiros to the world. She hated being at loggerheads with Hanook, for she liked him – not just because he was kin, but even more poignantly, he reminded her of her dead husband.

Alaron would be in the library at the other end of this floor, or maybe upstairs in bed by now. She wished she'd had the chance to talk to him, but he was preoccupied with the training regime he'd started at the monastery; it invariably left him exhausted and abed early. Or perhaps he was avoiding her.

Is Hanook right? Am I being unreasonable because part of me just wants to run away with my loyal Goat, and damn the world? She was sure that wasn't the case, but the nagging feeling remained, that she was being selfish rather than strong. It undermined her resolve and weakened her will.

Tomorrow night I'll decide, she promised herself. *They will give in, or Alaron and I will leave.*

'Enough,' said Hanook, clapping his hands. 'We are almost there. The rest will follow tomorrow.'

The tailors stepped back, looking put out, but Ramita felt herself reel and had to catch her balance lest she fall off the stool. *Dear gods, I am tired.* She looked at Hanook gratefully.

'This sari accentuates the best features of your form and colouring,' he told her, waving the tailors away to the far corner of the room and lowering his voice. 'Mid-hues to downplay your darkness, fewer pleats and more flair to minimise your hips. Tariq favours skinny girls.'

And ones with nipples like flowers. 'He is a shallow child if that is all that matters to him.'

'Lady, he is a gentle soul, and you will come to feel affection for each other, of this I am certain. I believe the two of you represent the start of a new era for Lakh.'

'Have the Godspeakers been told yet?' she asked doubtfully.

'All in good time,' Hanook replied. 'There will be moderate members of the clergy present tomorrow night, noted for their flexibility and realism. Once we win them over, the majority will be swayed. The dream of Lakh supremacy will overcome their repugnance for the magi.'

The thought was a queasy one. Repugnance could turn to murder very quickly. 'If you cannot find a way to ensure my autonomy, I will not agree to this,' she reminded him firmly.

He went to reply, but his words were drowned by a massive *boom!*, like a giant heartbeat.

Then came a sound that hit her like a blow to the chest: she felt a mighty crash in her ears and through all her gnostic senses, throbbing through the whole palace, shaking the floors.

Like nightmares given voice, beast calls echoed distantly through the corridors.

Alaron was walking back to his room with the rolled-up notes in his hand and his head full of thoughts. So much was happening, soaking up the hours, and he still had much to decide. He was unravelling the Scytale, but what to do with it? Ramita and the mughal was another problem – and then there was the exploration of uncharted gnostic territory. He was keeping up his kon-staff practise on his own now Yash had gone to his new monastery. Alaron missed him; the young monk was the only person here whose company didn't come with an array of complications. Between the physical and mental stresses, he was exhausted, and more than ready for bed.

He had to admit that the gnosis-work was exhilarating, though. He was making breakthroughs with every session. All the old fears that had held him back now had no sway: he could summon spirits or use necromancy if he chose, without that mind-numbing fear that had plagued his Arcanum years. His aptitude for each Study was constantly increasing.

He felt sorry that Ramita wasn't being allowed the time to do the same, but she was tied up in the negotiations with Hanook and the mughal. She was being pulled away from him, back into the world of courts and harems, and that was the counter-balance to his excitement over the gnosis. He was losing her, and there was nothing he could do. It left him feeling sick with longing.

At least the Scytale work was paying off: his hand-drawn chart of all the runes and the ingredients they represented was completed, the last of the herbs and chemicals having fallen into place, but it was now clear that these were just additives, to some *master ingredient*, and he could find no clue in the Scytale for the nature of that base compound. He had learned so much, only to find out that there was more to find out – but he was now convinced that knowledge must be out there, and his determination to learn the remaining secrets was undimmed.

He still couldn't decide if he should reveal the Scytale to Hanook: the vizier's determination to see Ramita wed to the mughal was undermining his faith in him, Antonin Meiros' grandson or not. He appeared to have the mughal's interests far more in mind than Ramita's, or her sons.

He missed the time when it had just been him and Ramita. The time they had spent together was beginning to feel increasingly idyllic; now that he looked back on it from a comfortable manor in the city all the cold and hunger and fear seemed somewhat romantic. Those miserably uncomfortable nights pressed back to back beneath a blanket in the tiny windskiff, trying to sleep while petrified by every night noise: now that felt like the stuff of ballads. He badly wanted to talk to her, but he wasn't at all sure what he wanted to say. In the meantime, all manner of possible conversations played out in his imagination:

'Perhaps it is best if I just leave?' She bursts into tears and begs me not to go. We never see each other again. She's fine, I die of loneliness.

'I pledge myself to your service as your bodyguard.' She accepts my service, I save her life from assassins and we have a passionate affair, until we're executed together when discovered by the vengeful mughal.

'Come away with me, and we'll find your family.' She refuses, and I go off alone. I'm captured by Inquisitors and tortured to death.

'I'm going back to the monastery to become a Zain monk.' I die alone and miserable in a mountain retreat, the only white man for a thousand miles.

Happy endings were rare in his daydreams.

These depressing thoughts were filling in his head as he headed for his rooms. Ramita was being fitted for a dress suitable for a banquet with the mughal, but he could hear the distant squeals of the twins, and the footsteps of servants echoing along the marble corridors. He reached the landing for the top floor, where the stair carried on upwards to a roof garden. He was just wondering whether he should get some fresh air up there . . .

. . . the door exploded, and the concussion staggered him backwards, dazed and terrified. He grabbed the balustrade and gaped upward as billowing smoke poured down the stairs toward him.

For a moment there was silence, then someone on the roof bellowed in agony and someone else shouted – words he couldn't make out through the ringing in his ears – and a cacophony of beast noises echoed down the stairs.

A year ago, he might have frozen, but by the time the first shapes poured out of the smoke he was mentally broadcasting warnings as he ran towards his room.

The auras of the attackers were like tentacled blobs: the same auras as those who had attacked the Isle of Glass: *Souldrinkers!*

Ramita's eyes went wide and she spun around, ignoring the protests of the three tailors. 'Hanook? What is it?' Then inchoate warnings filled the aether: Alaron's mental voice, shouting for her to *run*.

The vizier's face was ashen, but he was already on his feet. 'An attack,' he said instantly, then shouted, '*Dareem!*' both aloud and with his mind.

The animal sounds were muffled by the carpets and tapestries covering the marble floors and walls, but to Ramita they sounded horribly close, and *horribly* familiar; she knew at once who it was. *Huriya.* White light kindled in her hands, fuelled by fury and fear, and the tailors backed away from her in confusion and then terror at this visible manifestation of the forbidden gnosis.

'My children!' She leaped from the low table, the heavy weight of the sari jingling. She ignored the tailors squawking in protest, her mind fixed only on Nasatya and Dasra as she stormed towards the door.

'Lady Meiros!' Hanook called, striding after her, and the tailors stared: even to the naked eye he was enmeshed in faint skeins of light, and the sapphire he always wore on a chain at his throat was glowing. Two of them dropped to their knees and wailed prayers, Jindas-sahib shrieked '*Rakas! Rakas!*', then they all ran for their lives.

Ramita hurried towards the nursery, ignoring Hanook shouting after her: nothing else mattered but getting to her boys. But between her and her children was the main stairwell, right ahead of her, and smoke was filling the shaft.

Darikha-ji be with me! she prayed as she ran down the corridor.

Malevorn Andevarion descended the stairs slowly, feeling horribly exposed and mortal without any gnostic shielding. Hessaz leaped past him, an arrow nocked and her eyes blazing, vanishing into the smoke followed by a jostling pack of jackals and wolves, snapping at each other in their eagerness to reach the enemy.

Blue light stabbed out of the glowing air from the right and one of the jackals was illuminated bright enough to see its skull, then it thudded onto its side, stunned or dead.

Mage-bolt! Kore's Balls! If one hits me . . .

Hessaz flattened herself against the balustrade and kindled light on her arrow before spinning and firing into the smoke. Malevorn heard a faint roar as it exploded, but no sound of pain. The Lokistani woman cursed and readied another arrow as Malevorn edged up behind her and pressed himself into cover. Around him, the shifters yowled and poured towards the source of the mage-bolt, then another flurry struck the nearest Dokken and a wall of flames ignited, trapping the next wave. They were all shielding now, but some less than effectively, for he heard semi-human screams as the front rank were flung backwards out of the smoke, their bodies dead and burned black.

The remaining shifters howled in fury.

'Release me!' Malevorn demanded of Huriya. 'I can kill him for you!'

'Move, Inquisitor.' She flung him aside like a discarded toy as light flashed past him and shattered on her shields. She shouted in Keshi and the pack charged forward again, and this time those with Firegnosis breached the flame-barrier. Huriya blasted air along the corridor, dissipating the smoke enough to see that there was just one man there – but he dodged through a side door as Huriya released mage-fire. A shifter in bear shape ran forward and began to batter the door down, while the jackals yowled and ran on, seeking easier prey.

Malevorn looked left, where the corridors continued deeper into the interior, as a dark shape appeared, tearing along the corridor towards him with a gaggle of beasts on his tail. He raised a hand to blast the newcomer then dropped it, snarling, '*Damn this!*' But in that instant, the runner reached a lamp which illuminated his face.

Alaron Mercer.

Ignoring Huriya, Malevorn sprinted towards his old foe.

The Scytale must be here!

Alaron ran down the corridor towards his rooms and the Scytale. Ramita was still on the floor below, and probably Hanook too. He thought he was the only one on the top floor, and he had a pack of jackals on his tail. He skidded around a corner as a servant put his head out of a door, his dark face wide-eyed with fear. 'Sahib?' the man called, then the jackals swarmed around the corner behind Alaron and he slammed the door shut again.

Twisting as he ran, Alaron fired a mage-bolt behind him and caught the lead jackal. Energy crackled around its shielding, making it skid on the slippery marble and giving Alaron a moment to kindle Fire-gnosis at the end of one ghost-arm, and hurl a ball of flame behind him. It gulfed the next pair, throwing them backwards, yelping and ablaze. He punched another mage-bolt into the first jackal and this time it burst through the shields and the beast rolled over, stunned.

It was the first time he'd used his new skills in real combat, but that was lost on him in the urgency of the moment. He needed to protect the Scytale and his notes, and he needed to be downstairs. *Ramita will get to the twins and I'll join her after this*, he promised himself, sprinting towards his room. He glimpsed movement ahead of him on the main stairs: more bestial shapes, several of them bipedal, and among them a bearded man in rough chainmail. They all saw him, roared wordlessly and charged in his direction, the beasts at the front, the Keshi following.

He'd had a thought about what to do if they encountered shape-changing Dokken again ... morphic-gnosis was an Earth and Hermetic combination: its opposite on the gnostic spectrum was Air and Theurgy: illusion. He hurled illusory mage-bolts at the heads of the pair of Dokken in front of the bearded Keshi; they went straight through their shields unchecked and frazzled their brains. Both dropped, and the Keshi ducked for cover.

That bought him the time to reach his door and dart inside, reaching ahead with the gnosis and cancelling the wards over the Scytale even as he spun and slammed the door shut with telekinesis, right in the face of the foremost Dokken, a shaggy bipedal man with a face like a wolverine. *Wards!* He kindled already primed shields on the doorframe and backed away. Claws raked the wood, but the door held.

Without a backwards look he engaged Earth-gnosis and wrenched up the marble tiles while he grabbed his pack and stuffed his notes and the Scytale case inside. He shouldered it whilst he gestured towards his sheathed sword, leaning against the wall. It flew to his waist and belted itself; he gestured again, and his Zain staff flew to his hands. Part of him was marvelling that he could keep so many threads of the gnosis active, but the greater part was already planning the next move: sixteen motes of gnostic light were now alight around his aura: sixteen ways to fight.

Something tore at the window shutters and a fist punched through the bars, smashing the glass. He glimpsed red glowing eyes outside. More blows struck the door to the room and his wards began to go turn from blue to purple as the force against them built.

I've got half a minute, and I'm trapped – or am I?

He looked down at the floor and gathered his Earth-gnosis.

Huriya Makani was wrong-footed by Malevorn's sudden lunge to the left and she lost sight of him. His absence left her feeling naked and vulnerable, without a man-shaped shield before her. She spat a curse and went to go after him, until a bellow from Wornu, who'd gone after the mage she'd confronted, transfixed her with indecision. She'd never been in a real fight before, and neither had Sabele. The Seeress had fought duels but never in battles, where an attack could manifest from any direction. With a flush of self-recognition, Huriya realised that she was actually afraid.

Cursing herself, she flooded her shields with power and began to edge down the stairs, listening with all her senses for any sign that something was about to be launched at her. Her brood shrieked for her to help them, but her thudding heart and trembling legs would not let her go faster than a limp.

'Seeress! Here!' Hessaz shouted. 'There's a magus!'

I know, bitch! Huriya reluctantly went that way, although she could see that there were bodies strewn along the corridor – and all of them her Dokken. A quick check showed most were just stunned, but at least three were dead and a storm of light was stabbing through a broken door like a celestial swordsman at bay. She saw Wornu caught in the midst of it: his shields were being shredded by skilful blasts and as he staggered aside, she saw his chest was a mess of criss-crossed burns and the left of his face was seared like roasted meat. His eyeball was gone. He was trying to use sheer power to storm forward, but his more skilled opponent was cutting him to pieces.

'Seeress, help us!' Hessaz was cowering the shadows, her arrows gone and her thigh charred. 'He's too good.'

'There's just one?'

Hessaz scowled bitterly. 'Yes.' She admitted, whimpering over her burned leg.

Something had to be done: Wornu was barely defending himself. Huriya gathered kinetic energy and pulled him from the fray, sending him sliding behind her down the blood-slick marble of the corridor.

One man. I can face one. Sabele has experience of duelling ... Though surrendering too much control to her alter-ego was as frightening as facing the mage himself, she pulled the old Seeress to the forefront of her mind and stepped into the line of fire.

A blast of mage-fire flashed against her shields, making her cry aloud, but they held. She peered at her foe and her Sabele-memories identified his facial stamp as being kin to Vizier Hanook. She immediately realised the implication: *the Vizier of Lakh is a mage.* Then a barrage of attacks drove everything but survival from her mind.

The vizier's son was clad in a nightgown and stood in the midst of a lounge filled with stuffed birds and bats, clutching a green periapt and a rod of carved ivory. His calm face shone with exertion.

Mage-bolts stabbed her shields, but the real battle was unseen. He was primarily a sorcerer, and his strongest affinity was mesmerism; he must have been ripping into Wornu's mind even as he fired his mage-bolts. Sensations of fear and pain enclosed her too, as if she'd fallen into venomous thorns, and the psychic barbs started ripping at her composure as her shields wavered. A blast of mage-fire struck her left knee and she shrieked as her skin blistered. She was almost lost in that instant, for her body was unused to real pain and her mind, never before invaded by another, began to yield before the man's clinical attack.

Then Sabele reared up inside her, she who had dwelt at the margins of civilisation since the time of Corineus. She had been cornered by magi before and had fought like a cornered rat to survive then – and mesmerism was her own forte, her weapon of choice in combat. She recognised the mage's techniques and after walling off the mind she shared with Huriya, she began to nullify them. For a second Sabele's wizened visage filled Huriya's head, but she slapped her back down and took over the shields the old Seeress had so flawlessly erected and started gathering in the strands of power she held.

Right, you . . .

Huriya went on the offensive.

She met the vizier's son's eyes and assaulted him with the same mesmerism he had employed against her. She had no finesse – and was too scared to open up to Sabele again, lest she couldn't shut her down this time – so she fought her own way, screaming abuse and invective as she sought to flood his senses with waves of hurt, using raw power against technique.

It didn't immediately work; the mage was an illusionist as well as a mesmerist and he fought with dogged skill. It seemed to her that her skin was boiling off her in red strips, her sight was flashing and throbbing, and every sense was overloaded. She could barely block his bolts, and every step was agony. Three of her jackals tried to aid her, but the first rolled over with its teeth bared in a rictus of agony and went limp and the other two soon backed away in terror, unable to intervene between the unseen forces.

But she had Ascendant strength and for all his skill, she was by far the stronger. 'I'm coming for you,' she screamed. *'I'm going to rip your eyeballs out.'*

He began backing away, then the ivory rod in his hand suddenly blazed to life as he changed tactics, going defensive against her mental attacks but launching something new.

On every side, the stuffed animals on his walls came to life, turning their heads and stretching their wings, then launching themselves at her. She slapped at them with contempt, but to her utter amazement they manifested their own wards and started flapping in slow motion *through* her shielding, claws extended, eyes burning with unnatural intelligence. For the second time she lost her composure, and they almost reached her.

But again Sabele spoke in her mind. *Wizardry*, her dry mental voice croaked. *You destroy them like . . .* this.

Power flared inside her mind and as one the skulls of each of the birds and bats exploded and the twice-dead corpses rained to the floor as she staggered. She gained a momentary respite as he retreated, and now she could sense desperation in him. She staggered him with a pure kinetic blow, then followed up with another and another, shrieking in hatred and battering at him with inefficient but overwhelming force. She stormed closer, step by step, until she gestured and the ivory rod snapped. He blanched and tried to back away, his face suddenly fearful.

<FATHER!> he called. *<HELP ME!>*

'Yes, call your daddy. I want him too!' She flung the vizier's son backwards against the wall and pinned him there, helpless as his wards wavered and vanished. Blood smeared the cracked plaster behind his head and his eyes rolled backwards. She opened her hand and slapped with an avalanche of telekinetic-gnosis behind her, his head spun sideways as his neck broke and he sagged in her gnostic grip, his eyes emptying. She threw herself across the room, gripped his face and kissed him furiously, gulping in the smoky essence of the man and refilling the well of her gnosis.

Dareem . . . Son of Hanook. Born and raised in secret, in Hebusalim and in monasteries and palaces all over Ahmedhassa. A fussy and inflexible child taught humanity by a patient father, who revered his grandfather . . .

. . . Antonin Meiros.

Huriya felt Sabele inside her gasp in amazement and she felt much the same. *What have we stumbled upon?* But there was no time to dwell on this; she had also seen another face in the flood of memories that flowed past her as Dareem perished.

Ramita is here!

Her energies renewed, she strode to the door, where Hessaz clung to the doorframe. She was hobbling painfully but at least she had some arrows for her bow again.

'Hessaz! Come with me!' Huriya snapped. 'The vizier and Ramita are here and I want them alive!'

Ramita reached the central stairwell overlooking the reception hall with Hanook a few paces behind her. The sounds of the intruders came from her left, where stairs rose into darkness, black smoke billowing from them. The balcony to her right curved around the stairwell and she took that way as black shapes poured down from above – first, beasts, then two-legged shapes following. Most – a dozen at least – poured straight down the stairs, but some saw her and dashed around the balcony, yowling and roaring.

She quelled her fear, as trained responses took over. Spreading her arms, she drew power from her core and readied elemental gnosis, the simplest to use. What little practise she'd managed would have to be enough. Her whole frame tingled with potentiality, fuelled by her fear for her children and Alaron Mercer.

'Lady, beware!' Hanook shouted as a bat-headed man with membraned wings on his arms leapt into the air and glided across the stairwell towards her. She threw kinesis at him, smacking him against the wall, but he gripped a torch-holder and hung on, then swung over the railing and into her path, baring massive fangs.

Behind her she heard snarling and barking, and a quick glimpse over her shoulder told her that Hanook had stopped to confront two more shapeshifters. But she had no time to worry about that: Bathead was coming right at her. She shoved kinetic force at him again, but his wards engaged and he staggered on. So she stamped her foot and poured destructive Earth-gnosis into the stonework, the tiles crumbled and Bat-head fell through.

To her amazement he again showed his agility by grasping a wooden beam to stop his fall. He bunched his limbs, ready to leap at her.

She snapped the beam with sylvan-gnosis and he plummeted away as behind her, Hanook blasted through the shields of a wolf and shattered its face. Then a great cat sprang past its stricken comrade and hammered into the vizier. Its teeth bared, it lunged—

—and flew sideways and hammered into the wall as she hit it with a panicked burst of kinesis. The cat landed on its feet, but its legs wobbled and it slumped, stunned. Hanook rolled onto his side and blasted a mage-bolt at its head, searing the shifter's skull to the bone.

He climbed painfully to his feet as Ramita sought a new route: she'd all but destroyed their way forward and more shapeshifters were coming, shielded, this time, and much more cautious.

She peered through the gap she'd smashed in the balcony; there were more of them below, including Bat-head, bruised and furious.

The nursery was on the other side of that gap. She was readying Air-gnosis to carry her over and into the teeth of more Dokken when Hanook gripped her arm. 'This way!' He thrust open a door beside her, which led to a beautifully appointed sitting room. There was a door on the left-hand wall and she went for it when suddenly Hanook stopped, clutching his chest.

Oh sweet Parvasi, he's having a heart seizure!

She reached for him, wondering what to do, when Hanook spoke in a pained whisper. 'Dareem! Oh no, my son . . .'

She understood, and her own heart broke for the old man and his loss, but it only intensified her fears for the twins. 'Please, come . . .'

'Dareem . . .'

Something slapped against the broken balcony outside: Bat-head, clambering over the railing with murder on his ugly bestial face. He lifted one hand, blue fire kindling in the air.

No! She unleashed more Earth-gnosis and collapsed the rest of the balcony. The Dokken's mage-bolt blasted the plaster ceiling above her head as he vanished in a rumble and crash. Beyond where he had stood, the top of the stairway was again revealed and she saw clearly who was stepping onto the top of the stairs one flight above.

Huriya Makani.

Their eyes met, and the Keshi girl bared her teeth.

Ramita gasped, and clapped her hands. The doors flew closed, blocking off the outside world, and she sealed them with the strongest warding she could conjure. A second later the doors bulged and almost shattered as a massive force struck them, but she grabbed Hanook's arm and wrenched him towards the door. A second blow struck the main door and almost shook it to pieces, but fear gave her wings. They burst into a smaller sitting room lined in books and ornaments and she slammed and warded the door behind and ran on. The vizier was moving in a daze, barely functioning. There was only one exit, leading back to the main corridor, but beyond the stairwell. She threw it open and looked left, saw a lean Lokistani woman with cropped hair and a drawn bow; an arrow was nocked. Both moved at once: the Lokistani tried to shoot; Ramita just *shoved* with the gnosis, as hard as she could.

The Lokistani flew backwards and over the edge of the broken stairwell railing, her arrow spilling impotently away. Ramita panted at the backlash of unleashing so much gnosis in so short a space of time and swayed dizzily for an instant, and this time it was Hanook who protected her, pulling her clear as blue fire flashed from a small figure at the opening of the corridor. The bolt struck his shielding, which flashed red, and he staggered. His eyes were clear again though, and Ramita marvelled at his courage in the face of such overwhelming grief. Then she spun away and dashed down the corridor, screaming for her children. Behind her, more gnosis-light flashed, and Hanook shouted defiantly, but her attention was on the nursery and that alone as she burst inside.

There was a gaping hole in the floor and another in the ceiling.

The twins were gone.

She screamed.

Alaron drew his sword, shifted the kon-staff to his left hand and crept back to the door, his gnostic senses vividly alive. Something was hammering at the barrier and it was too damned strong for his wards. He reached the side of the door and placed his blade against it, right beside the flap of the viewing slot – Hanook had installed them in many of the bedroom doors. Then he used kinesis to flip it up.

He glimpsed amber eyes that shone from a goat's head with coiling horns and called, 'Hey!' The goat-thing stopped in the middle of pulling back its hands, presumably readying itself to pour more energy into breaking the door-wards, and stared at him from a foot away.

He slammed the sword through the slot and straight into the creature's mouth, simultaneously feeding gnosis-energy into the steel so that it would punch through any shields, but there weren't any and the blade went right through the back of the thing's skull. The shifter slid off his blade, already dead, but there so no time for satisfaction. Someone – or some*thing* – hit his sword so hard it snapped off at the hilt, which spilled from his hand as he bent over in agony at the blow to his wrist. That convulsive movement saved him from the flame that burst through the viewing slot until he slammed it shut with a gesture. He started backing away as more blows hammered into the door, but they were weaker now. He'd bought a little more time.

With his kon-staff in his left hand and healing-gnosis repairing his right, he returned to the task he'd set himself. While he rebuilt the door-wards, he was also channelling power into Earth-gnosis, using it to carve a circle in the floor. The beam of amber light he conjured up sliced through the marble as easily as butter, but for all his haste, he worked carefully: he could not allow the disc of stone to fall into the nursery below.

The door behind him began to come apart and even through the thick wood he could hear snarling and bellowing as the Dokken started threatening what they would do to him. The words were in Rondian. Without stopping his Earth-gnosis work, he called upon mesmerism to create a whip from the gnosis and cracked it at the mental signatures beyond the door. Without eye-contact it didn't do that much, but he felt at least three of the shifters reel at the unexpected blow, and that brought him a few more moments, enough time to lift the three-foot-wide disc of stone clear, revealing the wooden sub-floor and beneath that, the ceiling of the nursery.

Then suddenly a hole was punched in the door behind, and it caved in. He turned as a human-sized lizard head peered through.

Using telekinesis he flung the enormously heavy stone disc he'd pulled from the floor. It burst the lizard-man's shields and struck the creature full-on. Its head pulped against the wall and it smeared down the plaster, but Alaron didn't wait to see whatever was coming next. He reset the door wards one last time, then dropped through the floor into the room below.

I've got the right room! He spared a second to breathe an enormous sigh of relief, then realised the children's ayah – their nursemaid – a grey-haired Lakh woman of indeterminate age, was staring at him with terrified eyes. She was clinging to the twins, her mouth opened to scream, but he called as quietly as he could, 'Ayah! It's okay, it's me, it's Alaron—'

She screamed anyway.

Damn it! She doesn't speak Rondian . . .

He used mysticism to send *calm* to the woman and she stopped shrieking, then he laid a hand on her forehead and spoke directly to her mind <It's okay. We're going to be all right. I'm here to help you,> he sent, letting her brain translate his Rondian into Lakh. He let the calming energy leak into the twins as well, soothing them. He felt oddly free of fear for himself; it was everyone else he was terrified for. Maybe that was helping, for he felt incredibly focused and his spells had never been more incisive.

'Stay calm,' he told the ayah again, and she *believed* him.

He began to carve another hole to the next level down, the connection to the Earth-gnosis even smoother, though he could hear shouting and snarling in the room above as his door-wards finally gave way. He wrenched the floor tiles up, then turned suddenly and using kinetic energy again, flung them through the hole in the ceiling and upwards into the room he'd left.

Something cried out, and blood-spattered shards fell back, but his focus remained on carving the new hole, all the while maintaining his grip on the ayah's emotions: three gnosis-effects at once – he could almost see Master Puravai's wrinkled face smiling in praise. His aura was shining like a Corineus Day tree, glittering with every hue of the rainbow.

He dropped the last tile through the floor, smashing a hole in the ceiling of the room below, then widened the gap with a thought. He checked to make sure the ayah still had a firm grip on the twins, then pulled her to him, enfolded her and the babies in his arms and dropped through the hole. She held him tightly, her eyes wide in mute terror, but they landed safely, cushioned by telekinesis, his eyes already seeking an exit.

Then a woman screamed in the nursery they had just escaped from.

Malevorn bellowed in frustration. *These Dokken are fucking useless! Even bloody Mercer can take them!*

With his own gnosis free he would have had that damned door down in seconds and Mercer gutted a moment later, he knew it, but here he was, absolutely powerless. He glared at the goat-headed body at his feet: Kraderz, his damned pure-blood gnosis wasted – and why? Because he'd forgotten to shield while attacking the door!

Forgotten to fucking shield?! Did anyone train these fools?

Another of the Souldrinkers had sprung on Kraderz as he lay dying, so at least the pure-blood strain had been preserved, but absorbing new power took valuable seconds and Mercer was escaping with the Scytale.

Then something slapped his mind, and with nothing to shield him he almost blacked out. It was just a simple mesmeric strike, one they called 'The Whip', delivered blind, but without the gnosis he was left horribly dazed. When he regained his senses he realised the Dokken around him evidently knew little or nothing of mental attacks because they had been just as badly affected. So more valuable seconds lost while he gathered himself and once he could stand straight, started roaring at the frightened Dokken, '*Get that bloody door down!*'

When did Mercer become an illusionist or a mesmerist? What the Hel is going on?

A bipedal lizard smashed a gnosis-strengthened fist into the timbers, and this time he punched right through and Mercer's wards began to come apart.

Finally!

Then the fool put his head through – and something smashed his lizard head into pulp. As the body slumped to the ground, the other Dokken lost no time in dragging him backwards, and one of them fell on their fellow to gain his energies. More time lost.

But there was no way he was going to go through that door to confront any mage, not even one as inferior as Alaron Mercer. *Damn you, Huriya! Give me back my powers!*

Then a shifter with a wolf's head gripped his shoulder. Darice's ample chest was heaving and her eyes gleaming with the new energy gleaned from Kraderz's soul. She shoved him aside and burst through the milling Dokken and into the room, howling like a Schlessen berserker. Others followed her, and Malevorn tailed them into a bedroom, completely empty – with a round hole in the floor. A few of the Dokken peered down the hole, then yelped and ducked for cover as a hail of tiles shot upwards through the hole, battering and slicing through those nearest. Malevorn cowered with the rest, and more time was lost, until finally it seemed safe. He strode to the edge of the hole and peered down.

Mercer was nowhere to be seen, but he gaped anyway: Ramita Ankesharan was directly below him, standing beside another hole in the floor of that room. She began shrieking with loss.

Malevorn turned to Darice and pointed a finger down, yelling, '*Get her!*'

Huriya strode along the corridor, only a dozen yards behind Ramita and the fleeing vizier. Inside her, Sabele was ranting, but she kept the old Seeress clamped down. Her blood was up and she wanted the vizier in her grasp – she wanted to rip him to pieces for daring to strike at her.

But here at the death, she found her feelings for Ramita more ambivalent. They had grown up as sisters, shared almost every moment of each other's lives from their childhood on. She knew her bloodsister's shape, her smell and her moods, as well as she knew her own. Ramita still mattered to her, and Sabele had divined that their futures were entwined in complex ways.

I will make you one of us, sister. You shall be my handmaiden and we'll be together for ever, as we always wished.

She raised a hand, but Ramita darted inside a door and Hanook interposed himself, blazing fire at her – illusory fire; she smiled and swatted it away, not reacting to the pseudo-pain that seared though her. But he'd slowed her, and he used that stolen moment to slam and seal the door.

Behind her more of the pack poured into the house, now led by Elando in his fanciful bat-guise; an idiot, poorly trained and reckless – and that, she was beginning to realise, was the same for most of the pack. She'd not known how poorly equipped the Dokken were to deal with properly trained magi. They'd been raised in the wild in small numbers; they were self-taught and most were illiterate. They couldn't use periapts to focus their power, and many of them had only a very basic knowledge of the gnosis.

'The city watch are coming, Seeress!' Elando gabbled at her. 'There is a patrol in the plaza outside!' He had absorbed the soul of Medelos on the rooftop, but she doubted Elendo had the wit to use the pure-blood gnosis well.

'Then we must finish this,' she told him. Behind the door, she heard Ramita cry out in despair. 'Break this down,' she commanded. *And take the first blows for me.* Elando and his shifters leapt to do her bidding.

She wondered vaguely where Malevorn was.

When a bulky wolf-woman dropped through the hole in the roof, Ramita froze in shock – but the Dokken had misjudged, and went straight on through the hole at Ramita's feet, vanishing into the room below. For a second Ramita just gaped, then someone roared outside the room behind her and everything happened at once.

Hanook had just entered, his face a mask of cold purpose stretched thinly over grief. But he acted with alacrity, strengthening the wards on the door while Ramita concentrated on the hole in the ceiling. When the next dark shape leapt through she was ready. She slapped her hands together, employing Earth and sylvan-gnosis on the timbers behind the plaster.

Even as the attacker began to drop through, her spell caused the whole roof to ripple like water and flow inwards, slamming the hole shut. She was too late to prevent the first shapeshifter coming through, but the closing stonework caught the second as he was halfway through and crushed his midriff. His legs thrashed then went limp, as the first attacker landed, a lion-headed man, who roared—

—then died in a wave of mage-fire from her hands, and Hanook's. The charred corpse crumpled and fell smouldering to the tiles, even as something hammered on the door like a battering ram.

Then from below, clearly audible through the still-open hole in the floor, the wolf-woman bellowed in fury, what sounded like a ton of crockery smashed, and a young male voice shouted in pain.

Alaron!

Then the sound of two infants bursting into tears reached her as well, freezing her heart.

Alaron had opened his mouth to call up to Ramita when something dropped past her, straight through the hole in the ceiling, and landed before him like a falling statue. As the ayah recoiled, the twins still wrapped in her arms, he confronted the newcomer: a massively muscled naked woman who was shaking her wolf-head. She was dazed and bloodied from the fall, but as he watched, she physically pulled herself together – then she growled, and leapt at him.

He couldn't dodge, not with the ayah and the twins behind him, so he stood his ground, though the shifter was far bulkier than him and howling in bloodlust. She was cloaked in shimmering shields, vivid in his gnosis-sight, and there was a non-too-subtle blast of mesmeric-gnosis in her howl that would have paralysed any normal human.

But he had been pummelled constantly by Malevorn Andevarion and his obnoxious pure-blood friends at college, and the past year had been one terrifying encounter after another. If there was one thing he was good at by now, it was ignoring terror. Instinctively he blocked her mesmeric-gnosis and fed his kon-staff with energy, planted his feet as Yash had shown him and launched into a driving lunge. The staff struck her shields with a blast of concentrated force as she slammed into him – and kept going. He felt like a bush in the path of a boulder.

Kore! She's got to be a pure-blood!

The impact drove him staggering backwards into a wall of shelves that collapsed behind him in an avalanche of smashing crockery. The shifter battered him onto his back with head-slamming force, and only his automatic back-shielding kept his skull from fracturing on the stone floor. But his staff bent almost in half, then pinged back, barely still in his grasp. The woman loomed above him, and with a terrifying backhanded blow, tore out the ayah's throat. The nursemaid went down silently, even in death shielding the twins with her body.

The two infants wailed in terror, and the sound galvanised him. He rose and thrust with his staff, slamming the wolf-woman backwards. Perhaps it was just the unexpectedness of the blow, but it was enough to hurl her into a heap of broken crockery with a crash.

She climbed to her feet, salivating, as he gripped the staff and kindled gnosis. *She's a shifter, she'll be all Earth and hermetic . . .* He sought the point where Air and theurgy met again – *illusion* – conjured an illusory knife, and threw it at her heaving breasts. She shrieked as the 'blade' seemed to imbed in her chest, reeling backwards. Such an attack could induce heart failure, and as she reeled, clutching at her chest, he thought for a second it might work. But all it purchased was a moment in which he put himself between her and the twins again. The giantess swiped away the blade, the illusion winked out and her amber eyes locked on his. Something like words rasped from her bestial maw as she bunched her muscles to leap at him again.

Then with a smash that filled the air with billowing dust and shook the floor like an earthquake, half the ceiling dropped on her head.

*

The door and walls were giving way and Hanook looked shattered. The ceiling above was beginning to crumble from the shapechanger's assault and Ramita could feel Huriya's mind inside her own: *Sister*, she was calling, *do not fear. I have come to help you.*

What makes her think I'm that stupid?

The twins' voices below were tearing at her and when she looked down, she could see the huge beast-women beginning to clamber towards a defiant Alaron. She did the only thing she could think of: she used Earth-gnosis to collapse the floor onto the head of the wolf-woman and used kinesis to ride it down as it dropped.

She felt rather than heard the woman's cry as she was crushed beneath the tiles.

Hanook fell with her, keeping his balance with surprising grace. Even as the floor shattered on impact, she was spinning to face Alaron, who was surrounded by fragments of stone and wood and plaster, all hanging in the air about him as his shields protected him and those behind him.

Ramita heard herself wail with desperate elation as she launched herself at the twins, lying in the dust behind Alaron and screeching for her.

She was sobbing deliriously, the boys in her arms, when Alaron regained her attention. 'Hey!' he shouted, 'Ramita, we've got to move.' He pulled Nasatya from her reluctant grasp. 'Come on!'

'Shukriya, Al'Rhon bhaiya,' she babbled, overcome with relief. 'Thank you so much!'

He saved my babies . . .

It took a few seconds for her to push her emotions aside and realise again what was happening. The rumbles and crashes from every direction told her the building was being torn apart from all sides as Huriya and her Dokken tried to reach them. Some still hammered on the door to the room above, where they'd been until she collapsed the floor. Then she noticed the poor ayah was lying by the crushed wolf-woman, her head almost torn off. She clutched Dasra to her. 'Dear gods . . .' she whispered, utterly appalled.

'We must escape,' Hanook said, composed again. 'Follow me!' He led them through the scullery and out into the kitchens, then down the corridor beyond. When she turned to the stairs leading up, the vizier gripped her arm. 'No,' he said, 'we must go the other way.' He looked Ramita in the eye. 'To the palace.'

From above, the sound of a door splintering jolted through them.

'Of course,' she replied, wondering if even the mughal's soldiers could protect them. They hurried after the vizier, Alaron taking the rear. He had Nas clasped to his chest, a satchel over his shoulder and his staff in one hand. His sword appeared to have been lost.

They took us utterly unprepared, she thought, shuddering. *It is a miracle we are still alive.*

They hurried after Hanook through the silent halls of the servants' quarters. Though they saw no one, they could hear voices: the screaming echoed down through the whole level. 'My people,' Hanook gasped, 'they're being slaughtered—' For a moment he was overcome, but then he shook his head and set his jaw. 'We must see you safe, Lady. *Come!*'

Hanook led them to the same hidden door he'd taken Ramita through before, to meet the mughal. He opened it with a gesture, and after they'd entered, sealed it behind them. He turned to Ramita and Alaron, his face almost preternaturally calm. 'Lady, you know the way.' He pulled a key from around his neck – the one that opened the door at the other end of the tunnel – and gave it to her.

'No,' she protested, 'you *must* come too.'

The vizier shook his head. 'They will find this door and they will break it down in seconds if there is no one to maintain the wards. The tunnel is only half a mile long, and they can move much faster than us. Someone has to remain to slow them down.'

Ramita and Alaron stared at him. Then Alaron, his face utterly white, took a step forward. 'Then I will do it, sir. You are too valuable.'

She felt her heart thud with terror at the thought of losing him.

Hanook shook his head. 'No, young man, I am old, and you have all your life.' He turned back to the door with a grim look on his face. 'And you have reasons to live. They killed mine.'

Ramita seized his hand and kissed it. 'I wish we could have had more time.'

'I too, widow of my grandfather. I too.' He smoothed her hair affectionately. 'Now go.'

Huriya stalked the vizier's palace in absolute rage while her remaining kindred, while seeking the fugitives, wrecked everything they could lay their hands on. The servants were all dead now, their souls gone to replenishing the pack's gnosis, but she was furious with the surviving pack-members, and she made sure they knew it.

How could they have escaped? Those outside had seen nothing – no shutter or outside door had been breached. She was shaking with anger, so livid she could barely think. *We've lost more than a dozen in here, and they've still escaped!*

'Huriya,' Malevorn Andevarion called to her.

She whirled to face him and spat venomously at him. 'What is it, you slugskin *bakrichod*?'

He didn't flinch. 'You're wasting time and effort: they've gone to earth – literally! It's the only place they could have gone: downwards. Bring all the pack downstairs and look there. There must be an escape tunnel.'

Her rage boiled, but she had to admit he was making sense. And there were soldiers outside now, with archers and spearmen. Those of the pack who'd been stationed out in the plaza had been driven inside and a full-on assault was inevitable.

'Very well. Do it!' She turned, seeking Wornu and Hessaz, and found them timidly hovering in her wake. Their usual bravado had been completely undone by the terror of facing actual, real magi.

'Get everyone down here,' she ordered them. 'Look for a tunnel!'

Malevorn dared to speak to her again. 'Free my gnosis,' he pleaded. 'I'm one of you now.'

She whirled on him and stabbed a finger. 'I still don't know if we even need you, Inquisitor! Perhaps your soul might better serve us as food after all?'

'Oh, fuck off, Seeress,' he sneered. 'Impressed with your kin? Half of them can't even shield while casting another spell. Even the most incompetent novice ever – *Alaron bloody Mercer* – has been carving them up like *humans*!'

It felt too much like truth. 'We're doing our best! Bu—'

'Your best? Well, *bravo*, you! Don't you see? You people aren't anywhere near as powerful as you think you are. You're only up against some street-girl and Alaron *fucking* Mercer and you still lost!' He jabbed his finger into her chest. 'You *need* me, Huriya. I'll swear any oath you like, just for Kore's sake, free my gnosis!'

'For *Kore's* sake?' That word killed any momentary temptation she had felt. 'How can I trust any oath you might swear to your false gods, Inquisitor? Come with me!'

Malevorn threw up his hands in utter disgust and fury and stormed away. But he didn't go far, instead hovering like a moth about her fire. She summoned the pack with her mind and set them, yammering in frustration and fear, to scouring the lower floors.

Yet it was still Malevorn who found the secret entrance, even without the gnosis. He pointed a finger at a blank wall and said, 'There.'

'There?'

He ran his mailed hands over it, his eyes closed, and grunted in satisfaction. 'Arcanum training, Huriya: they teach us to penetrate illusions, even if your gnosis is blinded to them. You close off your senses and use touch alone, filtering out all other senses.' He reached out and seized her hand, then pressed it to the blank door. It encountered a door knob she could not see. 'Feel that? Hidden by illusion, but it's there.'

She scowled and wrenched her hand away, then glared up at him. He looked so smugly knowing that she wanted to slap him – but he'd found what they sought. *Kraderz and Darice are dead. Wornu is broken. I'm surrounded by beasts and idiots. And him.*

Still she shrank from trusting him. Instead, she turned to the blank wall and wiped away the illusion. The door appeared, and wards immediately sprang into life around it. Even though she battered at them with all her power, she could feel them being renewed, and then she sensed another presence on the other side.

Someone is there, waiting for us.

Fear of what Dareem had almost done to her made her flinch and step back. She glanced at Malevorn, knowing that he could most likely have the door down in seconds, but it was fear of that very competence that continued to hold her back.

Let them do it, she thought. She turned to the pack. 'Tear it down.'

37

Without the Gnosis

The Scytale of Corineus

After the Ascension and the overthrow of Rym, Baramitius gradually retired from public life. But he emerged in the later years of his life to present Emperor Sertain with the Scytale of Corineus, which preserved the secrets of the Rite of Ascendancy. The Scytale is the greatest treasure of the empire, worth more than every ounce of gold and every gem ever to be found on Urte. It is the greatest gift a ruler has ever received.

THE ANNALS OF PALLAS

Baramitius was, to all intents and purposes, the world's most celebrated drug-pedlar, a man for whom no amount of suffering was too great a price to pay for knowledge – provided someone else did the suffering for him.

ANTONIN MEIROS, HEBUSALIM, 793

Teshwallabad, Lakh, on the continent of Antiopia
Rami (Septinon) 929
15th month of the Moontide

Alaron hurried along the tunnel, lighting the way with a gnosis-light affixed to his staff. Nasatya was cradled in one arm and the satchel containing the Scytale and his notes was slapping against his thigh. How on Urte he was going to be able to fight when burdened like this he didn't know.

Better hope I don't have to.

Ramita followed, rattling off prayers under her breath. She'd been teary-eyed since Hanook's decision to remain behind, but she was holding together, and her gnostic aura was formidably bright. Then they heard the first beasts, howling in the tunnel behind them, and he thought of Hanook, his serene and kindly face, his intelligence and wisdom.

Ramita's face was stricken.

'Did we do right?' he asked, slapping the satchel holding the Scytale. 'Should we have told him?'

She shook her head. 'I don't know.'

'Can you run?'

The brick tunnel was well-made, square-cornered and fairly straight. Alaron kicked into a trot, and Ramita tried too, though she wasn't a natural runner and the heavy gem-encrusted sari impeded her movements and left her gasping for air after just a few seconds. And the twins were a burden to both of them, awkwardly heavy and thrashing about. They were covering ground, but Alaron was increasingly frightened that they weren't going anywhere near fast enough. Then they rounded a gentle bend, and he saw light at the end of the tunnel.

Ramita cried out in hope—

— and from behind them came an echoing cry, the many-throated voices of the pack, boiling after them like rats along a flooding drain. He threw a glance over his shoulder and saw low shapes bounding into view. 'Run! Run! For Kore's sake,' move!'

He let Ramita pass so he could guard her back, loping behind her with his every instinct screaming in warning. Every glimpse behind showed the beasts getting closer. He realised it was his turn to do as Hanook had done: to sacrifice himself so that she could go on. He grabbed Ramita's shoulder. 'Listen, you've got to—'

She immediately understood – and refused. 'No! No more! We stay together!' Her face was adamant, freezing his protests. 'Together, bhaiya!' She stepped past him, faced the darkness and reached for Earth-gnosis, and he understood immediately what she was trying to do, but unlike at the palace, with its clear layout, she was unsure how to proceed. He linked hands with her and used mysticism to link their minds, and her eyes widened as she felt his gnosis link to hers.

<See?>

He pulled her awareness with him, and suddenly the earthworks above began to reveal themselves. He could see the pressure points and the buttresses. This wasn't something he could sustain for long – he was only a quarter-blood – but then her strength came in behind him, dwarfing him, and he rode that wave, expanding their awareness together.

<There! And there! See?>

She called amber-coloured gnosis to her hands and sent it into the roof of the tunnel. He provided the guidance, she the raw powerand with the two of them working as one, as the amber light surged upwards. He shielded his mind– her strength scared him, and he couldn't help feeling like an egg in her grasp. She dropped his hand and snapped, 'Now we run again!'

The snarling, yowling beasts got closer and closer and he looked back again as the pack reached the spot where they'd paused, barely sixty yards away. Their eyes and teeth were gleaming in the lamplight and their howls echoed, savage and unearthly in the confined space.

'*Now!*'

Malevorn ran in the wake of the barking, yelping brutes, counting as he went. Huriya had only sixteen of the pack left. *Sixteen.* There were a few more of them outside in the street, perhaps, but more than thirty had entered the vizier's palace and now half were dead – at the hands of four enemy magi. He was grudgingly impressed. *Damn you, Mercer. I didn't think you capable.*

Without access to the gnosis running in chainmail was hard, and it made him realise how much he depended upon his magic in all he did. There was a silent place inside his skull which had always been pumping energy to his limbs, or drawing information from all about him. Now the silence inside was deafening and deadening.

Huriya did not deign to run: she floated beside him, sparing her little legs but burning gnosis like lamp-oil. *Yes, run through all your energy, little princess. Then you'll be helpless and I'll snap your neck.*

The pack stormed along the tunnel ahead of them both, their calls louder and more eager—

—until he heard a violent *crack!* that reverberated through the enclosed space. He was an Earth-mage and recognised it instantly, even without his gnosis.

He stopped dead, grabbed the startled Lakh girl and threw them both to the ground, then he rolled so that she was on top, because if one of them was going to die it might as well be her. With a roar, the lights vanished and the tunnel before them filled with noise and dust and the screams of those who had gone before them.

His luck held: they were outside the main collapse. Huriya shielded them, keeping rocks as big as their bodies from crushing them, and his last sight before all light vanished was of her face above his, her eyes filled with so much hate and fear it paralysed him in the darkness.

Alaron stared at Ramita as the roof collapsed. Her mind was still fused with his and he could feel her emotions as if they were his own: protective fear for the twins and for him, and absolute determination not to be taken. Her almost savage will to survive was tempered only by her cool practicality.

She was staring at him with glowing eyes, seeing more than just his physical form. 'Sivraman,' she breathed. 'You are my Sivraman.' She was trembling with primal ferocity.

He fell utterly in love. Her face, full of protective fire, was instantly imprinted onto his soul for all time.

Then dust engulfed them as they clung together, using Air-gnosis to call fresh air to keep them alive for the coming moment. They bowed together, turned away from the onrush of dirt and dust, shielding as they pulled all the air they could into a tiny bundle of space containing the two of them and their tiny shrieking burdens. Linked still, she fed more power into the shields, and once again her sheer strength awed him. He wondered how she could possibly be so

728

strong – it was as if she was made of the same stuff as the rock beneath their feet.

They clung together and weathered the storm of dust and debris until, gradually, it ebbed and they could dimly sense the lamp they had been making for. Wrapped in their bubble of air, they began to edge forward. The twins were kept from full-blown panic only by Ramita's use of mystic-gnosis to calm them. He pulled energy from everywhere as they went: Air-gnosis to breathe, Earth- and sylvan-gnosis to solidify the roof above, healing for scratches and cuts, even divination, to predict any incoming threats. There were holes in the roof from the collapse, even the dim light shone from the moon shining through the dust, and distant shouts from the street above, fearful or in pain. He could not even begin to imagine what damage they'd wrought up there. The air wasn't good, but it was enough, and they staggered onwards, retching and spitting out dust, until they emerged into the golden haze of a glowing lamp before a door. His eyes were streaming, but his heart was dancing.

I will do anything to see her safe.

Ramita produced the key and unlocked the door, they stumbled through and she shut it on the thick dust swirling behind them. He caught his breath and inhaled the wondrously clean air. 'We did it,' he gasped. He reached for more gnosis to lock the door.

And found nothing.

What? He clutched at his periapt and tried again.

Ramita saw his bewilderment and patted his arm. 'Calm, bhaiya. I have been here before. This palace has a barrier that prevents use of the gnosis.'

'What?' he asked, astonished. 'How?'

'Something my husband devised, to protect the mughals from the magi. Hanook brought me this way when we met with Tariq.' She walked to the next door and pulled a bell-rope. 'We must gain entrance to the palace. I fear that Huriya will still find a way to reach us.'

'Your *sister* is here?'

'*Adopted* sister,' she corrected curtly. 'I saw her during the attack.'

'Then it's the same group who attacked us at the Isle?' Alaron was astonished. 'They've chased us a long way.'

Ramita was cooing in Dasra's ear and he tended to Nasatya, stroking his head and sending soothing thoughts. The baby stopped wailing, looked up at him with wide, serious eyes.

Don't fear, little one. I'll protect you.

At last a panel opened in the inner door and a man spoke in Lakh. Ramita stood, faced the panel and bowed slightly as she answered. A few words passed back and forth, then the door opened. An impressively attired guardsman admitted them to another room beyond: a hall of white marble, with a balcony above.

Ramita touched his arm, pointed. 'Archers,' she whispered.

He looked up and saw the dozens of slots in the stonework, and the arrowheads that tracked them around the room.

He instinctively went to shield, then remembered that he couldn't. 'What's happening?' he asked her, trying to silence the bell of joy he felt just from looking at her.

'I've told them something terrible has happened,' she replied. 'Mughal Tariq is coming himself, to hear our story.'

He exhaled heavily. 'Well, he better not take too long. And tell them to guard that door.'

When the dust settled, they were still alive, alone in the darkness. For no good reason Malevorn reached up and kissed Huriya's mouth. Despite being only a Noorie, she tasted like any other girl, until she bit his lip so badly his mouth was filled with blood and he could barely think past the pain.

'Do you think you're funny, slugskin?' She pushed off him, kindling gnosis-light. When he tried to rise, she slammed him back onto the rubble-strewn ground hard enough to wind him. 'Stay there, bakrichod.'

'What's a bakrichod?' he asked as he gasped for breath in the choking dust.

'It's Lakh for goat-fucker, which is what you are, slugskin. Don't touch me without permission.' She climbed into a shaft of light that coated her in silver like one of Kore's angels descended from on high, then he realised it was just moonlight, pouring from a long rift in the roof of the tunnel that reached the surface.

He wiped the blood from his mouth and sat up. The lure of the Scytale was goading him on, despite all the loathing for felt for his enforced companions. As Huriya climbed the rubble he staggered upright and went after her.

Every second revealed more of what had happened: the tunnel roof had collapsed – probably brought down by Mercer or his Lakh bint – and most of the remaining pack-members had been right under it. He wondered if any still lived. They emerged into the moonlight to find that the tunnel had been following the route of a street, presumably to avoid the weight of buildings above.

As he watched, the rubble about him shook, and suddenly Wornu emerged, half-mad and roaring in bewildered rage. Hessaz followed him, shrieking triumphantly at still being alive. Both were caked in dust and blood and looked ready to tear apart the rest of the city in vengeance. Half a dozen other mounds slowly rose and hands started clawing a way to the surface. An animagus was usually also an Earthmage, so the capacity of the shifters to survive such an attack did not altogether surprise him. But there had been sixteen Dokken in the tunnel, and only seven emerged from the rubble.

He joined Huriya and she called the rest of the pack, those who'd stayed outside the vizier's palace to keep the soldiers out. A dozen winged shapes flapped down and joined them. He scanned the area, seeking their prey. The whole of the street running from the vizier's palace visible at the far end to the glowing Dome of the Mughal's Palace towering above was in a state of semi-collapse. Bells were ringing and torches flaring on the battlements. To the left and right he could see people peering from ruined houses, and even as he watched, more came down, amidst screams from those trapped within.

'Brethren!' Huriya called to the pack as they settled about her. She gestured furiously towards the Mughal's Dome. 'We must go on! The prize is here, right before us. We have lost many, but the ultimate goal is in reach and we *must not* flinch now!'

He half-expected that they would tell her to piss off, that nothing was worth the trail of death she had led them to, but he underestimated the depth of longing the Dokken felt to escape their condition, for they obeyed instantly. Huriya looked back at him, at Wornu and Hessaz and the few left from the tunnel collapse who were fit to go on. 'Come!' she shouted at them, her eyes ablaze. She looked deranged to his eyes, unhinged, a figure of Lantric myth come to life: Luna, the Mad Queen of Heaven.

But Mercer is here, and so is the Scytale.

He found himself clambering through the rubble in the pack's wake.

Ramita placed Dasra against the wall and Alaron put Nasatya beside him, then they both stood. She looked at the staff he carried and murmured that he should leave it by the wall as well. 'There are archers, and it is a weapon,' she told him. She wanted to take the young Rondian mage's hand and ask him what he'd seen in her face just before, for something had blazed through him like wildfire. But there was no time.

Before Alaron could discard the staff, the far doors flew open and half a dozen soldiers strode through, tall lean men with immaculate moustaches and silk uniforms, armed with gilded spears and gleaming sword-hilts. After the terrifying Souldrinkers, these men looked like toy soldiers, and about as threatening. But the shaven-skulled bodyguard Kindu was with them, and he looked like someone who could rip up trees. Then the young mughal himself appeared, and she fell to her knees, because Tariq had to do exactly as she needed and she couldn't afford him to stall over protocol. She tugged at Alaron's knee, but he remained standing, his face pale and truculent.

'Please, Al'Rhon!' she hissed softly. 'We need his help!'

Reluctantly, the Rondian youth dropped to one knee, his look making it clear it was only because she asked him to. He placed the staff on the floor at his own feet. They were both caked in dust and dried blood, him in a tunic and breeches, her in the ruined sari. *We must look like beggars.*

'Lady Ramita?' Tariq looked severely put out. He was dressed in a red turban and an ivory and gold coat that glowed in the lamplight, but they were rumpled, as if he'd just thrown them on. Maybe he'd been asleep, or frolicking with his pretty little wives. There was no fondness in his face for her. At his shoulder was a white-robed man with a long curling grey beard and a face like iron: the Amteh Godspeaker Vahraz, already whispering in his ear.

'What are you doing here, Lady? Where is Vizier Hanook?'

Her voice caught as she replied, 'Exalted Lord, your vizier is dead.'

Tariq went pale, his hand going to his mouth. 'Dead?'

Behind him, Godspeaker Vahraz's face lit up.

'He was murdered. His house was attacked. Only we escaped, with these two' – Ramita thought swiftly as she indicated the twins – 'infants from the nursery.'

Tariq barely registered her words, for he had just realised that the man with Ramita was white. 'Rondian?' he gasped.

The word was universal.

Alaron raised a defiant head. 'Noroman,' he said. 'And a mage.' He picked up the staff and stood, and the tension in the room redoubled. Ramita wavered between pulling him back to his knees or standing: she chose to rise also.

Tariq probably understood only one of the four words Alaron had said: *mage*. He swallowed, while his six soldiers aligned their spears protectively about their ruler. Ramita realised that everyone here knew of the wards that suppressed the gnosis. They knew that she and Alaron were helpless.

'Why is a Rondian mage here, Lady?' Tariq demanded, clearly on the point of ordering his men to attack. Vahraz plucked at his sleeve but he ignored the Godspeaker, staring at Alaron in fascination.

'He is a Zain novice. He is not a Crusader.'

'A Zain?' Tariq's eyebrows shot up. 'A Rondian mage sworn to the Zains?' His voice was incredulous.

'Yes, Exalted Lord. He is protecting me. I trust him with my life.'

The Godspeaker whispered urgently in Tariq's ear and the mughal said, 'Godspeaker Vahraz reminds me that any magus discovered in my lands must instantly be put to death.'

'But he is my protector,' Ramita protested.

'That might mitigate his punishment in Shaitan's demesne,' Vahraz replied coldly, looking down at her with chilling eyes. He turned to Tariq. 'Who is this woman?'

Tariq hesitated as the deeper implications of Hanook's death struck him. 'Where is Dareem?' he asked her, lifting a hand to Godspeaker Vahraz to forestall answering his question.

Ramita bowed her head as she felt the threads of Hanook's plans come apart. 'I believe he is also dead, Exalted Lord,' she said in a small voice.

The triumph that flared in Godspeaker Vahraz's eyes was perhaps the most hateful thing she had seen that night. Alaron saw it too, and his jaw hardened. He stared along the spear-shafts pointed at him with a fatalistic fearlessness that scared her.

'Do nothing,' she begged him, in Rondian. 'Please, do nothing.'

'Who is she?' Vahraz persisted, eyeing Ramita with distaste, seeing her dark skin, grimed with dust and sweat. 'What is a half-dressed peasant girl doing in this place?'

She looked up at Tariq and realised that their lives were in the fourteen-year-old's hands. *If he tells him, without Hanook to protect us, they're going to kill us both.*

Alaron could see it too, judging by the way his hand changed grip on the staff. Sudden violence lurked in everyone's stance.

Only an Ascendant can use the gnosis here, Hanook had told her. *But I'm even stronger than that, as my husband said I would be.* She dropped her eyes and reached inside herself.

It was hard, like trying to dive deeply into water when your lungs were already bursting, but it was there, suppressed by the wards that had been built into the bones of the building – but she could reach her powers if she had to. She looked up again, the realisation that she wasn't helpless after all thrilling through her.

The young mughal's eyes met hers. Without Hanook to champion her, it came down to his desire for a mage-bride against his fear of the

Godspeakers. He made the answer clear with his next words. 'This is the widow of Antonin Meiros,' he said in a disdainful voice. His eyes trailed to the twins beside the wall. 'And it would not surprise me if those brats are his.'

Godspeaker Vahraz's mouth went round in surprise and excitement. This would surely be the coup of a career, to be the one who condemned Lady Meiros to death for her sins. 'She must go on trial,' he announced triumphantly. 'Arrest them!'

Alaron rose and stepped in front of her, his kon-staff gripped firmly and his pale face full of desperate courage. She reached for the gnosis, through the oppressive wards . . .

Despite his belief that she and Alaron were unable to reach the gnosis, Tariq stepped back timidly and let the six spearmen close ranks before him. From above she heard a dozen bows creak as they were bent.

Then there came a great *boom!* that reverberated through the open door behind her, a blow upon the outside door, and it splintered with a deafening crack. That sound was still echoing through the chamber as a jackal howled.

Huriya sent her kindred along the line of the collapsed tunnel while she flew behind them, careless now of who saw them. Though both were wounded, Wornu and Hessaz led the way. To her eyes, Wornu was being pulled along in Hessaz's wake, his spirit crushed by his failure in the fight against Dareem.

Malevorn Andevarion still followed her, blood trickling from his mouth where she had bitten him – the least the chodia deserved for his temerity. She just wished one or two of the pack had even half his skill and nerve.

Those few citizens stupid enough to get in the way were battered aside by the remaining pack members – just a dozen of them – storming along the collapsed street, seeking a way back into the tunnel beyond the rockfall. Soldiers began to appear on all sides, but they backed away at the sight of the beasts – and more especially at her, gliding through the air aglow with the gnosis.

They found another hole, about eighty yards short of the palace walls. The pack milled about, snarling at the soldiers and keeping them at bay. The bells still rang from all around as the temples and Dom-al'Ahms awoke to the calamity. Growing crowds of people were emerging to aid the trapped and injured.

'Down, down,' Huriya shouted, 'into the tunnel!'

'Huriya,' Malevorn interjected, 'leave some up here, to keep our exit clear. Otherwise we could be trapped below.'

Would that leave enough to capture Ramita and her Rondian? Huriya bit her lip, then nodded. She grabbed Wornu's shoulder. 'Leave four up here, Wornu – they must hold this exit. Take the rest below. I'll be with you.'

The massive packleader bellowed orders while beside him Hessaz was testing the pull of a bow she'd come across somewhere. She went to follow her mate down into the darkness, but Malevorn stopped her. 'We'll need an archer up here,' he snapped. 'You'll have no field of fire below.'

The Lokistani woman glowered at him, but he was right again. 'Do as he says,' Huriya ordered.

The two women glared at each other for a second, then Hessaz grimaced sourly and took up a stance beside the hole. 'Do not forget to return for us,' she snarled through gritted teeth.

Huriya tried to reassure her. 'We will prevail.' *I need her, she's the only competent woman I have.*

Hessaz met her eyes, then leant forward and whispered in her ear. 'Wornu is a broken vessel: widow me.'

They shared a look of understanding, then the Lokistani woman nocked an arrow and with her fellows, faced the gathering crowds. Huriya turned and glided down into the tunnel in the wake of Wornu and his group. The passage was still intact here, leading to a doorway lit by a single oil-lamp. The pack members slavered and whined, while Wornu dithered. 'Is it warded?' he asked, as if he had no means to work it out himself.

Hessaz is right: he's lost his nerve.

She pushed through the dozen pack-members and laid her palm

against the door. Extending her senses, she found nothing: no wards – just a dulled absence that was puzzling ... but there was no time to contemplate it, so she shrugged it off. *If it's a trap, it's a trap. The Scytale lies beyond.*

'Break it down,' she told them.

'Use that fallen beam as a ram,' Malevorn suggested in his coolly detached voice, and yet again the packmates muttered and growled, then did his bidding. Trying to reassert himself, Wornu organised the ramming, taking the lead as they hefted the beam. The rest lengthened their claws and teeth or cradled their weapons, preparing to pour through as soon as the door was breached.

She had thought it might need several blows, but it took just one. Fuelled by raw strength and the gnosis, the beam smashed the door to kindling and those who had wielded the ram dropped it and staggered through the opening. Beyond she glimpsed a small room, an open door and a larger space, but that was all there was time to see before Wornu roared and led the warriors of the pack through and into the fray. She let them go until there was only the Inquisitor left beside her. He drew the scimitar she had given him.

'Another kiss for luck?' he asked archly, licking his torn lip.

'You push your luck, slugskin. Get in there and die.'

He gave an ironic bow as the first cries of battle welled back to their ears, then followed the Dokken into battle.

Alaron never took his eyes from the six spears thrust in his direction, not until each one wavered and the eyes of the soldiers went to the commotion behind him. Then he moved, stepped back and sideways, out of thrust distance, and pulled Ramita towards the twins, trying to shield her with his body as he went. Ramita's face looked like she was caught up in some kind of inner struggle; it reminded him of how she had looked in early labour ... or straining to use a gnostic skill. But there was no time to consider it further: the archers on the opposite balcony above were standing and taking aim at them – then a burst of dust and splinters preceded a flood of shapechangers into the chamber.

The first man through was massive, six foot and more with the build of a wrestler – but he had the head of a bull, complete with a pair of thick horns, and he held a giant war-spear in his hands. Behind him came more giants, the largest of the Dokken in semi-human forms of varying horror, and all of them were roaring and snarling—

—and changing.

Alaron realised instantly what was happening; not only was the gnosis that supported the Souldrinkers' shapes being negated, but they were being stripped of their shielding wards. He saw fangs and nails shorten and bestial faces begin to turn more human – and it was hurting them too, warping their bodies as their shapes altered.

The charge faltered.

Someone above shouted, and a dozen arrows flew. Most struck Bull-Head, in his chest and belly and shoulders, and one went right through his left eye. Hammered by blow after blow, he toppled backwards, and the two behind him went down as well, yowling in disbelief. The fourth, a bat-headed man, roared in fury even as his throat changed and his enraged cry instead came out as a plaintive and very human, 'Argh!'

But still they came on, mostly men, and all naked and changing, carried by momentum into the fray. This second wave held blades and axes, boiling through the smashed door and slamming into the line of six spearmen.

But one of the Dokken came straight for Alaron: a man his own height, yowling as his flesh and bones warped and ran like melted wax. A horrific visage like a burn victim tried to reform into something more human even as he swung a curved sword at Alaron's neck. Alaron blocked with the kon-staff, then launched into the sort of counter-attack he and Yash had practised so often: low with the left and dashing the other's blade aside, then up at the right, slamming the iron-shod heel of the staff at the bewildered Dokken's temple.

He struck flesh and bone and felt it cave in as the man toppled. More arrows flew, though now the spearmen were engaged, the archers had fewer clear targets. The doorway continued to disgorge

Dokken, all reeling in pain at the changes wrought upon them and gradually becoming human again, even as death rained down.

'Alaron!' Ramita shouted in his ear. She was shielding the wailing twins with her body. 'Which way?'

'Further in,' he shouted back, pointing to the double doors through which the mughal had entered. The ruler of Lakh was backing towards them even now, with the Godspeaker, and the shaven-headed bodyguard was shielding them both. 'That way!'

Another Dokken came at him, a wiry man with a sword; he battered the man's blade aside almost effortlessly, then slammed the staff into his nose. Bone and cartilage crunched, and blood erupted in an arc as the man went over backwards. He didn't get up. Alaron saw two spearmen impale another Dokken, but then one of them was overborne and had his head smashed in with a hatchet. Kindu the bodyguard hacked at the back of the victorious Dokken's neck, almost decapitating him. More arrows whistled around them, shaving his cheek and slicing a gash in his shoulder.

Alaron turned to warn Ramita . . .

. . . as blue light flashed around her and an arrow broke on her wards.

'The gnosis?' He reached inside, but he could still feel nothing.

'I can reach it!' Ramita shouted. 'Just a little!'

He suddenly had hope again.

A tall shape entered the fray behind the Dokken: the Keshi mercenary he'd glimpsed at Hanook's mansion – but then he looked again, and almost dropped his staff.

Malevorn Andevarion.

He felt a choked cry leave his lips as his Arcanum nemesis darted sideways to avoid the arrows from above, then launched himself at a spearman.

Ramita pulled at Alaron's sleeve, dragging him with her, and he let her. She had to be his first concern. They were beneath one balcony, their backs to the wall so the archers above their heads could not see them, but the ones opposite were now beginning to concentrate their fire on Ramita, as if her wards drew their hatred. She was coping, but the strain of reaching her gnosis in this place was clearly showing.

Then another girl stepped into the maelstrom, a tiny keshi, with a curvaceous body and a seductive face that was contorted with blood lust. He recognised her from the Isle of Glass, and from Ramita's stories: Huriya Makani, her lifelong friend, her blood-sister – and now her bitterest enemy. The air about the Keshi girl was alive with glimmering light and distorted air. *She can reach the gnosis too . . .*

With a look of utter disdain, Huriya raised both her hands and made a vicious cutting gesture. Coruscating light blazed in every colour, like twin rainbows being born in her hands, and ignited over the balconies with dazzling light. The archers opposite Alaron's position threw up their hands as their retinas were all but burned out.

Huriya's eyes swivelled and found Ramita. '*Blood-sister! Stay right there!*'

Malevorn ploughed into the mêlée, leaping at a spearman who'd just skewered one of the pack. With his spear jammed in the Souldrinker's body, the guardsman was helpless and Malevorn severed his hand, then whipped the blade across his neck, splitting the leather throat protector and laying his jugular open. Blood gushed, and the man went down.

Even as he did this, Malevorn could feel something strange inside, like a bubble bursting. It felt like an enchantment failing, but the only enchantment on him was Huriya's Chain-rune, and when he tried to reach the gnosis there was nothing there. There was no time to explore this mystery; two spearmen had just gutted another Souldrinker and were turning on him.

The pair thrust simultaneously, trying to leave him no room to parry or dodge, but they were ponderous movers and he was already gone, swaying to one side then leaping in as they tried to adjust to his position. He blinded one with a slash across the eyes, kicking him aside even as he caught the other's spear-shaft with his left hand. The man failed to react quickly enough, presenting an easy thrust to the throat. Three down in three heartbeats. The Dokken had slain another and now the remaining two spearmen blanched and gave ground, stumbling through the tangle of dead and dying. Blood was running everywhere, making the tiles slick and treacherous. The pack were almost all slain, shot down from above, mostly, only a handful still able to fight. Another went down to the shaven-headed man's massive sword. Behind him, the richly dressed boy – the mughal, he presumed, with a grim-faced man who must be a Godspeaker – reached the doors.

He heard screams from above and guessed Huriya had dealt with the archers. No further bowstrings thrummed. The combat was thinning out, allowing him to look left, then right, at—

Alaron Mercer!

He shouted a war-cry and raised his sword as Mercer lifted a staff of all things to block him. But the Lakh bint behind Mercer moved faster, and an unseen blow to the chest cracked his ribs and sent him skidding across the room, air belching from his lungs. He thudded into the far wall, gasping for breath.

Holy Kore!

Now he remembered: at the island, this girl had skewered a fully shielded Inquisitor with a thrown mast. Counting himself lucky to still be alive, he staggered to his feet. Mercer was across the room now, and holding off a Dokken who'd snatched up one of the guardsmen's spears. The boy-mughal had reached the doors leading deeper into the palace, but the Godspeaker was already gone, leaving his ruler behind. Bells were clamouring from within.

Huriya gestured, and the doors slammed shut in the young mughal's face, making him wail in terror, then she launched some kind of illusion and mesmerism attack at the Lakh girl – *Ramita*, that was her name. The Lakh girl was struggling too, half her mage-bolts going astray as if she were befuddled. But those which did strike home were bizarrely strong, making Huriya's wards crackle red at the stress. Malevorn would have happily seen either or both go down.

He lurched to his feet, still struggling to breathe, and looked up. The archers were obviously blinded and out of the game – in fact, so was almost everyone in the room. The remaining spearman went down under three Dokken, who all had weapons now. One of the shapeshifters went for the mughal, but was cut almost in half by the giant bodyguard. The hammering on the inner doors suggested reinforcements were imminent. Mercer was still on his feet, warding off a Dokken warrior with surprising skill using just a wooden staff, but he wasn't using the gnosis, so something was definitely happening here; there was some reason why all the Dokken were fighting in human shape ...

But before he'd fully grasped the thought it was swept away as his eyes fell upon the satchel Mercer was wearing: a leather bag, from which poked the top of a scroll-case.

The Scytale? It must be!

He gripped his scimitar anew and charged.

38

A Child's Life

The Value of Life

There is no greater glory than to hold your child close to you, basking in the unconditional love the child feels for you, and to return that a thousandfold. How could I deny myself such a moment in my life?

SISTER MYRETTA OF DELPH, DISGRACED KORE NUN, 872

The price of a life? Why, the same as the value of anything else: whatever you can get for it on the day!

KANN BENTYK, VERELONI SLAVE-TRADER, 911

Teshwallabad, Lakh, on the continent of Antiopia
Rami (Septinon) 929
15th month of the Moontide

<You're weak, Bloodsister. Yield, before I really hurt you.>

Huriya's contempt echoed inside Ramita's head as she staggered backwards, barely able to focus on the blinding lights and mesmeric words that were freezing her brain. She felt her will to fight, to resist at all, wavering as Huriya drove her backwards towards Tariq, who was huddling beside the big doors.

Then the screaming of her children made her focus: they were right behind her, flailing about blindly. She tried to counter again, throwing another bolt of energy, the best she could muster, but Huriya's mental attacks pounded into her head, disorienting her, and she missed again. Terrified one of her wayward blasts would strike Alaron

743

by accident, she abruptly stopped firing and instead concentrated on her defences.

Her vision cleared: Alaron was fighting in the centre of the room, using the staff like a Zain monk, a blur of movement and balletic poise she'd never have thought him capable of. He hammered another blow into the midriff of his attacker, leaving the Dokken dazed. But Huriya was edging closer to her, webs of light in her hand.

<Where can you run, 'Mita? There's nowhere I cannot find you.>

Ramita suspected that only the inhibited gnostic use in the chamber had kept her alive. It wasn't that Huriya was stronger than her – she wasn't – but she had found herself unable to strike whole-heartedly at her Bloodsister. Some part of her still wanted to believe that they were, deep down, still the some girls who had grown up together and had sworn everlasting friendship. Then her heel struck one of the twins and she realised there was nowhere else to go.

She played her last trick. As she stepped from beneath the end of the balcony she blazed Earth-gnosis into the balcony above Huriya's head and with a great crack, the stone gave way and rained down upon her head, along with half the blinded archers, who came smash-ing down in a roar of stone and dust, sending shards of stone blasting through the chamber.

Alaron's staff cracked against the temple of another Dokken who'd clearly never had his mettle honed by Yash. He stepped back and almost fell against the young mughal, who was hammering impo-tently against the doors. Someone was striking from the other side as well, but he could see blue sparks crackling around the frame, bind-ing it in place.

The big bald bodyguard swung his head and glared sternly at Alaron, but he'd evidently noted they were both fighting the same people, for he did no more than tap his own chest. 'Kindu.'

A greeting? His name? 'Alaron,' he said, tapping his own chest, then looked at the remaining four Dokken and swallowed heavily. He'd never fought more than one man at a time without the gnosis, and he doubted he had the skill. He stepped carefully out of the swing-space of Kindu's massive two-handed scimitar and looked for Malevorn. He spotted him moving towards Kindu's flank.

Huriya was advancing on Ramita when amber light flashed and the balcony collapsed. Ramita stepped out of the reach of the falling stone and with a gesture sent the twins spinning across the floor behind her. For a few seconds the Keshi girl vanished, but she staggered out into the centre of the room just a couple of seconds later, bleeding from a gashed forehead and covered in dust. She shrieked a furious command and the remaining four Dokken threw themselves at him and Kindu while behind him, the ruler of Lakh wailed fearfully.

Only one Souldrinker came at Alaron; a middle-aged man wielding a Brician longsword. He attacked cautiously, crabbing forward and lunging, then darting away, forcing Alaron to fight defensively, and though he blocked and parried furiously, he couldn't do much more than jab at his foe, coming up short each time.

The other three had gone for Kindu, the more obvious threat, who responded with a roar of his own and swung his huge cleaver in a massive arc that went straight through the wooden haft of a stolen spear and almost cut its wielder in two. But the blow had left Kindu exposed and the other two Dokken lunged in.

Kindu ducked under one thrust, produced a dagger from somewhere and buried it into the throat of the attacker, but he took the third one's sword in the side. He bellowed painfully, his limbs convulsed and he fell to one knee. His attacker rashly lunged in to finish him: Kindu caught the man's wrist and wrenched, the weapon clattered on the tiles and the pair fell into a bloody wrestling match, each holding knives, fighting to keep the other's blade at bay. Alaron tried to intervene, but his own foe lunged in again, overextending in his anxiety to protect his fellow; Alaron cracked him across the temple and dropped him – but it was at the cost of a slash to his ribcage. Blood began to soak his shirt as he turned, but too late: Malevorn reared up from behind the mughal's empty throne and thrust his blade straight-armed into Kindu's throat, even as the bodyguard plunged his own knife into his foe's chest. The guard roared, the mughal screamed and Malevorn stepped away, his face a mask of calm composure.

'I guess it's just you and me now, Mercer. Just like college. Remember?'

Alaron remembered all too well: so many beatings he could not count them; so much pain, and in all that time he'd barely landed a blow.

His legs were shaking, but he raised his staff and prepared for another round. The last one.

Malevorn came at him hard, his sword a blur as it flashed left, then right, forcing him to parry, then moving too fast to riposte – then the scimitar stabbed low inside his guard and pain knifed through his right thigh and he staggered back, hit the doors beside Ramita and almost slid down them. Red blood began to pump from his thigh, staining his leggings, while the wound in his chest seemed to be tearing wider.

Malevorn drew off, his eyes intent. Behind him, the Dokken Alaron had stunned slowly rose to his feet. In a few seconds it would be two on one. He swallowed and sought some way to live through this, some way to win.

During the breif flurry of blows, Huriya had renewed her assault on Ramita. Though her brow was cut and bleeding, she was obviously gaining the upper hand. Ramita's lack of recent training time was telling: she'd not been able to fully integrate the new configuration of her gnosis the way Alaron had and now she was huddled before her children, encased in shields that were turning scarlet and flickering. Her face was lined with strain and fear.

Then Huriya slammed Ramita aside with a casual flick of her wrist, sending her careering into Tariq, and they both fell in a heap. Alaron cried out in fear for her as the Keshi girl stepped forward, snatched up Nasatya and put a knife to the child's chest. She spoke in Rondian, presumably for Malevorn's benefit. 'Stop now! Everyone, stop!'

Ramita wailed and began to move, then froze as the knife scoured the child's chest. Alaron felt his guts churn. Malevorn stepped across and grabbed Dasra. Behind him the last of the Dokken men groaned and looked about for his weapon. Tariq whimpered and hid his face.

Kore on High! Alaron stepped in front of Ramita and raised his staff protectively, his heart thudding. 'Back off,' he warned.

Huriya gestured again, but Ramita was swift enough to lay a hand on his shoulder and held him in place, beating off Huriya's gnosis with surprising firmness. Ramita's face, after the initial panic, had gone coldly furious. 'Give me back my children,' she told the Keshi girl in a voice like stones grating together.

Huriya slowly shook her head, clasping Nasatya to her chest.

Malevorn spat a bloody wad of phlegm through his split lips. 'Mercer, the Scytale. Throw it to me.'

The door into the palace thudded suddenly, the timbers bulging and cracking, and Tariq shouted in desperate hope. Huriya scowled and reinforced her warding, but Alaron saw the blue lights of the door-wards flash through violet to red as they began to wear down. She too was almost exhausted. *A minute, maybe two, before the soldiers get in.*

Huriya had made the same calculation. She looked at Ramita menacingly, spat a curse and raised the blade. 'Five seconds, or this one dies and we take the artefact off you anyway.'

Alaron looked at Ramita. They could not communicate mentally, only by eyes, but they had been together for so long now that he could almost read her thoughts anyway. They were her children, flesh of her flesh.

Nothing is so important to her as them.

'Five.'

But the Scytale is the treasure above all treasures . . .

'Four.'

The door hammered again, harder. A battering ram. The timbers cracked and almost broke.

'Three,' Huriya went on.

Alaron tore his eyes away, then back to Ramita. She was pleading with him to do . . . *something.*

'Two.'

'All right! Okay! You can have it!' He reached down, grasped the cylinder containing the Scytale. 'You can have it. Just release the children.'

Ramita sagged with relief.

Malevorn showed him Dasra. 'All right, Mercer. Here's how we do it. I'm going to put the child down here. You can come forward, put down the Scytale and I'll take it. Then we give you the second child.' His voice was cold and hard as he placed the infant down just out of Alaron's reach.

'No. Both at once.'

Huriya snarled, 'I'll kill this one now, and then we'll see about the other! Hand over the Scytale!'

Ramita choked back a sob. Alaron raised his hand. 'Okay.' He stepped forward, scooped up Dasra and handed the child to Ramita, who made a sobbing sound and squeezed the boy to her chest. He put down the Scytale and watched mutely as Malevorn picked up the case and examined the Scytale inside. Alaron didn't expect Malevorn knew much about it, but his old antagonist sounded confident when he said to Huriya, 'This is it.'

Huriya gave a low, throaty laugh, stood and backed away, Nasatya still cradled in her arms.

Ramita stepped towards her. 'Give him to me, Sister! Please!'

The Keshi girl snickered and kept retreating, her blade still pressed to the child's chest. 'I think not, Blood-sister. I don't want you coming after me, so here's what I'll do. I'll keep hold of this one until I decide that you deserve his return.'

'Huriya, please!' Ramita fell to her knees. 'I am begging you!'

'That's all you're fit to do: grovel and beg.' Huriya's face filled with contempt. 'Beggar-girl.'

'I don't understand! I *loved* you, Sister! There was nothing I wouldn't have shared with you.'

Huriya smiled condescendingly. 'I was never who you thought, 'Mita. Sabele visited me hundreds of times through spirit-sendings, telling me all the things I could be – things so far beyond your dreams. Silly Kazim just wanted an ordinary life with you, but Sabele promised me so much more! And look, it's all coming true: I'm going to be queen of the whole world.' She kissed Nasatya's forehead. 'Don't follow me, Sister, if you ever want to see this one alive again.'

Ramita sagged, her eyes streaming. 'Mercy . . .'

With the Scytale in his hand, Malevorn brandished his blade and backed away towards the door. Huriya followed, her eyes flickering from Ramita to Alaron to the mughal.

'Exalted One,' she said to Tariq, her voice heavy with irony. 'So good to make your acquaintance.'

'Who . . . who are you?' the young man asked in a frightened voice.

Huriya laughed. 'Your next queen.' Her eyes went to Ramita. 'Don't come after us, Ramita.'

She stepped through the doorway and was gone. The half-stunned Dokken went after her, clutching at the doorway as he exited, followed by Malevorn. The young Inquisitor gave an ironic salute. 'Until next time, Mercer. If there is one.' Then he too was gone.

Tariq screamed for aid, and the inner door broke open in a crash of timber.

As he stepped through the broken door into the tunnel it took Malevorn Andevarion two seconds to realise that somehow, some way, the Chain-rune that had bound his powers was gone.

So that was what I felt when I first entered the chamber . . .

All his gnostic perceptions returned in a flood, plus another set of senses that ignited in his head: his gnosis was now finite, like a Dokken's, and it made him desperately hungry, ravenous in a way that food could never fill. He had just the tiniest reserve, the barest residue, and that for now was crucial. He ran gnosis-fire down his blade and plunged it into the back of the sole surviving Dokken. The man stiffened, groaned, and fell on his face.

Malevorn saw smoke billowing from the dead one's mouth and he bent, as he'd seen the Souldrinkers do, and inhaled it. The energy coursed straight into him and he felt that sense of hunger fade, even as he dealt with a sudden rush of images from the man's life. He blanked them, stood and twirled the Scytale. Suddenly he felt magnificent, better than at any time in his life despite the cracked ribs and cuts from the fight. He had all his old strength as a pure-blood, fully charged and brimming with vigour. He conjured wards and shields, felt his gnostic aura blaze into life around him.

Huriya had gone ahead. Now she looked back at him, her face lit by the oil lamp, and suddenly more than a little tentative. She saw. She *knew*.

You won't be kicking me around again, you Noorie slut . . .

She clutched the child to her, her pupils dilating.

'So,' he said. 'Perhaps it's time to renegotiate our relationship?'

'In what way?'

I've got the gnosis back, but I'm now a creature of anathema. I need this Scytale, to become my old self . . . No, better – an Ascendant. He recalled what Adamus Crozier had said about the Scytale of Corineus: that the artefact was not an instant answer. It required understanding and knowledge he didn't have. And he was a Souldrinker now, and the Inquisitors would kill him on sight. He needed allies . . .

Why not her?

'A new deal,' he said, looking her in the face. *Her gorgeous, hedonistic face.* 'Equals,' he said, laughing internally at the very word. *I have no equals, girl, but I'm prepared to pretend.*

'Equals?' she sneered. 'I have the—'

'Powers of an Ascendant. I know. But you don't know how to use them and you don't know how to fight. However, you do know this land, and you know your Dokken secrets. We need each other, Huriya.' He tapped his chest. 'You've made me one of your kind, and that has perforce altered my loyalties. I won't pretend I don't resent it, but it's done. We move on. You are the Alpha Female of your kind. I'm going to be the Alpha Male. You need a partner, and so do I.'

There were noises coming from behind him, wary footsteps. Pretty soon they were both going to have to run or fight. He didn't care which – he felt strong enough to take down a legion – but it would be wasted energy. He wiped his bloody mouth and applied a little healing-gnosis, just enough to cleanse and close the wound; it wouldn't prevent a scar as he'd never been a terribly good healer. Then he tapped the Scytale impatiently against his thigh.

Huriya stroked the stolen baby's head and licked her lips. 'You and me? You despise me, slugskin. You always will. And it's mutual.'

'You're wrong. I'd have done exactly what you did to me, in your place. We think alike, Huriya. We're practical and ruthless. I even admire you a little. We could work well together.'

'How could I ever trust you?' she demanded. 'You think it beneath you to have any dealings with me.'

'Maybe, but there's nothing I won't do to win.' He tapped the Scytale impatiently again. 'Come on, Huriya: decide. Do you want my partnership, or do you want to fight me, right now?'

She glowered, then, narrowed her eyes. 'Throw me the Scytale first. Then he'll see. *Partner.*'

He considered, then casually tossed the artefact to her. He walked cautiously towards her. 'You asked if there is some way that we can trust each other. I know one.' He lifted a hand and kindled gold light on it. 'Touch my hand.'

She frowned warily. 'Why?'

'Just do it. I swear, all you need to do if you don't like what I have to say is to let go.'

She looked at him curiously. From somewhere above and behind her, Hessaz called out, 'Seeress? Is that you?'

'We're coming,' she called over her shoulder, without taking her eyes off Malevorn. Then slowly she lifted her hand and placed it against his palm.

The golden light in his hand coursed through them both and he felt his heart jolt and thud. He gasped despite himself, and she did the same. He met her eyes as the gnosis continued to hum through them both, coiling around each other's hearts. 'Feel that?'

Her eyes were huge in the pale light. 'What are you doing?'

'I'm aligning our hearts – it's a tricky little spell involving healing and mysticism – neither of which are strengths but I can just about reach them. It takes about twenty seconds and at the end of that, our hearts will, quite literally, beat in time. Linked. That means we're bound together: if one of us dies, the other will too, about six seconds later, and there is nothing the survivor can do to stop that.'

She stiffened in fear. 'You are serious?'

'Deadly. This spell is almost never used, because most consider what is gained not worth it, but I don't think there is any other way we'll ever trust each other.' He tapped his chest. 'Can you feel it?'

She nodded fearfully. 'But why—?'

'You want to be able to trust me? You'll have that, in another fifteen seconds. If you want it to stop, just pull your hand away.' He met her eyes. 'Then I'll have to kill you.'

She swallowed. 'You'd do this? With a "mudskin"?'

'Oh, you have your charms, Huriya. And so do I, for a slugskin.'

She swallowed, and so did he, because he hadn't really been sure she would go through with this, or if he even wanted her to. But otherwise it would be a fight to the death and she had Ascendant-level gnosis, though he had the training. He had no idea who'd win, and that made the risk too great.

'Time's running out. Are you going to go through with this?' He thought about Raine Caladryn, the brief dreams they'd harboured. Strangely, though she'd been as ruthless as he was, he'd felt a better person when he was with her. He'd never feel the same for this Keshi harlot; life with her would be a form of torture. But if he was to get what he wanted, this was the required price.

She looked away, no doubt filled with her own misgivings. Then she looked back at him, closed her eyes and kissed him as the spell bonded. Her lips were full and soft and her tongue deliberately teased his raw lip, making him wince. 'Done.' She stroked the Scytale. 'I like a man who gives me something long and hard,' she purred, then stepped away. She thrust the whimpering baby at him. 'Let's go then, "Heart of my Heart".'

One of the mughal's soldiers went after the intruders, but Ramita doubted he'd tried very hard to catch up with the dreaded 'afreet'. In the meantime, she and Alaron waited, holding Dasra, as the chamber filled up with Tariq's soldiers, who stationed themselves in front of them: a fearful wall of steel. A tongue of fire was dancing on Ramita's palm and that was holding them at bay.

Beside her Alaron gripped his staff wearily and tried to look like he could do the same. She appreciated the gesture, but she knew he was on his last legs. Hand-to-hand fighting was incredibly draining, and he'd been fighting for his life.

Please, she thought, *just let us go.*

Godspeaker Vahraz had returned and was earnestly berating Tariq, who was visibly wavering. She picked up a few words: *Rakas. Afreet. Sacred Duty.* To her it sounded like they were building up the nerve to order the soldiers to attack.

She didn't know if she had the strength or skill to kill them all, but she knew she had the will. Whether they deserved to die didn't matter: she had to live if she was ever to get Nasatya back.

Tariq edged through the soldiers, right to the front of the line, barely four yards away from her. His manner was changed: fear still lingered, but there was a new respect for her. He'd seen what she could do, but he had also seen that she had protected him. That was reflected in the new deference in his voice.

'Lady Ramita, what is happening? Why did you come here?' Tariq was anxious, and she could understand why: the Godspeakers were listening with avid ears for evidence of heresy and evil, and she did not doubt that they could bring down even a mughal if he uttered a misjudged word here.

She glanced at Alaron, who didn't understand Lakh. There was not time to confer. 'Exalted Lord, my intention here was honest, and as stated by the vizier. But he is now dead, with nothing resolved.'

There, I've given you a way out. You clearly want one.

Tariq seemed to understand. 'I would never have agreed to what was proposed by the vizier,' he said slowly, ensuring that Vahraz heard him clearly.

'Nor I,' she could not resist saying, although right now he was doing far more to raise himself in her eyes than he would ever know. 'And now it is impossible.'

Tariq nodded slowly, aware of the faint insult – but he'd seen what she could do and he was afraid. 'You will leave now?' It was framed as a question, but she knew it was a command.

We saved your life, boy. But she didn't truly feel angry, only dread for Nasatya, and the urgent need to be gone. *We brought the danger here*, she acknowledged silently. *And you've been stripped of the best advisor and protector you could ever have had.* 'We will leave immediately, Exalted Lord.'

The only exit they were offered was the tunnel; they had to hope Huriya was long gone. She looked up at Alaron: exhausted, sweat-stained and bloodied, but steadfast. *He gave up the prize of prizes for the sake of my child.* Her heart quavered at the thought.

She lifted her head, faced Tariq, ignoring the Godspeakers and soldiers who made evil eye signs and either glared or squirmed under her gaze. 'Farewell. We depart in peace. Please do not follow us.'

On the street above, Alaron lifted his cowl and peered about. The Souldrinkers were gone, and he was deeply thankful, because he was exhausted. Ramita asked one of the crowd of milling people where they had gone, and those who responded pointed up into the skies. A line of rubble ran half a mile back to the vizier's mansion. The mughal's archers surrounded them, uncertain and afraid.

Ramita whispered to Alaron, 'In our folklore, mortal weapons cannot harm an afreet, and that is what these soldiers think they face.'

He nodded, then said, 'We need to get back to the skiff.' He spotted a mounted officer and began to walk towards him, lighting his shields. The crowd fell back, and when he kindled light in his hands, everyone ran, except the horse, because he had gripped its mind with animagery. The officer panicked, leapt from the saddle and fled, but the horse stayed.

He turned to Ramita. 'We'll have to share.'

'Shukriya, bhaiya.' She levitated calmly to the horse's back and sat side-saddle, the ruined sari draped around her. She had nothing else, just her child. She hugged Dasra to her while Alaron scanned for danger, terribly aware of the thousands of eyes on them. He stowed his satchel in one of the saddlebags; it still held his notes. *But not the Scytale*. The loss throbbed inside his brain. *We lost the Scytale. Kore forgive us!*

He slid his kon-staff beneath a strap and secured it, then climbed up behind Ramita and slid his feet into the stirrups. He had to put both arms around her to grasp the reins, which felt unavoidably inappropriate, but what else could he do?

He clicked his tongue and nudged the horse into motion. 'Where do we go?'

'To get my son back,' she whispered. 'The Scytale too.' She looked up at him. Their noses and mouths were almost touching; he could feel her breath on his face. Her eyes held so much intensity he couldn't look away. 'Will you come with me, bhaiya?'

'Of course. You don't have to ask.' *Ever again.*

Burned Bridges

A Meditation on Dawn

Night follows day, and day follows night. No season is eternal, all things pass. But the sight of the sun rising, the shafts of pure light breaking through the wall of darkness, is our most potent and ancient symbol of hope. Who, witnessing dawn, can deny its power to lift our spirits, no matter how dire the day to come may seem?

ANTONIN MEIROS, HEBUSALIM, 854

Teshwallabad, Lakh, on the continent of Antiopia
Rami (Septinon) 929
15th month of the Moontide

Ramita Ankesharan walked down to the ghats where the River Imuna flowed by the monastery. It was here that Yash had come after delivering them to the vizier, and the Zain monks had opened their doors to the fugitives when they came knocking. Holy Imuna, which sprang from the eternal Nimtaya Mountains and joined Teshwallabad, Baranasi and the north with the distant south, was the artery that flowed through the heart of Lakh. The tide was high, lapping at the stonework hungrily, and it wasn't safe to bathe, so Ramita just sat and watched the waters flow past.

Yash and Alaron were in the shade not far away, playing a game with little Dasra that involved a lot of face-pulling. The baby boy was giggling and chortling, but she knew he would cry again soon, when he remembered that the other half of his heart was gone.

Nasatya, where are you?

Her eyes went back to Alaron. He looked so grown-up, so different to the youth who'd flown into the Isle of Glass that night nine months ago. He was broader, taller, more assured. The puppy fat had been chiselled from his face, leaving a pleasing, honest visage. And the way he looked to her gnostic sight sent a thrill of recognition through her: four arms holding the elemental forces; many faces crowding behind his own, and a lion pelt across his shoulders. To her Lakh eyes, it was clear: *Sivraman is with him.*

This is Destiny. Even the theft of my son . . . all these things are fated and so I will not fear.

Oh, but it was dreadfully hard not to be scared when she thought of tiny Nas, caught up in Huriya's hands. Or when she remembered that sneering, hateful Inquisitor, the darkness to Alaron's light. *Malevorn . . . an ugly name for an ugly soul! And he's got the Scytale . . . If Al'Rhon and I don't stop them, they'll wake Shaitan himself . . .*

She sighed heavily, and climbed to her feet. She had only one other solace: that the Gods might hear her prayers. There was nothing else to hope for. 'Al'Rhon,' she called softly, 'I'll be in the temple. Just for a while.'

He looked up, holding Dasra on two wobbly legs, showing him how to be upright, and nodded.

The Zains had been keeping their presence here a secret but that wouldn't last long, and they'd promised the Master that they'd be gone by dawn. Alaron said he had an idea, a place they could go, and that was enough for her, for now.

There was a small Omali temple inside the monastery – the Zains were not Omali, of course, but they kept a shrine here, as at Mandira Khojana in the mountains. She rang the bell over the arch, entered the temple and fell to her knees. No one else was here and she was grateful to be alone. She didn't want others here, not when her grief was so fresh. She lost herself in prayer, taking comfort in the rote words and the benevolent gaze of the statuary that crowded about her. 'Vishnarayan-ji, Protector of Man, hear me! Aid me! Darikha-ji, hear me! Help me, Queen of Heaven! Hear me, Dar-kana-ji,

Demon-Slayer! Come to my aid! Makheera-ji, Goddess of Destiny, alter your weaving to save my son!'

Ever since she got here, she'd been more than praying, for she had begun to think that if magi and Souldrinkers were real, then surely the gods could hear her. She prayed not just with her words, but with the gnosis too: she called upon heaven with her voice and her mind, sending her prayers up, into the heavens, willing the gods to be real and to come down and find her child.

But the only answer thus far had been heaven's silence.

Finally she had cried and prayed herself into numbness. The only sounds were distant ones, from the river and the city outside. She rose and and turned to leave – as the statue of Makheera-ji moved, and she froze in shock.

The statue had blue skin and six arms, and snaky black tresses. Fruit and knives and a cup and other symbols of power were held in her hands. Her eyes of burnished gold caught the lamplight and gave back more. Those eyes pierced Ramita through, burning into her heart, as she stepped down from her pedestal and glided towards her.

She fell to her knees, mouth opening and closing until finally she whispered, '*Makheera-ji?*'

The statue laughed, and changed again, to an utterly unexpected face and form. 'If you wish to speak to me, use my real name,' she said. 'Call me Corinea.'

Southern Kesh, on the continent of Antiopia
Rami (Septinon) 929
15th month of the Moontide

Ramon Sensini poked a finger into the tiny hand of the infant in his lap. She was gurgling blindly, her rosebud mouth blowing kisses into the air. The little hand batted at his finger, then gripped it, and he felt tears well up and tried to blink them away. *I have a daughter.*

'Ooo, look at the big brave man who doesn't cry,' Severine teased gently. It was the fondest she'd been for months, let alone the last few hours, during which she'd screeched abuse at him for ruining her body and implanting the creature that was about to kill her as it ripped its way out.

'I love you,' he said, to her and to the little piece of them both lying in his lap.

They were in the kitchen of an abandoned farm house they'd found on the march towards the Tigrates. The tiny building was now at the centre of the Southern Army's camp. He'd been preparing to go and view the Vida Bridge when Lanna Jureigh had shouted into his mind, <*Sensini! Sensini! Your wife – the baby is coming!*>

So he left Seth to handle things for a while.

The next twelve hours had been among the most harrowing of his life, and that included the battle at Shaliyah. He'd seldom felt as truly helpless as he had here. He had no healing-gnosis, nor know-ledge of what to do, so all he could do was bathe Sevvie's brow whilst whispering words of encouragement and soaking up her abuse. He didn't mind her words – he'd had worse, and for worse reasons – but the helplessness was agony.

Occasionally he thought of Cym and tried to picture her going through this, and then decided he'd rather not. *A mage pregnant to a Souldrinker . . . what did that even mean?* Thinking of her led to thinking about Alaron, and wondering if his hapless friend really was some-where in Lakh. The Alaron he knew could barely leave his front door without tripping over his laces. And what the Hel could he hope to do with the Scytale in Lakh? *I bet it's that Lakh girl pulling your strings! She'll have you wrapped around her little fingers.* He beamed at his daughter. *Girls can do that to a man. You'll learn that too, little one. You'll practise on me.*

He heard boots outside and looked up as the scout Coll came in, struggling to avoid looking at Severine, who had her body covered but was otherwise not at her glamorous best.

'Sir? I have a message.'

Ramon held up the child. 'I have a daughter.'

Coll forced a quick smile, and said, 'Congrats, Magister. Ma'am.' He bobbed his head at Severine, then thrust a piece of paper at

Ramon. 'From the General, sir.' He saluted and hurried away, probably worried that he'd be given the baby to hold if he stayed.

Ramon noted that his daughter was still making divine little kissing movements with her tiny mouth. 'She's hungry again,' he commented, giving her to Severine. They shared a look, a moment of warmth, then while she put their child to her breast, Ramon gave his full attention to the note.

It was brief, just ten words that changed everything:

The Inquisitors have destroyed the bridge at Vida. Come quickly.

Southern Kesh, on the continent of Antiopia
Rami (Septinon) 929
15th month of the Moontide

Zaqri of Metia hunched over the cooking fire, turning the roasting partridges on a spit. The hillside was far above the net of campfires of the refugee camp, three miles down the valley. He'd had to leave, now his heritage had been revealed to the refugees. Though the legions had gone, Salim's army was still days away and those left inside the pen were reverting to the laws of beasts.

Cym lay on the other side of the fire on a dirty blanket, sipping an astringent tea, her deep-set eyes and narrow face rendered gaunt and ancient by the flickering firelight. She'd spent days in a sweating, torrid delirium and he was certain she would have been murdered for what she was if he'd not managed to get her out. He couldn't begin to guess what she was going through. He'd been terrified of infection, but the legion's healer, a patient, gentle Rondian women called Lanna Jureigh, had cleansed her before the army left. After that, Cym's life had been in his hands, some measure of payback for the months she'd spent tending him when he'd nearly died. It felt like they were always paying off debts to each other and he was sick of it.

After they'd eaten, he studied her face, and decided she was ready for the conversation they had to have. 'Cymbellea, why? Why kill our child?'

She turned her head away. 'You know why.'

'It was my child – you had no right—'

'It's *my* body and I have *every* right. And you killed my mother.'

'Do you think that killing our unborn child makes that right?' he snapped. 'How can you think that?'

'A life for a life,' she replied, 'that's what the oath of vendetta states. It doesn't try to balance the worth of those lives.' Then she paused before saying, 'There is a war going on, and my friend is lost in Antiopia with the greatest treasure on Urte. I need to be able to run and fight, not waddle around like a cow. And I didn't want your child anyway.'

'You're my wife! You can't make a decision like that without my consent.'

'No, I'm your *mate*. I don't really know what that means, but you know under what circumstances I agreed to be such a thing. I am not beholden to you for every action I take. You say you love me: but if you don't support my choices, it's not me you love, just some idea of me you've conjured in your own head.'

Her harshness stung him, making him wonder what it was he actually loved in her – no, it was still there, that tenacious vivacity, the coltish vibrancy . . . but it was being filtered through bitterness right now.

'Perhaps I don't know you at all, Cymbellea. I thought you were someone who loved life, but you've just killed our child.'

'Rich, to be condemned by a Souldrinker. How many lives have you taken lately, Dokken?'

He looked away. *Is she right?* He didn't know any more. Didn't know anything. *Let Pater Sol or Kore or Ahm work it out. It's beyond me.* For a moment he missed Ghila and the simple, uncomplicated anger that had fuelled her; it had made her explicable and knowable – then he recalled that her lack of mystery had been one of the things he'd been impatient of. Compared to Cym, Ghila had been made of clay.

Is it the mystery of love or the love of mystery that keeps bringing me back to you? The old Rimoni lament had it spot-on. *I don't know the answer to that either.* 'So, what do we do now?'

'We?' She looked at him.

He nodded slowly, solemnly. 'Yes, *we.*' It might take years to forgive her; it might never happen. But he was sworn to her: pledged and mated. They needed each other, even if she didn't yet recognise that fact. And he had no other reason to go on: she was all that was left.

She looked at him thoughtfully, her face shrouded by black hair and shadows. She seemed carved out of moonlight; Mater Lune come to life: Queen of Magic and Madness.

'I'll be able to get up again tomorrow,' she said at last. 'The Keshi are coming, and your people are with them – leaderless, if what Ramon said about Arkanus is true. And Seth Korion's name will see us given audience with the Sultan, Ramon said.'

'How will that help your friend Alaron?'

'I don't know, but we are so far behind the chase now that we need to try anything to catch up, even if that means using Salim or your people to help find him.'

He breathed deeply, in and out. As plans went, it was pretty desperate. 'The Keshi lock up magi in breeding dens. And I'm packless, with no standing among the Brethren any longer. The Keshi would take the Scytale off your friend and kill him without remorse.' He shook his head. 'It is not a good plan.'

'Do you have a better one?'

Hytel, Javon, on the continent of Antiopia
Rami (Septinon) 929
15th month of the Moontide

Queen Portia Tolidi screamed as if sound alone would drive the child from her body. Her maids and midwives clustered on the far side of the room, scared of the uncontrolled winds that ripped through the chamber, tearing the shutters from the window frames and rattling the furniture, and the light that was seeping from her fingertips. They had been warned that the queen had been cursed with the dreaded gnosis of the magi, but they'd never seen anything like this before and they were utterly terrified. Only the presence of the Sollan priest in the corner gave them the courage to stay in the room.

Every time the queen's contractions paused and the magic died down they would scurry in and swaddle her in wet cloth and bathe her brow – then flee as the next crisis of labour began.

Alfredo Gorgio had not touched her since the day she'd emasculated him. She had no idea if she could restore him even if she wanted to, but the hint that she could was enough to have him bowing and scraping and doing her bidding in an eye-blink. That all she really wanted was to be left alone made that easier; he wasn't forced into any corners and neither was she. Hytel continued to produce its tribute of metals and stone to be shipped south, and Dorobon magi visited occasionally and gave her rudimentary lessons in the gnosis. Alfredo concealed his humiliating injury so no one except the two of them knew – she guessed his wife and the girls he victimised were just grateful to be left alone.

'Sol et Lune,' she gasped as another burst of agony wracked her and she felt something begin to tear her in half at the hips. She was completely exhausted now, and no light flared, no winds blew or threw furniture about, so the midwives took heart and came forward to swamp her in reassurance and firm, gentle hands.

'Breathe,' they told her, so she breathed. 'Push,' they ordered, and she pushed, and then, 'Stop,' they said, and she paused and breathed in deeply until they commanded again, 'Push . . .'

The baby came easily in the end, in a gush of blood-smeared flesh and fluids that soaked the bedclothes and her thighs. When the child wailed, her heart burst. 'It is a boy,' someone told her. 'A little boy.'

Some part of her had assumed that she would hate it, that she would physically and mentally reject it, because hate was her most powerful emotion and this creature had been planted in her by *him*, and it was enemy and it was alien.

But Francis is dead now. I'm a widow. I'll never have to be anyone's whore again.

So instead of hate, she felt a strange ambivalence as she took in her child's knowing eyes and serene face. She recognised him as a piece of herself as well, and quite unexpectedly, love of the little being came flooding into her and filled her, through and through like purest light.

Lybis, Javon, on the continent of Antiopia
Rami (Septinon) 929
15th month of the Moontide

Gurvon Gyle felt Elena Anborn's hand touch his shoulder, the first physical contact they'd had since his capture. 'Wait here,' she said softly, her eyes on the far end of the bridge.

He followed her gaze. Perhaps Rutt Sordell would try something, though he doubted it; Rutt didn't have the imagination. At the far end, he could see a dozen men and a wagon. Rutt Sordell's 'Guy Lassaigne' body was easy to see: he was the only one in battle-mage robes, surrounded by mail-clad legionaries. The bridge was over a ravine outside Lybis – he remembered crossing it on the first day of his trek into the mountains, with Arnulf Rhumberg and his men. They were now just ash in the lamiae's valley, or strips of smoked meat in their larders.

He shuddered.

It was three weeks since he'd fallen into Elena's hands, but they'd not spoken again. She refused to engage in conversation, though she'd visited him every day, to ensure he was still penned and that her Noorie lover's Chain-rune held. It did: he could feel it constraining him so thoroughly that he was beginning to wonder if Rutt would be strong enough to break it. They fed him, and let him wash in a cave-pool, but he'd not been allowed near a razor and the stubble irritated his sense of self. He'd not had a beard since the worst days of the Noros Revolt. The last week they'd returned by paths through the mountains that were far more direct than those he'd found on the way in, just he and Elena, her Noorie and a handful of lamaie. The snakemen were out of sight, but he knew they were close by.

Looking at Elena now, he was sickened by how damned *well* she looked. Her blonde hair had been bleached almost white by the sun, and she was letting it grow. Her skin was brown and healthy, her face freckled and youthful. Her body was toned and limber – age was certainly not biting yet, showing only in the crow's feet at the corner of her eyes and a few lines on her brow.

'He's half your age, Ella,' he commented, glancing back at Kazim Makani.

'Gurvon, I can still gag you,' she said coolly.

'He's a Dokken, for Kore's sake! He's leeching off you! He's killing you slowly!'

'Mmm. Yes, I feel so deathly at the moment. I'm just wasting away.' She snorted dismissively. 'Come on, Gurvon, you can do better than that! Where's that old snide magic gone?'

'We made plans,' he reminded her. 'We dreamed together—'

She spat over the parapet. 'Plans to rob and kill undeserving victims. I've moved on.'

'You're going to fight for a treacherous little bint who's already sold you out once. You'll never be able to trust her. She doesn't care about her little brother – he was never anything more than a pretext. She only wants the power – she got a taste for it and she'll never let it go. You'll see.'

He watched, smiling inwardly, as these words struck home. She really did *want* to able to trust Cera Nesti.

That old snide magic.

She stomped away, then came back and snarled, glaring at him, 'Listen well, Gurvon. These are my last words to you. Get out of Javon, because if you stay, you will die. The Javonesi are going to take back what is theirs and you're not going to be able to stop it happening. So if you don't want to waste the lives of the last few sentient beings who still trust you, you'd better run.'

Before he could respond, she stalked onto the bridge. At the far end, the wagon lurched into motion, carrying all the gold he and Rutt had managed to collect. It sickened him to be giving it away, but at least it meant he kept his head.

He'd tried telling Elena that it wasn't about the money. 'That's just one way we keep score,' he told her.

She'd smiled and told him that was fine: he was losing fifteen thousand to nil.

He spat sourly over the parapet and prayed Rutt didn't cock up this exchange. He had a lot to do to win this game.

It's never over, Elena . . . It never will be, until you're a corpse.

Elena peered at the pallid mage driving the wagon. Different body, same bastido, she decided. 'Rutt. I'd recognise you in any body.'

The face twitched with the telltale tick of someone imperfectly controlled by a scarab. 'This body's pure-blood, Elena,' he replied. 'I've upgraded.'

'I bet you miss your real body, though. All your normal senses are distorted, aren't they? Taste, touch, smell – they all feel second-hand, don't they?' She fixed him with a hard smile. 'I hear Betillon's arrived in Brochena.'

Sordell flinched, as she knew he would. Someone in Rykjard's legion had panicked when they'd lost contact with Gurvon and Rhumberg, then some Imperial informer had got wind of the crisis and now the Butcher of Knebb was in Javon. He'd flown in with a legion of Kirkegarde, and direct orders from Lucia to take over.

The phoney war is over. Thank Kore I got Timori out. Gurvon had wriggled and pleaded, but he'd been forced to concede both the money and the boy-king in the end. *I just wish we could have given Kekropius something for all he's lost.* All she could promise him was that their existence would be very delicately raised, and she'd ask that the lamiae be given their own lands and left alone.

'Sure, the Butcher's in Brochena now,' Sordell sniffed. 'But we've got Endus, Adi, Hans and Staria in play. Betillon might think he's in charge, but he won't be for long. Either way, we've got magi everywhere, and you've got what? Two? You're doomed, Elena.' He looked towards the far end of the bridge. 'Let me see the boss.'

'Of course.' That was the arrangement: an inspection of the goods before the exchange. 'Don't do anything silly, Rutt. Kazim is ten times the warrior you will ever be.'

'I will conduct myself correctly. See you do the same,' Sordell snapped.

Elena watched him carefully as they crossed, then approached the wagon. *If I was pulling some kind of stunt, there would be men in the wagon, crouching in the boxes, or even clinging to the underside.* But there was no trace of gnostic activity, and no interlopers. Elena ran a hand over the flanks of the horses, scanning them too, because you really couldn't be too careful. Only then did she turn to the two young Nesti, huddled in the back.

Timori dropped from the cart and ran forward. 'Tante Ella!' The boy-king leapt and clung to her as she struggled to cope with his weight. He'd grown so much – he was almost up to her chest now, and a lot heavier. 'I've missed you so much, Tante Ella,' he whispered.

She lightly touched Timi's mind and found only the wide-eyed innocence she'd always found there, albeit with a little more maturity and a lot more fear. *Poor boy, hidden from sight, kept as a prisoner. But not abused, thank Kore.* She squeezed him back, then lowered him down to the ground. 'It's good to see you, Timi. Please wait here a moment while I see to Cera.'

She turned to the princessa.

So many emotions, all at once: anger and bitterness warred with a desire to find a reason to forgive, but she couldn't, not yet. Her fingers twisted into claws just to look at her. It didn't matter that the princessa looked miserable, lifeless, broken down by the weight of all she'd seen and done.

You sold me to Gurvon, you little piece of . . .

Their eyes met . . .

Deep breath. Deep breath.

'Cera.'

'Elena . . . I'm so sorry.' Tears began to well from the young woman's eyes. 'Please, please, *please* forgive me.'

She was conscious of the weight of Timori's gaze, the way the boy was holding his breath, not really understanding, but achingly aware of the unexpected hostility in the air when he'd expected only joyous reunion.

But she couldn't lie either.

'I don't know if I can,' she replied, then for Timori's sake she added, 'but I'll try.'

Pontus, on the continent of Yuros
Rami (Septinon) 929
15th month of the Moontide

Vannaton Mercer was playing tabula with one of his guards, a bluff, middle-aged man named Pol Tannor. After nine months of being cooped up with each other they were something like friends. Tannor was affable enough, more than happy to open the wine or bring eastern delicacies from the markets. Goods from Antiopia had been flooding into Pontus for months now, the harvest of conquest, and the markets were going insane, with prices spiralling and gold coin becoming harder and harder to find. The fact that the plunder was far less than expected had driven the prices even higher.

'They say the Imperial Treasury has stopped issuing hard coin,' Tannor was telling him. 'Ain't got none, way I hear it.'

'Dubrayle's a smart man,' Vann replied, stretching his legs. 'I'm sure he knows what he's doing.'

It was hard to get enough exercise here in the protective custody of the Merchants' Guild. The courtyard was barely sixty yards across, and there were no gardens – the building was just another small, anonymous house crammed into the trading district of Pontus, a city that went mad four years in twelve, then was left virtually derelict for the rest of the Moontide cycle.

Vann would dearly have loved to be allowed to go for a walk: anywhere. Escape wasn't on his mind, not at all, but despite being a 'guest', his movements were very much curtailed. *For my own good, or so they keep telling me.*

'Aye, sure Dubrayle knows what he's doing,' Tannor grumbled. 'He's stringing the guilds along and praying he can ride this out, same as last time. But it ain't like last time, I'm telling yer.' Everyone associated with the Merchants' Guild fancied themselves as men of business, even the guards. Tannor slugged back his ale and was about to launch into another of his discourses on the duplicity of Imperial Treasurers when the door swung open, and Jean Benoit entered, his face grim.

'Vann! We need to talk. Pol, you may go . . .'

Tannor stood, and all levity left his face. He flashed Vann a sympathetic look, then scurried out, meek as a serving girl. Vann swallowed, then indicated the now vacant chair.

'I'll stand,' Benoit said, not quite meeting his eye.

Vann slowly stood also, wondering. Benoit's normally confident, genial face was rigidly set. *Bad news, or unpleasant tidings then . . .*

'Vann,' the Guildmaster began, 'we've hidden you from the empire these past nine months. The Quizzies want you, but I've never questioned your story, not once.'

Vann felt his mouth go dry. 'I'm grateful, Jean. If there is any way I can repay you, you know I will . . .'

'I know, Vann, I know,' Benoit replied, his voice a little choked and uncomfortable. 'But the thing is, I've finally gained a greater insight into why the Inquisitors have been hunting your son.' He put his hands to his hips and took a deep breath. 'The fact is, new information has come to light.'

Vann felt the ground shift beneath him. 'No, Jean . . .' He threw up his hands. 'Kore's Blood, man, you *know* these people! You know the lies they tell!'

And the gold they sometimes share . . .

Nine months, and I'm sure he's been touting me around every dealer-in-secrets from here to Pallas . . .

I knew I didn't trust you, you silk-stocking full of shit.

The door opened again, and a stiff-backed woman entered, her haughty face of faded beauty framed by severely tied grey hair. Her eyes glittered like diamonds. The cassock she wore was so deeply

...rple it was almost black, and chains of gold hung about her neck and waist. A key emblem was embroidered on her left breast, a sign he'd been told of but never before seen. His heart crumbled.

'My name is Delfinne de Tressot,' the woman said in a cool, brittle voice. 'Do you know what I am?'

Vann nodded, his eyes caught by hers. Benoit's change of heart became all the more explicable. 'You're a Keeper, Lady; one raised to the Ascendancy as a reward for loyalty and service to the empire.'

In fact, you're the bitch who ran the Imperial Orphanages ... while your husband Lord Aldemar ran a chain of brothels.

'Quite so.' She prowled a circle around him, then gestured dismissively at Benoit. The Guildmaster fled whilst looking at *anything* but Vann.

Dear Kore ... will I ever leave this room again?

Delfinne de Tressot motioned for him to sit, and he was too frightened to refuse.

'Well, Master Vannaton: I believe you and I have much to talk about. Let's start with your son Alaron, and his Arcanum thesis that postulated the theft of the Scytale of Corineus during the Noros Revolt.' She bent over him, and her eyes flashed like those of a vulture. *'Tell me ... who the Hel told him so?'*

Ebensar Heights, Zhassi Valley, on the continent of Antiopia
Rami (Septinon) 929
15th month of the Moontide

Kaltus Korion urged his khurne to halt and the beast did so with silent obedience, standing rock-still and waiting as he stared down the long slopes of Ebensar Heights at the blackened sands and smouldering bodies.

For eight days, Emir Rashid Mubarak of Halli'kut had thrown men at his First Army, masses upon masses, trying to smash through with sheer manpower. It had been slaughter on a grand scale, uphill and into the teeth of the Imperial magi.

Did they think my magi were like Echor's, nothing but low-blooded provincials?

Kaltus Korion had the elite of the battle-magi, armed with construct beasts and siege engines, all bolstered by the gnosis: five hundred years of Rondian Empire knowledge, invention, experimentation and expertise, distilled into a perfect instrument of military magic and placed at his command. He had gnosis-guided exploding ballistae bolts; fragmenting fireballs launched from catapults more than half a mile away; flying constructs who breathed fire after the manner of the dragons of legend. And all this firepower had been concentrated on a narrow front where half a million men had thought to break through. The results had been catastrophic for Rashid's Keshi.

Korion liked to imagine there were just the two of them, standing like gods over the battlefield, avatars of Kore and Ahm hurling men at each other like spells. *And I am clearly the better man*, he mused. *And the greater god.*

A nervous aide approached. 'Sir, here are the latest despatch memos received via the relay-staves.'

Korion saluted the young man, well aware of his effect on the junior officers. Worship shone from the eyes of the men he gathered to his command tent, all dreaming that he would notice them and advance their careers.

He turned back to the view. Even his most senior commanders didn't know why this place had been chosen to defend.

This ridge was on the west flank of the Zhassi Valley. On his charts, Ebensar Heights was marked very specifically, and it pleased him to be the only man in the army to know why.

Korion accepted the two despatches and studied the seals – unbroken of course, though the transcribing mage who'd taken the communications would know the contents – and wondered which to open first. He chose Tomas Betillon's: news of betrayal, rogue mercenary legions and disarray in Javon. *Gurvon has botched it, so they've sent Tomas in. Hah!* He wasn't surprised. Noromen had always been provincial muck, with no head for the heights of leadership.

Maybe now we'll finally execute Gyle, as we should have done after the Revolt.

The second despatch was from far to the south, from the commander of the garrison at Vida, a Brician legion initially assigned to Echor's command and assigned garrison duty.

What news could there possibly be from down there?

He had to read the note twice to believe his eyes.

Some of Echor's Second Army survived? And they are commanded by . . . my son?

He rubbed the grit from his eyes. *Seth?*

He had to pause to picture his only legitimate son's face: uncertain, weak-chinned, too much baby fat. Certainly not the face of a hero – not the face of a *real* Korion. The paperwork to officially legitimise another son was on his desk, selected from his string of male bastards. He re-read the note: *Seth led a retreat from Shaliyah? My Seth?* For a moment he felt something like pride, then he paused and scowled. *What does he know?*

The thought spoiled his mood somewhat, especially as he read on. The bridges had been destroyed and this remnant of Echor's force was trapped on the far side of the Tigrates River. It didn't say how the bridges had been destroyed, or by whom. The commander wanted guidance – an army of Keshi was closing in on the younger Korion's forces, and he didn't know whether to aid him?

He stared off into the distance and thought about that. *No. Let my son forge his own legend. And if he does know of how Echor came to be defeated, let it die with him.* He scrawled a reply and handed it to the aide, almost sent him on his way, then paused as a thought hit him.

'Tonville, isn't it? I believe we had a wager on how many days the Keshi would keep coming? Yours was seven or under, was it not?' He held out his hand. 'My bet.'

The aide looked abashed, but pleased to be remembered. He fished out a piece of paper. 'Will this do, sir? Redeemable from the Treasury, it says here.'

Is this one of the notes Dubrayle was fussing about? Korion held out his hand, examined the paper, frowned, stared, and looked again. 'Where did this come from?'

'I don't know, sir, but there are more of these in circulation than all the coins in existence. Crusader notes, we call them.'

'Is that Dubrayle's personal seal?'

'Yes, sir.'

'But Dubrayle hasn't even set foot in Antiopia – the army can't issue notes with a Treasury seal.'

It's just as Dubrayle suspected: someone has been using his name and seal. Serves the smug prick right. He still didn't see how this so-called promissory note crisis could be worth getting flustered over.

Tonville shuffled uncomfortably. 'It's the Treasury seal that gives it its worth, sir. Shows that it's genuine. There's a lot of rubbish notes out there, right enough, but these ones are guaranteed – look, it says so on the bottom here. But I can probably scrounge up some coin if you prefer?'

Korion shook his head slowly, turning the note over in his hand and examining the signature: not Dubrayle, obviously. The first name seemed to start with 'R', the rest was just a squiggle. 'No, your debt's discharged, Tonville. But I'd like you to look into the origin of this note.'

'Right away.' Tonville looked puzzled as he saluted and left. Korion turned back to the slopes and the view out over Rashid's army. The plains were still thick with Keshi, despite all the casualties littering the slopes, and the hymns still rose from below, like a million Brevian washer-wraiths calling the dead to their graves. There'd been plenty of corpses, enough to appease even a Schlessen war god, but the wailing never ceased.

It's nine months until the end of the Moontide, he mused, *when we change this world for ever.*

773

THE END OF BOOK THREE OF THE MOONTIDE

The story concludes in

ASCENDANT'S RITE

Book IV of The Moontide

Acknowledgements

Thanks are due! Firstly to my brave test readers: Paul Linton, Kerry Greig and Heather Adams. Readers will not be aware of how many deranged and ill-judged ideas make it as far as the first draft, and these are the three troopers who read that draft, shake their heads, then pour exactly the right amount of cold water on them and me. This series is *so* much better for your efforts.

Heather is of course also my agent (alongside her husband Mike Bryan): thank you for fighting my corner and getting me this opportunity. I still bless the day we all met (in the hospitality tent at the polo in Delhi, obviously). An auspicious day indeed.

Mega-thanks to editor and publishing goddess Jo Fletcher for her expert judgement, knowledge and experience, and supportive nature throughout. It's been a long epic and we're only halfway through the second half! Continued gratitude and respect. Also thanks again to Nicole Budd and Andrew Turner at Quercus, Emily Faccini for the maps, art designer Patrick Carpenter and artists Paul Young and Jem Butcher for the cover, and all the rest of the JFB/Quercus team.

Biggest hugs to my wonderful wife Kerry, she of the eagle eye for detail, especially continuity, and fearless red ink. When someone loves you enough to tell you where you're going wrong, you're loved indeed. She also does supportive encouragement too! I'm a very lucky person.

Lots of love to my children, Brendan and Melissa, my parents Cliff and Biddy, and all my friends, especially Mark, Felix and Stefania, Raj, Andrew and Brenda, and Keith and Kathryn.

David Hair
Auckland, July 2014
HTJI

DRAMATIS PERSONAE

Unholy War

As at Junesse 928

In Yuros
Imperial Court, Pallas

- Emperor Constant Sacrecour: Emperor of Rondelmar and all Yuros
- Mater-Imperia Lucia Fasterius: the emperor's mother, a Living Saint
- Cordan: son of Constant, heir to the throne
- Coramore: daughter of Constant
- Lord Calan Dubrayle: Imperial Treasurer
- Arch-Prelate Dominius Wurther: Head of the Church of Kore
- Adamus Crozier: a bishop of the Kore
- Natia Sacrecour: Constant's imprisoned elder sister
- Ervyn Naxius, former Ordo Costruo mage
- Delfinne de Tressot: A Keeper and Ascendant mage
- Jean Benoit, Merchant Guildmaster
- Orly, a thief

Eighteenth Fist of Kore's Holy Inquisition

- Elath Dranid: Fist Second
- Raine Caladryn: an Acolyte
- Dominic Rysen: an Acolyte
- Malevorn Andevarion: an Acolyte
- Virgina Purfoyl: an acolyte [deceased]

Thirty-Second Fist of Kore's Holy Inquisition

- Fronck Quintius, Commandant
- Artus Leblanc: an Acolyte
- Geoffram: an Acolyte

Twenty-Third Fist of Kore's Holy Inquisition

- Ullyn Siburnius: Inquisitor and Fist Commander
- Alis Nytrasia, Fist Third
- Einar Perle, an Acolyte
- Delta: a Souldrinker mage

Norostein, Noros

- King Phyllios III: King of Noros
- Vannaton Mercer: a trader
- Tesla Anborn-Mercer: mage, wife of Vannaton Mercer [deceased]
- Alaron Mercer: mage, son of Vann and Tesla
- Relik Folsteyn, courier
- Captain Jeris Muhren: Watch Captain [deceased]

Silacia

- Mercellus di Regia: head of a Rimoni gypsy family [deceased]
- Cymbellea di Regia: Rimoni gypsy, daughter of Mercellus
- Anise: a Rimoni orphan
- Pater-Retiari: a criminal clan-lord

Turm Zauberin Arcanum, Norostein

- Lucien Gavius: Principal of Turm Zauberin (Arcanum College)
- Darius Fyrell: a tutor at Turm Zauberin (deceased)
- Agnes Yune: a tutor at Turm Zauberin

Gurvon Gyle's Grey Foxes (based in Noros)

- Gurvon Gyle: a mage-spy
- Rutt Sordell: a mage, whose soul is currently in the body of Guy Lassaigne
- Mara Secordin: a mage

- Yvette ('Coin'): a child of Mater-Imperia Lucia
- Symone: a fictitious identity of Coin
- Madeline Parlow: a mage

In Pontus

- Pol Tannor: Merchant Guild guardsman

Ordo Costruo (Mage Order based in Hebusalim)

- Antonin Meiros: Arch-Magus and founder [deceased]
- Justina Meiros: Antonin's daughter [deceased]
- Rene Cardien: missing mage
- Ramita Ankesharan: Lakh widow of Antonin Meiros
- Dasra and Nasatya: twin sons of Antonin Meiros and Ramita

Hebusalim

- Tomas Betillon: Imperial Governor of Hebusalim

Crusaders
The First Army (Northern)

- General Kaltus Korion: Commander of the Armies of Rondelmar
- Tonville: aide to General Korion
- General Rhynus Bergium, Korion's second-in-command
- Tomas Betillon: Imperial Governor of Hebusalim
- Enott: a battlemage
- Tribune Gestryn: maniple commander

The 'Lost Legions' of the Southern Crusade

- Baltus Prenton: Windmaster of Pallacios XXIII
- Lanna Jureigh: Healer of Pallacios XXIII
- Tyron Frand: Legion Chaplain of Pallacios XXIII
- Severine Tiseme: Legion Farseer of Pallacios XXIII
- Seth Korion: a battlemage of Pallacios XXIII
- Renn Bondeau: a battle-mage of Pallacios XXIII
- Hugh Gerant: a battle-mage of Pallacios XXIII
- Evan Hale: a battle-mage of Pallacios XXIII
- Fridryk Kippenegger: a battle-mage of Pallacios XXIII
- Ramon Sensini: a battle-mage of Pallacios XXIII
- Storn: Tribune of the Tenth Maniple of Pallacios XXIII

- Coll: a scout of the Tenth Maniple of Pallacios XXIII
- Sigurd Vaas: Argundian battlemage
- Jelaska Lyndrethuse: Argundian battlemage
- Carmina: Argundian healer-mage
- Gerdhart: Argundian chaplain and mage
- Lysart: Noroman battlemage
- Sordan: Noroman battlemage
- Mylde: Noroman battlemage
- Wilbrecht: Brevian battlemage
- Runsald: Brevian battlemage
- Hulbert: Hollenian battlemage
- Kyrcen: Estellan battlemage
- Penn Magro, a ranker

Lukaz's cohort; Pallacios XXIII (Ramon's guards)

- Lukaz: pilus (commander)
- Baden: bannerman
- The Front Rank: Serjant Manius, Dolman, Ferdi, Trefeld, Hedman, Gannoval
- The Second Rank: Serjant Vidran, Bowe, Ilwyn, Holdyne, Gal Herde, Jan Herde
- The Flankman: Kel Harmon, Briggan, Kent, Ollyd, Neubeau, Tolomon

In Javon
In Forensa

- Paolo Castellini: a Nesti guard commander [currently missing]
- Harshal ali-Assam: a Jhafi noble
- Pita Rosco: Master of the Royal Purse
- Luigi Ginovisi: Master of Revenues
- Comte Piero Inveglio: a Rimoni nobleman
- Ivan Prato: a Sollan drui
- Borsa: Nesti family nursemaid

In Brochena

- Cera Nesti: co-Queen of Javon
- Timori Nesti: Crown Prince of Javon

- Solinde Nesti: Princess of Javon [deceased]
- Francesco Perdonello: Chief of Royal Bureaucracy
- Tarita: Cera's personal maid
- Acmed al-Istan: Senior Amteh Godspeaker
- Talfayeed al'Marech: a Ja'arathi Godspeaker
- Josip Yannos, High Drui of the Sollan Church
- Ilmaz: a Godspeaker
- Mustaq al'Madhi: a criminal lord
- Hazmani: a man of Brochena
- Mukla: a woman of Brochena
- Oviya: daughter of Hazmani and Mukla
- Kiraz: a girl of Brochena

The Dorobon monarchy

- Octa Dorobon: matriarch of Dorobon Family [deceased]
- Francis Dorobon: son and heir of the Dorobon line
- Olivia Dorobon: sister to Francis
- Craith Margham, mage-knight
- Roland Heale, mage-knight
- Jedyk Luman, mage
- Guy Lassaigne, mage (possessed by Rutt Sordell)
- Etain Tullesque: Kirkegarde Grandmaster
- Elissen: a Dorobon officer
- Rhinus: a Dorobon guardsman
- Jacquo: a Dorobon guardsman
- Tholum: a Dorobon guardsman

Gorgio Family of Hytel

- Alfredo Gorgio: a Rimoni lord of Hytel
- Portia Tolidi: co-Queen of Javon, sister of Fernando
- Fernando Tolidi: a nobleman of Hytel [deceased]

Other Javonesi

- Seir Lorenzo di Kestria: a Rimoni knight [deceased]
- Lord Stefan Aranio of Riban
- Emir Mekmud bin al'Azhir of Lybis

Gyle's Mercenaries

- Endus Rykjard: a mercenary commander
- Arnulf Rhumberg: battlemage of Rykjard's legion
- Niklyn Vardel: battlemage of Rykjard's legion
- Hetta Descholt: battlemage of Rykjard's legion
- Adi Paavus: a mercenary commander
- Hans Frikter: a mercenary commander
- Staria Canestos: a mercenary commander
- Leopollo Canestos: Staria's nephew and adopted son
- Kordea Canestos: Staria's adopted daughter

Renegades

- Elena Anborn: mage, former Grey Fox and Nesti guard
- Kazim Makani: a Souldrinker and assassin

Among the Lamiae

- Kekropius: an Elder male
- Kessa: mate of Kekropius and Elder
- Simou: an Elder male
- Herotos: an Elder male

In Kesh
Sagostabad

- Salim Kabarakhi I, Sultan of Kesh
- Latif, one of the Sultan's impersonators
- Rashid Mubarak, Emir of Halli'kut and Ordo Costruo renegade
- Alyssa Dulayne, renegade Ordo Costruo mage, Rashid's mistress

Among the Hadishah

- Jamil: a mage assassin [deceased]
- Molmar: a Hadishah skiff-pilot
- Gatoz: Hadishah mage and commander [deceased]
- Haroun: an Amteh Scriptualist [deceased]

Zaqri's Pack

- Huriya Makani: a Souldrinker, sister of Kazim
- Zaqri: a Souldrinker and packleader
- Ghila: a Souldrinker, wife of Zaqri [deceased]
- Perno: a Souldrinker [deceased]
- Hessaz: a Souldrinker, wife of Perno
- Sabele: a Souldrinker seer [deceased and soul taken by Huriya]
- Wornu: a Souldrinker male
- Kenner: a Souldrinker male
- Darice: a Souldrinker female
- Elando: a Souldrinker male
- Kraderz: a Souldrinker male
- Tomacz: a Souldrinker male and Elder
- Federi: a Souldrinker male and Elder
- Medolos: a Souldrinker male
- Fasha: a Souldrinker female
- Chasander: a Souldrinker male
- Rayle: a Souldrinker male

Souldrinkers in the Sultan's army

- Yorj Arkanus: a Souldrinker warleader
- Hecatta, a Souldrinker, Arkanus' mate
- Zsdryk, a Souldrinker male
- Kadimarah, a Souldrinker female
- Brennan: a Souldrinker male
- Tynbrook: a Souldrinker male

In Khotriawal
Ardijah

- Amiza al'Ardijah, Calipha of Ardijah

In Lokistan
Mandira Khojana monastery

- Puravai: a Zain master
- Yash: a Zain acolyte

In Lakh
Teshwallabad

- Tariq Srinarayan Kishan-ji, Mughal of Lakh
- Hanook: Royal Vizier
- Dareem: son of Hanook
- Jindas-sahib: a royal tailor
- Kindu: bodyguard of Tariq
- Varhaz: Godspeaker, adviser to Tariq

Baranasi

- Ispal Ankesharan: trader
- Tanuva Ankesharan: Ispal's wife
- Jai: Ispal's son
- Keita: Jai's lover
- Vikash Nooradin: market trader

From the Past

- Johan Corin ('Corineus'): and Messiah of the Kore
- Selene Corin ('Corinea'): sister and murderer of Johan, personification of feminine evil
- Baramitius: Ascendant mage and creator of the Scytale of Corineus
- Olfuss Nesti: a deceased King of Javon
- Jarius Langstrit: a Noros general
- Belonius Vult, deceased Governor of Norostein
- Nasette Ledoc: only person in history known to have been transformed from a mage into a Souldrinker
- Heward Ledoc: Nasette's father and killer
- Attiya Zai: Omali holy man, founder of the Zain order of monasticism
- Adric Meiros: deceased son of Antonin Meiros